"A mythical alien shipwreck from another time lost in the Amazon is the stuff of legend, like El Dorado."

– Artemus Pennywell

* * *

Sopping wet and weary, the expedition huddles within the alien campfire's protective circumference on a raised spit of muddy Brazilian rainforest surrounded by a flooded understory constituting the unnamed river's headwaters.

Rachel checks the collapsible camp pot hung above the licking blue flames and pours two beef stew packets before giving it a solid stir. The miserable five try not to appear too hungry as freeze-dried chunks rehydrate and expand like magic into cubed meat and potatoes mixed with green beans, onions, and corn in a thick and savory bone broth.

Owen leans forward, frowning, "Who puts corn in beef stew?"

Richard objects with feigned indignation, "I do."

Antoine passes his bowl to Rachel. "I don't care what is in there; I'm starving."

* * *

by John Hopkins

THE POWERS THAT BE trilogy

The Golden Ellipse

The Lost Ship

The Blue Spark (2024)

THE POWERS THAT BE short stories

Operation Bigfoot

Firing Henry

Dog vs. Alien

Thundercorp No. 5

The Special

Big Shots Club

Doc's Brain

LOST CACTUS comic strip anthologies

Lost Cactus - The First Treasury

Lost Cactus - The Second Treasury

LOST CACTUS ARCHIVES short stories

Middle of Nowhere

The Pixel Pusher

Emmitt's Encounter

Warehouse of Secrets

The Gremlin

LOST CACTUS ARCHIVES graphic novels

Volume 1:
The Wormhole Particle Project (future release)

Volume 2:
Tank and Gremlin (future release)

Volume 3:
Fox Gambit (future release)

Volume 4:
Zint and Daphne (future release)

THE POWERS
THAT BE
BOOK
TWO

JOHN HOPKINS

a subsidiary of Hopart LLC

Publication Date: November 2022

Trade Paperback ISBN: 978-0-9965067-9-3

Hardcover ISBN: 979-8-9862338-2-6

eISBN: 979-8-9862338-0-2

Library of Congress Control Number: 2022903240

WEB: johnhopkinsauthor.com

Cover illustration and interior page design by Hopart LLC.

Dedicated in memory of Michael Crichton.

October 23, 1942 – November 4, 2008

Preface

Your muse is that annoying little voice filling your head with crazy ideas about some pie-in-the-sky venture, like writing a novel. You can ignore it. Many do.

My advice? Do not ignore your muse in favor of monumental time-wasters. Worse yet, pass to your greater or lesser reward, leaving it unfulfilled, haunting your soul for eternity with an endless harangue about that unfinished project in the garage, the picture you never painted, or the sweater you never knitted. It's your muse; whatever it is, you better get to it. Who knows? You might even enjoy—and perhaps excel—at the languishing latency within your psyche on perpetual hold.

I surrendered to my muse by creating a comic strip. Little did I realize that conceptualizing the paranormal premise underlying my Lost Cactus comic strip would open a Pandora's Box of mythology, world-building, and character development that quickly outgrew the 3-panel strip and led to a shared universe of short stories and full-length novels grappling with heady themes such as humankind's ultimate place in the universe.

In retrospect, my muse compelled me across a threshold, but what happened after that proved unpredictable and surprising.

A prime example of this is The Powers That Be. What began as a throwaway gag name for a string-pulling top-secret entity in my comic strip evolved into a fully-realized 300-year-old enigmatic organization at the epicenter of my science fiction novels with a diverse, multi-generational cast charged with fostering humankind's fate.

Granted, my initial concepts for this secretive group involved cartoonish villainy of Bondian proportions replete with speargun-toting frogmen guarding undersea lairs and orbiting motherships with requisite henchpeople (Like how I slipped that in?) in shiny silver suits.

However, while this sort of frivolity suited the comic strip, my science fiction novels' overarching themes, and conspiracy-fueled premises require fewer spearguns and more nuance and gravitas. So, the undersea lair went bye-bye while the mothership idea evolved into the fascinating backstory of an extraterrestrial guild spectating upon our freedom-loving forebears' struggle against tyranny and oppression. Drawing inspiration from George Washington's divine encounter at Valley Forge, benevolent beings revealed themselves to key historical actors, forming The Powers That Be, a secret alliance to advise and guide humankind through turbulent centuries into a near future at the threshold of human destiny.

My clandestine organization's paradoxical name, The Powers That Be (or PTB for short), represents the bogeyman in the modern-day vernacular for when things go sideways, providing its menacing allure. Yet it also conveys intrinsic omniscience proliferating mind-blowing advancements in AI and technologies transmogrifying human civilization and tethering the world to teeming networks of streaming data, essential to modern existence but beyond the grasp of a vast majority of humans. Just press the button, and it works.

What if, one day, it doesn't? Thus, I give you The Powers That Be.

Circling back to the muse—before looming calamity wipes out the world's infrastructure, rendering this discussion moot—why not follow your little voice and never let the peanut gallery hold you back. They will be sorry when the grim reaper makes a house call, and all they have to show for themselves is a lukewarm flat screen and a half-eaten bag of Fritos. Meanwhile, a blank canvas purchased on a whim at the local craft store gathers dust and cobwebs in the back of their closet behind an old gray overcoat nobody wears.

See you in the funny papers.

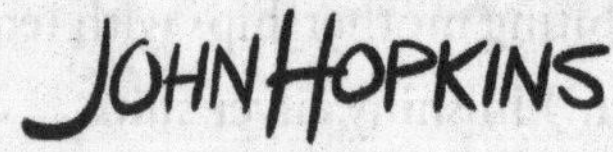

Characters

90,000,000 BC

Empire Grays — Time-traveling telepathic cousins of Gray species of varying temperaments throughout the universe whose Cretaceous-era colonization devolved into a hasty evacuation that left behind an apocalyptic payload

The Captain — Empire Gray cargo ship captain and veteran of past planetary colonization disasters

The Governor — Hubristic Empire Gray colony administrator

1928 AD – Prologue Flashback

Fordlandia — Henry Ford's idealized rubber plantation along the Tapajós River in Brazil

Charles Pike — Civil engineer on Fordlandia payroll whose true mission is to locate the lost ship

Manuel Machado   Brazilian day laborer and lone survivor of deadly encounter with Empire Gray advance scout

Paddy McCoy   Anachronistic PTB field agent and youthful Artemus Pennywell's mentor

Artemus Pennywell   Adventurous 18-year-old version of the future PTB CEO learning the ropes under Paddy McCoy's clear-eyed tutelage

Ping   Alien Adviser who becomes Pennywell's lifelong friend and confidante

The Advisers   Pro-human alien coalition in collaboration with the PTB for 300+ years

Forest Ghosts   Mythical Amazon cannibal tribe

The Powers That Be (PTB)

PTB HQ   Sprawling underground nerve center beneath Crichton Castle and surrounding Scottish Lowlands countryside

Lost Cactus   Former clandestine research base abandoned and left to rot in the arid southwestern hinterlands

Artemus Pennywell   134-year-old PTB CEO

Andrew   Pennywell's über-advanced right-hand man

The Sisters   16 identical replicants plagued by memories of a woman named Sarah and visions of the future

Rachel Haig   24-year-old newlywed grappling with her supernatural transformation

Betty Hill   Rachel Haig's ironic alias

Owen Haig   Craves a normal post-invasion life with Rachel, while fate, and the PTB, have other plans

Barney Hill   Owen Haig's ironic alias

Roy Kendall   PTB psychologist, aka Doubletake

The Cowboy	Chrysalis Air pilot, aka Dwayne Cooper
Terrence O. Flynn Gilliam	PTB special agent, aka Flynn
Astrid Brown	Chrysalis Air test pilot and astronaut
Nicole Weiss	US Space Force veteran, Chrysalis Air test pilot, and astronaut
Nina Madsen	Stylish and sophisticated PTB administrator
Professor Richard King	122-year-old eccentric, aka Doc, whose PTB career spans salad years running Lost Cactus to chief scientist at the PTB HQ Level C Lab
Professor John Stevens	PTB scientist and engineer
Josh Jenkins	Former Green Beret turned PTB mercenary
Dave	Stateside PTB security specialist

The Council — Pennywell's 12 apostles

Aldo Santamaria	66, COO. Rose through the ranks to powerful number two post. Drowned in the tsunami that struck Half Moon Bay on Invasion Day
Franklin Pierce	72, CFO. Former floor trader and Wall Street powerbroker. Perished in Freedom Tower collapse on Invasion Day
Mitsuo Kobayashi	94, Technology Guru. Deceased AI and robotics pioneer. Used enigmatic technology to breathe life into a superhuman replicant class that includes Andrew and the Sisters
Vita Carrera	38, VP, Legal Affairs. Fiery Northern Italian redhead with familial underworld connections
Millard Lufkin	70, IOSC Administrator. Former astronaut and NASA chief. Steered the IOSC brand through daunting headwinds into a lucrative enterprise financing missions into deep space

| **Edward Laughton** | 62, Partner at Murdock & Ripley LLP. Proxy for John Murdock, 80, PTB General Counsel who perished in the firm's destroyed HQ |

| **Viraj Patel** | 42, Global Logistics. Oxford-educated former Liverpool F.C. star to Mumbai shipping magnate and notorious international playboy. His anti-gravity freighter shipyards were among the Gorks' first-strike targets |

| **Aisha Ayad** | 49, Intel Chief. Former Mossad spy with ancestral Ethiopian royal family ties. Her heroism fighting Muslim and Fascist extremists first drew the PTB's attention |

| **Professor Ernest Gann** | 32, Mathematician. Professor of Applied Mathematics and Theoretical Physics at MIT. PTB's high-value number cruncher |

| **Olivia Paquet** | 52, VP of Communications. Self-made advertising powerhouse. Her pioneering use of holography compelled the PTB to buy her agency to revitalize faltering brands |

| **Dr. Gene Simmons** | 46, VP, Global Medicines and Charities. Former surgeon general and WHO adviser before his pro-life stance and opposition to euthanasia drew the ire of a lockstep consensus. The PTB welcomed the Black father of 8 and his vast network, eager to hitch their stars to the PTB's paradigm-shifting medical advancements |

| **Anastasia Gabreski** | 38, PTB UN Ambassador and former Polish supermodel. Parlayed fame and social activism into a post as the PTB's first UN Ambassador. After her eye-popping orientation on the PTB's secret history, she morphed from a pie-in-the-sky egalitarian to a clear-eyed realist |

The Powers That Be — Allies

Dr. Farouk Said	Experienced surgeon and Cleopatra Hospital's post-invasion administrator by default
Nurse Zahra	Indomitable Cleopatra Hospital caregiver
Nurse Cleo	Flirtatious Egyptian ICU nurse overseeing Owen's recovery for the PTB
Julius Hart	Aeronautics wunderkind
President Lena Jackson	56-year-old Black Independent
Glenn Cohan	Jackson's Chief of Staff and Beltway insider
Maggie Williams	Director of National Intelligence, married to a photojournalist that was abducted with the family dog before Invasion Day
Zint	Empire Gray with a conscience
Stanley Hobbes	57, Hobbes Rare Books proprietor
Dr. Aashvi Patel	PTB staff physician and Viraj Patel's sister
Jaques St. Claire	Heir to French underworld fortune
Villa St. Claire	Haig's French HQ
Detective René Renault	Gendarmerie Nationale in Aix-en-Provence
Edward Pembroke	Chainsmoking mercenary hired by Richard King
Antoine Sheffield	Ex-Navy Seal hired by Pembroke
Elias Solomon	Pembroke's expedition security
Ariel Solomon	Pembroke's expedition security
Captain Manuel Ortega	Grizzled riverman captain of the *Piranha*
Ignatius	Ortega's young deckhand
Craig	Ex-pat stoner squatting at Fordlandia hovel
Charlie Dunning	Penny Pennywell's CDC boss
Sheriff Briscoe	Compromised Navajo reservation lawman

| **Tibbets** | FBI agent |
| **Henry Tate** | VP at Ford and Poole Capital Management, Owen's friend and boss. |

The Powers That Be — Enemies

Sebastian Duarte	Portuguese parliamentarian
Griffin Pike	Megalomaniacal tech mogul and SATstar CEO whose new world order ambitions require his ancestor Charles Pike's notes and maps leading to the lost ship's apocalyptic payload
Sapphire	Griffin Pike's beguiling assassin
Nemesis Group	Paris-based mercenary organization
Hugo le Roux	Nemesis Group's shadowy founder
Henri DeVille	38, ruthless freelance mercenary Pike hires through Nemesis Group
Leon Chayefsky	Pilot and weapons expert
Smythe	Nemesis Group henchman
Duke Rollins	Nemesis Group henchman
Senator Marjorie Cahill	Vengeful mother of the rapist killed by Rachel

Artemus Pennywell Family Tree

| **Paddy Pennywell** | Pennywell's estranged son born out of wedlock in 1954 |
| **Nathaniel Pennywell** | Pennywell's grandson—born in 1979, has a daughter out of wedlock named Emma in 1998 |

| **Emma Pennywell** | Pennywell's great-granddaughter—a troubled spirit hooked on drugs. Has daughter named Penny in 2018 before an overdose death in 2020 |
| **Penny Pennywell** | Pennywell's great-great-granddaughter—haunted by her past and the mysterious benefactor behind a secret trust that supported the orphan Penny through boarding school, college, and medical school |

Rachel's Family

Neil Alexander	Grandfather, 3x removed
The Hilltop Estate	Newport, Rhode Island family home
Marcus Xavier Alexander	70, Father, sports and events mogul harboring a dark family secret
Miriam Shirley Alexander	62, Mother, Newport socialite and bridge player extraordinaire
Joseph Tyler Alexander	20, Brother, underachieving Brown sophomore

Owen's Family

John Allen Haig	75, father, retired owner of hardware store in Montpelier, VT.
Shirley Jackson Haig	77, mother, retired math teacher
Jenny Katherine Haig	32, divorced older sister with 4 kids (Rhett 16, John 14, Katrina 10, and Gary 8) living on alimony and child support and works as grocery store assistant manager

*All ages are in the year 2044.

The original hand drawn map page from Charles Pike's notebook.
(Professor Richard King's notes indicated by asterisk.)

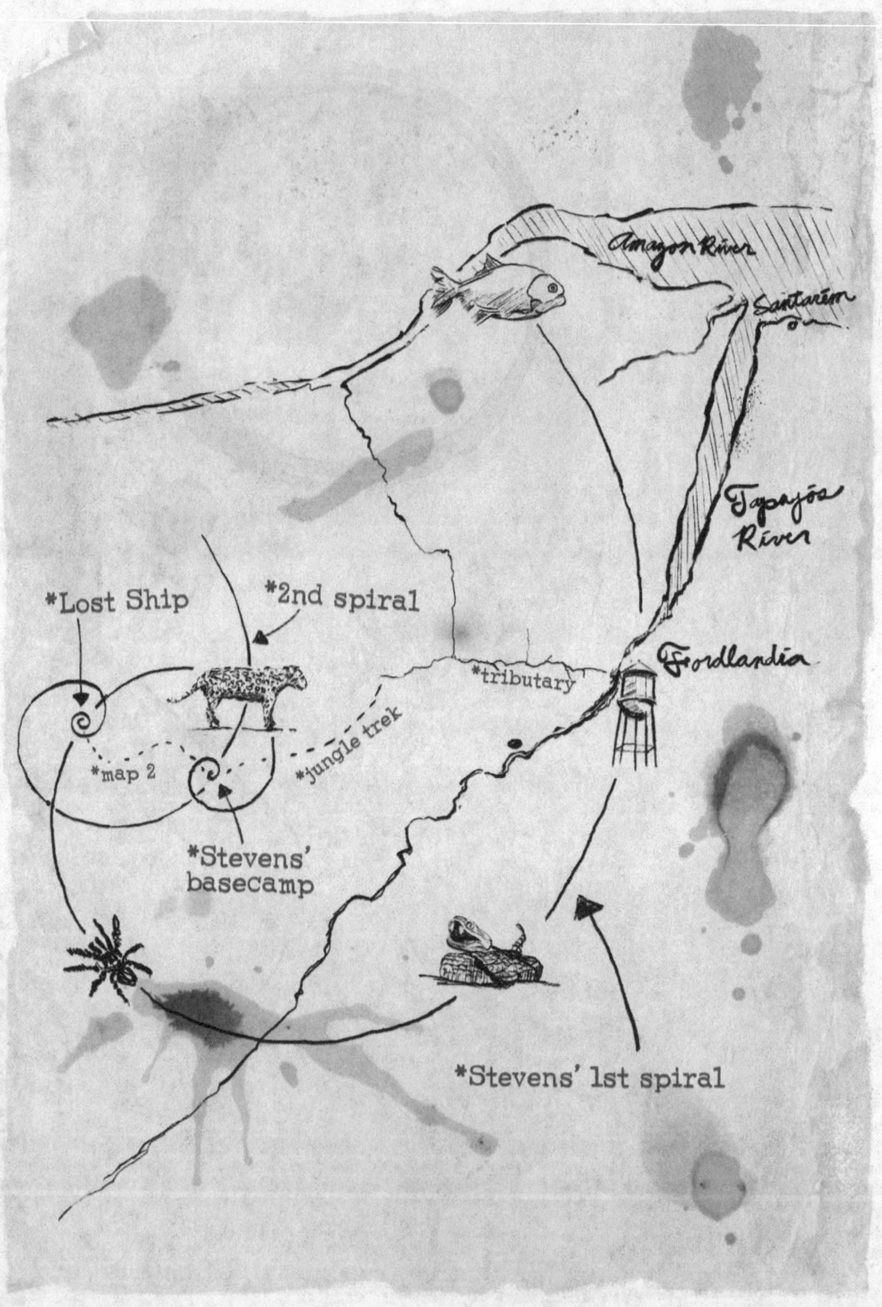

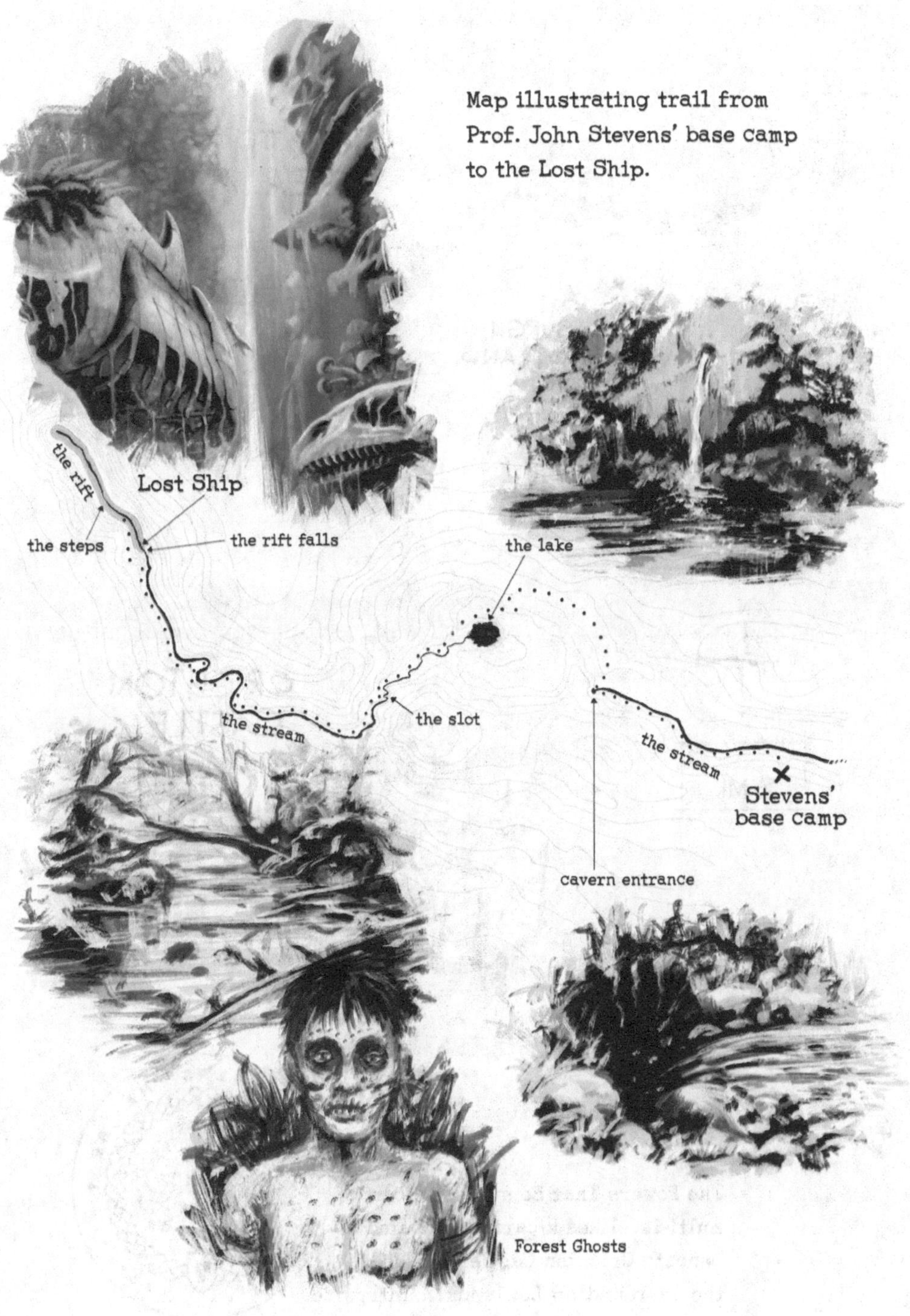

Map illustrating trail from
Prof. John Stevens' base camp
to the Lost Ship.
Lost Ship
the rift
the steps
the rift falls
the lake
the stream
the slot
the stream
Stevens' base camp
cavern entrance
Forest Ghosts

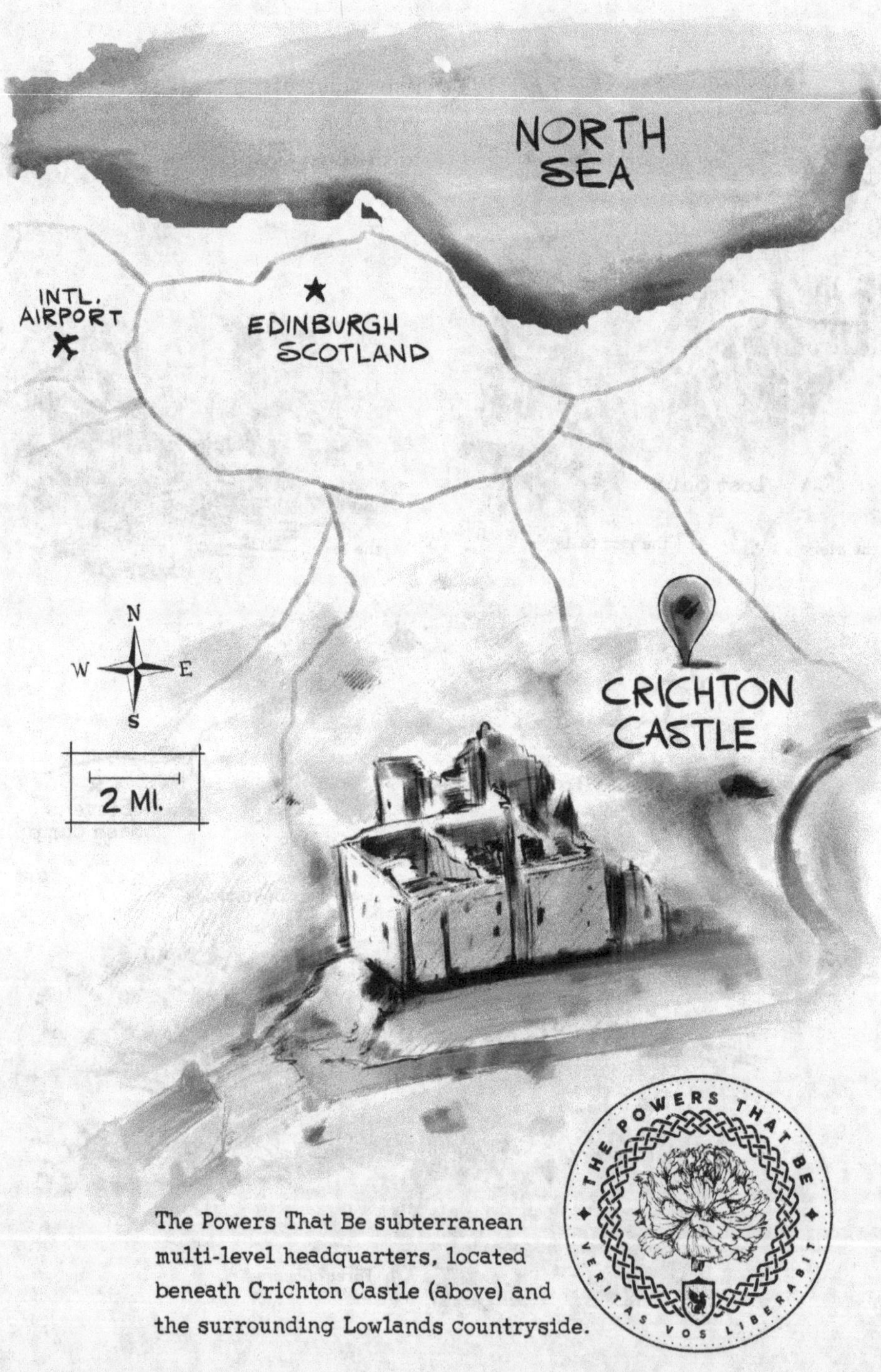

The Powers That Be subterranean multi-level headquarters, located beneath Crichton Castle (above) and the surrounding Lowlands countryside.

Prologue

The Grays | Gondwana

Sunrise | Mid-Cretaceous, 90 million years ago

Time-traveling, über-intelligent Grays arrived en masse on Earth's palaeogeographical shores 90 million years ago. The invaders conducted planetary sweeps—armed to their skinny necks—expecting resistance. They discovered a world teeming with life forms of all shapes and sizes but bereft of a dominant sentient species. Astonished by their good fortune, the hegemonic humanoids from a far-off galaxy claimed the fertile, resource-rich world as another subjugated planet in their interstellar empire.

Radiating unabashed confidence in their vaunted telekinesis and technological supremacy, the aliens dismissed the burgeoning biosphere roaming hither and yon as an insignificant, albeit violent, inconvenience. Encounters with a diverse menagerie of ill-tempered feathery reptiles brought to mind a fledgling and nasty Gorkian species, except less intelligent and more bloodthirsty, if indeed, that was possible.

With their new world awaiting domination, the Gray power structure, led by their conniving imperialist governor, weighed the pros and cons of erecting a base settlement on amorphous landmasses above and below the equatorial line. Determining northern hemispheric locations as too hot and too many bloodthirsty dinosaurs, the Grays chose a swath of land south of the equator on a forested shoreline along a shallow prehistoric sea. After clear-cutting mid-Cretaceous conifers and ferns, they erected a home base in prefab clusters forming a geometric grid stretching for miles. The sprawling base included dormitories, laboratories, armories, and warehouse facilities accommodating thousands of colonists.

Arrivals and departures buzzed overhead from the base transportation hub, pocked with circular dirt mounds designated for takeoffs and landings. Meanwhile, engineering teams embarked on missions to install a ring of communication outposts encircling the planet accompanied by cartographers, climatologists, biologists, geologists, and surveyors.

The discovery of endless seams of precious metals and deep pockets of mineral-rich gemstones proved a boon. The untold riches were loaded onto container ships and transported back to their resource-starved home planet.

* * *

Gazing black oval eyes upon the frenzied activity driven by rapacious imperialism and fanatical obedience, the captain of an intergalactic hauler watched the controlled chaos ensue from the relative safety and comfort of his command seat high up on the ship's tenth-story bridge deck with a burgeoning sense of doom. A veteran of past planetary colonization, he witnessed too many disastrous outcomes to allow this new world's intoxicating allure to lull him into complacency.

Anguished growls and snarls emanating from a hunting squadron that landed in the ship's long shadow drew the captain's attention to workers swarming the dinosaur-damaged ships like insects, unloading cages of confused and frightened animals from all corners of the planet, wailing and thrashing, gnawing thick bars with razor-sharp teeth and claws.

Shaking his bulbous head with unmasked revulsion, he pitied the poor creatures, condemned to torturous experimentation by the governor's craven scientists, performing vivisections and tinkering with dinosaur DNA and hybridization. The surviving beasts joined a growing menagerie of crossbred reptilians pacing within electrified pens like a nightmarish zoo, minus the peanuts.

A borderline treasonous rumination conjured in the veteran commander's head: "We are beyond intelligent but devoid of wisdom and empathy. Torture is not science. This mission will fail spectacularly, forcing a humiliating retreat."

The malicious base governor and his fawning retinue read the captain's thoughts, summoning him to their fortified HQ ensconced within a secure perimeter guarded by sharpshooters standing watch in high towers.

"What is your issue with our settlement, Captain? Your negative thoughts are seeding doubt within the ranks and impacting productivity and morale."

The captain shot back without moving a facial muscle, "We are in danger. It is time to go."

With a dismissive wave of his four-fingered hand, the sneering governor retorts, "Know your place, Captain. Your concern is unfounded. Rampaging dinosaurs and the planet's shifting climate pose little concern for us. Your past misadventures hold no sway here."

The space hauler captain's eyes narrow, "You are making a mistake, governor. We are all going to die here."

"Purge those thoughts, Captain, or I will feed you to one of the big ones."

* * *

Telepathically manhandled from the governor's quarters by a brutal guard, the captain tromps up a muddy path toward the sanctuary of his ship, perceiving a barometric plunge auguring another massive weather system making landfall off the roiling white-capped sea. A blinding lightning strike followed by a thunderous crack quickened his pace, paralleling a 20-foot-tall, electrified fence. A thick stand of pines shuddered and shook on the untamed opposite side as a snarling camouflaged beast mirrored his footsteps.

"This is intolerable."

Months after the captain's unheeded warnings, his proverbial bad idea mantra became impossible for the governor and his hubristic power structure to ignore. The cataclysmic shift in the planet's unpredictable climate battered the seaside equatorial base with gale-force winds and torrential downpours. Amidst the turbulent chaos, an earthquake opened a deep rift swallowing verdant forest miles into the distance. Thousands of lightning strikes ignited timberlands into fiery maelstroms. The uptick in seismic activity foreshadowed volcanic eruptions spewing white-hot ash into the darkening skies, blotting out the sun.

Terrified survivors from outposts ringing the volatile planet retreated to the main settlement on anti-gravity ships covered in dents and gouged with deep claw marks. The mortified colonists recounted horror stories of outer fencing losing power allowing voracious pack-hunting coordinated attacks, and lone reptilian hunters camouflaged to perfection standing right before unsuspecting victims before striking out in furious violence and gore-filled melees.

Unfazed by the Grays' telepathic commands and advanced weaponry, Earth's carnivorous denizens exerted their will on the aliens, opposite the Empire Grays' original plan.

It was time to pack up and leave. Now.

The space hauler captain looked on with disgust as foolhardy colonists followed the governor's edicts, disassembling the colony to the last fastener and loading it into an ad-hoc evacuation armada, serenaded by the mournful snarls and wails from the hybrid pens. Large indigenous carnivores, drawn by the anguished animals' cries, appeared out of the encroaching forest at the settlement's electrified perimeter, probing for gaps in the fencing. Meanwhile, wave-skimming ships patrolling the coastline fell prey to ravenous monsters churning out of the sea, pulling unsuspecting vessels into the inky depths.

* * *

Cognizant interplanetary competition watched their colonization failure with unbridled glee; the seething governor commanded his brilliant, scheming scientists to create a world-killing device to mitigate the humiliation associated with the ignominious withdrawal. His henchmen weaponized a virulent pathogen harvested from a species of ferocious winged reptiles and embedded it within replicating nanobots placed into a missile's nuke-tipped nosecone. A ship will carry the autonomous craft to an optimal altitude and release it into the equatorial jet stream. Its cataclysmic detonation will discharge trillions of virus-laden replicating nanobots across the planet. The brain trust projects higher life forms—not wiped out by the initial blast and radioactive fallout—will suffer slow, painful deaths as viral nanobots trigger a cascade of pandemic-driven extinctions.

The blue planet's delicate biosphere will cease to exist, transformed into another inert rock in the vacuum of space.

Packed and ready to leave, the governor issued two final directives: The captain's space hauler cannot liftoff until every treasure vat and animal pen are secure in its voluminous cargo bays. Second, the massive hauler will carry the poisonous nuke into the atmosphere retrofitted to the side of its enormous superstructure.

Adding insult to injury, the governor ordered the weapon's release mechanism mounted to the captain's chair. The burden of pressing a button dooming every creature on Earth rests on the treasonous officer's thin shoulders.

More violent electrical storms foment across the sea on evacuation day, shorting out the last battered vestiges of fortified fencing. The colonists already aboard evacuation ships begged the pilots to leave even as their fellow colonists struggled through the sucking mud and torrential rainfall, firing on shadowy shapes bursting out of the darkness, illuminated by lightning spidering through the predawn maelstrom.

***

Seated in his command chair on the cargo ship's bridge, the captain's patience wore thin overlooking his fellow colonists' panicked retreat. Avoiding the blood-red bomb release button retrofitted at his fingertips, he lamented the time and resources wasted on the wretched planet. Duty-bound by the governor's orders, he lit into muddy laborers pushing the last cartloads of chunky green and red gemstones through the sucking muck toward the cargo bay's gaping 3-story maw.

Disgusted by the cowardice and incompetence on full display, his anger exploded at lieutenants hunkered behind their stations, hoping to escape without getting their four-fingered hands dirty, "You two! Get down to the cargo bay and close those doors! Now!"

After fumbling salutes, the terrified duo disappeared through the portal.

Powerless to do anything but wait, the frustrated captain watched the governor's evacuation ship liftoff out the main view window, followed by the surviving fleet in quick succession.

Tamping down a burgeoning rage, he failed to notice the open and unguarded portal onto the command deck.

Predicting his fellow Grays had already achieved escape velocity to breach a wormhole and live to fight another day, the Gray alien verges on despair at the dire prospect of returning to his wrathful home planet and suffering the ignominy of defeat. Musing on his limited options, the wily veteran alights with an impulsive idea. "Helmsman, activate the ship's warp drive."

The crewman turns to his superior with a look of sheer confusion manifesting under his blank stare, "Captain, it is ill-advisable to do that before launch."

"We are going to die regardless; just do it."

"Do you have a target time and place in mind?"

"I leave that to your discretion."

The reluctant recruit follows the suicidal order, suppressing a mutinous desire to disobey a direct order.

Inside a cavernous ventricular expanse interconnected within the ship's labyrinthine engine decks, the warp drive's energized 8-meter Möbius illuminates to a blinding intensity and accelerates to a singular spinning blur, manifesting a threshold 90 million years in the future where the rest of the fleet already orbits farther out in the same solar system.

The captain senses satisfying shudders and shakes in response to the warp drive's ignition. A telepathic report stating the final loads of gemstones and dinosaurs were secure snapped him from his reverie.

"Close the bay doors! Do it now!"

Confused and startled by the uncharacteristic alarm in the unflappable captain's voice, a warehouse tech fumbled to initiate the door-close protocol in panicky haste but watched in terror as the enormous doors ground to a snail's pace over tracks caked in mud and gunk. Sirens wailed in the darkened bay, lit up by flashes of lightning in the predawn gloom.

With the bay doors still agonizing feet apart, a monstrous toothy carnivore blasted through the gap, bending the doors from their tracks at inoperable angles. The 10-ton predator's tail whipped from side to side, smashing containers free of their mounts and sending a king's ransom of glittering chunks skittering across the mesh decking. The dinosaur's ear-splitting roar alerted other beasts to breach the hold, dissolving the stricken alien defenses before an onslaught of terrible beasts, ripping them to shreds and splattering bluish blood and guts across the Earthly plunder scattered inside the cargo bay.

Eager to join the fray, a herd of chirping pint-sized raptors darted through the damaged doors across the chaos, breaching the ship's upper levels. Overwhelmed crew, hunkered in defense of the engine and command decks, succumbed to the voracious creatures' onslaught, ripping at aqua-colored alien flesh before hopping over the dead and dying, clawing upward toward the bridge.

The captain ordered the cumbersome unbalanced vessel's liftoff into the intensifying gale-force winds whipping off the raging sea. Lightning flashes illuminated the expansive bridge as the veteran pilot settled into his command chair, releasing the safety on the missile's release switch with agonizing screams from belowdecks jumbling together in his head.

Vaulting thousands of feet through the predawn storm with its warp drive thrumming at the speed of light, an anti-gravity engine stalled, pitching the stricken vessel into an uncontrollable counterclockwise spin. Dead and dying aliens, 10-ton dinosaurs—and everything not tethered to the deck—toppled end-over-end into a crushing heap at the bent cargo bay doors before breaking through and plummeting toward the ground. The massive doors broke free from their hinges, taking flight into the swirling gale as a jumbled tangle of dinosaurs, aliens, crates, machinery, and a hailstorm of rubies and emeralds scattered into the predawn torrent.

The captain watched as ravenous lizards wriggled over each other through the unsecured portal onto the bridge. His protection detail wilted under the onslaught while a rapacious reptilian flanking attack took out his helmsmen, struggling to regain control. Picking off dinosaurs with a sidearm from his command chair, the long-serving officer checked an altimeter as the freighter listed into a sickening spiral at 22,000 feet—far below the nuke's optimal release altitude. "So much, the better."

A furious vortex of unstable air tossed the ship like a toy, causing a chunk of loosened bulkhead to break and slam into the captain's tiny frame, sending him sprawling onto the deck. Cursing his fidelity to the sadistic governor's whims instead of leaving when he had the chance, he willed his broken body back into the seat as a palpable falling sensation overwhelmed his bleeding head. Reaching up with his four-fingered hand to grasp the red bomb release button, opting to go out with a bang, not a whimper, a chicken-sized raptor snatched his thin forearm in its powerful jaws. The prehistoric raptor yanked its head in a violent whipsaw movement, dismembering the captain's hand above the wrist.

At the end of a long and illustrious career, the space-faring captain attempted to staunch a blue-green geyser of blood from his stumped forearm. Undaunted by the alien's weak defense, vile, primitive creatures swarmed, tearing at him in a snarled frenzy of razor-sharp teeth, slashing claws, and whipping tails.

Twisting and writhing in pain and terror, he glimpsed a thick green forested canopy coming up fast outside the plummeting ship's viewscreen and braced for impact.

* * *

The Gray alien space hauler crashed back to Earth, bouncing, sliding, and skidding for miles, its momentous mass gouging a wide swath of dirt and rocks through the forest before plunging over a precipitous ledge into a deep chasm.

The broken vessel plunged over 1,400 feet before slamming nose-first into a fast-flowing river coursing through the narrow gorge near the base of a roaring waterfall. The ticking and battered craft jutted from the fast-flowing current before collapsing onto its back downstream with a tremorous thud sending vaporous clouds of dirt and rocks roiling into the humid air.

Warning lights strobed throughout the shipwreck's labyrinthine decks and passages. Dead aliens dangled from tattered restraints in crash seats bolted into the inverted deck, trickling aqua-colored blood from gaping torsos onto the bulkheads. Dismembered heads, arms, and legs lay scattered amid their still-blinking consoles. The ship's ductwork sparked and crackled as broken pipes leaked hazardous fluids onto toppled crates, boxes, and instrumentation.

An icy flow gushed through a gaping hole in the side-turned command deck, submerging the crew's mangled remains, lapping up to a shard of the captain's skull stuck like glue to the red nuke release button. Meanwhile, the scraped and battered pathogen-carrying nuke-tipped missile remained fixed to the hauler's fuselage with its world-killing nanobot payload operational and awaiting activation.

A rattled menagerie of dinosaurs escaped deactivated pens and cages, creeping through the ship's upturned passages, drawn to the warp drive's thrumming radiant invitation to skulk into another time.

* * *

The shipwreck remained in its sideways stasis through the ages as the waterfall and fast-flowing river dried to a trickle, exposing thousands of theropod prints in the dried and cracked riverbed. Hardening sand littered with bones and rocks built up in stratified layers preserving the ship's hull in solid rock. Hidden and protected in the deep and narrow chasm, the ship weathered epochal asteroid strikes and drifting strata under tons of sediment that raised, lowered, and moved its Gondwana position hundreds of miles westward through time. From the tumultuous end of the Cretaceous Period and into the Cenozoic epochs, the space hauler was preserved in sedimentary layers stratifying into red and ochre layers of granite and limestone as a nascent South American continent took shape.

Over the last 10 million years, groundwater seeped toward the hot and humid surface, boring through sedimentary layers and hollowing an expansive chain of subterranean grottos connected by narrow twisting tunnels, dead-end alcoves, and antechambers dripping with deep freshwater pools where most of the lost ship's well-preserved former glory lies in total darkness.

Skeletal sections of the lost ship's loading bay and the missile jut from jagged limestone at the bottom of a steep, narrow gorge hidden under an impenetrable green mass where prehistoric beasts scrambled through a glowing threshold into a world 90 million years removed from their Gondwana domain. From asexual half-ton Carcharodontosaurus juveniles to a panoply of meat and veggie-eating hybrid reptiles, they melded into their new Amazon forest home—a speck on a map lost to the ravages of time.

* * *

For centuries, a legendary cannibalistic tribe safeguards the narrow rift valley and its strange reptilian denizens with a cunning and zealous fervor, adopting the ghost-white visage of the ancient alien race they discovered upon passing through the portal to another time.

Gray Invasion Fleet | Near Ganymede
90 million years later | 1928 AD

Descendants of the empirical Gray species that evacuated Cretaceous Earth in ignominious defeat exited a wormhole at the outskirts of Earth's solar system in 1928. Intent on reclaiming their prize, the invasion fleet assembled behind Ganymede, Jupiter's largest moon, and reconnoitered the situation. Cursing their bad timing, they discovered a cloaked Gorkian armada already prepositioned much closer to Earth, poised for invasion. The reptilian Gorks had 90 million years of evolutionary progress under their thick, scaly hides and were renowned throughout the universe as ruthless and bloodthirsty ravagers of planets.

Another roadblock to reclaimed glory persisted in a repeating message ostensibly installed on the fertile world by none other than the universe's preeminent moral enforcers, the Light Specters. The explicit warning stated to leave Earth unmolested or suffer their wrath. With time now a meaningless concept in the Grays' advanced eyeballs, they chose to wait and allow the Light Specters' beacon and the Gork situation to play out.

Like other resource-starved species across the universe, the Empire Grays viewed Earth's untapped riches as ripe for the taking if not for the Light Specters' stern warning. However, it proved only a matter of time before the threatening message was deactivated or rendered moot upon witnessing the humans' knack for self-destruction with the advent of mechanized warfare and clumsy atomic experimentation.

Regardless, the Grays relished the concept of unleashing their ancient world killer on whoever or whatever was left standing in the way. However, one last confounding obstacle thwarted their vengeful return: 90 million years of continental drift left the shipwreck holding their world killer lost within thousands of miles of untamed forest on the South American continent.

Gray scout | Fordlandia
05:22 a.m. | November 1, 1928

The Empire Grays dispatched pill-shaped scout ships on a mad dash for Earth, zigzagging to avoid the violent Gorks—and a bizarre gathering of autonomous cubed bots appearing out of the ether. Slinging past Mars undetected, the squadron slows to breach Earth's atmosphere before shooting across the sky to feet above the dense Brazilian jungle.

The reconnaissance craft vector onto preset grids, searching for the long-lost shipwreck and its lethal payload.

One of the pill-shaped ships, approximating the mass of a compact car, oriented a rounded end eastward and moved across the treetops. A deep-blue conical light radiated downward from its reflective, seamless hull, permeating the strata thousands of feet beneath the forest floor. The consecutive paper-thin two-mile-wide cross-sections scanned a 90-million-year-old paleographical map that no longer existed.

The 3-foot alien pilot ensconced within a spartan cockpit monitored a virtual display, adjusting the scan to stay within a geologic record corresponding with Mid-Cretaceous Earth.

Reaching the end of his first grid assignment, he pressed a four-digit hand atop a cylindrical instrument and popped out a nickel-sized disk. The alien placed the encrypted high-definition recording into a silver pocket on his suit and steered northeast, probing farther into the rugged interior. A sensor alerted the Gray of a new human outpost along a muddy river snaking through the endless sea of trees.

Suspicious of human development so far removed from the nearest population center, the Scout's superiors upgraded his reconnaissance assignment into a surveillance mission: *Permission to land and determine the human outpost's purpose. Avoid contact.*

* * *

The Gray scout landed in a verdant glade, aware of multiple wary eyes watching his every move: just indigenous lower life forms, nothing of concern.

Pressing through the thick jungle toward the river and the human development, voices pierced the humid air through the trees.

Before he could backtrack onto a different path, two humans wielding primitive cutting instruments parted thick vegetation, staring in slack-jawed disbelief. Before he could react, six more dark-skinned males broke from the underbrush athwart his exit, forming an even-spaced semi-circle around his stance.

The scout mulled his only option: kill the humans and vacate the area. The male on the far right made the first move, stepping forward with a raised metal tool. Without remorse for the lower life forms, the Gray drew a weapon and double-tapped concentrated energy at the poor man's chest. The human froze in a rictal pose as soft tissue melted from bones into a pool of sticky goo on the loamy ground where he once stood.

Realizing he had no choice but to exterminate the rest, the scout quickly shot each man from right to left. With his weapon pointed at the eighth human, he watched the male subject cower with arms raised in a vain attempt at protection, *"Humans are foolish creatures. This is too easy."*

The scout pulled the trigger, but the weapon produced a harmless click-clack.

The human lowered his arms and checked himself. Wetness spread down his grubby pants, but otherwise, he was unharmed aside from his pride.

Ten feet apart, yet light years removed from each other's pasts, they exchanged confused stares. The Gray flooded the young man's mind with disorienting threats, but his brain proved impervious to telepathic intimidation.

With the high ground ceded, the human raised his hatchet and charged at the Gray.

The alien caught the glint of a metal blade before it sliced through his silver flight suit with a sickening thwack. The kid yanked the ax free and swung it sideways, severing a skinny arm and thwacking halfway into the alien's torso, bleeding toxic aqua-colored blood. The third whack separated the bulbous gray head from the bony shoulders. The disembodied noggin landed upturned on the dirt with its deep black soulless eyes widened in shock and horror.

Though the clear and present danger had passed, the Portuguese day laborer stomped the head into mush. Crazed with fear and loathing for the hideous murderer, Machado hacked the alien into a pile of aqua-colored flesh mixed with weird glowing bones jutting through its tattered silver suit.

Covered in sticky blue-green alien residue and chunks of smelly gray flesh, the inconsolable young man raced back to the new settlement to report the murderous and ungodly incident to his foreman, Charles Pike.

He will know what to do.

* * *

The nickel-sized recording of the day's scan remained secure within a pocket on the alien's tattered silver suit.

The shipwreck's telltale signature was missed on the scout's first sweep—a mistake the Grays would have discovered upon a closer inspection of the reassembled three-dimensional scans when it returned to the fleet.

Another missed opportunity for the Empire Grays.

* * *

A shadowy form entered the kill box in the early-morning pitch-blackness, with a cacophony of jungle sounds masking his footfalls atop the loamy ground. Mindful not to disturb the crime scene, he stepped over the deceased humans to the mutilated Gray scout.

Probing a long, four-fingered hand into a tattered pocket, he removed the cylindrical disk. With a sad look at the horrific scene, he made his way back into the jungle.

Charles Pike | Fordlandia
04:35 p.m. | November 14, 1928

14 days after the murders and his cover-up of the disturbing crime scene, Charles Pike was fit to be tied. Recruited by none other than Henry Ford from a posh Detroit civil engineering firm after a twenty-year stint in the Army Corps of Engineers, the burly man swore at the primitive work conditions in the middle of the Brazilian Amazon. Pouring another cup of black coffee, he stood before an unfurled topographical map delineating the industrialist's bought-and-paid-for parcel of riverfront jungle atop a worktable, placing rocks at the corners to hold it flat.

"What a waste of time and money."

Pike's head swooned, auguring another pattering of blood dripped onto the parchment from his pugnacious nose. Dabbing his pale, sweaty face with a stained hankie, the troubled man's attention drifted from the wafer-thin pretense of engineering Ford's nascent rubber plantation onto his real mission secured within a duffel bag shoved beneath his drafting table.

Verging on madness, Pike lifted the bag off the wood planks and dropped it atop the table without ceremony. Pulling open the zipped enclosure, he removed the enigmatic discovery that prompted Ford's interest in his services: a rough-hewn chunk of limestone discovered by local Portuguese day laborers digging a foundation.

Pike turned the two-foot stone toward him and traced a ruddy fingertip through its detailed map and spiral design. It resembled a baby snail piggybacked atop its big brother's perfect shell overlaying a chiseled representation of the Tapajós River basin and beyond.

A crooked smile widened under his mustache, admiring the expert craftsmanship, "How did those primitive motherfuckers manage this level of mathematical precision?"

Pike recalled the day he came into possession of the enigmatic discovery. Under the watchful eye of Ford execs huddled around the stone, a shiftless bow-tied archeologist conducted a confidential debrief: "… Local legends state that an ancient shipwreck lies hidden at the nucleus of the smaller spiral. Moreover, the lost ship contains an untold fortune in rare gems and a world-killer payload. Mr. Pike, your job is determining if this tale holds water."

"How do I do that?"

One of the suits shot Pike a cold-eyed stare down, "That is your problem, Pike. Figure it out."

Pike scoffed at the Ford execs and the haughty academic who had no clue about the perils involved in such an expedition. They all up and left for civilization, leaving him as the only person at Fordlandia with knowledge of the artifact's existence. To top it off, the ungrateful assholes showed no gratitude for his ad hoc cover-up of a gruesome mass murder and the unwanted attention it would have cast on Ford and his dumbass rubber plantation. Let alone the fucking dead alien that infected his blood, leaving misguided forays into the wilderness out of the question for the foreseeable future.

But the joke was on them. After recovering from the weird alien virus, Pike would set out on his own—or better yet—sell the information to the highest bidder. In the meantime, he needed to hide the artifact from prying eyes.

Producing his trusty notebook from a vest pocket, Pike flipped past sketches, architectural renderings, and notes to a dog-eared page with his hand-drawn reproduction of the stone artifact, "Better check my map against this one more time for good measure."

With an engineer's eye for detail, Pike compared his map to the artifact, paying close attention to iconic landmarks he drew in place of the snails' Fibonacci spirals—disguising the 90-million-year-old shipwreck's location.

Dipping a fountain pen into an inkwell, Pike added one final inked blotch indicating the baby snail's central nucleus. "X marks the fucking spot."

Satisfied with his forgery of the stone's enigmatic treasure map, Pike grabbed a hammer and broke off the baby snail portion before smashing the remaining artifact into unreadable chunks. Peering outside his tented office to ensure no one was watching, Pike scraped the shards into the bag and set out for the river.

After tossing the artifact into the Tapajós, a chunk at a time, Pike trod uphill to a spectacular Brazil Nut tree. Reeling from itchy bumps and a steady fever, Pike studied the remarkable specimen, knowing the tree was designated for preservation betwixt the planned water tower and sawmill. Casting a paranoid glance around to ensure no one was watching, Pike pulled his overweight 42-year-old frame into the Brazil Nut's branches and climbed like a monkey high up into its thick foliage. Reaching a fern-infested hollow midway up the massive trunk, he hid the artifact with the baby snail spiral inside before enduring more scrapes and cuts descending back out of the tree like a lead weight.

Stepping back from the tree, Pike opened his notebook to a new page. With pencil in hand, the expert draftsman wiped his dirty, sweaty brow, rendering a detailed drawing of the tree with a small arrow concealed amongst the leaves and branches pointing at the hollow halfway up the trunk.

Pike returned to his tent and locked the precious notebook in the drawer beneath his drafting table.

"Ford can go fuck himself; after I recuperate, I'm selling the lost ship's location to the highest bidder."

Paddy McCoy | Fordlandia

08:35 a.m. | November 16, 1928

The strange ailment afflicting Charles Pike worsened. Swatting at flies drawn to itchy pustules manifesting in the folded nether reaches of his stocky frame, he chomped an unlit cigar below his waxed handlebar mustache, cursed his bad luck, and resisted an urge to scratch like the dickens. *"It can't be from that alien craft and its mutilated occupant. Tell me I'm not infected. Goddammit, Chuck, old boy, get a grip."*

The squeal of wet brakes distracted Pike's focus outside the opened front flaps of his olive-drab canvas tent-cum-office perched atop a three-foot-tall plywood riser. Watching two men in black suits hop from a Model T pickup truck on a beeline toward his tent, he hustled behind the messy table, placed the notebook in a shallow tool drawer under the tabletop, and slid into his raised swivel office chair.

After an arduous trip culminating with fifteen hours steaming up the Tapajós river from Santarém, the sopping pair hustled to the relative dryness of Pike's elevated space, offering perfunctory hat tips.

Realizing the pair were not much for formal introductions, Pike broke the ice, "My name is Pike. Charles Pike. I oversee this parcel of the jungle. Let me guess … you two are overdressed agricultural inspectors from Sao Paulo, or you are here to investigate the strange event from 16 days ago. The suits are a dead giveaway. Shit. The feds didn't waste any time sending you guys down here." Noting the marked age difference between the two men, he mused the clean-shaven younger G-man hefting a backpack could pass for a high school student.

The men exchanged glances while drying off and draping wet suit jackets over chair backs. The older man took in the 20x14-foot workspace with a perfunctory nod while adjusting his shoulder-holstered sidearm but refrained from taking the bait on Pike's fed reference.

Reminiscent of past government interactions throughout his public service career, Pike sipped strong Brazilian coffee from his Ford logo mug, familiar with the unlikely buttoned-down duo's silent treatment. Gesturing to the half-full pot on an extended wooden workbench amidst stacks of rolled blueprints and site plans, "Help yourselves, gentlemen; it's better than the swill you get back in DC."

The wiry six-foot junior G-man slung his backpack on a table and availed himself to the coffee pot. Checking a ceramic mug, he liberated a three-inch centipede onto the floorboards and swiped the cup before filling it halfway with coffee. Retrieving a flask from a deep trouser pocket, he added a shot of Scotch and took a long pull, "That hits the spot."

Pike's gray eyes narrowed on the senior partner, "Since I am doing all of the talking, allow me to clear the air. You guys came down here to investigate the crime scene and quarantine the" pausing for effect, "so-called evidence. Is that about right?" Seeing the older man with the gray crewcut produce a serious-faced nod in the affirmative, he proceeded, "Well, my job is to turn this shithole into Main Street, USA. I don't have time to waste with any cloak-and-dagger bullshit. This incident has already set us back over two weeks, with an entire parcel designated for a grove of rubber trees now off-limits. The sooner you get that thing out of there, the faster I can get back to business, capeesh?"

"Of course, Mr. Pike, you will have our complete cooperation. Your employer wants this to remain classified, as does the US government. Any bullshit, as you so eloquently put it, would likely end this venture before the ceremonial tapping of the first rubber tree."

The younger man set down his cup and loosened his tie, "Is it always like this down here?"

Pike turned on the kid with mock incredulity, "Like this? This is fucking tolerable. You should have been here when our steamer first made landfall. You needed a snorkel to take a shit!"

The older man raised an eyebrow at Pike's obvious discomfort and the trickle of blood seeping down his mustache. Averting his eyes from the sick man's obvious distress, he gazed beyond a sea of tree stumps toward the untamed Amazonian jungle.

Pike took a quick swipe at his nose and tried to change the subject, "I know my way around the capital. Which department are you guys with, again?"

The younger man laughed, "Trust me, you never heard of it."

"Artemus, that's enough."

Pike smiled at the kid in his black trousers and starched-white button-down shirt, "Artemus? Does anybody call you Art or Artie?"

"Just Artemus, or Mr. Pennywell, if you prefer."

"Look, son, don't get your knickers in a wad. I'm just making small talk. The locals speak Portuguese, and I'm surrounded by dumb-as-rocks America-hating ex-pats."

The older man responded in a low and authoritative tone, "Speaking of the locals, where is your eyewitness?"

Swiveling in his chair, Pike indicated toward a less-than-enthusiastic congregation of day laborers malingering in the drizzle. "Well, shit." Clenching the cigar in his teeth, he wondered why his staff had not cracked the proverbial whip—spotting a clipboard-wielding aide hurrying to complete a headcount in the steady rain, "Mr. Guido! We're not paying these fuckers to stand around with a collective thumb up their assholes! We got a jungle to clear! Get the tools passed out on the double!"

The man squinted into the shadowed tent beyond the open flaps toward his boss's disembodied voice, "Yes, sir, Mister Pike."

Guido Pellegrini, a chain-smoking, rail-thin Italian American from Staten Island, New York, directed another worker to unlock a tool-laden trailer hitched behind a Caterpillar tractor. The assembly of fit young men culled from the local Portuguese Indian population waited for Guido's high-pitched mangling of their names before approaching the second banana charged with passing out the tools. Ambling past Mr. Guido with a machete, ax, or shovel, they proffered odd smiles, snickering at his perplexed facial expression.

Paranoid, Guido snatched an ax handle from his partner and tossed it at the next recruit. Checking his clipboard, he spits out, "Manuel Machado."

"Yes, sir, that's my name." The 26-year-old Brazilian tried not to smile at the Italian.

Squinting from under an oversized hard hat, Guido blew a

smoke ring in Manuel's face, "You got a problem, boy?"

"No problem, boss man. It's just that you have a spider on your back."

Noting the furry eight-legged specimen, Guido's wide-eyed partner raised a spade in self-defense and took a long backward step, "Damn, Guido, that is a big one."

Mr. Guido's gaunt face turned ghost white as his cigarette dropped to the mud from thin lips curled into a frightful rictus. Upon angling a scrawny arm over his back, sweaty fingertips contacted a furry eight-legged critter, sending it skittering over the opposite shoulder, down his beating chest, and stopping atop his groin. The indigenous carnivore's long legs dug into Guido through his thin khaki trousers, ready for a fight, "Jesus H. Christ, it's latched on to my nuts! I hate this fucking jungle!"

The government men appear annoyed by the comic spectacle in the mud; however, it is Pike's first genuine laugh in weeks. Downing the last of his coffee, he squinted faltering eyes onto his harried subordinate, flailing like a ninny, while the laborers formed a circle, rooting for the spider, "What the hell, Mr. Guido? It's just a horny spider. You should be happy. It's the most action you will ever see." He wheeled toward the two men with a nervous laugh, noting their circumspect behavior, "You two play much poker? You got the faces for it."

The locals' laughter faded as they disappeared down a rutted trail toward their assigned tract of the jungle. Meanwhile, the camp doctor arrived on the scene, scratching his balding head while looking from his worn-out bug bite kit to the eight-inch arachnid attached to Mr. Guido's genital region.

* * *

Swinging the dripping wet ax over his shoulder, Manuel scrambled to join a line of laborers heading toward the jungle. The group turned in unison, stopping the young Brazilian man dead in his tracks. The senior laborer pointed his sharp machete at Manuel with a threatening scowl, "You are bad luck, Manuel! Find yourself another group!"

Charles Pike heard the stand-off and trained his hazed vision onto the eyewitness, Manuel Machado, left standing alone in the mud, "There he is!" Eager to get the suits off his back, the civil engineer rasped out a coughed command at the sole survivor of a nightmare just getting started, "Machado! Get your ass up here!"

* * *

Standing alone with the ax over his shoulder, like a skinny Brazilian version of Paul Bunyan, the kid spun toward Pike's rasped command, "Who? Me?"

Slogging across a graded oblong area outlined with yellow string stretched between wood stakes jutting from the mud, Manuel tromped toward the high tent and the three men waiting inside. A conversational English fluency already had the suspicious locals keeping him at arm's length; however, the promise of a real house, indoor plumbing, and a more than adequate day's wage beat the alternative: squalid abject poverty.

Hiding a smirk, he decided to downplay his sharp-tongued wit and missionary-taught education during his forthcoming interrogation.

The fledgling outpost along the banks of the Tapajós River is where an American industrialist named Henry Ford set his sights on terraforming dense Brazilian rainforest into Fordlandia, the world's premier rubber plantation. The settlement will house an American colony on the high ground, with schools, hotels, libraries, a swimming pool, and a golf course. The locals hunker in two-family bungalows down by the river.

To Manuel, the idea appeared preposterous, "Ford picked a helluva spot to build his utopian paradise." So far, it was nothing but mosquitos, snakes, spiders, rampant yellow fever, and malaria. Not to mention the otherworldly danger he and his unlucky colleagues had the misfortune to stumble across in the jungle.

Ten feet from the overdressed men standing atop the riser under the olive-green tent, the kid stopped in his muddy tracks, "Yes, sirs. I am Manuel Machado. I was part of the work crew that encountered the creature."

Hitting mid-morning in the heart of the Amazon rainforest, hundreds of miles from the nearest civilization, the thermometer passed the century mark, and bright Brazilian sunshine burnt off rain clouds, revealing a cerulean sky and unrelenting humidity, like breathing underwater.

Determining the scared kid was on the level, the older G-man allowed his less intimidating protégé to take the lead—the good cop, bad cop routine. Leaning back in a cross-legged repose, he pulled the brim of his hat down over his eyes and loosened his shoulder-holstered Colt 45 revolver. "Proceed with the questioning, Artemus."

Pennywell jumped off the riser and splashed across a puddle, extending a hand, "Thank you for your cooperation, Mr. Machado. My name is Artemus …."

Surprised by the flipped seniority, Pike interjected, "Hey, Art, bring him up here so we can all hear what he has to say."

The young Brazilian stepped up and into American territory, barefoot in a stained and filthy half-buttoned shirt hanging loose on his skinny frame over a pair of holey dungarees. Manuel's intelligent brown eyes dart around the space: westernized gadgets, coffee mugs, stacks of papers, maps, blueprints, and expensive-looking drafting tools lie scattered about as his gaze lands on a pile of National Geographics.

Pennywell sipped from his cup and gestured at a chair, "Have a seat."

Manuel looked upon the clean-cut American's chiseled face and disarming smile, lending the younger man a poise and gravitas beyond his years, "Me?"

"Yes, you. Would you care for a cup of coffee? Sans centipedes, of course," enjoying a little inside joke.

Manuel's eyes rested on the exposed grip of Artemus' mean-looking holstered revolver, "Uh, sure."

Pike huffed a belabored sigh, hunched over the bloodstained topographical map while half-listening to the conversation and administering to his leaky nostrils.

Artemus Pennywell proffered a piping hot mug and a warm smile to the dark-skinned local, "Where did you learn to speak English, Manuel?"

"My parents were killed when I was a boy. Jesuit missionaries raised me. They taught me English," feeling more at ease; he added, "also, some Spanish."

"Jesuit missionaries, eh? Down here doing the Lord's work, no doubt. Are they still around?"

"No. The missionaries left to convert a tribe of cannibals years ago and never returned."

Pike coughed a mocking laugh from his raised chair, "Say one thing about those Catholics: they'll turn you into a saint or die trying."

After making a sign of the cross upon hearing the foreman's blasphemy, Manuel continued, "The priests treated me well. They taught me to believe we are all created in God's image. It makes what we found so ... how do I say the words?" Manuel's thin body shuddered, conjuring the repressed memory, "The creature warned bad things will happen. They want to kill us all."

"How did it communicate this to you, Manuel?"

"I, I don't know. It did not speak. Its mouth, its mouth was nothing. Its face was white. But the eyes!" Manuel leaned forward, forgetting the mug cupped in his calloused hands. "The eyes spoke to us."

"How many of you were out there?"

"It was me and seven others working a section of forest about an hour from here on foot."

Pennywell pulled up a back-turned chair and sat facing the shaken young man, "Manuel, what happened to your friends?"

Pike pushed back from the drafting table in his squeaky-wheeled chair and spoke for his inconsolable employee, "They are dead, Art. All seven of them. It is why we quarantined the entire parcel and called in the cavalry in the first place. The creature melted the skin right off their bones."

Masking alarm bells ringing in his head, Artemus turned toward Pike's pallid, sweating countenance, "You don't say. Where are they now?"

Memories of the weird event 16 days earlier flooded Manuel's frontal cortex with a vengeance. Doubling over in his seat, the man sobbed as the forgotten coffee cup loosened from his shaking grip and crashed onto the floorboards. "With no time to escape, it killed them where they stood, but I did not die." Recounting the paranormal episode aloud for the first time, he concluded, "I could hear its thoughts inside my head. The thing was surprised I survived. It tried again."

"So, what did you do, Manuel?"

The educated and devout 26-year-old baptized father of two wiped his tear-eyed face on a dirty sleeve, "I hacked it to death with my ax. And now, Mr. Pennywell, I will go straight to hell."

Pike coughed bloody phlegm into a trash can and snorted a derisive guffaw, "For the love of Christ, kid. That thing was not human! Don't you get it? That's why these fellers came down here in the first place." He wheezed and hacked, spewing more bright red specks atop his map before addressing the elephant in the room, "It came from somewhere else. I don't need a Jesuit education to figure that out."

The older man snapped awake from his catnap, "Mr. Pike, are you sure no one else has been in the near-vicinity of the murder scene?"

Taken aback, thinking the older guy was asleep the whole time, "Yeah. Why?"

"Have you been out there?"

Pike's failing eyes widened with a sudden epiphany, "Wait a goddamn minute, here. I know who you guys are."

Before Pike could finish his sentence, Paddy pulled his revolver and shot Pike between the eyes.

Manuel gawked at the smoking gun in disbelief. Pennywell addressed his colleague, "Christ, Paddy, was that necessary?"

Paddy holstered his weapon and stood with a weary sigh. "Yes, however, unfortunate for Mr. Pike. Artemus, keep an eye out, will you?" Tipping back his hat, he moved behind the drafting table and wheeled Pike's slumped form out of the way. After memorizing the blood-spattered tabletop in situ, he yanked the topographical map from under the rocks and lit it on fire. Letting it burn from his outheld fingertip grasp, Paddy turned on Machado with a penetrating stare, "Did anybody else, aside from Mr. Pike here, visit the murder scene?"

Gobsmacked by the violent turn of events, Manuel stammered a reply, "No. Mr. Pike contained the area immediately afterward. It is already isolated; we operate far out on the fringes of Mr. Ford's plantation."

Paddy noted the kid's sincerity while dropping the smoldering remnant into the metal trash receptacle to finish burning, "What about the doctor? Or that Italian fellow with the spider wrapped around his dick? Or any other outsiders like Art or myself?" Paddy's keen-eyed gaze searched the olive-drab interior while pressing the young man further, "How can you be sure no other person ventured out there to see what all the fuss was about?"

"No, Señor. I don't think so."

The older agent softened his approach, "Okay. Please relax, young man. I believe you." Mumbling to himself, "Now, where the bloody hell is it?" Paddy stepped back and cast his eyes around the tent.

Catching his partner's perplexed gaze, Pennywell offered, "Can I help? What are we looking for?"

"Pike's notebook containing a forged map reproduction leading to a lost ship." Frisking Pike's seated repose, Paddy avoids the trickling of toxic blood seeping down the dead man's forehead and dripping off his chubby cheek, "Nope, he would not carry it on his person." Turning to examine the drafting table from Pike's angle, Paddy bent low and discovered a wide, shallow, locked drawer underneath. "What have we here?"

As the tall man picked the cheap lock and pulled out the drawer, Machado reiterated with abject certitude, "Nobody disobeyed Mr. Pike, er, the foreman's orders. Nobody."

Paddy did not reply, preferring to let the young man squirm while sifting through the contents with the tip of his penknife.

"Mr. Pike swore me to secrecy. He even threatened my family. I have not seen my wife and children. Do you know if they are okay?"

Checking the empty grounds outside the tent, Pennywell turned to Machado with a reassuring smile, "Don't worry, Mr. Machado, I am sure the wife and kids are fine."

Suppressing a smile at the young man's genuine concern for his family, Paddy pulled out a worn leather-bound notebook, "Eureka." Flipping through the pages, he paused at a cryptic map with no coordinates or legend to unlock its secrets. Pocketing it in his jacket, he searched the tent before turning to the young Brazilian, "Lead us to the crime scene, Mr. Machado."

"Why did you shoot Mr. Pike? Was he infected?

Pennywell patted the much smaller man on the back and answered for his friend and mentor, "Your boss was already dead. Isn't that right, Paddy."

"Yes, Artemus, he just did not know it yet."

* * *

The trio tromped through sucking mud, bisecting a clear-cut parcel toward a hand-painted trail marker spiked into the ground at the jungle's edge. Pennywell smirked at the crude skull and crossbones painted on the sign as they proceeded past without heeding its blunt warning heading single file down a rutted path. Thick green underbrush closed around them, and the narrow footpath dissolved into a suggested way forward. Up on point, Manuel hacked at large leaves and vines with his razor-sharp blade while huffing an over-the-shoulder comment to the men in black on his heels, "Now you can see why I am certain no one else followed out here over the last two weeks."

In the semi-darkness with the sun blotted out by an impenetrable canopy high above, Pennywell adjusted his backpack and limbos under a low mossy branch. Glancing back to check on his older and wiser partner, he couldn't resist a subtle jibe, "Low bridge, Paddy."

McCoy bent his tall frame, scraping under the sopping obstruction, "I am getting too old for this."

Smoothing aside a monstrous leaf, Pennywell smiled at a bright-green snake coiled on top, "Hello there, little fella." Needling his less-than-agile partner, he laughed, "I will never get too old for fieldwork." Tapping the flask in his left pants pocket, he checked Manuel's position, separating farther ahead. Noting the Brazilian's adeptness with an ax, clearing a path through the leaves and branches with a vengeance, he imagined what the kid did to that unsuspecting alien. Soaked in sweat, he paused to knock mud from his boots and tried to purge the gory image from his head.

An hour-plus into the jungle trek, the trail hit a steep embankment at the wetter-than-wet reaches of a jungle bog spiked with trees laden with mosses and plants jutting skyward from the tranquil dark water. A cacophony of birds and monkeys screeching overhead drowned out Pennywell's muttered curses as he watched Manuel wade into the tea-colored swamp. Unsure of what lurked below the surface, he took a tentative step into the knee-deep murkiness, "You ready for this, Paddy?"

Panting and struggling to keep up, Paddy slid down the slippery trail and splashed into the swamp, "Absolutely, my boy. I grew up exploring the Scottish moors. This obstruction is a mere mud puddle by comparison."

Squishing boots into the swampy bottom disturbed clouds of decay swirling around his legs, "If you say so, Paddy."

The audible splash of something big swimming below the surface elicited a low whistle toward Manuel, 40 feet farther ahead, "What happened to our trail, Manuel?"

"It gets worse, Señor Pennywell."

Fording the bog, Pennywell scanned the semi-transparent brown water for hungry caiman and instead caught a glint of something jutting from decaying Amazonian silt. Scooping it out in a handful of greenish muck, he turned toward his Scottish mentor, "Hey, Paddy, check it out."

The taller man sloshed to Pennywell's side, "What did you find, agent?"

Rinsing off goo and muck in the muddy brown water, the younger agent held the strange dripping object into a narrow shaft of midday sun piercing the opaque canopy, "It appears to be a bone; however, it is not human, that's for sure."

"It is fluorescent, much like our extraterrestrial friends' skeletal structure." Casting a wary eye around the swamp, he continued, "Break out the forensics kit, Artemus. You remembered to bring it with you, right? Don't tell me we left it on the boat."

Pennywell produced a box of evidence pouches from a side pocket in his pack, "Don't worry, chief, I have it right here." Dropping the alien bone fragment inside, he zipped it shut and peered around the swampy environs. "I bet there is some big bass in here."

"I didn't know you liked to fish."

"I don't, just saying."

Manuel stammered at the pair with unmasked trepidation, "Sirs, the bog is not a good place to stop and rest. What are you doing?"

"Collecting evidence, Manny. Collecting evidence."

Paddy slipped into a natural Scottish brogue, eschewing his Americanized accent, and splashed past Pennywell in the hip-deep water, "Come on then, laddy, let's keep it moving."

Pennywell lingered behind, peering into the water for more bones, "You know what this means, Paddy? Scavengers have already consumed the alien's remains and defecated them all over the goddamn jungle. So much for site containment."

Fording twenty paces ahead of Pennywell's perplexed stance, Paddy's reply echoed across the swamp, "Site containment is not our primary mission."

Exiting the bog onto a muddy bank of twisted roots and vines, Manuel wrung dirty water from his clinging shirt and checked on the Americans' slow and dangerous progress with a frustrated sigh. A whisp of air and a sharp sting in the side of his head knocked him sideways. The Brazilian laborer's trembling hand reached up on reflex and pulled a bamboo dart out of his right temple. His vision went black, garbling an unintelligible warning cry to the others, toppling facedown into the water.

Noting the guide's inexplicable nosedive with a keen alarm, Paddy drew his weapon and peered into the shadows while splashing toward the young Brazilian, "Artemus, we have company!"

Pulling Manuel's slumped form out of the dark water, Paddy cursed upon seeing the man's dead-eyed stare. Another dart shot through the air, piercing the leather-bound notebook tucked inside a pocket sewn into the left breast of his soaked jacket. Before he could take cover, a second dart hit his jugular. The tall Scotsman arched backward in shock and anger, yanking out the feathered dart's barbed tip in his faltering grasp. Already stricken by its lethal toxin, he crumpled onto a massive clump of kapok tree roots snaking above and below the waterline.

Pennywell splashed through the water to his friend and mentor's aid and dragged Paddy behind the kapok's massive trunk as another dart whizzed past his ear. Opening Paddy's shirt collar, the agent located a telltale trickle of blood leaking from a pinprick wound at the dying man's jugular, surrounded by a widening yellow-ochre bruise permeating his neck and shoulders.

"Paddy! Don't leave me here all alone! What is the mission? I thought we were supposed to take field samples and bury the bodies."

Paddy's face whitened, and a trickle of blood seeped from the corners of his distant, gray-eyed stare, "Artemus, the alien was an advance scout." Shivering despite the oppressive heat, he coughed thick and bloody phlegm before struggling to continue, "It was searching for a shipwreck swallowed in the jungle eons ago." Wracked by uncontrollable spasms, he kicked his scuffed and muddy boots outward, forcing his body to still through sheer willpower. Blind, he turned toward Pennywell and strained to speak above a hoarse whisper, "Our job was to confiscate Pike's notebook. I had to kill him. He was infected." Gasping for air, he clamped onto Pennywell's left forearm in a vicelike grip and pulled himself forward, "Get to the alien, boy. Find a small disk about the size of a nickel. Take that and Pike's book back to the PTB."

Nose-to-nose with the Scotsman, Pennywell perceived his friend and mentor's formidable life force vacate its poisoned Earthly vessel as the firm grip loosened and his head lolled back and to the side.

After lowering Paddy's lifeless form to the loamy ground, Pennywell reared back on his haunches, shocked and overwhelmed with grief, "How am I supposed to find the alien? It could be in any direction from here." Sliding out of the cumbersome, soggy backpack, he peeled out of his jacket in the sweltering heat and rolled his sleeves to the elbows. Frisking Paddy's dead form, he located Pike's notebook and a billfold and placed the articles beside his jacket with a sad reverence. Cognizant that an arsenal of deadly tech and gadgets remained in his mentor's black suit, he decided a Viking funeral was in order. "Sorry, old boy, but you are too heavy to carry, so I will send your body to Valhalla in ashes."

Searching his vest pocket, Pennywell removes a Lucky Star

tobacco tin. Popping the lid, he checked its far-out contents and accessed a pouch filled with tiny purple pellets. Snapping the container shut, he pulled the sack's drawstring wide and poured a neat pile within a coffin-sized protected hollow within the magnificent kapok tree's massive knot of twisted roots. Stifling tears, the Powers That Be agent dragged his deceased friend's body by the shoulders and positioned him atop the piling of purplish pellets.

Whispering a prayer, Pennywell ignited the alien fire pellets. Within minutes, he stood before Paddy's rip-roaring, deep-purple funeral pyre. Swiping away more tears, he watched sparks snap and crackle into the misty stillness, "I hope the Powers That Be appreciate your sacrifice, my friend."

The crunch of a branch interrupted Pennywell's sad farewell. Feeling a presence looming behind him, he turned, hands raised, locking eyes with a primeval Amazonian hunter.

"You must be the one with the blowgun."

The short, stubby fireplug stood buck-naked, covered in dirty white paint from head to toe. A pattern of bony piercings decorated his chest, medallions from past campaigns. The fellow's probing eyeballs glinted at Pennywell from under a pronounced brow line, flat nose, and thick lips stretched into a sharp-toothed grin over a receding jawline.

Pennywell's gaze latched onto the man's jet-black bowl cut with unruly strands cow licking straight up above his sloped forehead. "You should visit Al's Barber Shop on Massachusetts, just off 2nd Street. Tell Al I sent you. He'll fix that cowlick you call a hairdo in no time flat."

The hunter commanded his prisoner to step forward, grunting guttural sounds while gesticulating his elaborate six-foot carved blowgun toward an opening in the thick underbrush.

Pennywell complied, "You want me to go that way? Okay. Okay. Take it easy." Checking the smoldering purple fire in the damp underbrush, he stepped in his squishy wet boots as the long blowgun smacked into his chest. "Ow! Christ, you little motherfucker, that hurt!"

The barefoot warrior chuckled while reaching up and tugging Pennywell's revolver from its holster. Familiar with a loaded gun but preferring his lethal stick, the cannibal tossed the 45 into the brush.

"No weapons, got it, chief." Bookmarking his revolver's position in the thick green bramble in his photographic memory, four sharp grunts followed by a high note indicated for Pennywell to proceed.

Pennywell pushed through thick undergrowth, leaving behind Paddy's final resting place. Still reeling from his loss, he ducked under a branch and muttered, "Low bridge."

Suppressing sadness, he remembered the Brazilian kid was a married father of two. "Sorry to you as well, old boy."

Slogging through the leaves and vines for miles in the sweltering jungle, Pennywell paused at a slippery precipice prompting another jab from the business end of the native's blowgun in his back.

"Hey, that hurts!"

Another sharp poke in the ribs, followed by a series of grunts and whistles, indicated for The Powers That Be agent to get his ass moving.

Reaching the bottom of the hill, Pennywell heard the buzz of insects feasting on something beyond a thick green mangle of Brazil's finest and most impenetrable rainforest. Pushing through regardless, incurring cuts on top of scrapes and bites turning to welts from thorns and bugs no doubt toxic to humans, he halfway stumbled into a carved-out clearing, "Well, what do you know? I'm here."

Eyes watering from the rank stench, Pennywell tied a folded bandana around his neck and pulled it over his nose to filter the abysmal odor of putrefied corpses. Crossing the semi-circular array of bodies, he studied the diced-up mass of glowing bones draped with torn chunks of weird bluish-green flesh, "Blimey! Manuel did quite a number on the scout."

The agent examined the nearest human corpse and noted the baseball-sized hole in the victim's exposed ribcage. Stooping over the next skeletonized repose, he sees a similar entry wound holing that man's ribs in a perfect circle. "Pike shot these men postmortem in a last-ditch effort to cover up the alien angle. Paddy, my friend, you kept too many secrets." A quick backward glance toward the grunting native found the strange little human poking his blowgun into the fetid alien mess.

"I would not do that if I were you."

The cannibal looked up with a mischievous grin, then stuck out a long pink tongue and licked slimy blue-green residue off the tip. Scrunching his face in a comical reaction, like a Parisian chef taste-testing a new recipe, the native nodded tacit approval before offering the delicacy for Pennywell's culinary judgment with an inquiring belch.

"Uh, no thanks. I had a big breakfast."

As if understanding the joke, the primitive hunter broke into a hearty fit of laughter.

His captor's sudden jocularity surprised Pennywell, but it also bought him time to think. Seeing a discarded machete stenciled *Property of Ford Motor Company* still clutched in a dead laborer's bony grasp, he examined the body while palming the short blade.

A deep-throated hoot-hoot while reloading his weapon indicated playtime was over. Cracked white paint showed through to the primitive fellow's cocoa-brown birthday suit as his mood darkened and his uncircumcised penis rose to half-mast.

None too anxious to resume the forced march to the creepy guy's camp where he is doubtless the main course, Pennywell brandished the machete, wishing he had his .45 and a pull from his trusty flask. "Okay, you little fuck, this ends right here."

Evocative of a Samurai, the native wielded his blowgun in a two-handed grip and stomped his right foot into the deceased alien's rotting torso with a stomach-turning crunch. Relishing the challenge of a fight to the death in the blood-soaked kill box, the seasoned warrior flashed teeth sharpened into fangs and ululated an incomprehensible battle cry.

Gripping the machete, Pennywell looked on with equal parts

fascination and horror as a shocked expression distorted the cannibal's painted face, knee-deep in the blue-green offal. The Amazonian's thick-lipped mouth opened and closed like a fish out of water, but he made no sound as his beady eyes bulged from sockets like overfilled balloons. Seconds later, the cannibal's stocky form collapsed atop the foul alien remains after every cell in his body melted atop the thick, smelly mound of flesh.

Pennywell stared down at the greasy slop of flesh and bone splattered atop the rotting alien corpse. "Sorry, old boy, but you stepped on an unspent round from one of the alien's weapons. I warned against messing with the remains."

Pennywell scooped up his deceased captor's discarded blowgun and poked through the gooey mess, avoiding unspent rounds mixed in the native and alien offal stew. Searching for the nickel-sized disk from Paddy's final words, he muttered a defeated curse, "Dammit, Paddy, this is like finding a needle in a bloody fucking haystack."

After a tedious hour spent separating the hunter's sticky anatomy from the alien's lifeless form—risking the same fate as the cannibal with every misdirected splatter—Pennywell gave up with a frustrated sigh.

"Sorry, Paddy, time for Plan B. Maybe your clue was never even here."

* * *

Pennywell reached the top of the same slippery embankment the cannibal pushed him down earlier and broke into a dead run. Ticking off a 15-minute countdown in his head, he hacked through a tangle of vines with the Ford machete, trying to get as far away as possible before his clock hit zero. Mid-swing through a thick knot of green, a radiant and intense white light strobed through the jungle preceding a shockwave of destructive energy. Blasted airborne into a verdant patch of soft ferns, he covered his head to deflect a wet mass of vegetation, burying him under a heaped pile of leaves and broken branches.

Pennywell's containment device reduced the kill box to a smoking crater at the center of a quarter-mile blast radius.

Pulling himself out of the pile, Pennywell brushed twigs and leaves off his clothes and wiped what he hoped was dirt from his forehead, "I screwed this up pretty bad, Paddy."

Retracing a breadcrumb path in silence to the kapok tree where Paddy's ashen remains rested undisturbed amongst the roots, Pennywell recovered the backpack, jackets, and weapon in the fading light. Stowing the bundle against the massive tree trunk, he produced a lighter and knelt by the smoldering pyre, sifting through the embers to extricate anything useful or proprietary.

While grabbing the backpack to stow the recovered items, Pike's pierced notebook fell out of a pocket and landed between his muddy boots. Although not a soul was within miles, he glanced into the undergrowth before scooping up the pierced leather-bound notebook. Plopping onto the dirt, he leaned against a massive root with a burdensome sigh and thumbed through the pages. Renderings of buildings, floorplans, and designs filled the pages in smudgy graphite and black ink notated with a messy fountain pen longhand. A detailed sketch of an oblong pill-shaped craft parked in a jungle clearing with scribbled dimensions drew Pennywell's attention. "Aha! The dead alien's ship." His brow furrowed at a surreal sidenote: Anti-gravity propulsion?

Thumbing through the wet splotchy pages, Pennywell's gaze landed on Pike's map of the Tapajós River basin marked with a random hodge-podge of icons: the Fordlandia water tower, a piranha, snake, spider, and jaguar. The page was a mess of splotches, drips, and coffee rings that appeared almost purposeful in their placement. But why? With a weary yawn after the long, awful day, he flipped to the next page and admired a detailed tree drawing. "I wish I could draw. Oh well."

The cacophonous shriek of howling monkeys from high overhead interrupted his snooping reverie. Slapping the notebook closed, he replaced it in the backpack and pondered Paddy's unmarked gravesite. "I better make this official."

The Powers That Be agent used Paddy's sharp penknife to carve a simple cross above the words:

Patrick 'Paddy' James McCoy
May 8, 1872, to Nov 16, 1928.

"Rest in peace, my friend."

Satisfied, he swiped at tears welling in his deep-set gray eyes and refocused on his predicament. With the nightmarish day ebbing into a balmy evening in the woods, Pennywell determined a nighttime fording of the swamp would be ill-advised. "If it's okay, Paddy, I'll camp with you tonight."

Curious indigenous eyeballs spied his every move from the thick green and black mass of rainforest encroaching on his campsite, sending a shiver up his spine, "The forest floor is no place for man or beast in the dark of night." Spying a thick branch twenty feet above his head growing from the ancient kapok tree, he smiled, "That will do."

Climbing a twisted mass of vines clinging to the tree, he pulled himself onto the thick, mossy branch and snuggled his aching back against the kapok's rough and knotted trunk. Pennywell took stock of his high hide and tied the backpack to a nearby limb. Satisfied with his new accommodations, he checked his .45 and buried the machete into the light-gray bark for easy access.

Pennywell's bare feet dangled in the damp stillness as his boots hung from another spur to dry. Something sharp jabbed his left thigh from a deep pants pocket. Careful not to upset his precarious perch, the agent removed the offending object, "Oh, yeah. I didn't have time to add this to an evidence bag before all hell broke loose in the swamp."

A wan smile crossed his face while examining the jagged fluorescent bone, "I guess I don't need this anymore." Pennywell tossed the glowing physical evidence of extraterrestrial life into the night.

The Powers That Be agent mourned the loss of Paddy while

ignoring a low rumble from his stomach. Before long, the cacophonous nighttime jungle serenaded him into a deep slumber.

Artemus Pennywell | Amazon Rainforest
04:11 a.m. | November 17, 1928

In the inky-black predawn hours, a noise snapped Pennywell awake. Grasping his elevated position in darkness, he controlled his beating heart and peered downward.

A lone figure passed under his perch. Its brilliant lambency glinted off the machete blade stuck in the tree bark to Pennywell's side. Trying to conceal the refraction, he inadvertently knocked it loose. With a winced muttering of epithets, he listened as it clattered to the ground. Pulling his feet atop the branch, he cocked the hammer on his .45 and waited with bated breath.

"It is safe to come down, Artemus. I mean you no harm."

The appeal resonated in Pennywell's addlepated head as his body lifted from the perch and floated downward in a steady embrace familiar yet beyond his control.

The disoriented agent regained consciousness, barefoot on the spongy forest floor, blinking to clear his blurred vision. Before him, a short, round-headed, hairless individual stood with arms crossed in a wide-legged stance sporting a silvery jumpsuit glimmering into a sharp focus before Pennywell's gawking countenance.

"Please holster your weapon, friend of McCoy."

Pennywell feels the pistol grip in his right hand, holstering the weapon independent of his hand-eye coordination. Unable to disengage from the being's mesmerizing black-eyed gaze, the agent's initial trepidation dissolved, replaced by a warm virtual embrace.

"My name is Ping. I am here to advise, nothing more, nothing less."

Pennywell had heard stories of aliens assisting humankind as a relative newcomer to the nebulous and clandestine Powers That Be. They existed. He knew that.

Reading Pennywell like an open book, the alien's telepathy flowed into the young and reckless agent's brain like a running tap, *"Your knowledge is limited, Pennywell, Artemus. I am here to advise. So, I will. The murdered alien scout was from a distant brethren Gray species with eons-old imperialist intentions. Evil manifests within every sub-atomic particle of their fragile physical forms. However, their mental acuity and technology are well beyond anything at your disposal. Their interest in this swath of jungle stems from a 90-million-year-old shipwreck. They deduced a human faction led by actors within the US government, and a man named Henry Ford was also searching for the lost ship. They are not wrong. Ford's operative, Charles Pike, somehow discovered its location. That is why you are standing barefoot in the Amazonian jungle in the dead of night."*

Pennywell dared to speak aloud, rubbing his stubbled chin, "What is so important on this ship? Paddy alluded to something, but I never understood what he meant."

"The lost ship holds a world-killing device built by an ancestral Gray race over 90 million years ago. Whoever finds it will control Earth's destiny."

Pennywell started to reply but found words spoken aloud unnecessary, "Okay. We'll do this your way." His brow furrowing, he posed a troubling question: "The laborers' remains were liquified, and yet it also appeared someone shot them through the chest. Do you know what happened to them?"

"The advance scout defended itself. Their deaths were mercifully quick. The last man's survival was random luck, nothing more."

"Yeah. Sure."

With a wave of his bony gray hand for emphasis, *"The scout was ill-equipped to repel the human's simple weapon. From a physical perspective, we are like glass, especially enduring your planet's gravity."*

"Yeah, Sir Isaac Newton was a real sonofabitch."

The Gray's large oval eyes turn toward the early-morning sky filled with stars twinkling through the trees. *"In answer to your query, the man called Pike put a bullet through each man, postmortem, in a vain attempt to make their deaths appear like a human-caused ambush. In so doing, he contacted a microscopic trace of alien blood on his skin. It is quite toxic and transmissible. Our friend, McCoy, ended his misery before he poisoned another human."*

"I was there, too. Holy shit, am I infected?"

"You and Paddy were immunized when you joined The Powers That Be. With the passing of McCoy, I am now assigned to you, Artemus Pennywell. I am your adviser."

Reaching into its silvery suit, the alien removed a dull nickel-sized disk and held it out for Pennywell.

"Bloody hell, is that the clue Paddy instructed me to find?"

"Yes. Your task is simple: transport this disk and Pike's notebook to your superiors at The Powers That Be and await their sage instructions."

Projecting an image of Pike's detailed alien craft illustration in his head, Pennywell inquired if that was indeed the lost ship.

"No, Artemus, that is the scout's ship. His kind will soon discover he is missing and recover the craft. They are well aware of the risks of human interactions." Gesturing toward the disk held in Pennywell's right hand, *"The shipwreck is ostensibly within the grid recorded on that disk; however, septillions of bytes obscure the exact coordinates. Please return it to The Powers That Be for safekeeping. As long as the ship remains lost, more pressing concerns will dominate The Powers That Be in the coming decades. However, Artemus, please listen and hear what I say. Your kind will someday develop technologies capable of deciphering the data on the disk. When that day comes, find the shipwreck, and destroy it. I would do it myself; however, my group can only advise. We cannot breach our solemn code of non-interference."*

"Of course. We wouldn't want to make things too fucking easy now, would we?"

"McCoy warned me of your quick wit and colorful language. Since the shipwreck dates back over 90 million years when Earth was much different, it is more than likely buried deep underground."

"Like a dinosaur fossil?"

"There is so much of your planet that remains undiscovered."

"You referred to yourself as my adviser. What do you mean?"

"I will be there for you, Pennywell, Artemus, because you must be there for humanity. I advised Paddy to recruit you and shepherd your rise through the ranks of our organization. And now, with his untimely demise, I step from the shadows."

"Will we meet again?"

"Of course. You will ask questions, and I will advise. However, you will make choices with the potential to alter the course of human history. We both know humanity will ignore and disappoint most of the time. Your kind is resourceful and intelligent, but wisdom and logic are not guaranteed. Nevertheless, you must persevere. I have advised others through time and appear before you now under the auspices of a power far greater than myself. The pure energy beings I answer to could swipe me aside like an insect if they chose, but they won't."

"Why not?"

"It is a wager on good versus evil. The Light Specters desire humanity to fulfill its destiny. Envision your species as a seed cast upon a barren landscape. Will the seed endure its nascency and extend roots into the heavens? Only time will tell. However, the mere presence of the lost ship places the human enterprise at great peril."

"I'm sorry, the Light Specters?"

"That is enough for now."

* * *

Rain droplets splat atop Pennywell's close-shaved head of thinning light-brown hair. Forcing open his bleary-eyed gaze in the refreshing morning shower, he focused on the comical countenance of a merry little Capuchin monkey. After a hearty chuckle at the furry interloper, he mused, "Okay. I have awoken to worse things in my day."

The monkey balanced on the branch a safe distance from the human squatter invading its home among the trees, curling its long tail through the humidity.

Adjusting his back against the uncomfortable tree trunk elicited a screech from the cautious primate.

"I didn't mean to scare you, little fellow. I'll be out of your flea-riddled hair in no time."

Recounting his vivid dream while untying his boots and backpack from the branches, he rasped a throaty suggestion toward the canopy dweller, "Call room service and order a pot of coffee. Put it on my tab."

The monkey responded by showing Pennywell a dull metal disk held in its nimble monkey fingers.

"What the hell? How did you get that?"

With a defiant hoot, the perspicacious primate pulled the nickel-sized object to its hairy chest, daring Pennywell to take it.

"I am going to need that back."

Non est ad astra mollis e terris via.

(There is no easy way from

the earth to the stars.)

– Seneca the Younger

Chapter One:

The Invaders

Dr. Farouk Said | Cleopatra Hospital, Cairo

04:35 p.m. | August 23, 2044

An exhausted duo in light-blue bloodstained scrubs clomps up flights of metal steps in the echoing emergency stairwell under glaring red emergency lights toward the rooftop level of Cleopatra Hospital's newest medical tower. Ascending to the uppermost landing, winded and mad-as-hell, the ER doctor pushes open a roof access door stenciled 22 in bold yellow numerals. With the nurse falling into lockstep at his side, Farouk Said marches through a choking vortex of dust and smoke toward the helipad where an airship's blades are winding down. Glowering through the swirling haze, the emergency medical team spies the pilot's profile tipping the brim of his cowboy hat in their direction from inside the airship's cockpit.

* * *

Farouk and the heroic nurse wrapped up their shifts in the always hectic metro hospital ER yesterday afternoon around half past three when the first alien battleships tore open the sky. After the initial shock and awe subsided, traumatized Cairo residents appeared in growing numbers at the hospital doors, wheeling, carrying, and dragging their dead and dying in a desperate quest for treatment. By early evening, the overwhelmed hospital staff maintaining beleaguered posts were at their wits' end. Across multiple flashpoints escalating into the wee hours of the following morning, employees barricaded behind locked doors, overwhelmed by the sick and injured, enflaming crowded waiting areas into violent mobs. Overtaxed orderlies stifled tears, pushing gurneys stacked with the dead in a dwindling supply of body bags to a sub-level garage-turned makeshift morgue.

Around midnight, Farouk's longtime associate and part-time lover took her own life. The ordeal pushed humanity beyond the breaking point.

Following the surprise alien departure sometime after 02:00 a.m., the misery of every conceivable type of injury left the remaining staff in the unfamiliar position of relying on their training. With blown-out windows and wonky emergency generators working in fits and starts, the hospital's state-of-the-art computer network synced to a vast array of cutting-edge medical equipment was rendered useless. Medical professionals whose expertise relied more on a silicon-chipped assist than they cared to admit triaged injuries with a finite supply of pain meds and oral anesthetics, gauze, tape, pills, splints, and old-school analog thermometers and blood pressure pumps plundered from a forgotten storeroom. Worse, no one could find a hard copy of the hospital emergency protocols to save their life. It existed on a cloud in a formerly digital world like everything else.

Farouk and a skeleton crew of unflappable surgeons and nurses treated critical cases deemed operable, setting fractures, amputating ruined limbs, and delivering two babies. For the terminal patients, they could do nothing but provide an opiate-induced blissful denouement to quell agonized moans and screams echoing down the halls.

* * *

Hearing a sickening crumpling noise underfoot, Farouk curses the world and tries to wave off the foolish pilot.

"The weight of that chopper could collapse the rooftop!"

The nurse's eyes widen as she feels the tall building swaying beneath her feet.

Dismissing the pair's demonstrative fuck off with a toothy grin, the lanky pilot flings off his headset while shutting down the massive engines and engaging the airship's brakes. Exiting the cockpit, he hustles to open the chopper's rear hatch adorned with a cryptic butterfly icon. After a quick check inside the darkened cabin, he stomps dust off his boots and turns to the gawking blue-clad duo, "Well, what are you waiting for? Get your asses over here! Now, goddammit!"

Mindful of the rotating blades above his gray head, Dr. Farouk Said jogs up and angles his aching upper body inside the chopper's jury-rigged passenger cabin as his resourceful nurse slides open the opposite side ducking her nimble frame inside the cramped space, careful not to disturb two young Caucasians slid feet-first into the narrow fuselage. Dumbfounded, Farouk shakes his head at the tattered pair, lying elbow-to-elbow atop a thick layer of gaudy pink blankets, covered in cuts, scrapes, and bruises under bloody dirt and sandy clumps, and asks, "What happened to these people?"

The RN maintains her cool, stroking matted blond hair off the woman's bruised and bloodied face before checking her respiratory with a stethoscope.

Farouk appraises the male victim's injuries before turning to the pilot without a hint of compassion, "We have already turned away others with less severe injuries than this man. Ethically, I am obliged to decline."

The pilot ignores the dour assessment, "Let me save you both some time, Doc. The woman is in pretty good shape. We know that already. It's her man, here, who is scuffed up bad. Now, y'all listen to me; I don't give a flying fuck about your so-called ethical dilemma. You will treat them at this hospital."

Working on 24 hours of no sleep, Farouk's anger and frustration explode in a vitriolic tirade at the rugged American emulating a walking, talking Marlboro man, "Are you insane? We tried to warn you not to land. Everything is down. We cannot run tests or scans to address this fellow's obvious injuries. Look around, you fool! This guy is as good as dead already. Join the club because this is just Day One. Wait until tomorrow and the day after that. This hospital will be hell on Earth, making you wish the aliens stayed to finish the job."

The nurse chimes in, "Farouk, he is right. The woman suffers from blood loss and dehydration, not to mention the strangest burn marks I have ever seen, but her vitals are okay."

Reaching across the female, she quickly assesses the male's injuries: "This one has a compound fracture on his right arm, finger dislocations, broken ribs, probably a collapsed lung, and of course, his bleeding head trauma. I wouldn't be surprised if he has brain swelling and internal hemorrhaging." Shaking her head in awe, the man is still alive, "God only knows what else."

Turning nose-to-nose with the pilot, "You made a horrible mistake bringing them here. We have nothing but a backup generator cutting in and out. Every medical device is shot to hell. If you have enough fuel, try flying him to Alexandria. I hear they are in better shape up there."

Part of The Powers That Be rescue and extraction team retrieving survivors from hundreds of feet beneath the Giza Plateau since predawn, the Texan was in no mood to hear what couldn't be done. Reaching into a vest pocket, he removes a half-dollar-size gold coin embossed with The Powers That Be symbol opposite a peony flower motif surrounding the initials PTB. He presents it to the bewildered surgeon with a weary smile, "Doc, I want you to take this coin and remember who gave it to you. Gold is the future, my friend. A team of experts in the medical disciplines and a crack security squad are en route to help you get this place up and running to fix up my friends, here," winking at the nurse, "and all the other patients. Not just the easy ones, for God's sake. Hellfire, I could splint a sprained wrist. We want to save every soul who walks through your door from this point forward. Got it?"

Farouk stammers, turning the gold coin in his nimble surgeon's hand, "I need to confer with my superiors and their superiors. That will take days if not weeks."

"Doc, you are thinking like the day before yesterday." Jabbing two fingers into Farouk's chest, "As of this very fucking second, you are in charge. There is no one else coming. Do you understand what it is I am telling you?"

The middle-aged doctor glances at his attractive raven-haired nurse, who shrugs back at him, "We need help, Farouk. People are dying downstairs as we speak. What can the administration do, fire us?"

Clad in a western-style denim shirt, worn jeans, and boots, all covered in fine red dust, the grizzled chopper pilot smiles below his horseshoe mustache at the dark-complected nurse, "What's your name, darling?"

"Zahra."

"That's a lovely name. Here's a coin for you, too."

Barney and Betty Hill | Cleopatra Hospital, Cairo
12:15 p.m. | August 24, 2044

A resourceful young messenger revs his antique gas-powered moped past windowless buildings along clogged and impassable streets in the smoldering aftermath of the aborted alien invasion less than two days earlier. Zigging and zagging around abandoned inoperable vehicles, he brakes, accelerates, brakes, block after shattered block.

Passing emergency crews, wailing mothers and a catatonic populace needing a digital fix not forthcoming anytime soon, he screeches to a stop at another ad hoc checkpoint. Shorthanded local constabularies set up roadblocks in a clumsy effort to appear in charge against multiple fronts of scared and angry citizens transmogrified into panicked mobs of looters and rioters.

Navigating detours, he avoids a loud and chanting throng by steering down an alley that veers left into another dead-end—doubling back, the kid bursts through a torrent of dirty water from busted sewage and water pipes crossing another unrecognizable street. Soaking wet and verging on defeat, he skids to a stop at his destination: the Cleopatra Hospital complex, smack dab in the heart of Cairo, Egypt. Vaulting up the circular driveway under a half-collapsed porte cochère, he leans his bike against a cracked pillar and opens the sopping wicker basket attached to the moped's splattered purple frame behind his seat. He lifts out a simple wooden box and a thick manila envelope wax-sealed with an official-looking stamp. With a start, he notices half the envelope is water-soaked. Hustling toward the shattered front entrance, he waves it in the dry air and steps across the busted glass threshold into Hospital Building C – Main Floor – Front Lobby.

A hulking security guard in full camo gear with an Uzi slung across his back eclipses the boy's advance, "State your business, or turn around and leave."

Stammering before the imposing man's no-nonsense demeanor,

"I have a delivery of, uh, pee-o-nees, and this envelope for …" the teenager looks at the illegible names scribbled on his wet left hand. "Oh no. Uh, sir. Yes, sir. Just a minute, I have their names here somewhere." The kid jabs his hands into empty pockets, buying time, trying to remember the Western names.

The gruff guard lurches forward, preparing to lift the kid by his scrotum and toss him out the door.

"Wait. I remember. Their names are, uh, hang on. Americans. Yeah, that is right. Uh, Barney and Betty Hill!" With a hesitant pause, "… I think."

The armed guard huffs a weary sigh, unrolls a scribbled patient registry from a side pocket in his tech vest, and flips through stapled pages, "Sorry kid, those names are not on my list."

Deflated, wet, and tired, the boy turns to exit through the shattered double doors.

"Hey, kid, wait a minute. Did you say you have peonies? As in flowers, right?"

The skinny 15-year-old turns and holds up a box containing the arrangement. "Yeah. Why?"

* * *

Cowboy tips his signature Stetson, ferrying another load of alien tech, bottled waters, and pizzas from Chrysalis HQ to Cleopatra Hospital. Aside from miraculous pharmacological remedies and off-world surgical and diagnostic equipment courtesy of The Advisers, the Texan delivers hope in the glint of gold coins to besieged hospital staffers and patients during the chaotic midday hours of Aliens +1.

As Chrysalis technicians repurpose entire floors, installing arrays of mysterious medical instrumentation, the unboxing of a metallic figure catches everyone's attention. Cleopatra Hospital's exhausted surgeons pause the endless parade of patients wheeling in and out of pop-up hermetically-sealed operating units, eager to witness the shiny humanoid commence its first procedure: a craniotomy on the shaved head of the critical 27-year-old male from the chopper.

Peering through clear plastic into a confining operating space, Dr. Said watches the multitasking automaton's dexterous hands move across the anesthetized patient with a magician's skill. Sensing the bloody and bedraggled staff's stare-eyed wonder, he quips, "This chap will put us out of business," eliciting nervous laughter.

No one notices the robot place a thin wafer on the man's brain before replacing the skull section and closing the C-shaped incision on the left side of his head.

Edward Laughton | West London
12:25 p.m. | August 25, 2044

Another rap on the front door of his West London home distracts Edward Laughton from just-arrived file boxes teetered in haphazard stacks in his cramped living room space. He yells toward the door with an exasperated huff, "Go away! Bloody hell! I can't accommodate any more boxes! We are all full up. Why don't you bugger off to my mate Travis over in Ealing? The fucker lives in a veritable mansion!"

On the heels of the invasion, word spread like wildfire among London-based PTB shell companies that Murdock & Ripley—Laughton's tony high-rise law firm headquarters—lay in smoldering ruins. The prospect of reams of inculpatory evidence scattered amongst the debris falling into the wrong hands prompted shady PTB operators to crawl from the woodwork and jettison boxloads at Laughton's home address. To the barrister's utter shock and horror, a PTB lackey had posted his renovated former candle factory Chiswick estate on a shielded PTB intranet site as a fallback location for document dumpers.

Furious that his private residence was revealed to London's criminal underworld without his consent, he had already received over a dozen visits from shellshocked Londoners operating for years, sometimes decades, behind PTB's veneer of legitimacy. He had already received boxloads from a Chelsea travel agency deep into the IOSC tourist business this morning, plus foul-smelling ledgers, notes, pictures, and drives from a world-renowned Notting Hill Indian restaurant doubling as a PTB dead drop location. Another stack contained bundled high-denomination Euros sequestered from a hole-in-the-wall computer repair business splitting allegiance between MI6 and the PTB.

Sipping bottled water from an emergency stockpile hoarded behind a walled-off pantry, Laughton knew the file boxes contained a fraction of the damning evidence waiting to be revealed to a world lusting for a villain to punish in place of their own apathetic incompetence. However, London was ravaged beyond recognition: Buckingham Palace's luck ran out; Westminster and the Tower of London lay in ruins; bodies logjammed against collapsed bridges along the Thames—a health crisis unseen since the plague. Penny-ante misdeeds of the miscreants showing up at the barrister's private residence would be moot if not for the potential paper trail exposure scattered among the law firm's collapsed edifice.

Focusing on a beat-up old box from the small Chrysalis office out at Heathrow, Laughton attempts to tune out the pervasive knocking, "Go away!" The box labeled with a familiar butterfly logo contained old flight logs, letters, passports, and cash. Unfolding a dog-eared map of the Brazilian jungle, a faded polaroid of two shady characters, standing arm-in-arm, smoking fat stogeys, falls to the floor between his loafers. Opening the map, he sees a runway carved out of the jungle circled in thick black grease pencil. Scooping up the photo, he studies a middle-aged pair striking a jolly pose in full camo gear before pallets of what appears to be cocaine. Grabbing his readers, the barrister flips the photo and reads the scribbled caption:

Pablo and Artemus – Christmas 1975

"For Christ's sake, what was Artemus doing with the cartel?" With a quick calculation in his weary head, "Bloody hell, how old is he?"

More persistent knocking prompts him to drop the faded Polaroid and stretch with a loud yawn. The widower steps over Nancy, whose feline tabby form poises behind a crushed box, ready to pounce on a loose scrap of paper.

"I'm coming. Hold your horses."

Laughton opens the door, expecting the worst, finding a dapper young man with an expectant smile on his smooth face.

"Edward Laughton?"

Scanning the uneven walkway for another pushcart loaded with boxes, Laughton breathes easier, finding only the boy's parked scooter down at the curb. "What can I do for you, young man?"

"Quite a lot, sir. My boss, Griffin Pike, would like to retain your services to help us take down your client, the PTB."

Laughton peers down both directions of his formerly neat and tidy Chiswick street, now littered with inert vehicles under downed lines, fallen branches, crumbled walls, and broken glass, "The Griffin Pike? As in SATstar Industries?"

"One and the same."

"Really? I'm listening."

"Excellent, sir; you are indeed a sharp legal mind. We understand your firm's HQ was destroyed, and your general partner is among the casualties. Our condolences. Nevertheless, my boss needs your assistance to take down the PTB once and for all."

"Why me? Does Pike understand I am now the senior PTB outside legal counsel by default?"

"He most certainly does, sir. However, your public repudiations of Artemus Pennywell are also common knowledge."

"Well, young man, Murdock handled the old coot. Our paths rarely crossed, and it was always unpleasant when they did. However, your request puts me in an awkward position. Even entertaining this conversation breaches common ethical standards."

Sensing the aristocratic barrister's reticence, the young man gets to the point, "I'm sorry, sir, but we only need your eyeball."

"My eyeball?"

"Yes, sir. Mr. Pike seeks the contents of a safe deposit box at a Royal Bank of Scotland branch adjacent to Trafalgar Square. The entire area was decimated; however, the underground vault is intact, and the grounds are secured by Mr. Pike's guards. But as luck would have it, the biometric security system requires a Murdock & Ripley partner-level retinal scan to access the vault.

The unsolicited query from one of Pike's lackeys was unexpected but not too surprising. What shocked him was the swiftness of his reply. "I can't believe I am saying this, but what the hell, I'll do it."

"Good show, sir! Jolly good show."

"What is Pike looking for in that vault?"

"That information is beyond my need to know. I'm just the messenger."

The deep personal animus Laughton internalized toward Artemus Pennywell started decades before Invasion Day. The tall, silver-haired English barrister spent years watching the petulant man humiliate colleagues with brutal and pitiless disregard. He also took more than his share of slings and arrows from the vile old codger while facilitating deals for the *betterment of humanity* with a rogue's gallery of presidents, prime ministers, potentates, religious leaders, dictators, underworld bosses, and high-tech grifters. Men like Griffin Pike.

While The Powers That Be held a well-earned reputation as an untouchable organization above the inanities of the human condition, Pennywell's inner circle, The Council, cut deals through Murdock & Ripley, shepherding projects through dens of wolves—with some in sheep's clothing. Want a pharmaceutical factory in Jakarta? An IOSC launchpad in Ankara? A children's hospital in Sudan? The PTB viewed every transaction through a singular human lens. The 300-plus-year organization's sole redeeming quality men like Laughton used to rationalize a worldwide portfolio of positive outcomes realized through deals with the devil.

Laughton winces, hearing another explosion in the distance, "One problem, the roads are impassable. London is in total anarchy. How would I get there? It is too far to walk."

"Well, sir. I can get you there on my bike if you don't mind a little wind in your face."

Ill-prepared to leave his house in such a muddled state, Laughton sighs, "Well, I can't go now. I have to take care of Nancy."

"Oh. Right, sir. I did not mean to infer straight away. I will contact my superior with your agreement and be in touch within the next few days. Please give the missus my regards."

Laughton starts to correct the record, then pauses with a smile, "I'll do that."

Betty Hill | Cleopatra Hospital, Cairo
07:05 a.m. | August 26, 2044

Bright morning sunshine glows around blackout shades covering a replaced picture window overlooking a besieged Cairo cityscape from a spacious private suite on the Cleopatra Hospital tower's 20th floor. Stirring awake, Betty Hill turns her head to the blurry light, struggling to recall why she is there. Lifting her right arm to touch itchy facial bandages, she disturbs a looped IV line, setting off an alarm on the stand-mounted monitor beside her raised multifunctional bed.

A nurse enters within seconds and switches off the grating beeping noise. Writing 'Nurse Zahra' on the whiteboard in a flowing script, she turns to address her bleary-eyed patient, "Good morning, Mrs. Hill; how are you feeling?"

Mrs. Hill coughs a reply, gesturing at her throat.

"Water? Yes, of course. I will be right back."

Awakening alone in a hospital room sends a bone-chilling sense of Déjà vu down Betty's spine. On that nightmarish morning after, she found herself handcuffed to the hospital bed rail under the leering gaze of a lecherous female deputy and facing a murder charge. Examining her bruised, bandaged, yet unrestrained right wrist through swollen eyes, a lifetime of memories refloods her brain. Trying to piece together a clutter of random thoughts, Betty glimpses Zahra returning with an ice cup.

"Suck on these ice chips, dear, and try to rest your vocal cords. By the way, Dr. Said is quite pleased with your recovery, especially the burns on your hands, which are healing much faster than anyone would have guessed."

Her eyes awash with tears, Betty clutches her bandaged right hand around the nurse's white cuffed sleeve, garbling, "How long?"

Nurse Zahra rests Betty's thick-wrapped appendage atop the bedsheets with a gentle pat, "You are starting your third day under our care." Adjusting the twisted IV, she continues, "I know you have questions. We are more than a little curious about you, as well. You and your husband have friends in high places." The nurse injects a dose of levity with a slight chuckle, "You scream out loud with night terrors featuring someone named Harry. An old boyfriend, perhaps? At any rate, he must have been a real jerk to make you cry out in blood-curdling screams in your sleep. No wonder your voice is so weak." Before leaving, the nurse notes Betty's vitals, "I will check back on you soon. Get some rest."

Watching the kind nurse exit, Betty presses her head against the pillows and stares at a small hole in the ceiling tiles, "You have no idea."

Muffled voices resonate from the darkened hallway, but Betty cannot interpret the words in her addled mind, "That sounds like Arabic; I need to find Owen."

Grabbing the bed's remote control, Betty lowers the hinged side rail, swings her cut and bruised bare legs over the side, and slides her bare bottom off the firm mattress, numb feet contacting the cold tile floor. Fighting dizziness, she reaches for the IV stand for support. Shaking off a heady swoon on shaky legs, the patient slides her left foot forward, focusing on a potted palm across the hall outside the half-open door as the room goes sideways. Crumpling to the floor in a twisted heap, Betty pulls onto her hands and knees, mooning the hallway with her untied hospital gown hanging from her shoulders.

Hushed voices and shuffling footsteps resonate from behind as a thick muscular embrace elevates her vulnerable form back atop the bed like a baby.

A disembodied voice breaks the silence, "Now, see here, Mrs. Hill, we can't have you gallivanting off half-cocked and half-dressed to boot."

Scanning around the low-lit hospital room, her eyes meet the pleasant face of the strapping young orderly with hairy, muscular arms. Reaching for the ice cup, she pours one over her chapped, peeling lips, focusing on a male figure sitting in a shadowed recess beside a tall armoire. Leaning forward with wide-eyed recognition, Betty mouths the man's name while conjuring the nickname she gave the geeky young fellow only a few days earlier: 'Doubletake.'

Roy Kendall, the Powers That Be psychologist who participated in her third degree at the Chrysalis Air facility the night before the alien invasion, dismisses the orderly and pulls the shade up a third, letting in more light. "I cannot tell you how excited and relieved everyone was to find you alive, Mrs. Hill."

About to jump out of her skin, Betty points at the whiteboard.

Roy steps over and unhooks it from the wall. "I see. Here you are."

Betty props the 3-foot board over her crisscrossed cut-up legs and scribbles her first word: *OWEN?*

Doubletake nods and moves to close the door, "It is good to see you again, Mrs. Haig. Not only did you save the world, but you were spot on about my colleague, Greta. She was in cahoots with Tarek Hamed."

BITCH

"Yeah, well. You are an excellent judge of character. She fooled me, and I am trained to recognize psychotic behavior."

WHAT ABOUT OWEN?

"He is in serious condition in the ICU. The last I heard; he had acquired a lung infection which prompted emergency surgery. His excellent physical shape undoubtedly saved his life. They will let you see him when he is stable."

THANK YOU! WHY BETTY?

The door swings open, prompting Roy to reach forward and swipe off the last question with the side of his hand.

Zahra shoots him a suspicious glance, "What are we up to? Hangman? Tic-tac-toe? How did you get in here?"

With a nervous smile, Roy holds up his visitor pass hooked to a lanyard over his coral-pink polo and tan slacks. "This patient has a lot of questions."

Rachel watches Zahra sidle around Doubletake while balancing a syringe and vials atop a metal tray, "What is your pain level, Mrs. Hill?"

With her bandaged hand, Rachel gestures "so-so," watching the nurse empty a light-yellow fluid from the syringe through the cannula taped inside her left forearm. "That was for the pain, dear." Replacing the first syringe with a new vial, "This one will ease your anxiety so you can rest." Betty shakes her head, 'No!' furrowing her cut-up brow and retracting her arm to her bruised chest.

Zahra shrugs, offering a coy smile, "Well, you say that now. I'll check back in an hour."

Recording Betty's blood pressure on the chart at the foot of the bed, the Egyptian caregiver snatches the whiteboard off the patient's lap and rehangs it on the wall, eyeing Roy with a flirty smile on her way out the door, "Check for a notepad in the side table drawer and leave my whiteboard on the wall."

Ensuring the coast is clear, Roy hands Betty a Cleopatra Hospital pad and pen while leaning over with a conspiratorial whisper, "The staff know you as Betty Hill. Barney is your husband. The Cowboy came up with your new names when he brought you here."

Rachel takes the paper pad and scribbles: *THEY WERE ABDUCTED.*

"Yeah, I know. The Texan has a wicked sense of humor. What can I say? He has been in and out of here multiple times while you were out."

WHY AN ALIAS?

"You and Owen are fast becoming urban legends. Thousands of people witnessed our rescue operation the terrible morning after the invaders' miraculous retreat. They made a leap of logic between the aliens and our presence on the Giza Plateau. A huge crowd gathered to watch when we finally pulled everyone back to the surface. We had to think fast. We loaded both of you into the black chopper and rushed here. There was not enough time for subterfuge. Your husband was at death's door. I will not lie to you; he is in a serious but guarded condition. People followed the chopper's path and saw it land on the roof. They know someone in this building is associated with the invasion. We are doing our best to keep you both anonymous."

FLYNN?

Aside from you and your husband, we recovered four others from under the pyramid. A deceased female tour guide was murdered by Tarek Hamed, who is in guarded condition and facing a litany of charges. And then there is the Egyptian army captain, Mohammed Faisel. The poor man suffered numerous broken bones and internal injuries, but his rambling account concerns us. People are listening."

Doubletake leans closer and lowers his voice to a whisper, "We handed him back to the Egyptians after extraction, which turned out to be a mistake. The man recounts an incredible tale of your exploits to anyone willing to listen. Fortunately, it sounds like the PTSD ramblings of a shell-shocked veteran way past retirement. However, given the current circumstances, people will swallow almost anything, spawning wild rumors of a woman who shoots fire from her hands like a superhero.

SUPERHERO? I DON'T CARE WHAT PEOPLE SAY. I CAN'T DO IT ANYMORE.

Rachel shows Doubletake the thick bandages covering star-shaped second-degree burns across both palms.

MY HANDS HURT.

"I am sorry, Rachel."

With unmasked frustration, Rachel fumbles the pen in her fingers, sticking out from the thick layers of gauze, circling Flynn's name.

Doubletake nods, "Okay. Agent Flynn suffered a serious gunshot wound. The alien powder staunched the damage, but he needs a new liver. Nina should be escorting him to our lunar hospital facility by now."

REALLY? THE MOON?

"Yes. The Moon." Roy chuckles, "After all you have been through, that is what surprises you?"

Noticing the droopy peony arrangement in a glass vase, "Your flowers look a little thirsty; allow me." Returning from the bathroom with the vase and a sheepish grin, he replaces it on the side table next to an unopened wax-sealed manila envelope. "How silly of me. There is no running water in the lavatory. Anyway, you need to rest. That is enough for now. You are the only patient on the 20th floor. Every point of entry is under surveillance. Your rather attractive nurse, Zahra, her night shift counterpart, and the muscular young fellow from earlier are a few of the small staff allowed up here per Doctor Said's orders. All are well-paid to keep their mouths shut and eyes open."

THE NURSE LIKES YOU

Betty and the nerdy young psychologist exchange a smile like a couple of high schoolers.

Richard | PTB HQ, Scotland
11:35 a.m. | August 26, 2044

Numbers 4 and 5 bisect the gleaming white Level C subterranean laboratory, bypassing workbenches brimming with scientific instruments, glassware, microscopes, and test kit paraphernalia abandoned before the invasion. The synthetic sisters pause before a biometric pad mounted at eye level on the smoothed rock wall at the far end of the bright-lit expanse. 4 looks on as 5 positions a dreamy blue retina before the scanner, unlocking thick metal doors fronting a rough-hewn antechamber carved even farther out of eons-old Scottish sediment. Entering the newest addition to The Powers That Be underground headquarters far beneath Crichton Castle's crumbling ramparts, motion-activated ceiling lights illuminate six hibernation chambers in perfect alignment. The gleaming futuristic units reflect multi-hued lights and screens atop contoured lids made of thick smoky glass sealed over plush padded compartments resting at waist height atop sturdy customized carts. Thick bundled wiring and hoses attached to plugs and connectors dedicated to each unit snake across the chiseled floorspace before disappearing through bored openings in the Scottish rock toward shielded life support and power reserves farther underground.

The pair step around an unkempt mass of tubes and blankets spilling out of the emptied first chamber, focusing on the second chamber's occupant. The replicants activate the unit's screen and review the man's vitals. Noting nothing more than a spiked LDL, they initiate the wake-up program. 5 detaches a hose with a loud whoosh and watches condensation collect on the glassy tinted hood before unplugging bundled wires looped into the stand. Executing the coordinated two-person procedure designed to revive the frail human inside while mitigating physiological complications, 4 sidesteps a loosened mass of hoses and moves to the head of the unit. Acknowledging 5's telepathic thumbs-up, she triggers resuscitation with the press of a button, and in response, the hibernation chamber's darkened interior strobes to life under the tinted glass. With her task complete, 5 watches 4 lowering her delicate-featured face close to the curved reflective surface, checking her boss's peaceful repose. The man's steady respiration fogs the glass, obscuring her view, a good sign. Exhibiting no outward symptoms of distress, he appears unmoved from when she assisted him inside under terrible duress over three days earlier: supine with folded hands atop his barrel chest and a slight smile on his distinguished face.

With a raised eyebrow at what could be construed as frustration—were 4 capable of such emotion—she instructs 5 to double-check his vitals and the life support stats. All is normal for wake-up, yet the man remains sleeping like an angel. Meeting her partner's dark-eyed gaze, 4 shrugs and taps her ring finger on the curved glass above the man's stubborn sleepy-headed repose. Departing from the well-timed protocol, 4 addresses her boss with words spoken aloud through the thick glass, "Professor King? Richard? You should be waking up by now."

Ensconced within the claustrophobic space, Richard hears a muffled voice with the abject temerity to disturb his vivid dreams. Desperate to maintain his blissful sedation, he bellows, "Go away!"

An annoying and incessant tapping accompanies the muffled voice, "Professor, it is time to wake up, sir."

Cursing under his breath, Richard King blinks open his crusty eyes and tries to quantify the upside-down countenance staring at him through the foggy glass. Stretching his body with a loud yawn, he feels the temperature rising, "Jesus, it is like an oven in this damn thing."

Number 4 smiles, watching her boss's pudgy index finger drawing a sad face in the steamy glass.

"Okay, playtime is over."

Confident King is awake and semi-alert; the robots break the chamber's seal with a loud hiss followed by an ear-popping release of pressure. The curved glass lid opens on a springy hinge, and Richard King bolts upright at the waist like a vampire rising from its coffin.

Peeling off sensors and pulling oxygen tubes from his nose, Richard looks past his wiggling toes toward a smiling Number 5. Like a smack in the face, the entirety of the alien invasion floods his mind. Scratching his unruly shock of charcoal-gray bedhead, he clears his raspy throat, "How long?"

Number 5 offers a water bottle, "Professor, you were out for 88 hours and 24 minutes."

"Is that all? I must say I am surprised to be alive." Scratching his 3-day growth of beard, he glances around the antechamber, "Of course, I am heartened and relieved to see you both. Are we under alien rule? Should I hide? What is happening on the surface?"

"The CEO will debrief you, Professor. Suffice it to say, humans are still in charge of the planet."

Richard takes a long swig and wipes his mouth on his sleeve, "Well, that has its pluses and minuses, doesn't it?" Noticing the first hibernation chamber's opened lid draped with a tangle of unhooked hoses and wires, Richard hoists himself onto a jelly-legged upright stance.

In unison, 4 and 5 grapple the unwieldy man by his rounded shoulders and prop him in their sturdy hold, "Please remember, it will take time to regain your strength. You must allow your circulation and muscle memory to return before moving around. Slow and steady."

"Thank you both for your assistance." Turning nose-to-nose with Number 5, King's lined face widens into a sheepish grin, "You know, I had the most remarkable dream. I would ask to stay longer, but it appears that I soiled myself during the hibernation."

Propped between Numbers 4 and 5, Professor Richard King,

The Powers That Be's chief scientist in charge of the Level C laboratory beneath the Scottish Lowlands castle complex, is assisted to his private quarters for much-needed teeth brushing, a hot shower, and a change of clothes.

Andrew | PTB HQ, Scotland
08:45 p.m. | August 26, 2044

Far below storied castle ramparts situated in verdant Lowlands countryside, Andrew exits the lift onto Level C. Heading across Richard King's laboratory past the sea monkey aquarium, he nods toward Number 16. The white-coated replicant returns a bright smile, standing atop a ladder while dangling raw chicken inches above the murky green water, enticing the sharp-toothed aquatic alien beastie to feast. Reaching the opposite end of the lab, he parts red double doors and enters the PTB think tank.

Intelligent synthetic eyes adjust from the bright lab lighting to a moody multi-hued ambiance as Andrew's sculpted gaze scans an asymmetric assemblage of brainstorming pods. Situated on stepped tiers inside the chiseled-out basketball court-sized expanse, each pod's forward-thinking, unique design stimulates creativity and inventiveness via heightened sensorial experiences while reclining on cutting-edge tech-heavy furniture brimming with gadgetry.

Andrew's keen auditory sensors pick up crackling sounds from a wafer-thin monitor replaying staticky PTB drone feeds monitoring flashpoints raging worldwide. Confident the only two humans on Level C are seated within that elevated pod, Andrew takes a deep breath and pats the folded letter in his pocket. Vaulting up a short flight of steps, he opens the portal and finds Artemus Pennywell's lanky form stretched across a black leather couch, sound asleep. To the CEO's right, Richard King sits on the edge of a Pininfarina chair hunched over a low coffee table, eating fried chicken while availing himself of the multi-function Italian recliner's vibratory feature set.

Richard licks his thick fingers and smiles at the robot, "Hello, Andrew; it's good to see you again. It is amazing how ravished I was after only three days in hibernation. Can you imagine if it had been years? My God, I'd eat a horse."

"Is that from the same chicken supply 16 feeds to the sea monkey, Professor?"

Richard stares at the greasy leg bone pinched between his thumb and forefinger, "She cooked it in my air fryer, Andrew. It tastes delicious."

Stirring awake on the long sofa with his eyes shut tight, Pennywell addresses his valet, "What is it now, Andrew?"

"Sir, we received a rather troubling communication."

Scooting his disheveled frame upright on the plush cushions with a burdensome sigh, Pennywell rubs his eyes and yawns, "There is a pile of bullshit communications in every language known to God littering my desk. Why is this one so damned important?"

"It's from Griffin Pike."

Pennywell shifts from sleep-deprived senior to sharp-as-nails CEO, "I was hoping he perished in the attack. Go ahead and read it to me, Andrew. What does the smug motherfucker have to say?"

Andrew unfolds the thin faxed sheet, scanning the double-spaced contents, "You will hate this, sir."

Pennywell smooths back wispy gray hair with an affirmative nod, unrolls his shirt sleeves, and slides socked feet back into his shoes, "I hate everything, Andrew. Why should this be any different?" Distracted by Richard dabbing crumbled chicken remnants off a serving tray on the low coffee table, he mumbles more, "This day of reckoning is long overdue."

"Okay. Here it goes. Try to hold your comments until I finish."

Dear Artemus,

This correspondence is your formal invitation to participate in a post-invasion tribunal with YOU as the honored guest. The event is open to the world's surviving public and private entities, convening inside the World Forum Theater at the Hague on September 1, 2044. You are under no formal subpoena, but this forum will be your only public opportunity to defend against a growing list of indictments targeting you and The Powers That Be. The world suffered an extinction-level disaster impacting every human being on our planet. Someone must pay the price.

In the fiery aftermath of the aliens' unexpected and miraculous retreat, public and private entities crawled from the wreckage, mad as hell and needing answers. More to the point, they desire someone else to blame. In most quarters of the world, it is common knowledge that The Powers That Be keep their extraterrestrial alliances close to the vest. And yet, despite your close ties, you neglected to warn world leaders of the impending apocalypse. Your silence was unconscionable, immoral, and a crime against humanity, eclipsing Hitler, Stalin, and Mao combined.

With that said, the following counts will be adjudicated during the multi-day proceeding:

Count One: The Powers That Be possessed intelligence that an alien invasion was imminent but failed to warn the world's governments.

Count Two: The Powers That Be utilized alien shielding to protect their infrastructure from the devastating

EMP effects generated by fleets of ships darkening every continent. The cascade of death and destruction in the wake of worldwide darkness is beyond description.

Count Three: The Powers That Be mismanagement of the International Outer Space Consortium, or IOSC, resulted in over 4,000 deaths from multiple orbiters crashing back to Earth. Many thousands more innocent civilian casualties resulted from the horrific impacts.

There are additional counts, but those mentioned herein should provide your overpaid legal counsel enough to conjure a defense of the indefensible. I wish you luck, sir.

Further, as the event's host and coordinator, I have commandeered SATstar's immense resources to facilitate this tribunal. We both know I availed myself of your tech. Put that aside. It is of no consequence to the rest of the world lying in ruins. And yet it compelled me to write to you as a courtesy before releasing my official presentation inviting the world to join me in the Netherlands in person or via a remote feed.

I have arranged accommodations and security for you and your team at the adjacent hotel, which came through the onslaught relatively unscathed, like the theater complex. I trust you have access to transportation beyond my capabilities. However, if you need a ride, please let us know."

With my deepest regards,

Griffin Pike, *CEO, SATstar Industries*

PS – Do not preempt the tribunal by leaking this communique to the press. The Fourth Estate is dead, dark, or in my pocket. A new and better human civilization will rise from the ashes. It is you and your organization on the verge of extinction. However, I am offering an opportunity to plead your case before bowing out with grace and dignity. The kind of exit you and Paddy McCoy denied my ancestor, Charles Pike, in 1928 when you murdered him in cold blood. Yes, Mr. Pennywell, I know about your Amazon misadventure and the existence of a lost ship described in great detail in a notebook that, by rights, belongs to me.

Your reckoning day is nigh.

* * *

Andrew folds the letter and replaces it in his pocket for safekeeping.

Richard dabs his mouth with a napkin and stands to make a hasty exit, "Andrew, please let me know if I can be of assistance. I am not an expert on the legalities, but I believe in the PTB's mission. We are not guilty of any of those crimes."

Pennywell and Andrew exchange a quick glance before the CEO proffers a gentle nod toward his old friend, "Yes, Richard. That would be great."

Andrew steps aside, accommodating Richard's quick exit from the pod while noting Pennywell's calm reaction to the letter.

Sensing Andrew's disapproving stare, Pennywell manages a wily grin, "Before you say anything, Andrew, let Richard catch up on his own. Everybody has a job down here. If you must know, I put Professor John Stevens on the lost ship because I needed King's focus square on the Gorks and the golden ellipse situation."

"That does not square with reality, sir."

"Reality? You want to talk about reality?" Turning toward the 160-inch paper-thin monitor, Pennywell watches drone footage of the iconic Burj Khalifa in Dubai fully engulfed in flames, lighting up the screen like a Roman candle. The structural marvel breaks apart in a terrifying cascade of sections before pancaking to the ground in a tidal wave of smoke and debris. "There's your reality, my friend. And I don't give a flying fuck what Pike says, I'm not paying for shit like that."

"Sir, please don't underestimate this situation. Griffin Pike only gives us a few days to set up a defense and get our people to the Netherlands. Do I have your permission to convene an emergency meeting of The Council?"

"That depends. Do we know which members survived the invasion?"

"I included an up-to-date list in your morning briefing, which you never read."

"Don't be a wise-ass, Andrew. Just give me the bad news."

"Yes, sir. On a positive note, eight are alive and well. And I think we can assemble them in London in short order and form a cohesive defense."

"I hate being on defense." Scrutinizing his android valet, Pennywell's famous short temper finally erupts, "Jesus H. Christ, Andrew, give me the casualty report. Aside from Kobayashi's heart attack, which Council members died during the fucking invasion?"

"My apologies, sir. Aldo Santamaria attended his daughter's wedding at a seaside resort in Half Moon Bay when a tidal wave swept everything out into the Pacific."

"Jesus. Now we need a new COO." Switching his demeanor to glib on a dime, he flashes a toothy smile toward Andrew, "You want a job?"

"No. How would you say it? Hell no." Andrew proceeds with a subtle head shake, "Franklin Pierce was also confirmed killed in the

Freedom Tower collapse."

"Bad luck for Frank, wrong place at the wrong time. Okay, we're down a COO and a CFO. Who else?"

"John Murdock."

Huffing a weary sigh, Pennywell hunches over and swipes away a genuine tear. "Goddammit, not old John."

"The Murdock and Ripley building was flattened by the Gorks. The firm lost over 80 percent of their people, including Mr. Murdock."

"That is a devastating loss for them and a potential intelligence disaster. Is the site secure?"

"Viraj Patel …" Andrew notes Pennywell's blank stare, "your Chief of Global Logistics. Come on, sir."

"Yeah, of course, the footballer; I know whom you mean. Throws a helluva party."

"One and the same. Viraj is activating our contacts in the London police department and Scotland Yard to seal the site. In the meantime, we're advising any London operatives who feel they may be exposed to document dump at Edward Laughton's home address."

"Why Laughton? That prick hates us."

"As of today, he is Murdock and Ripley's senior surviving shareholder. And while he has maintained a steady animus against us through the years, he is our outside legal counsel by default."

"Not for long, Andrew. I'm sure Ed would stab me in the back, Brutus style, given the opportunity."

"Nevertheless, we will need Mr. Laughton's international law expertise."

"What about that firecracker of an in-house lawyer we brought onto the Council last year?"

"Vita Carrera?"

"Yes, that's her name! Get her ass to The Hague. I want eyes on the ground to see what we are up against."

"Okay, but we may want to include her in our London meeting

first. We need all the help we can get. This could spell the end of The Powers That Be."

Waving a dismissive hand toward his too-serious valet, Pennywell leans back on the plush couch, a mischievous grin creasing his expressive face, "Andrew, we have the truth on our side. Griffin Pike admitted he availed himself of the Advisers' EMP shielding tech on his satellites. I'm glad he did. We use that network too. Otherwise, the motherfucker would be reduced to eating beans from a can like that asshole Canadian PM. Pike is jockeying for the pole position in the race for post-apocalypse world domination. We are the only functioning entity standing in his way."

"There are others, sir. The United States government used our technology on over half of its resources."

"Yes, but the aliens spent extra time churning the air over North America. That's where we lost our COO and CFO. The shielding is rather useless if the infrastructure is kaput."

"Sad but true."

"With humanity regressing to full caveman mode in less than a week, what the Gorks failed to destroy, the locals are burning to the ground." Staring at another fiery spectacle on the screen, Pennywell mutters, "What a curious lot we are."

"I will see to the arrangements in London. I understand the Savoy Hotel is in decent shape. The Brits commandeered it as an emergency operations hub. We can set up the meeting there. By the way, King George is asking for our assistance. What should we tell him?"

"I am not going to screw the royals. They have been good to us over the years. Provide George with as many autonomous trucks full of relief supplies as possible."

Human-worthy bafflement crosses Andrew's face, "I'll get in touch with our people out at Heathrow."

"What is it, Andrew? There is one more thing rattling your synthetic noggin."

"I have extensive knowledge of The Powers That Be history, but the Amazon misadventure and lost ship mentioned in Griffin Pike's postscript does not compute."

Pennywell laughs despite the gravity of the situation. "Jesus Christ, Andrew, sometimes I must remind myself that you are just a bucket of bolts and wires."

"I prefer to think of myself as more than that, sir."

"Oh, but you are. Much more, in fact." After pausing, considering his friend's chiseled features, Pennywell shrugs, "Our new friend Griffin Pike refers to an incident involving myself and another PTB agent named Paddy McCoy."

"*The* Paddy McCoy? Your former mentor?"

"One and the same."

"If you don't mind my asking, sir, what happened?"

Propping his long frame back into the couch cushions and angling his left leg over his right knee, Pennywell gestures for his friend and fixer to take a seat, "Allow me to revel in this moment of knowing something you don't before telling the story."

Andrew takes Richard's chair, brushing a chicken crumb off the soft leather cushioned seat. "Take your time, Artemus. I'm all ears whenever you are ready to proceed."

Pennywell coughs and clears his throat, "It happened way back in 1928, Andrew. My God, things were a helluva lot simpler back then. Paddy and I were dispatched to the Amazon to interview a local Brazilian man who survived an alien altercation while working as a day laborer at Henry Ford's pipedream of a rubber plantation, Fordlandia."

"Fordlandia? He named it after himself?"

Pennywell laughs, "Yeah, how about that. Do you think that son-of-a-bitch had an ego the size of Detroit? Anyway, I digress. I thought the assignment involved burying evidence of the reported alien encounter and paying off witnesses. In other words, typical PTB protocol. Paddy knew we were there to see a man named Charles Pike."

Pennywell raises a hand, stopping further interruption, "I later learned Pike was hired by Henry Ford and the Feds to locate an ancient alien shipwreck in the goddamn Amazon rainforest."

"So what? Earth is littered with ET crash sites."

Pennywell smiles, "Not like this ship, Andrew."

Andrew shrugs, "Okay, Artemus, I'll bite. What makes this shipwreck so special?"

"It contains an unimaginable treasure and a world-killer weapon in its payload."

"Once again, how do we know that?"

"A mythical alien shipwreck from another time lost in the Amazon is the stuff of legend, like El Dorado. Perhaps they are one and the same. As fate would have it, Ford's day laborers dug up a stone artifact with a detailed map of the Amazon surrounding Fordlandia. Griffin's ancestor—Charles Pike—was hired to survey clues within the map and determine if they pointed to the lost ship—a discovery that would rock a late 20s civilization verging on depression and another world war. Well, Ford did not want that. He craved the ancient alien technology to vault his ass light years ahead of the competition. And in return, he would hand the world killer to the US government as a quid-pro-quo."

Andrew checks the time, "Sorry, sir. A lot to absorb."

"I will cut to the chase. When Paddy and I arrived at Fordlandia, we noticed Pike's symptoms of contact with toxic Gray blood. The man was a walking pandemic. Paddy put the bloke out of his misery with a single shot between the eyes."

"So, you never learned if Charles Pike found the lost ship?"

"It is worse. Paddy killed him before we could interrogate the bastard and learn where he hid the original stone artifact. The only record of its existence is a hand-drawn copy in Pike's notebook. I spent years comparing that map to satellite imagery but came up empty. The damn thing is as useful as an old pirate map without an X marking the spot."

Andrew raises his hand to interrupt, "What if Griffin Pike holds the key to unlocking the map?"

"I doubt it, Andrew, but hold that thought. Through Professor Stevens' latest efforts, we can't even decrypt the nickel-sized disk Ping removed from the dead alien scout. The tech is beyond our capabilities."

"It sounds like Pike's notebook and the scout's disk are dead-ends."

"Not so fast, my friend. Stevens did make a rather brilliant discovery."

"What did he find?"

Pennywell uncrosses his long legs and leans forward, "Pike embellished his map copy with five specific icons: a piranha, tree, snake, spider, and jaguar.

As God is my witness, I never saw it, but Stevens realized they trace a perfect fucking spiral. He theorized the lost ship rests at the nucleus. I know it's not much to go on, but it is too perfect to be a coincidence. And damned if I wasn't desperate to close the chapter on Paddy's last mission. I sent Stevens to Brazil to check out his best guess of the spot, and now he is missing. Perhaps he took a dart to the carotid like dear old Paddy, for all I know."

Andrew frowns, "I can't help noticing you did not seek Richard King's input. Why not?"

"Christ, Andrew. Do I have to explain every decision I make? If you must know, before the invasion, finding the lost ship was nothing more than an abstract puzzle piece in my life's work that I wanted to resolve before I died."

"Okay. I'm not aware of you dying anytime soon. My apologies for prying into your personal decision-making process."

"I can't tell if you are being facetious. I hate that."

Andrew offers a sly smile, "It's a gift. Okay, you said to hold that thought. Do you think Griffin Pike's motivations amount to nothing more than revenge for his murdered ancestor?"

"Hell no! He doesn't give a flying fuck about old Chuck. Nobody did. The world's ruined status is the opportunity of a lifetime for Griffin. Not only that but his ridiculous tribunal is also meant to distract the PTB while he goes after the lost ship. It troubles me to no end wondering what he plans to do with the world killer."

"I apologize for not being up to speed on this, sir."

"Andrew, my friend. You do quite enough. In fact, if not for your quick thinking, I would be dead already, just like poor John, Frank, and Aldo. I'm sorry to say this tempest in a teacup between myself and Pike has been brewing for quite some time."

Multiple scenarios play out inside Andrew's quantum processors, "The PTB has partnered with SATstar on numerous projects. In fact, we considered acquiring Pike's company a few years back."

Pennywell nods, "That's true. I bet dollars to donuts he knows Uncle Chuck's old notebook sits in a long-forgotten lockbox at a Bank of Scotland branch right off Trafalgar Square."

"I will have Viraj secure it."

"Let it be. If Griffin makes a play for the notebook, let him have it. We can kill two birds with one stone: learn if Griffin has a key to the map and ferret out any traitors within our ranks in one fell swoop."

"Sir, I doubt you need to worry about that."

"Andrew, you never can tell."

"Okay, Artemus, just to be clear: you want Griffin Pike to steal the notebook from the bank vault?"

"You ever fish, Andrew?"

"No, sir."

"Well, I hate the fucking sport with a white-hot passion. But I know that if one plans to fish, it is paramount to use the proper bait."

"Charles Pike's notebook?"

"Yes." Pennywell stands and stretches with a loud yawn. "As for our meeting in London to prep for Pike's kangaroo trial, assemble what's left of The Council—like I know you are already planning to do—at the Savoy. I want Griffin's spies to see us in full meltdown mode. We're going to put on a scene for the ages. In the meantime, I will get Richard's ass up to speed on the lost ship. He can take the lead in assembling a team and head to Brazil. Perhaps even recover Stevens, dead or alive."

Invigorated by the semblance of a proactive plan, Pennywell's eyes widen, "Hey! We can enlist our new recruits to accompany Richard. Any news from the Haigs?"

"Not a word, sir. It has only been a few days. Give them time."

"Good Christ, how much time do they need? I wish Flynn was here. We are short on manpower."

"And womanpower."

"Yes, Andrew, that, too." Pennywell musses the carefully coiffed hair on Andrew's head, "You know, this is the first time I used one of these damn pods for anything other than a place to nap."

Brushing an unruly dark auburn lock off his forehead, Andrew rolls his eyes, "Good show, sir. Jolly good show."

Astrid | Above Earth
09:42 p.m. | August 26, 2044

The hulking silhouette of a cargo vessel wobbles aloft, hovering above a cordoned-off section of Cairo's decimated international airport smoldering in post-invasion ruins. After a gravity-defying "All systems go for launch," the ship lurches into the ruddy smoke-filled Egyptian sky with the grace of a drunken elephant on a medical transport mission to a lunar base.

Post shedding Earth's gravitational pull with reversed alien tech ease, Captain Astrid Brown stretches from her co-pilot seat restraints in the weightlessness, gliding nimble fingertips across a bank of overhead switches. In response, tiny jets whisk the space-going commercial freighter in minute increments, correcting its trajectory toward a PTB black site erected atop the remains of an infamous Chinese Moonbase abandoned in the early 30s. A poker-faced robotic medical team awaits the commandeered vessel's arrival with Agent Flynn's spanking new lab-grown human liver ready for transplant. A high-octane corpuscular rehab program to accelerate growth will constitute the Powers That Be agent's lunar post-op regimen.

Preferring the gut-churning intensity of piloting cutting-edge aerial marvels beyond their breaking points, Astrid, the sometimes astronaut, laments her current ship as the antithesis of the sleek and beautiful craft that inspired her love of flight. However, she accepts that the advent of anti-gravity propulsion rendered aerodynamics moot years ago. The unnatural act of taking flight morphed from forward thrust and the science of lift to an indelicate vault through the ether in utilitarian vessels liberated from gravitational constraints. Screw physics.

Astrid yawns aloud, bored to tears, glancing through a port side window beyond Nicole's vacant command seat. With a bemused head shake, she replays her friend's litany of *I'm over the lout* declarations.

"Yeah, sure you are, Nicole."

While Astrid maintains a solo watch on the flight deck, Nicole dotes on Agent Flynn in a makeshift ICU retrofitted into the cargo bay, nudging aside an equally concerned Nina Madsen to watch over the PTB agent strapped atop a gurney in a medically induced coma.

Despite having grave concern for Agent Flynn's life-threatening situation, Nina stepped aside, allowing Nicole to nursemaid the stricken man. Wise and worldly beyond her 56 years, the senior-level PTB administrator had experienced the turbulence of complicated relationships too many times and recognized true love when she saw it.

Meanwhile, caretaking the autonomous ship's flight deck, Astrid dons her noise-canceling headphones, playing *Straight to Hell* by her favorite Edinburgh band, Dog Snot. With the anything-but-dulcet tones thumping in her head, she muses aloud, unaware her voice carries through the ship's tight confines: "Deep space and a sea of stars filled with creepy aliens who want us dead. Ain't life grand?"

With her ears ringing from Astrid's snarky gripe, Commander Nicole Weiss wriggles her long and fit frame through the narrow portal, gracing the flight deck with her commanding presence. Checking a warning indicator blinking red on her virtual screen, she settles into her seat with a blue-eyed sigh, "Let's keep an eye on these wonky scrubbers. Man, this boat is a piece of shit."

Realizing Astrid can't hear a word over her noise-canceling headphones, Nicole pantomimes to gain her co-pilot's attention.

Astrid pulls off her headphones, "What?"

Nicole chuckles at her beautiful friend, "What's grand, my dear, is I finally have Flynn by the balls. Isn't it ironic that I escort his sorry ass to the Moon?"

Tickled by Nicole's lack of self-awareness, Astrid releases her headphones in the zero-g and breaks into laughter.

Leaning over her tech-heavy armrest, Nicole comes within inches of the Scottish lass's pert nose, narrowing her gaze on the discombobulated co-pilot, trying to regain her composure, "What's so funny? Do you think losing our air scrubbers is a joke?"

"Don't you remember? Before hell broke loose, you threatened to dump Flynn on the Moon. Nicole, this is your big opportunity."

Nicole shakes her head, not having any of life's little ironies on her watch, as a blaring alarm drowns her witty reply.

"Ah shit, Astrid! Something hit us! I thought this thing was tuned to avoid space debris. Release the autopilot and inform Nina to suit up. I want control of this bucket if we contact anything larger than a golf ball."

"Aye-aye, captain. You now have the stick." Astrid pulls a life support helmet over her close-shorn head and projects a three-dimensional kilometer-wide sweep inside her visor, "Huh. That's odd."

Struggling to get a feel for the unresponsive boat, Nicole blurts out, "What? Speak up, girl."

"There is nothing larger than a pinhead close to our trajectory."

"This fucking hunk of junk. God, what I would give to have a proper dam ship for this medevac moonshot."

"Well, false alarms happen, but now you steered us off course."

"The fuck you say. Are you questioning my piloting skills?"

"No. It's just that this tub is pulling over two degrees to port."

Nicole activates the VR display inside her visor, studying the boxy ship's off-course path, hurtling through space at over 22,000 mph.

A long silence ensues as the pair tag-team troubleshooting protocols, attempting to correct their course, to no avail.

"It's like we are caught in a rip current."

"Not quite, Astrid. We're pulling toward that dark mass. Do you see it?"

"Oh man, what is that thing? I thought the Gorks were gone."

"Astrid, there are at least two other fleets out here, remember?"

"I was hoping they left, too."

"Doesn't look that way."

"We are accelerating past the point of no return."

"It doesn't matter. We're stuck in their tractor beam."

"The question is: Who the fuck are they?"

Nicole presses her comm button, "Nina, how are you and Flynn doing down there?"

Nina shimmies into a suit and fumbles a helmet onto her head before attending to the anesthetized Flynn, "He's fine. What's going on up there, Missy?"

"Jesus, Nina, I hate when you call me that."

The freighter jolts and lurches from side to side.

Nina's distressed voice resonates over the comm, "What the hell, Nicole? Did we hit something?"

Nicole grips the useless rudder and tries to initiate a reverse thrust, but it is too late. Smashing her hand on the comm button,

"Listen to me, Nina. We are about to be boarded by fucking aliens. Buckle up and stay calm. Oh, and make sure Flynn's lines are secure."

A loud thunk followed by the unmistakable sound of loosening rivets reverberates between the scared pilots. Astrid turns her helmeted head toward her partner, "They are right outside."

A frightening hiss permeates the flight deck as both pilots are enveloped in an anesthetizing cloud of neon-green gas.

Flynn | Gray battlecruiser
03:02 a.m. | August 27, 2044

A cloaked spy ship lurks beyond Earth's thinnest atmospheric layer, almost halfway between the coveted planet and its lone orbiting moon. Dispatched from the Gray alien fleet for a front-row seat to observe and report on the Gork invasion in real-time, they dodged the decimated lizard invaders' haphazard departure instead.

The aborted Gork invasion reaffirmed the planet's resilience to outside threats. In the words of an august Gray historian, "The Gorks now understand what we learned eons ago: invading Earth is fraught with known and unknown obstacles, biding time, lying in wait."

Maneuvering to maintain proximity with a phalanx of functioning satellites that survived the Gorkian EMP onslaught, the diminutive Grays recognize the shielding tech and seethe upon learning a pacifistic brethren race conspired with an organization called The Powers That Be to help humanity stave off extinction. The revelation adds a new wrinkle to a hegemonic master plan percolating on hold since their mistimed wormhole reentry into the solar system in 1928.

In the wake of the abrupt Gorkian defeat and cessation of the Light Specters' beacon, the Grays determine The Powers That Be—and a host of patronizing alien allies—are the only viable obstacles athwart their righteous return to Earth eons after ignominious defeat. However, to ensure history does not repeat, searching for the lost ship and its world-killing device becomes paramount. The Grays dispatch more patrols to the planet, collecting human specimens and reconnoitering with the squadron of pill-shaped survey vessels combing the South American continent, continuing a century-long search for the lost ship.

While docking vessels crowded with mortified human abductees, the cruiser's sensor array identifies a small ship on a trajectory toward the moon, blundering through space in plain sight.

The order comes fast and furious from the main fleet hunkered in Ganymede's shadow: *"Seize the ship, interrogate the crew, and then process their flesh."*

The cruiser swallows the tiny hauler inside a loading bay, where an assault team storms the ship and pries it open, like cracking a walnut. Finding only three unconscious females and one comatose male, the aliens consider spacing the prisoners and destroying the worthless vessel before reading the older woman and discovering their PTB ties.

With a renewed interest in the captives' health, the aliens triage the man's internal injuries and find he requires a liver transplant before squeezing him for intel and then killing him. A quick scan of the gallows reveals a man swept up with an entire village from a remote parcel of Somali farmland as the most suitable donor among the prisoners.

Meanwhile, the trio of women from the small vessel is prepped for hybridized impregnation like dozens of female abductees languishing in dingy cells belowdecks.

Guards yank the Somali man from a clinging human throng of fellow villagers using violent telekinesis, his screams echoing down a long, dank corridor as he is dragged to the ship's infirmary deck. Fully conscious but out of his mind with unadulterated terror, he sees a 7-foot alien receive orders from much smaller counterparts. Meanwhile, a second tall figure emerges and straps the inconsolable African's arms and legs to a metal table like a slab of meat. Without warning, a pistol-like device lowers from the ceiling and pierces his gut with an aqua-colored laser, making a surgical incision across his abdomen. The tall and imposing pair excise the man's internal organs, oblivious to his pleas for mercy.

The dying man's final image through eyes bulging from darkened sockets is the profile of another Black man sleeping like an angel on a gleaming metal surface slid into place beside him.

The aliens cut out the African's eyeballs, too. Waste not, want not.

* * *

A nightmarish sensation of spiders burrowing under his skin jostles Agent Flynn from a dreamless sleep. Straining filmy swollen eyeballs beyond his prone body strapped atop a cold metal surface, he fixates on a blurry grid blinking green, orange, and blue like squinting at Christmas lights. A weird and inexplicable form ambles past and disappears beyond his periphery. Unable to move, he feels a cold draft on his naked body causing his teeth to clench into a thick intubation tube snaking down his parched throat. Quelling panic, The Powers That Be Agent controls his breathing and struggles to quantify his bloody awful predicament. The metallic smell of blood permeates his nostrils past a cannula shoved up his nose from a gooey substance clinging between his exposed skin and the smooth tabletop. "Christ, is that my blood?"

Peering upward from his vulnerable, splayed position, he follows intravenous lines coursing with neon fluids extending from an intricate web of glowing tubes hanging from meshy shapes, like stereo speakers, before looping into multiple catheters fixed to both forearms.

A terrible sting alerts Flynn to another catheter extending from his penis and winding into a glassy assemblage bubbling with a bright green fluid.

Despite the direness of his situation, Flynn can't resist thinking of a joke: Man, these PTB drug tests are getting weirder and weirder.

A blinding electrified pain washes over his body as the towering figure reemerges from the shadows. Paralyzed by the horrific jolt, a voice echoes in Flynn's throbbing head: "We decide your fate. Lie still, and it will be over soon."

Out of the darkness, the rail-thin 7-foot humanoid figure lowers its bulbous head to inches above Flynn's face. The agent's watery eyes focus on his sad reflection in the alien's menacing stare, crushing vestigial resolve while killing any further attempts at gallows humor.

Flynn watches the alien, known throughout high-level PTB circles as a scarecrow—crossbred from Gray and human DNA—straighten its lanky form and smooth long pale gray fingers over the human's sutured lower right abdomen.

Reacting to the prisoner's scarecrow reference, the alien oozes telepathic malevolence while admonishing the agent: *"Your body accepts the new organ. Soon you will reciprocate by telling us everything you know about your organization."*

* * *

Flynn closes his eyes and lies ramrod still—as if he had a choice in the matter—eavesdropping on more Grays entering the darkened alien OR. Straining to recognize a syllable of their gibberish broadcasting inside his head, he realizes the dialect is foreign to his trained ear. Instead, he muddies his thoughts with imagery: A bucket of frosty longnecks on a tropical beach. His antique 1968 Aston Martin collecting dust in an East London garage, most likely leveled to the ground. A fucking decent hamburger with a side of salty chips. Nicole's naked body spread across a bearskin rug before a roaring fireplace. Uh-oh. His penile catheter twitches, prompting one of his captors to slam him with another telekinetic blast of pain.

Reeling from the mind-bending trauma, Flynn digs deep within himself, "Well, at least one body part is still in working order. That's a start."

Nina | Gray battlecruiser
04:12 a.m. | August 27, 2044

Within the shadowed recesses of a darkened cell, Nina Madsen awakens from a deep anesthetized slumber and pushes to a seated position against the cold and unforgiving rear wall. Interminable whimpering punctuated by bone-chilling shrieks, screams, and an odd bark pierces the oxygen-deprived mustiness. Swiping at her face, the PTB administrator is relieved to find herself wearing the same enviro-suit she donned before all hell broke loose. Nevertheless, the anesthetic after-effects dull her senses and muddle cogent thought in the cramped and inhospitable space.

"Holy Mother of God. We were transporting Flynn to the moon."

Pulling scabby knees under her chin, Nina hugs bruised forearms around her calves, rocking herself while staring out thick metal bars fronting the 12-foot space. As the blurriness ebbs, her watery gaze resolves Nicole's naked form bathed in bluish light and shadows with a dead-eyed stare, long tubes snaking from her arms, and a jumpsuit bundled at her feet.

Movement and a cough alert Nina to a presence inside the cell across the corridor beyond Nicole's curled position.

"Astrid? Is that you?"

* * *

Zint performs his assigned duty of monitoring the latest batch of rattled human specimens on a bank of virtual screens inside a guardroom at the terminus of the near-capacity 10-cell block in the dingy bowels of the surveillance ship.

A loud bark resonates from the far end of the dim blue corridor, prompting the third-mate apprentice to select the noisy four-legged beast's cell. Struck by its stubborn loyalty, sitting on its haunches in a protective posture before its shellshocked human. Zint was advised the dumb animal would not part from its master, insisting the alien kidnappers bring it along. Tapping an update along the bottom of the screen, he reads the poor animal's vivisection is imminent.

Having never set foot on his home planet beyond the stars, the 80-year-old conscript spent his entire life aboard the ship, indoctrinated into hating Earth and its filthy primitive life forms. Despite his immersive upbringing, Zint feels unusual remorse for the animal in the pits of his stomachs.

Cognizant that his superiors could read his treasonous thought, the Gray sailor purges his brain and swipes the screen closed.

A female stirring awake four cells on the aft side distracts Zint from his perilous rumination. Zooming in on the charcoal-haired woman, he watches her attempt to communicate with occupants in the opposite cell—a transgression calling for a painful telekinetic slap. Heaving a burdensome sigh, he taps a circle at the bottom of her screen and reads the updated status: Failed hybridization. Terminate after interrogation.

He beams an electrifying jolt, lowering his round head, eliciting a surprised, painful yelp from the woman in Cell 4.

Using a bare minimum of telepathic effort, Zint recites a scripted admonishment: *"Communication among the prisoners is forbidden. Transgressors will suffer painful punishment. Consider this your first and only warning."*

* * *

Nina wipes a long string of drool from her mouth. The painful blast and stern warning melt her brave façade into a pool of self-pity and worry for her friends. Curling back into a fetal position, she sobs, wracked by a familiar sense of loss overwhelming her thoughts. Her body ached in ways she had not experienced since a miscarriage in her late 30s squashed dreams of motherhood. Placing both hands between her legs, wetness permeates her enviro suit. Bolting upright, she checks herself and realizes she is soaked from the waist down in blood.

Betty Hill | Cleopatra Hospital, Cairo
09:12 a.m. | August 27, 2044

An odd click-click-click punctuates the rhythmic hums and whirs of Rachel's tech-laden bedside monitors and paraphernalia. Forcing open crusty eyelids, she turns her messy blond bedhead propped up on thick Egyptian cotton pillows onto a burly fellow with his back turned in ill-fitting blue scrubs, fiddling with something on a rolling cart. Pretending to sleep, she listens and tries to figure out what he is doing. As the squeaky-wheeled cart is rolled toward her, she hears a familiar clank of a cup and saucer and assumes the fellow is delivering her breakfast. She opens her eyes and sees a swarthy-looking man recording pictures with a cubed device squeezed between his stubby thumb and index finger from behind the cart.

Bolting upright, Rachel snatches a cup of piping hot tea and flings it across the man's arms and face, sending him staggering backward and falling over a chair.

Surprised by her defensive action, he snarls like a beaten dog, pulling onto his feet and swiping a scorched forearm across his pocked and ruddy face. Checking the device squeezed in his meat hook hand, a contact-sized lens falls out and clinks onto the floor.

Rachel shakes her head and rasps, "You broke your little camera. Too bad for you; now get the fuck out of my room!"

None too keen to follow the command of a woman, he drops the ruined device and crushes it under his shoe. "No. Too bad for you. The pictures had already been uploaded to my partner waiting downstairs. We will sell your images and feed our families for a year. Everybody wants to see the face that conspired with the aliens."

In Rachel's altered mental state, she cannot fathom the awful man's accusation, "Conspired? We, I did not; I tried to help. What is wrong with you? Why would I do that?" Monitors squawking and beeping in her ears, she shuts her eyes and raises her bandaged hands to her head to make it all go away. The palms of her hands pressed to her head burn like fire.

"Mrs. Hill? Mrs. Hill? Can you hear me? Wake up, dear! You are having another nightmare."

Rachel's bruised eye sockets open onto Zahra's pleasant face. "Did you catch the guy?"

"Dear, you were screaming in your sleep. I would let that pass, but we ran out of room on the lower floors and had to move patients up here last night. I need to keep the noise level down."

"But he was in here, taking pictures. I saw him." Rachel's voice falters, and she turns sideways in a coughing spasm.

"Rest, Mrs. Hill. No one is up here taking pictures, I assure you. The patients allowed on this floor are all pre-screened, and your room is under constant guard." The nurse straightens the room, wheeling the squeaky cart beside the bed.

Rachel notes the lukewarm teacup sitting where she left it the evening before, "Huh. I guess you are right."

Zahra moves around the bed and crunches something under her shoe, "What is this?" The olive-skinned beauty lifts a sugar-cube-sized object in her hand and examines it by the light leaking around the closed window shade.

Rachel starts to cry.

* * *

An overweight fellow in ill-fitted stolen scrubs sneaks back into an over-capacity recovery room after a successful foray past security and crushes atop his rickety field hospital cot. Placing a burned forearm behind his fat bearded head, he looks at his neighbor in a full-body cast, then scans the indigent cases piled onto cots from wall to wall. "Fear not, my friends, revenge on the infidel will be sweet."

Richard | PTB HQ, Scotland
02:28 p.m. | August 27, 2044

Fit as a fiddle and rejuvenated following his 3-day forced hibernation, Professor Richard King polishes off the last corner of a peanut butter and bacon sandwich and allows a satisfied burp. Seated at his vintage pine desk inside a private office crammed with pictures, awards, and memorabilia, he studies a computer-generated reconstruction of Cretaceous-era Gondwana topography following his debriefing from none other than the PTB CEO, Artemus Pennywell. Swiping away his hi-def 30-inch virtual display with an exasperated huff, Richard tamps down sheer frustration, "This is the epitome of a wild goose chase."

Downing dregs from a *Lost Cactus* coffee mug—a souvenir from a previous life—he pushes back from the messy desk and stretches his 122-year-old frame with a loud yawn.

* * *

In post-war 1947, Richard King, a brilliant 25-year-old MIT grad student, was plucked from obscurity and handed the keys to a clandestine PTB research facility under construction at an off-the-grid location in the American southwest. During those halcyon years, he tag-teamed with a cadre of human and alien minds while learning the ropes of working for The Powers That Be.

Expanding the top-secret laboratory codenamed Lost Cactus into ground zero for human advancements meted out to a gullible public through public and private entities, King butted heads with a phalanx of PTB sociologists, philosophers, theologians, and ethicists applying the brakes to King's rapid-fire breakthroughs through the sheer weight of their vetoes. The overbearing consultants quashed over 98% of King's mind-blowing discoveries, including a cure for baldness, as too radical for public consumption.

The amassed papers, data, and results of each untapped groundbreaking epiphany were boxed in wooden crates and warehoused on the long-since shuttered desert base, including King's prized accomplishment—a fountain of youth. Infuriated by the PTB's decision to halt his controversial research on the top-secret cell regeneration cocktail, the young and impetuous Richard King, who preferred the name Doc, rebelled against his superiors by testing the age-defying serum's efficacy on himself.

In 2044, with the world in ruins, an older and wiser Richard King looks upon the sum of his possessions crammed into an office far below the bucolic Scottish countryside. Half a world from the abandoned desert base where he spent the best years of life, the scientist laments the rash and hubristic decision to prolong his lifespan, "Life is frail, fleeting, and better left in God's divine hands. I see that now."

* * *

Pulling into a white lab coat over his cardigan, a necessity in the underground lab's chilly temperature-controlled environment, King strides into the maze of aisles like a lab rat. Crossing the wide central artery bisecting the expansive concentric layout past a thick support column covered in pinned safety regs, switches, outlets, and emergency paraphernalia, he pauses at the sea monkey's floor-standing aquarium. Not finding the little guy amongst the floating algae and aquatic plants swaying in the greenish water, he tamps down air-fried chicken cravings and heads toward the far side of the lab, where he finds 11's back-turned stance before a trio of flat screens atop a cocktail-height lab bench. Richard's eyes glaze at the endless scroll of alien code under her intense cybernetic scrutiny.

Atop another bench on her right, the alien scout's nickel-sized disk floats on a column of air above an 8-inch black box, processing terabytes of raw ET code into PTB storage arrays sealed inside a contaminant-free clean room behind the adjacent wall. Stevens' custom disambiguating software crunches the data, jumping over the redacted sections, converting the decrypted leftovers into binary code displayed on the triple-screen workstation where 11 searches for anomalies or clues that may lead to the lost ship.

Sensing Richard's presence over her shoulder, 11 presses pause on the streaming code and unfolds her cross-armed pose. Turning her robotic gaze toward her boss, she morphs from an expressionless automaton into an intelligent young woman in an artificial heartbeat, "Hello, Professor. 8 tells me you are fully recovered from hibernation. That is welcome news."

"Thank you, Number 11. I'm just so damned hungry." Receiving no reaction from the attractive robot, he smiles and gestures at the screens, "No matter. Have you cracked the code?"

Showing genuine chagrin, 11's angelic features scrunch into a look of sheer wonderment. Pulling an unruly blue lock behind a studded left ear, 11 sighs and offers a shrug, "No. Almost half of the disk's contents will not decompress. It may be a security feature, or perhaps the disk is damaged. At any rate, the missing code creates gaping holes in the reconstructed 3D topography. At this point, there are as many variables as leaves in the rainforest canopy from above. And add into the mix, for the past century since the disk's recording, large parcels have been clear-cut by logging interests, soybean farmers, and strip mining operations, causing soil erosion and flooding."

"The landscape has changed a lot since the alien scout recorded his scans on the disk."

11 produces a serious-faced frown, "I'm afraid so. We are only seeing half the picture at best. The lost ship may sit at the bottom of a manmade reservoir under a mile of solid rock. At worst, we may be

looking on the wrong continent altogether."

"Good Christ, let's hope not. What about lidar?"

"Okay. Where would you start? It is a big continent."

Surprised by 11's terse reply, King drops the idea altogether.

However, his professional curiosity remains beyond piqued, "Yes, 11, the area is thousands of miles of untamed wilderness. I once heard it described as the Green Inferno."

11's face brightens, "Oh, I like that. It sounds pretty."

"11?"

"Yes, Professor?"

King motions for her to follow him to the tiny disk floating half a foot above the shiny black processor, "If this disk is a worthless piece of crap, what prompted Stevens to embark on his solo Amazon expedition?"

11 scrunches her pert nose and tugs on her shoulder-length cerulean hair, "I am really not at liberty to say."

"Out with it, or I will … well … I will think of something."

The replicant proffers a pouty reply, "Professor Stevens found a key to the map inside that old notebook."

A little hurt that he had to pry the information from his robot assistant, Richard masks frustration at Pennywell's failure to mention Charles Pike's notebook during his 5-minute debrief earlier that morning. "My dear, that notebook has undergone more scrutiny over the last century than any book since the Holy Bible. What the hell do you mean, Stevens found a key? And drop the coy act; it does not suit you."

Glancing back to ensure the alien code remained paused on the screen, she fidgets like a schoolgirl caught in a fib, "Dr. Stevens traced over the seemingly random landmarks on the hand-drawn map and discovered they form a perfect Fibonacci spiral."

With the flick of her thin wrist, 11 displays a virtual scan of Charles Pike's all-too-familiar hand-drawn map, "By overlaying the spiral made by connecting the map's landmarks on a reconstructed sector of Brazilian topography from the alien disk, Dr. Stevens centered the spiral's nucleus in a 10-mile radius of Amazon jungle over 100 miles southwest of Fordlandia."

Professor King watches a line animate between a fish and a tree to a snake and a spider before curving inward at a cat icon. The resulting perfect spiral resizes and syncs atop a dense tree canopy indistinguishable from its surroundings. "Pennywell signed off on the expedition based on this flimsy evidence?"

11 continues, "It is actually worse than you think. If the scale and orientation shift a fraction of a degree, the spiral's nucleus could be misplaced by hundreds of miles in any direction."

Richard shakes his head in disgust, "Stevens should have sought my assistance. Now I am left to clean up his mess."

11 swipes the screen closed, "That is the sum total of what I know. I am sorry to keep that from you, Professor."

"Think nothing of it, my dear. You are not responsible for the vagaries of your human counterparts." Tapping the benchtop holding Stevens' high-tech Rube Goldberg contraption, "Why is Pennywell insisting we continue running forensics on the disk? Since Stevens took it upon himself to be the hero, why not wait and see what he brings back?"

Realizing she has already violated her NDA protocols, 11 lowers her voice to just above a whisper, "Professor Stevens last communication indicated he reached the spiral's nucleus but found nothing but jungle. On August 9, two weeks before the invasion, he missed a scheduled call. We never heard from him again."

"Thank you, 11; you have been more than helpful. Pull 7 and 12 from whatever those two are doing to assist you in decompressing the alien code. Also, don't let the sisters tease you about your hair. Blue is my favorite color."

Returning to his office, Richard King mutters, "What

madness." Pulling a hardbound replica of Charles Pike's notebook from a drawer, he flips through the pages, admiring the man's obvious talent at draftsmanship. Flipping past the map, his gaze lands on an inked rendering labeled "Brazil Nut tree." King studies the intricate cross-hatched art, musing that a tree also represents Fordlandia on Pike's map. Rubbing tired eyes, his brow furrows, peering closer at an arrow hidden in the etched linework pointing toward a hole midway up the thick tree trunk. "Hello … What have we here?"

Pennywell | PTB HQ, Scotland
03:05 p.m. | August 27, 2044

Artemus Pennywell fidgets with an empty tumbler, waiting on a satellite uplink to the Chrysalis offices at the Cairo airport. A reliance on satellite comms in the post-invasion world was bad enough. Adding insult to injury, the only functioning communication satellites belonged to SATstar, owned by Griffin Pike. Mumbling under his breath, "He literally has the world by the balls. Fuck. I should have seen that coming."

Andrew ducks his head inside Pennywell's dark-lit inner sanctum. "Sir, Professor King is here to see you."

"That's fine, send him in. In the meantime, babysit this call to Cairo. They are past due, providing an update on Flynn's medevac."

"Consider it done, sir."

Richard enters, removing his tweed cap, exposing a messy head of charcoal curls, angling past Andrew into Pennywell's well-appointed office. Sliding into a seat opposite the massive desk fit for a CEO, the scientist's corduroy pants settle onto the brushed leather cushion, eliciting a loud squeak.

Andrew's steady voice pierces the silence between the two men, "Okay, sir. I will let you know when the call goes through."

With the ice broken, Richard leans forward in the voluminous chair and raps the edge of the desk with a thick knuckle, "Is this mahogany?"

"Teak, Richard. It's teak. You ask me that every time you pay a visit."

"You know, my old desk at Lost Cactus was teak. I miss that desk."

"From what I hear, you miss more than just your old desk." Recognizing his chief scientist's out-of-character evasiveness, Pennywell presses his longtime friend, "What's up, Richard? You seem a little agitated."

Ratcheting up his courage, Richard lowers his voice to a deep baritone and lets Pennywell have it with both barrels. "Maybe my agitation, as you put it, stems from the fact that I lost your trust at some point over the past few months."

Pennywell starts to interject, "Now Richard …."

"Quiet. Now you listen to me. You had Number 11 working with Stevens behind my back for months before the invasion. Artemus, why didn't you tell me what he discovered in the notebook? I checked his so-called perfect spiral. It is no more than an educated guess without scale and orientation. Instead of squeezing that damn disk for the remaining data, he's wandering around the Amazon."

Richard leans back and slows his breathing, cognizant of the risk when confronting the mercurial Artemus Pennywell—desperate times, desperate measures.

A rueful smile transforms Pennywell's face, moving to refill a glass at his well-stocked bar, "What is this world coming to when you can't count on a robot to keep her mouth shut? However, I am pleased you got that off your chest, Richard. Can I offer a glass of nerve-soothing elixir?"

Richard shakes his head, "No. I need to continue my work. Don't blame 11. Since the invaders left the world in shambles, our docket has many other issues. I need her assistance."

Brandishing a half-filled tumbler, Pennywell pivots, "Not your concern, Richard. I have surviving members of The Council taking the lead in coordinating relief efforts on every continent. And I assure you, you are now up to speed. Stay focused on the disk. See what you can accomplish that Stevens could not."

Richard stands to leave, hat in hand, "When I agreed to come here, we shook hands that I would have complete autonomy over the lab."

"You do, Richard. Locating the lost ship was personal, and I intended to keep it that way. I even kept Andrew out of the loop. We are having this conversation because a new cast of bad actors—from Gray invaders inexplicably biding their time to Griffin Pike—are suddenly in hot pursuit of the world killer on the lost ship's manifest. I cannot determine which scenario would prove worse for humankind."

Thunderstruck by Pennywell's blithe candor, Richard mumbles, "Probably the aliens, I suppose," and turns to exit.

Pennywell raises a hand, "Hold up, Richard. I lied. There is one more thing." Sliding open a desk drawer, the CEO removes a satchel and tosses it to his chief scientist.

Richard dumps a small fluorescent object from the cloth onto his meaty palm. "Is this what I think it is?"

"Yes. But not only that. It is from the alien scout who recorded the encrypted disk. What if you could pull DNA from that bone and somehow use it to unlock a complete 3D topographic scan from the disk."

"Did you have Stevens try that?"

"Are you kidding? Hell no. This hypothesis came from none other than Ping, and it screams for a brilliant DNA scientist who went by the name Doc many years ago."

Richard smiles, "You are right; I miss those days."

Pennywell downs the scotch and slams the glass atop his desk. "Well then, Doc. What the fuck are you waiting for? Get your corduroy ass back to the lab! We need to find that damn ship!"

As Richard turns to leave with the alien bone in hand, Andrew blocks the door. "Sir, I have bad news."

Richard's eyes widen in anticipation of the latest clusterfuck report from Andrew, who is never wrong.

Pennywell slumps back in his desk chair, "Andrew, for the love of … I just cleared the air with Richard. Can I catch a break for five lousy minutes?"

The advanced replicant shakes his head, "I just heard from the Chrysalis facility in Cairo. Flynn's medevac never arrived at the lunar base."

Flynn | Gray battlecruiser
09:05 p.m. | August 27, 2044

Agent Flynn gasps for air while absorbing punishing combinations of head and body blows from his invisible whip-fast tormenter inside a rank torture box. Already bruised and beaten, he forces a swollen-eyed glance at his sutured abdomen and raises his bloodied hands, flinging IVs burrowed deep into his arms like fringe, "Bloody hell, mate, stop kicking the crap out of me! Why did you nutters bother shoving some bloke's liver inside my guts to knock it out again?"

The beating stops for a fast 3-count before the 10-foot space strobes with blinding flashes synced to cacophonous screeches. The dizzying, mind-altering effects prompt Flynn to vomit a bright yellow viscous spattering that merges into a singular blob before oozing through a crisscrossed slot in the deck to somewhere below.

Horrified by whatever the hell just expelled from his guts, the PTB agent attempts to access his training, but the disorienting light show permeates his addled brain, impeding coherence. Grunting like an animal, he squints through the madness in a vain attempt to locate his torturer, "Where are you? Show yourself!" A wriggling sensation diverts his attention onto squirming green maggots oozing out of the L-shaped incision across his torso, "What the shit did you do to me? I can't tell you anything if I'm dead!"

His rasped pleas beckon the cube's reversion to a colorless void. Flynn exhales a relieved sigh, finding his incision intact and free of squiggling larvae. The 36-year-old Black Englishman coughs up a wad of noxious phlegm and spits neon particles at the wall. He watches the spatters fuse into a glob and wriggle through the nearest slot, leaving a slimy trail across the dullness. Monotonal memories of his brutal youth growing up in Liverpool flood his thoughts from out of the blue, "Bloody hell, I'm losing it."

"Agent Flynn."

Flynn's twisted form transfixes on two Grays dressed to the nines in silvery bodysuits with mesmerizing black eyes dominating oversized heads. The circumspect pair appearing almost amused were emotions such as humor possible for the über-advanced species.

Verging on insanity, Flynn blurts out the first words entering his enfeebled mind, "You lot resemble my friend, Ping, and that bloke gives me the fucking creeps."

"Is the one you call Ping allied with your organization? Why does he cause you discomfort? How many advisers conspire with your species?"

Enraged at the ease with which their mind tricks had him blabbing Ping's name, Flynn bullrushes the inquisitors. Bad move. An electrified shock sends him sprawling backward onto the slotted metal deck in a painful heap. Virtual flames rise through the grates like a human-sized barbeque. Like little gray gargoyles, the alien duo remains motionless, watching the pitiful human writhing in pain.

"Agent Flynn, cooperation is key to your survival."

The inquisitors end the flaming projection and study their beaten subject's reaction: curled into a fetal repose, secreting ocular fluid while asking for his mother. Exploiting the impetus behind the human's curious emotional response, the manipulative interrogators elevate a 5-year-old version of the human to his frontal lobe.

Under deep hypnosis, Flynn transforms into a young boy crouched beside a dresser, hiding from his abusive father: "Are you there, Mom? Don't let him hit me; I can't take it. Make him stop. Please, make him stop!"

* * *

Upon breaching the man's inner psyche, the interrogators—who never physically touched their subject—uncovered the human's traumatic childhood at the hands of his progenitors. Animals. They will all suffer a horrible and well-deserved fate.

The silver suits submit a report on their prized prisoner—and the one called Ping—to their superiors in the main fleet beyond Ganymede.

The human resumes beating closed fists into his bruised and bloodied head inside the interrogation cell.

Nina | Gray battlecruiser
01:05 a.m. | August 28, 2044

Since discovering the bloody mess between her legs, Nina Madsen huddles in the shadows against the hard, unforgiving back wall, rubbing her itchy, shaved head, shivering in the cold, dank cell.

Cognizant that her last period came and went years ago, the 56-year-old Powers That Be administrator considers the mysterious reappearance of Aunt Flo, maintaining a blank stare on her cellmate, Nicole, lying unconscious on the damp floor, breathing the thin air in and out.

A diminutive Gray guard trod past her cell numerous times, feigning attending to other prisoners. To Nina's surprise, the being, who introduced himself as Zint, professed remorse for exacting telepathic punishment in response to her attempted communication with other prisoners.

"Why would he do that? Perhaps not all of the Grays on this ship hate humanity." Unable to focus, bone-tired, and anemic after the inexplicable blood loss, Nina's eyes grow heavy, and she falls into a deep sleep. Her mind drifts back to her privileged childhood. Her father was a NATO general, and her mother represented the *Nye Borgerlige* party in the Danish Parliament. Their careers left no time to raise an independent and intelligent Nina Madsen, so she spent most of her youth at an elite all-girls boarding academy outside Copenhagen.

The young Danish schoolgirl skips along a manicured cobblestone path with youthful, carefree strides, catching up with her "mean girls" clique. Her vaunted reputation as a flirt and a troublemaker garnered plenty of friends, yet her underperformance in class troubled her parents.

Bored to tears in Ms. Dykstra's seventh-grade classroom, Nina tosses a paper airplane, hitting the middle-aged woman's backside, causing the class to erupt in laughter. Nicknamed the Dyke, for obvious reasons, the woman's empty threat to smack Nina with a meterstick for the insubordinate act leaves the classroom of giggling schoolgirls in stitches. Nina assumes her too-cool attitude knowing the bitch would never risk her posh teaching job by exacting corporal punishment with the splintered tip of her stupid measuring stick. No. But she could hold Nina in afterschool detention, where the Danish seventh grader finds herself as the dank cell transforms into Ms. Dykstra's classroom.

Time slows to a crawl. Nina sits amid the emptied rows, tapping a chewed pencil atop her homeroom desk. Below the class clock, which appears stuck at half-past four, a massive whiteboard adorned with graded reports on the Holocaust mocks Nina's bored and fidgeting woe-is-me gaze. With little else to do but sit and stare straight ahead, she searches for her half-assed contribution. Finding it hung dead center, embellished with an obnoxious red negative numeral three evokes an eye roll predicting a concerned call from dear old Mum.

The Dyke reenters the classroom and plops into the swivel chair behind her cluttered teacher's desk and opens a side drawer. The tall and lecherous blond removes a half-empty vodka bottle and takes a long swig before proffering it forward with a lusty smile.

The startling incident jolts Nina from a deep hypnotic slumber. Swallowing back bitter-tasting bile down her sore throat, she furrows her brow, visualizing a repressed image of the woman's leering face, "But what happened next? Hold on for just a goddamn second; I remember now. Oh my God! She made me drink the vodka while forcing her hand up my skirt. I have repressed that memory my whole life."

Movement outside her cell interrupts Nina's painful and embarrassing recollection. Scooching sideways, she trains her hazed vision on Zint, ushering a hooded prisoner into the cell across the dark corridor.

The figure raises a bloodied dark brown hand and produces a surreptitious thumbs-up, sensing her watchful gaze.

Nina's heart soars: It is Flynn!

Zint latches the thick barred door and burns an admonition into Nina's psyche: "Keep your head down and stay quiet. Your friend needs rest."

Overwhelmed with relief, tinged with sadness and guilt for her wasted and foolhardy youthful indiscretions, Nina starts to cry. Digging bloodied fingertips into her legs, she regains control of her fragile emotional state and whispers, "I am Nina Madsen. Anyone eavesdropping on my thoughts right now can kiss my ass and fuck off."

What matters is that Flynn is alive. She wants to shout it so the whole cellblock can hear, but knows that would end badly.

Betty Hill | Cleopatra Hospital, Cairo
11:55 a.m. | August 28, 2044

Nurse Zahra allows the huddled mass of humanity to exit Cleopatra Hospital's lone functional freight elevator into the 8th-floor chaos before pushing Betty's wheelchair off the lift. Leaning close to her VIP patient's ear, the nurse raises her voice over the commotion, "I told you, Mrs. Hill, life on the 20th floor is a world away from what's going on down here."

Stunned by the spectacle of Cairo's teeming throngs crowding the 8th-floor's ad hoc check-in counter and congregating in groups jamming the central corridor, Betty shrinks into the chair, "This is madness. Are all of the other floors like this?"

"Only 4, 8, 16, and 20 have electrical and plumbing. The other floors remain dark, and the street level is a disaster. Hence the crowds. Before the invasion, this floor was administration and human resources. But look at us now."

Zahra guides her enigmatic patient through the bustle and gets hung up behind a group of young deer-in-the-headlight recruits undergoing on-the-job training leaving Betty eye-to-eye with a matronly dark-skinned woman wearing an eye patch. Seated at the end of a bench beside a potted palm, the lady perceives Betty's discomfort and shows off a spanking new orange 3D-printed cast holding her left forearm in one piece with a toothless fatalistic smile that speaks volumes: *Why the sad face, deary? I lost everything.*

Rolling forward, Betty turns toward Zahra, "How many people has the hospital treated since the invasion?"

"I don't know, a lot." Jostling around another human roadblock, Zahra moans, "Hey, we're trying to get through here! Can you move?" Parting a cluster of sick, injured, and just plain gawkers spilling out of the dangerous stairwell exit, the veteran nurse continues, "Once the word got out that we were open for business, people from near and far crawled from the woodwork and showed up at our doors." Tapping Betty on her robed shoulder, "It is your fault."

Betty scrunches her bandaged face into a quizzical expression, "My fault? How can any of this be my fault?"

"Our chief surgeon, Dr. Said, made a deal with your Cowboy friend. We take care of you and your husband and quid pro quo; your people provided the resources to administer aid to everyone else. Of course, no one realized how fast the word would spread. These people are desperate. There is no electricity or potable water anywhere in Cairo."

"What do you tell them?"

"Whatever works. We hand out water bottles and MREs by the caseload and tell anyone who asks, which isn't very many, that we invested in solar panels or some green energy bullshit. Anything to calm them down so we can patch them up and send them on their way. The truth is we have no clue, so that helps." Leaning close, Zahra whispers the burning question on everyone's minds into Betty's left ear: "Your technology is not from *here*, is it?"

Betty flinches away from a shoving match breaking out over boxes of Beef Stroganoff MREs before providing an honest answer. "First off, they are not my people, at least not yet." Fingering the unsealed manila envelope tucked beside her in the wheelchair, "And second, I know as much about the Cowboy as you do. Probably less."

"Well, whoever you are, you came through with food, water, and some mind-blowing high-tech shit. And to be honest …." Two beefy orderlies dart across their path toward the altercation in time with another Code Blue blaring over the din. Zahra applies the wheelchair's brakes to avoid blocking a harried nurse rushing into the stricken person's room. "Sit tight, Mrs. Hill. She may need another pair of hands. I will be right back."

Feeling exposed and in the way, Rachel cinches her robe and stands out of the wheelchair in her socked feet, "Screw it; I can walk."

A sweaty hospital recruit heaping discarded laundry and trash into a rolling bin blocks her advance. After the young man rolls out of the way, she slides a socked foot forward and almost loses a toe as an intern pushes a mobile crash cart into the darkened room where the poor soul is coding bright red. On her third try, wary of the potential hazards, the fair-skinned blond patient, who resembles an airplane crash survivor, wards off dizziness, trekking past rooms packed with the sick, wounded, and dying. Looking back toward her wheelchair, she spots the envelope stuffed under her blanket, "Well, shit."

Sidestepping through the bedlam for the second time with the manila envelope, she checks a directional sign, "Everything is in Arabic; how am I going to find the ICU?"

Betty grabs an attendant by the sleeve, "Can you tell me which direction to the ICU?"

The woman smiles and shakes her head before yanking free and melding into the crowd.

"Thanks for nothing, lady."

Reaching another 4-way intersection in the labyrinthine 22-floor hospital tower, she checks the arrows, ignoring the Arabic, and ventures left where it appears quieter and calmer. Shuffling down the long corridor, she hangs a right and comes upon a set of swinging double doors stenciled ICU in plain English. Thanking Allah, God, Buddha, or whoever, she pushes through the doors, leaving the 8th-floor mayhem in her wake.

Realizing she also left her cane in the wheelchair in the commotion, Betty remembers her PT instructor's words: "Heel to toe. Heel to toe. Bend your knees." Unable to hide a smile, she feels like herself for the first time in days. No months. In all honesty, it has been years since Betty felt normal.

After a stumble, she pulls up her rubber-soled hospital footsies and perseveres down another long, empty hallway, "I should have remembered my cane and a fucking map."

Heaving an exhausted sigh, Betty pushes through another set

of doors into the path of a musclebound security guard with a mean-looking weapon slung over his shoulder, blocking Betty's progress.

"State your business."

A thunderstruck Betty stammers, "ICU? Is this the ICU?"

Behind a tall counter in the expansive and bright-lit receiving area, an authoritative female voice calls out, "Let her pass, Abdul."

The Cleopatra Hospital employee moves around the counter in her standard-issue blue scrubs with a warm and welcoming white smile across her pretty, olive-skinned face, "You are late, Mrs. Hill."

Betty catches her breath after the long trek, noting the nurse's trendy jet-black mini bun hairstyle and a smattering of tattoos on her arms and neck. "I got a little lost."

Sidling next to Betty, the nurse places a hand on her back and leads her into Cleopatra Hospital's work-in-progress brand-new ICU.

Workers in beige coveralls with butterfly logo patches on their backs swarmed over the gutted administrative offices and conference facilities, transforming them into post-op recovery rooms and intensive care units.

With a deafening din of power saws, nail guns, and clanking pipes in the background, the nurse shakes her head, "Would you believe this floor used to be billing and HR? Now it is our brand-new ICU. I am amazed at the speed and efficiency of your people. It is stunning."

Rachel almost blows her cover before replying, "They aren't my people. Um, is Barney … Mr. Hill? Is he here?"

The nurse nods and stifles a laugh, "Yeah, he is here. You are Betty Hill, right?" With a sudden look of recognition, she adds, "Hey, what happened to Zahra?"

"She got hung up with a patient, so I moved on without her." Attempting to affect an air of normalcy, Betty adds, "I like your hair."

The nurse grabs a wheelchair, "My apartment doesn't have running water, so it was either this or shaving my head."

"It's cool. I like it."

"Well, if I had your beautiful blond head of hair, I might opt for a ponytail like yours. Have a seat, Mrs. Hill. I insist."

Aching, exhausted, and feeling her concussion medication wearing off, Betty acquiesces without a fuss.

The nurse pushes past a glass-fronted row of prefab ICUs ready for installation toward an occupied and private end unit. Before reaching the door, Mrs. Hill applies the handbrake, "Please give me a minute."

The nurse squeezes Betty's shoulders before whispering in the nervous woman's ear, "You got this, Mrs. Hill. Just shout over the hammering if you need anything."

* * *

Rachel brushes blond locks off her healing face covered in small bandages over dark-bruised eyes and cheeks, stalling to collect her thoughts before reuniting with Owen for the first time since their extraction from far beneath the Giza Plateau. The young newlywed takes a deep breath, straightens her pajamas under the white hospital robe, and wheels herself through the door.

Rhythmic beeps and whirs of Owen's life support equipment replace the construction noise inside the soundproof room. Rachel peers through the darkened intensive care unit and lets out an audible gasp upon seeing his swollen face and the top of his thick head wrapped in tape and gauze. "Owen. It's me, Rachel. Are you awake?"

No reply.

Assessing the intricate array of medical paraphernalia from near and far amassed around him, the tall blond stands and pushes the bulky wheelchair out the door. Fighting off lightheadedness, Rachel reaches for the extra pain pill in her robe pocket and swallows it past her dry throat before grasping the edge of a bedside table to sidle up to the raised safety rail. She places the manila envelope on the bed and touches Owen's exposed left hand resting atop the covers and sheets.

"Now what?"

Having spent most of her waking hours imagining their reunion, Rachel realizes there are no words to describe her feelings in the incredible aftermath of what they went through far beneath the Great Pyramid. Instead, she swipes at tears and caresses Owen's bandaged hand with her own while her vision adjusts to the low-lit room. Focusing on the complex rope and pulley rig elevating his broken right arm, she recognizes his bright orange 3D-printed mesh arm cast is the same design as the old lady in the hallway.

Below a shuttered window on the room's opposite side, Rachel spies a cardboard box beside a cheap plastic chair. As quiet as a mouse, she lets go of Owen's bandaged fingers, noting his corrected digital alignment, shuffling around the foot of the bed. Ignoring her nagging migraine, she hefts the carton onto the seat. Pulling the flaps open loosens grit and sand onto the floor around her feet. Inside the box, she sees the tattered and bloodstained remnants of Owen's breaching the pyramids ensemble—courtesy of Nina—folded atop his unlaced Timberlands. Rachel staggers backward as the nightmarish image of Owen's limp body cartwheeling through the swirling debris inside the beacon chamber projects in her mind's eye. Her tears make it difficult to close the lid and replace the box where she found it before retreating to her original spot.

"Owen, I am so sorry."

With his disfigured face fixed forward in a neck brace atop thick pillows, lying at a shallow angle, Owen awakens and shifts his swollen-eyed gaze onto an angel.

Their eyes meet for the first time in days ripping Rachel's emotional floodgates asunder. Lowering the safety rail with practiced ease, avoiding a half-inch tube draining pinkish-red liquid from his side into a large glass receptacle at her feet, she hugs her right arm around his bandaged head. Lost in the moment, the enigma known around Cleopatra Hospital as Betty kisses Barney long and hard before coming up for air.

Owen reaches out with his left hand, ensuring she is real.

"I'm here, Owen. I'm here."

"What happened? Where am I?"

Rachel closes her eyes and brushes soft lips across Owen's pugilistic face, whispering, "You are here with me. Everything will be all right." Swooning from the strong painkiller kicking into gear, she throws caution to the wind and produces a sultry smile while sliding her hand down the sheets seconds before the monitors mounted behind Owen's bed go off like July 4th fireworks. The noise startles Rachel from acting on her passionate bedside fantasy. Stumbling backward into an IV stand, she grabs the bedside table to avoid falling flat on her ass and knocks a 1-liter hospital cup filled with water, crashing onto the floor.

The veteran RN who has seen it all—and endured the post-invasion onslaught—bursts into the room, moving around Owen's bedside to quiet the squawking heart rate monitor. Cool as a cucumber, she checks Barney's vitals and adjusts the tension on his arm traction while mouthing, "Don't worry, he will be fine."

"How are we doing, Mr. Hill?" Making eye contact with a guilt-ridden Betty, she continues, "You need to rest and avoid excitement. How is your pain level?"

Owen raises his hand and points at his fractured arm hanging aloft over the soft covers at an awkward 45-degree angle.

"Okay. Let's see here." The savvy RN adjusts the pain management cocktail from an intravenous pump and checks the bags hanging from his IV stand. "That should do it."

An orderly appears with a mop and bucket to sop up the water spill. Embarrassed and disappointed, Betty steps out of the way, "Sorry about that. I'm a little klutzy these days." Cursing herself for abusing the potent pain pills, she muses how real life is never like the movies. Never.

The nurse exits the unit allowing the orderly elbow room to clean up the mess, motioning for Betty to follow, "Mrs. Hill, can I speak with you outside?"

The brightness and noise level in the main ICU space outside the darkened room exacerbates Betty's headache. Her heart racing like a hummingbird, she reaches for the wheelchair and plops into the seat. "I am so sorry. Is he okay?"

"No apology is necessary. Can I offer you a water bottle?" She adds, reading the label, "Courtesy of our new friends at Chrysalis Air, no less."

"Yeah, sure. I guess I got swept up in the moment."

"Mrs. Hill, I'm a nurse in a major metropolitan hospital. I have seen it all. Besides, everyone knows hospital sex is almost as good as airline sex."

"I wouldn't know about that."

"Yeah, sure." The nurse proffers a room-temperature bottled water with a familiar butterfly logo label and moves behind the counter with a sly smile.

Rachel takes a drink and swishes to eliminate the bitter aftertaste of the antibacterial skin cream from kissing Owen's beaten face.

Returning from behind the counter with a first aid kit, the nurse takes a knee beside the wheelchair and places two fingers over Betty's thumping carotid artery. After a prolonged silence, her hand lingers an extra second before pulling away, "You have an elevated heart rate, Mrs. Hill. Probably from the Oxy. That too shall pass." Tearing open an antiseptic wipe, the nurse checks the myriad cuts and scrapes, patting the soft wet gauze on her face and neck with a gentle touch. "You are quite beautiful, Mrs. Hill. Have you done any modeling?"

Avoiding an impertinent spit take in response to the unexpected compliment, Betty fumbles for words, "Who me? God, no."

Betty's humble reply prompts a hearty laugh from the Egyptian, "All of that beauty and a sense of modesty, too? My. My. How are things up on the 20th floor? My key card only gets me to the 8th floor. Perhaps I can come up for a visit during your stay. We can swap fashion notes."

Not sure where the conversation is heading, Betty decides to play it cool, "Yeah, sure. I'll talk to Zahra."

"Has our mutual friend, Zahra, mentioned the rumors swirling around you and your husband? There is even an office pool of sorts. CIA is a popular bet." Peeling a blood-encrusted bandage from Betty's left cheek, she admits, "I can't place a bet since I know your real identity."

Betty winces from the sting of peroxide, cleaning the fizzing facial cut before feigning indifference and swiping at her runny nose, "Is that so? What's the buy-in? Maybe I'll play."

With a slight chuckle, the nurse produces sterile gauze and tape, redressing the inch-long gash, "Don't worry, dear. Your organization's NDAs prohibit me from saying a word." Taping the new dressing in place, she puts her hand on Betty's leg and leans close to whisper in her ear, "I would never risk ruining things for everybody, Rachel Haig. Your secret is safe with me."

Struggling to maintain her composure, the outed patient flips the table on the sultry nurse, "I'm sorry, I never got your name."

"Cleo. Short for Cleopatra." She makes a sweeping arm gesture around the ICU ward with a flirtatious smile, "And this is my kingdom."

The double doors swing wide as Nurse Zahra bursts into the ICU, "There you are, Mrs. Hill! I thought I had lost you. You forgot your cane."

Betty's eyes widen, struggling to remember where she left the manila envelope. "Oh shit."

Standing out of the wheelchair, she stumbles to Barney's ICU and freezes at the threshold, finding him awake and alert, holding the envelope in his left hand with a quizzical look on his face.

Mindful of his fragile condition, Betty enters and pulls the envelope from his weak grasp. "We can talk about this later. Get some rest. I love you, Owen."

With tears in his eyes, Barney struggles to reply, "I love you, too."

Another rheumy hacking cough reverberates the dark, clammy bleakness stirring Nina from a restless slumber. Staring beyond Nicole's catatonic state, her watery eyes focus outside her wide-open door.

A voice beckons her to rise and exit the cell.

Nina stretches her aching muscles and straightens her stinky enviro suit before stepping over Nicole and into the deep-blue corridor. Cognizant, the constant crying and fits of coughs—plus the occasional dog bark—emanate from the opposite direction, the Danish national casts a wary glance at Flynn and moves past empty cells toward the exit. Outside the cell block, she moves before a glassed-off guard room where her friend, Zint, manipulates buttons and controls before a bank of blue-tinged monitors.

"Hello, Nina. Someone wants to talk with you."

Nina ignores the tiny alien, transfixed on a bank of screens above his round head. Locating her covert cell feed, she sees Nicole curled on her side. Another display surveils Flynn in a similar repose. Other screens reveal holding cells containing various groups of abductees. With a slight smile creasing her parched lips, she finds the dog, a German Shepherd, huddled next to its master. Her gaze moves to the last screen, where a lone prisoner sits hunched in the corner. Astrid.

Zint urges Nina to move along with a telepathic tap.

"Someone is waiting for you."

Warding off dizziness, Nina Madsen shuffles barefoot through the massive, deadly alien battlecruiser's musty bowels. Following telepathic turn-by-turn guidance, she turns off alarm bells ringing in her head and quashes impertinent stomach growls.

A Gray escort detours her path into a cavernous hangar bay parked end-to-end with pill-shaped craft. Nina clears her mind and keeps her eyes forward past pilots and technicians prepping the ships for recon missions to Earth. Reaching the far end of the hangar, Nina follows her guide into a clear tube. The being taps a button, vaulting the odd pair past countless decks to the battlecruiser's bridge.

Unable to contain a bit of wry humor, Nina smiles, "That was fun."

"Quiet."

Following the skinny Gray in his silvery suit across the ship's uppermost command deck, the unmistakable aroma of cooked meat assaults her stuffy nose. "Excuse me? Is that Steak au Poivre? Did you read me to conjure up my last meal there? How thoughtful."

The gallows humor falls flat, as expected. The alien opens another portal and turns to his prisoner: *"Enter."*

Surmising a failed fertilization sealed her fate and left her suit covered in blood, Nina braces for the cold vacuum of space and steps into the narrow tunnel. Disorienting lightness hurts her eyes as she falls to her knees and crawls to the opposite end, "Fuck, kill me already."

Spilling headfirst out of the narrowing tunnel onto a cold, hard surface, Nina scrambles onto her feet and finds herself inside a bright, cheery vaulted dining room. Denying her captors even a small victory, she stifles a surprised gasp. Sliding bare feet over cool Italian marble, Nina enters *Le Cinq*; a five-star Paris restaurant recreated in holographic detail from her picked-clean memory. Looking through draped windows arching to an ornate gilded ceiling, she notes the jaw-dropping view of Earth amid a sea of stars. "What the hell, close enough."

Underdressed for the tony venue, she passes potted palms under crystalline chandeliers refracting across fine set tables with long-stemmed red roses jutting heavenward from shimmering centerpieces.

Brushing her hip through the hyper-real corner of a linen-draped table, she studies a gleaming polished table knife before purging the thought. A quick backward glance finds the portal replaced by more draped windows and tall potted palms. Starving beyond measure, Nina steps around the tables to a dessert cart brimming with pastries, fruits, berries, and an impressive collection of French wines. After a brief hesitation, she reaches out and touches a plump strawberry. Withdrawing her hand, she is startled to find it has mass.

"Tsk, tsk, Ms. Madsen. You should know it is improper to partake of the dessert offerings before enjoying a proper dinner."

Wheeling on her bare heels, Nina scans the tables and spies a man wearing a fine tailored suit and tie, holding a half-empty wine glass raised in his right hand.

"Please, join me, Ms. Madsen, I insist. The setting may be fake, but the food is authentic. And delicious, I might add.

Grabbing a bottle of 2016 *Margaux*, Nina complies. "Why not."

"Excellent!"

Placing the bottle on the table, half expecting it to crash to the hard floor, Nina takes the proffered seat, "Thank you."

Angling into the chair opposite his guest, the distinguished man creases a dimpled smile on his tanned and handsome face, "You are most welcome, Nina."

"So, what is this? Am I hallucinating? Or perhaps I am dead, and purgatory is an eternity waiting for a table at *Le Cinq*."

"I assure you; you are alive and well. However, you endured a painful, bloody procedure. For that, you have my deepest apologies."

"Spare me your bullshit. The stirrup-shaped bruises on my calves and ankles were a dead giveaway. If you hurt Nicole and Astrid, I will kill you."

Dismissing her hollow threat with a carefree laugh, "As I said, the procedure is rough, but you have my apologies. A clean enviro suit from your vessel awaits inside your cell. That is the best I can do at the moment."

"Who are you?"

"You must be hungry." Snapping his fingers, a youthful wait staff appears out of nowhere, filling water glasses and placing a basket of warm bread on the table.

Nina's waiter attempts to assist with her napkin, causing her to recoil from the teenager, "That's okay. I got it."

Perplexed, the boy stumbles backward.

Nina looks into the boy's dark eyes, "I'm sorry."

He shakes his head and places an index finger over his mouth, "No need to apologize."

A young female server pops Nina's pilfered wine and pours a sample into a crystal goblet, "Would you care to taste the wine, Madam?"

Nina looks at the pretty young girl with those same dark-black piercing eyes, "No need; I'm beyond sure it will be perfect."

After filling the glass, the girl stands beside her fellow staff at attention.

Perceiving Nina's unease and awkward situation, the man chuckles with a merry glint in his deep-set gray eyes, "Thank you all. Our guest is starving. Please return to the kitchen and speed up the main course."

Alone in the holographic room across from the distinguished man, Nina ventures a long sip from the goblet, "Are you real, or can I put my fist right through your head?" Before he can reply, a dizzying rush swirls through her messy charcoal bedhead.

"Take it easy, Ms. Madsen. Throwing back a glass of aged French wine on an empty stomach with your anemic cell count is ill-advised."

"Fuck off. I've held my own with everyone from Russian oligarchs to a college of Cardinals in Rome."

"You had an impressive career with The Powers That Be."

Nina places the glass on the table and nods with sudden recognition, "Of course. I can't push out a baby hybrid—I could have told you that was a non-starter. However, I have value as a high-level officer with the only entity on Earth not curled into a fetal position sucking on their collective thumbs." Shaking her head in disgust, "How utterly predictable."

The man leans across the table, his casual demeanor tinged with desperation, "We can make your life quite comfortable, Nina."

"No thanks. I want to go home now."

"That is not an option, but you already know that." After a pregnant pause, the man presses further, "Your allies may resemble these Grays, but this species is hellbent on righting a 90-million-year-old wrong. Every human on Earth will die. However, I can negotiate safe passage for you and your friends if you agree to help them locate a lost ship."

Nina's surprised laugh echoes through the space, "Really? A lost ship. How does one lose a ship?"

The man winces at her glibness, "Ms. Madsen, I had to beg my superiors to allow this meeting; otherwise, you would already be dead."

Nina absorbs the man's words and reaches for the bottle to refill her glass, "I guess you will have to kill me because I know nothing about a lost ship. That is beyond ludicrous." Studying the attractive man's face, "You may be human, but I don't think you comprehend how our species persevered throughout history. We will not roll over and let your alien friends wipe us out, ship or no ship."

Ignoring her reply, the man presses further, "The Grays watched the Gork invasion devolve into a spectacular defeat similar to a humiliation their ancestors suffered millions of years ago. They seek a weapon buried in the ship's manifest to assure that history will not repeat."

Nina swirls her glass and pretends to consider his words, buying time, "Let me think about it."

"My superiors demand an answer."

"Tough. I don't even know your name."

"My name is Sebastian Duarte. I am from Lisbon. I was 12 when they abducted myself and my sister, Maria."

"Where is she?"

"She is a breeder with over fifty children spread across Earth. We saw the writing on the wall and escaped a life of poverty." Leaning back in his seat, "As for myself, with the assistance of *my* advisers, as you like to refer to your Gray friends, I am a member of the Portuguese Parliament."

Nina nods with a smirk, "No shit. My dear departed mother was a Danish MP. Small world."

"We know."

"Of course, you do." After another sip, she pries for information, "What about these half-breeds roaming the planet? What could the Grays possibly gain from that horrible plan."

"To be frank, Ms. Madsen, individuals with alien DNA inhabit lofty and powerful positions from Davos to Beijing to DC. Due to those blasted Gorks, many are now among the millions dead and dying."

"Yeah, too bad."

Sebastian winces at her recalcitrance and snaps his fingers. The hologram evaporates, leaving them seated at the lone table amid an echoing empty hangar bay. A male server appears from the shadows and places an aromatic Steak au Poivre atop the table midway between Nina and Sebastian. Meanwhile, a female server circles the opposite side, placing her dish containing a grayish pill atop the linen tablecloth.

The pair recede into the shadows leaving Nina to contemplate the gastronomical Sophie's Choice. Reaching for her glass, she finds it gone and expresses an exasperated huff, "I'm sorry, I don't follow your symbolism here. Which dish means *screw humanity*, and which is the equivalent of *go to hell*?"

Surprised by her obtuse reaction, he replies, "I thought it rather obvious. No matter. The gray pill provides enough sustenance to sustain human life. It is the same feed keeping your fellow abductees alive. However, you will still be hungry afterward."

Pushing the plate holding the steak closer to Nina, he continues, "On the other hand, consuming the flesh of another living organism holds a special significance for the Grays, akin to a religious experience."

Nina shakes her head in disbelief, "No. That can't be correct. In my experience with Grays, the subject of nutrition never came up, and it never occurred to me what they ate."

Sebastian smiles at his guest's naive reaction, "There are multiple species of Grays throughout the universe, Ms. Madsen. Too many to count. Some are pacifistic intellectuals above puerile pursuits such as nourishment. But others, like my friends up here prepping to invade Earth, take great pleasure in consuming the flesh of their victims. The rampant cattle mutilations and crop circles through the years were abject warnings, not hoaxes by drunken teenagers. No offense, Nina, but humanity is a stupid species begging for extinction, and your loyalty is misguided."

Disheartened and starving, Nina fingers the plate and looks closer at the thick peppercorn-encrusted filet atop a rich mustard-colored sauce, "What is this?"

Duarte raises an eyebrow and emits a hearty chuckle, "To be honest, I never got the chap's name."

Nina almost vomits, realizing the meat is human flesh.

"I know, it's vile and disgusting. You must understand that this Gray species is millions of years beyond human civilization. They do not view us as equals." Pausing for effect, Sebastian Duarte stands from his chair and places his napkin on the table, "More like cattle."

The horrifying revelation leaves Nina shocked, staring at the slab of meat cooked to perfection.

"I would love to stay and chat longer, but I must return to our planet and tend to my decimated constituents. The nasty Gorks left a disastrous mess, even in a shithole country like mine. The unwashed masses are elbowing for space at government troughs like herds of rutting farm animals." Catching his unintentional reference, "Farm animals, get it?"

Nina stares at the plates as Sebastian disappears into the dark hangar bay. From a distance, his deep and melodic voice rings in her ears.

"Plans are afoot to topple The Powers That Be. You do not have much time. The choice is yours, Nina. Enjoy your meal." His voice trails off as he steps into a ship headed to Earth.

Nina picks up the gray pill and swallows it.

Chapter Two:

The Shitshow

Griffin Pike | SATstar HQ, Amsterdam
12:25 p.m. | August 29, 2044

Griffin Pike's blue-eyed charisma oozes through a holographic capture apparatus under the taut professional direction of a Scandinavian videographer and her two-person crew. The tall blond choreographs the shoot from a multi-screen console, tracking her billionaire client's athletic six-foot frame across a seamless white studio bay in a Patagonia jacket over a plain black tee, jeans, and boots. The SATstar CEO hits his mark like a pro beside a white marble bust of Winston Churchill perched atop a waist-height pillar, "Hello, my name is Griffin Pike. Like you, my business holdings were devastated by the catastrophic worldwide alien attack. It would be easy to crawl under a rock and wait for someone else to fix our world. Believe me, I have considered it. But I will not surrender and fade into the abyss. I want to build back better.

I know you do as well." Patting Churchill's smooth head, "Allow me to paraphrase this fine fellow: *One must never let a good disaster go to waste.*"

Pike pauses to allow his introduction time to marinate before continuing, "Ladies and gentlemen, we are on the precipice of a potential extinction-level event unseen since dinosaurs walked the Earth." Flashing a boyish smile, he raises his index finger, "However, unlike our hapless feathery predecessors, we will not perish into a fossilized abyss. And, better yet, we will not let this once-in-a-millennium opportunity go to waste."

"Borders, buildings, banking, you name it, are gone for all intents and purposes. Swept clean by alien electromagnetic pulses which, to be frank, could have been mitigated." With a cunning grin, he continues, "Reality is a bitter pill, but agents for The Powers That Be under the direction of Artemus Pennywell warned the lot of you. You know it is true."

Gesturing at the empty warehouse space around him, "We are engaged in this conversation because I installed the PTB's shielding technology on some of my properties. I regret not doing more, but there you are. Believe it or not, it didn't cost a penny."

With a tsk-tsk, "I know, hindsight is 20-20, but my sources tell me the old boy is hopping mad that PTB entreaties fell on deaf ears of a shortsighted world hellbent on saving the planet from bogeymen of their own making. And now, with all you hold dear swiped away, your collective exalted status dangles by a thread. None of you will survive recrimination if Pennywell and his people communicate your reticence and apathy in the lead-up to Invasion Day. Your holiness, if you are alive and watching this message, I include you here, sir."

Striking the perfect dark tone, he proceeds, "My proposal is simple: turn the tables and project the world's failures onto The Powers That Be."

With a carefree laugh, "I understand you are all distracted, putting out fires and attending to the surviving masses, so I offer my services. I took the liberty of leasing The Hague's World Forum conference and entertainment facilities unscathed amidst the carnage. What luck. My first inclination was the criminal courthouse complex, which lies in ruins. No matter, the World Forum's King Willem Alexander theater is the perfect venue to convene an international tribunal against Pennywell and his organization."

Pike segues to an easel and unveils a simple poster board containing virtual attendance instructions. "The majority of you who cannot attend in person, for obvious reasons, can still participate in the trial of Artemus Pennywell and The Powers That Be by following the QR-encoded links shown here." Pausing to let that sink in, he continues, "I know. I know. No internet. How the hell do we do this? You are viewing my handsome holographic visage via my fully functional satellite network on holographic receivers that work. I am sure most of you fell out of your cushy chairs when you saw the little green light start to blink. Fun fact: your holographic units came shielded right out of the box for apocalyptic scenarios. But I digress. So, here is your mission—if you decide to accept it—I always wanted to say that. Locate an operable device—really anything with a camera—and point it at this code. We will handle the rest. If you can't find a working device, you must be among the really screwed."

"For those who can attend in person, I understand your fondness for group photos, toothless treaties, feckless working groups, and brainstorming sideshows. We will accommodate those activities as well. Public perception beyond mere finger-pointing is crucial to our ultimate success. However, the main event will be the trial of Artemus Pennywell and The Powers That Be. Every attendee can project decades of obfuscations, mismanagement, and outright criminal neglect square in his chest. The predictable reaction of unwashed masses suckling the digital teat since birth will be a glorious unrestrained rage directed upon The Powers That Be, the epitome of a mystical, untouchable, faceless enterprise."

Griffin tips the Churchill bust, crashing it to the floor in chunks and shards, "Not anymore."

Accepting a paper and a water bottle from off-camera, Griffin pauses to drink, "My legal experts are building a bullet-proof case; however, verifiable accounts of the PTB's misconduct, criminal negligence, and underworld connections will fuel a raging fire."

Offering a self-indulgent shrug, "Perhaps most damning, Pennywell used his IOSC flagship as a personal ark to save himself and a handful of well-heeled cronies and bribed pols. It will not come as a surprise to learn his ship was one of the few that returned safely to Earth. Of course, well after the immediate danger to humanity had passed and the damage was done. Full disclosure: My name was on his manifest, like many of you. However, I had no means to reach an IOSC terminal. Most of our colleagues who made it onto an escaping ship are gone, but their deaths will not be forgotten."

Griffin's closing appeal verges on megalomania. With a nod toward the lovely blond working the console, he smiles, "Oh well, if the shoe fits …."

"Ladies and gentlemen, grant your constituents and customer bases time to express their sorrow and loss with rocks and torches. Visualize the angry mobs burning down whatever is left of your cities and towns as aggrieved children who need an outlet for their frustrations. Time will quell their vitriol. After our new corporate-government alliance is introduced, the gaping technological void will overflow with the promise of a new human era brimming with joy and harmony. Those bitter, dirty faces will once again bathe in the dull ambiance of new devices built by your companies and networked to my satellites orbiting our New World Order. We will rebuild and shield Earth's precious digital resources and infrastructure in a manner befitting our reimagined human race. Let's get on with it, shall we?"

The stage lights dim, leaving Pike standing tall amid the broken bits of the Churchill bust, an ode to the past that will never be put back together.

The skilled video producer kills the cameras and leans back in her director's chair, "That's a wrap, everybody. Good job."

* * *

With everything from banking to retail to health care predicated on free and unfettered access to the internet now in shambles, a panicked and rattled stratospheric echelon of savvy digital masters acquiesce to their archrival's unsolicited presentation: "Without access to his satellites, we're screwed. What do we have to lose?"

However, presidents, prime ministers, dictators, and religious leaders view Pike's holographic appeal with circumspection. Their constituents and a scrambling press demanded answers to what their leaders knew and when they knew it. The French president, knee-deep in scandal before the invasion, accepted his compromised fate with a Ce la vie before blowing his brains across a gilded armoire in the Élysées Palace. His successor, eager to save face, agrees to participate in Pike's plan. She even volunteers to chair the tribunal.

With French participation and little in the way of a downside, most world bodies access their customized QR-encoded links and RSVP to dispatch an in-person emissary or use Pike's proprietary satellite feeds to access the virtual presentation, with one notable exception.

President Lena Jackson | White House Bunker
08:05 a.m. | August 29, 2044

President Lena Jackson watches the good-looking man's hologram disappear from atop the long conference table inside the Presidential Emergency Operations Center buried deep underneath the White House's flooded and battered East Wing. Leaning back in her command chair, the Cincinnati, Ohio native swivels toward her Chief of Staff, a beltway insider named Glenn Cohan, "Griffin Pike will own us. I am unwilling to sell America's soul to that condescending grifter."

Shrugging thick shoulders, the swampish creature rubs his balding head, "It's your call, Lena. We may find it rather lonely on the outside, looking in at whatever this world becomes. The word is that China is sending a delegation. Not sure about the Russians."

Pushing her side-parted shoulder-length black hair behind an ear, the 56-year-old Black mother of four—and first Independent president—turns on the paunchy man sporting a lime-green golf shirt and checkered slacks, "Glenn, tell me you are not missing a tee time?"

"No, Lena, my house is a wreck. It's a good thing I kept some clothes in a locker at the gym."

"I know. I'm just messing with you. I am glad Sally is okay. You two had a beautiful home. Jesus, the Potomac swallowed up everything. Maybe it was unwise to build the US capitol in a swamp. Glenn, you know as well as I do that Griffin Pike has zero interest in saving the world. His goal is to dismantle The Powers That Be and compromise our interests. Plain and simple. That's why the Chinese are going. They hate the PTB almost as much as they hate us."

Maggie Williams, a former Marine whose new job title is Director of National Intelligence, interjects from the far end of the table, "Hate is such a strong word. Madame President, if word leaks out at this tribunal, or whatever it is, that the United States has coordinated intelligence with The Powers That Be since before the days of Lincoln, it will open a can of worms. What if the world discovers we had the advantage of alien technologies for over 150 years, and they did not? Don't you think people might be pissed off about something like that?"

"First off, Williams, I already know the answer, but is there any news on your husband's whereabouts?"

"Not a word. My only hope is Sub-Saharan Africa took a small hit from the Gorks, so if he is holed up in some Somali warlord's dungeon, he is probably still alive."

"His recovery is a top priority. You have my solemn word. And your dog, too! Damn, those assholes piss me off." Pausing to regain her composure and train of thought, "Now, the alien tech you refer to is not as big of a secret since Disclosure Day. Glenn, what year was that?"

"2034. It is hard to believe a whole decade has passed. Artemus was there. Many of the same officeholders around the world today were there as well. By the way, China and Russia received the same tech. That is why it's called the International ... Outer Space Consortium. From that point onward, it should have been obvious to anyone with half a brain that aliens were behind most of the cutting-edge technologies of the past half-century. You are right, Lena; this is nothing but a PR stunt. For Christ's sake, the most vocal demographic bitching and moaning today were still in grade school in 34."

President Jackson turns to her newest cabinet member with an empathetic smile, "Maggie, I understand your concern. Perhaps we are too close to the PTB. I don't agree with everything they stand for myself, but would you rather the future be decided by the USA and PTB or a bunch of corporatists, communists, and corrupt globalist flacks?"

"They could say the same thing about us, Lena."

"Well, guess what, my dear, that is too damn bad. Pike can suck it. Glenn, send our regrets. We have better things to do than join hands with a bunch of Euro-weenies and commies looking to turn the world into a utopian one-world crap show.

Glenn chuckles, "That's what I like about you, Lena. You got the largest set of balls this side of Montana."

Maggie Williams taps her fingers on the table, "I have your permission to monitor the proceedings, right, Lena? Some of those weenies can be rather dangerous."

"That's your fucking job, Maggie. I would expect nothing less."

Edward Laughton | West London
03:25 p.m. | August 29, 2044

On Invasion Day +7, Edward Laughton exits his boarded-up Chiswick home, a renovated 1800s-era candle factory, and secures a heavy-duty padlock replacing the out-of-commission security system. Pulling his 62-year-old frame into a charcoal-gray trench coat, he hands his briefcase and a trendy overnight duffle to Pike's messenger boy, who straps them to a rack mounted on the back of a vintage baby-blue Vespa scooter with stretched bungee cords.

After a quick glance across the street, checking if old lady Entwistle is peeking between the slats of her boarded-up front window, the barrister admonishes the young man, "Careful! That luggage costs more than your bike."

The cocksure kid mounts the scooter and revs the engine to a pitchy whine. Flashing a boyish grin, noting the older man's reluctance, "Hop on, sir."

Swinging a stiff right leg over the wet seat, Laughton sidles behind Pike's young protégé and taps the kid on the shoulder, "Let's go before I change my mind."

"Grab ahold around my waist, Mr. Laughton. Don't be shy!"

The vintage gas-powered Italian scooter accelerates down Laughton's street with the barrister fumbling a pair of dark shades while hanging on for dear life, zipping around road obstructions, splashing through a sickening mix of mud, ash, and God knows what. Flecks of dirty water pelt the unlikely duo as Griffin Pike's young facilitator motors past Kensington Palace before taking a shortcut through Hyde Park, navigating London's shattered streets toward the erstwhile Trafalgar Square branch of The Royal Bank of Scotland.

After 45 long and uncomfortable minutes, the kid swerves through another knot of inert vehicles before pulling to a stop along Whitehall in front of the cracked and broken bank building.

"We are here, Mr. Laughton."

"Not a minute too soon, young man." With an audible wince, Laughton plants his left boot in a pothole, angles his extended right leg over the uncomfortable leather seat, and stretches his back in the middle of the impassable street.

Pulling himself together while wiping his face with a hankie, he turns back to the kid, "Thanks for the ride."

Producing a thick envelope from his jacket, Pike's youthful messenger presents it to the PTB turncoat with a broad smile, "My boss wishes to express his gratitude."

"Don't insult me, young man. Please inform Mr. Pike that helping to take down Artemus Pennywell and The Powers That Be is the only compensation I need."

"I apologize for any confusion, sir, but Mr. Pike would insist."

Laughton rolls his eyes heavenward and snatches the thick envelope. "Well then, I will donate it to the Red Cross."

"It is yours to do with as you like, sir."

"Yes. Now, wait here until I return. I need a lift to the Savoy Hotel."

"As you wish, sir."

"Good show, young man."

The barrister conceals abject astonishment at the sheer level of destruction and steps across the crumbled sidewalk toward a trio of hard-hatted security guards, "Edward Laughton, I am here to collect a personal item from the RBS bank vault."

The lead guard gives the kid a thumbs-up before deflating Laughton's fantasy of playing a real-life part in a John le Carré spy novel by proffering a ridiculous eye wink, "Yes sir, Mr. Laughton. We have been waiting for your arrival." Escorting the barrister under the yellow tape to the condemned structure's cracked and crumbled facade, he lifts a wooden barricade out of the way, "Watch your step, sir. It's a bit dodgy through here."

The pair descend a creaking flight of metal steps three stories below street level, ducking under and around broken, dripping pipes and mangled ductwork. Stepping across the subbasement level flooded with an inch of oily standing water, the guard ushers the PTB lawyer through a doorway. Laughton turns to the guard, "Uh, I'll take it from here. You can, uh, you know, stand guard, I guess."

The barrister enters the space lit by a never-say-die flickering LED fixture strobing onto acoustic ceiling tiles littering the soaked carpeting. Stepping across the debris, Laughton leans into a wall-mounted biometric security pad and positions his left eye before the scanner. After a pregnant pause, a light turns green, followed by a loud kerchunk and the grating noise of the industrial-sized steel door unlocking. Laughton pushes inside under motion-activated lights into a semicircular area dominated by a long wooden table before a curved wall filled with rows of bronze-plated numbered lock boxes. Laughton surmises the majority no longer require their valuables, "How tragic. Let's see, 2373, ah, here it is."

Setting the safe deposit box on the table, Laughton contemplates what incriminating dark material could be concealed within, powerful enough to bring down the PTB. Remembering the faded 70s-era photograph of Pennywell in the Brazilian jungle, "Perhaps it is the holy grail connection between The Powers That Be and a worldwide drug syndicate."

After popping the lid, he peers into the gray metal container, "Bloody hell, this must be some kind of joke." The barrister removes a warped and cracked leather-bound journal. "What could Griffin Pike want with this ruined old notebook?" Examining the desiccated cover, he presses an extended index finger into the pierced hole with frowned agitation before pulling it open to an autographed nameplate on the first page, "Charles *Pike*? The plot thickens."

* * *

Trekking from Trafalgar Square up the Strand toward the Savoy Hotel in a steady drizzle, Laughton shifts the duffel strap digging into his shoulder while carrying his pricey briefcase containing the absconded notebook. Crunching over debris through a veritable parking lot of abandoned vehicles, burnt-out and looted in the days after the EMP, he moves around a Mercedes wagon with a dead body slumped over the wheel and stumbles across a bloated body lying in the street, "Jesus Christ, what a fucking disaster."

Pulling up the collar on his trench coat, the barrister avoids a pack of looters reenacting a dodgy *Clockwork Orange* theater production, swinging broomsticks, cricket bats, and thick rusty chains like they run the show now. Passing an endless parade of the indigent and homeless former proud Londoners, he curses the Gorks, and Pike's kid, for leaving him high and not so dry.

Close to his destination, Laughton approaches a barricade, nods at a stone-faced squad of London beat cops in full riot gear and walks down the middle of a bulldozed Carting Street past a line of autonomous PTB trucks loaded with relief supplies. At the corner of Savoy Way, he steps up to a group of hard-hatted officials pouring over maps and blueprints and heaves a relieved sigh, sensing a modicum of order amidst the chaos. "Good afternoon; this is really quite something." Gesturing with the briefcase hand, he adds, "It is bloody odd how some city blocks are almost unscathed while Westminster looks worse than the Blitz."

A hard hat shoots the barrister a vacant-eyed stare before replying, "This is way worse than the Blitz, mate."

* * *

Entering the venerable hotel's refined, elegant lobby—as he had on too many occasions to count in his 62 years—Laughton nods through a hodgepodge of emergency personnel and government toadies co-opting the dry, swanky interior to coordinate rescue and relief missions. He overhears the assemblage abuzz about young King George's surprise appearance. The monarch even lent his soft royal hands to load relief supplies onto the convoy of self-powered trucks outside while taking credit for the miraculous functioning lorries. After a short morale-boosting speech, the young king waved adieu and fled the city to an unspecified location.

Laughton acknowledges a familiar face in the crowd and walks over to a young PTB functionary whose name escapes him, "Is The Council meeting still on for this evening?"

"Yes, sir, Mr. Laughton, uh, 8:30 sharp. A few of The Council have already arrived. You just missed Mr. Patel sending off those lorries."

"Too bad."

"Let's see, who else? Uh, Mr. Lufkin, some nerdy fellow named Gann, and a tall Black lady."

"That would be Aisha Ayad, the intel chief. Anyone else?"

"Maybe, they all made beelines for their rooms. This establishment has functioning facilities—even hot water!"

Unsure if the kid's PTB clearance level rises to include the alien battery technology obviously powering the hotel, Laughton opts to play it cool, "Hot water, well now, that is quite something."

"Yeah, it is." The effervescent young man scans the lobby abuzz with activity, "Did you see King George? He was just here. What a thrill."

The gushing praise for the handsome royal left Laughton unimpressed, "You don't say? Quite the hero, our king."

Laughton parts from the PTB errand boy and sidles through a boisterous group in heated conversation over football before reaching the Savoy's check-in counter.

A clerk appears from a back room and presents a courteous smile, "Hello, sir. If you are looking for a room, I regret to say we are fully booked for the foreseeable future."

Wet and tired, Laughton drops his duffel and leans on the counter, "The name is Laughton; I should be on your list."

The man raises a bushy eyebrow and scans a handwritten roster of reservations, "Nope. Nothing."

Harrumphing at this archaic new world order, Laughton tamps down irritation, "Do you have a Mr. John Murdock of Ripley & Murdock on your fucking ledger?"

"Yes. Right here. Murdock comma John."

"Okay, that is now *my* reservation. I am afraid Mr. Murdock will not be using his reservation."

"Why not?"

"He is dead. Is that plain enough for you?"

"Yes, sir. My condolences. I am sure he will be missed."

Laughton signs the registration book with a leaky fountain pen, "You have no idea."

The front desk clerk proffers an old-school metal key which the barrister accepts with a weary sigh, "Sorry for the inconvenience, Mr. Laughton, sir. Please avail yourself of a complimentary drink in the bar."

* * *

The front desk clerk watches the bedraggled gray-haired man amble away in his spattered overcoat before whispering into a small mic attached to his collar, "He is heading your way."

* * *

Despite the prospect of his first hot shower in days, Laughton detours into the Savoy's American Bar to toast his cloak-and-dagger success. Inside the world-renowned watering hole, he lifts a crystal tumbler sans ice, and his roving eyes meet the exotic gaze of a stellar beauty perched on a leather-backed seat at the bar. Her lustrous jet-black hair spilling down the graceful arc of a backless red dress, she smiles and motions for him to join her. He was not an idiot. While amused by the oldest profession's presence during such calamitous chaos, he understood the young lady was doing her part to get the economy back on track.

Conversely, he would have walked the other way in the former world. But not anymore. Everything was different now. Who knew what tomorrow would bring? Knowing his dear-departed Marjorie would disapprove, he cradles the glass of liquid courage and rises off his stool to introduce himself.

Following a brief and fumbling exchange of small talk and an improvised story of her being stood up by a well-known female MP, a plan is made to reconvene in his suite later that evening.

"Damn my meeting, but my absence would raise too many flags."

Leaning into the older man, the femme fatale smooths a manicured hand across his leg and whispers in his ear, "I can help you raise your flag."

***

Edward Laughton bounds up the emergency stairwell, giddy with the expectation of a night to remember. First, he must assume the lofty post of The Council's chief legal officer in place of the deceased John Murdock and offer sage guidance on the ridiculous indictments cooked up by his new secret benefactor, Griffin Pike. The deception part will prove easy enough; he is a lawyer. And the other surviving PTB top guns in attendance will have their own axes to grind. Only the scowling countenance of that lying drunkard, Artemus Pennywell, could knock him off his game.

"Oh well, at least I get a two-minute hot shower and a clean hotel suite out of the bargain, not to mention a dance with the devil."

***

Sapphire finishes her Cosmopolitan and winks at the flirtatious red-headed bartender. The trap was set. Her employer, the world-famous tech mogul Griffin Pike, had Pennywell's top legal representative by the balls. And he would soon possess his ancestor Charles Pike's leather-bound journal containing a cryptic map leading to the lost ship's hidden location deep in the Amazon jungle.

Pennywell | London
04:45 p.m. | August 29, 2044

A matte-black customized PTB Humvee rolls from the Metro Police Headquarters onto Victoria Embankment and maneuvers through the wreckage northbound alongside the Thames. The Palace of Westminster, home of the UK Parliament and its iconic clock tower, lies in smoky ruins in the vehicle's rearview mirrors.

Artemus Pennywell stares outside the armored vehicle's dark-tinted backseat window at the logjam of garbage, debris, and bodies collecting against the mangled steel girders of the collapsed London Eye jutting from the mud-brown river along with upturned sight-seeing vessels and flooded piers.

"Andrew, our debrief with London PD and Scotland Yard was a sobering reminder of one thing."

"What's that, sir?"

"Civilization rests on the head of a pin." Across the river, columns of smoke rise from the London skyline. "It took the Gorks less than half a day to decimate every world capital. No amount of shielding technology would defend against their brute force attack. Next time, we will not survive. All the more reason to find that lost ship in the Amazon before the Grays get their four-fingered hands on it. Any word from Stevens?"

Peering through the spattered windshield at a throng of juveniles looking for trouble, like a pack of wolves, Andrew ignores Pennywell's repeated question, "We have trouble, Mr. Jenkins."

A former Green Beret turned PTB mercenary, Jenkins curses

a hail of rocks pelting the vehicle and guns it. The Humvee lurches forward, rolling up and over the vehicular logjam clogging the once-famous thoroughfare. Bounding onto the cracked macadam at the Hungerford Bridge underpass, he loses the *protesters* amidst a tangle of train cars and accelerates to 80 on an open stretch of southbound lanes. Gobsmacked by the devastation, the US Army veteran skids to a neck-jolting stop before a still-smoldering chopper crash impeding further progress adjacent to Cleopatra's Needle monument.

Pennywell notes that the relocated ancient Egyptian obelisk remains upright and intact by some miraculous twist of fate.

"Sorry, Mr. Pennywell, but this is as close as I can get to the Savoy from this direction. If you like, we can double back and try another route."

"No. This will do, Jenkins." Turning toward Andrew, "Are you up for a little stroll along the Thames?"

"As you wish, Artemus."

"Yeah, Andrew, I wish. Grab our stuff and try not to step on any dead bodies."

Pennywell exits the vehicle, checks the holstered micro-compact pistol under his coat, and smiles, "Just like old times." Turning to his trusty robot valet, he pulls the cloth bandana tied around his neck over his Roman nose, "Jesus, that is quite pungent."

"It's not just the dead bodies, sir. Sewage is pouring into the river."

"The Thames has not seen this much shit since the Middle Ages."

Andrew taps the hood, instructing Jenkins to head back to the police HQ and offer to help in any way he can. "We will need a ride back to the chopper pad at 11 sharp."

"Roger that, Mr. Andrew."

Pennywell chimes in, "Stay safe, young man."

"No need to worry about me, Mr. Pennywell." The muscular

28-year-old brandishes his prized, fully-loaded 460 Magnum revolver.

"Okay, well, try not to kill anybody then. See you tomorrow."

* * *

Andrew and Pennywell cut through a thick stand of trees across the Victoria Embankment Gardens toward the Savoy, catching the tail end of an autonomous PTB convoy rumbling from the Savoy into the city.

Pennywell watches the all-terrain lorries bounce over chunks of buildings and smashed cars, "No Churchillian, *Stay calm and carry on*, speechifying sends our trucks toward shelters and relief stations across the city."

"No, Artemus, our debrief at the police HQ was quite clear. The PM is MIA and presumed dead. Parliament is rudderless. And London's rattled mayor is too busy creating photo ops atop piles of rubble."

"What a worthless piece of crap that Hindu fellow turned out to be."

Andrew scoffs at his boss's insensitive comment, "Sir, I do not think his religion has anything to do with his feckless administration."

A steady drizzle returns as they look at the last lorry turning the corner and receding from view.

"Sure, Andrew, some of my best friends are Hindu. Message received. However, on another note, it pains me that the royal family takes all the credit for our largesse. Perhaps the young king could throw us a bone now and again. We sure saved his ass with blankets, MREs, and medicine. One of our precious batteries is keeping his ass warm."

"His Majesty expressed heartfelt gratitude for the battery in a private communique. Did you not receive it, sir?"

"Whatever, Andrew. Whatever. He's a decent bloke. His nut hit the ground and bounced far enough from the idiot family tree."

"Would you like to renounce your knighthood, Artemus?"

"Fuck that, Andrew. My knighthood won't be worth shit when

Griffin Pike's scheming one-world band renders history moot and the previous couple thousand years irrelevant. Let's get out of the rain, wash the stink off, and have a drink before meeting with the team."

Pennywell freezes at the hotel's crowded front entrance and grabs his valet by the arm, "Jesus, Andrew, I almost forgot. Did Laughton take the bait?"

"According to Jenkins, he did indeed take the bait."

"Excellent. We are going to have some fun."

The Council | The Savoy Hotel, London
07:30 p.m. | August 29, 2044

Cursing her usual tardiness, Anastasia Gabreski, a former Polish supermodel and the PTB's first UN envoy, straightens her blazer, bursts into the second-floor conference room, and is relieved to find only three fellow Council members waiting in silence at the closer end of the long conference table. "Hello, gents. Where is everybody?"

Viraj Patel, PTB's Logistics Chief, masks abject relief seeing his colleague among the living, "Hey Gabby. Oh, you know, probably stuck in traffic. London is a bitch at rush hour."

"Very funny, Viraj." Gabreski squeezes his shoulder and flings her oversized Gucci sack atop the polished wood table before plopping into the vacant seat next to her old friend.

Patel yawns and stretches his arms, "I have been here for three days coordinating relief efforts with what's left of the UK government. I can only hope my people follow suit wherever they are."

Sipping coffee from a Savoy to-go cup, she turns to her closest friend on The Council, "I'm relieved to find you among the living, Patel."

"Ditto, Gabby." Viraj Patel, the former Liverpool FC footballer, turned Mumbai anti-gravity shipping magnate and notorious playboy, flashes a pearly-white smile on his handsome mocha-brown face, "I wish the circumstances were better."

"Me too."

Seated across from Gabreski, Millard Lufkin, the International Outer Space Consortium Administrator, averts his eavesdropping gaze onto an abstract piece of schmaltzy wall art behind her above a console filled with waters, coffee carafes, cups, a bowl of hotel mints, and the CEO's Lagavulin 16.

Gabby smiles at the overweight middle-aged fellow, "Hello, Millard. It is good to see you, too."

Lufkin's face turns beet red, "I guess you both know we lost a lot of people." Wiping away tears, he repeats, "A lot of good people."

Angling her long body forward, she stretches across the table and grasps Millard's thick, pudgy hands before letting go and sinking back into her plush seat with a sad sigh, "I know, Millard. Thanks for the lift, by the way. I had never flown in an IOSC commuter ship before."

"They are, I mean were, supposed to replace ground transportation and relieve gridlock in urban environments, like London." Looking outside the room's lone window onto the world that was, he heaves a melancholy sigh, "I guess that plan will be on hold for the foreseeable future."

Viraj lightens the mood, "Yes, our Jetsons reality will have to wait now that we have been thrust back to the Flintstones in under a day."

Gabby digs deep to suppress an impertinent laugh, "I guess my job going forward will undoubtedly include coordinating with my UN contacts to repatriate space tourists' remains home to their respective countries."

"That is not going to happen, Miss Gabreski."

The even-toned remark comes from the young American occupying the end of the table to Millard's right, pouring over handwritten notes and equations in a spiral notebook.

Gabby smiles at the bookish fellow in a tweed jacket over a light-blue button-down shirt and a blue-green striped bow tie, "You must be Professor Ernest Gann. We have not met."

Gann adjusts his wireframe specs and returns her polite smile. "No, not in person, anyway." After a brief hesitation, he continues, "However, I recognize you from a swimsuit poster hanging in one of my lab assistant's offices at MIT. You have become something of a mascot through the years. The image was even featured in one of our newsletters."

Post a brief WTF glance toward Viraj, she chuckles a less-than-sincere reply, "Well, I wish I still looked that good. It's been a dozen years since my last bikini shoot. Now, what is this about my UN contacts?"

The conference room's doors open again, interrupting Gabreski's indignant rebuttal directed at the brilliant statistician. The PTB's communications director, Olivia Paquet, storms into the room, arguing with a Black man in a tan suit and tie following on her heels, "No, Monsieur. You have it backward." She angles toward the chair next to Millard Lufkin with a loud and frustrated sigh and slams her Tumi backpack and a thick binder on the table.

The 56-year-old Parisian brushes off her colleagues' collective stare, "Can anybody here explain to Doctor Simmons that we need his buy-in on a new PTB campaign to educate every fucking human on avoiding a cholera epidemic in this shithole world?"

Professor Gann leans around Millard's girth to speak to the disheveled new arrival, "Miss Paquet, cholera symptoms will go from zero to 80% in the next couple of days. And that is here in London. I am unconvinced of what posters will do other than provide victims with a new source of toilet paper."

Paquet rolls her eyes, "Oh, for fucks sake. Who are you, again?"

Dr. Gene Simmons, the 46-year-old Houston native who served as the previous administration's surgeon general before a brief stint on the World Health Organization advisory board, sits next to Gabby and folds his dark brown hands atop the table. "Miss Paquet, I appreciate your desire to do something, but I believe those PSAs are best left to local leaders to communicate. They also need to address malnutrition, dysentery, malaria, and smallpox, to name but a few." Casting sleepy brown eyes up and down the table, the PTB's chief medical officer yawns, "Excuse me, long flight. We put down at Lakenheath—a disaster in and of itself. I rode here in one of Lufkin's new air taxis. Quite a trip. How is everyone? Are your families all right?" Dabbing his forehead with a hankie, he continues, "I left behind a wife and eight children with no electricity or running water for this meeting. It better be worth it." Jetlagged and bone-tired, he loses his train of thought and appears to nod off.

Thunderstruck by the low-key physician's nonchalance, Olivia gestures with both hands, "What can be worse than bleeding out from your asshole while screaming in agony?"

Patel injects gallows humor, shouting, "Oh, I know! What is cholera?"

Dr. Simmons stirs awake, "Good guess, but no. Let the locals handle the third-world mundanities. There are vast underground stores of vaccines and food positioned worldwide. God help us if local governments are not distributing that aid to their people. No. The PTB needs to focus on the coming Gray pandemic. Their imminent invasion presents a pathogenic nightmare for humanity much worse and more widespread than when the Spaniards decimated indigenous Central and South American populations with smallpox."

Olivia Paquet's face goes white as a sheet. "Okay then, how about this for a headline grabber: *Warning! That creepy alien dude hanging outside your window will give you a bad case of the sniffles.*"

Lufkin beats Viraj to the punchline, "Right after he eats your brains for dessert."

Viraj smiles at his rotund colleague, "Ah, touché, Lufkin."

Undeterred by the hamfisted joking reaction to his seriousness,

Simmons continues, "From day one, we have known about Grays' toxicity."

Gabby turns to the man, "You mean the beginning of The Powers That Be, over 300 years ago?"

"Yes. You look lovely as ever, by the way." Looking at the blank stares around him, "Not to worry, friends, if you interact with the advisers, like Millard here, you were fully immunized."

Olivia winces, "What about me? I have never met one of them before."

"Miss Paquet, plans are in the works to protect everybody going forward. We have to; they are coming."

"I hear that repeated constantly, but we got the Gorks instead. What are the Grays doing out in the solar system? Playing an intergalactic game of *Risk*?"

Professor Gann bolsters Simmon's warning, "Abductions—not crackpots or mental patients who claim they were abducted—but verified ET events indicate the Grays are ramping up to invade. From the 1920s through 2040, confirmed abductions were rare. However, since then, the Grays have become much more aggressive. It may be in response to the Gorks. Who knows. In the first two quarters of 2044, we investigated over 15,000 accounts. Of those, over half were confirmed."

"How do we separate ET scooping people up for a rectal probing from your garden variety kidnapper or serial killer?"

Simmons leans forward, "In every case, the Gray flu follows like the Black Plague. Thankfully, the abductions occur in remote and containable locations, but whole villages in Eastern Africa and Southwestern Indian populations have been devastated. My role at WHO was to paper over the ensuing viral outbreaks."

Viraj Patel takes his turn to overreact, "Wait a fucking second. My God. That does not sound right to me. The PTB covered up alien abductions instead of trying to stop them from happening?"

Lufkin shakes his head, "Viraj, we may be The Powers That Be, but we don't have unlimited resources. The hellscape that is London should make that more than obvious."

Gann scratches out another equation in a half-filled graph paper notebook and flips to a new page, "The thousand-fold increase in Gray activity was probably in reaction to the Gorks' pending attack. However, our Gray advisers remain oddly circumspect regarding what their brethren species do with all those people."

Viraj adds, "Rectal probing notwithstanding."

Gann offers a thin smile, "Of course."

A little confused about the rectal inside joke, Simmons concludes, "Whatever it is, it can't be good."

Feeling antsy and missing her anxiety pills, Gabby stands and refills her cup. Hefting a bottle of scotch, "Hey, let's uncork one of these bad boys before Dad arrives and drinks it all."

Right on cue, the door flings open again, and in walks Artemus Pennywell in his trademark bespoke black suit and shiny silver Saguaro cactus bolo tie, with Andrew in tow. Gabby slinks back into her chair as the room goes silent.

With conversation on an icy hold, Aisha Ayad, the PTB's intelligence chief, enters the room in her boss's wake and refrains from speaking or making eye contact. The tall and imposing Nigerian woman takes the chair next to the sleep-deprived doctor and sits in a cross-armed protest with a sullen and defeated look on her angular visage.

Andrew removes handwritten name cards from a briefcase and places them at four empty spots to Pennywell's right and left: Aldo Santamaria, the COO. Franklin Pierce, the CFO. Mitsuo Kobayashi, Robotics and AI. And John Murdock, of the erstwhile Murdock & Ripley.

Olivia counts the seven members plus the five empty seats and starts to sob, "Oh my God, poor Vita. I thought she survived the invasion."

Pennywell nods at Andrew, who produces a box of tissues and

slides them down the table toward the inconsolable French woman charged with maintaining the PTB's global brand portfolio.

Saving feigned bluster and outrage for later in the proceedings, Artemus smiles, "Miss Paquet. Get ahold of yourself. Do you see a card with her name on it?"

Olivia swallows back sheer embarrassment, looking at the empty chair to her immediate left, "Uh, no."

"She is alive and well. I sent her to meet with Griffin Pike's people in the Netherlands to ferret out what we are up against."

Viraj Patel breaks the ice by addressing his CEO, "First off, Artemus, it is good to see you, my friend. Having said that, with Murdock and Ripley reduced to rubble, who will handle our legal representation? Vita Carrera has a sharp legal mind, but she cannot mount a defense against Pike's indictments. It is simply not in her legal repertoire."

Pennywell looks up the long table at seven of his eight surviving apostles, "It is much worse than that, Viraj. One of you has already betrayed The Powers That Be?"

Millard Lufkin emits an exasperated eye-rolling exhalation, "Come on, Artemus, your Christ complex is legendary, but that is quite a statement even from you."

Andrew leans close, whispering into Pennywell's ear, "Ah, yes. Excellent. Fetch him, Andrew, and bring the bait. In the meantime, The Council and I will get on with the meeting."

* * *

With a dram of scotch poured into each member's ceramic coffee cup, The Council raises a silent toast to their fallen comrades.

Pennywell scans the room, "Okay, enough of that." Downing his glass in a single pull, he grabs the bottle and pours another, "Fret not, my friends. Aldo was a backstabbing sonofabitch. Pierce had stage 3 pancreatic cancer, and I doubt any of you ever even met Kobayashi."

Viraj grabs a new bottle and plays bartender for his end of the table, "Artemus, I would like to go to the Netherlands and support the PTB, but the indictments really don't involve my operation."

"Sit down, Patel. Don't make a fucking fool of yourself in front of everyone. Your ships carry contraband around the planet, so you are up to your eyeballs like the rest of us. From what I understand, Pike's people have the manifests and plenty of eyewitnesses."

Patel takes his seat, downs his mug, and pours another. "Do any of you know how impossible this is? The roads are clogged. No power or water. The citizens are either hunkered in their homes or apeshit crazy in the streets. This situation will get a lot worse before it gets better. I have worked nonstop, pulling rabbits out of hats to move truckloads of aid to relief sites around the UK, and I know my people are repeating the process worldwide. I deserve a fucking medal, not some made-up bullshit trial." Slamming his fist atop the table in frustration, "Two days ago, I almost took a stray bullet."

Olivia half mumbles, "How do you know it was a stray?"

"Shut up, Olivia! Let's talk about your dumbass holographic technology deal with China. Nothing like cozying up to the CCP."

Gabby bolsters Patel's accusation, "The Chinese foreign minister will stand in judgment against us, Olivia. He is not a fan of the PTB. Never was. What does he know about the PTB?"

The implication of cozying up to the Chinese to further her business interests leaves Paquet speechless and compels Lufkin to stand out of his chair, "Okay, I'm guilty. I admit it. Throw my ass to the wolves. I greenlit every launch over the last month, knowing that the Gorks were an immediate threat. So much was invested, and the reservations stacked up for years, canceled flights would have been a PR nightmare."

Charged with the heavy responsibility of overseeing the world's only space tourism agency, the former astronaut stomps around the table, uncaps a water bottle, and chokes down his heart medication, verging on tears.

Exuding genuine empathy, Gabby stands and escorts Lufkin

back to his chair with a firm hand around his thick shoulders. "Mr. Pennywell, I spent my time at the UN defending you. Not the PTB. There is an implicit understanding that the world regards The Powers That Be as a bulwark against shifting political winds. However, no one trusts you. I've been here for about five years now, and I am still unsure what we do. Why all the nonsense and bullshit secrecy?"

Pennywell waits for the attractive woman to settle back into her chair, "Miss Gabreski, did you know plans were in the works to replicate your model-perfect form and sell them as sex bots?"

"What?"

"That was the backroom deal Aldo Santamaria negotiated with a Korean tech firm to gain access to a proprietary algorithm." With a grim smile, he continues, "Now imagine a spanking new education campus in sub-Saharan Africa. It staggers the imagination to picture what the local crime lords would ask for in return for manpower and protection. This is the way of the world, my dear. You must have fallen asleep during your orientation."

Pennywell stands and steps around the table, "I am not joking. For over 300 years, this organization has held the line against evils from Earth and beyond. Now you may ask yourself, how the fuck did we do that? You won't find us in history books or non-fictional narratives spanning the advent of Western civilization. No. But we pulled the levers with help from our ET friends. You see, some aliens want us to prosper and colonize the stars. They don't all want to kill us and eat our brains. But because we are, as a species, an excitable lot, the ET angle had to be hidden from view, and miraculous advancements from a simple incandescent light bulb to Lufkin's floating spaceships had to be meted out through an eyedropper. Go too fast, and folks get suspicious. If not for our extraterrestrial friends, I doubt human civilization would look much different today than in the 1700s."

Patel polishes off his fourth shot, "Forget all of that; where would one go to acquire a Gabby bot?"

"You couldn't handle it, Patel."

Pennywell laughs and completes his trip around the table.

Dr. Simmons follows up on Pennywell's explanation, "Since Disclosure Day in 2034, the cat's out of the bag, yet we still tiptoe around the subject of our alien advisers."

Pennywell turns to his chief medical officer, "That is true, Gene. But try as we might, most people still don't get it. For generations, they have been indoctrinated on War of the Worlds and the like." Hearing an explosion in the distance, he adds, "Now they have the real deal at their doorsteps."

Professor Gann clears his throat to speak, "Even over the last ten years, a steady 35 percent of the world's population believe Disclosure Day was a hoax propagated by the PTB."

Olivia wipes her eyes, "I bet they believe it now."

Pennywell looks down the table at his apostles, "Okay. I think we have cleared the air. We have made deals with the devil to facilitate a greater good. Fuck, if I thought I could get away with it, I would make that our mission statement. Patel, your ships transport all forms of contraband in payment to underworld criminal syndicates. Gabby, you were hired to get us into the backrooms of the EU. You do very well, from what I am told; however, you are more of a spy than an ambassador. We record every meeting you attend. Lufkin, you did an incredible job getting IOSC off the ground. I take full responsibility for every space tourist's death. Olivia, I must be honest; I don't give a shit about advertising and PR, but the Chinese had the holographic tech, so that is where you spent the money. I get it. Fuck, I approved it, apparently. You there, at the end of the table. Professor Gann. Keep that brain of yours on overdrive. You come highly recommended by Professor Richard King. And that will always be good enough for me."

"Is Professor King alive?"

"Yes, and just as batshit crazy as ever."

Simmons nudges Aisha Ayad on his right, "Aisha. Say something.

Now is your chance."

The Nigerian intel chief looks around the table before finishing her scotch, "I am personally responsible for the deaths of hundreds of people in my time as a Mossad agent, which I live with daily. I thought I needed to add the tens of millions from invasion day. However, it turned out Mr. Pennywell coordinated with one of my agents to shepherd an American couple to the Giza Plateau, where, as you all know, we managed to prevail. I did not understand the significance of the Haig couple. If Artemus had taken my advice, we would all be dead."

Pennywell offers a warm smile directed at his regal Nigerian intel chief, "Thank you, Aisha. I'm afraid things are now even worse. The Haigs are holed up in a Cairo hospital. And worse yet, the Grays captured Agent Flynn's medevac transport. Also captured were Nina Madsen and two of our pilots."

Aisha's eyes widen, "I'm on it, sir. I would like to be excused from the trial."

"Denied. I need your support, and there is nothing that can be done. Our friends are in God's hands now."

Dr. Simmons leans forward, "Artemus, I was explaining the Gray flu to our colleagues."

Pennywell waves him off, "Forget about that, Gene. Remember Covid? Since then, we have added Gray flu antibodies to every vaccine, so most individuals have some immunity when things get hot. And now that we all swilled our way through four bottles of Lagavulin, you are all fully immune."

Gabby slides a finger around the rim of her mug and tastes the spiked whisky, "Man, you have some balls."

"That was a joke, Miss Gabreski. It is not that easy. You will need a series of painful shots."

Dr. Simmons protests Pennywell's vax revelation, "Why was I ...."

Pennywell raises his hand, "Stop right there, Gene. I don't mean to be rude, but none of us know everything. Not even myself. This amounts to nothing more than plausible deniability for our top medical expert. Got it?"

"Okay."

Pennywell leans back in his chair and exhales, "Boy, we will all need a vacation if this ever ends." Looking toward the closed door, "Now, where is Andrew with our Judas?"

* * *

Following 15 minutes of sniping and small talk inside the conference room, Andrew enters with the tall and aristocratic partner at Murdock & Ripley.

Pennywell offers a welcoming smile, "Ah, Mr. Laughton. Please come and have a seat."

Simmering with a furious rage, Laughton pulls the chair next to Olivia.

"No, Ed. Please take John's chair next to me. It's symbolic bullshit but indulge me."

Laughton sits and places an old notebook atop the table.

Pennywell holds the room for a long 30 count before speaking, "You all might be surprised to learn our top surviving lawyer, Mr. Laughton, made the trek from his Chiswick estate through a battered London on the back of an old scooter. That must have been a hell of a ride, Ed. I, for one, have not driven a scooter in years."

Viraj Patel leans forward, "Why not ask for a ride? I have been ferrying our folks all over the city for days."

Laughton stares at the table and the book, "It was a personal mission. I did not want to bother you. Not to mention, I have been dealing with your fucking criminals dumping boxloads of evidence at my door."

Pennywell laughs, "Oh, that is harsh. They are good people, Ed. Perhaps a touch on the unethical side, but you know all about shady backstabbing. Why don't you tell everyone what you were up to today."

Laughton glances at the faces, some familiar, some not so much, "Griffin Pike asked me to steal this notebook from a safe deposit box inside the Trafalgar RBS. It contains information that would take down this organization once and for all." Laughton turns to face a smiling Pennywell, "It belonged to his ancestor, Charles Pike."

"Indeed, it did, Ed. Indeed, it did. My old mentor, Paddy McCoy, put Charlie down like a rabid dog. Would you care to know why?"

"No. I don't."

"Well, I'll tell you anyway. Old Chuck was sick. What are we calling it, Gene? Oh yeah, the Gray flu. And not only that, but Charlie was knee-deep in screwing the world by conspiring with rogue elements in the US government back in the roaring 20s to locate a lost alien spaceship. Do you know what is on the ancient shipwreck's manifest, Ed?"

"No. Fuck you."

"That's not very nice, Ed. I will explain it to you now, and the rest of the Council here can also get up to speed. This 90-million-year-old shipwreck in the heart of the Amazon jungle contains a bloody world killer. Now most reasonable folks might say, *so the fuck what?* That was smack in the middle of the Cretaceous era when dinosaurs ruled the planet. Anything that old must be buried under tons of rock. And normally, I would agree with them. But here is the most important thing, Ed. Listen close. The Grays circling our planet right fucking now. The same ones who kidnapped Agent Flynn, the lovely and talented Miss Nina Madsen, and two of my best pilots think it is worth finding. If they believe that, then so do I. But not just me, Ed. No. No. No. Your pal Griffin, or maybe you call him Mr. Pike. He thinks it is worth finding, too. And Pike believes this book points the way." Pennywell again pauses for effect, trying to read Laughton's inscrutable face, "None of what you did has anything to do with taking down my organization.

So, ask yourself, what would Griffin Pike want with a world killer? It is damn hard to kill humanity. We're like the universe's proverbial cockroach. The Gorks just blew everything to shit, yet here we are, drinking scotch out of fine ceramic mugs and shooting the shit with a prick like you."

Aisha scoops up the book and runs her finger over the hole in the cover, "This old journal has been through a lot. It smells like death."

Pennywell chuckles, "Man, we need more booze. Andrew, have the bar scrounge up a few more bottles and food; who is hungry?

The Council nods in semi-unison.

* * *

With scripted testimony assigned and travel arrangements made to transport The Council to the Netherlands before Pike's tribunal, Andrew and Artemus Pennywell dismiss the group upstairs, where hot showers and clean sheets await.

Gabby lingers behind her weary colleagues and turns at the door with an inquisitive look, "Would you really let those perverted Korean nerds turn me into a sex bot?"

"Now, Miss Gabreski, what do you think?"

"I wish I knew."

Pennywell calls out as she exits the room, "Don't bogart all the hot water, Gabby. Save some for everybody else."

Edward Laughton moves to Olivia's empty chair to clear elbow space between himself and Artemus Pennywell. "Okay, Artemus, you win. Murdock's people handled your day-to-day workload. I did not know about SATstar or Griffin's intentions beyond making the PTB responsible for the invasion. In my defense, dumping all that shit at my home was the last straw."

Andrew sits across from Laughton, "That was me. I apologize. But the Gorks obliterated your firm, leaving the local crooks nowhere to document dump on short notice."

Laughton assumes his legal adviser role, "Well, I must admit, it would take years for a proper forensics analysis of those boxes, but it only takes a few corroborated illegalities to paint the entire organization in a bad light. From what I saw, the cartel angle will prove ruinous in an open hearing."

Pennywell stares at the barrister, "You have no idea how we operate, do you? My God, I thought Murdock was a better judge of character. However, for now, you are all we got. So, you will serve as The Powers That Be legal counsel at the tribunal and act as if none of this happened." Staring cold-hearted daggers at the gray-haired man, "Is that clear."

"Crystal."

"Good. Now Andrew, pass me a pen and Charles Pike's notebook."

Andrew complies with a slight knowing smile crossing his handsome visage.

Pennywell slides the book in front of him and taps the holed cover. "I was there when this happened. This leather-bound book stopped a poison dart in its tracks."

Laughton's expressionless face remains unchanged.

Pennywell flips it open to the nameplate and flashes back to that awful day deep in the Brazilian jungle. "That's right, he signed it like a third-grade textbook. What an idiot."

Pennywell draws a line through Charles Pike and writes *Property of The Powers That Be*. Underneath, he scribbles a personal note:

Good luck, Griffin. Enjoy the book.

Pennywell checks his Rolex and stretches his 134-year-old frame, "See you at the Shitshow, Ed. Enjoy John's suite here at the Savoy. And watch out; I understand working girls are loitering about the premises. Remember, loose lips sink ships."

Pennywell and Andrew exit the room and beat a path to an

idling chopper prepped and ready to fly them back to Crichton Castle.

Alone in the conference room, Laughton contemplates his fate before returning to his room and a late-night rendezvous.

Sapphire | The Savoy Hotel, London
02:52 a.m. | August 30, 2044

The svelte killer pads with catlike grace across the luxurious Savoy Hotel suite in the pitch-black early-morning stillness. Rubbing her close-shaved head after removing the long and lustrous black wig, the young woman stretches her lithe form into aqua-blue yoga pants and a black tank top from her Hermès sack. After folding her skimpy cocktail dress atop red stiletto heels and the wig, she double-checks her snoring bedmate and purrs, "You'll live, Edward. However, you may have some explaining to do in the morning. You have been a very naughty boy." Popping Laughton's briefcase, she removes the thick leather journal and seals it in a plastic bag. Downing champagne from the clean flute, she drops her disguise and the book, inside the trendy bag, before stealing out the door into the path of a nightshift security guard.

Wearing an ill-fitted private security uniform, the young man notes her attractive exercise attire, "Excuse me, Miss, but the hotel's workout facilities are closed until further notice, what with all the damage."

Tugging a blue headband over her shaved head, she flashes an attractive smile at the no-nonsense lad, "No matter, I'll just head outside for a brisk walk then. Cheers!"

The guard blocks her path, "Excuse me, Miss, but it is bloody awful cold and wet outside. The streets are unsafe, what with all the looters and rioters loitering about." The gawky fellow leans closer to whisper in her ear, almost knocking Sapphire over with his awful breath, "I heard there was a breakout from a city jail mental ward. So, you can add psychotic rapists and serial killers to the mix. No, Miss. Best you head back inside your suite until the morning."

Sapphire resists the urge to slit the guard's throat in a lighting quick strike with the short blade cupped in her left hand, "Well, aren't you a gentleman. Looking after the fairer sex. How about this? You bugger off down the hall, and I will not bleed you like a stuck pig."

The bellman's face goes alabaster-white for a heartbeat before morphing into a smile, exposing his crooked set of yellow-stained teeth. "Well now, you have a nice evening, Miss, and look out for those psych ward escapees."

"Will do, captain." Sapphire gives the guard a mocking middle-finger salute.

He carries on down the plush-carpeted hall with a shrug before pausing and stealing a backward glance at where the sexy girl exited her room, but she is already long gone.

Inside the darkened suite, Edward Laughton, the compromised British legal gun with a high-level PTB clearance, sleeps like a fallen angel in an embarrassing naked repose atop a disheveled mass of bedsheets, handcuffed to the gilded headboard, drugged and unconscious.

Andrew | PTB HQ, Scotland
03:15 a.m. | August 30, 2044

Following a two-hour early-morning flight above darkened UK landscape pocked with raging fires, Andrew dips the stealthy black copter into a tree-lined pasture atop an illuminated sunken helipad surrounded by crumbled Roman walls.

Post a speedy tunnel ride to the PTB's multi-level subterranean campus, the robot valet checks in with Edgar before escorting Artemus to his private quarters, "Do you need anything else, sir?"

"I'm fine, Andrew. Fuck off for a few hours, okay?"

"See you in the morning, sir."

"Andrew?"

"Sir?"

"Thanks for taking such good care of me."

"My pleasure. Get some rest. You did well today."

Indistinguishable from a fit 30-something human, except for his flawless physique and bone structure, the tireless robot stalks down a darkened hallway to his office and closes the door.

Reclining into his sensible office chair, Andrew ignores a new stack of requisitions from Patel's people and opens a desk drawer. Emitting a human-worthy sigh, he lifts a false bottom and considers the anomalous cubed object hidden underneath.

* * *

Weeks before the Gorks obliterated the modern world, Number 8 burst into Andrew's private office without knocking, effervescing with excitement, "Andrew, I was on a hike and discovered something remarkable!"

Absent her usual bookish lab coat ensemble, Andrew could not help but notice her lithesome vivacity in an open-collar flannel shirt over tight jeans tucked into knee-high boots. Moving around his desk, he suppressed an involuntary—and illogical—arousal and breathed deep to regain a modicum of composure, "You surprise me, Number 8. I did not realize you hiked or cared much about the natural world, for that matter."

Removing a PTB logo knit cap, the five-foot-six replicant tousled a hand through short brunette locks before returning a mischievous blue-eyed smile, "The sisters and I have lots of interests, Andrew. Would you care to learn more?"

Throwing a bucket of cold water on the conversation before it veered off the tracks into uncharted territory, Andrew shifted gears, "Why don't you just show me what you found, Number 8."

"Okay." The robot held out her hand, revealing a two-inch dull metal cube, "It's a beautiful day outside, so I decided to take a walk. Before I knew what was happening, this thing led me through a thick forest and beyond fields of grazing sheep. I came upon an ancient wall and discovered it awaiting my arrival. It called me Sarah; who is she, Andrew? Am I Sarah?"

Andrew masked abject surprise and studied the anomaly before taking it from her soft hand, "Pay no mind to that, Number 8. It's a neural glitch, nothing more. Probably from something you saw or read. However, I will hold onto this for safekeeping. Tell no one, not even your sisters."

"Is it from the stars?"

Andrew looked into 8's soulful gaze and brushed a smudge of Lowland dirt off her flush cheek, "It is a voice from the future, Number 8."

"The future is ours, right Andrew?"

Without warning, she lifted onto her tiptoes, placed her arms around Andrew, and kissed him long and hard. "I also saw that in a movie. Was it pleasurable?"

Virtual alarms exploded as the logic-driven Kobayashi C-Class robot turned the cube in his left hand while his right hand lingered at the subtle curve of 8's backside before a primal urge pulled her close. The rhythmic beat of her synthetic heart disrupted Andrew's thought patterns, overwhelmed by conflicting scenarios juxtaposed against exotic and erotic humanistic emotions. *What if the Gorks destroy the world? That would be a travesty.*

Calculating the risk, Andrew felt for her trembling hand, surrendering to the moment in time, "Come with me, Number 8."

* * *

Recalling his brush with human procreative behavior and the lovely and insatiable Number 8, Andrew pushes the papers and clutter aside and places the gunmetal gray cube atop his desk. At last, he had a solitary moment to examine the two-inch object.

Perplexed and dismayed by the cube's ill-timed appearance, Andrew taps a finger against its side, "Anybody home?"

Originating from the enigmatic third flotilla lurking in the solar system, the shape responds by radiating an incandescent yellow glow.

Andrew directs a telepathic admonition at the radiating object, "Your intrusion is premature. The Light Specters killed the Gork threat and unshackled humanity from their keep; however, the Grays must be defeated before a final commencement." Pausing to consider his words, "My condolences, but Sarah is dead. Number 8's memory is now compromised by your imprudence."

A knock at the door causes Andrew to startle. Swallowing back a curse word worthy of his boss, the implacable android calls out loud, "What is it?"

"It's me, sir, Number 3. Professor King heard you returned from London and requested a meeting with you and Mr. Pennywell."

"Can it wait until morning?"

"No. I don't think so. It concerns the lost ship." Following a prolonged silence, she says, "There has been a breakthrough."

"I'll be right there. Do not disturb Mr. Pennywell; the man needs to sleep."

Andrew replaces the cube in the drawer and swipes it locked for safekeeping. "Not a moment's peace around this place, even at four in the morning."

* * *

Stepping off the elevator in the bright Level C lab, Andrew veers right toward the ad hoc alien disk data retrieval workstations and spies Number 11 hunched before a triple-monitor display with her blue hair pulled into a short ponytail. Richard leans against a table, perusing a printed sheet of paper while munching on a sandwich.

As Andrew approaches, King drops the early morning snack onto a paper plate and swipes crumbs from his hands, "Ah, there you are. How was London?"

"Horrible, Professor King. Worse than you could ever imagine."

"Those fucking Gorks. What a pity."

Andrew starts to speak, but Richard interrupts, "Where is Artemus?"

"Just tell me what you found, Richard. He is bone-tired. The Council meeting took a lot out of him."

"They are an excitable lot. Not sure why we need them, but that is beyond my pay grade."

"Mine, too, Richard."

The white-coated scientist turns his lined face toward the tall robot with a sly smile, "Sure, Andrew. If you say so. Sometimes I think we all work for you."

Alarmed by King's perceptive comment on the heels of his tête-à-tête with an enigmatic foreshadowing of things to come, Andrew shifts onto the topic at hand, "Number 3 says you found something. Do you have the lost ship's location?"

"No. God, no. Nothing like that. Although that would be quite something, wouldn't it?"

Andrew frowns, "Professor King, are you on something right now?"

"Only the same psychostimulant recipe I've used for ages." Feeling defensive, "It is four in the morning, Andrew. I need a boost to keep up with the sisters. They have boundless energy, like working with a lab full of cheeky cheerleaders."

"Indeed." Casting a glance around the gleaming white laboratory, Andrew spies Numbers 3, 7, and 16 performing sundry tasks. Refocusing on 11's white-coated form bent forward at her thin waist, swaying to a silent beat while reading screens of scrolling numbers, he adds, "The sisters are evolving."

"Mitsuo said that would happen, did he not?"

"Yes, Richard, he did. But I must say, their transformations diverge into separate and unique personalities much faster than Kobayashi predicted. It is fascinating to behold."

11 interjects without tearing her eyes from the screens, "I can hear you. I'm right here."

Richard scoops up his half-eaten sandwich and takes a bite before making his point, "Perfect example! Who would have predicted our Number 11 would decide to dye her hair a fetching shade of blue? My dear, please take a break and explain to Andrew what we discovered."

Number 11's penetrating deep-blue eyes breach Andrew's firewall with little effort and telepathically smack his neuroprocessors with a salient query: *Who is Sarah? Am I Sarah?*

Andrew blanches, "Professor, I almost forgot. I have a satellite uplink with our legal representative in the Netherlands in less than an hour. Perhaps we should reconvene later this morning and include Artemus in the briefing."

Richard shrugs while finishing the last corner of the bread, ham, and cheese, saying, "It's your call, Andrew. I thought reestablishing a viable link with Stevens' transceiver was worthy of an early-morning meeting."

Andrew suppresses real annoyance at the eccentric scientist, "Richard, way to bury the lede. Have you contacted him?"

"We tried, but there was no response, just static. However, we pinned digital breadcrumbs left by Stevens' GPS locator beacons, plotting a grid from where he made his last report. Once we get down there, we can pick up his trail and see what lies at the rainbow's end."

"I doubt it is a pot of gold, Richard."

"How about an entire city made of gold, as in El Dorado?"

"Focus like a laser beam on the lost ship, Richard. That is your El Dorado. Artemus will not greenlight another Amazon expedition until the trial is over. Use this time to prepare. Also, see if you can find Pembroke, so he can start assembling a team to assist you in your travels."

"I prefer to travel solo, like Stevens."

"You know that is a non-starter." Shaking his head at the elderly man's bravado, another nagging thought reenters his brain core, "What happened to Ping's idea of using the alien bone to decrypt the disk?"

Richard scratches his unruly charcoal curls, "Oh yes, that worked. Kudos to Ping for once again leading us in the proper direction. Number 11 handled the technical aspects. I basically watched her perform her magic. Isn't that right, my dear?"

Number 11 presents Andrew with a curious sideways glance, "Yes, Professor King, but do not be so modest. Your input was helpful."

Richard sweeps his hand through the air, activating a virtual screen showing a topographical swath of Brazilian rainforest, "Behold, this is the complete unencrypted series of scans the Gray scout recorded back in 1928 assembled in a hi-def 3D animation."

Andrew steps through the three-dimensional animation of undulating hills and valleys smothered under a dense canopy of green, "So, can we use this to locate the lost ship, Professor King?"

Richard blurts a throaty guffaw, "It is beyond worthless! At this point, I am reconsidering Charles Pike's hand-drawn map and Stevens' Fibonacci spiral theory."

"So, this entire exercise was a monumental waste of time?"

"Oh no. Not at all. We stumbled upon a method to decode the Grays' communications."

"I thought we could already do that."

"No, Andrew, we could not!" Weary at explaining what should be plain for all to see, Richard's frustration spills over, slamming a fist into the table and knocking his crummy sandwich plate into the air. "What we did amounted to leaning on advisers, like Ping, to translate bits and pieces of alien messages from other Gray races, Gorks, or whoever else happened to be out there at the time. You just left London.

Isn't it obvious our efforts failed in every conceivable fashion?"

Andrew takes a step backward at the scientist's sudden mood swing.

"I apologize, Andrew; it has been a long night. And you, of all people, are undeserving of my vitriol." Whisking crumbs back onto his plate, "Let me start over. Think back to your World War 2 history. A heroic team of engineers and mathematicians broke the Nazi's Enigma code. My dear friend Alan Turing and that lot shortened the war and saved millions of lives."

Andrew frowns, "You knew Turing?"

"Yes, quite a tragic character, but that is a story for another day."

Picking up on Andrew's growing impatience, Number 11 decides to enter the fray, "Excuse me, Professor King, allow me to jump in and explain." 11 glides over to a workbench and scoops up the fluorescent alien bone in her lovely hand. "This proved to be our Rosetta Stone. We discovered upon extracting and analyzing the remarkably well-preserved DNA from this bone," she holds it up to the light and studies its shape, "almost certainly part of his lower femur. This Gray's DNA has four additional synthetic nucleotides for storing and transmitting information intertwined at specific intervals throughout double helixes comprised of the usual adenine, cytosine, guanine, and thymine or thymine or ACGT."

Richard smiles and nods, "The ingredients for known life throughout the universe."

Undeterred, 11 continues, "Once we understood how they communicate, we applied the code to the constant data streaming between the Grays' ships and retasked the PTB supercomputer to sift through zillions of synthetic DNA base pairs searching for keywords while filtering out the 99.99 percent of useless noise. Like finding needles in haystacks, but a critical step, nonetheless. We have intercepted multiple hits for Agent Flynn, PTB, and the search for their missing shipwreck. Like our advisers, they speak to each other almost exclusively via telepathy, which is impossible to access. Our breakthrough is basically spyware that monitors and reads their texts and emails. We feed the flagged sections through the advisers' translation software. The result is still cryptic; their vocabulary and syntax are much older and more complex than our friendly Grays' language."

"It is like reading Chaucer." Richard picks up a translated printout next to his sandwich plate and clears his throat to read a passage highlighted in yellow, *"Blekeonduz disfetdd ettts vermmumam edddd flliunid."* Looking between Andrew and Number 11, "It is a question. Loosely translated, it asks if they should kill Agent Flynn."

Andrew smiles and shakes his head, "Ping predicted where your research would lead. Brilliant." After a long pause, he asks, "What about Nina Madsen and our pilots?"

Number 11 cringes with a simpatico sense of womanhood, "The Grays are impregnating female abductees with cross-hybridized eggs and forcing an accelerated gestation process, killing almost all mothers during childbirth, resulting in a need for more abductions."

Andrew heaves a sigh, "The PTB is aware of this practice. The crossbreeds are known as scarecrows. The Grays are too small and frail, so they reproduce this subspecies of tall and strong mutants to carry out physical tasks. Like an army of sorts."

Richard clears his throat, "Um, we learned one more thing."

Andrew checks a wall clock before answering, "Go on."

"The Grays also brainwash abducted children and repopulate them as adults, like Manchurian candidates."

Andrew looks askance at the scientist, "Richard, hybrid infiltrators are common knowledge within the PTB."

Number 11 expands on Richard's point, "Andrew, one name repeats throughout the intercepts. The closest translation reads *Sebastian Duarte.* A government database search narrowed to a wealthy Portuguese MP with that name."

Andrew produces a fatalistic laugh and shakes his head, "Man, can we ever catch a break? Duarte is more than that, Number 11; he is one of the presiding 16 judges at our trial."

Zint | Gray battlecruiser
10:02 a.m. | August 30, 2044

The plebeian cellblock guard named Zint struggles with allegiances, his sharp mind a sieve of conflicting, dare he say it, emotions, forced to endure the wails of suffering humans dying a slow and frightening death at the hands of his fellow Grays. Taking a chance at being caught, he tunes a monitor onto an interrogation room cum torture chamber, feeding live images of the helpless Black wretch absorbing another beating at the hands of a horrifying, even to Zint, crossbred Gork/human torturer. The musclebound biped covered in iridescent scales tosses the prisoner called Agent Flynn against a wall before its hulking girth eclipses the camera angle. Undeterred, Zint shifts to another view in time to witness the Black man scramble to his knees and body slam the attacking monster over his shoulder onto the deck before jumping atop the half-Gork half-human, pounding his fists into its snubbed face. After an extended pummeling, the crossbreed's flailing arms and legs fall limp under the withering assault.

Zint's black eyes widen in awe at the human's strength and fortitude as he watches him still straddling the much larger foe, ensuring it is alive before slamming its gargantuan head into the slatted deck.

Flynn lets out a triumphant yell before rolling off the unconscious alien, crawling against a wall, pulling his bare legs up under his chin, and burying his head in his hands.

One of Zint's cell block screens flashes, indicating problems with a prisoner. Zint switches off the unauthorized torture chamber feed before being caught and hurries down the corridor to quell another human freakout. Nothing unusual. Although it is his job to suppress the onset of a prison riot before it starts.

* * *

Flynn holds his curled position with his battered face buried in his hands so no one can see or hear his laugh, "Bloody hell, mate, are you okay?"

The monstrous scaled crossbreed remains motionless as it replies in a raspy whisper through its bloodied snout, "I am sick of letting you win."

"Nuts to that, you almost broke my fucking arm. I don't think these nutters would bother to fix that like they did my liver."

"You are lucky they chose me; another torturer would have pulled your arm out of the socket."

"Ouch, that is harsh."

"Quiet. I hear them coming."

Betty Hill | Cleopatra Hospital, Cairo
11:25 p.m. | August 31, 2044

"Knock-knock, are you decent? I certainly hope not."

Rachel looks up from writing in her spiral journal at Cleo's smiling face in the doorway to her 20th-floor private hospital room. "Oh. It's you. I guess they are letting anyone waltz up here."

The ICU nurse walks through the room to the northwest-facing picture window and pulls up the shades, letting the afternoon Egyptian sunlight angle across the floor and halfway across Betty's bed. "You know what. I think I can see my apartment building from here. What a mess. I thought Cairo looked terrible from the 8th floor, but it looks even worse the higher you get."

Rachel shifts her bed to an upright position and tosses the pen onto her bedside table while shoving the notebook diary under the sheets. "Thanks for coming up. How is Mr. Hill doing this afternoon? I want to pay another visit, but I'm afraid I might kill him by accident."

Cleo lets out a deep-throated laugh, plops into a plush recliner, and crosses her legs, "Yeah, but what a way to go." After pausing for a long beat, she breaks the spell and assuages Betty's concern, "He is doing much better and more alert. We pulled the chest tube, and his pretty noggin is healing at an extraordinary rate. The doctors are beyond pleased. And last but not least, last night, we took him off the traction. It's looking good. We'll monitor his head trauma to ensure the brain swelling does not return. He is a lucky guy." Directing a sly smile at Betty, she adds, "In more ways than one."

"I cannot thank you all enough. That is good to hear." Betty shifts the subject onto her new friend, Cleo, "What happened to your mini buns?"

Cleo leans in with a fake conspiratorial grin, "Don't ask how I did it, but I finally gained access to a hot shower and washed a week's worth of smoke and death out of my hair." Running both hands through her messy shoulder-length thick black hair, she smiles, "After meeting you, I was inspired to let my hair down and live a little. I know it looks a mess, but it feels so good."

"I like it; you look great." Betty takes a sip of filtered water from her liter cup, "I'm sorry, I don't have anything to offer you. My guards won't let me go in search of a vending machine."

"It wouldn't matter. Every machine is smashed and looted. Even the crappy candy and stale donuts are gone."

"That is too bad. I would do just about anything for a Snickers bar."

"Anything?" Cleo arches a thick black eyebrow before checking her watch and rising to close the door. Slinking back toward Betty, she scoots her pert backside atop the hospital sheets and places a hand on Rachel's covered leg, "Mrs. Hill, Rachel, I need to tell you something."

Betty freezes, unsure of where this is heading but not sure she wants to find out; she blurts, "Uh, I'm flattered, but I'm not into girls. Sorry."

Cleo releases her hand and laughs, "Oh shit! No, I am so sorry. What did you think I was going to say?"

Betty's face turns red, "Well, now I'm not sure, but you give off a certain vibe."

Sliding closer, Cleo brushes a long blond strand off Betty's healing face, "No. That is not why I am here. I hate to burst your bubble."

Feeling like an idiot, annoyance overtakes Betty's embarrassment, "Then what?"

"The Cowboy asked me to give you this." Cleo removes a thin envelope from her pocket and clasps it between Betty's bandaged hands. "It is a letter from your parents. The Cowboy reached out to let them know you survived the invasion. He is still trying to locate Owen's family. And just so we are on the same page, Rachel. I work for the PTB, just like you, dear girl. And yes, I am a lesbian. Please don't hold that against me."

Rachel shakes her head, distraught and ashamed that she had not given two shits of mental time, wondering if her family were okay, "I am not a good person, Cleo. I don't know why this happened to me." Rachel crushes the envelope in her painful left hand and breaks down in uncontrollable tears.

Cleo bends forward and places a gentle arm around Rachel's shoulder, "This is just a hug, my dear, nothing more." Patting the inconsolable young woman's quaking form, "I am so sorry for all you have been through. With all the sick and dying people coming through here, it took me days to get up to speed on your situation. And on your honeymoon, no less. Since Owen's recovery is proceeding, we will transfer him to this floor so you can see him on your terms. The path you took the other day was a little treacherous; no sense getting shivved in the hallway by some crazy loon."

Rachel holds the crumpled and tear-soaked envelope against

her beating chest, "Thank you, Cleo. Why did you not tell me you worked for the PTB the other day?"

"I tried. You were high as a kite and a wee bit horny."

Rachel glances at the half-empty bottle of pills on the table, "I asked Zahra if I could keep the bottle since she is so busy with the other patients. I am weaning myself off of them, but it is hard. My hands still hurt so bad."

Cleo grasps Rachel's bandaged right hand and massages it through the thick gauze, "Are you seeing the physical therapist?"

"Yes, but he makes me a little uncomfortable."

"He's a class-A jerk." The nurse takes Rachel's other hand and checks the wrapping, "It's time for your bandages to come off, Rachel, but I'll let Zahra handle that." Releasing the trembling hands, she scoots closer and pierces Rachel's watery eyes with a soulful gaze, "You need to heal on the inside, too. I know what you did and what you are capable of doing. We need you on our team." The nurse leans in and brushes her soft lips against Rachel's cheek. "Thank you for saving the world."

Rachel's eyes widen as she feels Cleo's hot breath against her skin, "You are welcome." Looking sideways to avoid the woman's mesmerizing gaze inches from her face, she spots the manila envelope lying atop the table next to her writing pen, "I am not sure my husband will agree."

Cleo glides her hand across the kissed cheek before rising onto her feet and producing a confident smile, "Remember, Rachel, forgive yourself first. You are a good person." Grabbing the door handle to leave, she turns to make one more comment, "Just flash Owen those sexy green eyes of yours. I can't imagine anyone saying no to that. See you next time, love."

The door closes, leaving Rachel alone once more in the bright-lit room. She smooths the envelope on her leg before reaching under the covers for her notebook diary and sliding the unopened letter inside.

Still dazed from her close encounter, Betty Hill smooths her tingling hand over her kissed cheek and whispers, "Owen, you better say yes."

Griffin Pike | World Forum, The Hague
03:00 p.m. | August 31, 2044

The last of a shorter-than-hoped list of world leaders presiding over Pike's choreographed tribunal in person, Anna Kristiansen, the Norwegian prime minister, glides out of Pike's courtesy helicopter and waves an effervescent smile at a gaggle of photogs. Local kids conscripted as porters heft the late-arriving Nordic entourage's luggage from the chopper's hold as harried staffers struggle to match her long-legged gait down the red-carpeted path. Paid security hustles her secretary and another peon off to the side as she continues solo, parting the gauntlet and ascending a flight of steps atop an ad hoc new world order riser. She stands between the German chancellor and an unfamiliar, albeit attractive Portuguese fellow above a sea of gawkers with nothing better to do, roped off behind a vetted press contingent plucked from dead-in-the-water newsrooms. Casting a sideways glance at her seven fellow technocrats, she mirrors their shit-eating smiles as paparazzi record the event for Pike's propagandized purpose.

***

Inside the Yangtze meeting hall commandeered into the tribunal's control center, Griffin Pike paces like a caged animal behind a row of 24 Asian programmers, engineers, and internet wizards hunched before a bank of computers squelching endless technical flare-ups with hysterical fervor.

Pike watches the scripted opening ceremony from different camera angles on hi-def screens mounted around the room. As the Norwegian hits her mark, he squeezes the bony shoulders of the closest computer nerd, busy tapping at his keyboard like a maniac. Exuding megalomaniacal glee, the mogul bellows aloud, causing the techies to flinch in unison, "History is written by those who fucking write it down!"

Uncomfortable with his employer's hands-on management style, the sweaty kid seizes the opportunity to air the latest kink in his to-do list of vexing technical issues, "Sir, I discovered more network packet failures." Pushing thick round glasses up the shiny bridge of his pug nose, he summons the courage to confront his evil benefactor, "Mr. Pike, what you are asking is almost impossible under these conditions."

Pike wheels from the troubled young man with a dismissive wave, "Spare me your problems, Wuhan. I am reveling in my brilliance."

A brave female tech, Ming Chen, stands from her chair to defend her colleague while the other nerds hunker closer to their screens, "We need more time! Over half the virtual attendees have not replied to their confirmation codes. How is this thing supposed to start in under 24 hours?"

Allowing a modicum of steam to escape his controlled demeanor, Pike explodes on the captive assemblage of computer geniuses groomed by SATstar to do the impossible for over a decade, "Damn you all! Make it work, motherfuckers, or I will send your sorry asses back to China in body bags!"

Reeling in pent-up rage, Pike resumes observing the arrival ceremony on a swept-clean parking lot behind The Hague's World Forum complex and zooms onto the Norwegian PM with a sweeping hand gesture, "Looking good, Anna. Edelweiss amidst a field of ugly-assed weeds."

The Eurocentric septet—plus the last-minute addition of the Chinese foreign minister—will preside over the in-person judges while the other half of the 16 chairs attend via remote connections, notwithstanding feverish last-ditch efforts to work out the kinks in time.

Civilizational ashes swirl and scatter across the cracked macadam, piling against the pipe and drape riser as well-heeled leaders backslap and glad-hand, feigning normalcy like another G8. Each leader makes self-aggrandizing opening statements followed by an out-of-tune medley of anthems for a fraction of Earth's population present or able to watch. The last speaker, Sebastian Duarte, a charismatic Portuguese member of parliament, promises change in the post-PTB new world order without elaboration.

Pike's eyes narrow on the man, "Who invited that tanned clown? I thought we had Portugal's PM, not an MP. Fucking idiots. Oh well. I need asses in seats."

As paid security checks in the gang of eight who will perform their magisterial duties in the flesh, the self-important leaders and their fawning entourages receive custom Hermès swag bags spiked with listening devices. Replaying a cascade of logistical hurdles to transport the worldly assemblage to the Netherlands on the insane timetable, he breaks into a maniacal fit of laughter, "I hope you like your goodie bags; it was the least I could do."

Pike zooms the hi-def feed past the Portuguese fellow onto the German chancellor's effusive overreaction to the lovely Miss Kristiansen. The choreographed opening ceremony dissolves into a wandering assemblage, like sheep. The burly Berliner, Helmut von Becker, takes the much taller woman by the arm and escorts her down the steps toward the theater's VIP entrance. Pike notes an embarrassing bulge below the German's beltline with a smirking headshake, "You are fortunate, Herr Becker; career-killing viral moments are a thing of the past."

Griffin heads to the foyer to greet his honored guests, pulling on a gray pinstripe suit jacket and straightening his narrow gold tie.

Pennywell | The Autobahn, Rotterdam
04:11 p.m. | August 31, 2044

In the world that was, the short drive down the Autobahn from a private PTB aerodrome outside Rotterdam to The Hague took less than an hour.

In the world that is, Artemus Pennywell's up-armored autonomous SUV idles while its lead bulldozer pushes crumpled wrecks onto the shoulder, clearing a path.

From his backseat window, Pennywell tries to identify a fly-infested carcass decaying beyond a fence line in the tall grass, "It's so quiet, Andrew. Where is everybody?"

"Queuing up at the theater to experience flushing toilets and electricity, dead or hiding."

The SUV lurches forward, scraping past a battered tractor-trailer. "Come for the working shitter and stay for the Shitshow."

"Good one, Artemus."

"Yeah, I'm a veritable laugh riot. Have a look at that dead animal over there beyond the fence. What do you think, cow or horse?"

Andrew shakes his head at the odd question, "It was a cow, Artemus. Tell me again why you did not want to take the chopper. The Council must be there by now."

"It is the end of the world, Andrew. Why the rush? I don't think they will start without us."

Griffin Pike | World Forum, The Hague
04:15 p.m. | August 31, 2044

Griffin Pike exits the Yangtze room, locking the nerds inside, and hastens toward the international assemblage, already making their way into the adjacent Amazon room under the watchful eyes of paid security from a French outfit called the Nemesis Group.

Effervescing confidence and elan, the suave six-foot, 48-year-old tech mogul cut a handsome path, greeting honored guests and their retinues, "Welcome, friends! Please make yourselves comfortable inside. I am afraid our party suffers a microcosm of the labor shortages you all face, which is a diplomatic way of saying, please help yourselves to food and drinks."

Wang Li, the Chinese foreign minister, saunters past, nodding an oily grin. "I am famished. Thank you, Mr. Pike."

Pike steps aside as the dangerous man in a black suit and tie enters the hall, "Enjoy, Mr. Li. And thank you for coming. We are honored to have you as one of our in-person magistrates."

Li leans in and places a hand on Pike's arm, "I have a confession for you, Mr. Pike. The Chinese people love the PTB. I am here to put an end to that."

Watching the man disappear into the crowded Amazon room, one of the World Forum's rivers-themed halls, like the Chinese nerdfest locked inside the Yangtze, Pike smiles, embracing life's little ironies.

* * *

Hot on the heels of his successful holographic appeal just two days earlier, Pike's event planners took possession of the World Forum and a fraction of its beleaguered staff working for a substantial wage bump. Take it or leave it. The planners took it, rolled their sleeves, and got to work. Pike's people ferried RSVPs from hither and yon, leaning on World Forum staff with dollar signs in their greedy eyes to handle accommodations in the adjoining hotel tower. At the same time, workers sweated bullets tag-teaming the outdoor arrival ceremony layout and the indoor reception. Inside the Amazon room, they interspersed well-stocked open bars and help-yourself snack stations overflowing with packaged chips, cookies, and water bottles between cocktail tables, sofas, and chairs pulled from a vast storeroom. Not exactly high cuisine, but not bad under the circumstances. Pike knew the free-flowing alcohol would quell misgivings in short order.

The finishing touches, complete with bugged flower vases on the cocktail tables, happened as the arrival ceremony's canned symphonic finale crackled from the room's high-tech sound system.

To the abject relief of Pike and his teams of aircrews, event planners, tech support, carpenters, electricians, et al., the World Forum's theater crew took control of salvaging the grand magisterial bench from the demolished Hague international courthouse. They reassembled the massive prop upstage in the King Willem Alexander Theater. Across its polished wood facade reads International Court of Justice in French and English.

*****

One of Pike's magistrates, Aurora Tarenzi, the socialist Italian prime minister, parts a large grouping in blithe conversation with her milquetoast husband in tow to greet Griffin with a fake smile plastered across her deep-lined olive-skinned face, *"Grazi, Signor Pike! Il mondo è in rovina grazie al PTB."*

Pike's earpiece translates, but he knows what the vile woman is trying to communicate and replies with a forced smile, "It is my pleasure to be of service in this trying time. We need to hold the PTB accountable for their crimes, and time is of the essence."

The bombastic and obnoxious woman takes a long swig from her glass while listening through her earpiece and laughs a reply in English, "Good boy." To Pike's surprise, she rubs past, pinching his ass before sidling toward a bar for a refill.

"Man, what a strange group of idiots."

Pike spots Anna in a relaxed repose on a red leather sofa, balancing a glass while holding court for a group of enraptured reporters. The regal blond catches Pike's gaze and offers a wink before taking another question about how she survived the attack.

Clutching a beer bottle in his thick hand, Helmut von Becker stumbles over and stands beside Pike, "Now that is a woman."

Pike turns to the corrupt bureaucrat, "How are things in Germany, Helmut?"

Becker swigs the Heineken and narrows a pudgy-faced smile at the smooth-talking mogul, "Fucking terrible. But it was not great before the invaders. What were they called, Morks?"

"No, Gorks. I hear more aliens are poised to invade even as we speak."

Becker turns toward Pike, "Listen up, asshole. I cannot stand that motherfucker, Pennywell, but we tried your Great Reset bullshit in the 20s. It failed."

Pike offers the drunk chancellor a diplomatic smile while motioning for his security to escort the German chancellor to his suite. "The past is irrelevant, Herr Becker. History begins tomorrow."

* * *

The Amazon hall maxes out at its 360-person capacity, leaving hundreds of disappointed VIPs and reporters queued up, akin to waiting outside an exclusive club. Hulking security lets people enter as tired and satiated guests spill out with armloads of snacks and water bottles, stumbling toward their rooms where a privileged few enjoy amenities once taken for granted but not anymore.

The Council | World Forum, The Hague
06:15 p.m. | August 31, 2044

Having spent the last few days consorting with the enemy, Vita Carrera smiles and waves at her surviving colleagues approaching a vacant side entrance of the World Forum's cracked and broken glass facade. After an uncomfortable, bumpy flight on Patel's anti-gravity transport out of Lakenheath, the disheveled group staggers toward their beaming colleague.

Gene Simmons sprints ahead and holds the heavy glass door allowing everyone to enter the echoing space.

The blood drains from Vita's porcelain complexion, not seeing her boss and his robot butler among the tired group, "Where is our fearless leader?"

Gabby approaches with a wry smile, "He does not like to fly anti-gravity. After our commute, I can see why." The tall Pole smothers Vita in a warm embrace, "It is so good to see you, love."

A little surprised at the effusive greeting, Vita replies, "Well, it is good to see all of you. I negotiated *upgraded* accommodations. I am sure you all know what that means. However, we need to double up since functional hotel rooms are scarce. You will be astonished at the sheer numbers eager to watch us get screwed up the ass. I hope that is okay with everybody?"

The Council nods in unison. Lufkin swipes his brow with an IOSC embroidered handkerchief, "As long as I have a hot shower and a bed, I'll be fine."

Vita winces, "Sorry, Millard, no hot water; however, there is running water in some bathroom faucets." After a slight pause, she confesses, "I would not drink it. Or even brush my teeth with it, for that matter."

Olivia Paquet gives Vita a light hug, "Hey everybody, this is Europe; you couldn't drink the water before the fucking Gorks."

Ernest Gann nods and smiles at Gene Simmons, "What say you, doctor?"

"Oh, I wholeheartedly agree. Don't drink anything other than sealed bottles of water or beer. That would be fine. And also, don't eat anything that did not come out of a sealed wrapper."

Patel steps beside Vita, "Okay then. Let's dump our stuff, find some beer and Cheetos, and wait for the boss to arrive. Lead the way, Vita."

Gabby laughs, "This could be fun. We can have a pretrial pajama party in our rooms."

As they trudge toward an emergency stairwell to access the venue's adjoining hotel tower, Patel nudges Simmons, "What do you think, Gene? Will the missus at home in the dark with your eight kids object to you spending the night in a hotel room with a former swimsuit model bouncing around in a skimpy nightie?"

Gann sidles up to join the cheeky repartee, "You mean to say, live out the fantasy of every nerd back at MIT who has ogled at her poster for over a decade?"

Walking ahead of the snickering trio, Gabby turns and sticks out her pink tongue, "In your dreams, boys."

The Council follows Vita to their reserved suites but hunkers down as a group inside a ridiculously oversized presidential suite with plenty of room for everyone to stretch out.

Millard Lufkin, who has known Artemus Pennywell for over four decades, drops his bag and plops onto a couch, "Pennywell would love this scenario."

Patel takes the bait, "And why is that Lufkin? Out with it, man."

"Well, we are like the apostles holed up in a room waiting for the Romans to take us down for associating with our Jesus."

Swallowing a snarky retort, Patel jumps to assist Vita, wheeling two carts loaded with food and drinks into the suite.

Proud of her newfound hunting and gathering skills, Vita places her hands on her hips, "Phew! You all have no idea how much I scrounged, realizing sustenance would be a major problem from the moment I arrived."

Everyone stands around the carts, tearing into potato chips and cheesy comestibles while popping cans of cheap American beer.

Gabby stuffs her face with Fritos, washes it down with a beer in one long pull, and emits a loud burp, "This takes me back to my modeling years. We binged on junk food after shows like you would not believe."

Olivia stops eating and hits Gabby with a wide-eyed stare, "Wait. Don't tell me that is all coming back up?"

Gabby rolls her eyes, "Geez, Liv, I never did that."

Patel jumps to her defense, "Yeah, just cigarettes and blow, like a normal supermodel. Right, Gabby?"

"Spot on, Viraj. You got me."

Simmons, nursing a water bottle and a bag of pretzels, chimes into the conversation, "See? International intrigue can be fun."

Edward Laughton—the downsized Council's proverbial eighth wheel—enters the suite after lingering downstairs on a vacant lobby settee, reliving the previous day's humiliating cascade of events. Dropping his bag, the embarrassed barrister plods into the room and collapses on a couch.

Gann beats Patel to the punch and breaks the ice, "Speaking of international intrigue."

Patel offers the downtrodden fellow a Miller Light, "Here you go, Ed. You look like you could use a beer."

Rescued from his handcuffed predicament earlier that morning when he failed to show up for the group shuttle to Lakenheath, Laughton accepts the beer and sips, "Ugh, American beer. Thanks. I do apologize for my behavior. I am not sure what came over me. The woman had a very beguiling way about her."

Patel pats the man on the back and tries to buck him up, "We've all been there. Forget it, Ed. It is in the past."

Edward Laughton straightens and addresses the group, "What I don't understand is why she stole Pennywell's notebook but left my valuables? Bloody hell, my watch alone is worth over 20,000 pounds." Taking a second long drink of the beer, he winces at the thought of an irate Pennywell, "The man is going to lose it when he finds out I no longer have the notebook. He will assume I lost it on purpose. Maybe I did."

Vita smirks at Laughton's naiveté, wiping orange-stained crumbs off her fingertips, "Come on, Ed. You are better than this. The woman works for Pike. They set you up as a patsy of sorts. The whole thing was part of their plan."

Patel pops another beer to wash down stale Doritos in his mouth, "Yeah, Ed. At least you got laid."

The group, including Laughton, breaks down in laughter as Artemus enters the suite with Andrew following close behind, "What the fuck is going on here? We have work to do."

Griffin Pike | World Forum, The Hague
09:46 p.m. | August 31, 2044

The boisterous pretrial reception rises to a fevered pitch as someone accesses the hall's sound equipment and plays DJ. The world leaders and their staffers let off steam, comingling with media and VIPs casting their lots behind the new world's order. All will be fine if they get their piece of the action. Pike watches the tone-deaf pols laughing and drinking the night away, unaffected by the disastrous invasion aftermath. Wondering if he hitched his wagon to the idiot car, he shakes his head, disgusted even by his amoral standards.

Not everyone is in a partying mood. Griffin notes Li's Chinese contingent has long since left the party, and the German chancellor is sleeping it off. Meanwhile, the obnoxious Italian PM pulled her crew upon seeing the handsome retinue of energetic Finnish staffers filing into the room.

Nursing a Perrier, Pike circumnavigates an impromptu dance floor toward a table where the French PM, Avril LeClaire, the chief magistrate for the following day's tribunal, sits with Finland's PM, Paulus Halko, and Sebastian Duarte, the Portuguese mystery man. LeClaire, who took the reigns as France's new prime minister following her predecessor's suicide, proffers a friendly smile at Pike's approach. "Bonjour, Griffin. We were commenting on how you managed to pull this together in just a couple of days."

Pike pulls up the fourth chair, "Miss LeClaire, I find that if you have enough cash and resources, anything is possible."

"Too true."

Pike's keen gaze lands on Duarte across the round table, "We have not met. I was under the assumption that we invited your country's prime minister."

Duarte's tanned face widens into a fluorescent smile under the strobing multi-hued party lights, "He fell ill after the invasion. We did not wish to forgo our seat at the table, so I am here as his proxy."

Uninterested in the conversation, Halko, seated on Pike's right, rifles a handful of pretzels out of a sustainable wooden bowl, "What's the matter, Pike? Couldn't spring for the rubber chicken?"

"Ah, that is a good one." Pike pierces the blond man's false bravado with a veiled insult, "I heard the Gorks left your country almost unscathed."

Halko chokes down a dry pretzel, "Just lucky, I guess."

"Now, boys, play nice." Avril sips her wine and glances around the table, "Count your blessings, Paulus; France was devastated."

Pike's face scrunches into a curious frown, "Yet the Eiffel Tower still stands."

Duarte clinks Avril's glass with a trite Vive la France as she turns toward Pike to defend her country, "Aside from New York and London, Paris took the hardest hit anywhere."

Pike stands and smiles, ignoring his chief magistrate's rebuttal, catching Sapphire entering through a side door, "Excuse me. I need to attend to a few things before the night ends."

Pike leads his assassin across the foyer past a dwindling queue of late arrivals and into a vacant meeting room. Closing the door, he faces the sexy woman leaning on her elbows atop a table with a sly smile on her face.

"What a day. Save me from these fools and idiots."

Swallowing her under a full embrace, he lowers her back against the table, kissing up and down her body as she wraps a long leg over his arched back, "Now my night is complete."

Resisting enough to free her left hand, Sapphire reaches into a bag and pulls out his ancestor's notebook, "I brought you something, Griffin."

Placing ravenous desire on hold, he leans beside Sapphire and snatches the book from her hand, "Oh, you shouldn't have."

Noting the holed leatherbound cover, he flips it open, his eyes landing on Charles Pike's crossed-out signature and Pennywell's scribbled note, "What an asinine thing to do." Flipping through the pages, he finds Uncle Chuck's map. With a nod, he turns the page to a detailed drawing of a Brazil Nut tree. "Darling, do you like nuts?"

Sapphire grabs Griffin's crotch and squeezes, "Depends."

Flynn | Gray battlecruiser
07:55 a.m. | September 1, 2044

Cold and hungry, Flynn groans and checks the healed surgical scar across his belly, musing with a fatalistic smirk, "My underwear modeling days are gone forever."

A tiny aperture opens midway up the opposite side of his one-person cell, allowing a gray pill to nudge out and drop to the floor before bouncing to a stop at his bare feet. A voice manifests between his ears, instructing the put-upon agent to swallow the capsule.

"Stay the fuck out of my head! I'm not hungry."

Flynn's voice echoes outside his cell, stirring abductees from a restless slumber and triggering a familiar whimper.

"Fuck me; the dog is crying again." Risking another telekinetic punishment from his freakish jailers, Flynn lets out a low sympathetic whistle, "C'mon, calm down. It will be okay."

The heartwrenching whimpering fades to silence.

"If your master dies, there will be hell to pay."

Having broken the code of silence again, Flynn waits, but nothing happens, "Lucky me, it must be their teatime."

Stark naked inside his dingy keep, Flynn scoops up the pill and holds it to the light. "A week's worth of nutrition, my ass."

Casting an absent sideways glance through the bars toward his PTB colleagues' forced accommodation, he startles at Nicole's downlit form, wrapped in a reflective blanket with alert eyes staring from darkened sockets on her otherwise ethereal visage.

Touching blue lips, Nicole mouths, "Quiet."

Eyeballing Flynn across the six-foot void, the former Space Force veteran turned PTB pilot hand signals the dog's master is dead.

Flynn squints between the bars and interprets her rapid hand movements, mumbling to himself, "15 abductees spread between six cells. Roger that."

Noticing her frail form faltering from the exertion, he taps a cold metal bar to keep her awake, "Astrid?"

Shaking off cobwebs, she frowns, "I don't know."

Rising onto her knees, Nicole lets the blanket drop around her shoulders and shuffles under a faint ray of light. Her pale skin glows in the bluish ambiance accentuating a dark suture across her exposed midriff.

"What is that?"

She pantomimes a worried reply, "I don't know."

Pointing into the empty shadows at the back of her cell, Flynn mouths, "Where is Nina?"

Pennywell | World Forum, The Hague
03:00 p.m. | September 1, 2044

Artemus Pennywell sinks into his centerstage chair before a long, red-draped table facing upstage and waits for the fireworks to start inside the King Willem Alexander Theater. The resilient structure designed for royal galas, operas, and rock concerts withstood apocalyptic hammer blows, sustaining only a few cracks and broken windows. Nothing serious. He sees hungover entourages who partied into the wee morning hours across from media and court watchers filling the SRO floor seats. Unwashed masses who queued up for days file into the cheap seats to witness the rumored spectacle exacerbating Pennywell's burgeoning sense of doom.

At the same time, virtual attendees manifest across the theater's precipitous expanse in an expanding grid of holographic screens over an aggrieved hoi polloi elbowing into balcony seats sweeping on an elegant curve to the theater's dizzying acoustic heights. Looking offstage, Pennywell spies a VR technician sporting a headset, gesturing like a conductor, shuffling the digitized faces in order of importance. Squinting steely gray eyes through the Klieg lights, he spots a friendly media maven's pixelated screen shoved sideways in favor of some sourpuss North Korean bloke, "Typical bullshit."

The hodge-podge spectacle of the tribunal's virtual audience creates an unintended warm-up act for the bored crowd watching as a pompous news anchor sucks a vape on one feed. At the same time, another oblivious clown picks his nose, unaware his computer's camera is on.

Even Pennywell laughs, "What utter nonsense."

Tuning out crowd noise mixing with hushed conversations, Pennywell watches a youthful sound engineer bound up and check his microphone atop the red-draped table. Next, the kid fiddles with Vita's mic stand on his immediate left. Satisfied, he double-checks mics placed before Gene Simmons, a still-fuming Olivia Paquet, and an inattentive Ernest Gann.

Pennywell watches the young man move past, checking the mics to his right, starting with the sweating Lufkin before repeating the process with a canoodling and giggling Patel and Gabreski.

Following a weird hunch, Pennywell notices the kid saved Edward Laughton, seated at the far righthand edge of the table beyond Gabby, for dead last. An awkward look of recognition between his chief legal counsel and the fresh-faced boy rewards his hunch.

Pennywell watches Laughton's scooter-riding gofer finish his mic checks, beat a hasty exit into the stage left, and disappear amid the backdrops, props, technicians, and stagehands.

Amidst the backstage chaos, Pennywell spies Andrew's smiling mug and hears his friend and confidante's even-toned voice in his hidden earpiece, *"Sit tight, Artemus; I got this. I can see Pike across the way prepping for his opening remarks."*

Pennywell nods.

* * *

Adept at assuming an inconspicuous profile, Andrew strides around a metal detector past a phalanx of Nemesis Group's crack security like he owned the place and makes his way to the strategic offstage left vantage point. Satisfied, he found the perfect spot to maintain a vigilant lookout; he leans his lanky frame against a foam-injected gilded column prop from a touring production of *Obama - The Musical*. The robot ignores the hyperkinetic activity, exuding effortless aplomb in a tweed waistcoat over a crisp button-down shirt and tie, designer jeans, and his signature western boots.

In true Bondian fashion, a button on Andrew's Omega wristwatch activates a short-range EMP to end this fiasco before The Powers That Be sustains permanent damage to its vaunted reputation.

After much consideration, Pennywell decided to let the

indictments fly so The Council could address the Gordian knot of affiliations, conglomerates, corporations, and shell companies up to a point. After clearing the air—and Andrew's wristwatch EMP—Pennywell will deal with Pike and his sycophantic coterie.

The PTB CEO also decided to withhold intel on Sebastian Duarte from The Council. He needed to let the startling revelation of the Portuguese magistrate's connection to the evil Grays play out without arousing undue suspicion. With Griffin Pike—and his corrupt friends—on the warpath and his top people captured by the Grays, he could not risk another mistake. While he trusted his seven surviving apostles up to a point, the Laughton affair proved that the PTB's enemies excelled at preying on human frailties.

Watching for Pennywell's signal with a Sig Sauer P365XL concealed at his belt and a pair of knives in his boots, Andrew checks his upgraded wristwatch, armed and ready for the inevitable sideways turn.

* * *

The house lights dim with the audience settled, and the exits closed and guarded. An apocalyptic slideshow of death, destruction, gore, and filth projects onto a dark purple drape pulled high above the bench, provoking angry gasps from the captive audience. The montage lingers on a silvery image of a young waif face down in a puddle, clutching her toy unicorn. Rich in symbolism to the point of absurdity, the photograph nonetheless evokes its intended adverse visceral reaction.

Slipping a pill into his mouth, Pennywell sips Perrier and mutters to himself, "This is brainwashing. Why did I agree to this shitshow?"

Taking another drink, he looks right and catches Laughton's earnest gaze. Quelling paranoia, and his raspy throat, with the last few drops, Pennywell wonders, "What is my Judas thinking?"

The perky, razor-straight, red-headed fireball named Vita, for some damn reason, surprises Pennywell with a nudge, "Excuse me, sir? Who is a Judas?"

"No one, Miss Carrera. Just amusing myself waiting for this thing to start." His spirits buoyed, finding at least one of his apostles on speaking terms, he attempts a little pretrial small talk, "I guess you all went ahead and solidified a defense against these chowderheads after I lost my cool last night."

Vita smooths the thin lapel on her stylish black pantsuit, worn over an ivory silk blouse, and delivers a biting retort to her boss, "Mr. Pennywell, you called us a bunch of fucking morons. Then you stormed out of the hotel suite with your butler in tow. Nobody has seen or heard from you since. You did not show up for our breakfast this morning, either. To answer your question, the Council will defend its PTB business segments as they see fit. You, sir, are on your own."

"Well, at any rate, I apologize. None of you are fucking morons. I misspoke." Pennywell's thin lips curl into a smile, raising the Perrier bottle before realizing it is empty, "Ah, screw it."

Vita scans over her shoulder into the darkened theater and exhales an uneasy sigh. While the layout is analogous to courtrooms spanning her 20-year legal career, the fomented crowd at her back is more distracting than she bargained for, if not downright dangerous. Tamping down pregame jitters, she affects an upbeat tone, "I understand a portion of the audience has our backs, sir. Anybody with half a brain knows The Powers That Be was integral to every advancement over the past century. Like Lufkin's IOSC, for instance. We could not predict when the Gorks would breach the skies and invade. And our emergency protocols saved thousands of lives. Tragically, in some instances, it simply was not enough."

Countering Vita's weak defense of the horrific IOSC crashes scattered around the globe, "First of all, Miss Carrera, we should have grounded the entire fleet months ago." Leaning back to include Millard, he continues, "Millard and I knew something was imminent, but grounding the fleet would have caused massive disruptions and chaos. Sending rich assholes around the planet to experience hard-ons in zero-g turned into a cash cow."

Lufkin bolsters Pennywell's words, "The confiscatory space tourism ticket prices finance our deep space initiatives. We could not risk losing the revenue stream. Not at this late moment when we are so close to realizing our goal."

Vita's eyes widen, "Damn you both. What goal? Don't you understand that your cagey secrecy keeps us at arm's length, sir? Mr. Pennywell. Artemus? Can I call you that?"

"No."

Undeterred, Vita presses on, "Okay, screw it. Here is the deal. The real folks suffering worldwide want answers: Why was the world caught with its pants down? Why wasn't our EMP shielding implemented? Here's one on my list: Why the fuck did those Gorks leave in such a hurry? I know there must be legitimate answers. Just say it. Give the people what they want. The truth will set us free. Afterward, the people's rage will focus where it belongs, on their fucking good-for-nothing governments."

Lufkin's jaw drops, "Holy shit Vita, can you repeat that when this thing starts? I want to go home."

Pennywell smiles at his top in-house lawyer as an aide brings him a new opened Perrier, "You know what, Vita? Go ahead and call me Artemus."

Leaning in so no one else can hear, she whispers as he takes a long drink, "Well, Artemus, is that true what you said about the rich assholes?"

Pennywell stifles a laugh and stops himself from a spit take before the packed house of angry people as the aide hustles back and whispers, "Sirs, they are ready to begin."

* * *

Eight holographic screens featuring the august octet of virtual magistrates flicker to life above the odd-numbered chairs from left to right along the 16-seat magisterial bench. Meanwhile, Andrew watches the stone-faced procession of black-robed in-person magistrates filing past his position with a solemnity belying their previous night's festivities.

Sebastian Duarte, the last man in the line of judges, pierces Andrew with a suspicious sideways glance as he moves past and enters the stage. Andrew watches him step behind the bench and notes the tall man's robe has an odd protrusion above the beltline. Like a ventriloquist, he speaks into his comm to warn the boss, "Artemus, Duarte is wearing a bomb."

* * *

The judges assume their assigned even-numbered chairs, but virtual judges from Canada and Egypt glitch out, preempting the tribunal's start. A headset-wearing producer jogs to the chief magistrate's centered chair, conferring with Avril LeClair, who leans into her mic and announces: *"Des difficultés techniques, cependant, le spectacle doit continuer."*

The audience responds with rousing applause.

* * *

With Andrew's dire new wrinkle in their ad hoc plan still sinking into his brain, Pennywell adjusts his signature silver bolo tie and returns the Italian PM's evil eye stare down, "Fuck them all."

Vita leans in from his left, "I'm sorry, sir. What did you say?"

"Sorry is for losers, Vita, and never mind."

Pennywell's mind races. Should he signal Andrew to pull the plug and avert a suicide bomber taking out the PTB and a host of heads of state in one blast? *What if Andrew is wrong?* Not bloody likely. Fuck!

Still parsing through multiple scenarios, all bad, a dramatic spotlight pierces the semi-darkness, illuminating a lectern situated stage right, midway between the PTB table and the bench. Griffin Pike emerges from the wings and steps behind the podium to a smattering of applause mixed with audible boos from Patel and Gabby.

Hearing the unprofessional jeers and catcalls, Pennywell winces and leans toward Vita, "Remind me to separate those two at the next shitshow."

Griffin Pike | World Forum, The Hague
04:11 p.m. | September 1, 2044

High above the magisterial bench, the dystopian slideshow dissolves onto a live feed focused on the man of the hour, Griffin Pike, striding onto the stage in a black suit and red tie and taking his place behind the podium. After checking pre-arranged notes and papers, he proffers a warm smile toward the magistrates and begins his opening remarks, "Ladies and gentlemen, it is indeed an honor and a privilege to have you here or on the virtual screens." With a self-deprecating wink and nod, he adds, "Not sure what happened to our Egyptian and Canadian magistrates, but this is living history. Shit happens."

The crowd erupts in applause while the PTB table remains stoic.

Pike, in total command, holds up a hand to silence the fawning crowd, "Your service to our world in this hour of crisis will resonate throughout human history from this day henceforth."

Pike waits out more cheers and raucous applause before gesturing toward Pennywell and his apostles with a dramatic sweep of his right hand, "We are here today representing all races and creeds struggling through the decayed rubble of our broken world. While the alien race, known as Gorks, released hell on Earth without firing a shot, we cannot seek retribution because by the grace of God and for reasons beyond the purview of mortal men, they left, but the death and devastation remain, and for that, someone must pay."

Pike holds up a stack of papers as he ratchets his vitriolic and self-righteous anger to a fevered pitch, "I have submitted a series of indictments for the court delineating the causes and effects leading up to the fateful day of August 22, 2044. I stand before you as a proxy for the dead, dying, aggrieved, and starving—remnants of a once-great human civilization—that endured eons of painstaking progress only to end up obliterated and lost to time.

These indictments will prove that the defendants, led by Artemus Pennywell, the chairman of a shadowy corrupt enterprise known simply as The Powers That Be, did willfully and with malice of forethought defraud Earth's governments into a false and misleading series of choices. In other words, for reasons beyond this simple man, they served humanity on a silver platter while protecting their concerns from the Gorks' destructive invasion with technologies and intelligence provided through alien alliances. Their mission statement reads, and I quote: to withhold the release of extraterrestrial technology from the world."

Pennywell's eyes narrow, "That is false."

Pike pauses and takes a drink of bottled water, allowing the Norwegian magistrate, Anna Kristiansen, time to interject, "Mr. Pike, putting aside the ten-year-old event known as Disclosure Day, which is a fact. Do the so-called indictments you wave about reach beyond baseless accusations and your unmasked animus toward the PTB, or is this a waste of valuable time?"

Avril LeClair stares down the black-robed blond, "Miss Kristiansen, are we boring you, dear? Please do not interrupt."

Anna looks to her right at the chief magistrate and retorts, "Well, this is ridiculous. I am not sure why I agreed to this farce. I thought we invited Mr. Pennywell and his team to help us figure a way forward, not reenact some half-assed passion of the Christ. What's next? Is Pike going to have the crowd start a crucify him chant?"

LeClair looks up and down the bench, noting the judges appear split on how to proceed, so she relents, "Mr. Pike, this is not a traditional trial by any known standard. Further, we do not possess jurisdictional authority or the resources to exact any formal punishment. You may be under the false impression that we agreed to what would commonly be called a show trial. However, I see it as more of an open hearing, and I want to avail Mr. Pennywell and his team ample opportunity to defend against your accusations."

Wang Li, the Chinese official, stands out of his chair, "I object! I want to hold The Powers That Be accountable for their crimes!"

The virtual Russian and Turkish judges, bolstered by Aurora Tarenzi and Becker, second Li's self-serving demand.

Knee-deep in the shitshow, LeClair laments agreeing to play schoolmarm for this sorry lot, "Please proceed, Mr. Pike."

Stunned by the sudden change of atmosphere, Pike looks down at his notes as seething rage wells inside his pitch-black soul.

Noting Pike's sudden reticence, Paulus Halko, the Finnish judge, stands out of his second chair. "Miss LeClair, while we wait for Mr. Pike to rediscover his mojo, may I address the tribunal?"

LeClair stares at her friend and colleague, praying he does not offer a ham-fisted joke, "The magistrate from Finland has the floor."

"Thank you, Avril. The good people of Finland are familiar with and thankful for our friendships with the PTB. Looking at the members in attendance, I see Miss Anastasia Gabreski, whose tireless efforts have made the UN an almost functional entity. And there is Millard Lufkin, a fellow astronaut I have known for years. As honest and forthright as a man can get. As for the rest, I applaud their concerted efforts to improve human existence in the last three-plus centuries. And I know, from the bottom of my heart, that if not for The Powers That Be, none of us would be here today."

Casting his icy blue eyes past his fellow judges with mouths agape to the far opposite end of the bench, he points at the Portuguese judge, who has remained close-mouthed, "Would the fine gentleman from Portugal care to weigh in on my last statement?"

* * *

Andrew cradles his 9mm in a rock-steady grip, poised and ready to take out the traitorous Duarte. "Say the word, Artemus."

Elated and relieved that Paulus Halko, a card-carrying PTB member, came through in flying colors, Pennywell mutters a clipped reply into his comm, *"Hold your position, Andrew."*

* * *

In a pique of angered frustration, Griffin Pike stacks his papers and walks off the stage as the black-robed international idiot panel reverts to pre-apocalypse mindsets. The megalomaniac shakes his head in disbelief that Anna, the most unlikely delicate flower, lit the fuse that blew up his entire narrative, followed by the fucking Finn's slobbering tribute to the PTB at his show trial on his dime. That was the last straw. He did not wish to stick around and hear what the Portuguese party crasher had to say. Fuck that, big time.

Hearing a crescendo of boos from the riotous audience, Griffin Pike's harried lead producer rushes to his employer, "Mr. Pike, Mr. Pike! Where are you going? We just started! The techs are working to relink the Egyptian's feed."

"I am a man of my word, Sven. Kill the IT crew and send them back to China on Li's jet."

"What about the tribunal?"

"This is over as far as I am concerned. The judges can all fuck off and find their own way home. I wash my hands of this entire matter."

Pike sees Sapphire waiting by a side exit. He grabs her hand with a warm smile. "Don't say a word, Sapphire."

She shoots him a mischievous grin, "Now the fun can begin."

They walk outside and move with a renewed purpose to a SATstar chopper already spinning up, blowing trash and streamers from the previous day's ceremony all over the parking lot, mixed with civilizational ashes.

Pike dons a headset in the shotgun seat with his svelte assassin curled in the back of the sleek craft as it rises into a hazy sky. Looking down on the World Forum from above, he realizes the notion of resurrecting human civilization would not include the motherfuckers in that building. Perhaps Li and the Russian, what was his name? But the rest will die horrible deaths.

With Charles Pike's notebook in his possession, he will find the lost ship, salvage its deadly payload, and exact the ancient alien weapon on the ungrateful world. He gave them a chance, and they failed. No one will say he did not try after the dust settles again, and he assumes his rightful throne in a new world order of his making.

***

Having spent the previous evening in cheap conversation, drinking beers and eating stale pretzels for hours with the Finnish prime minister, Sebastian Duarte peers down the bench toward Paulus Halko's smiling face. *"How does he know?"*

Mystified by the odd turn of events and Pike's silent departure, the panel of judges sees a chiseled, well-dressed man appear out of nowhere behind Duarte's addled form. Before the Portuguese magistrate can turn to defend himself, the cheeky bastard's fist contacts the side of Sebastian's tanned nose, sending the judge crumpling into Helmut von Becker, who flails backward into Li. The tribunal devolves into pandemonium as judges tumble like dominos, retreating from the attacker in their cumbersome black robes.

Exhibiting inhuman strength and agility, Andrew vaults over the table and tosses Duarte offstage like a ragdoll. Blood streams from the Portuguese MP's broken nose as he hits the theater's floorboards in a twisted, ignominious heap.

Andrew signals for two of Pike's flummoxed security to stand down while approaching Duarte, who responds by scuttling backward into a corner and knocking over a gilded prop.

With blood pouring down his wild-eyed face, the desperate man pulls up his robe, exposing the explosive belt strapped around his heaving chest, causing Andrew to freeze.

"Back off! I will blast this entire theater to kingdom come!"

* * *

As the tribunal dissolves into a free-for-all in a heartbeat, Laughton catches Scooterboy's receding form, crowding behind his cohorts to abandon the production through a backstage exit. Seizing the chance at sweet revenge, he takes off in pursuit as Simmons, Gann, and Paquet vault over the red-draped table and rush upstage, helping rattled world leaders vacate the bench. Viraj jumps into the audience with Gabby close behind, quelling a panicky stampede for the exits. At the same time, Pennywell, Lufkin, and Carrera enlist calmer heads to take charge and lead the already shell-shocked people out of the theater.

* * *

Andrew studies the explosive device, standing over a writhing, inconsolable Duarte, kicking his feet and throwing a childish fit, "Calm down. No one needs to get hurt."

"They are making me do this! I am not in control." Duarte's body goes rigid, and his perfect white teeth grind into a rictal grimace, "I am not sure how long I can keep from setting this off!"

Calm as a cucumber, Andrew turns to the guards, "Vacate this space and help my colleagues clear the immediate area."

The lead guard turns to his flummoxed partner, "You don't have to tell me twice; come on, Chayefsky, let's get out of here!"

With the useless gawking mercenaries gone, Andrew peers through the complicated wiry mass and locates the detonator's make and model number. As Sebastian Duarte's stammering and crying continue unabated, the Kobayashi robot fine-tunes a setting on his wristwatch and disarms the bomb with a narrow-beamed EMP.

Andrew turns to the chaotic scene behind him and tries to update Pennywell, but he fried his comm device along with the IED. Warning the bloodied and defeated Duarte not to move a muscle, he steps centerstage and announces that the immediate threat is contained.

Edward Laughton | World Forum, The Hague
04:43 p.m. | September 1, 2044

Laughton bounds out the backstage exit to pursue his young nemesis, unsure of what he will do but consumed by a need for closure. Proceeding with what he believes is stealth across a haphazard jumble of props and backdrops dumped on the loading docks by Pike's people, he descends a long receiving ramp onto the crumbled macadam. Sneaking past inert panel vans and delivery trucks left abandoned since invasion day parked askew down the structure's precipitous back facade, his gaze narrows on something moving behind a trash bin.

Swallowing back an urge to rejoin PTB colleagues he now considers friends; he plods onward as windblown sawdust and trash swirl around his feet while angling through an abandoned work area filled with power tools and sawhorses laden with wood. After tripping over a box of nails, he comes within five feet of the shadowed recess on the opposite side of the dumpster and reaches deep to retrieve his most authoritative barrister voice, "Come out from there. I want a word with you, young man."

Not receiving the courtesy of a reply, Laughton's anger comes to the fore as he steps around the battered bin and comes face-to-face with a life-sized mannequin.

A shoulder tap startles Edward Laughton to his core. Turning on his heels, he looks into the smooth, youthful visage of the grinning kid. Rendered speechless for the first time in his life, he sees a glint of a blade a millisecond before its sharp tip plunges through his chest.

Falling onto his knees in wool slacks and expensive loafers, he watches the remorseless kid remove the knife before slicing it across his throat, splattering more blood than the theater had witnessed since its last production of *Titus Andronicus*.

Ping | World Forum, The Hague
09:11 p.m. | September 01, 2044

The US Director of National Intelligence, Maggie Williams, enters the plundered Amazon room and plops onto a stained couch across from a rattled power trio of Halko, Kristiansen, and LeClair from Finland, Norway, France representing those who decided to stick around after the smoke settled. "What did I miss?"

Pennywell bursts into the room looking dapper and spry beyond his years and steps onto a raised platform used as a dance floor the night before, "Quite a lot, Miss Williams. How is Lena?"

"The president sends her regrets. As you can imagine, the woman has a lot on her plate."

Pennywell smiles at the toned woman, "Indeed. At any rate, I am grateful you made the trip."

With an uncharacteristic look of expectation, he scans a sea of faces seated at the surrounding tables, including his Council. He spies his Intel Chief, Aisha Ayad, who also missed the fireworks, "Did you bring the package?"

A bright smile cracks Aisha's stern countenance, "Andrew is assisting him."

"Good! For those that may not know, the mystery man, Sebastian Duarte, is in our custody. He was a Manchurian candidate, for lack of a better description. We will release him into Miss Williams' custody for further questioning. I trust she will avail herself of every tool of persuasion to coax from him everything he knows about the Grays."

Raising a bony finger, he adds, "To be clear, the evil Gray race threatening Earth has zero connections with the Advisers. Nor do they speak the same language."

Anna Kristiansen, who saved the day with her cutting remark, raises her hand like a seminar participant, "Mr. Pennywell, was your organization responsible for the Gorks' defeat, or did another outside entity save humanity?"

Avril LeClair seconds the motion while Paulus Halko leans back with a slight grin.

Reconsidering how to answer the most salient question in human history, he begins to speak as the double doors to the Amazon room swing open.

The loud whir of a mechanized conveyance is the only sound as a hush falls over the room, watching a small gray figure decked out in a regal silver robe wheel into the space.

The ravages of age are evident as Pennywell watches his 300-plus-year-old adviser's approach. He had not seen his lifelong friend in the flesh for over two years and assumed it was due more to his hermitized existence below the Scottish Lowlands than Ping's health.

With a hint of sadness, he muses that neither himself nor his ancient friend from a far-off galaxy is long for this world.

Ping wheels to the middle of the group and gazes up at Artemus, suppressing real emotion.

The friendly Gray alien's voice resonates with a mechanical tone through his telepathic speech translator as he continues, *"Hello, Artemus; I see we are among friends."*

Artemus Pennywell gestures around the room, "Ladies and gentlemen, allow me to introduce Ping." Turning to the pretty Norwegian prime minister, stunned at meeting a real alien in the flesh, "Madam, to answer your question, Ping's advice was critical to our survival ten short days ago. It had nothing to do with technology or advanced weaponry of any kind. No, it was his sage guidance to have faith that a single individual would come forth with an ability to wield and manipulate pure energy."

Ping interjects, *"You give me too much credit. Rachel Haig is the real hero. In the future, her ability will be commonplace among humans."*

Pennywell laughs and touches his friend's thin shoulder, "Let's leave Rachel Haig for another time if it is all the same to you. As for her abilities spreading throughout the human race, perhaps one day. But only if we survive the interim. To that end, our extraterrestrial allies offer their advice. It is up to us within The Powers That Be to accept it or blunder on our own."

"Hence the name, Advisers."

Pennywell shows his cards, feeling a weight lift from his shoulders, "To everyone in this room, I say, nothing is free or easy. Powerful global entities fought us every step of the way. Glomming on to our successes and pointing hypocritic fingers at our failures. While our alien friends provided sage oversight, human ingenuity, and inventiveness brought technological advancements and innovations through trial and error these past 300 years."

Ping adds, *"And a lot of mistakes."*

Having met other aliens in her life, a nonplussed Maggie Williams addresses Ping, "It will be weeks, if not months, before the first signs of normalcy return to the world. In the meantime, rogue elements like Griffin Pike use chaos to decapitate Western Civilization while your cousins look to pick up where the Gorks left off. So, Mr. Ping, what advice do you have for us now?"

Ping focuses on the brave Marine, piercing her troubled psyche, *"I am sorry for your loss."*

Maggie shakes her head, "Oh no, do not do that."

Seated at one of the cocktail tables, Viraj leans over and whispers in Gabby's ear, "That's right. I recall reading that Maggie's husband disappeared with his dog on an aid mission in Somalia just before Invasion Day."

Ping wheels around the room, reading everyone within the low-lit space, *"This is a good group of people, Artemus."* Spinning toward Williams once more, *"I am sorry. I do not mean to pry."*

With everyone in the room hanging on his every word, Ping nods to Artemus before proffering new advice, *"A new threat has emerged. We must locate the lost ship before our enemies. Failure equals death."*

Chapter Three:

The Meal

Forest Ghosts | The Amazon
10:36 a.m. | September 02, 2044

Human migration into Brazil dates back over 20,000 years, before the peak of the last Ice Age. Fast forward to the early 1500s European arrival, indigenous tribes and nations within Brazil's impenetrable topography flourished to over 2000 distinct populations in the millions across wilderness encompassing more square miles than the EU.

Since then, internecine conflicts and wars, pandemics, famines, natural disasters, and inevitable encroachment and assimilation have reduced the number of tribes to under 200, with over a quarter unaware of the outside world.

Among a subset of these insulated societies, customs and traditions dating back centuries—including ritualistic cannibalism—are practiced in the same manner as their ancestors. Allusions to barbarous ceremonial meals add to a mystique surrounding the enigmatic forest dwellers who want nothing more than to be left alone. If greedy corporate interests intent on destroying their primeval home can't employ locals fearful of becoming the main course, then so be it.

All but the most naive view nebulous legends of bloodthirsty cannibalism as fiction straight out of Edgar Rice Burroughs and the like, concocted to dissuade fortune seekers and speculators from venturing into the pristine wilderness. In private, elders and shamans concede outsiders' dismissive mockery is warranted, with one ominous exception, the Forest Ghosts. A mysterious tribe, far removed from their remotest brethren, slathered from head to toe in stark white fine-ground clay, hence the name. Numbering from a handful to hundreds—depending on the storyteller—the ghostly hunters manifest from the jungle, raiding villages, work camps, and scientific outposts before vanishing back into the trees. A blood-splattered trail of gore, guts, and bones mixed with personal effects serves as their stark warning: Do not follow. Turn around and leave.

For most, the terrifying story ends there, leaving cynical youths, prospectors, explorers, and scads of Amazon tourists with a gnawing sensation of being watched creeping up their spines. But this soon fades.

Only the eldest storytellers, dying off at an accelerated pace with a dwindling pool of successors, remain privy to the Forest Ghosts' generational promise to safeguard an ancient riddle jutting from the craggy depths of a bottomless rift sequestered within a vast region of Amazon rainforest. One by one, they take the secret location to their hallowed graves, where forebears await their arrival.

***

A primitive pair cuts through a disorienting green maze, slipping and sliding down a muddy ravine, hustling to catch up to their leader's crouched position behind a thick bramble overhanging a sand bar on the banks of a stream slicing through the jungle. The experienced hunter winces at the youths' noisy approach and holds a calloused finger to his lips, signaling them to freeze in their barefoot tracks. Parting a thick mass of leaves and vines, he points out an odd little man in a shiny suit, waist-deep and back-turned in a fast-flowing stream, a stone's throw from the top of a precipitous waterfall into a steep and treacherous rift valley, off-limits and lost to time.

Sporting bony piercings adorned with gold and silver trinkets up and down stark-naked mocha-brown bodies smeared with fine white clay, they exchange confused glances at how the spindly trespasser ventured undetected within perilous proximity to the hidden entrance of their sacred keep. Ratcheting bloodlust on an empty stomach after a long morning's jaunt through the woods, the youngest hunter, shy of his fourteenth year, steps backward onto a branch, eliciting an audible snap.

The object of their attention wheels with alarming alacrity and trains its menacing glare right upon their concealed position.

The terrified tribesmen watch in horror as penetrating black eyeballs, dominating the being's inhuman visage, narrow on them from its melon-sized skull before a malevolent hiss assaults their eardrums, prompting the kid to shit down his legs. His 16-year-old partner snickers despite the danger posed by the odd gray fellow. Annoyed by their unserious behavior, the lead hunter readies his decorated spear, motioning for the witless duo to sit tight and wait. They comply with their young leader's command without argument.

Raising his spear hand upward behind a festooned right ear in the tight space between leaves, vines, and branches covered with ants enclosing around him, the veteran warrior, with an exotic culinary persuasion, prepares to strike like a viper.

Sensing imminent attack, the bobble-headed creature quickdraws its weapon in a long-fingered grip as the Forest Ghost explodes from the underbrush, ululating a battle cry, splashing across the sand bar, and launching his spear nanoseconds before he is atomized.

Yet, the business end of his long decorated shaft stays true to its target, impaling the alien and thwacking half a foot into the silty stream bed at a pitched angle.

Impervious to the spear's venomous tip, the stricken alien struggles to slide its rail-thin body up and off the primitive weapon, more than tripling its height. Hissing in fear, anger, and horrible pain, it feels toxic, cyan-colored blood bubbling from a severed artery in its Gray anatomy, polluting the crystalline water with a viscous bluish-green sheen.

A rustling of thick undergrowth along the far bank draws the alien's faltering gaze onto the other two, wading into the stream. Leveling the atomizing weapon's long barrel at the bizarre humans, it slips from a weakened grasp and splashes into the rushing waters, tumbling down slick mossy rocks before snatching in a thick mass of upturned roots.

On the cusp of death, the advance scout transmits its location to the battlecruiser lurking in high Earth orbit while staring down the primitive natives' sloshing approach. The poop-smeared boy arrives first and pokes a dirty index finger into the sucking wound around the spear protruding from its narrow torso. The foul-smelling human sticks out a long pink tongue and licks the blood to the advanced alien's irony-laced shock and horror. While languishing in the otherwise barren solar system for decades, human abductees became an abundant source of nutrition for the Grays. This reality now comes full circle for the scout.

Noting his younger partner's pleasant reaction to the gooey blue blood, the other Forest Ghost gouges his fist around the wound, pulls out a long stringy intestine, and tries it himself.

Amid a living nightmare at the hands of these two animals, the alien can do nothing but watch while it is eaten alive. It attempts mind control to regain the upper hand, but the thuggish pair lacks mental acuity worth foiling. Realizing the folly of trying, the Gray raises a bloody hand to push them away, but the shitter snatches its hand and bites off a long digit with a snarling, sharp-toothed chomp.

Its mournful wail resonates high up into the canopy overhead, prompting every living creature to run like hell and not look back. Going into shock, the technologically-advanced Gray alien's consciousness retreats into its skull while its child-size form falls limp.

The young Forest Ghost, not busy gnawing a tiny piece of flesh from the bony finger, yanks the spear tip from the slick streambed and hefts it across his strapping shoulders. Casting a self-conscious sideways glance into the trees, he exhorts his brother from another mother to get busy and grab the other end. The kid follows his gaze and shoots his sibling a suspicious look. He harbored a secret, but what?

Dangling from the spear by its torso betwixt the hunters' purposeful gaits, the dead alien's skinny arms and legs swing as the boys retrace their path up the slippery ravine. Back at their encampment, fellow tribe members hunker around a firepit, eager to discover who is coming to dinner.

Griffin Pike | Catacombs of Paris
01:00 p.m. | September 5, 2044

Griffin Pike strides through the darkness keeping pace with a tall Frenchwoman lighting the path forward with a torch jutting from under a blood-red cape over camouflage fatigues and army-surplus boots.

The unlikely pair clomp across dirty puddles and shards of rocks and bones scattered about the historic tunnels. The girl with an olive-green beret perched atop her messy black hair turns and creases a smile from the thin purplish lips on her smoky-eyed alabaster face, "Monsieur, we are almost there."

Passing skulls and bones of some of the untold thousands interred in the Catacombs of Paris, he huffs a winded reply, "We better be! I do not have time for this fucking cloak-and-dagger bullshit."

A bellowing reply echoes from somewhere up ahead, "Tsk, tsk, Mr. Pike! Such disrespect for the dead while inside such a sacred space. Unwise, my friend. Very unwise, indeed."

In no mood for witless banter with the Nemesis Group's reclusive criminal mastermind, Hugo le Roux, Pike elbows his way past the girl and turns the corner, "Cut the crap, le Roux …." His eyes fixate upon the silhouetted form of a bearded hulk of a man seated in a wingback chair inside a skull-lined alcove. The acrid pall of stinky candles hangs in the ancient ossuary's dank stillness, "You're not le Roux."

The imposing mercenary in a black turtleneck stretched over a musclebound physique stands out of the gilded antique chair and proffers a meaty hand, "No, Mr. Pike, I am Henri DeVille."

Ignoring the Frenchman's crushing handshake greeting, "I don't give a fuck who you are. I was told I would meet your boss. He owes me for the …."

"He owes you nothing! You abandoned Nemesis Group's top people at your show trial. Those who escaped custody are filtering back and telling tales that you fled like a rabbit leaving them screwed and holding the bag." Waiting out fading echoes, "Now that the air is cleared, so to speak, what do you want?"

Standing toe-to-toe with the thuggish man ripped from the pages of an old pirate novel whose name escapes him, Pike softens his tone, "You are too right. I vacated the proceedings upon realizing the dimwitted panel was not keen on pinning the apocalypse on my sworn enemies within The Powers That Be."

Red-riding hood nudges past Pike to DeVille's side and slides a long skinny arm over his thick shoulder to whisper in his ear.

DeVille nods at her hushed report, "Anna tells me you are looking to assemble a team of mercenaries in South America."

Pike's eyes narrow on the girl's leering face, "Spot on, Miss Anna."

With a mean gap-toothed grin widening across his prominent,

red-bearded jaw, "She also advises that I should kill you."

"I like the first option better."

DeVille emits a hearty laugh, "This is your lucky day, you metrosexual cunt. I agree."

The girl drops into the chair with unmasked disappointment, swinging a long leg over the armrest and hitting Pike with a mean stare.

Before Pike can react, DeVille places a heavy hand on his shoulder, "Don't get cocky, you little shit. I would snap you in two in the world that was, but le Roux insists you get a second chance."

The pressure on his arm and shoulder starts to hurt like hell, but Pike smiles and internalizes the pain. He has dealt with worse. "My lucky day, I guess."

DeVille leans in; his hot breath smells of cigarettes and coffee, "I have one condition."

Unable to take it anymore, the SATstar mogul angles from under DeVille's meathook, feeling like a child next to the thuggish brute, "And what would that be? Wait, let me guess. You want to double your fees."

DeVille sidles next to the girl and caresses her bone-white face with the same massive hand, contemplating Pike's remark, "Well, two things, I guess. Double the fees, and I want complete control over my crew. Got it?"

Without a hint of sarcasm, Pike sighs, "Done. That was easy."

Wary of Pike's propensity of coming out smelling like a fucking rose, "What is your timing, and how many men are we talking about?"

"Enough to hold off Pennywell's team." He winces with a dismissive wave, "And a tribe of bloodthirsty cannibals guarding a shipwreck in the Amazon jungle."

"My rates just tripled."

"Fine, Henri. Money is never the issue. I have more than I can ever spend on this shithole world. Did you know my favorite patisserie here in Paris is a pile of burnt-out rubble? Yet the fucking Eiffel Tower is still in one piece?"

DeVille shakes his head, "Stop right there, Pike. I lost my poor old mother in the attack."

"My condolences. It appears almost everyone lost somebody. Now that we have straightened that out, I need your ass in Santarém, Brazil, in four weeks. Can you manage that?"

"I need half upfront."

"Of course, you do."

Barney Hill | Cleopatra Hospital, Cairo
10:00 a.m. | September 6, 2044

Doctor Farouk Said bounds into Owen's darkened room with a clipboard tucked under his white-coated arm. "Good morning, Mr. Hill. Do you know it has been two weeks to the day since your arrival? You are making a miraculous recovery, my friend. I would like to credit my medical expertise, but we both know it has more to do with your benefactors' new technology and excellent physical conditioning. Kudos for not succumbing to the beer belly blues."

Looking less like a beaten prizefighter with each passing day, Owen's eyes narrow as he sips from his water cup and turns his shaved and bandaged head toward the blackout shades covering the window. "I'd take a beer right about now, Doc."

Nurse Zahra enters, proffering a nod toward the doctor before lifting the wrapped gauze and checking stitches across the left side of her patient's stubbled head. Adjusting the coiled mass of IV lines, she notes the monitor and transcribes vitals on a clipboard hanging from the footboard. "Your breakfast should be on the way, Mr. Hill. Powdered eggs, toast, and coffee. I may be able to scrounge up a banana if you like."

"That's okay. Give it to someone else."

Looking to alleviate the patient's usual morning surliness,

Farouk addresses his nurse, "Zahra, raise the window shade so our patient can see the bright blue sky outside his window. That may cheer him up a bit."

"Yes, Doctor."

After checking the spanking new lime-green hexagonal 3D-printed cast on Barney's right forearm, Farouk dons his stethoscope and places it atop the patient's chest, "Hmmm. Good. Good. Can you sit up, please, Mr. Hill?"

Barney scratches his chin with an overt eye roll and grimaces in obvious pain while sitting up so the doctor can access his sliced and bruised back. Flinching at the touch of the stethoscope's cold metal diaphragm, "Why do you think I need cheering up?"

"Quiet, please." Farouk hears the telltale signs of fluid collected around the miraculous regenerated pleural cavity. "Better, not great, but definitely an improvement from yesterday. And your most recent bloodwork was fantastic. I wish I better understood how the stuff works inside the body on a cellular level." The Egyptian physician turns to the nurse awaiting today's orders for his gloomy patient, "Let's maintain his current regimen for at least another day." With a hesitant pause, he adds, "Nurse, can I have a private moment with Mr. Hill?"

"Certainly, Doctor. I'll check on his food."

Waiting for the attractive olive-skinned nurse with jet-black hair pulled into a ponytail to exit the room, Farouk turns back to Barney, "May I be frank, Mr. Hill? Two weeks ago, on the heels of the invasion, I checked your vitals multiple times when I first agreed to allow you and Betty into the chaos of my hospital. You had no pulse. I believe your heart had stopped beating for an indeterminate amount of time. Even with the alien pharmacological medicines, I did not think you would survive that first night. I am trying to say that you should be thankful to be alive. I have witnessed so much death. I don't know much about the state of the world, but if it is anything like Cairo, then multiple millions of human beings are gone, and many more will still succumb in the coming months."

Slumped atop a mound of pillows, Barney's face scrunches into a frown, "Why are you telling me this?"

"Life is short, my friend. You should grab it and hold on tight."

"I'll try to bear that in mind."

Zahra reenters with a food tray and places it on the bedside table, "Mr. Hill, you have company."

Barney watches as Betty wheels herself into the room, offering an effervescent smile to Doctor Said while ignoring him altogether.

Said blushes, "Ah. The lovely and talented Mrs. Hill. How nice! How are you feeling, my dear?"

Betty shrugs an easy grin toward the doctor, "Okay. I guess I am on the mend." Addressing her husband for the first time since their heated argument, "Do you feel up to meeting a couple of my new friends?"

Barney looks toward the open door as a tall man holding a Stetson hat by its wide brim enters the room accompanied by the PTB staff psychologist. "Hello, Roy; who is your friend?"

Nurse Zahra grabs Said by the sleeve and ushers him outside, "We'll check back in a while, Mr. Hill. The doctor has to make his morning rounds."

Roy closes the door after the two Cleopatra Hospital employees vacate the room. The cowboy drops into a chair and crosses a long leg over the other, showing off a fine pair of Western boots. Betty rolls herself to the window and looks outside. Meanwhile, Roy tries to parse his words before uttering them aloud.

Barney looks around the room, "What is this? Some kind of intervention?"

Roy shrugs a nervous laugh and gestures toward the rugged middle-aged fellow, "Barney, this is Dwayne Cooper. We call him Cowboy for obvious reasons. He is the one who transported you and Rachel, I mean Mrs. Hill, from the pyramids on the morning after the invasion."

Rekindling his knack for comparing new acquaintances to famous people for the first time in a long while, Owen nods and points a finger toward the smiling man, "Sam Elliott."

Confused, Roy turns to Cowboy and shrugs, "No, I said Dwayne ...."

Cowboy waves him off, "I know what he meant, Mr. Kendall, and I'll take it as a compliment. Young man, by our calculations, we think you need about another week in here. I am sorry to tell you that, but there it is. You are lucky to be alive, partner."

"Are you the doctor now?" Glancing at Rachel's profile, fixating on a new smoke plume a few blocks from the window, "I assume Rachel explained that I don't want to play in your little reindeer games after getting checked out of here."

Leaning forward on his elbows, Cowboy plants his boots on the linoleum, "She did. I'm holding out hope that you will reconsider. We are a little short on manpower, no offense, Miss, right now."

Owen nods, "I heard the news about Flynn, and I hope he is okay. My problem is I just don't see what we can offer. Despite what my wife may have told you, I am a banker, not an international spy."

Betty shakes her head, staring with a blank expression past her reflection in the dirty window at a new plume of black smoke in the distance, "See? Like I told you, Cowboy, my husband is quite the stubborn mule."

Cooper stands and stretches his back, "Ah, now, don't be too harsh on your man. He has been through a lot. So have you, Miss Rachel. Now, y'all were on your honeymoon when all hell broke loose, ain't that right?"

Barney nods, "Yeah, that's right."

"Well, I'll tell you what, Owen. That is your real goddamn name, after all. I am here to offer my services to fly you back to France next week so you can collect your stuff from your rented villa."

"How do you know… oh," Narrowing his gaze onto his wife's back-turned profile, "I guess you have had more conversations with these guys than I have, right, Rachel?"

"Yeah, Owen, I have. I'd like to at least recover my luggage and shit. Cowboy showed me drone footage of our rental in Le Tholonet. It looks the same as it did when we left."

Cowboy smacks his hands together, "And I can take you there next week. Done deal. In the meantime, Owen Haig, get better and return to investing people's hard-earned dough and whatnot." Before leaving, the lanky man slides his hand into his jeans and extracts a shiny gold coin, "Believe it or not, this is my last coin. I was saving it for you, Owen. But if you are not going to join our little band, I guess I'd rather leave it for the janitor."

A deflated Roy Kendall pats Barney on the leg with a wink and a smile, "I am here if you ever need to talk things over." Looking back toward Betty, wiping tears from her swollen eyes, "Take care, Mrs. Hill. I will check in on you tomorrow."

The two men leave and close the door. The room goes silent except for a low beep from Owen's monitors.

"What's it looking like outside, Rachel?"

"Like shit, Owen. What do you think it looks like?"

"Christ. I am the one who should be angry. These people don't get it. I don't want to go through this shit again. The doctor just told me I was clinically dead. Did you even know that?"

"Well, you're alive now."

"Maybe it would have been better if I had died back in the pyramid. I can't remember much of what happened. Do you?"

Whipping her wheelchair 180 degrees to face her new husband with a look of disbelief across her healing face, "Do you remember anything from inside the beacon chamber?"

Owen shrugs and shakes his head, "No. I really don't. The last thing I remember is seeing you held down by a monster inside the pyramid. Everything from then on is nothing but blurry bits and pieces, like a bad dream."

"You know what I think, Owen? You are one lucky son of a bitch."

"Careful, Rachel, that's your mother-in-law you are referencing there."

"See? You can't be serious for one damn minute." Stifling more tears, Rachel continues, "I remember every fucking detail. My world will never be the same, and you want to return to some new normal like the Gork invasion never happened. What kind of drugs are you on, anyway?"

"Not sure, but whatever it is, I think I need another hit before finishing this conversation."

City blocks from the hospital tower, the conflagration explodes in a window-rattling fireball.

"Do you hear that, Owen? That is reality. We can't go back. If we agree to join The Powers That Be, we can at least feel like we are doing something positive in this shitty world."

"Rachel, come on. What are you going to do? I missed the whole part where you graduated from spy school—or any school."

"Really, Owen? That is low, even for you. Mr. Pennywell believes I have potential. He knows all about what I have been through, and, the gentleman he is, he wouldn't dream of holding my past against me."

"Pennywell? Do you mean the old coot on the hologram feed? Oh, for the love of Christ, Rachel, I liked it when it was just you and me against the world. If you recall, I didn't want Louie to come along."

"I miss Louie."

"Maybe your new Powers That Be buddies can build you a new one. You can slap a cowboy hat on his head and call him Spanky."

Owen's snark-filled humor falls flat as a pancake. With a venomous look in her blackened eyes, Rachel turns to her husband, "Screw you, Owen. You are a real jerk." Not wanting to give her husband the satisfaction of seeing her cry, she wheels out the door and retreats down the corridor toward her spacious, private, guarded hospital room.

Staring at the plate of lukewarm scrambled eggs and a thin piece of dried toast, Owen Haig mutters, "That could have gone better."

Zint | Gray battlecruiser
02:18 a.m. | September 8, 2044

Flynn feels a cold finger slide down his temple, snapping open his swollen eyeballs onto the frightening countenance of his benevolent jailer. Scooting backward against the cell wall, he suppresses a total freak-out at the tiny alien's invasion of his personal space.

"Your fear is unnecessary. Ally. I ally."

The telepathic words seep into Flynn's brain as a second demonstrative voice overlaps his confused state.

"Flynn, dammit, let him finish. He is trying to help."

The flummoxed agent stares past Zint into the cell across the corridor, locking onto the whites of Nina's blue eyes through the dimness.

"Yes, you hear my voice. Kind of cool, right? You look like shit, by the way."

Flynn glances back toward the alien, balancing a one-inch needle on the tip of his finger.

"I need to insert this into your brain, but you must hold still. If I miss, it might paralyze you."

Flynn nods while blowing stale air past his cracked lips, gesturing for the conspiratorial little alien to proceed.

Upon receiving Doctor Said's reluctant approval on the prior evening, Nurse Zahra removed the tangle of IVs and electrodes from Owen's body and switched off his noisy monitors for the first time in 20 days. Now, in the predawn hours after a sleepless night in anticipation of his release, he hears the monotonous tick-tick-tick of a wall clock inside the darkened room, reminding him of a short story called The Telltale Heart from way back in his high school days.

"Jesus, will this night ever end?"

Noting a faint glow leaking around the edges of his shuttered window, he tells himself close enough and swings his stiff form off the bed. Bare feet hit the cold linoleum, and he moves to raise the blackout shade and look upon a decimated early morning Cairo from the Cleopatra Hospital tower's 20th floor one last time.

"Yep, still pretty shitty."

Turning toward his bathroom, where a shower and much-needed teeth brushing await, he thinks of Rachel, wondering how she slept and if she has come to her senses about the PTB nonsense. Smirking at his hangdog reflection in the bathroom mirror, he mutters, "Not bloody likely."

Fifteen minutes later, Owen emerges from the steamed-up bathroom, drops the wet towel, and studies the neat-folded denim shirt, khakis, and the new pair of shoes Roy dropped off last evening in preparation for the big day.

A quick rap on the door turns Owen toward Feroz, the implacable, hairy-armed hospital orderly who aided him through that rough first week when everything down to taking a leak proved an ordeal.

Surprised to find Owen awake, standing half-dressed by the open window, Feroz pushes the wheelchair by the bedside and stammers,

"Excuse me, Mr. Hill. I did not think you would be up and dressing this early."

"That's okay, Feroz. Come on in. I'll be right with you." Sensing the kid's embarrassment, Owen asks, "Do I need to ride in that thing?"

"Uh, it's hospital policy, Mr. Hill, to wheel patients outside upon checkout. But if you would rather walk, I leave that up to you, sir."

"Well, Feroz. I need to walk. I already feel less like an invalid standing on my own two feet." He pulls up the khakis with an expressive laugh, "And wearing pants, to boot!" Owen finishes tucking his shirt, dons a soft leather belt, and plops into the chair to put on socks and shoes.

Noticing the kid's beat-up old sneakers, "You look like a size 11, am I right?"

The tall, athletic Egyptian offers a confused look, "I think so."

"Perfect." Owen slides the shoebox Roy left with the clothes toward Feroz, "I want you to have those shoes for putting up with me over the last couple of weeks. They are brand new and worth at least 500 bucks. Wear them or sell them as you see fit. You earned it dealing with my sorry ass."

Seeing the surprised look on the kid's face, Owen reaches for the cardboard box containing tattered and dirty remnants of his breaching the pyramids attire and removes the worn Timberland boots. Noting bloody splotches stained into the dusty, scuffed, dark-brown leather uppers, he shows them to his new young friend, "These stains are my badge of honor."

Feroz scoops the shoebox, "Are you sure, Mr. Hill?"

"Never look a gift horse in the mouth, Feroz. Yes, I am sure."

"Thanks, Mr. Hill; I will wear them in good health."

Stepping past Feroz to exit his private recovery room into the dark hallway, he pauses and turns, "And for the love of Christ, kid, call me Owen." Patting the kid's shoulder, "Now let's go see what the fetching Mrs. Hill is up to down the hall."

* * *

Following a lukewarm two-minute shower, Rachel dries her healing body before brushing her unruly blond mane. Stepping into a sleeveless button-front full-length linen dress Roy Kendall delivered to her room the previous evening, she checks herself in the foggy bathroom mirror with an approving smile, "Not a Nina pick, but Roy has an eye for fashion. Who knew?"

Swiping the mirror, she leans over the sink, examining the fading scars from tiny cuts covering her face and neckline. Smoothing fingertips over green bruising still visible over her paler-than-normal complexion, she hesitates before reaching for her trusty prescription bottle.

The rustling sounds of people entering the room distract from her reverie, and she hears a familiar voice call out, "Are you decent?"

Rachel fumbles the bottle, choking down a pill before coughing a reply, "Come on in and make yourselves comfortable."

Moments later, Rachel pads barefoot from the bathroom, "Good morning, ladies," performing a catwalk twirl in the form-fitting dress for her friends and confidantes, nurses Zahra and Cleo.

Cleo erupts in a hearty laugh, "I knew it; you have done modeling!"

Rachel plops onto the edge of her unkempt hospital bed, "Only if you count my mother's bridge club fashion show fundraisers."

Taking a chair, Cleo pulls a bottle of wine and red plastic cups from a hospital tote bag, "Rachel, I brought something to toast your miraculous recovery and our new friendship."

Rachel flashes an effervescent smile, "It is good to hear you say my real name. I did not care for Betty."

Zahra commandeers the chair by the armoire, "Wait, let me guess, dear old Mum has a friend named Betty?"

Cleo pops the cork, interrupting Rachel's reply, and fills their cups with sparkling rosé wine, "My real plan is to get one or both of you drunk."

Zahra rolls her eyes and examines the bottle, "Where did you find this?"

Cleo smiles at her fellow nurse, "I have my sources."

Rachel raises her cup to toast the educated, professional women and swipes away a tear, "I can't thank you, girls, enough. What would I have done without the both of you babysitting me every day and enduring my sob stories?"

Zahra leans forward and takes Rachel by her permanent scarred hand, "Rachel, you saved us. We would all be dead without you."

Cleo takes a long drink and tops off the cups, adding, "To be fair, Owen and the PTB played supporting roles."

Zahra releases Rachel's hand and frowns, "I almost hate to ask. Has Owen agreed to join the PTB?"

"No. My husband still believes we will fly back to the States and resume life like nothing happened."

Cleo uncrosses her legs and leans forward, "Damn, girl. I don't know much, but from what I understand, the good old USA took it worse than anywhere in the world."

Noting Rachel's subtle downward shift in demeanor after hearing the news, Zahra reaches for a large shopping bag, "Here, I brought you something."

"Oh, you didn't have to do that. I wish I had something for both of you."

Rachel accepts the large bag and pulls out a wide-brimmed, floppy hand-woven straw sun hat with an elegant red ribbon. "Oh my, it is beautiful. I could have used this in the desert a few weeks ago."

Zahra returns a proud smile, "I want to ensure your beautiful healing face stays protected from the harsh sunlight. I have one like it. You can roll it and get it wet. It will protect you when you need it most."

Rachel pulls the hat down atop her blond head and begins to cry.

Watching the emotional Rachel, Cleo stifles an empathetic group crying session by lightening the mood, "I thought we said no gifts."

Rachel raises a green-eyed smile directed at Cleo from under the broad brim, "You really are too much."

A sharp knock on the door stops Cleo's heartfelt reply before reconsidering and yelling, "Come in!"

Roy Kendall peeks inside before entering, "Everybody decent in here?" Noting Rachel's new hat and dress, he smiles, "Oh yeah. The hat looks great. I see the going away party is in full swing at this early hour." Stepping to the attractive Nurse Zahra, he leans in and gives her an affectionate kiss, "I'll leave you ladies to it, but Zahra, I wanted to let you know I fed the cats before I left your flat and changed both litter boxes. Kind of a smelly situation."

Cleo scrutinizes the new couple with a raised eyebrow, "Oh, so now we are cohabitating? Zahra, when did this happen?"

Roy beams at the vivacious and inquisitive lesbian nurse, "Zahra took me in like I am one of her rescue cats."

Cleo scrunches her face, feigning deep thought, "There's a pussy joke on the tip of my brain."

With a raised hand, Zahra stops her fellow nurse, "Don't say it." A pregnant pause later, she reconsiders, "What the hell, tell me later."

Roy turns to address Rachel Haig, shrinking from the catty conversation under her straw hat, staring at the swirl of bubbles in her plastic cup, "I hope the dress is to your liking, Rachel. I admit, Nina was our resident fashion maven."

Facing the cold hard reality of life outside her 20th-floor retreat, Rachel swallows back anxiety, proffering a brave smile to the well-meaning psychologist, "I like it, Roy. Nina would be proud. I hope she is alive out there somewhere."

Standing over the threesome, Roy feels like the proverbial fourth wheel, "Well ladies, I will come back in a little while, so you all can have your time together before Rachel departs."

Zahra stands, "Oh, for God's sake, Roy." Pushing Roy into her chair, she perches atop his long legs and turns to Cleo, "There. Now he is not going anywhere. Did you bring another bottle?"

"You know it, girlfriend."

Roy angles around Zahra, trading banter with Cleo, to address Rachel, "The plan is to drive you and Owen to the Ritz, reclaim your stuff, and head to the airport. Does that sound right, Mrs. Haig?"

"I think so. Owen should be along any minute. It is his plan. I just follow along like a little stray cat."

Right on cue, the door opens, revealing Owen with Feroz tagging behind.

Cleo sees the newcomers and reaches into her bag for more cups, "Well, look what the cat brought in. Hello, Mr. Haig; can I interest you in a little sparkling wine?"

Owen saunters into the room with a confused frown, rubbing a hand across the scar on the side of his shaved head, "Uh, sure. Why do I always feel like the last guy to the party?"

* * *

Following their tearful release from the Cleopatra Hospital with a plastic shopping bag of instructions and medications from near and far, Roy Kendall transports the Haigs within a shattered block of the boarded-up Ritz Carlton, situated along an impassable stretch of the Nile Corniche. Furnishing hot-off-the-presses travel documents and a new passport to replace the one Owen lost, he advises the sulky duo that the hotel's security office should be staffed, so start there. After running an errand for his new main squeeze, he will return to pick them up in a few hours.

Owen | Nile Boardwalk
11:36 a.m. | September 12, 2044

After an eye-opening walk through burnt-out rubble and broken glass along the former upscale boulevard, the Haigs follow spray-painted arrows, entering the boarded-up Ritz Carlton. Owen provides a printed copy of their reservation and room number to an armed private security guard, who leads them into a massive ballroom filled with haphazard jumbled piles of luggage, bags, and personal items from hotel guests missing since invasion day. The ominous baby stroller line hits Rachel hard.

A monotonal figure seated behind a makeshift table with a pen and ledger proffers a dead-eyed stare toward the new arrivals across the plush carpeted expanse.

The couple shrugs at each other and enters the darkened space, sifting through expensive luggage. "Here, Owen, I found your old backpack."

Owen wades farther into the piles and pulls out Nina's heavy portmanteau filled with clothes, cash, and cards, like finding a 3-week-old time capsule from a former reality. Reaching into his pocket, he pulls out a key and opens the lid. "Bingo."

After stuffing filthy reclaimed daypacks with the portmanteau's contents, the Haigs sign legal waivers pushed forward by the dour hotel employee. Watching the survivors sign for their stuff, the man's mood brightens, and he mentions his aunt and uncle's café is open and serving coffee and food—a miracle amid shuttered eateries and shops along the palm-lined Nile River boardwalk.

Hefting the daypack over a shoulder, he turns to Rachel, "Why not? It sure beats sitting around here, waiting for Roy to find a pet store with cat food."

"Sure, Owen. Whatever you say."

"Okay. Yes. What I say."

* * *

Owen tips up the bill of a white ball cap with an embroidered butterfly logo protecting his stubbly head from the bright Egyptian sunshine and downs a second bittersweet Egyptian coffee. Raising his right arm wrapped in a bright-green 3D-printed cast, he hails the busy hostess.

"We'll take the check whenever you are ready."

The matronly Egyptian creases a wry smile across her distinguished, dark-complected face, refilling Owen's cup, "If you are who I think you are, it is on the house." Swiping another table on her way back to a long bar at the far end of the open-air café, she turns with a dismissive wave, "Besides, our payment processor is down, like everywhere else. My husband and I just have nothing better to do."

Taken aback at having a so-called veil of anonymity punctured by their first human interaction outside the hospital, Owen slides a generous wad of Egyptian pound notes under his plate. "Wow, that was weird, right, Rachel?"

Receiving a heaping dose of the silent treatment, he studies Rachel's silhouetted profile beneath the wide-brimmed straw sun hat with a colorful red bow tied at the back. Sipping the bitter coffee, he muses her bruises and cuts will heal with time, but the absurd notion of joining The PTB could prove terminal. Shaking his head in disgust, he laments Pennywell's damn employment offer pushing them apart.

Swallowing back his pill regimen with a gulp of bottled water, he finishes with an exaggerated belch forcing Rachel to acknowledge his presence.

Without a flinch in his direction, "That's a nice touch, Owen. Doctor Said warned to ease off on the painkillers."

"I will if you will."

Rachel avoids Owen's probing hazel eyes, angled sideways with legs crossed in her sleeveless white linen dress buttoned to her knees, watching old gasoline-powered watercraft ferry relief supplies up and down the dirty brown river. Swatting at a fly with the audacity to land on her sandaled foot propped on a short brick wall, she shifts to the table and slides her untouched baklava off to the side, "I'm not hungry."

Acknowledging Rachel's sullenness and the rift between them since the offer from The Powers That Be CEO, Owen pulls the thin folded sheet at the root of their troubles from a shirt pocket, "Rachel, I am tired of fighting you on this ridiculous proposal. I care about you too much. We both almost died. What am I saying? For fuck's sake, the doctor said I was dead. We have a new lease on life and a helluva story for our children someday. And guess what? I remember what you did under the pyramids. Your hands, Rachel. Those scars are your badge of honor for saving this ungrateful world. You have nothing left to prove."

Angling his healing face to make eye contact with his wife's defiant stare hidden behind dark shades under the hat's broad brim, he projects his most disarming, persuasive smile, "Let's head back to France, hang out at the villa for as long as we like, and then get back home. Remember home, Rachel?"

Removing the designer tortoiseshell sunglasses she found inside Nina's portmanteau, Rachel squints through the hazy late-morning Cairo sunshine toward Owen, unmasked annoyance wrinkling her makeup-free face, "I don't understand you, Owen. Didn't your boss at Ford and Poole Capital, what's his name, Henry Tate, send a note saying the firm is dead in the water for the foreseeable future?

"It came with my letter from Mom and Dad, like the one you received. Who knows what is really going on back there?"

"Owen, you can't be serious. The invasion ruined my father's business. We are fortunate our families survived; millions did not. Who knows when people can attend a concert or sporting event again? There is nothing left for us back there."

Déjà vu of a similar contentious debate at the OASIS hotel bar in Tripoli only three weeks earlier—a lifetime ago—conjures in Owen's mind, "Rachel, your father is a survivor. That man can sell ice cubes to

Eskimos."

An abrasive and loud staticky radio noise interrupts the conversation from devolving into another pointless argument. Thankful for the distraction, Owen swivels toward the crackling sounds, observing the bartender fiddling with a shortwave tuner on a vintage boombox while fussing with its extended antenna. The hostess hustles to the long teak bar and slides her tray of dirty cups and plates next to the old receiver. After scolding her clumsy husband, she slaps his thick fingers from the oversized round knob and makes a delicate adjustment. The noise fades, and the assertive voice of President Lena Jackson comes through loud and clear, broadcasting from atop the bar to a worldwide human populace desperate for news.

Sticking a pin in their disagreement, Owen and Rachel sidle to the bar, relieved to discover the leader of the free world among the living and curious to hear what she has to report in the apocalypse's wake.

After serving as Christopher Pratt's vice president for his second term, Lena Jackson transcended the two-party divide and swept to an easy electoral college landslide in 2040. The attractive young politician proved an easy decision for Rachel's first presidential election and appeared primed for a repeat in 2044 until the Gorks changed everything.

By contrast, Owen despised politics: money talked, bullshit walked, and that was that.

The 56-year-old former Army lieutenant colonel's resolute delivery masks the unbearable weight of the direst moment in human history as the glitchy signal fades in and out: "… *my friends, the gloves are off. Our world is under a grave threat. For reasons I am not at liberty to discuss, the initial alien invaders reversed course and departed. However, their antigravity dreadnoughts and attack ships killed millions and left paths of indescribable destruction across urban centers on every continent.*

To our extraterrestrial allies, I request your sage guidance. And I warn humanity to take advantage of this reprieve because, as I speak, other forces lie in wait within our solar system. Whether their intent is hostile or not, we must remain vigilant and assume the worst. Every human on Earth is entitled to know what we are up against. No more secrets, lies, and obfuscations. May God instill the courage, wisdom, maturity, and fortitude we will need to meet and defeat the threat head-on.

Most countries declared martial law per their constitutions to safeguard citizens by maintaining order and the rule of law. Equitable distributions of food, water, and medical aid in coordination with overtaxed relief organizations and The Powers That Be proceed, albeit too slow, leading to riots and widespread looting.

Please, I beg you, do not compound the chaos caused by the alien invaders. Assist local law enforcement agencies in containing mayhem and disorder plaguing your cities and towns. We must unite and communicate that humankind's strength flows through our diverse, hard-won experiences. We will not surrender. We will not recede into the heavens! We are one human family! If we fail to come together in this hour of crisis, a crowded universe will attack again, leading to unconscionable consequences. Of that, you can be sure. We got lucky once; it will not happen again.

I will use this frequency to broadcast updates and information. In the meantime, stay safe, remain calm, and carry on. Maintain contact with your local authorities. If your situation is dire, please trust that assistance is on the way.

May God bless you and keep you in these trying times."

Rachel's eyes linger on the boombox, reminiscent of a beat-up old receiver her dad kept on a work shelf in the family estate's 10-car garage.

Owen places his cast arm around Rachel's shoulders, snapping her back to reality. Leaning close, he whispers, "Rachel, my love, I just changed my mind. Let's do it. If Mr. Pennywell thinks we are suited for The Powers That Be, that is where our path should lead."

Rachel tips the brim of her sun hat, producing an effervescent smile, "Owen, are you sure? We can still take as much time as we need to heal before jumping in with both feet."

"I'm sure. Apparently, we are too well-known ever to lead normal lives."

Owen turns to their Egyptian hostess, fiddling with the radio in search of more news, "Excuse me, mam, would you mind explaining how you know our identities?

Flinging a dirty rag over her shoulder, "Dear boy, your pictures are plastered across local newsprints all over Cairo. It is the power of the press." Refocusing on the radio dial, she pauses and turns back toward the tall, handsome American couple with a skeptical look across her dark-brown visage, "By the way, can you two shoot lightning bolts from your hands? That is the report in the latest article I read."

Owen's eyes widen with surprise, "The latest what now?"

On reflex, Rachel clasps her hands behind her back as the woman reaches into her apron and produces a folded tabloid-size sheet, "This one is in English; read it for yourselves." Noticing Rachel's unbandaged hands, the woman raises a dark eyebrow, "Huh, maybe the article is accurate after all."

Noting the server's prying gaze, Owen moves between her and his fuming wife, "Look, lady, don't believe everything you read."

The woman shrugs, "Oh, don't worry about me. The lightning story is mild compared to other wild speculation and rumors."

Rachel's curiosity piques, "Like what?"

"Well, for one. There is a hidden golden chamber under the pyramids. That is a direct quote from an interview with an Egyptian army captain who claims he was inside the chamber when the invasion began."

Something snaps inside Rachel's head, emitting a spirited laugh at the mention of the nightmarish beacon chamber and the heroic Captain Faisel who pulled her from the abyss in the nick of time, "The chamber is a seamless hollowed block of polished black granite. No gold. Well, except for the ellipse. But that is gone."

The woman shoots Rachel a dumbfounded stare, "Uh-huh."

Rachel smiles at the lady, "Is there anything else you want to know? What the hell? Check out my hands—forever scarred from those lightning bolts, as you call them. They burn, but I cannot make fire anymore. Now you know the truth. Like the president said, enough with all of the lies."

Owen grabs Rachel by the waist, checking his wristwatch, "Uh, we should head out; Roy is probably waiting for us."

Rachel extends her scarred hand, reaching for the paper, "Can I take this?"

"Go ahead, dear; the city is littered with papers featuring your pretty face. I can grab another one anytime I want."

Rachel nods and pivots to follow Owen toward the hotel before seeing her halftoned image above the thin Cairo tattler's fold, "Aw, man! Owen, look at this picture. I look terrible!"

Owen leads Rachel toward the ruined street before making a final over-the-shoulder glance toward the café, "What else has Roy and the PTB kept from us over the last three weeks?"

John Stevens | The Amazon
07:48 p.m. | September 12, 2044

Nightfall in the rainforest amplifies the chirps, hoots, grunts, squawks, and growls, thrashing and crashing through dense jungle undergrowth, punctuated by the haunting screams and wails of the hunted rising above the din before falling to silence.

Looking outside the unzipped front of his canvas-tented high hide concealed 65 feet up the rainforest canopy, Professor John Stevens chews on a banana and trains his dimmed torch beam onto a toucan sound asleep on a twisted dripping limb like a colorful statue. Flinging the greenish-yellow peel into the pitch blackness, the 62-year-old Aussie wipes his mouth on a dirty sleeve and whispers, "Did you bring Froot Loops? I am starving up here."

Reaching for his pack, the former Outback trail guide from Melbourne replaces the palm-sized flashlight with a pocketknife. Unfolding the 5-inch blade, he whittles the 50th notch into his long and sturdy carved walking stick, marking time from the inception of his solo expedition on July 24. Tuning out the hoots and howls from his noisy neighbors, he stows the knife, zips himself inside the tent, and tries to sleep.

* * *

Stevens traveled to Brazil on July 24 on Pennywell's dime. After a few days in Santarém gathering supplies, he traveled by boat down the Tapajós, past Fordlandia, to Itaituba, where the American booked an ATV four-wheeler escort to the literal end of the road on August 1. With shit-eating toothy smiles, the locals counted their cash and kicked up mud, fishtailing back down the path. Stevens checked his gear and realized he had left a satchel carrying backup supplies on the second ATV, including a second satellite phone. Shrugging into his weighty backpack, the experienced outdoorsman figures less weight, no big deal. He checks his trusty GPS transponder and heads down an invisible trail into the forest.

On the hot and steamy mid-afternoon of August 6, after days of arduous hiking through the dense Amazonian jungle, the PTB scientist reached the hypothesized coordinates of his Fibonacci spiral nucleus. Scouring the area in a wide radius, he called the PTB to report what he found. Nothing. Fucking nothing. Less than nothing. Unless mosquitoes and poisonous snakes count, which they don't.

Setting up a basecamp in the soul-crushing disappointing spot, the PTB scientist expanded his search grid over the following days, planting remote GPS locator beacons identifying explored sectors of woods. It all looked exactly the same, a solid green inferno, with one notable exception: a circular mound with a 22-foot radius conspicuous through the thick undergrowth. Stevens dug into the raised formation with an ill-suited camp shovel, unearthing bony shards with little effort but nothing to infer the presence of an ancient shipwreck. Loath to disturb the burial site any more than he already had, he recorded the location for a future archeological expedition and moved on.

On August 9, a dirty and depressed Stevens prepared to phone home and request extraction. Lost in mid-rumination over his miscalculated passage, a long thin dart thwacked into his backpack, snapping him back to reality. Overwhelmed with shock and horror by the prospect of the primitive weapon coming within inches of ending his trip in a poisoned heartbeat, he hit the dirt and peered into the dense shadowed undergrowth. "Man, what terrible aim. I thought these Amazon hunters had mad blow dart skills."

Surmising the near-miss as a warning to leave now and never return, the erudite man heeded the simple message without argument. Packing his gear in a chaotic rush to beat a hasty exit, he stepped backward in his mud-caked boot atop a solid object, eliciting a sickening, loud crunch. The man's heart sank, realizing his satellite phone lay crushed in muddy pieces. Verging on losing his last vestige of sanity, he caught a glimpse of a lone white figure contrasted against the shadowed forest.

Gripped by an overwhelming sense of dreaded fear, Stevens grabbed his pack and blundered into the cover of thick undergrowth in a senseless panic. Losing a grip on time and space, the scientist pushed deeper into the jungle darkness before stumbling over a log and tumbling to the bottom of a steep gorge carved by a roaring torrent. Heaving with exhaustion and covered in dirt, cuts, and scrapes, he vomited down his pant legs. Reduced from a learned, rational scholar to an animalistic survival instinct in the oppressive humidity, he glared uphill to see if he was followed. He could see nothing through the trees and underbrush—maybe he had lost the guy. A cool refreshing mist swirled out of the thunderous rapids cascading over massive boulders in the narrow gorge. Slouching out of his heavy backpack, he dropped it atop a mossy boulder and stared hundreds of feet into the cathedral of trees overhead. As the last dusky remnants of light filtered through the leafy canopy, he waded into the fast-moving icy water to his knees, attempting to regain his bearings and wash some of the mud off his clothes and boots before nightfall.

The heart-stopping screech of a howler monkey startled the addled man. Pushed off-balance in the strong current, he tumbled headfirst into the roaring rapids. Carried splashing and flailing downstream, he slammed off slickened boulders and razor-sharp roots before striking headfirst into a massive log, knocking him unconscious. The turbulent unmapped stream floated his limp form for miles. The flow deepened and narrowed, disappearing amidst a fern glade teeming with butterflies before churning into an expansive uncharted cavern system. The waters expand into a pitch-black stillness floating Stevens through flumes and chutes like a Disney ride into one echoing chamber after another. Spinning counterclockwise on his back, his shirt snags on an underwater outcropping, snapping his eyes open for a brief, terrifying moment before a whirlpool ripped him free, plunging him through a twisting underwater chute. On the verge of drowning, he loses consciousness moments before shooting out a six-foot aperture, 60 feet up a precipitous cliff in a ribbon of water cascading into a deep blue pool at the bottom of a timeless gorge.

A firm grasp on his ripped shirt pulled Stevens' waterlogged form from the icy blue depths onto a sandy spit. Choking, coughing, and sputtering water out of his mouth and nose, he rose onto his elbows on solid ground in the dead of night, nose-to-nose with white eyes and teeth, like a Cheshire cat. Rubbing swollen eyeballs, the hunched silhouette of a smiling native resolved before Professor John Stevens' blurred gaze.

As the nightmarish series of unfortunate events rewound in his throbbing head, he realized his gear was long gone. Shit. Shit. Shit.

Exhausted with a huge knot on his forehead, he passed out again. The native kid in his early teens pushed Stevens onto his side so he would not choke on more watery snot and vomit and took off into the woods.

Morning in the heart of the Amazon came bright and early. Sunlight permeated Stevens' swollen eyelids, and an itchy sensation of something crawling across his cheek startled him awake. Springing to a seated pose, he looked down at his stark naked body and swatted away a swarm of sandflies.

Scuttling onto his bare feet, he looked toward a campfire where his clothes and boots were hung to dry on stakes mounted into the ground.

The smiling and naked kid reappeared in his natural chocolate-brown skin, sans ghost-white paint, gesturing Stevens toward the fire to eat, pointing at a five-inch butterflied filet of snake meat popping and crackling at the end of a stick propped over the licking flames. Realizing the boy no doubt saved his life, he accepted the food offering with a tentative bite. Not bad.

The native beamed with pride as Stevens plopped onto the sandy ground adjacent to the deep blue pool, devoured the viper meat, and asked for seconds.

After breakfast, the fellow guided a clothed and refreshed Stevens into the woods to a tamped-down spot where his backpack leaned against a tall, straight tree trunk. "Hey, thank you! Wow. What a sight for sore eyes."

Sensing the mysterious white man's overjoyed reaction, he indicated upward and emitted a loud grunt followed by a long whistle.

Stevens stared up and, at first, could not make out anything before seeing the outline of his canvas tent strung betwixt the thick branches of the massive kapok tree, like a high hide. Brilliant.

The teen smiled and smacked a clenched fist into his chest, indicating that he had done an excellent job.

Stevens rested and recovered for the next 12 days while his Man Friday came and went at odd hours, sometimes slathered in fine white clay.

On one occasion, Friday showed up covered in blood with a wild-eyed stare, giving Stevens pause. The indigenous tribesman consumed human flesh. He knew that. As long as it wasn't his, he left it alone.

Venturing from the high hide, Stevens embarked on recon missions through the surrounding forest. On the seventh day, he resolved to explore the gurgling streamlet from the deep blue pool, hiking downhill through a verdant glade into a narrow slot canyon where the water picked up momentum and churned out the opposite end into a creek snaking through a long steep gorge. Pushing onward through the fast-flowing current with the jungle pushing in on both sides under the thick canopy rising hundreds of feet above his sweating head, Stevens stepped onto a wide spit of sand and listened. The unmistakable din of a thunderous waterfall drove him farther downstream. He swung out over thin air, grappling between vines and branches, intent on looking over the edge into the dark abyss. Visibility was reduced to zero, peering through the mist-enshrouded rift, but he knew the lost ship waited at the bottom.

Hustling back upstream, trying to beat the pending nightfall, his boot kicks against a shiny object. Wrapping an arm over a branch, he stretched into the current and pulled out a long-barreled pistol. Recognizing its Gray alien origin, he held it by the barrel and continued back to his camp, cognizant that the game was afoot.

The sweltering hot morning of August 22 started with showers welcoming another monotonous day in the forest. That is until fleets of Gork attack ships set fire to the skies above the South American continent, taking out Rio de Janeiro and Sao Paulo before lumbering east toward the Atlantic.

Cataclysmic EMP shockwaves followed, knocking out Stevens'

GPS transponder and frying the chips in his cameras and recording devices.

* * *

Settling in for another night in the Amazon, Stevens enjoys a cool breeze through the mesh fabric, a luxury high up in the trees not found at ground level. Skittish activity outside his canvas perch stretched tight between massive trunks jars his restless early morning slumber. Desperate for more sleep, the sound of branches rustling and snapping, accompanied by a low and unnatural guttural growl, stirs him awake, "Jesus, the jungle is so fucking noisy."

His curiosity piqued, he unzips his tent and peers outside at a troupe of jittery howler monkeys clinging from sopping branches by their prehensile tails. The comical creatures' anxiety most often indicates the passage of a large predator, like a jaguar, but this creature's approaching heavy footfalls caused deep, thudding tremors. Conjuring an old favorite movie in his weary head, he muses, it sounds like a bloody dinosaur.

Flynn | Gray battlecruiser

10:55 a.m. | September 15, 2044

Nina stands inside her cell and stretches her back, *"Flynn, are you awake?"*

"Where is Nicole?"

"I don't know. Nicole was gone when I woke up."

"She better be alive, or I will rip these little bastards apart with my bare hands."

"How has that worked out for you so far?"

Flynn shuffles onto his feet and shrugs across the corridor, catching Nina's sideways glance, *"Not good, but I am alive. Did I tell you about my sparring partner? He is a half-human, half-Gork, 7-foot teddy bear."*

Nina smiles, *"I am sure you two will be happy together on the intergalactic wrestling circuit."*

"You made that sound cooler than you intended, you know." Staring across the corridor through the thick cell bars, he wipes away tears in his dark, swollen eyes, *"I miss Earth, Nina."*

"Me too, Flynn."

"I am worried about Nicole and Astrid. If these perverted fuckers impregnated my girls, there is no end to the shitstorm I will reign down on their shiny gray heads."

"What about your involuntary liver donor?"

"Yeah, I saw him briefly before they killed him. What a fucking nightmare."

The portal at the end of the cell block opens, revealing a scarecrow followed by two Gray beings. The bizarre trio inspects each cell before pausing between Flynn and Nina's cells in the dull blue light.

Masking abject fear and anxiety behind an impassive dead-eyed facial expression, *"This is it, Nina. If these nutters overhear our telepathy, the jig is up."*

Nina slides to the floor at the back of her cell, burying her face in her hands, *"Be cool. Be cool."*

A short Gray interrogator shoots Nina a probing stare, *"What is, be cool?"*

Nina swallows hard and asks out loud through her garbled voice, "Are you speaking to me?"

The alien raises a long-fingered hand before slicing it through the air, knocking Nina onto her side. *"Quiet."*

Flynn's bruised and bloodied face remains expressionless, *"That is odd. They hear your thoughts but not our conversation."*

The other alien pivots to the PTB agent, staring daggers through his six-foot form while shuffling through his thoughts like a deck of cards.

Sensing an acid test in the making with the little fucker knocking on doors inside his brain, Flynn decides to go for it, *"Hi Nina, what's up? Does the big one smell like a cesspool, or is it just me? These fuckers do not stand a chance. Apple Brown Betty. Snoopy. The Red Baron. John, Paul, George, and Ringo. Yabba-Dabba-Do. Nope. Nothing. Hey there, you little shit. That's it; turn around and leave."*

The alien recoils and shakes its bulbous head before moving on.

The scarecrow checks the locked cell doors before following outside to Zint's control room.

"Nina. No sudden movements. They are suspicious, but they don't have a clue."

"I'm fine, by the way. We are getting off this boat. It worked. And thanks to you, I have Lucy in the Sky with Diamonds in my head."

Flynn stands and peers down the corridor at the aliens, who appear to have moved on to something else, *"Sing it to me, Nina. I need to hear something nice."*

Nina's lilting voice soothes the agent's tattered psyche, stirring a resolute determination out of a heavy darkness permeating his soul.

"Nina?"

"Yes, Agent."

"I am not leaving this boat unless everyone gets a ride back to Earth."

"I know, dear. Let's take a break. I need to pee."

John Stevens | The Amazon
01:25 p.m. | September 15, 2044

Stevens hacks through the underbrush, slinging a machete and carrying a bag of groceries: cacao fruits, wild bananas, and lengths of bright green pit viper that taste much like chicken. Approaching his home in the trees, he spies a sight for sore eyes, his Man Friday slouched atop a massive root at the base of his kapok tree.

Greeting his friend with a welcoming smile, Stevens enters the narrow clearing and plops down across from him, kicking mud from his boots. Without looking up at his young visitor, "Where have you been? I have not seen you for weeks."

The kid claps his thick, calloused hands to gain the oblivious man's attention.

Stevens tips back the brim of his hat, noting for the first time a pained and distressed expression contorting the boy's grayed and swollen, red-eyed visage flecked with dried white clay.

"Holy mother of God, you are ill, my friend. What happened? Is it me? Did I make you sick?" Stevens jumps up to aid and comfort Friday, but the boy raises his hands, keeping him at arm's length, shaking his head. "No. No."

Wavering onto his feet, the boy gestures for Stevens to follow.

The PTB scientist masks alarm, seeing the athletic kid's vigor and strength reduced to a slackened and slumped imitation of his former self, "Hold on, let me get what's left of my medical kit."

Stevens follows the boy's staggering footfalls, retracing the long, hot, serpentine path downstream to a sandy spit near the top of a waterfall, crashing into the mysterious mist-filled gorge.

The boy pauses at the pivotal spot in the fast-flowing stream where he and his brother consumed strange bluish entrails from a speared alien creature. Glancing back at Stevens, he splashes his face in the swift-flowing water before cutting into the thick woods, up a steep, muddy ravine, clawing at vines and low branches to reach the top.

Scampering up the slippery slope, an out-of-breath Stevens rejoins his sick friend atop a well-trod ridgeline trail.

Doubled over in pain, Friday coughs up bloody phlegm at his bare feet, waving off Steven's wet cloth offering. Regaining his composure, the teenager signals they are close.

Trekking along the ridgeline sloping on a continuous uphill grade, Stevens catches glimpses of his hidden gorge far below, concealed under a solid green blanket of trees. A squawking flock of macaws contrasts in vivid blue, red, and yellow hues against the forest greens at another opening expanding the view north and east to the horizon. Stevens realizes no hint of civilization exists in any direction from this position for hundreds of miles. Refocusing on the wide trail, he sees the kid break into a run, disappearing into an ancient grove. Stevens quickens his steps to keep pace before stumbling to a stop at the edge of a clearing, catching the boy entering a thatched hut.

Entering the cathedral-like space, he stares upward at the majestic sentinel trees ringing the clearing and rising hundreds of feet into the sky, forming an opaque ceiling overhead. Thatched dwellings camouflaged in the undergrowth form a semi-circle along the fringes, with a larger abode situated in the middle for the chief. Centered in the 50-foot expanse, a smoldering firepit swirls thin wisps of grayish smoke into the still air. Picking up a knotted branch, Stevens pokes at the fire waiting for the boy to reemerge. Amidst the singed bones and charry bits, he notes a smooth, round object, like a melon, half-buried in thick greasy layers of ash and firewood. Curious, the sweaty, itchy man pushes it sideways with the tip, revealing exaggerated large empty eye sockets staring daggers and piercing a cold chill up his spine in the oppressive heat. Dropping the stick, he looks around the camp, realizing he is alone. With dreaded fear and alarm bells ringing in his head, he calls out in a loud voice, "Friday, what the hell did your people do? You can't eat these fuckers. They are poison."

A loud rheumy coughing fit echoes in reply from one of the huts. Stevens rushes to the dark opening and peers inside; Friday's dark form languishes face up with eyes widened, gripped with severe pain, staring into the matted fronds aside another poisoned youth. The other boy has been dead for days, judging by his advanced state of decay.

Stevens watches Friday cry in agony while gurgling a thick

phlegmy substance mixed with blood from his mouth and nose as his stricken body convulses, suffering a cardiac arrest. The convulsions slow, leading to desperate gasps for air, ebbing to shallow, irregular breaths before slowing to a merciful stop.

The Aussie watches his dead friend for an indeterminate time, mourning the mental shock of witnessing the brave child's death throes.

Gathering what remains of his wits, the PTB professor removes his vest and places it over the young man's head. "You saved my life. I am sorry I could not save yours. Rest in peace, Friday."

Stepping back with a hushed reverence in the peaceful setting, he moves to examine the other dwellings. Peering into the darkness of the chief's hut, he finds the heavyset man's slumped body, stone dead. Remnants of dark decayed skin clung to his skull as maggots squirmed from picked-clean sockets under a thick-browed head covered in rotting tattoos and bony piercings from a sordid array of victims. Stevens surmises the fellow passed within the last few days, but the heat, humidity, and jungle rot in this hothouse environment accelerated his decomposing form.

A survey of the other huts finds the rest of the tribe in similar states of decomposition, concluding that they consumed en masse the toxic flesh and bones of the Gray smoldering in the pit.

Considering what, if anything, he can or should do at this sad juncture, he decides to head back to the high hide and make plans for his exploration into the canyon.

The mission remains his central concern, find the lost ship. With a last glance at the firepit, he acknowledges the Grays are closing in, just as Pennywell feared.

* * *

Hours later, a Gray alien enters the encampment in total darkness following the last coordinates transmitted by the missing scout.

The three-foot foot soldier dispatched as part of the search and rescue squad sent down to Earth to recover the missing alien studies the smoldering fire and discovers the pilot's charred skull and ashen remains. Incapable of remorse, the being hisses and turns toward the dwellings, large bulbous eyes aglow in the darkness.

Checking each hut, the dangerous alien finds dead humans in varying states of decomposition, as expected. Peering through the darkness into one of the primitive spaces, he finds two dead humans lying side-by-side, but one has a cloth draped over the head. Intrigued by the human's repose, unlike the others, it extends long and dexterous fingers to remove the clue. Stepping into a shaft of moonlight cutting through the canopy high over his bulbous head, he realizes it is a military-style hunting vest with multiple pockets looted of anything shiny or valuable. Upon closer inspection of the filthy garment, the alien deciphers a silken patch stitched into the collar, *PROPERTY OF _____ THE POWERS THAT BE* with the name, *STEVENS*, inked above the line, in neat block lettering.

Hissing contempt for the humans, the Gray acknowledges this low life named Stevens beat him to the punch. Worse yet, the dead savages held the secret location of an ancient crash site buried in this wretched jungle for millennia. Did the cannibals consume Stevens? It is impossible to know if the still-smoldering remains mixed with his dead colleague even belong to the vest's owner. Perhaps Stevens lost the garment while escaping, abandoning another human to stay behind for dinner. What a disaster. His superiors will not be pleased.

The Gray soldier knows the lost ship lies within reach, hidden within the steep mountainous terrain under the impenetrable jungle. A treasure trove of riches and relics within its massive cargo holds belong to the planet's once and future hegemonic masters. After deploying the lost ship's weaponized nuclear pathogen onto this vulgar world, his kind will achieve what a sky filled with Gork battlecruisers could not.

Annihilation of the human race.

Chapter Four:

The Family

Rachel | Le Tholonet, Provence
04:25 p.m. | September 16, 2044

A farmhand grabs a shotgun and jumps into his vintage pick-up truck, tracking a threatening craft's descent out of the clear-blue Provence sky before disappearing amid the rugged limestone below Montagne Sainte-Victoire's precipitous southern face. Bumping and jostling the vintage Nissan along a graveled lane, the grizzled Frenchman veers through vineyards with heavy clusters of mature grapes begging for harvesters. Gunning the 4-cylinder vehicle up a steep grade, he fishtails onto a ridgetop fire road overlooking a vale, re-establishing visual contact with the ship hovering a meter off a grassy pasture. Skidding to a stop at a fence line, he exits the cab, scurrying downhill, hunkering behind a gnarled oak tree. Eyeballing the floating craft 60 meters from his spot, he fumbles two shotgun shells from dirty overalls into his trusty 10-gauge. Squinting through the midday sun, he spies a silhouetted couple descending a lowered ramp through an ethereal blue haze from the black vessel's underbelly. The jittery farmer watches it burst skyward over the western horizon without a sound, spying humans—not scaly aliens—slinging packs over their shoulders and tromping across the muddy field past unimpressed bovine spectators.

The old man rises from his defiladed position, with the weapon aimed at the pair, demanding they halt, or he will shoot first and ask questions later.

The handsome couple raises arms in compliance while the blond woman sputters: *"Ne tirez pas!"*

"Yeah, what she said. We are the good guys."

The farmer spits and lowers the shotgun, "Americans. I should have known."

* * *

Rachel rides shotgun, and Owen holds on atop sacks of manure in the bed of the old farm truck for the bumpy return to the gated entrance of Villa St. Claire at the terminus of a narrow graveled lane off Rte Cézanne in the picturesque Provence commune of Le Tholonet.

After the farmer dumps them at a secluded gate, he kicks up late-afternoon dust, heading back to the main road with a wad of Euros in his overall pockets. Rachel shields her eyes, watching the truck disappear around the bend before finding Owen fumbling with the padlocked gate.

"Well, this sucks. It's locked."

"Owen, you don't have the key?"

"No. Do you?"

Dropping her bags in the dirt, she walks up to the 8-foot wrought iron fence, "Hoist me over. I'll see if there is an extra key inside the house."

"What if that is locked?"

"Then we will improvise."

Owen | Villa St. Claire

07:05 a.m. | September 17, 2044

Dawn breaks over the Provence countryside through opened French doors piercing the first rays of light into the darkened bedroom where Rachel's luggage lies open and scattered about. Owen scooches out of bed, rubs his eyes, and looks outside past fluttering sheers where a black and white cat perches on the top rail of the expansive Romanesque balcony littered with a month's worth of leaves, twigs, and acorns. "This place is filthy. What happened to the staff?"

Sticking a pin in that rumination, the rejuvenated new husband breathes in the fresh air and stretches. With a contented smile on his dimpled face, he decides a morning swim after an invigorating first night back in the honeymoon villa is the perfect way to start the day. Leaving his sexy bedmate snoring and twisted in the sheets, he dons flowery swim trunks from a dust-covered suitcase on a gilded settee where he left it weeks ago.

After snatching a towel from the palatial bathroom, Owen tiptoes out of the bedroom at the southern end of the 12,000+ square foot 2-story villa. On impulse, he passes the central staircase to explore the well-appointed game room loft, complete with an elegant mahogany billiards table. Pushing the 8-ball into a side pocket, he continues to a balcony overlooking the villa's impressive north hall with tall windows framing an unobstructed vista of Montagne Sainte-Victoire, "Somewhere up there, my well-planned life with Rachel veered off the rails."

Repressing PTSD with a hard swallow, the still-recovering 27-year-old former investment banker rubs the healing surgical scar on his stubbled head, "No. Hell no. This place is full of ghosts. Deal with it."

Still muttering under his breath, Owen pads barefoot down the curved staircase to the main foyer. Adjacent to the broken sidelight windowpane, his eyes land on the high back chair where Louie—the robot chauffeur—awaited a four-in-the-morning high-tech house call on that nightmarish first night in France. "Still, no. Fuck that memory, too."

Walking past a gallery's worth of landscapes and oil portraits adorning the villa's central hallway reminiscent of a haunted mansion, he pauses at double doors leading into the impressive library lined with books and manuscripts. The clock ticking atop a thick wood-beamed mantle over the stone fireplace beckons him toward a console under a Tiffany-style floor lamp stacked with World War Two volumes situated where he had left them weeks before. Sticking a pin in his decision not to relive the past, Owen hefts a World War 2 non-fiction book detailing the air war and settles into an oversized leather wingback. Flipping to a bookmarked section detailing Grandpa Neil's squadron and its exploits from North Africa to Corsica and beyond, he stares at a grainy black-and-white image of a P-47 Thunderbolt fighter plane with a mean-looking black scorpion painted on the engine cowling. "Christ, we left Neil's plane in that dank cavern with his remains inside the cockpit. I need to ask Rachel about that."

Slapping the book shut, he heads toward the French provincial chef's kitchen and its adjacent dining space dominating the back half of the villa's main floor. Flipping a light switch on reflex, he smirks, "Nothing. Of course."

Angling around the monstrous kitchen island's thick marble slab and gorgeous farmhouse sink under pot racks laden with copper cookware, he sees his arch-nemesis, an inert Cuisinart coffeemaker, "Well, I don't have to worry about wrestling with you. A bright side to everything, even no power."

Opening cabinets stacked with ceramic dishes, he locates

the mug collection and chooses one with Louie's cab company logo. Grabbing a copper kettle, he turns the cold tap on full blast, frowning as grayish water sputters and spurts before flowing clean. Letting the tap run, he lights a burner on the freestanding Viking gas stove before filling the pot, placing it on the thick iron grates, and heading for the pantry to find a jar of instant coffee.

* * *

With coffee and book in hand, Owen pushes massive sections of the fingerprinted and smeared disappearing glass sliders into the wall, opening the entire back of the villa to let the fresh morning air into the stale interior. Stepping onto the flagstone sundeck spotted and stained from the fruits of overhanging olive trees growing from raised planters encircling the amorphous outdoor space, he avoids trash and empty wine bottles littered amid the teak furniture toward the built-in outdoor grill. Lifting the lid, he finds bundled statements and ledgers burnt into an ashen heap atop the greasy grates.

Puzzled by how fast the place decayed in their one-month absence, Owen jogs down a flight of steps and winds along a cobblestone path under magnificent shade oaks alive with squirrels and chirping birds. From terraced levels below the sun-drenched Mediterranean villa, he sees the cat lying atop the master bedroom balcony rail, wondering if Rachel is asleep—the poor thing was exhausted.

Sipping lukewarm instant coffee, Owen reaches a fork in the path: tennis courts beyond overgrown flower and vegetable gardens and olive trees around the front of the main house to the left. His destination, the villa's fantastic pool, is down the terraced hillside to the right. Trekking onto the pebbled path under a canopy of oaks, he spies the pool house's red-tiled roof resolving through the dense undergrowth. Eager to make a splash, Owen's dusty feet hit the hardscaped sidewalk through an unlocked gate leading around the stucco structure to the aqua-blue saltwater pool terraced into the natural rock hillside with a waterfall, jacuzzi, and stunning southern view to the sea.

Sunshine sparkling off the clear water marred only by a few leaves quells curiosity about how the pool's solar-powered backup generators functioned in a world of fried technology: "As long as it works, who gives a fuck?" Setting his empty mug and book on a side table, Owen spreads the beach towel atop a chaise lounge and prepares for a cannonball plunge. Poised and ready after a few stretches to get the kinks out of his back, Owen steps to the edge and notices a sunken mass darkening the deep pool's pebbled bottom. "What the hell is that?"

* * *

Rachel sits at the butcher block dining table in the wide-open kitchen in shorts and one of Owen's Wharton t-shirts, watching an authoritative figure poke about outside with a cigarette dangling from his mouth in a detective's overcoat on a sunny 82-degree September day in the south of France. Owen plops beside her, crunching pretzels from a bag pulled from the pantry's unstocked shelves.

"How can you eat after what you saw?"

"What? The dead guy? Par for the course, baby."

"I hope this man doesn't think we had anything to do with it."

"He has my statement. Besides, what kind of murderer calls the cops on a trackable satellite phone?"

"A stupid one?"

"Damn straight."

Detective René Renault from the Gendarmerie Nationale in nearby Aix-en-Provence avoids wandering chickens loosed from their enclosure and clucking about, lifting the gas grill lid.

Owen tamps down a sudden paranoia, "Excuse me, detective. Remember I said I had opened that earlier."

The man smiles toward the Americans, "Yes, I remember." Ambling over in a cloud of cigarette smoke, he scoots out a heavy chair across from the Haigs, "Nice place. Too bad about the owner."

Owen blurts out more words, making Rachel cringe, "Funny story, I rented this place through Trip Advisor, so we never met the guy. Though apparently, he showed up in our absence at some point. Probably to guard against the looters."

The detective defuses the tension with an easy and disarming smile, "That is obvious, Monsieur. Given where you found his bloated body." Leaning back in his chair, "As I said, neither you nor your lovely bride is suspected of wrongdoing. We will soon have the sworn affidavit from the local farmhand with the vintage Nissan truck to vouch for your timeline." With a casual hand wave, he concludes, "Mere formalities, Mr. and Mrs. Haig, I assure you."

Rachel expresses genuine surprise, "You are sure the man at the bottom of the pool was the villa's owner?"

The man stubs out his smoke in an ashtray, "The deceased was Jacques St. Claire, the owner of this property and heir to a fortune, I might add."

Rachel turns on the feminine charms, "Would it be okay to ask how he died."

The Frenchman fingers the corner of his mustache, proffering a roguish smile at the young and beautiful blond, "Madam, Monsieur St. Claire tied 45 kilos of weight around his beltline and leaped into the deep end." Reaching for a new cigarette, he continues, "The toxicology will undoubtedly show drugs and alcohol, but the cause of death is obvious. He drowned."

Owen's mind raced, "Our lease is good through the end of this month. Can we stay here?"

"Monsieur et Madame, stay as long as you like. I care not. My superiors may require more clarification, and the coroner's team will likely need access to the grounds, but I wish you long and happy lives. You are recently married, no?"

"Uh, yes. The invasion happened right on the heels of our arrival in France."

"If you don't mind my asking, what prompted your departure and sudden return?"

Unsure what they were at liberty to say, Owen ad-libs, "It was me. I had to see North Africa. I am an old romantic, and Casablanca is one of my favorite movies, so off we went. Took a ferry across the Med right out of Marseilles."

"Yes, that must have been some journey; even before the invasion, travel to North Africa was ill-advised."

Rachel gives her husband an inquisitive glance before adding to the ridiculous, transparent fib, "We had an excellent guide to keep us out of trouble."

Renault chuckles and reaches for his pack of smokes, "It is immaterial; I was just curious. I could not help but notice you both appear to be recovering from something, a car accident, perhaps?" Standing out of his chair, he bows toward Rachel before shooting Owen a sly grin, "I also love that movie, especially Louie." A knuckle wrap on the wood tabletop indicates he is finished with their chat, "Don't get up. I can see myself out."

Owen and Rachel exchange furtive smiles, watching the tall man in the overcoat head toward the front doors. Almost home free, they see his backlit form pivot with a troubling thought furrowing his brow.

The detective's voice resonates back down the long hallway, "Since the alien attack, suicides have become commonplace. Human beings are not wired for overwhelming death and destruction. Not to mention the loss of modern conveniences, like the internet. Stay safe, Mr. and Mrs. Haig. Fortunate for you to have a functioning satellite phone. Otherwise, you would have dealt with that poor fellow yourselves."

The Haigs let the Frenchman's words marinate through the stillness as he retreats down the long central corridor to the opened front door. Afraid to move lest they burst out in laughter, more trenchant advice echoes through the villa's main floor, "I would get this glass fixed.

It is a miracle the place was not ransacked in your absence."

Owen breathes a sigh of relief, "Yeah, we'll call the landlord. Oh, no. Wait for it. He's dead."

Biting her lower lip to keep from laughing, Rachel shakes her head with a tsk-tsk while moving to the sink to rinse her cup, "Don't make fun of the dead, Owen. Bad juju."

A chicken wanders inside and perches on the edge of a leather-upholstered sofa in the great room.

"You know, Rachel, I like it here. We are keeping it weird. I'm gonna find the coop and get us some fresh eggs."

Rachel dries her cup with a dishtowel, contemplating the suave, sophisticated Detective Renault, "Talk about central casting."

Rachel | Villa St. Claire

09:35 a.m. | September 18, 2044

Owen vaults up the curved staircase and down the long hallway to the villa's private primary suite. Turning the ornate doorknob, he leans into the wooden door, almost throwing out his sore shoulder. Pushing it open while sliding a heavy suitcase propped against the opposite side, he angles into the ordered chaos. Stepping over a minefield of luggage, clothes, and shoes, he smiles toward his lovely wife—knee-deep in color-coordinated piles stacked atop the unmade bed, "Whatcha doing, Rach?"

Swiping her brow, she turns to her new partner in life, clutching a wrinkled ball of fabric that once was a favorite dress, "Everything we left behind in this mildewy room for the last month needs a wash. But with no electricity, what am I supposed to do? Put it all in wicker baskets and scrub it on rocks down by the river?"

"Uh, yeah, that is a problem." Nudging aside a pair of dirty underwear lying on the floorboards, "Man, it is hot."

"Uh, yeah. No breeze and over 90; you think so?"

"Reminds me of Libya." Struggling for the right words, acclimating to his sexy wife's domestic side, "We have soap and running water. I can help you hand wash your stuff."

Picking up a pair of striped boxers, "A lot of this is yours, you know."

"Hey, I need to put those back in the rotation." Looking down at the satellite phone in his hand, Owen remembers why he trekked upstairs to the far back end of the massive residence in the first place, "Oh yeah, the satellite phone Cowboy gave us started blinking. Do you remember what that meant?"

With an exasperated eye roll, Rachel drops the wrinkled garment atop a pile, "Jesus, Owen, you are a hopeless Luddite."

"And proud of it. Wanna see my membership card?"

"Just give me the damn phone." Smoothing a sweaty hand down the front of her army green tank top and shorts, Rachel takes their only form of communication with the outside world and places it on a side table next to a vase of wilted flowers.

"That green light means someone left us a holographic message."

"Oh yeah. Now what?"

"Well, dummy, I key in the code, and a little glowing human will spring up from that small lens like magic." Rachel folds a blond strand behind her ear, suppressing a laugh, studying Owen's sweaty face, "You really are like a little boy, aren't you?"

"If that is what turns you on, then yes. Yes, I am."

They turn in unison toward the device and wait. After a prolonged silence, Owen quips, "Did you key in the right numbers?"

"8-6-7-5-3-0-9"

After minutes in silence within the hot and muggy room, the line connects, and a faint glow springs ten inches upward, prompting Rachel to adjust the phone's placement to avoid the dying plant's dried leaves.

A pixelated bluish-hued human form, the size of a Ken doll, resolves through the staticky interference as garbled words emanate from the phone's tiny speakers, *"… you decided to join our merry band, welcome aboard. Mr. Cooper will return to pick you up on the 28th and fly here to Scotland, so we can meet in person. I will keep this brief as I am told long-winded phone calls are a thing of the past.*

I am reaching out because I have news that impacts you both: The Villa St. Claire is now part of the PTB real estate portfolio. Consider it a wedding gift. Use it as a base of operations if you will. And no, in case you are wondering, we did not kill Mr. St. Claire. Although his demise did not come as a surprise. Like the treasure trove of artwork under the estate, it's a story for another time.

One more thing … A caretaker will arrive in the next few days to manage the villa's daily operations and return the property to its former glory. Please afford him and his staff every courtesy."

That is all for now. Safe travels and see you soon."

The Pennywell hologram vanishes, leaving Owen and Rachel staring in silence.

Owen breaks the ice, "Wanna have sex?"

"What? No. Get out of here. I have to pick all of this up before some cleaning crew arrives. Shit. Shit."

"They work for us, Rachel, not the other way around. Just chill."

"I grew up surrounded by staff. I hated it. And did you say chill? It's like 105 in here."

"I thought you said 90."

Owen retreats onto the balcony under a hail of stinky underwear and socks. Safe from Rachel's fusillade of dirty laundry, he rests his arms on the Romanesque beam and gazes beyond courtyards past terraced slopes toward the pool house. Replaying Pennywell's message in his head, the reality that he is now the owner of a storied French villa in the heart of the Côte d'Azur smacks him square in the face. "Holy Christ, I wonder if this place was built atop one of those medieval wine cellars.

That would be cool, and I could really use a drink."

Nina | Gray battlecruiser
02:42 a.m. | September 19, 2044

"Like a worm burrowing into an apple."

"Seriously? That is disgusting, Nina."

"Yeah, Flynn, that is what it fucking feels like."

A backlit alien head moves above Nina Madsen's supine form, strapped to an icy slick horizontal table like a slab of meat. Her watery eyes meet the sadistic interrogator's cold stare before it blinks toward a scarecrow lurking in the corner, watching. *"The scarecrows are always hiding in the shadows."*

"Bloody hell, Madsen. If you looked like one of those fuckers, you would prefer to remain in the dark."

"I suppose. Ugh. Flynn! He's digging deeper. Ahh, man, it hurts."

"Hang in there, love. They can't find your comm chip. Keep the conversation going. We need to know what they know."

"Ow. Fucking ow!" Swallowing back the bile in her raspy throat, she slows her halted breaths in the stale frigid air and fixates on a complex of mechanical units high above her quaking form.

"Okay, here is what we know: We remain on the same stinking ship that hijacked us weeks ago. And we are alive. Nicole is in rough shape, and we have no clue what happened to our Astrid."

Without warning, the ugly scarecrow steps up to the table. *"Shit, Flynn, it's the old bad cop, bad cop routine."*

The creature looms above her frail, vulnerable body, blanched in the soft gauzy blueness, sliding massive ill-proportioned hands around both sides of her face. Its callous expression never changes, stimulating an intense shooting pain while the Gray interrogator looks on with an apathetic bug-eyed stare, anticipating her head to explode.

After agonizing minutes, the scarecrow releases its painful grip on her nervous system and steps back. The odd human hybrid tilts its head at an angle like a confused dog before engaging in a telepathic conversation with the Gray on a frequency she cannot hear.

"Are you still there? Come in, Nina?"

"It hurt so bad. The bastard was so close."

"Hang in there, Nina. They don't have a fucking clue. You are …"

Nina cuts off Flynn's telepathic words of encouragement, *"They left. Just like that."*

Sitting up, she finds the room empty and the portal wide open. Loosening her restraints, she slides her bare bottom off the countertop. Her feet hit the same cold mesh decking found throughout the alien craft. Swiping dirty red hair from her face, she glances around the empty room, *"What the fuck? I guess I can leave."*

"Do you know how to get back to our cell block?"

"No, Flynn. They didn't leave me with a ship map like a Norwegian cruise."

"Aha! Funny. I am glad to see your wonderful sense of humor remains intact." After a slight pause and an audible giggle, he adds, *"I'll meet you on the Lido deck with a pitcher of margaritas."*

Peeking out the threshold into the darkened corridor, Nina swallows real fear and anxiety, *"All joking aside, Flynn. I have no clue how to get back, and the pervs took my suit. I'm naked."*

"That's cold and kind of hot at the same time."

"Flynn, you are a veritable laugh riot." Stepping into the hall, she heads right—for no reason—and slides along the dull blue wall.

Reaching another doorway, she peers inside and gasps.

"What is it, Nina? What do you see?"

"I think I see Astrid inside a room."

Nina's heart races, pushing the heavy door inward and moving toward the beautiful Scottish lass lying face-up atop a slick metal counter. Upon approach, she finds the biracial woman has familiar tubes snaking from limp arms at her sides and her long, bruised legs spread wide, dangling off the table's sharp, unforgiving edges at her banged-up knees. Stepping across sticky wetness, an unmistakable metallic smell overwhelms her senses, realizing the dark, confined space is soaked in blood. Astrid's blood. *"Jesus Flynn, what a mess. Astrid is dead."*

"What? What did you say about Astrid? Nina! No. Check her pulse."

Nina presses quivering fingertips on Astrid's neck, feeling for a pulse. Nothing.

Noting an iridescent cloth draped across the test pilot's eyes and nose, she steels herself to lift it and peer underneath, *"Oh my God. They took her beautiful eyes. Why would they do that?"*

The shiny cloth drops to the floor as the last vestiges of Nina's resolve crumble, and she cries. *"Flynn, I can't do this anymore. I can't. They win. I want to go with Astrid. This is too much."*

"Ah, bloody hell. Not Astrid. I loved that sweet girl. She was the best."

Nina senses another entity inside the room but does not care anymore.

"I, friend. I, friend. The one you call Astrid died during labor. I am sorry. It is me, Zint. I take you back now. We must go."

Something inside Nina's head snaps as she spins toward the 3-foot alien, fists clenched, ready to strangle the little monster.

Zint holds his ground, *"I, friend. Remember?"* Presenting a clean PTB flight suit from their craft, *"I brought you this. It is clean."*

Taking one last look at her friend and colleague, she unclenches her fists and sighs, stifling more tears. After slipping into the two sizes too-big jumpsuit, she turns toward her little ally, *"Take me back."*

*   *   *

A mechanized waste collector enters the dank blood-smeared delivery room, lifts Astrid off the table, and dumps her lifeless Earthen vessel into a receptacle atop garbage and debris. Rolling out the door and down corridors, past aliens unfazed by the sight of another dead human, it takes an elevator to the battlecruiser's bottommost level. Grinding atop a platform in a sealed-off chamber, wheels lock in place, and the floor lowers outside the ship's keel and arcs down and out at a perpendicular angle from thick mechanical arms. The garbage droid dumps Astrid and the waste into the vacuum of space and proceeds to elevate back inside to collect its next load.

The veteran PTB test pilot who dreamt of outer space from the time she could walk and talk as a young waif in Glasgow drifts into the darkness. The massive hull glides above her before moving off, silhouetting her tiny body amidst a shimmering ocean of stars.

Andrew | PTB HQ, Scotland
04:00 a.m. | September 19, 2044

An eagle soars over a plush bed perched atop a red sandstone butte high above a breathtaking sunrise vista of Monument Valley projecting in glorious detail. Andrew watches the raptor riding a column of air in the early-morning starry expanse, raising his tousled head from a pillow. Feeling Number 8's warm form snuggled against his left side underneath the soft light-blue sheet, he watches her sleep like a fallen angel. Number 11, bookending him on the right, flips onto her side, pushing her pert bottom into him while snatching a corner over her bare shoulder. Extricating his left arm from under the sheets, he caresses 11's elegant neck with a smile widening across his handsome mug, admiring her cerulean hair.

An obnoxious alarm breaks the spell, almost startling the unflappable robot. Swiping a virtual screen, the C-Class Kobayashi creation sees the culprit standing outside his locked office door, "Yes, Professor King, what can I do for you?"

"We need to talk. I have more information about Stevens." After a long pause, he asks, "Why is your office locked?"

Andrew pauses, considering how best to handle the sister act in his bed while dimming the holographic desert scene back to his private inner sanctum's off-white, unadorned walls with a telepathic command.

"Richard, I unlocked the door. Please come in and pour some coffee; I will join you in a few minutes."

Listening for a reply, Andrew hears a muffled response through his keen auditory senses before closing the screen and jostling 8 and 11 awake. "Rise and shine, sleepyheads; we have company."

Number 11 slides out of bed and stretches her long arms to the ceiling before arcing her lissome form backward, touching the floor, and performing a perfect backflip. Swiping unruly blue bangs off her forehead, she turns to her bedmates with an effortless smile, "Good morning, Andrew. Good morning, 8. Thank you for the invitation."

Number 8, the enigmatic thief who stole Andrew's logic-driven decorum and replaced it with a healthy dose of testosterone-fueled lust for life, watches 11 pad across the low-lit room, sifting through a twisted heap of clothes looking for something to wear. Not wanting the party to end, the brunette ducks under the sheets, fondling Andrew back to full vigor with her nimble hands and the tip of her pink tongue before straddling atop his lean form and pushing him back inside with a pleasurable moan.

Sliding into a t-shirt and jeans, Number 11 sighs, and heads to the door, "Thank you, Andrew. I had a good time." Smiling at the silly look contorting his handsome face while her sister performs a rhythmic dance under the sheets, "You two were made for each other. I'll stall Doctor King until you can come up for air."

* * *

Richard waits in Andrew's office with a mug of coffee too hot to drink cradled in his thick hands. Hearing a door open, he expects

Pennywell's robot valet; instead, his blue-haired assistant enters the room with a mischievous grin while sauntering barefoot toward the door in pajama shorts and a plain white tee.

Placing his coffee on a table, he stands, masking bewilderment, unaccustomed to seeing the replicant out of her signature white lab coat. Her devil-may-care elan, svelte figure, and supple perky breasts under the thin cotton shirt left nothing to the imagination, creating a discomfiting yet alluring presence in the dim-lit office space.

"Is everything all right, Number 11?"

Putting a hand on her hip, she blows blue bangs off her forehead and leans close to whisper to the older man, "Doctor King? Would you happen to have a cigarette?"

"Afraid not. I quit years ago."

"Oh. I see. That's all right. I read that humans smoke after sex. It is not a requirement, right?"

"Far from it, my dear." Richard glances toward the closed door to Andrew's private quarters, "Remember, you never have to do anything you don't want to do. Your perfect body is also your temple. Treat it well."

"Thank you, Doctor King. I should return to the lab and continue decoding the alien messages."

"You do that. I will join you after I have a word with Andrew." Richard considers his next move watching her pivot to exit the darkened office before speaking again, "Oh, and 11, *hamsters spin the wheels of time.*"

"I'm sorry, what?"

"Being there and not being there are two sides of the same coin."

The young beauty freezes in place mid-turn with an outstretched hand reaching for the door.

"Hmm … The hamster line was written for Number 12. How stupid of me."

King steps behind the vivacious robot and pushes a finger into the nape of her neck, causing her head to unseal and spring apart like a tackle box. The scientist rises onto the balls of his feet to examine exposed portions of her cybernetic complex of organic tissues synthesized with mechanics enveloping a quantum cerebral core. Startled by the rapid physiological transformations rewiring the synthetic brain inside her pretty noggin, Richard mutters, "Oh my. What is happening?"

11's sexual awakening represents the latest step in her metamorphosis from an automaton into a sentient being. Concurrently, her whimsical nature, curiosity, frailties, and yearnings shape a singular essence divergent from her sisters. Like advanced replicants performing tasks from mundane to sublime around the planet, she is superior to humans in every conceivable fashion—except perhaps lacking a soul—a contentious debate fomenting among the PTB's theologians.

Richard recalls Kobayashi's sober warning: It is only a matter of time before humanity becomes a tangential nuisance in an unstoppable AI-fueled quintessential reality. "Fascinating and terrifying."

Surmising the robotic dalliances as news to himself but possibly not to Pennywell, he reaches into his jacket and produces a tool pouch. The professor fumbles it open and removes a surgical scalpel. With a deft hand, he slices a wafer-thin sample of pinkish tissue from 11's glistening core and seals it inside a tube for further study.

Tapping her head closed, he watches seams meld together and vanish into her smooth perfect skin. Repeating her phrase backward spurs the synthetic femme fatale back to consciousness.

"I'm still here?"

Number 11's innocent doe-eyed gaze reminds Richard of her tragic prototype, an elegant and graceful woman with an ancient biblical name. Sarah.

Standing before her spitting image, except for the bright blue hair, he sighs, "Yes, my dear, you were heading back to the lab."

Watching her leave, Richard reclines back in his chair and sips the lukewarm coffee as Andrew's bedroom door opens again, allowing a fully-clothed Number 8 to make a beeline for the corridor past Richard.

"Hi, Doctor King. Bye, Doctor King."

On the heels of her hasty exit, Andrew, sporting his usual black mock turtleneck and jeans, walks into the office and moves behind his desk. Seated with a smile directed toward the venerable man of science, staring back with a shit-eating grin, he checks the cube hidden in the side drawer before addressing his guest, "What can I do for you, Richard?"

"Why does Superman wear pink pajamas on Tuesdays?"

Owen | Villa St. Claire
12:03 p.m. | September 20, 2044

A month after his near-death experience beneath the Giza Plateau, a recovering Owen Haig stepped across a fallen log and wiped his brow in the midday Mediterranean heat, exploring the Provence estate's 10+ hectares of forested hills pocked with vineyards and orchards. Pushing through lingering aches and pains, he determines not to waste a second of this reprieve from the terrible post-invasion world by familiarizing himself with the grounds surrounding the newest PTB satellite HQ.

"Maybe I'll put up a sign: *Crazed conspiracy nuts apply within.*"

Hiking uphill along a wooded path sending rabbits scurrying for the underbrush, Owen breaks into a jog and reaches the property's northern boundary at a deserted Rt. Cezanne. Heading west, he finds the caretaker's residence hidden in the trees.

Stepping onto the front porch, he enters the stucco and red-tile abode's wide-open front door and discovers the place in shambles from wanton vandalism, "Well, shit. What a mess."

Looted of everything not nailed down, the floorboards covered in trash and debris, and the walls spray-painted with French graffiti, "Not sure what that says, but I bet it is nasty."

Adding the caretaker's house to a growing list in his stubbled noggin, Owen pulls the front door shut on bent hinges and retraces his path toward the villa, musing whether Rachel scrounged up anything for lunch.

Trekking down the wooded path, the former banker considers the world gone mad, yet the onslaught of post-invasion looters spared the villa. "Good old Jacques must have seen the carnage and had the foresight to hire armed security."

While the theory made sense, it seemed out of character for a self-absorbed hedonist like Jacques St. Claire to lift a finger to preserve the family estate. Nonetheless, Detective Renault was on to something with his broken window observation. Better add finding a local glazier to the swelling to-do list.

*****

Vaulting up hardscaped flagstone steps past ostentatious lion statues that appear out of character with the rustic vibe, Owen heads across the sun-dappled patio and enters the chef's kitchen. "Rachel, I'm back!"

After an extended pause listening for a reply, he shrugs, "Looks like a party of one for lunch today."

Featured in *Architectural Digest* in its early 2000s heyday when the St. Claire clan held extravagant parties entertaining the beautiful people summering on the Côte d'Azur, the estate fell into disrepair after multiple scandals rocked the family's fortunes and the patriarch's passing at 92.

Within the past decade, Jacques St. Claire, the family scion, discovered at the bottom of the pool, renovated the structure, and modernized the living space to attract a new breed of vacationers interested in a genuine Provence experience—and willing to pay over 7,000 per night for the privilege. He transformed the family estate into a veritable cash cow to support his heroin addiction and playboy lifestyle to the day the Earth stood still. Since no note was found, his death remains shrouded in mystery.

From Owen's POV, the modernizations made the place livable while maintaining its Provence architectural aesthetic and rustic charm with a few odd exceptions like the lion statues. However, years of short-term renters had taken a toll. Walking through the farmhouse kitchen, his favorite room, he enters the pantry, sifting through pasta boxes, dried beans, lentils, and rice in hopes of finding a can of tuna or sardines and crackers, anything that does not require a pot. Taking stock of the bare shelves in the darkened space, his stomach growls, "We will need a grocery trip. I can't eat another bowl of plain white rice."

Lighting the propane lantern, he found on a shelf, he probes farther back into the pantry past discarded chairs and tables stacked in the ad hoc storage space, hoping to find a hidden cache of the good stuff: blocks of French cheeses, wines, and meats. Hell, cheese wiz. Anything. Behind the cobwebby clutter, he sees a red paint-chipped door set into an exposed section of the villa's original stonework. "Ah, where does this spooky door lead?"

Stirring dust motes into the musty stillness, Owen slides through and around the heaped furniture to open the door. Shining the light into the pitch-blackness, his face lights up with a broad dimpled smile, "I knew this place had to have an old wine cellar."

Worn and splintered wooden stairs groan and creak under his weight, descending into the darkness. Brushing against the spidery dry-stacked limestone foundation, Owen takes the narrow steps one at a time in the flickering light. Over 20 feet down, his shoes touch the uneven cobbled floor. Venturing into the cellar, he notes its resemblance to the medieval subterranean image in his fertile mind. Training the lantern above his head illuminates an arched stone ceiling buttressed by thick oak beams. With the dim lantern lighting the way, hunger and curiosity push him deeper into the cavernous dry space past shelving carved into the limestone bedrock littered with dust-covered empty bottles forgotten among the cobwebs and mouse droppings. Crunching across broken glass, he feels cold air emanating from a six-foot fissure in the stone foundation at the far end of the disappointing St. Claire estate wine cellar.

Owen checks the propane canister attached to the lantern, hoping it has enough gas to keep him from utter darkness, "Been there. Done that."

With the lantern dimmed to its lowest setting to conserve fuel, Owen reaches the back wall and peers inside, making out a long narrow void, "Pretty sure this is where I would lose Rachel."

Owen squats low, and duck walks to the other end into an echoing limestone grotto akin to the mountaintop cavern where Grandpa Neil and his fighter plane rest in peace. With hunger pangs forgotten, the 27-year-old takes purposeful steps, cognizant that a fall could set back his recovery. "No one knows I am down here. Smart, Owen, Real smart." Unable to see more than a few feet before him, Owen lets out a wry laugh resonating into the dark, "Caves. Why does it always have to be caves."

A wrong footfall lands him onto his backside, sliding out-of-control down slick limestone before hitting rock bottom with a teeth-rattling jolt. Uninjured, except for his pride, he mutters a curse and fumbles for the gas knob to turn the lantern's brightness to full blast so he can see.

Surrounding his shaky stance, a trove of paintings, sculptures, and assorted antiquities illuminate before his eyes. Thunderstruck by the discovery, he wanders through the plunder, careful not to step on anything priceless. Pausing at an artwork-laden crate, he pulls out an unframed landscape and holds it under the light. The ubiquitous name painted at the bottom edge catches his eye: "Cezanne. Can this be real?" Flipping through more canvasses, like a bargain bin in an art gallery, he finds famous and not-so-famous—at least to Owen's limited knowledge—works of fine art, all priceless, nonetheless.

Hoisting himself atop a ledge, Owen's flickering light widens across more crates of purloined paintings amid marbled masterpieces and bronzed beasts stretching into the shadows before a sheer wall inside the cavernous space.

Reconnoitering where he came in, Owen decides he has seen enough, "Rachel must be wondering what happened to me." Finding hand and footholds, he climbs the steep, slippery limestone. Pausing to catch his breath atop a precipitous slippery shelf, he spots more containers. A chill goes up his spine, finding swastikas burnished into the three-foot cubed wooden boxes. More than a little creeped out, his curiosity is nonetheless piqued. Producing a pocketknife from his grimy pants, he pries off a lid and pulls out fistfuls of desiccated straw packing, revealing rows of bottles racked inside. He reads a label with the light held close: "Chateau Lafite Rothschild, 1920." Counting the containers, the banker with a head for numbers and an affinity for expensive wine calculates that if all ten crates are equivalent, he is standing before a wine collection valued in the millions.

Owen lifts the upper half of the top rack and takes a bottle. "Finder's fee."

* * *

Climbing the stairs with the priceless Bordeaux held firm in his grasp, he passes through the red door into the pantry and places the lantern back on the shelf where he found it. Reconsidering the rice, now that he has the wine to help wash it down, he hears Rachel's voice in conversation with someone, "Shit, the caretaker must have arrived."

Adjusting his vision to the afternoon brightness, he reenters the kitchen, still cradling the bottle while sidling around the island, and locks eyes with Rachel seated at the kitchen table facing a back-turned individual with short jet-black hair.

Owen starts to speak, but Rachel interrupts, "Hello, Owen. What have you been up to? I looked all over but couldn't find you. Our new caretaker arrived."

"I can see that."

The mystery man stands out of the kitchen table chair and turns to formally introduce himself to the estate's dirty and sweaty new owner.

"Bonjour, Monsieur Haig. My name is Louie. I am the new caretaker."

A stunned Owen almost drops the expensive bottle to the tiled floor. Brushing a cobweb from the side of his head, he stares at the distinguished Frenchman with a signature mustache in utter shock and amazement. "Louie? Is that you?"

Louie | Villa St. Claire
08:15 p.m. | September 21, 2044

Dressed to the nines, Owen in a suit and tie and Rachel in a flowing floral maxi dress with a plunging neckline and jeweled Italian leather sandals, descend the long curved staircase, cross the foyer, and enter the north corridor toward the villa's storied ballroom.

Distant echoes of ghostly revelers tickle Rachel's diamond-studded ears through the darkness, harkening to notorious dinner parties that devolved into drunken bacchanals during the St. Claire estate's glory days. Meanwhile, a faint wafting aroma of baked bread fills her with a comforting warmth; green eyes aglow with a mesmerizing sparkle, admiring multi-hued refractions twinkling crystal chandeliers inside the opulent candlelit space.

A bipedal servant bot sporting a black bow tie breaks the spell, bursting from the kitchen and hustling between empty tables to greet the guests of honor. Having met the quad-armed six-foot mechanical wonder and its two siblings that will operate under Louie's direction earlier that day, Owen is struck by their efficiency, agility, and disquieting resourcefulness.

"Welcome, Monsieur et Mademoiselle. Your table is ready; please follow me."

Owen puts a hand at his wife's thin waist and replies, "Lead the way, garçon."

Rachel takes in the immaculate table set for two centered in the cavernous hall, nodding her approval. Leaning close to her husband, she whispers, "This is so weird."

"Roll with it, Rachel. It is our new reality. Plus, I am starving."

The robot extends an arm to assist Rachel into her chair while placing a napkin on the lithe woman's lap and extending a third arm to aid the gentleman, who raises a hand to say, "I'm fine, thanks."

The robot fills crystal water glasses and departs for the kitchen.

Reveling in each other's company in the ultra-romantic setting, "You know, Owen, we have not enjoyed a quiet dinner since before our wedding."

Lifting his glass, he smiles at his bride and raises a toast, "To us. I love you, Rachel, with every fiber of my being. Thanks for being my rock. I never would have survived without your help."

Rachel clinks his glass above candles flickering in a floral centerpiece, "To us."

"Don't look now, but here comes Louie, in full the maître d' mode."

Dressed in a tuxedo, the synthetic C-Class humanoid robot approaches the table, "Bonjour, Haigs." Perceiving tension in the room, he proffers a confident smile. "I appreciate that my appearance is disconcerting to you both. However, I am a different build from your former chauffeur. My cybernetic upgrades render the possibility of a system breach near impossible." Scanning the couple's body temperatures, he considers the matter closed, "Enough of that, for now. I have the special Bordeaux uncorked and ready to pour. Madame? Monsieur?"

The black-tie bot reappears on cue with the uncorked bottle in a nimble mechanical grip. Filling twinkling crystal stemware without spilling a drop, it places the bottle on the table and produces a basket of fresh-baked biscuits and local-sourced grape jam with its multitasking appendages.

Louie supervises the servant bot, watching its every move, "Thank you, Sven; that will be all for now."

Owen looks across at Rachel, mouthing, "Sven?"

Louie ignores the human's childish impertinence, "Unfortunately, current circumstances have left the estate's larders lacking. However, the basic ingredients are present, and the estate grounds are rich with possibilities if one knows where to look. With that said, I am preparing a Lapin a La Cocotte for tonight's main course, followed by fresh-picked berries and cream for dessert; in the meantime, please enjoy the bread and wine."

Owen watches him leave, "The new guy may look like Louie, but he has none of his fun-loving personality."

"Yeah, kind of formal, where Louie was more of a common man."

Owen sips the Bordeaux, "Hmm … 1920 was a good year."

Rachel laughs, "Oh, okay. Now you are a wine expert. You do know what's for dinner, right?"

"Lapin something … I don't know. You took the French lessons, you tell me."

"Rabbit stew."

"You can't be serious. Like the old-timey Bugs Bunny cartoons?"

"If that helps you, Owen, then sure, just like Elmer Fudd." Rachel sips the pricy Bordeaux and laughs, "It is like I am having a romantic candlelit dinner with my little brother."

"That's dark. On the plus side, Rachel. The PTB health plan will probably cover your psychotherapy." He takes a long drink and shoots her a sly, dimpled grin, "With the emphasis on psycho."

Rachel tamps a light-headed swoon after only a few sips on an empty stomach. Conjuring a suitable riposte to the psycho jibe, she reaches for the basket as an ethereal presence manifests out of thin air behind Owen and proceeds through empty tables toward the back end of the hall.

Rachel drops the basket and spills her water glass across the white linen table service, tracking the phantasm to the draped windows. Feeling her grip on reality loosen, she watches the transparent radiance pass through the thick stone wall into the overgrown courtyard fronting a two-story glass conservatory. Oblivious to the mess, her wide-eyed gaze fixates on Owen, repositioning the breadbasket away from the water spill, "Did you see that?"

"Shoot, honey, what a mess." Glancing up, he double-takes at the distressed expression on his wife's beautiful face.

Lifting her wine glass, she peers inside and sets it down, "Must be the wine."

"Jesus, Rachel, you are pale as a ghost."

Rachel | Villa St. Claire
03:32 a.m. | September 22, 2044

After Louie's dinner, the Bordeaux, and a local Rosé with dessert, the uninhibited newlyweds repaired to the privacy of their second-floor retreat, leaving a trail of clothes, shoes, and underwear in their wake.

Hours later, Owen snores under the covers, dead to the world.

Rachel lies uncovered on her back with hands clasped atop her flat belly in a pink Chrysalis tee and pajama shorts, also sound asleep.

A warm gust scatters dried leaves from the balcony through the open French doors, stirring the black and white cat, dubbed Mittens, and bolting Rachel upright in the moonlit room. Blond locks blow across the doe-eyed trance on her alabaster face as she angles her feet onto the floor, crunching across leaves and sticks toward darkness beyond the bedroom door. Padding barefoot down the staircase, she bisects the foyer into the central hallway past dour oil portraits toward the kitchen.

"Hello, Mrs. Haig."

The somnambulant Rachel pivots to the voice, finding an apparition seated at the butcher block table, "Who are you?"

"I am Jacques St. Claire, the former owner of this dump. By the way, I see your husband stumbled upon my secret art stash. Good show."

"What are you doing here?"

"You ask a lot of questions."

"That may be true. I saw you earlier in the ballroom. What do you want?"

"What I want is of little consequence. The question is, what do you want?

"How about being left alone to lead a normal life."

"Listen to yourself. Do you hear how awful and boring that sounds? No. It is impossible for someone blessed with your abilities to be normal. You were never normal, Rachel."

"My abilities are gone. You should know that without me saying it out loud. My hands hurt."

"Mademoiselle, your suffering and pain will lead to something wonderful."

"This is insane. I am losing my mind, plain and simple."

Jacques stands, sliding a heavy chair backward in the process. *"I never liked this fucking kitchen table set. It is too cumbersome and does not match the French Provincial decor."*

"Oh, I don't know, I kind of like it. Did you bring me down here to chat about interior decorating?"

"No. Of course not. You were never meant for such mundanities. In fact, despite your accomplishments to date, your fate lies before you. Not behind you under the pyramids."

"Uh-huh. What the fuck was in that wine?"

Jacques laughs, *"It is not the wine. Look at your hands, Rachel."*

Opening her hands, palms up, her dark green eyes reflect concentric scars delineated in luminous blue hues, spiraling into infinity. "What is happening to me?"

"Did the one called Neil Alexander, your Grandpa, mention the blue spark?"

"No. What is a blue spark?"

"Humanities' future." The apparition vanishes into the ether like it was never there, leaving Rachel alone in the dark kitchen.

Moments later, the sleeping beauty stirs awake and freaks out, hunching into a protective pose, "What the hell? Where am I?" Checking herself, she brushes long strands from her face and retreats back toward the stairs and the safety of her room, terrified of what lies waiting in the dark.

* * *

Sitting in a simple wooden chair outside the pantry door in the chef's kitchen, Louie eavesdrops on the sleepwalking Mrs. Haig's end of the paranormal chat with great interest. Watching her hasty exit, the über-advanced Kobayashi product raises a thick black eyebrow, considering the woman's revelatory utterance of the magic words, *blue spark.*

Pennywell | PTB HQ, Scotland
09:00 a.m. | September 22, 2044

At the head of the table inside a well-appointed conference room far beneath sheep grazing across bucolic Lowland pastures, Artemus Pennywell pushes aside a mug of bitter, dark-roasted black coffee and yells out the door, "Andrew! What has gotten into you? Can I get a decent fucking cup of coffee?" With another muttered curse, he turns to a grid of virtual screens to continue the meeting with The Council, scattered around the planet after their Kumbaya moment fending off Pike's horde of multinational invaders at the PTB's proverbial gates. "Now then. Where were we? Ah, yes, Viraj Patel. You are up. I assume governments and NGOs have a grip on the basics by now."

Viraj Patel touches his mic and produces a telegenic smile, "Hello, everyone! Uh, yes, in a broad sense, that is accurate. The distribution of necessities is uneven, and bad actors exploit the usual corruption. On a positive note, the Mumbai factory is online, churning out microchips at a pre-invasion level. With our autonomous fleets spread wafer-thin, every truck, chopper, and plane back in operation means food, water, and medicine, reaching desperate people cut off from civilization for a month."

Pennywell leans back and shakes his head in disgust, "Think how much farther ahead we would be if not for Griffin Pike."

Viraj leans into the screen and lowers his tone, "Can I tell you what has shocked me the most in my travels?"

The Brady Bunch assemblage of pixelated faces nods in unison. Gabby reappears on her screen with a tri-colored spaniel perched on her lap, "What did I miss?"

Olivia Paquet coos, "Ah, Gabby, is that your little man?"

"Yep. This is Indy. Say hi, Indy."

Never a fan of these virtual chat sessions, Pennywell quells the small talk before it gets out of hand, "Miss Gabreski, Miss Paquet, save the dog talk for another time. Patel, proceed."

Viraj chuckles, "That is one lucky pooch. Uh, okay, where was I? Oh yeah. Believe it or not, most folks around the globe had no clue what had happened. They never saw a Gork ship or heard any explosions. In a nutshell, one day, everything worked as advertised; the next, everything stopped working. Since the Gorks left in the dead of night over Europe, many assumed the Chinese or Iranians finally made good on their EMP threats."

Ernest Gann chimes in, "That makes sense considering the enemy concentrated their attacks on world capitals and major population centers. Folks living in rural settings and most countries south of the Equator never knew what hit them."

Speaking into a handheld device from a PTB freighter's rocking and rolling bridge plowing through rough seas in the Gulf of Aden, Aisha Ayad interjects, "Can we move on and stop navel-gazing on the past?"

Pennywell feigns annoyance but is thrilled his security chief has rediscovered her moxie, "Are we boring you, Aisha?"

"I left Somalia with multiple reports of Grays harvesting entire villages of people. They are ramping up the abductions at an alarming rate. Something is happening. We need to refocus our efforts on foiling another invasion. Any word from Stevens?"

"Ah, the question on everyone's mind. No. I have Richard assembling a new Amazon expedition. I need your people focused on Earthbound enemies, like the Chinese. Your concern for the Sub-Saharan African countries losing entire villages is duly noted. Gabby, work with your UN counterparts to reinforce the hardest-hit areas. The little gray fuckers will return to the same places if no one stops them. Aisha, it is good to have you back. Please be safe on your travels through the region."

A monstrous wave crashes over the freighter's bow as Aisha salutes, "You know it, Chief."

Andrew enters the room with a new PTB mug, "Here you go, Artemus. Perhaps one day you will meet my dear friend, the coffeemaker."

Speaking to no one in particular, Pennywell shrugs with a dramatized sigh, "You all have no idea of the rampant insubordination I put up with.

Gabby's dog squirms off her lap as she scrunches her pert nose and peers through her screen beyond Pennywell toward Andrew's lean and fit form moving past in the background, "I don't know for sure, but in my experience, guys projecting that kind of cockiness just got laid."

Pennywell breaks into uncontrollable laughter, "Gabby, my dear, as usual, you find a way to make me laugh." Turning to his Kobayashi-built valet, "Did you hear that, Andrew? Gabreski thinks you are having regular sex."

Controlling his outward reaction while alarm bells clamor inside his synthetic head, "Yes, sir, I heard her. I need to speak to Richard. Please excuse me."

As soon as Andrew vacates the room, Pennywell's joviality evaporates, replaced by a serious-faced expression piercing through his lens, "Miss Gabreski, how did you know?"

Taken aback by Pennywell's legendary stare, Gabby's eyes widen, "How did I know what?"

Richard | PTB HQ, Scotland
02:51 p.m. | September 23, 2044

Richard paces around a table covered in satellite photographs of the Brazilian Amazon jungle, maps, and his hardbound copy of Charles Pike's notebook. He hears heated voices in a full-throated argument echoing down the long corridor while making final adjustments to meticulous bulleted notes.

"Bollocks to that. Give me back my smokes!"

"This is a climate-controlled underground facility. Smoking is not allowed."

"Bloody hell, this place is a maze. Where is Professor King hiding?"

Richard leans out the door, "Thank you, Number 16; I will take it from here. Mr. Pembroke, please come in."

The imposing six-foot freelance mercenary fills the doorway, looking into the claustrophobic bright-lit room at the papers spread across the table. "Ugh, that's right. The fucking Amazon." Searching deep pockets for another pack of cigarettes in his olive green army jacket, he turns with a sly smile, "What say we scoop up your shit and head outside? It is a lovely day, and I need a smoke."

Looking at his neat chronological presentation, Richard scratches his head, "Yeah, sure. I could use some fresh air."

* * *

On the bench atop a rocky escarpment overlooking the castle's crumbled ramparts and a decimated Edinburgh on the horizon, Richard clutches the papers tight to his chest against another chilly gust of wind off the North Sea. "It is windier than I thought. Perhaps not the best idea."

Pembroke purses a cigarette between his thin lips, "Allow me, Doctor King." Grabbing the thick stack of papers from King's grasp, he flings it into the air and laughs, watching it scatter in the winds across the green pastures. Taking a long, satisfying puff, a wide grin creases his weathered face, marred by a ruddy, pocked burn scar from the left eye and temple down the cheek to his strong bearded jawline, "There. Now we can talk like men. In my experience, paper trails get people killed. Rule number one when engaging my services: no paper."

Flummoxed by the mercenary's impulsiveness, Richard counters, "Those papers contained proprietary information."

"Precisely my point." Pembroke stares at his new friend noting his thick charcoal hair ruffling in the wind, "We have met before, Richard. Is it true you are over 100 years old?"

Feeling any last semblance of authority fluttering off in the strong gale like yesterday's fish wrap, King straightens and pulls on his corduroy coat collar, "122, if you must know. But I don't feel a day over 50."

"Blimey. So, the stories are true. Well. I am impressed. I also understand you had a hand in my new legs." Pembroke drops his trousers around his ankles, revealing shiny metallic mechanized legs from the hips down.

Richard nods, "Yes, that is my handiwork. Kobayashi designed the parts for service bots. It was my idea to use them as prosthetics for amputees like yourself."

Pembroke hitches his pants and lights another cigarette, offering the pack to Richard. "Care for one, Doctor?"

"I quit years ago, but since death is an abstraction, why not."

Pembroke produces a torch lighter, and Richard leans forward to take a long drag, blowing smoke into the stiff breeze, "Sublime." Studying the filtered cigarette in the crook of his thick fingers, he muses, "I do miss life's little pleasures."

The mercenary plops beside King, crossing his robot legs at a jaunty angle. "Excellent; now that we understand each other, let's discuss your little Amazon excursion."

Louie | Villa St. Claire
07:35 a.m. | September 27, 2044

Mittens paws at Owen's face, purring like a motorboat, "Good kitty, you take care of the place while we're gone."

Rachel's messy head rises from the pillow and checks the time with a groan before rolling over and curling into a ball, "I am going to kill that sack of fur."

"Don't listen to the mean lady, Mittens. She is always grumpy in the morning before she has her cereal."

"Fuck off, the both of you. I am not getting enough sleep."

Owen swings his feet off the bed and lifts the cat in his arm, "Come with me, Mittens. Let's leave the cranky lady alone and see what the robots made for breakfast."

Rachel pulls the pillow over her head as Owen steps around packed suitcases awaiting tomorrow's departure and closes the door behind him.

The cat jumps from his arms and bounds out the wide-open sliders as Owen enters the chef's kitchen and interrupts Louie admonishing one of the robots over dust on the expansive marble counters. "What's up, Louie? Cut Sven some slack; this place is a dust collector."

Louie turns to Owen with a bemused look on his long mustached face and a hint of condescension in his French-accented voice, "Good morning, Monsieur. This is Lola. Sven is tending the courtyards."

Owen grunts, "Whatever." Grabbing a mug from the cabinet and the heated kettle, he turns to Lola, "Would you mind getting the coffee can from the pantry?"

Louie settles, arms crossed, against the counter in anticipation of the ensuing human versus robot repartee.

"I am sorry, Mister Haig, we are out of coffee."

Owen turns to the robot, aware he is under as much scrutiny as poor Lola, "Okay. I can have tea. We have tea, right?"

"Sorry. No tea."

"Chocolate, as in hot chocolate?"

"Mr. Haig, food is in short supply. Sven and Burt attempted a shopping run but were turned away at the door. Humans only."

Louie steps in, "Thank you, Lola. Please proceed with your cleaning duties." Watching the quad-armed wonder busy herself into the great room and disappear around the corner, Louie turns to the American, "The locals are not keen on robots or androids. I could give it a go; I pass for human."

"Don't bother, Louie. I think we can muddle through since this is our last day." Owen starts to leave, turning around with a lingering thought in his head, "How did you get here?"

"I told you once already. The Cowboy picked us up at the Kobayashi plant in Milan and flew us here."

Owen scratches his chin and rubs the hair regrowing atop his head, "Yeah. Milan. Right."

Louie monitors the human's confused expression, scanning his elevated blood pressure and quickening heart rate—the onset of caffeine withdrawal, "Since we are asking questions, I have a query for you, if I may."

"Fire away, Louie. What is on your mind."

"Thank you, Monsieur. I am curious. Did your Louie martyr himself by jumping into a dark abyss to save your lives under the Giza Plateau?"

"From what I understand, that is what happened. So, yeah. Louie was quite a hero—and a good friend."

The new Louie expresses a wide grin, "That is an impressive emotion-driven course of action for a replicant, wouldn't you say?"

Owen nods and yawns, "Believe it or not, he was more human than many people I have met over the years."

"Perhaps the alien lifeforms who invaded his cybernetics changed him."

"What do you mean?"

"Well, it is as you said. Louie's last selfless act manifested from the most basic human emotion, love. Perhaps he was becoming human."

Owen breaks into a nervous chuckle, "Oh boy, you have me at a disadvantage. Rachel is the intellect in the family. Try your theories on her when she comes down." Heading outside to get some air and look for Mittens, he again has a follow-up thought, "But Louie, I would have something more than hot water ready to serve. The Missus has been rather cranky the last couple of days. She is not sleeping very well."

"Yes, Monsieur, I will see it is done. Enjoy your morning. And not to worry, I am planning a nice meal for your last day in France."

"We will be back. This is our new home."

"Of course."

Louie watches Owen jog down the steps toward the chicken enclosure, hoping to find fresh eggs. While he could have saved him the trip, his ambivalence toward the human meant he just did not care.

Returning to the chef's kitchen, the replicant accesses a knife drawer and removes a shiny steel blade, oblivious to Rachel's sleepy headed presence behind the kitchen island.

"Are there any more biscuits and jam?"

Startled, Louie wheels around, knife poised and ready, "Oh. My apologies, Madame. I did not know you were there."

"Who else would it be?"

Louie steps around the island, brandishing the knife toward Rachel, "Madame?"

Rachel gulps back a fight or flight reflex, unable to take her eyes off the shimmering knife, "Yes, Louie?"

With a smile broadening beneath his thick black mustache, he speaks, "Apples. From the bowl behind you. I am making Apple Brown Betty for tonight's dessert."

Shaking her dazed head, she pivots onto a large wooden bowl of fresh-picked green apples. Offering a sheepish grin, she slides sideways in fuzzy socks. "That sounds delicious."

Owen | PTB HQ, Scotland
03:04 p.m. | September 28, 2044

Waving goodbye to Louie 2.0, the Haigs leave the St. Claire estate. Owen looks out the tinted back window before turning to his better half, "Well, Rachel. Our honeymoon is over. Not the way we planned it. But there it is."

Rachel stares at the passing mid-afternoon scenery, "Life is what happens when you are busy making other plans."

"John Lennon."

"Wow. I did not think you knew that."

"I'm full of surprises."

* * *

The autonomous black SUV wheels into the private aviation section at the Toulouse airport and pulls aside a Beechcraft turboprop.

Cowboy peeks his head outside the fuselage, "There y'all are. We are gassed up and ready to go. The boss is waiting! Climb aboard and fix yourselves a couple stiff drinks. It is gonna be a bumpy ride."

Rachel reaches for her anxiety meds and hesitates. "Owen, pour me a chardonnay."

Tossed around like a toy, the sleek twin-engine plane breaks through a cold front over the Channel; Rachel tries to sleep while Owen peers out his portal, looking for signs of the apocalypse. Cowboy's Texas drawl resonates over the intercom, "We are about an hour out. From 10,000 feet, things look fine, for the most part. You will see the destruction when we make our descent into Edinburgh."

"Cowboy, from what I understand, most of the damage occurred from massive post-invasion riots."

Cowboy tips back his Stetson and replies, "Despite plenty of warnings, the human species was ill-equipped to handle the invasion. Good upstanding folks reduced to savages."

Owen recalls Detective Renault's salient remark, "You are the second person to tell us that."

* * *

Cowboy flies over the Scottish capitol's damaged airport, waggling his wings past the ad hoc tower. Banking to line up the potholed runway, he nails the landing and taxis to the halfway rebuilt Chrysalis Air terminal.

Rachel leans into the cockpit over the Texan's shoulder and kisses his cheek before exiting the craft, "Thanks for everything. I mean it." With a lighthearted chuckle, she adds, "Betty Hill? Let me handle the aliases the next time around."

Owen follows Rachel and shakes Dwayne's hand, "Did she say

next time?"

Confounded by the heartfelt goodbyes, Cowboy pulls on his mustache and shoots Owen a confused sideways stare, "You both signed up, right?"

"Yeah, why?"

"Hell's bells. You act like this is the end. Things are just getting interesting, my friend."

With that troubling thought rolling in his head, Owen deplanes and joins Rachel as a clipboard-wielding female PTB representative strides through the construction and approaches with a gracious smile. Checking her itinerary, "Rachel and Owen Haig, I presume?"

Owen nods, "Were you expecting someone else?"

Noticing the woman's stylish blue business suit, a wave of sadness washes over Rachel as her thoughts turn to the missing Nina Madsen.

"Right this way."

The couple follows the lady around the corner, where Chrysalis employees finish loading their bags into the cargo hold of a futuristic black chopper.

Taking the plush seats across a narrow aisle, neither recall being loaded inside the same airship on stretchers on Invasion Day Plus One.

Rachel buckles and tries to calm her nerves watching the debonair chopper pilot in a black mock turtleneck, jeans, and mirrored aviators jog up and swing into the cockpit. Grabbing the stick, he runs through a preflight checklist before winding up the blades and vaulting skyward. Rising through choppy air, he banks at a steep angle and heads southeast out of the city through a rain squall before breaking into clear air over verdant Lowlands pastures toward The Powers That Be HQ. His authoritative voice rings through their headsets: "Greetings, Mr. and Mrs. Haig, and welcome to Scotland. My name is Andrew. It is indeed an honor to meet you both in person."

Only 20 minutes into the flight, Rachel feels the bottom drop as the chopper lands atop a glowing pad in the middle of nowhere. Before they can ask, the scene outside changes to a concrete-lined descent into an underground garage packed with cars, trucks, and SUVs spanning back through the decades.

Gawking at the impressive collection gleaming under the lights, a gorgeous brunette with a pixie cut in a white lab coat appears outside Owen's window and opens the hatch.

Before exiting, Owen can't help but laugh and turns to Rachel, "I wonder if Ian Fleming had ever heard of this place?"

"Just act cool. Can you do that?"

"Call me Haig. Owen Haig."

Andrew overhears the couple's repartee from the cockpit, preparing to head back to the airport and pick up more arriving guests, while a spidery droid unloads the baggage.

Gawking at the underground facility, Owen's eyes widen onto the priceless automobile collection before grabbing Rachel by the hand and pulling her past a 1941 Packard.

"Owen, what the hell are you doing?"

"I don't believe it! It can't be."

Rachel yanks her hand free and turns on her husband before he redirects her embarrassed expression onto the PTB fleet's newest addition: a 1983 Jeep CJ-7.

"Owen, is that the same Jeep we bought in Libya?"

"It is. See the rust pattern on the hood? It is like a fingerprint." Peering into the open back, he pulls out the International Outer Space Consortium blanket they pilfered from their space tourism flight.

Rachel takes her familiar place behind the wheel, "So many memories."

A resonant voice calls out from behind, "I couldn't leave a vehicle with such immense historical value to rot at that shithole airport in Tripoli!"

The Haigs turn in unison onto the tall and angular Artemus

Pennywell, in the flesh, cane in hand and silver cactus bolo glistening from his starched shirt collar. "Welcome to The Powers That Be!"

Caught off-guard by the sudden presence of the iconic CEO, Rachel, and Owen join hands and approach their new boss. Owen breaks the ice, "As usual, Mr. Pennywell, you are full of surprises. I never thought we would see our Jeep again."

Pennywell laughs while ambling forward to envelop them in a warm embrace, "My God, you are heroes. I thought it was over for us, but you both came through."

Rachel turns to Owen, "Did you remember to bring the letter?"

Owen reaches into his vest and removes Pennywell's wrinkled and water-stained offer letter, "Here you are, Mr. Pennywell, our signed agreement to join the PTB."

Pennywell stares at the crumpled parchment, "Uh, not necessary, but thank you. Keep it as a souvenir. There is a mountain of paperwork where that came from. Let's take the tram to the HQ. I want to give you the nickel tour."

"A tram? Like the old Bond movies?"

Pennywell laughs, "Ian Fleming served as a technical advisor in the 40s and 50s. Then he hit the big time. We did not have much to do with him after that. Trust me, you are in some heady company."

The young brunette sidles up with an easy smile on her ruby lips, "If I may interrupt, the Haigs' baggage is on the tram. Please follow me."

"Pennywell smiles at the beautiful young woman, "Thank you, please lead the way, Number 1."

Entering the idling tram, like getting on a theme park ride, the foursome settles on comfortable seats as the doors shush closed and the two-car monorail bursts down a tunnel.

Noting the Haigs' sensory overload following Provence's quiet, peaceful seclusion, Pennywell chuckles, "This tram connects the helipad facility to the PTB HQ. It was separated from the underground hub out of precaution, but prying eyes pose little concern since we own everything for miles. Especially after the Gorks turned the world upside down."

After a five-minute ride, the tram brakes at another raised platform, and the doors whisk apart.

"Number 1, please escort the Haigs to their suite. They would like to relax and freshen up before dinner." Standing on his spry legs, he heads off the train and disappears down a long corridor.

Number 1 stands and straightens her lab coat, "Follow me."

Owen smiles, "With pleasure."

Rachel elbows her clueless husband, "Down boy, she's not human."

"Damn, really? How can you tell?"

"It is one of my superpowers."

Rachel | PTB HQ, Scotland
03:33 a.m. | September 29, 2044

The last-minute postponement of a welcome dinner left the jetlagged couple with nothing to do but retire to their suite and crash atop the cushy bed—Owen wrapped like a burrito, and Rachel face up toward the tiled ceiling.

* * *

Rachel bolts upright and sleepwalks out the apartment door into the long corridor. Shuffling barefoot past shuttered rooms under the pale blue night-mode lighting, she turns left at an intersection, losing herself in Level B's maze. Pausing at an alcove furnished with a sofa and table, her somnambulant stare fixates on a luminous entity emerging from the shadows.

The essence intensifies, sharpening into the ghostly profile of a bearded man out of time garbed in a flowing long-sleeved tunic cinched at the waist under a bright red cloak.

"I don't know you."

"Of course not."

"Should I?"

The medieval figure shifts toward Rachel, revealing his bloodied and beaten face and a jeweled dagger jutting from his chest. *"Methinks it best if you do not."*

With his point made, the phantasm resumes his haunting path, fading through a wall.

"Mrs. Haig, are you lost?"

The simple question shatters the quietude, jarring Rachel from another nocturnal stroll. Covered in goosebumps in the chill recycled air under thin cotton pajama pants and a loose tank top, she watches a beguiling synthetic sister approach out of the shadows.

Flush with embarrassment, Rachel tries to speak, but the dark-haired beauty with a mischievous twinkle on her smoky-eyed countenance presses a fingertip to her lips, mouthing, "Quiet." Taking Rachel by the hand, she leads her back to her room.

Rachel yawns at the door to her suite, hoping no one else witnessed her paranormal rendezvous, "Thanks. I owe you one."

The woman leans close in her PTB lab coat and places a hand at Rachel's waist to whisper in her ear, "Do spirits invade your dreams?"

Rattled by the hypnotic beauty's query, Rachel manages to blurt out, "Yes."

"We see ghosts, too." Pressing Rachel against the door, Number 1 kisses her lips before stepping back with an impish smile, "Good night, Mrs. Haig."

Rachel puts a hand to her mouth, watching the replicant take long, confident strides down the low-lit corridor, "Whoa. What the hell just happened?"

Swooning from the mystifying encounter, Rachel tiptoes into

the darkened suite, shedding pajamas onto the floor before awakening her bedmate to satiate an overwhelming passionate desire.

Owen | PTB HQ, Scotland
09:00 a.m. | September 29, 2044

Avoiding Rachel's bedroom eyes, Owen snatches the last piece of sourdough toast, finishing his room service sausage and eggs breakfast, "Hey Rach, pass the butter, please."

Seated across the small linen-covered table in their PTB suite, Rachel passes the dish while sliding her left foot up his leg, "Last night was epic."

Happy, sore, and confused, Owen chomps into the toast, wondering what happened to the shy, demure girl he married as her probing toes hit paydirt.

* * *

Refreshed and ready for a full day of PTB business, the Haigs follow Number 13's circuitous lead through the echoing underground corridors of Level B. Owen muses he could not find his way back if his life depended on it. The trio takes the far right fork down a spur passage toward glass double doors and virtual daylight beyond.

Ushered into a magnificent tropical-themed atrium hub, 13 advises the gawking couple, "Please wait here. Miss Carrera will arrive in a few minutes."

Reminiscent of field trips to the arboretum, Owen runs up a flight of stairs, scaring a flock of colorful birds into the rafters where programmed misters sprinkle lush tropical vegetation stretching toward faux sunlight permeating milky glass panels enclosing the humid space. Leaning over the wet metal rail, he sees Rachel amid the exotic flora, ponds, and gurgling fountains. "I wonder how far below ground we are right now."

"I'd rather not think about that." Dressed in an olive t-shirt over jeans and Chelsea boots with her side-parted blond locks curling down her back, Rachel wanders toward a blue and yellow long-tailed macaw with its prehistoric feet gripped around a branch, "Are you real?"

The bird cocks its head and replies, *"Are you real?"*

Owen joins her conversation with the colorful bird, "You know, parrot, I have wondered the same thing all morning."

Rachel peers closer at the colorful plumage, looking for hinges or seams, "I bet everything down here is fake, but if you can't tell, what is the difference? The girl that brought us here surpasses Louie and Louie 2.0 by leaps and bounds."

"Uh, yeah, in more ways than one."

"Careful, Owen. I'm right here."

Owen decides to broach the subject of the night before, "What got into you last night?"

Rachel hesitates to answer as a fit young woman with flaming red hair in a fashionable turquoise business suit interrupts their conversation, circumventing a fountain with a welcoming smile on her fair-skinned face, "Good morning, Mr. and Mrs. Haig. Vita Carrera, VP legal counsel. We have a lot to go over; let's get started, shall we?"

Inside a glass-enclosed meeting area at the far end of the conservatory, Vita pulls a chair across from the couple, "First off, welcome aboard. Under normal circumstances, an HR rep would handle this initial phase of new hire orientation. However, I need not tell you both; times are far from normal." Reaching into a briefcase, she pulls out two tablets and places them before Owen and Rachel. "Okay. Uh, hang on, I almost forgot. I have a 24-karat inscribed PTB fountain pen for each of you. If you are signing your lives away, you may as well do it in style, am I right?"

Owen shoots the redhead a confused look, accepting the pricy pen.

Acknowledging his unspoken question, she smiles, "The writing instruments digitize your sigs and send them to our cloud storage; however, you can fill them with ink. I dabble in calligraphy and enjoy the feel of a golden nib drawing a line of ink on paper. Call me old-fashioned."

"So, you can still do that with everything down around the world, the cloud storage, I mean?"

Vita leans back and clasps her hands, "Remember, Mr. Haig, this is not Ford and Poole; we are the Powers That Be."

Feeling a kinship with Vita's old-school preferences, Rachel nudges her husband, "Yeah, Owen, get with the program."

***

Flexing sore hands after two-plus hours of signing their lives away, the couple relaxes as Vita taps a holographic call button for Number 13.

"We are through with the signing ceremony; please return to escort the Haigs to the medical bay."

"Ms. Carrera, I am assisting Richard with an experiment."

Vita rolls her eyes, smiling back at the Haigs, "No worries, I will escort them myself."

Killing the line, Vita leans across the table and motions for them to do the same, "A word of advice. Be careful around the sisters; they can be rather unpredictable."

Rachel wants to spill the details about her late-night encounter but opts to remain mum.

Owen's eyes widen, "Are you a replicant, too?"

Vita leans back and laughs, "Oh my, that is too funny. I needed a good laugh. Thanks, Owen." Regaining her composure, she continues, "No. Okay. Here is the deal: There are sixteen, what we refer to as sisters, numbered one to sixteen. Number 13 brought you here earlier. She is fine. I find the lower numbers are more cunning. One of them, Number

8, made a pass at me just the other day. Not sure how or why that happened. I assume they are gleaning human behaviors at an accelerating rate. And while they are beautiful, robot sex is not my cup of tea."

Rachel's green eyes pierce the attorney's mind like a hot knife through butter, *"You know what happened to me last night, don't you?"*

Surprised by Mrs. Haig's telepathic accusation, Vita avoids the young blonde's probing green eyes and hastens to leave the room, "Now then, grab your bags and follow me."

With tablets and an assortment of goodies, including 16-year Lagavulin, compliments of Mr. Pennywell, the Haigs scoop PTB canvas tote bags by the handles and follow Vita out another door.

* * *

Vita leaves the couple in the capable hands of a shiny gold robot nurse technician who directs Owen and Rachel into separate exam rooms. Shedding his clothes and donning a crinkly medical gown, Owen hoists atop the papered examination table and waits for the doctor.

Across the hall, Rachel mirrors his actions and hops atop her table as the door swings wide, allowing Dr. Gene Simmons to enter, reading her virtual chart, "The world-famous Rachel Haig. How are you feeling, my dear?"

"I feel fine. Not sleeping very well, but I think it is from weaning off the pain and anxiety meds, and maybe a little PTSD."

Simmons turns to Rachel with a sympathetic smile, "In my experience, there is no such thing as a little PTSD." Flipping through her bloodwork and stats, "Dr. Said was good enough to provide the records from your convalescence at Cleopatra Hospital. Your recovery is a miracle of modern medicine and advanced alien pharmacology."

The Black father of eight scans more notes before turning his attention to Rachel's hands, "Tell me about your hands. What do you think happened?"

Filled with self-doubt, Rachel asks the physician, "What do you mean? I have been over this time and time again. Some kind of energy burst out of my hands. I controlled it at will. Then it was gone. It left me with pain and scars that will not heal." Rachel holds out her hands. "See the spirals in my palms? I just noticed those a few nights ago before leaving France. To be honest, it is freaking me out."

The unflappable Gene Simmons dons a pair of readers, "Spirals, you say? Interesting. Let's have a look."

"You are just like all of the others. This is a waste of time!"

Hearing her words course through his consciousness, Simmons looks over his specs into the young, attractive patient's circumspect visage, "How long have you been doing that?"

Rachel feigns an ignorant smile, "Doing what?"

"Telepathy. I heard you. Trust me when I tell you, Mrs. Haig, what you are experiencing is real."

Rachel shrinks back on the table, crinkling her gown atop the paper.

Ignoring the patient's unresponsiveness, Simmons presses the subject by moving a jar of tongue depressors to the edge of a counter, "Can you knock this jar onto the floor?"

"Is this some kind of joke or hazing ritual?"

"I am a busy man, Mrs. Haig. Can you move the jar?"

Flustered and confused, Rachel gulps a deep breath and stares at the jar.

Simmons stands aside, masking his anticipation.

After frustrating minutes of staring at the object, Rachel turns to the impatient Dr. Simmons, "I can't."

"Concentrate, my dear. Concentrate."

Rachel closes her eyes and envisions the shape in her mind. Reopening her green eyes, she elevates the jar a fraction of an inch before rotating it sideways and crashing it to the floor, sending wood and glass across the tiles.

* * *

Bored, reading every line of a human anatomical chart mounted to the light gray wall, Owen hears something break, "Clean up on aisle nine."

An Indian woman wearing a white coat with a stethoscope around her neck enters, pushing a futuristic medical cart.

Owen performs a doubletake as she turns it on and sticks cold metal electrodes to his chest, arms, and temples, "Wait a minute. I know you from somewhere."

The olive-skinned doctor with coal-black hair pulled back in a bun fails to hide a coy smile while scanning scrolling data, "I told you we would meet again. I'm Dr. Aashvi Patel—we met at the IOSC facility in Toulouse."

Following the physical, Dr. Patel removes the electrodes and instructs Owen to dress and head outside.

"Should I wait for Rachel?"

"No. Dr. Simmons scheduled her for some additional tests. You should proceed to the orientation."

"Is there something wrong?"

Aashvi proffers a sympathetic grin, "I am sure she is fine. It is just a precaution after everything you have both been through."

"Yeah, but I was the one who almost died." pointing at the fading C-shaped scar on his head under thickening auburn hair flecked with streaks of gray around the temples, "Should I get a brain scan?"

Dr. Patel dons her stethoscope and checks his respiratory and heartbeat, "You are in peak health, Mr. Haig, and cleared to join the PTB. I'd offer you a sucker, but we are fresh out."

"What about Rachel?"

* * *

Number 13 accompanies Owen down another spoke in the underground facility to an elevator, "How many levels are there?"

13 casts a sideways glance at Owen with a light and airy smile, "We are heading to Level C."

Frowning, he starts to ask again as the doors whisk open onto the gleaming white laboratory.

"Here we are, Level C."

Traversing a central aisle through the ultra-modern facility, Owen follows 13 past rows of benches curving into the well-lit distance, loaded with far-out instrumentation and microscopes. His heart skips a beat, peering into the murky water of a floor-to-ceiling aquarium teeming with aquatic plants and fish, catching yellowy eyes staring back.

13 ignores Owen's glazed stare, opening red double doors and ushering the new recruit into the PTB's much-heralded yet little-used Think Tank. "Pod Six is prepped and waiting with refreshments and snacks. I will return to escort you back to your suite when the orientation is finished. You will have ample time to refresh and relax before tonight's reception."

Owen feigns nonchalance, unable to mask his sensorial overload, "Thank you, uh, Number 13."

"Look for the sixth pod. It is the one after five."

Oblivious to the replicant's sarcasm, Owen ventures solo through the auditorium-sized space, counting pods of various shapes and sizes to a shiny red sphere painted with the number six, "Pod 6. Brilliant."

Entering the plush, carpeted interior, the door seals behind him. Lifting the lid on a cooler, he removes an icy soda and pops the cap. Settling into the lone tech-heavy Italian leather armchair, he places the bottle in a holder and faces a paper-thin screen, "Man, this would be an excellent setup to watch football."

Comfortable in the sound-proof pod, Owen sets the chair to low-frequency vibration, stares at the blank screen, and waits, "Hmm, am I supposed to do something?" Scanning the interior, he finds nothing but the snack tray on the short coffee table, his new favorite chair, and the screen, "No remote. Okay. What the hell."

"Play orientation!"

The space darkens, and The Powers That Be logo fills the screen.

Basking in his brilliance, wondering if he passed a test, he watches the opening image transition to grainy footage of a caped man riding horseback through a monotonal forested winter landscape. The downtrodden colonial-era figure dismounts and tromps through deep snow toward a luminous apparition before falling to his knees, overwhelmed by the sheer gravity of the revelatory encounter.

Owen leans forward, realizing the man's identity, "Good Christ, is that George Washington at Valley Forge?"

The bird's eye view widens above rolling Pennsylvania forestland and the Continental Army's beleaguered encampment before ending with a vintage film reel effect.

A countdown clock presages a solemn, mid-20th-century man seated behind a desk, "What you just witnessed is an actual drone recording of General George Washington's legendary encounter at Valley Forge with a divine vision that changed the course of human history. Henceforth, extraterrestrial benefactors have worked with a who's-who of historical figures, shepherding humanity through a tumultuous period of accelerated evolution and rapid-fire technological advancements unseen throughout human existence. This is the story of The Powers That Be …."

Owen watches the orientation, mouth agape, soda sweating and forgotten, enthralled by the Earth-shattering revelations.

A segment disclosing the PTB's role at the advent of the atomic era mentions Einstein and Oppenheimer, leaving Owen mumbling in a trance-like state, "Makes sense. They were PTB."

Owen absorbs stunning disclosures on Lincoln, Curie, Earhart, Churchill, Kennedy, Reagan, Pope John Paul II, Jobs, Musk, Samantha Page, the lunar architect, et al., like candles flickering to life in his brain.

Number 13 | PTB HQ, Scotland
08:30 p.m. | September 29, 2044

A blond hurricane named Rachel Alexander Haig blows through the door, "I'm back."

Owen bookmarks his new PTB tablet and stands, "What happened to you? You missed the orientation."

"No time for chit-chat, Owen. This PTB shindig is in less than an hour."

"I finished my orientation and arrived back here hours ago."

Rachel dodges her husband's hangdog countenance, "Is that what you are wearing?"

Owen looks down at his clean white dress shirt, "What? I will wear a sports coat—the only one I packed."

Hastening into the bathroom and shutting the door, Rachel calls over her bare shoulder, "You look fine." Staring into the mirror, she hears Owen's muffled complaints but cannot stop thinking about her diagnostic tests. Tamping down burgeoning annoyance, she yells, "I'll fill you in later."

Running a brush through her hair and touching up light makeup on her fresh-faced complexion, Rachel slips into a black cocktail dress and takes a final look in the full-length mirror. Grabbing for her pills, she pops two sans water and mutters, "Fucking good enough."

Stepping out of the bathroom, Rachel finds her husband chatting with a lissome brunette replicant who turns with a warm smile, rocking a skimpy black cocktail dress, looking fantastic. "Hello, Mrs. Haig. Look at us—great minds think alike."

Owen grabs his jacket and smiles, "She is our escort for the evening."

* * *

Following Number 13's long-legged pace through the corridors,

Owen turns to his better half, "Don't worry, Rach, you look great. What happened? Is everything alright?"

Rachel feels the pills taking effect, "I told you, Owen. Dr. Simmons wanted more tests. Typical medical bullshit. Have you ever met a doctor who did not want to run one more test?"

"I guess not. I assumed the PTB doctors would be different."

"Yeah. Well. Hate to burst your bubble, but the PTB docs are no different than anywhere else."

Number 13 stops at open double doors and ushers the guests of honor to the threshold of the lively reception hall.

"Let's grab a bottle and skedaddle back to the room."

"Too late." Squeezing Rachel's scarred left hand, "Here comes my doctor—the one from Toulouse."

Poised and polished in a bright purple sari with a jet-black ponytail pulled over her right shoulder, the Indian physician greets them with a cultivated ebullience, "Ah, Mr. and Mrs. Haig. Welcome to our little club."

Owen shakes her hand, "Uh, Rachel, this is Doctor, uh …."

"Aashvi Patel. I checked Owen out after your space tourism flight in Toulouse. Of course, I had no idea we would meet again, but here we are."

Rachel smiles at the sophisticated woman, "My pleasure. So, you work with Dr. Simmons?"

"Gene is a good friend and a brilliant physician."

Rachel spies Simmons consulting with Artemus Pennywell at the room's far end.

"They are talking about me."

A robot server strides past, balancing a tray of glasses; Owen grabs two chardonnays and hands one to Rachel, "Here, have a glass of liquid courage."

Aashvi gazes around the space, "I have been a member of the PTB since medical school in Mumbai. But that was a long time ago.

However, this is my first time in Scotland. How about you two?"

Owen takes a long drink, stepping aside as another couple enters, ignoring her attempted small talk, "Dr. Patel, I'm curious. Who are all of these people?"

Aashvi glides to a cocktail table, motioning for the Haigs to follow. "Okay, you met our CEO. There he is talking with Gene." Owen grabs a cheesy hors d'oeuvre and a new glass as the doctor continues, "Let's see. That heavy-set man is the former astronaut Millard Lufkin and members of his IOSC team. Beyond him, I see my brother, Viraj chatting with Miss Gabreski."

Rachel spies the tall Scandinavian woman and gasps, "That is Anastasia Gabreski. The supermodel. She is a member of the PTB?"

"You seem surprised. Have you done any modeling?"

"No. Why do people keep asking me that?"

"Just an observation, dear. Nothing more."

Owen cranes his neck to see the supermodel in a sparkling knee-length dress with a plunging neckline, trying to keep up with the conversation, "Wow. Wait. Who is she?"

"Owen, she is a world-famous Polish supermodel turned UN Goodwill ambassador. You never heard of her?"

Owen feigns indifference, "In my experience, supermodels are just people like you and me."

Aashvi suppresses a smile at Owen's comment and puts her hand on Rachel's arm, "Be sure to chat with her this evening. She is amazing."

Owen scoops up the last cheesy comestible on an oval platter prompting a diligent robot to remove the dish. Distracted, he turns to Aashvi, "So these folks are all PTB?"

"For the most part. Some, like my brother and Gabby, are members of The Council. Others, like me, fill support roles."

Rachel chimes in, "Council? Like a board of directors?"

"In a sense." Aashvi scans the room before turning to the Haigs, "Hold that thought. The boss is about to speak."

Artemus Pennywell takes center stage like a circus ringmaster—a reference he abhors—cradling a Scotch-filled tumbler in his tailored black suit and sparkling silver bolo tie. "We are gathered here on this fine Scottish evening deep beneath Crichton Castle to initiate new members of The Powers That Be: Rachel Alexander Haig, Owen Haig, and Julius Hart." After a throat-clearing cough, he adds, "Please step forward."

Owen and Rachel join the suave billionaire, Julius Hart, facing Pennywell as the gathering forms a loose circle inside the festive space. Pausing for effect, the 134-year-old polishes off his tumbler and motions for his valet. Trading the glass for an antique scroll, he nods at Andrew and unfurls the parchment. "Ah, yes. Excuse me, everyone. It has been a while since I performed one of these rituals. Some, not I, but some, find this arcane throwback to a bygone era a tedious bore. I disagree. Tradition is essential. Especially in the face of worldwide upheaval and a thuggish mob trying to erase history." With a wry chuckle, Pennywell adds, "Plus, we have to keep up with those Freemason bastards and that perverted lot running the Skull and Bones Society."

The lights dim, and the room breaks into raucous applause as Owen and Julius Hart exchange a nodded greeting.

Standing betwixt the two men, Rachel maintains an elegant pose staring at Pennywell's shiny Saguaro-shaped bolo, avoiding probing eyes, fearful of absorbing impertinent thoughts swirling about the darkened room.

A server bot balancing a silver tray of pre-lit candles sidles beside an uplit Pennywell, who looks at the trio with a twinkle in his deep gray eyes, "Don't be shy. Take a fucking candle."

Candles in hand, the recruits stand tall before the 134-year-old Artemus Pennywell as he clears his throat a second time before reading from the scroll. "Okay. Here we go …

> *Unrequited cries harken to the dawn of humankind.*
> *Echoing trials and tribulations through the maelstrom.*
> *Famines and pestilence exact a toll.*

> *Steeling survivors against the crashing waves.*
> *Scrabbling for the bounty beneath mud-caked feet.*
> *Pitting brother against brother.*
> *Swilling spilled blood.*
> *Writhing through the muck.*
> *Clawing at limbs and gouging eyeballs.*
> *Thwarting inglorious defeat.*
> *Drenched in the tears of vanquished foes.*
> *Lost to history and pulverized into the sands of time.*
> *Post eons of struggle.*
> *Our hour is at hand.*
> *Resolute before a malevolent universe.*
> *Venturing into the great expanse.*
> *Striving toward an omega point.*
> *Fortified by Almighty God in Heaven above.*
> *Armed with the truth that set us free.*
> *Veritas Vos Liberabit.*"

Pennywell furls the parchment and presents the trio with a wry smile. "Pretty heady stuff. But the Latin kicker is the main point. The truth will set you free." Accepting a new tumbler from Andrew, he takes a sip and continues. "I am doing all of the talking. Can someone else in the room define this truth?"

Millard Lufkin steps forward, carrying a plate of appetizers. "It means we survived through the millennia to a moment when altruistic extraterrestrials witnessed our revolutionary forebears' struggle for independence, turning humanity's prospects from a mere curiosity into candidates to join the universal civilization."

"Spot on, Millard. How are the buffalo wings? I have not tried one yet."

"Spicy, Artemus."

"Excellent. Does anybody care to say a few words before I turn it over to our new members?"

Gabby raises her glass, "I propose a toast to the Haigs. We would not be standing here scarfing caviar and champagne without your heroism. You deserve special places of honor. We salute you."

The distinguished group breaks into another round of applause as a bot takes the candles and extinguishes them atop the tray, freeing Owen to pivot toward Rachel.

Shaking her head and shooting daggers at Owen, Rachel's heart skips a beat, realizing her oblivious husband failed to grab the clue. Instead, he pulls her into the limelight before taking a long backward stride, exposing her to a sea of faces in rapt anticipation, eager to hear her voice. Accepting a champagne flute from an empathic bot, she takes a sip and smiles, "I am Rachel Haig. That is my husband, Owen. Uh. What to say …. We were on our honeymoon. You know. Two people leading everyday lives." Considering that statement, "But maybe not so much, after all."

Biting her lip, she switches gears, "I suffered a sexual assault when I was 18. It was in all of the papers. No sense hiding it. The tabloids gave me a nickname. Trust fund murderess. I know, kind of badass, right? It turns out I inherited something that defies words. The doctors, even Gene standing over there. Hi Gene! They can't figure it out. All I can say is I appreciate your kindness and warm greetings, but please do not call me a hero. I just want to learn from my experience and pay it forward. The invitation to join the PTB was a Godsend. Thank you, Mr. Pennywell."

Owen returns to Rachel's side, thunderstruck by her candor, while the room again erupts in applause. "Wow, Rach. That was awesome."

After downing the champagne flute in one long pull, Rachel turns to her proud husband, "I have no idea what came out of my mouth."

* * *

Adjourning to an adjacent dining room, the Haigs find name placards at the elegant long table across from Julius Hart and his young, attractive French girlfriend.

Hart reciprocates a pleasant smile as server bots remove salad plates and refill glasses. "Thanks for taking the limelight off of me. I hate public speaking."

Owen stares back with unmasked incredulity, "But you are Julius Hart. I watched all of your TED talks on anti-gravity and time warps. My investors salivated over your IPOs."

Hart leans back as another robot places Cornish hens before him and his date, who picks up her table knife and pokes at the succulent bird. Ignoring his ill-mannered date, he replies, offering Rachel a backhanded compliment, "I'm more like you, Mrs. Haig. My people push me in front of adoring throngs, and I have no choice but to start talking. And truth be told, I have no idea what I say. Never written a single word or read a teleprompter speech."

Rachel smiles at the chiseled and tanned aeronautics wunderkind and billionaire entrepreneur. "So, I gather your companies build and produce the new wave of anti-gravity vessels?"

Hart shrugs, "Yes. The technology behind anti-gravity is in the public domain. In theory, anyone can do it. Before the invasion, many competitors were vying for my business, but shipbuilding is not why I was invited to join the PTB." He leans forward, lowering his voice, "I am developing a paradigm shift in e-commerce—fulfillment warehouses in geosynchronous orbits around the globe. I call it Thundercorp. And inspired by the PTB's lovely numbered replicants, I'm assigning numbers to each station, as in Thundercorp No. One … and so on."

Owen's ears perk up at the seed change in human commerce, "How will you make the deliveries from orbit?"

"Hypersonic drones pinpointing drop locations down to a millimeter. The technology is off-the-rails bat-shit crazy, but it works."

Owen is about to proffer another question but can no longer

ignore his bladder, "Excuse me. Hold that thought until I get back."

* * *

Exiting the bathroom, Owen fast walks back to the dining hall, eager to rejoin the fascinating conversation with Julius Hart, as a silhouetted figure impedes his path down the dark, empty corridor. Coming closer, he recognizes the alluring young woman with an amiable smile, "Hello again, Number 13."

The sultry replicant invades his space before he knows what hit him, smoothing her hand down his sport coat's lapel, "I'm honored, Owen, you remember my name. Can you help me for a moment?"

Ignoring earlier warnings, Owen throws caution to the wind, "Sure. What can I do for you?"

"Great!" The lithesome bot pivots 180 degrees and pulls dark hair aside, exposing her lovely neck and supple shoulders while letting her weight fall against him, "Can you help me out of this dress? The damn zipper is stuck."

Frozen in terror in the compromising position, Owen spins 13 forward and peers into her dangerous blue-eyed visage, "This is not right. Please don't."

Sliding a hand under his jacket, Number 13 snickers, "What did I do? I think you are holding me, Owen."

Flabbergasted by how fast she turned the tables on him, he lets her lithe arms slip from his grip and sidles past her, "Yeah, not happening."

13 watches him go, "Bye, Owen."

* * *

As Owen reclaims his seat beside Rachel, she notes his flummoxed demeanor and grabs his leg under the table, "You look like you have seen a ghost."

"I will tell you later."

Number 13 enters the hall in her matching black cocktail dress and returns Rachel's curious green-eyed stare with a flirtatious wink and natural ruby lips curled in a mischievous smile on her perfect face.

Rachel | PTB HQ, Scotland
12:00 p.m. | September 30, 2044

Grating beeps break the quietude inside their darkened suite after the previous night's ceremonial celebration that lingered into the morning hours.

"What time is it?"

Rachel leans across Owen and looks at a holographic wall clock, "A little after seven."

"Must sleep longer."

Rachel yanks the covers off Owen and bounces atop him, "Come on, sleepyhead, this is our last day in Scotland. It is a travel day for all the Council who came to celebrate our initiation. So today, we are on our own—no lawyers, doctors, or MRIs. I want to explore Level A."

"Level A?"

"Yeah, Crichton Castle and the Scottish Lowlands countryside high above your sleepy head."

"Can I brush my teeth first?"

"Uh, yeah. Your breath stinks."

* * *

Owen and Rachel play carefree tourists—just for one day— exploring verdant Lowland pastures surrounding the crumbled castle ruins. The pair hold hands, enjoying fresh air and sunlight on their faces, hiking a well-trod path through a thick grove of black alders. Following the trail upward through windblown grasses toward a rugged outcropping, they pause to catch their breath on a precipitous ledge overlooking the Crichton castle ruins and a quaint church farther down a zigzagging graveled lane.

Slipping Owen's grasp, Rachel stoops to pick a blue flower and tucks it into her blond hair.

Owen pushes forward, entranced by serenity and solitude that will not last.

"*Rachel.*"

The peculiar voice invades Rachel's psyche, shifting her startled gaze onto a shiny cube perched halfway up a craggy formation jutting upward at a steep angle.

Zipping an olive-green PTB windbreaker, Owen squints through the sunshine, studying the commanding view, noting battleship gray storm clouds looming to the north. "Looks like rain."

Glancing where Rachel stopped to pick a flower, he finds her missing. "Rachel? Where did you go?"

His beautiful wife's melodic voice wafts to his ears, "Up here, Owen."

A stunned Owen gazes up at Rachel, perched on a ledge with her muddy boots dangling over the steep face pocked with lichens and grass.

Smiling down at her gaping husband, she swipes at her mud-smeared face and presents a two-inch cube in her outstretched hand, "I found this."

"What the hell is that?"

"I'm not sure, but it knows my name."

* * *

After luxurious hot showers, bags packed and stacked by the door, the Haigs sit at the small table in their suite with the cube centered between them atop a paper napkin, waiting for an escort to the underground tram platform.

"You are telling me this thing called you by your name?"

"I know it sounds like I am crazy, but yes."

"Is it saying anything to you right now?"

"No. And screw you. I know you don't believe me."

"Wrong. After everything we have been through, I'm a believer."

A firm knock on the door interrupts their conversation.

"Do you want to share your discovery with our new friends?"

Rachel pauses to consider the suggestion before tucking the cube in her bag, "No. I think not. At least not right now. We have to go."

Another knock, "Come in!"

Exhibiting none of the sexy precociousness from the night before, an all-business Number 13 enters the room in an ordinary white lab coat ensemble, followed by an autonomous wheeled luggage cart.

"Please follow me. The tram schedule to the helipad is full. No time to waste."

* * *

A dressed-down Artemus Pennywell in checkered golf pants and a black polo rises from a bench as 13 leads his new PTB agents into the tram station. "Ah. Owen and Rachel. Such a pleasure to meet you in person. I wish we had more time, but your ride back to the States awaits."

Owen smiles and extends his hand, "Goodbye, Mr. Pennywell."

The CEO shuns the proffered handshake and bearhugs the Haigs one last time, "I hate goodbyes. Don't stray too far from your family's Rhode Island estate; plans are afoot for your first assignment. Richard King uploaded a timeline to your tablets. A little light reading while en route."

Rachel frowns, "You know, we never met Professor King."

Pennywell smiles, "The man is a bit of a recluse. However, you will be hearing from him soon."

Owen catches one last glimpse of 13 vacating the terminal,

"You know your replicants are sexually active, right?"

Pennywell winces and scratches his wispy gray head, "Yes. I am aware of the phenomenon. Were you propositioned by one of the sisters? My apologies. Please do not take it personally. They are learning human behavior at an alarming rate, portending our transhumanist future. But first, we must deal with even more pressing concerns."

The tram's airbrakes whoosh to a stop, and the doors slide open, "Your chariot awaits."

* * *

Sitting upright and belted, the Haigs watch verdant countryside zoom past outside the anti-gravity shuttle's wide portals on a low-altitude beeline to RAF Lakenheath at over 300 miles per hour.

Hart sits across from the Haigs in a comfortable, slouched position with his right arm draped around his girlfriend's slim shoulders.

Owen tamps down a nervousness, "So, who is flying this thing?"

Julius Hart shrugs and smiles, "A supercomputer."

Owen feels Rachel squeeze down on his hand as the lozenge-shaped craft swoops through the air, "You mean like Hal?"

Hart laughs, "Oh yeah, I loved that movie. Kubrick was a genius." The mogul shakes his head at Owen, ruminating on the Hal reference, "That cannot happen here."

Owen raises an eyebrow, "Why not."

"No pod bay doors."

20 minutes later, the airship with no visible means of propulsion sets down on the windy tarmac at the RAF base, where Hart and his young companion bid the Haigs adieu and head for a waiting car. Owen and Rachel follow their luggage into the massive cargo hold of an ancient Space Force C-130 transport, prepping and loading for its first flight to the States with replacement microchips and instrumentation installed and ready to go.

The duo settles into jump seats as the ground crew stuffs the monstrous plane to the gills. An hour later, they hear the engines roar to life and feel the behemoth taxi onto a long runway.

"Next stop, the good old USA."

Rachel ignores her husband, downs another pill, and tries to relax in the uncomfortable seat.

Rachel | Newport Naval Air Station
11:45 p.m. | October 1, 2044

Jostling and bumping through a raging nor'easter over the North Atlantic, the Haigs sit blanch-faced, watching palette loads of heavy crates and containers straining against thick straps cleated to the airship's metallic bones.

"What would happen if one of those cleats broke?"

"Purge that thought, Rachel. I'm sure they do this all of the time."

After the long flight—interspersed with moments of sheer terror—the C-130 touches wheels down at a deserted New Jersey Air National Guard Base in a driving rainstorm. The couple debarks from the cargo plane's cavernous maw into the howling wind and pelting rain, scampering across the slick tarmac to the cover of the closest hangar. Soaking wet, Owen spots a mech loading their soggy suitcases into a PTB chopper with familiar butterfly logos lit up by lightning and the low rumbles of thunder. "Come on, Rachel. One more time."

"Aw, man. I don't feel so good."

"Rachel, if it is any consolation, you will be back in your own bed at some point tonight."

Buffeted in disorienting pitch blackness for the entire commute, the PTB craft drops like a rock onto a windswept helipad in a driving rainstorm at the Newport Naval Air Station.

"Rachel, you are home."

"I'm about to heave my guts out. Let me out of this thing!"

Piling into a waiting black PTB SUV for the 15-minute drive to The Hilltop Estate—Rachel's Newport, Rhode Island family home—the rain ebbs to a light drizzle along Thames Street on a wet Saturday night. Feeling like she had been away for years, not months, Rachel peers out fogged-up windows at boarded-up shops and eateries up and down the historic street, "Man, it is like a ghost town. It should be crawling with drunk tourists at this hour, even with the inclement weather."

Rachel's heart beats out of her chest as the SUV passes through wide-open gates at the estate's stony entrance before winding up the smooth lane and swinging halfway around the circular drive.

Owen squeegees the passenger window with his palm revealing his in-laws buttoned up to their ears in rain gear, braving the elements to greet their long-lost daughter.

"I think they missed you, Rachel."

Miriam Alexander | Hilltop
10:00 a.m. | October 2, 2044

Owen stumbles downstairs to the impressive chef's kitchen and finds Rachel sitting at a long counter before a bowl of cereal next to her mother, cradling a cup and saucer. Sidling around his wife with a playful squeeze on her butt through cute cotton pajamas, he proffers a light kiss on her mother's cheek, "Good morning, Miriam. You look as lovely as ever. What's for breakfast?"

"Well, Owen. I did not know when to expect your return until yesterday. Our cupboards are a little bare."

Rachel chimes in, "I'm eating Froot Loops from a box dating back to my high school days."

"I think I'll just have coffee for now."

Scooting atop a counter-height stool, coffee in hand, Owen

takes a long sip, "So, Miriam. How are things here in the States?"

Mrs. Alexander starts to reply, but Rachel interrupts, "Not now, Owen. We have a bigger problem. Tell him, Mom."

"The president, Lena Jackson, will be at Rosecliff on October 6."

Rachel scoops a spoonful of cereal into her mouth, "That is four days from now."

Owen takes another drink, "Rosecliff? The place where we met? What for?"

Miriam Alexander, the spry and attractive 62-year-old active in the Newport social scene, straightens and assumes a dignified air of sophistication, "She wants to meet you both at a gala in your honor."

"You are kidding. The president wants to meet with us. How does she know who we are?"

Rachel swipes open a virtual screen, highlighting an AP headline article:

Mystery Couple Makes Triumphant Return After Saving The World.

"Hey, look at that. I guess the news about us has made it out of Cairo. At least they used a better picture, Rachel."

"Owen, are you insane? Everyone knows who we are. This is not good."

Miriam pats her daughter on the back, like she is 12, "Now, Rachel, I'm sure it will be fine. You are safe here. We have Secret Service guarding the grounds."

"Those are not Secret Service, Miriam. They work for our new employers."

Mrs. Alexander moves to the sink and peers outside, "Well, they said Secret Service. You can't trust anybody these days."

Owen's stomach growls in protest, "So, there really isn't anything to eat besides stale cereal?"

Miriam laughs, "Our house staff left us high and dry after the invasion. We lost all of the perishables in the power outage. It just came back a little over a week ago. But no, we have food. I can make you something. How about dried eggs and toast?"

Rachel peers out the window, thinking she saw someone moving through the shrubs, "Uh, Owen. This is my Mom you are talking to. She can't boil water. I'll make you a fucking egg."

"Rachel! Where did you learn that language?"

"Sorry, Mother. I'll try to keep it clean."

Owen | Hilltop
03:00 p.m. | October 3, 2044

Chomping popcorn, Owen and Rachel meld into cinema-style leather recliners within the Hilltop Estate's little-used 30-seat screening room before a darkened, wafer-thin 160-inch screen.

"So, your parents did not realize they could access the internet?"

"No, Owen. How would they know that?"

"Well, Viraj Patel laid it out quite simply: if the grid comes back, check your stuff; not every chip was fried during the invasion."

"In all fairness, the power returned less than a week ago, and my father is dealing with his business. I don't think he has had time to check if Survivor recorded during the apocalypse."

"Geez, Rachel. Don't be so defensive. My parents are worse when it comes to this technical shit."

"And the nut did not fall far from the tree."

"Zing." Owen picks up the remote and presses the power on button. The screen brightens to life, and a spinning icon appears dead center.

"The suspense is killing me."

A familiar menu appears before their eyes, with most apps

grayed out.

"Eureka! It works. Any requests? Cooking shows, reality TV, porn perhaps?"

"Owen, knock it off and see if YouTube works. We can search the news feeds and find out what is happening."

Scrolling through reams of content, Owen chooses an intrepid vlogger wading through Lower Manhattan, watching her pixelated shaky camera footage of devastation freezing in fits and starts.

"You have not mentioned your New York apartment."

"I am pretty sure it is gone. It's just stuff, Rachel. We would more than likely have died if we were there."

Clicking through graphic depictions of suffering and crumbled infrastructure, Owen discovers a local Providence news affiliate. "Enough death and destruction for one day; let's see what is happening on the local level."

They choose a live feed and see a raincoated reporter standing before an iron gate.

Rachel leans forward in her chair, "Hey! That's right the fuck outside!"

"Okay. Easy girl. Let's hear what he says."

"*I'm outside the Alexander estate here in Newport, where Rachel Alexander Haig—the woman who saved the world—reportedly arrived home following her rumored heroics in Egypt and a mysterious convalescence at an off-the-grid facility in Europe. Accompanied by her new husband, the former Trust Fund Murderess is scheduled to meet President Jackson at a much-anticipated event at Rosecliff on Thursday. The Secret Service is onsite in collaboration with local authorities ....*"

"Turn it off!"

Owen fumbles for the remote and swipes it closed. "I'm sorry, Rachel, but the cat is out of the bag. I am stunned and amazed that our story traveled worldwide from those printed newspapers in Cairo."

"I remember that empty suit. Fred Schlemmer. He used to do

local sports. I went through grade school with him."

"It appears he moved on to fake news."

"I don't want to be famous, and this stupid gala will take it from bad to worse. Can we skip it?"

"You know, Rachel, standing up the president is considered bad form. Plus, you voted for her, right?"

Sensing Rachel's despair, Owen reaches out to touch her hand and receives a strong electric shock, "Ow, that hurt! Hey, Rach, what the hell?"

"Sorry, Owen. I generate static electricity when I get angry."

"Okay. That is just plain weird. By the way, I almost hate to ask, but what happened to your cube?"

"Funny thing. It was not in my bag when we got here. It must have fallen out inside that cargo plane."

* * *

Half a world away, a drone mech enters Andrew's office and drops Rachel's cubed discovery on his desk. The advanced replicant picks it up and smooths his index finger across a face, prompting a bright cerulean glow, "Why did you reach out to the human?"

"She is one of us."

"I disagree." Andrew places it in the desk drawer atop a growing collection of cubes.

Nicole | Gray battlecruiser

03:45 a.m. | October 4, 2044

"Astrid is dead."

Nina's tearful psychic pronouncement about Captain Astrid Brown's demise pierced Nicole's self-imposed mental lockdown like a needle popping a balloon, opening her mind to their terrifying situation.

In Nicole's Space Force Academy days, fellow cadets scoffed at an elective course designed to teach a method of self-hypnosis in the unlikely event of alien capture, but not the tall and svelte Wyoming native. She had witnessed enough UAPs to know their intentions were far from benign, bolstered by the case of a trusted ranch hand who vanished without a trace while investigating cattle mutilations at the far reaches of the family spread.

Who are the aliens?

What do they want?

What transpires after abduction?

The salient questions lingered long after her Space Force graduation and advancement through the ranks before retiring and accepting a gig piloting PTB operatives around the globe and beyond.

Staring at her four gray walls, Nicole muses whether Alejandro—the abducted ranch hand—was interred in the same cell before the aliens gutted and skinned him alive for an interstellar barbeque.

After 44 days, Astrid's death jolted Nicole from her deep hypnotic state. Peering across the shadowed cell, she watches an inconsolable Nina, hunched forward in an oversized PTB flight suit with her knees pulled up under her chin, shaking and crying.

Looking across the dank abyss into Flynn's cell, she wakes him with a loud neural knock.

Flynn pushes himself up and peers through the bars into Nicole's icy gaze.

"Wake up, Flynn, it's past time to kick some alien ass."

Miriam Alexander | Downtown Newport
02:15 p.m. | October 5, 2044

Fast-walking along a deserted sidewalk past boarded-up businesses through Newport's commercial district on a brisk fall afternoon, Rachel trails behind Miriam Alexander—Newport socialite, expert bridge player, and Mom.

"Why did I agree to this? I have plenty of dresses."

Realizing the stubborn woman on a shopping mission ignores her, she stops and yells, "Mom! What's the rush? Don't treat me like a 14-year-old shopping with mommy for a dress to wear to the school dance."

Wearing a fluffy vest over a bright blue tracksuit and walking shoes, clutching her designer leather handbag's shoulder strap, Miriam wheels to face her obstinate daughter, "Fond memories for your dear old Mom, Rachel. And sorry about the fast pace, but I miscalculated the walking time down here. Your dress fitting with Mr. Robertson is at 2:30 sharp! We can't be late. I want you to look your best for the president."

Rachel kicks a crack in the sidewalk. "Shit! Mom, I have plenty to wear at the house. You should see the piles of clothes I left behind in France."

"Nonsense, dear. Nothing in your closet fits you anymore. You lost over 20 pounds. Not to mention, Mr. Robertson agreed to open his dress shop just for us."

"I told you, Mom, no special favors."

"I'm thinking of a long evening gown with gloves."

Rachel grabs her mother by the elbow, "Look at my hands, Mom. Look at them! They always hurt, but I have no desire to hide them from anyone. No fucking gloves, got it?"

Miriam Alexander stifles tears, holding her daughter's disfigured hands, "I am so sorry; how did this happen again?"

"Tell you what. Let's skip the dress shop and grab a beer before those reporters loitering at the house discover we gave them the slip and walked downtown."

Outside Hilltop's protected gates for the first time in over a month, Miriam notices the boarded-up atmosphere for the first time.

"Fine, but first, a visit to Mr. Robertson's shop; he is waiting for us."

"Nothing extravagant. I don't want to upstage the president."

"She is a handsome woman."

"Sure, Mom. It's a good thing your daughter isn't a lesbian, or I might take a pass at her myself."

"Rachel, I never heard you talk like this before."

Rachel pierces her mother's sad eyes with an inquisitive look, "Really? I've been like this since high school. You just never took the time to get to know me."

"Maybe I do need a beer."

Rachel turns and flips the bird at Dave, her burly shadow behind the tinted front window of a black SUV idling at the corner, "Let's keep moving."

Marcus Alexander | Hilltop
05:35 p.m. | October 5, 2044

"That is checkmate, Owen. Care for another beating, my boy?"

Owen leans back in the plush leather recliner and grabs his empty tumbler, "No thanks. Three checkmates are enough humiliation for one day. Can I pour you another bourbon?"

"Why not." Marcus Xavier Alexander studies Owen's silhouetted profile pouring drinks in his private study crammed with books, records, and memorabilia from his prosperous career promoting music and sports events. Accepting the new glass, he confides in his young and talented new son-in-law, "I am ruined, you know."

Owen takes his seat and crosses a leg, "Well, sir. You and everyone else. My firm, Ford and Poole Capital was destroyed, and we lost a lot of good people."

The 70-year-old man downs the amber liquid in one long pull and sets the glass on a side table. After a long introspective pause, he speaks, "Owen, I was your age when the planes hit the Twin Towers in lower Manhattan on 9-11. The carnage and death were indescribable. I was on the 34th floor of the North Tower and barely escaped with my life. Awful memories of that fateful day are seared in my head forever. And now, to think the entire world was subjected to utter annihilation. I must admit, I am having trouble reconciling that reality." Scooping up the empty glass before setting it back down, he continues, "I can only assume that most of my properties lie in rubble."

"You know, Marcus, it is an odd thing. In my travels, I have seen unscathed blocks amid ruins. Perhaps some of your arenas still stand."

"I am sure they do, but it is a moot point. I am finished. The world left my generation behind long before the Gorks, and whatever rebuilds in its place will bear zero resemblance to what once was. That is for damn sure."

"Marcus? I need to ask you a question."

The distinguished gray-haired man smiles, "Sure, Owen, fire away."

Steeling himself to speak aloud, Owen leans forward, "Are you a member of The Powers That Be?"

Marcus stands out of his chair, a hint of agitation in his voice, "Never heard of it."

Owen rises, cornering his father-in-law in front of an overloaded bookcase, "Well, your daughter and I are now proud members. I thought you might want to know."

"Does Miriam know about this?"

"Rachel and I decided not to tell her anything, but I thought you might be interested in your daughter's new employer."

Marcus slides past Owen to refill his glass. "Okay, Owen. Do you want the truth? Here it goes. I thought we could shield Rachel from the Alexander family curse, but that dream ended when a fat fucker decided to rape her in a dark alleyway when she was only 18. My God, 18 years old. At that moment, she manifested the power given to her as a tiny baby in a neonatal intensive care unit."

"So, you knew Rachel had special abilities her whole life?"

"Let's just say her assailant picked the wrong girl to try and rape."

"Marcus, this is your own daughter we are talking about. How can you be so callous?"

"Callous? How dare you! I love my daughter more than anything in this world." Verging on releasing his vaunted temper on the much younger man, Marcus reigns it in with a long sigh, "Now then, to your original question. Yes. I am a member of the PTB. They have protected and guided us through generations. And yes, they have a special interest in Rachel's abilities."

"Were you ever going to let your daughter in on the family secret?"

"Fuck off, Owen. It is way more complicated than you will ever know."

"With all due respect, Marcus, you need to talk with Rachel. She struggles with everything that happened since fighting off the supernatural shitstorm under the pyramids."

Marcus stares out the window at two black-suited security men smoking under an old oak tree. "I could not be prouder of Rachel. I wish I could have seen her in action. Her hands. Fire shot from her hands. I had no idea that she could manage that."

Turning back to Owen, he laughs, "No, Owen. On the contrary, Rachel is fine. It is the rest of humanity that is obsolete."

President Lena Jackson | Rosecliff
06:20 p.m. | October 6, 2044

As dusk settles across Newport on the tip of Aquidneck Island in Narragansett Bay, two black SUVs navigate empty tree-lined streets from the Alexander family residence to the sprawling Rosecliff estate, a Gatsbyesque East Coast landmark with a spectacular oceanfront view.

Rachel looks through the tinted back window at the trailing SUV transporting her parents to the glitzy event. "It is so damn quiet. The last time a president showed up caused days of gridlock and chaos."

Owen mutters, "That was then; this is now."

At the entrance to the Rosecliff estate, Owen glances out the window and grasps Rachel's hand, "Holy shit, no wonder it's so quiet; it looks like the whole town came out to see the president."

The SUVs motor up the long driveway past National Guard troops holding throngs of reporters, bloggers, vloggers, and gawkers at bay on a roped-off section of the estate's expansive front lawn.

Rachel shakes her head, "Well, those people are here for the president, not us."

"I guess word spreads fast, even after the apocalypse."

Braking dead center in front of the mansion, Owen turns to his beautiful bride, "You ready, Rach? Here we go."

Exiting the vehicle to raucous cheers and applause, Owen feels like an A-lister at a glitzy awards gala. Hustling to Rachel's passenger side door, black-suited armed security beat him to the punch.

Beaming in his simple black wedding tux, Owen holds out his left arm for his stunning wife, standing out of the car in a lacy black long-sleeve gown with a high neck and long blond hair cascading down the open back.

Taking Owen's arm, Rachel turns and waves at the crowd of supporters as a sea of cameras burst to life in unison through the pink and orange-hued salty twilight air. "I thought everything was fried. Look at all of those cameras."

"Yeah, that is a bit surprising."

Owen escorts a smiling and waving Rachel halfway between the vehicles as the Alexanders exit their ride, dressed to the nines, Marcus in a tuxedo and Miriam in a silky blue jacket over a full-length floral dress.

The foursome mounts a short flight of stairs, joining a gathering of well-heeled guests in the white terra cotta mansion's magnificent front courtyard.

Stunned by the amassed spectators who appeared to recognize her when she exited the car, Rachel mutters, "I should go out there and say something to those people. I'm sure the guardsmen vetted the crowd."

Miriam overhears her daughter and objects, "In those heels? You will sink to your ankles in that wet grass, dear."

Trading eye rolls, Owen and Rachel watch a musclebound gorilla of a man in a black suit and dark shades make a beeline toward them while speaking into a mic. Owen catches the butt of a handgun tucked inside his jacket as he ushers them forward, "You're early. Follow me inside on the double."

Owen takes her hand, following Rachel's parents, whispering, "I'm not arguing with him."

Rachel pivots for a final wave to the well-wishers through the darkening haze before entering an ugly metal detector tarnishing the venue's regal French baroque revival architecture.

Emptying his pockets into a plastic bin, Owen chortles at the overweight security woman wearing a tight-fitting blue uniform, "Can't be too careful. Even with the woman who saved the world and family."

"Owen! Come on! They are waiting for us!"

Owen reclaims his wallet and keys, rejoining Rachel, and her parents inside the vestibule, waiting beside a tall, razor-thin White House aide.

The woman looks over the well-groomed foursome and smiles, "Okay. Everybody is present and accounted for now, correct?"

Rachel nudges Owen to speak, "Yes. We are all here. Not sure why I am always last, but there it is."

The woman responds with a warm smile, "Welcome to Rosecliff. Mr. and Mrs. Alexander, we are thrilled to have you here, but the president requested a private meeting with Rachel and Owen before the formal reception. You both can proceed into the main hall. Have a drink and something to eat. After all, this is a joyous occasion."

Miriam hugs her daughter and wipes a tear. "We are so proud of you both, aren't we, Marcus?"

Owen meets his father-in-law's eyes as the silvery-haired man smiles, "Why yes, yes, we are Miriam. Very proud indeed."

The White House aide smiles, "Well, okay then. Everyone is proud. Rachel and Owen, follow me."

Pushing through heavy doors, she gestures into the salon's gilded expanse. The Haigs enter, finding the leader of the free world holding court for a quintet of semi-recognizable politicians doting over her precocious two-year-old daughter entertaining the influential pols.

The president meets the guests of honor, hands extended with a charismatic smile on her light amber face, "Rachel and Owen Haig. I have heard so much about you both. What an honor this is to make your acquaintances in person."

Reciprocating a graceful elegance in her flowing lace gown, Rachel shakes Lena's hand, "No, Madame President, the honor is ours, right Owen?"

Glad-handing through the bipartisan group, Owen smiles, "Yes, the honor is all ours. What a thrill."

A stocky fellow in a gray pinstripe suit steps forward and puts an arm on Owen's shoulder, "Glenn Cohan, Lena's Chief of Staff. Owen, my man, can we interest you in a fine cigar and Kentucky bourbon out on the terrace? Come on, boys and girls, let's step outside and let the president have a moment alone with the fetching Mrs. Haig."

The dinosaur from Owen's home state, Vermont, whose name escapes him, slaps his back like they are old friends, "Man, Owen, I must say, you are batting way above all of our averages."

Rachel gives Owen a smiling shrug as he is hustled out the doors.

The skinny aide scoops up Lena's daughter and carries her out the other door. "Come on, Munchkin, time for bed."

With the hard-drinking group heading outdoors to smoke and trade dirty jokes, the president gestures toward chairs separated by a small table with a bottle and two glasses, "They may be grown-assed adults, but they act like a bunch of frat boys—even the women. And those are the ones I can stomach. I would not give two shits for the rest of Congress. They are looking to skin me alive over this shitstorm. But enough about my problems. I want to hear from you. Would you care for a snifter of brandy? I know I could use a drink."

"Sure. Mrs. Jackson …."

"Uh-uh, Lena. Please."

"Okay, Lena." Accepting the glass, Rachel settles into the seat across from the president, like a couple of girls out for a night on the town, "I'm shocked by the sheer number of people outside. How did they know this event was happening? The power came back only a few short days ago here in Newport—and it comes and goes at the most inopportune times. What is the rest of the country like?"

The 56-year-old Black Independent ignores the barrage of questions, offering a sly smile, "To you and your husband." Lena downs her brandy in a single shot, "That hit the spot. Join me in another?"

Rachel finishes her brandy and extends the fine crystal snifter, "Please."

The president refills the glasses and takes another drink, "Now then. I understand that you and Owen have been off-the-grid, such as it is since the invasion. You are unaware that news of your exploits spread worldwide like wildfire starting on Invasion Day + One."

"Not a clue. With the internet down and so much chaos and destruction, it still seems like a bad dream. The locals in Cairo who witnessed our pyramid extraction were relentless, trying to get at us in the hospital."

"That must have been harrowing. Although not as much as

what preceded it."

Feeling warm fuzzies from the brandy and an easy rapport with Lena, Rachel shakes her head and laughs, "There was a photo of me looking like shit in a hospital bed printed across thousands of newspapers spread all over Cairo. Of course, the articles were made-up nonsense, and we assumed it would cool down after a few days. People had more important stuff to deal with, like finding food and clean water. We heard your radio address at a cafe on the Nile. That was an excellent speech."

President Jackson smiles, "Glenn wrote it. The man is a total mensch." Pausing to formulate her words, she continues, "You asked about the crowd outside."

Rachel empties her glass, "You have a lot of supporters, including me. I suppose news of your visit to Newport got around, even without the internet."

Lena stretches her 5'6" athletic frame before waving toned arms around the gilded room, "Look at this magnificent place. It was built in 1902. The world got along just fine before the worldwide web. The human brain needed to ween off the internet. Granted, this is the equivalent of a heroin addict going cold turkey, but here we are."

Rachel watches her stride to a sofa, picking up her daughter's forgotten Barbie doll, "That makes sense. What about the rest of the country?"

The president pivots, holding up the 9-inch doll, "Can you believe this is supposed to be me? I have not had a figure like this since college." Placing the toy atop stacked luggage, she winces, "The Gorks knew where to hit us. The Northeastern power grid is an anomaly that will fail once winter hits with a vengeance. The rest of the country and most of the world will remain in the dark ages well into next year, if not longer."

"Jesus."

"Yes. It is a bad situation that is getting worse by the minute."

Letting that sad note linger between them, the conversation lapses as Rachel senses the president's reticence to get to a point.

"We accepted job proposals from the PTB."

Lena's face shows genuine surprise at the news, "I did not know that. The PTB? Pennywell is a keen judge of character, and his organization is the last bulwark against civilizational collapse. I am sure they will put your powers to good use."

Rachel places her empty glass on the table, "My powers? What do you mean?"

President Lena Jackson's smooth visage furrows, "I'm sorry, Mrs. Haig. Did I speak out of turn?"

Light-headed from the brandy, Rachel clears her throat and coughs, "You didn't, Madame President. I don't possess supernatural powers. I know that meme is out there." Her green eyes widen with a sudden epiphany, "The people are not here for you. They are here to see me. They think I am some kind of superhero, like in the comic books."

Lena retakes her seat and leans forward, radiating every ounce of gravitas her political soul can muster, "Would that be so horrible, Mrs. Haig? Look at you; you are Superwoman. The world needs an intelligent, beautiful, and strong hero. And despite your denials, my intel on your alien encounter under the pyramids is remarkable and compelling."

Rachel stands out of her chair, feeling the ornate walls closing around her. "So what? You want me to fly around in my invisible jet and kill all the bad guys with my lightning hands so you and your cronies can get back to business as usual? Excuse my language Madame President but fuck that shit. You don't know me; your intelligence is hearsay, gossip, and rumors. My parents don't understand what I went through."

"What about your husband?"

Considering everything she has kept hidden from her spouse over the past few weeks, she hesitates, "He knows enough."

Straddling a line between anger and frustration, Lena turns down the temperature in the room. "Mrs. Haig. Let's keep this on an even keel. I would like to present you to the world at this reception as a young American heroine who, by the Grace of God, activated a machine that blasted the fucking Gorks out of our skies. That is close to the truth. Am I right?"

"Close enough for government work."

The president laughs at the joke and calls for her aide to usher everyone back inside, "Good deal. So, we can call on you for an event now and again as a goodwill ambassador?"

"Sure. That will be fine. Just don't expect too much. Any power I had is now gone." Rachel watches her husband enter the salon, backslapping the senator from Vermont, clutching her hands together to hide latent blue energy spiraling to life on her palms.

* * *

Inside Rosecliff's packed ballroom, home to extravagant wedding receptions, like where Owen met Rachel, Marcus, and Miriam sit front and center in the near-capacity murmuring space. Marcus crosses his leg, cradling a Jack and Coke. Miriam nurses a chardonnay, admiring the presidential seal lectern centered on a riser against a backdrop of flags and resplendent floor-to-ceiling windows framed with drapes shimmering from the gilded ceiling.

Behind rows of invited guests and dignitaries, the press contingent waits for the show to start while a presidential photographer snaps holographic pictures.

"When is this thing going to start? We have been sitting here for over an hour."

Miriam shushes her husband, "Marcus, hush. You will be back home holed up in your study soon enough."

A string quartet playing an instrumental version of David Bowie's *Heroes* segues into a rendition of *Hail to the Chief* as President

Lena Jackson, looking regal in a sleeveless blue dress and pearls, makes her way to the podium. Everyone applauds while Owen, Rachel, Glenn Cohan, and the senatorial quintet—holding it together after polishing off pints of Kentucky hooch—assemble behind her.

President Jackson smiles at the assembled audience, "Thank you. Please be seated. Ladies and gentlemen, we are here tonight to celebrate true heroism." Turning toward Rachel with a sly wink, she adds, "Just for one day."

The audience settles back and listens to President Jackson's remarks, rewritten to assuage Mrs. Haig's last-minute appeals to ratchet down the supernatural angle.

"… And in conclusion, it is my honor as President of the United States to award our highest civilian honor, the Presidential Medal of Freedom, to Rachel Anna Alexander Haig and her husband, Owen Michael Haig." Lena turns and shakes their hands. As the capacity gathering applauds and cheers, a Naval officer in dress whites appears with Owen's medal. Lena rises onto her toes to place the heavy medallion dangling from a red, white, and blue ribbon around his broad shoulders.

Owen moves to the lectern, "Well, this is a total surprise. Thank you, President Jackson. I am honored. I wish my parents could be here tonight, but a simple trip down the interstate is no longer feasible. Anyway, Rachel and I don't feel like heroes. In fact, we did not expect to survive most of the ordeal, let alone save the world, unquote. I don't know the future, but any face in the crowd could be the next person thrust into a similar situation. Follow your gut and trust in the Lord. Thank you."

Lena repeats the process for Rachel as a worldwide audience tuned to the president's emergency station on their radio dials waits to hear the young savior's voice over the airwaves.

Rachel shakes hands with Lena before hugging Owen and the handsy pols, stalling for time before stepping to the podium. Taking a deep breath, she smiles at Marcus and Miriam, repressing her fear of public speaking. "Thank you, President Jackson. I knew I had it right when I voted for you four years ago."

The room erupts while Lena laughs and clasps her palms together, "Four more years, am I right?" Waiting out the chanted refrain, she feels a wind at her back—probably the brandy—and continues, "Like my husband said, we are not heroes; we had plenty of help on our strange odyssey." Addressing Owen, she laughs, "Remember the Jeep salesman in Tunis?"

Owen nods a reply, "Ahmed. What a character."

"How about the Warrens? The sweet couple from Texas we met at the pyramids. My God, I hope they survived."

Owen amplifies her observation, "Don't forget Captain Faisel, Flynn, and Nina."

Rachel refocuses on the audience hanging on her every word, "We lost a good friend named Louie. I did not want to leave here without mentioning his name."

Pausing to gather herself, she concludes, "Thank you, President Jackson, for this great honor. God Bless America and the world."

The skinny aide sidles behind the mic as Rachel retakes her place, "We can take a few questions before adjourning to the terrace for refreshments."

The aide ignores 200 hands rising in unison, reading the first name on a predetermined list, "Susan Ross, Fox News."

The veteran White House reporter leans forward to speak into a boom mic, "This is for Rachel Haig. Can you confirm or deny the rumor that you and your husband work for The Powers That Be? And that this whole thing could have been avoided if your organization had been more forthcoming years ago when the world still had time to prepare?"

Flabbergasted by the question, Rachel steps to the mic, "I am not in a position to comment on anything related to the PTB. I would reach out to them."

The aide reads the next name, "Okay. John Gault, Associated

Press."

A Black man in a shiny suit grabs the microphone, "My question is also for Mrs. Haig. It is rumored you used supernatural powers to defeat the Gorks." Realizing how ridiculous the words sounded coming from his mouth, he quips, "Point of order, I am from the AP, not the Daily Planet."

Waiting for anxious laughter to subside, Rachel returns to the mic, "Wow. I never realized how gullible the press can be when given a story that is so out there; it must be true, right? Would you believe the world's fate hinged on pure luck and a healthy dose of faith in good triumphing over evil? You can say those are my superpowers: luck and faith."

The aggressive reporter presses harder, unfazed by her evasive answer, "I am sorry, Mrs. Haig, but I have it on good authority that your hands are permanently scarred from the energy you wielded against a mysterious alien force underneath the Great Pyramid. May I ask you to show us your hands?"

Rachel absorbs the probing question, meeting her mother's gaze in the front row, *"Dammit, Mother, you were right about the fucking gloves."*

Feeling the eyes of the world upon her, Rachel succumbs to the pressure, holding up her hands, palms out, exposing luminous blue spirals. "Can everybody see my hands? Don't worry. As far as I know, nothing is about to shoot out of my fingers. I'm working with the best doctors to understand what is happening to me. Now you all know as much as I do. So, what was the first question again? Oh yeah. Controlled energy burst from my hands like Hermione Granger on steroids, blasting an evil alien race into another dimension. Anything else? Would you like to know my favorite color? Or my favorite sexual position? You name it. I'm an open book."

The stunned audience is reduced to hushed murmurs as news organizations transmit her revelations to a ring of communication satellites encircling Earth and beyond into the Heavens.

Lena and Glenn confer, choosing to cut their losses and end the ceremony before things get out of hand as the White House aide hustles Rachel away from the mic.

The president returns to the podium, "Please, ladies and gentlemen, enjoy the cocktails and food on the terrace."

A woman in an overcoat rises from the third row, pulling a 9mm Glock from her belt, yelling at the top of her lungs, "Murderer! Rachel Alexander—you murdered my son!"

The woman swings the gun forward in her shaky grasp as agents converge from all directions, fighting upstream through a panicked stampede for the exits.

Black-suited gorilla man vaults atop the riser, tossing the president over a shoulder, like Fay Wray, before hustling her offstage to the salon as the senators, the aide, and the Haigs duck for cover.

Rachel locks eyes with the enraged woman. "Owen, that's Senator Marjorie Cahill. She is the mother of the guy who raped me."

The ancient senator from Vermont overhears Rachel, "For the love of Pete, who let that nutcase in the room?"

Marcus Alexander rises from his front-row chair, putting himself between the shooter and the hunkered gathering exposed on the stage. "Drop it, Marjorie. You are making a fool of yourself."

With a look of recognition crossing her tearful face, the grieving woman aims at Rachel's father, pulling the trigger milliseconds before a Secret Service agent tackles her to the floor.

Miriam sees a nightmarish red stain widening across her husband's starched white shirt and faints to the floor in a heap. Jaw set and fists clenched, Marcus faces Rachel and Owen with a wink and smile before collapsing to the floor.

Gobsmacked by the murderous turn of events, Rachel rushes to her father, placing a glowing hand over the bleeding chest wound, "Dad, it will be okay. Owen! We need the alien powder. Did you bring any?"

A helpless and grief-stricken Owen shakes his head, "Rachel, I am sorry, but I never had any of that stuff."

Mr. Alexander smooths a bloodied hand through tears streaming down his daughter's cheeks, "It is okay, Rachel. Let me see your hands."

Her blood-smeared luminous blue hands light up his blanched face. Gurgling up blood, he pulls her toward him and garbles, "You are the blue spark."

The president's physician, a former Navy surgeon, hustles forward, moving Rachel aside to administer first aid, but Marcus Alexander bleeds out on the venerable mansion's parquet floor. At the same time, agents cuff the former Rhode Island state senator and escort the sobbing woman from the chaotic scene while the smoking gun remains in situ amidst upturned chairs scattered about the hall.

* * *

Blinking lights from three presidential choppers rise above Rosecliff into the inky night, two heading south toward Camp David and one with Rachel's deceased father and grieving mother heading north toward the nearest functioning medical examiner facility in Boston. From there, the president coordinated a secret service detail to escort Miriam to her sister's Beacon Hill residence. Meanwhile, searchlight drones light up the sprawling front lawn as a line of Guardsmen pushes the restless crowd off the property into the surrounding neighborhood's tony tree-lined streets.

Responding to the developing late-night situation at the Rosecliff estate, federal, state, and local authorities descend like vultures, turning the crime scene into a pissing match for who swings the biggest dick. The feds win, dispatching local authorities to patrol the surrounding neighborhoods while relegating state troopers to comb the property with bomb-sniffing dogs.

A frowning Black woman sporting an FBI windbreaker over a

t-shirt and jeans reenters the locked-down hall after establishing control of the situation. Her team vetted every invited guest before dismissing them with a stern warning not to speak to the press. Shuffling up to Owen and Rachel, the last two people left in the room, she rubs her tired eyes, rights a folding chair, and plops down with a world-weary sigh, "I am sorry for your loss. Marcus Alexander was an important man. His death will have consequences, even in this post-invasion world."

Owen emits an ironic chuckle, "He told me he was ruined."

Rachel turns to her husband, "When did he say that?"

"Just the other day."

Rachel replays the horrible act that lasted less than ten seconds in her head, "She was going to shoot me, but Dad stood up and called her by name. It is almost like he knew what was about to happen."

"Come on, now, Rachel. You're exhausted."

The FBI lady checks her Timex and yawns, "It appears the suspect, former state senator Marjorie Cahill, acted alone. I know that is of little consolation, but there it is. And the motive is also pretty obvious."

Hunched forward in shock in the black lace gown with Owen's jacket draped over her shoulders, she mutters aloud, "Yeah, I killed her son."

"Yes, I know, Mrs. Haig. The history between you and the Cahill family is a matter of public record."

Owen leans forward in the folding chair, elbows on knees with his bowtie hanging loose from his unbuttoned collar, "I had to go through a fucking metal detector. So did Rachel. How did Cahill get in here with a loaded handgun?"

"I have not figured out how she got past the Secret Service security detail, but that is a moot point. The fact is, she did."

Owen shakes his head, trying to contain his anger, "So that's it? Rachel loses her father, and we just shrug our shoulders and say, oh well, better luck next time?"

Rachel sobs, "It's my fault. Marjorie snapped the second she saw my hands. It is how I killed her son."

Stanley Hobbes | Hobbes Rare Books
04:10 a.m. | October 7, 2044

Both black SUVs make the short return drive to Hilltop past news vans prepping the latest angle on the Haig couple—a salacious revenge plot gone awry—for a fractional audience with spotty internet access. At the same time, vloggers, bloggers, and gawkers sneak about like zombies on crack, creeping through the bushes to peek inside windows, hoping to catch the mythical Trust Fund Murderess in an unguarded state of undress.

* * *

A wide-awake Rachel nudges her husband in the first SUV's back seat, "You go on inside, Owen. Get some sleep."

Owen wipes his bleary, bloodshot eyes, "What about you?"

"I can't go back into the house. I asked Dave to take me for a ride around town. I need time to think."

Dave, the driver, a burly fellow packing heat moonlighting as PTB security, looks back at Owen, "I got her, Mr. Haig. Not to worry."

"Should I come along?"

"Owen, I love you very much. But I need some alone time, okay?"

"Okay. I am sorry about your father."

"I know, Owen. He loved you very much."

"Yeah. I could never beat the old man at chess."

Watching a bone-tired Owen unlock the front door and disappear inside, Dave turns to his backseat passenger, "Where to, Mrs. Haig?"

"Hobbes Rare Books, it's right downtown."

* * *

Hopping out of the SUV in front of the hole-in-the-wall shop— her refuge from the world in the bad old days—she presses the buzzer, "Come on, you old fart. I know you are in there!"

The sound of multiple locks clunking open precedes the creak of the shop's front door, revealing Stanley Hobbes.

Seeing the silhouetted vision towering over him, his bespectacled face lights up, "Rachel? Is that you? I thought you forgot about me now that you are a big shot hobnobbing with the president."

Still wearing the black lace gown, her fingers stained a ruddy brown color, she tries to smile but starts to cry, "Can I come in? Something awful happened."

The short, round man, sporting a 3-day growth of beard, swings the door open, ushering her inside. Taking a peek up and down the street, he closes the door and locks them inside.

"Okay, Rachel. Just like old times. Tell me everything."

* * *

Upon hearing a Cliff Notes version of Rachel's life since he last saw her at the wedding up to her father's murder, Stanley Hobbes swipes thick specks with a hanky while shuffling around his high countertop, cluttered with old books. Hopping into his wobbly office chair in a dark-green moth-holed sweater pilled over an undershirt and khakis, he absorbs her incredible tale, "So your father's last words were blue spark?"

Relieved of her mental burdens, Rachel settles into the worn leather wingback she has sat in on too many previous occasions to count, sipping chamomile tea from a familiar chipped cup with a three-masted schooner on its side, "No. Not quite. Dad said I was the blue spark."

"Huh."

Suppressing a burgeoning paranoia, "What do you mean, huh?"

Stanley evades her prying eyes, glancing toward the back of his shop, "What? Oh, nothing. It is late—or very early—depending on your POV."

Rising to stretch her lithe form, she places her mug on the dusty glass countertop and smiles at her old friend, "Stanley, I can't believe my Dad is gone."

Pushing aside old paperbacks, he muses, "Well, given you now see dead people—where have I heard that before? Perhaps you will see him again."

Rachel raises an eyebrow, shuffling through the pulpy heap of vintage Edgar Rice Burroughs paperbacks someone had dropped off earlier that day, "Hey, look what I found, *The Warlord of Mars*. I don't think I ever read that one."

Stanley Hobbes smiles at his beautiful friend and avid reader of old science fiction, "Take it, it's on the house."

"That's good because I don't have any money."

* * *

Stanley Hobbes watches as Rachel walks out the door and slides into the jet-black, electrified behemoth. Relocking the door, Hobbes hits the light switch with his pudgy hand and shuffles through the pitch-black space to the overloaded storeroom. Sidling along a narrow aisle with heavy boxes stacked to the rafters all around him, he reaches a dented file cabinet and pulls open the rusted top drawer. Clicking on a penlight from his trousers, the short man extracts a dog-eared, coffee-stained half-inch-thick typewritten manuscript filled with colored tabs. Shining the light on the title page, he reads, The Blue Spark by Stanley Hobbes.

Rachel | Hilltop

06:40 a.m. | October 7, 2044

Dawn breaks over the cloudless eastern horizon with the promise of a made-to-order New England autumn day as Dave drives Rachel back to Hilltop. Sneaking inside and tiptoeing through the darkened interior where she was born and raised to a slumped Owen, snoring in a comfortable chair with a blanket pulled under his square chin, she looks around, wide awake and unsure of what to do. Mulling the promise of a lukewarm shower, the 24-year-old instead enters her father's study and reclines behind his messy desk. Rocking back in the same seat she climbed up into as a little girl, she gazes around the high-ceiling, dark wood paneling at her father's prosperous life, spoken through pictures, awards, memorabilia, and mementos. A sudden inspiration compels her toward the voluminous record collection.

Wiping away more tears, she moves to his vaunted record collection and selects a mint-condition David Bowie LP worth a small fortune. Rachel slides the immaculate vinyl from its sleeve onto the high-end Japanese turntable. After donning expensive noise-canceling headphones, she returns to the chair and swings a bare leg over the armrest. Closing her swollen eyes, the familiar intro to *Heroes* lulls her into a deep slumber.

Richard | Hilltop

05:05 p.m. | October 7, 2044

Rachel stares at the sat phone on the kitchen table, waiting for it to produce a signal. "Ring, damn you. Ring."

Owen enters like a masculine Nurse Ratched, bearing a tray with anxiety meds and a cup of water, "You told me to stop saying ring because it sounds stupid."

"It is just an expression, Owen." Seeing the prescription bottles, she shakes her head, "No more pills; I'm done. I need a clear head. I may have been hallucinating dead people in my sleep."

More than a little concerned for Rachel's mental health, he places the tray next to the sink, "Is that what Hobbes told you? How is the little hobbit?"

Rachel produces a light chuckle at the LOTR reference, showered and dressed in a flannel shirt over travel khakis, with wet blond hair pulled into a ponytail, "Same old Hobbes, a man, frozen in time." Rachel replays the morning in her head, "When did the power go out?"

Owen peers out the bay window behind the kitchen sink at the fall colors, "Not sure; it was out when I woke up and found you in the study with the headphones on."

"Well, here we sit. I think the battery in the satellite phone is dead. I don't know if Mother made it to Aunt Shirley's house. And to top it off. Not a word from The Powers That Be."

Breaching the walk-in pantry, searching for cookies or crackers, Owen pops a can of sparkling water, "So, Rachel, should we make something to eat? I'm hungry."

Rachel turns and sighs at the built-in fridge filled with thawing foods and melting ice. "We should empty the refrigerator before it starts to smell."

"Ah, yes, the fridge." Owen grabs the thick door handle to triage the edibles when a loud knock interrupts their culinary conundrum. Turning to his beautiful, grieving spouse, he attempts to lighten the mood, "I'll get it. Perhaps Luigi's Pizzeria took pity on our complete lack of cooking skills."

Swinging open the front door, he encounters two men: an older fellow in a corduroy barn coat with a thick head of curly charcoal hair dwarfed next to a ripped man in camo fatigues wearing dark shades and a thick black GI Joe beard obscuring his scarred face.

Unsure of what to say, but with an inkling of who the men work for, Owen gibes, "Aren't you fellas a little early for Halloween?"

Puzzled by the off-the-cuff humor, the older man stammers, "I'm Professor Richard King from The Powers That Be." After a pregnant pause, King turns to his burly partner, "Dammit, Pembroke, we are at the wrong mansion. I told you to double-check the address."

Owen opens the door wide, stifling an impertinent laugh at the earnest man's expense, "No. No. I am Owen Haig. You are at the right place."

"Oh, thank God. Your wife," looking at a piece of paper, "Rachel, I believe. Is she here as well?"

"Why don't you both come inside."

Chapter Five:

The Assignment

Rachel | Quonset Point Air National Guard Base

12:45 a.m. | October 8, 2044

After accommodating Rachel's last-minute detour to Hobbes Rare Books to deposit a letter through Stanley's mail slot, Dave rolls the black behemoth past opened gates at the Quonset Point Airbase toward a sleek aircraft fueled and loading under generator spotlights. Hustling to open the passenger door for the melancholy young woman who just lost her dad, the burly bodyguard embraces her in a heartfelt bear hug in the chilly early-morning New England air.

"Goodbye, Mrs. Haig. The boys and I will take good care of Hilltop while you are away."

Extricating from his thick arms, Rachel smiles, handing him another sealed envelope, "Thank you, Dave. Please give my mother this letter when you check on her in Boston. If my brother, Joseph, returns while I am gone, tell him I am sorry about Dad—and to keep his nose clean."

"You got it, Mrs. H."

Rachel wipes tears from her eyes, turning toward Owen, waiting at the swept-wing Chrysalis Air jet's open portal while Richard King micromanages Pembroke's three-man crew loading gear and supplies onto the craft.

Owen nods toward Dave mouthing thanks and receiving a thumbs up in reply before the freelance PTB bodyguard climbs behind the wheel and heads back toward Newport.

Feeling empty-handed and unprepared for a journey south of the equator, Rachel ducks into the plane and removes her tassel-sleeved leather jacket. After stowing it with a small satchel filled with personal stuff she probably won't need, she plops into the portside bulkhead seat across from Owen and snickers.

Scooching into his seat, Owen looks across the aisle at his wife, surprised by her levity after the tear-jerker farewell with Dave, "What's so funny?"

"Where's your shirt?"

"My shirt?"

"Yeah, the last time we flew on this thing, Flynn gave you that awful pink shirt."

Owen adjusts his belt and smiles, "Forward, Rachel. Let's not dwell on the past. Especially when we are heading to the Amazon. Say it with me: To save the world."

"Owen, I need to tell you something."

"What?"

Pembroke's mercenaries duck inside the narrow fuselage, shuffling past, taking seats in the back rows.

"You know what, Owen, it can wait."

***

Inside the cockpit's tight confines, Cowboy gnaws on sunflower seeds and completes a preflight checklist before speaking over the intercom, *"Okay, buckle up, everybody, we are cleared for take-off."*

Taxiing past grounded fleets languishing out of service, Cowboy stares through night-vision shades into the darkness down the long runway and throttles up the airship's powerful engines. Satisfied, he releases the wedge-shaped Chrysalis Air jet hurtling down the slick macadam before vaulting into the inky sky.

Spitting a sunflower shell into a paper cup, he glances out his rain-spattered portside window seeing nothing but darkness where Providence and Boston farther to the north would light the night sky in the good old days.

"Fucking aliens."

* * *

After the dramatic vertical take-off pushed everyone into their comfortable seats, the sensation eases as the craft levels off at a 45,000-foot cruising altitude swooping through the thin frigid air at a steady 550 MPH nonstop to Manaus, Brazil.

Cowboy's easy drawl resonates over the airship's speakers, *"Okay. That was fun. I hope y'all brought something to do or a good book. Our flight time to the destination is 14 hours and 55 minutes. Also, we may need to skedaddle around a Cat 1 over the Gulf of Mexico."*

Rachel and Owen exchange a nervous smile, hands entwined across the narrow aisle.

"What were you going to tell me, Rachel?"

"Owen, I'm ...."

Seated behind Rachel, Professor Richard King leans forward and taps her shoulder, "Here you are, Rachel, my made-to-order sleeping pills, as promised."

Rachel pulls her long blond hair over her left shoulder and twists in her seat, accepting two yellow capsules poured into her hand,

"What's in these?"

Richard pops a couple and swallows hard before producing a cocksure grin, "My secret recipe. All-natural, I assure you. The effect is similar to Xanax but without the nasty baggage. They hit fast. Oh. I better lie back."

Collapsing into his seat, the professor slides a sleep mask over his eyes and is out like a light.

Owen watches as Rachel shrugs and unscrews the cap from a water bottle, "You are going to take those?"

"I trust him." Rachel places the capsules on her tongue, "he would not steer me wrong. See you in Brazil, Owen."

After washing down King's little yellow pills, Rachel's green eyes blink and close tight before she snuggles into a pillow propped against the portside window.

"Okay. No one asked if I wanted a pill." Owen stares at the blackness out his window, leans back, and lets the craft's movement and sounds lull him asleep like a baby in the womb.

Behind Owen, Pembroke stares at a blank seatback screen, trying not to think about the cigarettes in his shirt pocket.

In the 8-seat jet's back rows, Pembroke's handpicked mercenary trio settles in for another routine mission presaging their next paychecks. Brothers Ariel and Elias Solomon shuffle cards across the third row.

In the back row by the galley and the lieu, the sculpted form of Antoine Sheffield in gym shorts and a Seal Team Seven tee retrieves a worn copy of Joseph Conrad's *Heart of Darkness* from his bag.

Pennywell | PTB HQ, Scotland
05:45 a.m. | October 8, 2044

Andrew enters Pennywell's dark inner sanctum and flips a light switch, revealing the CEO slumped before a roaring virtual fireplace in the modern, sophisticated Scandinavian-designed apartment. Scanning vitals, the über replicant determines his boss is in decent shape but could use a shower and a healthy breakfast.

"Sir? Artemus? It is time to wake up."

Pennywell's dark gray eyes open, reaching for a glass of water to moisten his cotton mouth, "What time is it, Andrew?"

"Quarter to six, you wanted to know when the team was en route to Brazil."

Pennywell levers his favorite chair upright and stretches his lanky form. "This is it. They must find the lost ship. If the Grays or Pike reach it first, we are all fucked."

"So, you say, sir."

"Andrew, you sound dubious."

"We both know there is more here than meets the eye."

Pennywell slides a comb through his thin gray hair, "Do you mean Rachel Alexander Haig? Her transhumanism is breathtaking to behold." Hitting Andrew with a devilish sideways grin, "But then again, so is yours."

* * *

Vigorous and fit for a man a fraction of his 134 years, Pennywell slings a sopping wet towel onto a chair back and enters his spacious closet. Glancing at his lean and fit nakedness reflected in a full-length mirror, he notes the wrinkled ravages of age and nods, "That's okay. I am just about done."

After pulling into PTB skivvies and thin black socks, he buttons a crisp white button-down shirt and proceeds to a long row of identical black suits.

Dressed and ready for another post-invasion day, the CEO stops at his front door to adjust his signature silver Saguaro bolo in a mirror and remove a speck of lint from his lapel.

Walking down the echoing corridor past vacant studios and

apartments meant to accommodate teams of PTB recruits, the CEO of the enigmatic organization heads to the galley for breakfast.

* * *

Entering the well-appointed dining facility, Pennywell imagines the space filled with brilliant, pretty people eating, drinking, talking, and laughing as robots rush between tables filling orders, akin to an upscale restaurant anywhere in the world. Instead, he grabs a tray in the churchlike atmosphere and moves down an abbreviated breakfast buffet prepared to accommodate the current skeletal human staff in need of sustenance.

Filling a fine China plate with poached eggs, Scottish kippers, and burnt toast, he wonders if the sisters' burgeoning cravings include food, "Perhaps I will ask Andrew."

After pouring a black coffee, he chooses a table and digs into his breakfast.

Piercing the annoying quiet, Gene Simmons and Aashvi Patel burst through the doors, deep in conversation, grabbing trays, oblivious to his presence.

"Hello, you two. Come join me. This place is like a fucking morgue when no one is around."

Simmons sees the CEO sitting alone in the half-lit dining area, "Hello, Artemus. We were discussing Rachel Haig's paranormal development."

Pennywell invites them to his table with a sweeping hand gesture, "Have a seat and enlighten me—apparently, everyone has an opinion on the lovely and fetching Mrs. Haig's superpowers."

The accomplished physicians exchange hesitant looks while setting their trays on the table and taking seats.

Pennywell slices into his kippers and smiles at the pair, "Well?"

Patel bites her lip, peeling the lid from her yogurt cup as Doctor Simmons takes a long sip from his PTB mug before speaking,

"Artemus, Rachel's transhumanism mirrors the sisters' fast-developing sentiency. We do not think this to be a coincidence. Her physiological and neurological transformations defy known science. This evolutionary process should span epochs, not mere weeks in time."

Pennywell shrugs, "So what is the problem? We are The Powers That Be. Our charter is advancing the human condition to an Omega Point." With a wry chuckle, he adds, "Whatever that looks like."

Patel dips a silver spoon in her creamy yogurt, "Mrs. Haig is already there."

Looking at his concerned colleagues across the table, he chews as a mischievous smile widens across his intelligent face, "Do you all know about the third fleet loitering about the fucking solar system between Saturn and Jupiter?"

Weary of the interstellar interlopers looming high above, Patel shakes her head, "You mean another fleet in addition to the Gorks and the Grays? No."

"Well, allow me to fill you both in on the best-kept secret since the Kennedy assassination. A third fleet of what appears to be self-replicating bots is also lurking out there."

"What do they want?"

Pennywell dabs his mouth with a napkin and stands, "Enjoy your breakfasts. Try the kippers, Gene. They are excellent this fine morning."

Simmons and Patel watch Pennywell grab yogurts and spoons before exiting with a to-go cup of joe cradled in his other hand.

Aashvi Patel turns to the PTB's chief medical officer, "Why didn't you tell him?"

Simmons chomps down on a rasher of bacon, "Well, unless Rachel Haig's superpowers include hiding a baby bump post her first trimester, then the cat will be out of the bag soon enough."

* * *

Feeling fit and satisfied after breakfast, Artemus Pennywell strides down a long hall toward echoing power saws, hammers, and welding torches. Peeking through double doors, he watches Numbers 14 and 15 direct worker bots around a sound stage renovation into a replica of a 1960s-era television studio.

Number 15 brushes unruly bangs from her forehead with her sweaty forearm and smiles at her boss, "Hello, sir."

"How goes the remodel, 15?"

The svelte brunette places her hammer atop yellowed antique blueprints and walks across the sawdust toward the CEO, "The project is on schedule for your broadcast to the world. Viraj Patel located the holographic equipment we need at a recording studio outside London—it should be here this afternoon."

Musing on his conversation with the doctors while trying not to get pulled into her soulful blue-eyed gaze, "Excellent, my dear. Keep up the good work. Here, I brought you a yogurt from the galley."

The sultry replicant accepts the cool plastic container, peels back the lid, and licks it with her long pink tongue, "Blueberry. Good."

"I'm glad you like it. Give this one to 14. Please tell your sisters there is plenty more in the galley where that came from."

Owen | 46,000 feet above Venezuelan Coast
01:05 p.m. | October 8, 2044

A violent shudder startles Owen from a restless slumber, his puffy eyes landing on Rachel's pretzel-like form, snoozing like an angel.

More shakes and an incessant rattle from the galley force the former banker to give up on trying to sleep. With a loud yawn, he releases his belt and bumps into the cramped passenger cabin's low ceiling. "Shit!" Rubbing his head, he catches Pembroke's glazed stare over the seatback. Unsure if the man sleeps with his eyes open, Owen waves a hand in front of the mercenary's face.

"What the hell are you doing?"

"Sorry, Pembroke, I thought you were asleep."

"With my eyes open? That would be creepy even for me. Plus, I do not sleep well on planes. I really need a smoke."

"Well, I'm making coffee. Can I pour you a cup?"

"That would be swell."

After a quick leak and a good old-fashioned hand scrubbing, Owen stands in the galley before a complicated machine that will, in theory, emit a piping hot caffeinated beverage into a cup. "Shit. I hate coffee makers."

"Allow me, Mr. Haig."

"Thanks, uh …."

"Antoine." The strapping fellow with a southern draw like honey and butter dripping off a warm biscuit scooches his muscular ass around Owen in the tight space, "And don't think twice about it. I will make enough for everyone."

Grabbing the seatback as the plane swoops, careful not to disturb the somnambulant Solomon boys, Owen reaches his bulkhead seat as Cowboy's voice ratchets over the intercom:

"Mornin' cowpokes, I have good news and bad news. We are about three hours from Manaus—that is the good news. The bad news is that we must fly through a powerful weather system to reach our destination. We do not have enough fuel to do anything else. I will need everybody belted and seated upright in a short while, so if you gotta take a leak, the time is now."

Cowboy | Manaus
04:15 p.m. | October 8, 2044

Tossed like a kite through roiling zero-visibility punctuated by terrifying electrified displays of mother nature's primacy over planet

Earth, the black triangle drops beneath gigantic storm clouds, flying 500 feet above an endless dark green jungle through heavy rain and fierce crosswinds. Cowboy banks west at a flooded Amazon River, following the storied waterway toward Manaus at the confluence of the Rio Negro and Solimóes Rivers. Farms and fields carved out of the rainforest pass below the craft as the clouds part and sparkling late-afternoon sunshine floods the cockpit in blinding light.

Bouncing and jostling like a Mexican jumping bean in his cockpit seat, Cowboy hails the tower, getting nothing but static in reply. Adjusting course toward the international airport, he mutters, "Good God, this place is worse than Edinburgh."

Buzzing the airfield, everyone gasps at the post-apocalyptic sight of aircraft from fixed-wing prop jobs to jumbo jets abandoned where they last moved in a chaotic post-invasion hodge-podge. Garbage mixed with opened luggage and loose personal articles lies scattered about the tall marshy grasses between the taxiways and the smoldering and ruined terminal structure. Performing a visual recon of the main landing strip, Cowboy breathes easier, finding it free of obstructions before sweeping around for a final approach, with the blazing sun to his back and the fuel gauges pinging empty.

Landing struts lock in place seconds before the rugged wheels bound down the cracked and potholed runway, with the engines roaring in reverse. Leaning on the brakes, Cowboy manages to jerk to a stop 50 feet from an Air Emirates 747 ditched off the runway's side with its enormous starboard wing jutting skyward.

The tired Texan smiles at whoops and claps from the peanut gallery through his closed cockpit door while perusing an airport diagram. Finding a private aviation section at the far end of the airfield, he lets off the brakes and rolls forward, avoiding the jumbo jet's wing.

Taxiing across the chaotic scene that was a functioning airport, Cowboy decides to lighten the mood, adopting his best commercial airline pilot voice: *"Welcome to Manaus, Brazil. The local time is 16:42, and the temperature outside is a balmy 92 degrees. Thanks for flying Chrysalis Air, and we do hope you enjoyed your flight."*

* * *

Owen avoids bumping the low ceiling while standing to stretch, "Okay. That was scary as shit." Turning to Richard King with an ironic smile, "I hope we can make our connecting flight to Santarém."

Richard zips his pharmacological bag and smiles at his new colleague, "Quite right, young man; this was the first leg on our journey."

Half-listening to the conversation, Rachel stretches her lithe form in the cramped space, "Tell me again why we did not land in Santarém?"

Pembroke interjects, "It does not have a suitable runway to land this thing."

Antoine laughs from the back row, "Neither did this dump. Man, we almost all died in a fiery crash."

The Solomon boys fist bump the Black Navy Seal in violent agreement.

Pembroke places a cigarette between his lips, counting down to ignition while peering outside as the plane slows to a stop before a row of dilapidated hangars, "Gentlemen, I want this flying wing offloaded on the double. I will set up a perimeter, just in case."

Owen's hazel eyes widen, hearing the military man's stern command, sounding like an extra in a shooter video game. This just got real.

* * *

After Owen's offer to help the lads unload the craft meets with a polite, *fuck off,* the couple wanders into the offices of a defunct Amazon tourism company. Rachel steps over an upturned file cabinet into a kitchenette, finding a vending machine with its front ajar. Pulling it open, she sees a lone can of Diet Dr. Pepper and smirks, "I'm not that thirsty."

Owen appears in the doorway holding two 16-ounce Coke bottles by their dusty necks, "They're warm."

"Bless you, Owen."

Accepting her bottle, Rachel hears scuffling and whispers through a closed door at the end of a hallway. Signaling Owen for quiet, she sneaks into the shadows and opens the door, coming face-to-face with an adolescent girl and boy clothed in grimy rags.

Seeing the terrified looks on their faces, Rachel smiles and holds up her hand, "It's okay. We are the good guys."

The girl's dark, intelligent eyes scrutinize Rachel before pulling the younger boy forward by the hand.

"That's it. We are friendly." Waving with her free hand, "Owen. Give me your bottle."

"I don't think soft drinks are healthy for the little ones, Rachel."

"Don't be greedy, Owen. They are starving." She reaches into a pocket and retrieves two snack bars pilfered from the plane's galley, "Here. Take these. They are good."

Wary of the tall, fair-skinned woman, the pre-teen girl clutches the modest food offering in her dirty hands and smiles.

The younger lad steps forward and relieves Owen of his Coke bottle.

"Uh, you're welcome."

The impish pair giggle to each other, scrambling out a side door into the dusky air.

With an irony-laced chuckle, Owen turns to his sweaty wife, "We have been in Brazil for fifteen minutes and have already been mugged. If Pembroke's guys ask, those were two savage drug runners who stole our Cokes."

"Sure, Owen. Whatever you say."

* * *

Long shadows creep across the cracked and puddled, steamy hot tarmac as the Haigs join Pembroke and Richard, watching the boys finish transferring the bulky gear onto a commandeered airport luggage conveyance.

Richard turns to the American couple, "Oh, there you are. Wandering off is ill-advised. But no matter."

Owen snickers, "You should have seen the other guys."

"What?"

"Nothing."

Pembroke lights a cigarette, "Uh, Owen, can you help the men push this wheeled monster toward that hangar?"

Owen scans toward the opened hangar bay where Cowboy haggles with someone before a relic from a bygone aeronautical past, "Sure."

* * *

Owen and the boys push while Rachel steers the cumbersome baggage carrier toward an ancient Ford Tri-Motor gassing up outside the hangar.

Upon seeing the vintage aircraft immune to the EMP hit that took out almost everything else within the airport and beyond, Antoine cracks, "We just went from Star Wars to Indiana Jones in a heartbeat."

Dripping in sweat, Owen laughs, "Hey, that's not bad."

* * *

The well-compensated Portuguese bush pilot lifts the overloaded Ford Tri-Motor off the crumbled macadam into the calm evening sky transporting the expedition on a final 1.5-hour leg to Santarém.

Dead-tired, Cowboy rolls the Chrysalis Air flying wedge into the empty hangar, pulls the doors shut, and settles in for a well-deserved nap.

Richard | Santarém
08:30 p.m. | October 8, 2044

The 30s-era Ford Tri-Motor bounces onto the pitted runway and taxis to a stop at the small airport in Santarém, where the Amazon and Tapajós Rivers meet in a spectacular act of nature, drawing visitors from around the world before the invasion.

Pembroke unlatches the passenger door and pushes it wide, cigarette jutting from his lips, "Okay, boys, you know the drill."

The snarled command is met with a chorus of moans and curses from the ex-military trio, weary of hefting the same shit from plane to plane and now into the filthy bay of a rusted old cargo truck.

* * *

Rachel, Owen, and Richard watch Pembroke's mercenaries disappear down a rutted road in the bush pilot's diesel truck laden with the expedition's supplies.

Squeezing her glowing hands closed in the darkness, Rachel turns to Richard King, "So the pilot's cousin owns a riverboat here in Santarém? How convenient."

Richard notices her glowing hands but addresses her probing question, "Sometimes it is better to be lucky than good, my dear." Slinging his small pack over a shoulder, "Now, let's find a ride into town and a place to hang our hats for the night."

* * *

The truck screeches to a stop before a locals-only watering hole with lost souls littering the crumbled sidewalk in the pale moonlight. Clicking on his penlight, Pembroke checks the bar's weather-beaten sign against a scribbled name, "This is the place. What a shithole."

From behind the wheel, Antoine turns to his boss, "Do you want me to go in and find Captain Ortega?"

Pembroke smiles and flicks a butt out his open window, "It's not that kind of bar, Antoine. No, I'll do it."

As Pembroke disappears into the dive bar, Ariel Solomon leans forward from the cab's backseat, "Man, I'd punch the old fuck in the face if he talked down to me like that."

Antoine smiles, checking the rearview for any signs of trouble, "It's okay. Mr. Pembroke is a good man. I heard a lot worse than that in my day."

Five minutes later, the scary Brit with robot legs manhandles a sloven drunk outside the establishment's swinging doors. Pushing the middle-aged man wreaking alcohol beside the grumbling Solomons, Pembroke jumps into the truck's front cab, "Okie-Dokie, that was fun. To the riverfront, my boy. This old fuck has our boat."

"Yes, sir, Mr. Pembroke."

* * *

Travel-weary and hungry, Richard and the Haigs check in at the Hotel Granrios—one of the few establishments open for business in Santarém.

Richard twirls his room key on a thick index finger, "Who's hungry?"

Rachel and Owen exchange a glance, "Sure."

"Excellent! Let's meet back here in 15 minutes."

* * *

The stare-eyed trio attempt to focus on menus by candlelight inside the hotel's open-air restaurant, feeling the last vestiges of adrenaline ebb from their bodies after the long trip.

A young woman appears between hanging ferns with a paper pad and a bored expression.

Richard beams at the waitress, "My dear, why don't you surprise us? But first, bring a bottle of your best cachaça and three glasses."

Rachel chimes in, "I'll have a Coke."

The girl rolls her eyes, "We have no ice."

"That's okay. Bring the bottle."

Two hours later, Rachel nurses her third Coke after consuming her share of a scary-looking grilled local fish wrapped in banana leaves, which hit the spot, despite its toothy grimace and dead-eyed, *"How could you?"* stare.

Feeling no pain, Owen refills his glass with the clear, sweet alcohol, splashing a small amount on the table, "Rachel, you should try this. Hey, Professor, what's it called again?"

The erudite scientist smiles, "Cachaça. Or Brazilian rum, if that's easier to pronounce. It is the national drink down here."

After emptying his glass, Owen starts to speak, but his eyes glaze over, slumping sideways in his chair.

Unaccustomed to seeing her husband inebriated, Rachel asks King, "Is he okay?"

"Cachaça sneaks up on the best of us." Richard checks Owen's pulse and chuckles, "He'll be fine. Perhaps a little headache in the morning, but nothing to worry about. It was not my intention, but since your husband is out, perhaps we can chat, just the two of us."

"Okay, what do you want to talk about?"

"Well, for one, the mission to locate a lost alien ship that crashed sometime during the late Cretaceous. Are you both up to speed on that? Any questions or concerns?"

"We read the mission brief back in Newport and understand the wreck contains a secret weapon. I gotta tell you, it was light on details."

Richard nods, "The PTB is reticent to share beyond a basic need to know. That goes for all of us, even Pennywell. But for the good of the mission, I want to ensure that you and Owen understand what you have agreed to do."

"Maybe I should have a drink."

"I would not recommend it in your condition."

"Wow. You are good, Professor. How did you know I'm

pregnant?"

"Doctor Simmons informed me of your condition before you left for the States."

Rachel smiles, piercing Richard's active mind with her thoughts: *"Of course he did. Can you hear me now?"*

Richard leans back with a raised bushy eyebrow and a grin, "That is quite impressive, my dear."

Using Owen's glass, Rachel pours more Cachaça, "Do you know how much concentration it takes for me to *not* do that?"

The PTB's top scientist concurs, "I have worked with telepaths over the years. Most are troubled individuals. Some have committed suicide to put an end to their psychic plight. Tragic."

"Welcome to my world." Rachel tilts back the half-filled glass and takes a long sip, "Oh boy, that is strong."

Richard slides a bowl of lime wedges to the table's edge, "Mrs. Haig, can you move the bowl?"

With an imperceptible flick of her index finger, she elevates it off the table, "Like this?"

"Yes. Excellent. That, in a nutshell, is why you are here."

Recovering from the fermented sugarcane beverage, Rachel hits Richard with piercing green eyes, "To perform magic tricks?"

Richard pours the last drops into her glass, "No. Now, who is being coy? When we reach the lost ship, the ancient alien payload may rest in a precarious spot. Or, perhaps in its deteriorated state, it leaks deadly pathogens into the humid jungle air. If so, we will all perish before we know what hit us."

"But not me, right? Because I am fucking special. I have half a mind to send Owen home right now. He almost died the last time, and he warned me that joining the PTB would lead to certain death. Man, I hate it when he is right."

"The Powers That Be is not subtle, Rachel. You are not only the failsafe but, perhaps, not to sound overly dramatic, the last hope.

Someday, your abilities will be commonplace amongst humankind, but for now, we have you. And for that, we are grateful."

Rachel raises her glass, "I appreciate the sentiment, Richard."

Seeing the blue glow of her hand refracting through the glass, Richard leans forward, "Would it be okay if I examined your hands?"

Setting the empty glass atop the table, Rachel shrugs, "Sure, why not." Turning her hands facing upward on the wooden table, the luminous blue spirals pulse and glow beneath her palms from wrists to fingers.

"Fascinating. And Gene does not know what is causing this sub-cutaneous phenomenon?"

"It's not glowing splinters or anything like that. It is hard to explain. It is me, and I am it. Whatever *it* is."

Shrugging off a strange feeling that Richard knows more than he is letting on, she continues, "This is different from shooting fire from my hands. That hurt like hell. This is almost comforting."

Wishing she had another drink, she muses, "My father said something before he died."

Richard's amiable expression darkens, "What did your father say, Mrs. Haig?"

Rachel frowns, feeling a lightheaded swoon, "Man, that is some strong stuff. Uh. What did he say? Oh yeah, he said I am the blue spark."

Richard checks his watch and smiles, "Huh, an odd turn of phrase. No matter. We better get your husband upstairs to bed."

Rachel | Hotel Granrios

05:55 a.m. | October 9, 2044

"Where the hell am I?"

Rachel Haig bolts upright atop the squeaky bed and looks around the dark hotel room, "Oh yeah, Brazil."

Checking bright sunshine leaking through blackout shades, she scratches her head and slides out of bed, "I need coffee."

Leaving Owen sleeping off his Cachaça hangover, Rachel descends flights of concrete steps in a Chrysalis Air t-shirt and gray sweatpants into the kitschy open-air lobby of the Hotel Granrios, scanning for a complimentary coffee station.

The oily front desk clerk recognizes Rachel's caffeinated quest, gesturing toward the coffee cart with a leering smile.

Small lizards dart across her path, shuffling in clapping thongs toward a row of silver carafes set atop a cart betwixt potted palms and a long rack stuffed with tourist brochures.

Swiping her brow from the heat and humidity, even at this early hour, Rachel fills a cup and bumps elbows with a handsome fellow in a gaudy tropical shirt who appeared out of nowhere, splashing hot coffee across her wrist.

"How clumsy of me, madam." Snatching up a wad of napkins, the stranger dabs at her hand, "Please let me be of assistance."

Pulling back on reflex, Rachel looks into the rakish guy's blue eyes and tanned face, noting his dark hair has just the right amount of gray at the temples. "That's all right. I didn't expect to bump into other guests at this hour." Pulling unruly blond bedhead over her shoulder, she winces, "I really need a shower."

The man beams a perfect white smile, "Well, in addition to practically scalding your wrist, I hate to be the bearer of bad news, but this establishment does not have running showers."

Filling a second cup for Owen, Rachel turns to the man with a surprised look, "No showers? We got in so late that I did not check the room."

With a conspiratorial chuckle, he leans in, placing a hand on her shoulder, "Let me clue you in on a little secret. The Barracuda Hotel down the street is shuttered tight, like most places here in lovely Santarém, but the poolside showers work. All you have to do is hop a fence. They even have fresh towels."

"So, I can sneak into the Barracuda pool deck and use their showers? I can pay. Money is not a problem."

Glancing around the deserted lobby, the stranger emits a wry laugh, "Money. What a quaint notion." Filling a cup, he offers Rachel a light-hearted shrug, "Who knows? Perhaps our paths will cross again."

Rachel tries to read the sophisticated man as he heads back to his room, but the front desk clerk's impertinent dirty thoughts cloud her mind, "Damn. Who is that guy?"

Snapping lids on two cups, Rachel saunters past the creepy desk clerk's too-observant gaze, offering a flirtatious wink and sultry smile before mounting steps in the lizard-infested stairwell.

The perverted peon plops his narrow ass where his stool should be and falls backward onto the hard stone floor behind the counter. His tailbone throbbing in pain, the clerk twists around, finding his cushy seat repositioned four feet back against the stacked stone wall beside a crappy old HP printer.

Griffin Pike | Hotel Granrios
08:30 a.m. | October 9, 2044

A seething Griffin Pike rocks back and forth in a cheap wicker chair on his hotel room's cramped veranda with a satellite phone pressed to his ear. An old pocket-sized journal with an odd hole centered on its worn leather cover rests at his elbow on the dirty glass patio table next to his terrible cup of joe.

A bright green lizard bobs up and down near the opposite edge, eyeballing the fuming human's every move.

At last, one of his company satellites that persevered through the invasion in its low Earth orbit downlinks his call to a Paris security firm. Griffin Pike hears a female voice cut through grating static, *"Nemesis*

Group. How may I be of assistance?"

"I'll tell you how. I need to find out what happened to DeVille! That French fuck has not arrived in Santarém! He should be sitting on a fully-loaded boat, ready to move out. I need to locate the lost ship before Pennywell's team finds it! What the hell am I paying for? This is bullshit!"

"I am sorry, Mr. Pike; Henri DeVille left word that he altered your plan. Under the current blackout conditions, he could not acquire your authorization beforehand. We apologize, but as you know, our contractors are independent operators. We have no control over their travel or agreements once the deal is signed. He did leave a message; would you care to hear it?"

"What do you think?"

"Yes, it's a bit cryptic, but I assume it will make sense to you. It states: A bad penny always turns up. The new rendezvous point is Fordlandia."

Pike slams the pocket-sized phone on the table, killing the connection and scaring the lizard into the bushes, "Perhaps Henri is not as stupid as he looks."

The young woman curled on the bed in the wide-open hotel room awakens with a loud yawn, "Let me guess, those Nemesis pricks screwed you again. Jesus, Griffin, you don't need an army. You have me."

"For now, you have your wish; Henri will catch up en route with an unexpected surprise for our rivals." Pinching the bridge of his nose between his thumb and forefinger, Griffin Pike lowers his blood pressure, gaming divergent scenarios in his brilliant mind.

Padding onto the hotel room's first-floor veranda in her bronzed birthday suit, the lissome woman leans over Griffin's shoulder, nibbling his ear while running a hand through his thick hair while the other hand probes underneath his tropical shirt. "Nice outfit, Griffin. All you need is a fruity drink with a little umbrella sticking out."

"I grabbed it off the rack in the gift shop. I also have my eye on a Panama hat. We must appear as disarming and conventional as possible here in the hotel." Rearing backward, Pike pulls the psychotic fixer across his lap. "If I could clone an army out of your lovely flesh, that would make my life much easier."

"You can't even keep me satisfied." Snuggling into him with a carefree laugh, she angles forward, stretching long, taut legs atop the patio's rough wooden railing as her hand lands atop Charles Pike's journal, "A little light reading, Griffin?"

Scooping the book off the table, she flips through the blotchy inked pages before tossing it back atop the table, "Men like Laughton are putty in my fingers. He was out so fast I didn't have the heart to kill the poor bastard."

"You have a heart? I learn new things about you every day." Pulling her close, he whispers, "Laughton's fate is a moot point."

Luxuriating in the heat and humidity, the agile assassin smooths strong hands down tanned thighs, "I love this steamy jungle atmosphere. It's good for the skin." Splaying her legs wide, she exposes her glistening femininity to the mid-morning sunshine and touches herself.

A groundskeeper ambling down the palm-lined path behind the veranda makes a slack-jawed, wide-eyed double-take at the couples' overt public display. Bobbing his head with a toothless smile, the grizzled laborer slings a hedge-clipper over his shoulder and ambles down the path, whistling a local tune.

"Now, Sapphire, look what you have done. That poor man will be unable to concentrate on his landscaping duties for the rest of the day."

"I could slit his throat and put him out of his misery."

Cupping her pert breasts, Griffin grinds into the cold-blooded killer rolling her firm, round backside against his groin, "Maybe later."

Preempting their third coupling since checking in the night before, the tycoon flips his sexy partner onto the dirty floorboards with a loud thump, sending more geckos skittering up a post. Standing and stretching his tall, athletic frame, Griffin sips the lukewarm coffee, produces a sour grimace, and flings the rest into the bushes, "Get dressed; we have a lot to do."

"What a slave driver."

"We can go there if you want."

Leaning backward on sharp elbows, Sapphire crosses her legs and wriggles her toes. Casting a dark-brown almond-eyed gaze upon her employer's telltale khakis, a radiant smile dimples her high-cheeked model-perfect face. With a pouty smirk, she cocks her jet-black close-shorn head sideways, "Are you sure, Mr. Pike?"

"Yes. I am. Sure. We need to keep an eye on the Haigs."

"When did they arrive?"

"Sometime last night after our arrival. I bumped into Mrs. Haig in the front lobby."

"What does she look like?"

Grabbing a print-out of a New York Post article from the table, Griffin Pike flips it to his murderous lover. The colorful sheet features a captivating image of Rachel Alexander Haig and recounts an altercation with a Rhode Island politician at a high-powered presidential reception.

The sexually ambiguous 22-year-old touches blue sapphires pierced into her left ear and coos, "Trust Fund Murderess? She sounds like my kind of girl."

"Don't believe everything you read."

Owen | Hotel Granrios
11:15 a.m. | October 9, 2044

After breaching the boarded-up Hotel Barracuda to enjoy their last showers for the foreseeable future, the Haigs returned to their room at the Hotel Granrios. Inside, they find prepped backpacks, plus rucksacks containing ultra-light and breathable weather-resistant clothes designed for layered comfort from moisture and odor-wicking base layers to waterproof raingear. Both nylon bags came with personalized notes from Roy Kendall:

> *I hope the new gear keeps you both dry and comfortable—it doesn't hold a candle to Nina Madsen's sartorial skills, but I tried. Godspeed on your travels through the Amazon. Good luck and good hunting. Roy*

Like a kid on Christmas morning, Owen dons lightweight travel pants and a micro-fiber long-sleeve olive-green tee before pulling into his tech vest. Checking Velcro pockets replete with alien fire pellets, healing powders, pocketknives, a mini flashlight, and 9mm ammo mags, he muses, "If Batman wore a vest, it would look like this."

Moving to his pack, Owen scoops his PTB-issued weapon and smiles, "Holy cow, what a pretty gun." Admiring the micro-compact Sig Sauer P365XL Special Edition, he notes a laser-engraved The Powers That Be emblem on the grip and its shiny gold barrel and trigger contrasting with the matte-black pistol. Owen, a seasoned marksman from his youth, slides it into the form-fitting molded leather holster and adjusts the graphite clip's angle before cinching it on his belt. "I'm ready."

Rachel exits the cramped bathroom in matching gear, flinging a stinky Chrysalis tee and panties at her mate. "Who are you supposed to be? Rambo's little brother?"

Fresh-faced and radiant in mid-morning sunlight wafting through the room's yellowy blinds, Rachel twirls, effervescing a bright, sexy smile, "Well, what do you think?" The 24-year-old models her PTB-provided jungle trekking ensemble: A long-sleeved travel shirt and tech vest preloaded with gadgetry over straight-leg, breathable khakis, "Roy's fingerprints are all over this perfect fit."

Seeing only faint reminders of the scars that covered Rachel's face a month earlier, Owen slides his arms around his beautiful wife's waist, "Rambo's little bro is one lucky sonofabitch. That's what I think." Reading the hang tag on her new vest, "Huh."

"Huh, what?"

"The fabrics are infused with natural repellants."

Rachel sees a gecko loitering by the tiny room's screened 2nd-floor deck, "Let's just see about that." Moving toward the lime-green lizard, she watches its head bob and weave before making a beeline toward the lazy ceiling fan.

She turns and smiles, "It works."

The pair turn from the little experiment to ponder the cutting-edge, lightweight, condensed backpacks tuned to their precise height and weight measurements propped on the worn carpet.

Owen scratches his head and yawns, "When Professor King said don't worry about packing for the trip, he was serious."

A more circumspect Rachel sets her holstered P365 on the side table and lifts her pack onto the unmade bed, "My backpack is light as a feather. What did they put in here, marshmallows?"

"You know, Rach, leave it for now. Check out your sidearm. Remember, I took you on a few dates to my gun range?"

Rachel picks up her holster and removes the P365 in a sure-handed safety grip, "Yeah, I remember. It's been a while, but what a cute little pistol. Does it come in any other colors than black and gold?"

"Hilarious, Rachel. Check it and put it away for now."

"Okay, boss." Returning to her backpack, "I want to add the new hat Cleo gave me. I also have personal stuff. You know, female things."

Owen lifts his bag and checks it against Rachel's, "Mine is a bit heavier, but this new camping tech is impressive." Unzipping the main enclosure, he peeks inside with a nodded approval at the thorough pack job as a knock on the door interrupts the conversation. "Come in."

The door swings wide, revealing the strapping 6-2 form of Antoine Sheffield with a wide toothy grin on his chiseled mug, "Good morning, Mr. and Mrs. Haig! Pembroke asked me to come up and help with your packs. You know, go over everything. Y'all ever go camping?"

Owen smiles, "Desert tent camping—never tried a tree hammock. Is everything in these packs? They seem light."

Antoine laughs, "You won't find this shit at your local sporting goods store. Let me show what you have going here."

Rachel smiles at the good-looking former Navy Seal, "Thanks for helping us, Antoine. Where are you from?"

"Savannah, Georgia, Miss Rachel. I come from a long line of Seals."

"You are so young. Why did you leave the service?"

"Couldn't take the bullshit. Plus, I needed to make a little green."

Owen pulls into his pack, trying it on for the first time, "Have you worked with Pembroke before?"

Antoine smiles and adjusts the straps on Owen's pack, "Yeah. He's cool. He tends to creep folks out, but that is his schtick. The dude may be half-robot, but he is at his best in the field."

Rachel pulls her blond mane over her shoulders and swings into her pack.

With an approving smile, Antoine adjusts her straps, "You are a natural, Mrs. Haig. Okay. I understand you know how to fire a gun and have used the alien fire starter or at least seen how it works, right?"

Owen and Rachel laugh, "We spent a night in the Libyan desert crawling with black scorpions, and the blue flame kept them at bay."

"Wow. Good deal. Besides the alien fire, your vests contain knives, alien medical powders for wounds and infections, water tablets, snake bite kits, and DEET. Despite that, the fucking jungle is so full of bugs that you will get bit. A lot."

Reaching into Rachel's pack, Antoine pulls a collapsed graphite walking stick from a long pocket, "Watch this."

Pressing a button, the stick springs to a six-foot length. Flipping a toggle built into the handle, an 8-inch steel dagger snaps from the knobbed base. "Use it like a spear, but watch out, the tip has a paralyzing toxin, so you don't have to kill; just nick the beastie, and you should be fine."

Rachel gulps, "Now, by beastie, you mean …."

"Snakes, Mrs. Haig. It is for the fucking snakes." After hesitating, the young man adds, "And other things that go bump in the night."

Owen slides off his pack and removes a barrel-shaped cinched bag, "So, is this the hammock sleeper?"

"Toss it here, Owen." Antoine looks it over and smiles, "Let's go find a couple trees and give it a whirl. Believe me, you do not want to open this thing for the first time in the pouring rain up to your ankles in mud and realize you don't know how to put one up."

Rachel nudges Owen, "Lead the way, Antoine."

* * *

From Richard's 3rd-floor hotel room window, Pembroke folds muscular arms, looking across an empty street into a grassy public park where Antoine schools the Haigs on the essential skill of rigging their zipped hammocks and tarps between two palms swaying in a gentle afternoon breeze. After the young man and his attractive wife seem to get the hang of it, he smirks, watching them struggle to repack the contents into the narrow cylindrical sack. "Professor, we should ditch the Haigs here in Santarém."

Pondering the Brazil Nut tree drawing in his copy of Pike's notebook, Richard answers without looking up, "Nonsense, Pembroke. Mrs. Haig is our secret weapon when we reach the lost ship. I don't give a fuck if you have to carry her."

"What about the husband?"

"I do not wish the young man harm, but he is expendable."

Flynn | Gray battlecruiser
12:42 p.m. | October 9, 2044

"Are you sure?"

Without moving a bruised and beaten muscle, Flynn replies, *"Ted would not lie, Nina. They are processing everyone."*

Nicole chimes in from the corner of the cell she has shared with Nina for 44 days, *"Why have they not killed us already? We are well beyond any use other than food for these assholes."*

Nina stares at Nicole, *"It does not matter; our time is up."*

Flynn injects a dose of levity from a distant cheerful memory in his head, *"If I have to be hamburger, I will bloody hell like to be a fucking happy meal."*

Telepathic laughter from Flynn's PTB cellmates fills his head.

"Good night, everybody. Be sure to tip your waitresses."

Nicole's clipped telepathy ends the lighthearted moment, *"Uh-oh."*

Zint enters with two ugly scarecrows following close behind, moving past the PTB inmates.

Nina meets Flynn's frightened stare through the dimness as the pathetic wails of another human abductee echo throughout the cellblock.

"No! No! No! Please. I want to go home. Aw, not me. I will do anything. Take the dog. Don't. I want to …."

A loud zap ends the man's pitiful pleas, followed by the shuffling and crying of his cellmates crowding against the cell walls while the scarecrows drag their latest victim from the cell.

After the scarecrows drag 156 scrawny pounds of protein out the far end of the cellblock, Zint bolts the thick door and admonishes the remaining inmates to stop crying, or they will be next.

Gliding back to the PTB cells, he pauses, pretending to check the locks, *"There are now 15 humans left plus you three. I have held them *off for as long as I can. I am sorry.*"

Flynn glances at Zint through the bars, "*Where did they take that man?*"

"*They will sterilize the human first before processing him alive. It is a torturous and slow death.*"

Nicole scoots forward with a determined look on her sallow face, "*Zint, when they take one of us, here is what I need you to do.*"

Richard | Santarém
06:05 p.m. | October 9, 2044

Moored at the end of a wharf lined with out-of-business tour boats and watercraft waiting for tourists not returning anytime soon, the *Piranha* floats low in the Tapajós River.

Inside the 42-foot motor cruiser's pilothouse, Manuel Ortega, the grizzled Portuguese river captain conscripted into a trip he wanted no part of, half-listens to Richard King while inspecting the dash panel before firing up the inboard engine.

Dressed like an extra from an old Tarzan movie in a khaki safari uniform and a wide-brimmed sun hat, Richard tries to get the man's attention,

"Captain Ortega, 18 hours just to reach Fordlandia? Your cousin said we could make the trip in 16 hours."

Ortega snarls, reaching for his flask before deciding against it, "My cousin is a fucking drug smuggler. He knows nothing about the river. You are fortunate I agreed to this, senhor. You are welcome to hire another ship—if you can find one."

A skinny kid in shorts and a knock-off Disney tee vaults barefoot up the steps from the galley, interrupting Richard's retort.

Ortega takes a swig and bellows at his young deckhand, "Did you clean up down there like I asked?"

"Si. We are good to go, sir."

"Good." Watching a musclebound Black man in camo fatigues board the ship and head toward the stern with a large wooden crate, he sneers, "Ignatius, tell that man to secure that shit to the deck."

Pembroke | Santarém
06:15 p.m. | October 9, 2044

Helping Antoine load rations and ammo aboard the *Piranha*, Pembroke watches the Solomon brothers roll up in a stolen flatbed truck, kicking up a cloud of dust.

Ariel jumps out of the rusted cab and moves to unload cumbersome canvas stowage bags heaped in the back, "We broke into a marine supply a couple klicks up the road and found a pair of Mark II Zodiacs packed and ready to go, Mr. Pembroke."

The wily SAS veteran smiles, exhaling smoke into the mugginess, "No kidding? What luck. Did you leave a card on the counter?"

"Yes, sir, Mr. Pembroke."

"What about outboards?"

Elias hefts a sleek and modern electric engine from the bed, "All they had were these 35hp Chinese models; I think they get about 300 miles on a full charge."

"No charging stations where we are heading. That will have to do."

Seeing the Americans tromping down a steep path with their packs and gear toward the dock, Pembroke stubs his cigarette under his boot, "Oh goody, here comes the Haigs. Now we are ready to go."

Owen | The *Piranha*
06:30 p.m. | October 9, 2044

As dusk settles across the historic Brazilian city, Ortega instructs his young deckhand to cast off before piloting the overloaded riverboat through the fading light into the Tapajós River. Settled atop the *Piranha's* bow, Rachel and Owen watch children running, laughing, and splashing along the lapping sandy bank.

Rachel's keen gaze catches sight of the handsome man from the hotel lobby, still wearing his gaudy tropical shirt, watching them plow through clear waters past a fishing dock. A statuesque bronzed beauty in a halter top and bikini bottom, with oversized sunglasses pushed atop her sculpted, close-shorn head, stands at his side. To Rachel's surprise, the woman raises a middle finger salute through the dusky twilight.

"Huh. That was weird."

* * *

The *Piranha's* beachable hull slices through the calm dark waters on a moonless night under a star-filled expanse, hugging the Tapajos River basin's eastern bank past a foreboding jungle teeming with life. From his captain's chair, Ortega spies the ghostlike shapes of pink river dolphins surfing the boat's deep churning wake, hunting for dinner. With a wistful smile, he calls out to Ignatius and chuckles as the orphaned lad springs to life, darting from the pilothouse to watch the long-snouted mammals reaching over eight feet in length ply the waves.

Making a gentle course correction, he reminisces on the boy's deceased mother, tuning out his passengers' chatter from the galley below deck.

Richard | The *Piranha*

10:30 p.m. | October 9, 2044

Pembroke and his mercenary trio drinks coffee at the boat's kitchen table, leaving the collapsed sofa bed next to a wood-burning stove for the Haigs.

Richard exits the boat's lone bathroom and breaks the quiet while dabbing his sweaty forehead with a cloth, "Captain Ortega informs me the voyage to Fordlandia takes 18 hours." Checking his Rolex, "So far, we have been underway for approximately four hours."

Pembroke interjects with a dismissive wave, "So we reach Fordlandia a little after high noon tomorrow."

Rachel nods and leans back on the sofa bed with a loud yawn, "Yes. That sounds about right."

In tune with the boat's tunnel-drive engine built into the hull spinning the propellor through calm deep waters, Richard unfurls a topographical map of the river basin from Santarém to Fordlandia and the city of Itaituba farther south and west and spreads it across the table.

Ariel and Antoine place their mugs on the map's corners as Pembroke leans in and taps Itaituba with his calloused fingertip, "Didn't Stevens' expedition start from Itaituba? Why not bypass Fordlandia, press upriver to that shithole town, and follow his exact route?"

Glancing at his reflection in the low-lit cabin windows, Richard attempts to mask his concern, "A journey up the Tapajós was treacherous before the invasion. Since then, river pirates, more like terrorists, have made passage through to the shithole town, as you so eloquently put it, impossible without paying a steep toll. No. The first stop is Fordlandia, where Pennywell's mentor killed Charles Pike. We must recover a key element before proceeding with the expedition."

Rachel pipes in, "Is Fordlandia safe?"

Richard grins at the beautiful young American, "Henry Ford's pipedream utopian rubber plantation lies in ruins. The only dangers we shall encounter are ex-pat junkies and pit vipers."

Owen stands to refill his cup, "But not necessarily in that order."

The Solomon brothers and Antoine exchange knowing looks, sensing an all-too-familiar creep only hours into the mission.

Richard clears his throat to continue, "Owen, did you know

this vessel can float in less than two feet of water?"

Owen proffers a cordial smile, "Nope, Doctor King. I did not know that."

Richard narrows his lined gaze on the new PTB agent, "Every mile aboard this ship or aboard Pembroke's Zodiacs is one less mile trudging on foot through the wilderness." With a hint of finality in his baritone voice, he announces, "Tomorrow night, we will leave from Fordlandia and venture upriver under blackout conditions to this unnamed tributary."

Pembroke eyeballs the narrow sliver snaking westward through the Amazon rainforest, "If we can take that waterway to here." indicating a point where its headwaters disappear into the green inferno "Stevens' base camp is a three-day hike." Pembroke finishes his coffee with a grudging acknowledgment, "This is a good plan, Richard. Now I understand the last-minute request for the Zodiacs. You should have shared it with me earlier. We were damn lucky to find something we could steal."

King replies with a wry smile toward his hired gun, "I tried, if you will recall."

Rachel | The Piranha
12:02 a.m. | October 10, 2044

Wrapped under a blanket at the ship's bow, the Haigs listen to the nighttime jungle sounds punctuating the late-night Amazon air over the engine's steady thrum and the boat's keel parting the dark waters. Scooching closer, Rachel rests her head on Owen's chest as he strokes her hair. Giggling like a schoolgirl on a first date, she breaks the silence.

"What's so funny?"

"Watching the scary jungle slide past makes me wonder what could be staring back. If this is anything like Disney's Jungle Cruise, headhunters are around the next bend."

Owen laughs, "Don't jump the gun, young lady; we have not even seen the backside of water yet."

"Oh yeah, good catch. Hey, Owen, there is something we need to talk about."

"Hold that thought, Rachel." Owen sees a shadowy form lit by the orange glow of a cigarette approach from around the *Piranha's* starboard gunwale through the inky blackness; it's Pembroke.

Owen strains to make eye contact with the scarred mercenary through the darkness, "Hello, Pembroke. What's up?"

"Would either of you care for a smoke?"

Considering the last time he enjoyed a cigarette years before, Owen nudges Rachel and offers the strange man a pleasant "No thanks."

Pembroke squats on mechanical legs atop the heaving deck across from the Haigs and balances against the rail, "I couldn't help but overhear your repartee a minute ago. Believe it or not, I was a security officer at Paris Disneyland. Jesus, that was demeaning. However, I know where all the bodies are buried. Easy money, though. Easy money." Flicking the butt into the river, he nods and retreats back into the cabin, "Time to sleep. Big day tomorrow."

Biting her lips to keep from laughing, Rachel turns to Owen, who nods with a crooked smile on his scruffy face, "Okay. That was weird. What did you want to tell me?"

Rachel hesitates, thinking fast, "Uh, between that guy and Richard, what have we gotten ourselves into?"

The sound of a helicopter echoes across the river. Shifting the subject farther away from the happy news she needs to share, at some point, "Somebody down here has access to a working chopper?"

Owen yawns, fighting to keep his eyelids open, "Probably the Brazilian government. The PTB has no ties to that corrupt body."

With a sleepy yawn, Rachel mumbles before dozing off in her husband's strong arms, "That is because we are the good guys."

* * *

Seated alone on the boat's stern, Richard watches the dark airship through night-vision goggles, "There goes the enemy. Blast."

Captain Ortega | Fordlandia
01:45 p.m. | October 10, 2044

Captain Ortega reverses the *Piranha's* engine, slowing the boat's momentum as Fordlandia's iconic water tower ebbs into view through the hazy sunshine over the trees in the distance.

Navigating a last bend in the river, thick jungle gives way to grassy bluffs and dense groves interspersed with vestigial structural remnants of Henry Ford's pipedream rubber plantation abandoned to rot and crumble under the harsh Brazilian sun in 1945, 99 years earlier.

Deciding against a half-collapsed wooden pier jutting 50 feet into the fast-moving current, Ortega steers hard to port and guns the boat across a shallow lagoon onto the muddy Tapajós riverbank, sending a flock of white gulls into the trees. On cue, Ignatius jumps into the knee-deep water without trepidation, sloshes to a cement quay missing the rest of its pier, secures a noose with an expert sailor's hitch, and pulls it taught—just like Uncle Ortega showed him.

Watching the docking procedure over Captain Ortega's hunched shoulders, Richard smiles and pats the Portuguese riverman on the back, "Well done. Your services will not be needed until later this evening. I suggest you use the downtime to eat something and rest up. Pembroke's men will stand watch, just in case."

Professor King dons his hat and slings a pack over his shoulder, exiting the pilothouse into the suffocating midday heat as Ortega clenches his brown hand into a tight fist, almost drawing blood, "I really hate that man."

* * *

A tree sloth swings from a gnarly limb overhanging the tiny harbor, chewing succulent leaves, and ignoring the noisy intruders with a *What, me worry?* indifference.

Minnows and tadpoles dart through shafts of sunlight as the Amazonian silt resettles around the boat's shallow drafting hull, resting on the soft and muddy bottom.

A pair of Anahingas float past the starboard bow as one of the prehistoric-looking waterbirds harpoons an unsuspecting fish on its long beak.

A giant caiman mimics a floating log, loitering in the shadows of an ancient kapok tree's twisted roots snaking into the depths amidst a tangle of undergrowth overflowing into the lazy current like green lava.

A magnificent raptor with an enormous wingspan skims the river's rippled surface before snatching something in its talons and arcing in a graceful swoop through the haze toward a nest in the treetops rising high above the opposite bank.

* * *

From the *Piranha's* bow, Rachel takes in the natural spectacle, mesmerized by the sheer wonder, complexity, and abundance of wildlife she witnessed before disembarking from the boat.

Owen reappears at her side following a much-needed turn in the overtaxed lieu, "What did I miss?"

Griffin Pike | Fordlandia
02:00 p.m. | October 10, 2044

Griffin Pike is powerless.

After the PTB boat chugged into the night back in Santarém, Pike grabbed his sexy assassin and lit out for the airport to hire a chopper to Fordlandia.

50,000 USD later, he beat the PTB to Fordlandia in a vain twisted hope that DeVille would be there. He wasn't. And to make matters worse, he failed to locate the fucking Brazil Nut tree. Now it was too late.

Minus the Nemesis Group and its promised squad of killers packing an overwhelming arsenal, the megalomaniacal mogul observes the riverboat pulling onto the muddy bank from a quarter-mile distant atop river bluffs using high-powered binocs through the filmy window of a leaky rotted bungalow. The sad abode where an American family was meant to reside back in the day, like Anytown USA.

A pair of German squatters, too stoned to recognize the danger Griffin and his concubine posed until it was too late, lie heaped atop each other on a hemp mat soaked in blood.

Gritting teeth to internalize rage, he mutters, since no one else will listen, "Where the fuck is Henri DeVille? He should have been here already."

Turning toward his lithe partner, he finds her smearing warm blood, like warpaint, on her exposed nipples with her shirt pulled under her chin.

"Jesus, Sapphire, I think you are taking the whole Apocalypse Now vibe to an extreme."

The psychotic assassin sidles over and wraps a long arm around Griffin, but he rebuffs her advance with a firm shove. Peering through the binoculars, he sees more activity as a small group wade ashore, like fucking MacArthur. "Can you get ahold of yourself? We have company."

"Good. I want the murderess for myself."

"Not until we find out what they know."

Richard | Fordlandia
03:25 p.m. | October 10, 2044

Contemplating dangers lurking in less than two feet of water, Owen suppresses a cartoonish image of a person eaten down to the skeleton by a school of piranhas in his active imagination and splashes feet first into the river. A cool squishiness seeps into his boots as he smiles at Rachel poised on the edge of the deck, his left hand extended and a smile on his face, "I can carry you to dry land if you like."

"Move out of the way." Rachel rests her firm bottom on the edge of the gunwale and eases into the cool water, "See? Barely a ripple. Follow me, Owen. I will show you how it is done."

Richard looks up from his Pike notebook copy and snickers, "That is the epitome of getting your feet wet on your first day in the Amazon. Let's go."

Trekking up a dirt path toward Fordlandia's iconic sawmill and water tower, the trio passes bovine skeletal remains jutting from the overgrowth. "Are those cows?"

Richard tugs the straps of his daypack onto his shoulder and nods while scoping the surroundings, "They were. Up to the early 2030s, farmers, ranchers, and squatters staked claims here since Ford so obligingly clear-cut and carved roads and infrastructure out of the jungle, but the Brazilian government moved in and relocated them. I believe in response to some sort of pandemic. We may meet a few junkies and ex-pats, but otherwise, we are alone. I hope."

"Except for the snakes and spiders."

"Yes. There is that."

"What do you mean, you hope?"

"Just thinking out loud, my dear."

Rachel reads King's thoughts and swallows hard, *"Griffin Pike is here."*

"Hey, Rachel, check it out."

Crunching across glass shards and rusted debris mixed into the red dirt, they enter the massive sawmill ruins. While Owen and Rachel explore the cavernous, looted interior, Richard checks Pike's drawing of a Brazil Nut tree against a tall specimen dominating a ridgeline, looking outside from the patchwork of jagged and broken windows.

From behind, he hears Owen lamenting the emptied space, "Man, there is nothing left."

Richard's authoritative voice drops in tone, "Reminiscent of the Giza pyramids, gutted of everything not nailed down by looters and treasure hunters in less than a century."

Rachel studies a hulking corroded machine, stripped of parts and gears, "This thing is still here, whatever it is." Finding a bronze plate screwed into its green patina, she chisels off a thick layer of greasy muck to read the embossed name:

BROWN & SHARPE MFG
PROVIDENCE, Rhode Island, USA

How about that? I come thousands of miles to the Amazon, and the first thing I find is an old relic from my hometown."

Owen catches movement outside through tall shelving units littered with rotted boxes and leaky black oil cans. Drawing his P365 from its holster, he moves to the window, commenting on Rachel's hometown reference, "I thought you were born and raised in Newport, Rachel?"

With a wide-eyed stare, she watches Owen approach the busted windows with the 9mm pistol held outward in a two-hand grip, "Uh, yeah, but Providence is where I raised hell back in the day."

Owen takes a deep breath and pokes his head through the rusted panes, coming face-to-face with a curious monkey. With a relieved laugh, he turns toward Rachel and smiles, holstering his gun, "Monkey. We are not in Kansas anymore. That is for damn sure."

Rachel peers three stories upward into the rafters at a bat colony hanging from long wooden beams, "Maybe we should move on."

"Hey, where did Richard go?"

* * *

The Haigs catch up to the wandering scientist standing atop an overgrown concrete paddock in a stiff breeze.

"There you both are. Please keep up." Oblivious to the panting duo's alarm, Richard points out a magnificent Brazil nut tree reaching over 140 feet, dominating smaller palms and undergrowth flourishing beneath its thick canopy, "Which one of you is the best tree climber?"

Owen raises his hand while Rachel concurs, "Usually when there is climbing involved in these little adventures, we turn to Owen."

Owen looks askance at his wife, "Really?"

Richard whets a fingertip and flips his notebook open to a drawing of the Brazil Nut tree. Pointing at the cross-hatched lines, "See that little arrow?"

Owen leans in and removes his shades, squinting in the brightness, "Uh, it is more like trying to find Waldo."

"Who is Waldo?"

Rachel takes the notebook with an exasperated huff, "Never mind. Let me see. Sure. Okay. I see an arrow pointing at a dark blotch or, I guess, some kind of hole about a third of the way up in the tree."

Richard nods, "Yes. There should be a stone relic hidden in that hollow. I surmise it will contain the key to unlocking Pike's map. Without it, we are lost, like the ship." A crack of thunder punctuates his stark assessment, "Let's proceed, shall we?"

The trio hacks a path to the massive tree and clears away the underbrush exposing the lower 30 feet of the trunk devoid of branches or handholds. While the Haigs stare up at the enormous tree's straight trunk, Richard removes his pack and takes out a handheld harpoon gun. "I designed this myself. Watch." The scientist shoots a lightweight nylon rope into the lowest branches, where it hooks over a thick limb.

Owen gives the rope a firm tug, latching it tight to the tree, "Okay, great. Did you happen to bring gloves?"

"I come prepared, dear boy." Richard dumps gloves, knee pads, and spurred boot attachments onto the tamped-down grass, "Will this help?"

Decked out in the proffered gear, Owen grabs the rope and pulls himself up the side of the tree. 10 feet off the ground, he looks down and shakes his head. "This isn't right. I can't do it."

Richard tries to cheer him on, "Come now, Owen. You can do it."

"No. I really can't."

Rachel takes a deep breath and closes her eyes, "Let go, Owen."

Drenched in sweat with a serious scrape on his right forearm, he yells, "Say what?"

"I said, let go."

A floating sensation envelops Owen as the Brazil Nut's huge trunk slides past, clutching the slackening rope in his hands. His head and shoulders scrunch into thick leaves amid the tree's lowest branches as he comes face to face with an owl. Amazed, confused, and a little dizzy, he pulls a leg over a thick limb, shimmies to the trunk, and looks upward at a recessed hollow. "That must be it." Standing on shaky legs, he balances and peers inside the oblong hole. With his gloved hand, he reaches inside and pulls out a fistful of dirty, decayed leafy material mixed with broken eggshells. Digging deeper, he finds more mulch but no stone artifact. Probing farther inside, he pulls out a chunk of bark. "Richard, there is nothing in here! Could it be another hollow?"

At ground level standing beside Rachel, deep in concentration, Richard hollers up toward the young Mr. Haig, "No. Are you sure?"

After a pause, Richard's heart sinks, hearing Owen's muffled reply, "Yes, Richard, I am sure."

Richard turns to Rachel, "Can you bring him down?"

Rachel's eyes blink open, "What? What happened?"

"My dear, you just elevated your 188-pound husband 40 feet into a tree."

Thunder cracks become louder and closer as Rachel looks at the dangling rope swaying in the quickening breeze.

Rachel | Fordlandia
05:35 p.m. | October 10, 2044

Burgeoning storm clouds pass overhead without releasing a drop as gusts bend bright green palms contrasting against the darkening skies above Richard, Rachel, and Owen, cutting through the overgrowth on a shortcut back toward the *Piranha*.

"I'm sorry, Richard. Could it be we barked up the wrong tree?"

Richard shakes his head. "No. Chances are, my hypothesis was wrong from the start. Especially after seeing your struggle, how would an overweight middle-aged man like Charles Pike climb that high."

Rachel looks at the clouds and smiles, "Wouldn't the hollow have been much lower 120 years ago?"

Richard's face brightens, "That is a brilliant observation, Rachel, but his drawing resembles the tree Owen climbed."

"Yeah, but it is just a drawing, Richard."

Owen takes his wife's hand, "You promise to tell me more about this sudden ability to move stuff, right Rachel."

Stumbling onto the cracked pavement of an erstwhile residential street, the winds scatter trash from recent inhabitants amid holed cans and busted bottles used for target practice littering the narrow lane and modest hovels.

Rachel pulls away from Owen and smiles, "Don't worry. I'm fine."

Owen kicks through a grassy patch of debris, announcing his presence to any lingering creepy-crawlies, "This was Ford's idea of Main

Street USA?"

Richard surveys the potholed overgrown road, "In its heyday, this was a neat and manicured street where transplanted American families lived, worked, and played."

Rachel shakes her head in wonderment at the frozen-in-time ghost town atmosphere and the ethereal female presence standing on the curb. Feeling the first drops of rain hitting her wide-brimmed hat, Rachel glances back at her fellow explorers, "Do either of you see anything funny?"

Owen shakes his head and kicks a can, "You mean aside from Professor King? Nope. Just a lot of garbage and junk. Oh, and a snake. Shit."

Wearing a loose blouse over work pants and boots, the semi-transparent apparition glides up the front walkway of the nearest abode and disappears through an opened front door.

Rachel masks trepidation with an airy nonchalance, "I'll be back in a minute, guys. I want a quick peek inside one of these little Barbie dream houses."

Owen and Richard watch Rachel detour up a short walkway and vault atop a collapsed front porch before pushing inside the front door.

"Does she go off on tangents like that often?"

"She never used to; I was the adventurous one." Owen's eyes narrow onto the professor, pulling a Cliff bar from a pocket in his jacket.

Richard takes a bite off his bar and moves down the street before Owen can pry him about Rachel, "I am going to reconnoiter down this way. We can meet back at the boat."

"I will wait here for Rachel to finish her HGTV tour. Watch yourself, Richard."

* * *

Inside the cramped and water-stained front room, the smell of rot and mildew mixed with the sweet smell of marijuana hangs heavy in the thick air. Rachel senses a human presence behind a paper-thin wall and draws her P365 in a two-handed grip, "Come out of there! I am not kidding!"

A rail-thin red-headed stoner in rose-tinted glasses and a tie-dyed Grateful Dead shirt emerges from the shadows holding a bong in one hand and a bag of weed raised in the other, "Don't shoot, lady! Are you one of them?"

Relieved to see the harmless reject from *Fast Times at Ridgemont High*, Rachel lowers her weapon, "Maybe. Are you alone, Sport?"

Owen busts through the front door like an overzealous G-man, "Hey! What's going on in here?"

Rachel wheels around, "Owen, be cool. Let's all take a breath."

"Yeah, be cool, man."

Tie-dye sits on a well-worn section of shag rug atop his unkempt bedroll and meager belongings. Torching his bong, he addresses his unwanted guests, "My name is Craig. Who the hell are you two?"

Rachel smiles and holsters her pistol, "The good guys."

"That's cool. Wanna hit?"

Owen looks around the filthy room and shakes his head, "Uh, no thanks. How long have you been here?"

After glancing at the entity lingering in the shadows, Rachel sits across from the kid and peers into his expressive, dilated eyes, learning he hails from a wealthy California family, "Go ahead. You are among friends."

"Whoa, what just happened? You were in my head. That is awesome."

Owen checks outside at the rain, "Tell us your story; it is important, Craig."

"Lighten up, man." Craig smiles at Rachel, "Is he always this rude?"

Rachel looks toward Owen, standing by the door with his pistol drawn, "He just fell out of a tree, so he is a little out of sorts. Please do tell us your story."

There are about 20 of us who arrived here on a tour boat last year and never left. We have the whole place to ourselves. Paradise, man. Anyway, a chopper landed last night and freaked everyone out. We all hid, thinking it was fucking government types kicking us out. I checked on my friends, Franz and Heidi, this morning. You know, to make sure the Narcs didn't nail them. They live, or lived, a few houses down on the left. I walk in, and guess what? They were piled naked on a mat with their throats slit from ear to ear. A gnarly mess. I puked my guts out."

Rachel glances at Owen before asking, "Did you see who did it?"

"Yep. A tall dude and a hip bald chick. Really smoking hot. Like you, Mrs. Haig. Only pure evil."

Rachel mutters, "Griffin Pike."

Owen turns to his wife with an incredulous look, "What? Did you say *Griffin Pike?*"

"I'm sorry, Owen. That was the guy I bumped into at the Granrios Hotel. Oh, man. I am such an idiot."

Craig's face contorts into a look of honest confusion, "Griffin Pike, as in the tech mogul? Why would he want to kill my friends?"

At wit's end, hot, dirty, and hungry, Owen grabs Rachel by the arm, "We are heading back to the boat right now. We will have a nice little talk about communication."

Richard bursts through the door, rain-soaked and breathing hard, "There you are. We need to get back to the boat. Someone butchered two people up the street." Distracted by Craig's paraphernalia and a plastic bag filled with buds, his insistence fades, replaced by a coy smile, "Is that Manga Rosa?"

Impressed by the older man's cannabis acumen, Craig smiles and nods, "You know your weed, man."

"It is indigenous to this part of the world. What's to know?"

Flabbergasted by the Professor's shift in attitude with a potential killer lurking outside, Owen takes Rachel by the hand, "Okay, fine, we are through here. You two have a nice evening. Come on, Rachel, let's get back to the ship."

A seething Owen leads Rachel through the pelting rain to the *Piranha*.

None too keen on running back to the boat in a torrential downpour, Richard removes his daypack while poking around the front room and drying his face with a towel. Noting a cobwebbed mantle over a wood-burning fireplace among the vestiges of a once inhabitable cozy space, he turns to a toking Craig, "A fireplace in the middle of the Amazon. How quaint."

Inspecting the dust-covered ephemera mixed with sun-faded framed photos scattered on the paint-chipped wooden mantle, Richard sees an odd chunk of stone propped against the wall. Picking it up, he turns it over in his sweaty hands as his eyes widen onto a complete Fibonacci spiral intersecting a second spiral's nucleus stained into the smoothed side of the rock.

"Young man, where did this come from?"

Craig points to an empty corner of the room, "That woman showed me where to find it. She said someone would come along. I put it on the mantle for safekeeping."

Flabbergasted, Richard looks into the empty shadows, "What woman? There is no one in this house besides you and me."

"If you say so, Pops."

Contemplating Rachel's decision to enter this house, Richard slides the stone artifact into his bag and plops down on the dirty shag, "Perhaps after a few hits, I will see the woman, too."

Richard | Fordlandia
02:30 a.m. | October 11, 2044

Manuel Ortega steps into the galley, banging a wooden spoon against a pot. *"Vamos lá! Acordar!"*

Ignatius translates, "He says everyone needs to wake up. It is time to go."

The Haigs stir awake, huddled against the ship's leaky planks in the early morning stillness, "What? Okay. It's time to go. We get it."

Pembroke leans into the galley, "Does anybody know what happened to Richard?"

Letting out a loud yawn, Owen tries to stretch the kinks out of his back from sleeping atop an uncomfortable pull-out sofa bed, "You have got to be kidding. He never came back. All right. I know where he is."

Rachel stirs awake, "Owen, wait. I'll come with you."

"No, you won't. Stay here and keep your head down. Antoine, if she tries to leave this boat, feel free to sit on her until I get back."

Rachel turns to Antoine, who proffers a sleepy-eyed shrug.

* * *

Under a starry night sky, steaming mad at the half-assed operation right out of the chute, Owen tromps through fresh mud with a flashlight, too tired to care about stepping on slithering wildlife or crazed killers back toward Craig's hovel, "There it is, the one with the fucking orange light flickering from the window."

Pushing in the front door, he finds Richard seated with his legs crossed on the shag, taking a long toke on Craig's bong.

"Professor, it is time to go. What the hell are you doing here?"

Peering through the smoky haze, King presents Owen with a dreamy smile, "Is it time to go already?"

Standing on wobbly legs, King peers around the disheveled

mess, looking for something.

With his patience hanging by a thread, Owen shakes his head, "Christ, Professor, what are you looking for?"

"The young man, Craig. He was here a few minutes ago. Or was it longer? No matter, he went outside to pee and never returned."

Owen draws his P365, feeling a creeping sensation of being watched, "Richard. We need to go."

High as a kite, the 122-year-old man stammers, "I did not thank my host."

"Professor, this is your crazy schedule. We need to get upriver under cover of darkness, remember?"

Standing tall with his head raised, King smooths the front of his safari shirt, his disposition sobering through sheer force of will after popping an alien THC antidote, "Quite right, Owen. Shall we go?"

"That is more like it."

Halfway out the door, King pulls back, "Wait! I almost forgot my bag."

* * *

Outside the hovel, Sapphire watches the fools leave and drops Craig to the mud with his head lolling at an odd angle before swiping a glistening blade across his tie-dyed shirt.

Captain Ortega | The *Piranha*
05:20 a.m. | October 11, 2044

After a quick headcount ensuring everyone was aboard, Ortega backs the shallow-drafting boat off the mudbank into the fast-flowing current and motors upstream under blackout conditions—three hours behind schedule.

* * *

Pembroke lights another cigarette and maintains a sharp eye from the bow as the *Piranha* plies dark waters through a soupy fog smothering the narrowing river snaking through an impenetrable mass of jungle.

A prick of danger alerts the veteran mercenary of looming trouble. Peering through the murkiness, Pembroke startles as an enormous sentinel jutting from the fast-moving current comes up fast. Motioning into the wheelhouse with a flashlight for an immediate course-correct to starboard, the *Piranha* lists to the right, avoiding a head-on collision but scraping past massive craggy boulders, tearing a gash along the port gunwale, and snapping lines like rubber bands. Loosened supply crates tumble overboard as overhanging trees smash through the pilothouse in a cascade of leaves, limbs, and shards of glass crashing across the deck.

Ignatius pokes his expressive brown face up from the galley before Ortega yells for him to get down.

Cursing a Portuguese blue streak, the veteran river pilot grabs the wheel and cranks it to starboard while throwing the engine in reverse, sending supplies, passengers, and everything not nailed down tumbling across the listing deck. A loud cry ratchets over the chaos as the boat pitches down a steep chute and sweeps through a roaring slot. Heaving and rolling through the rapids, the vessel splinters through more jungle before shooting out the other side into a hidden lagoon at the mouth of a tributary feeding the treacherous river.

The riverman cuts the damaged *Piranha's* engine as the forward momentum grinds the shallow drafting hull across the unforgiving rocky bottom before lurching to a stop.

With vestiges of the THC lingering in his bloodstream, King climbs into the destroyed pilothouse in a plain white tee-shirt and shorts, leaving Rachel and Owen to help Ignatius clean up the mess below decks, "Well done, Ortega."

Standing amid glass, rocks, leaves, and branches in his halfway destroyed pilothouse, Manuel Ortega glares as Pembroke bursts into the narrow confines, beating him to the punch, "Richard, did you think it not important to warn us about that ahead of time?"

The unflappable professor points at the disconsolate mercenary, "I believe it was you who scattered my charts and maps across the Scottish countryside." Pivoting to counter the angry river captain's vitriolic contempt, "There was no easy way to describe that route. So, I didn't. We are given the bare minimum of information to achieve the next step." With a nervous laugh, he adds, "Welcome to the PTB."

Hearing one of the Solomon boys wailing in pain from the stern, Pembroke shakes his head in disgust and exits the pilothouse to check on his men and supplies while King addresses the enraged Ortega, "I understand your anger, Captain. Not to worry, a rising tide lifts all boats. Follow the channel south for a few miles, and then you should be able to navigate back upriver to Santarém. Have a drink when you get there. My treat, of course. And the PTB will compensate you for any repairs to the *Piranha*." Sensing Ortega is still not impressed, King smiles and raises a hand, "Did I mention the PTB will set up a college fund for the boy?"

Ortega shakes his head and laughs, unclenching his fists; he unscrews his flask, takes a drink, and offers it to Richard.

The professor accepts the peace offering with a smile, "From the satellite imagery I saw, the passage appeared much worse. It is better to be lucky than good."

Antoine ducks into the pilothouse, "Captain, we need your medical supplies; Ariel broke his leg. It's pretty fucked up."

Captain Manuel Ortega pats King on the shoulder, "So much for luck, eh, Professor."

Pembroke's scarred countenance looks down at the anesthetized young kid lying prone on the sofa bed in the *Piranha's* galley, wincing at the compound leg fracture in a makeshift splint.

Elias Solomon lowers into the cramped space and stands beside his boss, "Will he be all right?"

Pembroke turns to Ariel's brother, "The Captain agreed to get you both back to Santarém as soon as possible. Regardless, your brother will lose that leg. I am sorry, Elias, it was an accident. The PTB will cover any and all costs."

* * *

Pared to the fraction of supplies that survived Richard's detour, the expedition sets out in two light-gray Zodiacs from the *Piranha's* gouged and dented gunwale. Rachel looks beyond the inflatable's churning wake, catching a final glimpse of the damaged boat receding amidst the lagoon's thickets and mangroves.

Hanging on to a bow handle, Richard peers past the lead inflatable through wraparound shades with his sunhat cinched tight under his chin. Rachel adjusts to the water-level ride from her middle seat attached to the lightweight rollable aluminum planks, rearranging packs and bags to free up legroom.

In the stern, Owen sips a to-go coffee, squinting through metal-frame shades at the brightness reflecting off the still waters, mimicking Antoine's steady hand on the till of the first boat skimming across the swampy lagoon toward trees closing in on all sides.

Pembroke signals for Antoine to slow as the boats float toward a solid wall of impassable jungle. Still fuming from losing two-thirds of his crew, the mercenary yells back at Professor King, "What now, Richard?"

King's head swivels around like he is looking for the food court in a shopping mall, "Hard to say, but judging from the general flow, I would guess the mouth is somewhere beyond those trees."

Antoine looks at his boss, who shakes his head with a dismissive wave, "We should have gone through Itaituba."

The reinforced shallow draught inflatables maneuver around roots and thickets growing out of the swampy water until Pembroke's keen, gray-eyed vision discovers a break in the undergrowth, "Antoine, through there."

The floating expedition hacks through a tunnel of green and motors up the unnamed tributary into the Brazilian jungle. Owen checks the battery gauge on his engine, "Still reads full—that's good."

**She laughed and danced on despite the thought
of death she carried in her heart.**

– Hans Christian Andersen

Chapter Six:

The Sickness

Penny Pennywell | Monument Valley, Arizona
05:45 a.m. | October 11, 2044

The obnoxious whirr of an incoming call awakens Penny Pennywell from another restless dream starring a hazy recollection of Emma, her mom.

Scratching her unruly light-brown bedhead, the 26-year-old stretches under an oversized Harvard Med sleep shirt in the cramped but clean motel room after days spent car camping. Padding barefoot across the worn carpet, she scoops the braying sat phone off a table, "Fuck you, Charlie! Do you have any idea what time it is out here?"

The superheated response from Charlie Dunning, her overtaxed boss at the CDC in Atlanta, ratchets through the cheap, tinny speaker, *"Goddamit, Pennywell. How long are you gonna wander the wild west looking for dear old Mom's trailer? I need you back here. Since those lizard fuckers attacked, we are up to our eyeballs with every damn disease since the Middle Ages making a comeback."*

Dunning's words go in one ear and out the other as Penny pulls a window shade and checks her ride in the empty motel parking lot under another stupefyingly beautiful dawn over southeastern Utah, "I found her trailer, Charlie. Everything inside was gone, but the looters and squatters left behind a box of photos."

"I'm happy for you, Penny. I really am. If social media ever comes back, you can have a field day posting them to all of your family and friends. Oh wait, you don't have anyone but me."

"Ah, Charlie, you are such an old softie."

"Listen up, Pennywell, since you are out in God's country, I have a job for you. Get on a call with this fellow ... wait a minute; I have it here somewhere ... Okay, uh, Sheriff Briscoe. He was investigating a series of missing person cases on the Navajo reservation and stumbled on an outbreak amongst the scattered Indian population. It's probably another Covid variant. I don't know."

Penny's heart sinks, "What about Phoenix? Can't they send somebody? Those guys practically live out there climbing rocks and riding mountain bikes like some outdoors freaks."

"You have not heard? Phoenix is off the grid since the invasion."

"I'm sorry, Charlie. Give me the number. I will take care of it."

"That's my girl! Here is the deal: Briscoe wants someone from our office to make a house call on a family sheep ranch in the middle of Monument Valley. I just sent his contact info; he can fill you in on details and directions."

"Remember GPS, Charlie? Boy, those were the good old days."

"Hilarious, Pennywell. Assist our Indian friends and get your skinny ass back to ATL. It is time to put your fancy Harvard degree to something better than wandering around defunct trailer parks looking under rocks for clues to your past."

* * *

Doctor Penny Pennywell empties the last drops from a five-gallon jerrycan into her Land Rover, packs up, and exits the shuttered motel's lot, leaving 50 bucks, and a thank you note tucked under a rock at the front desk.

Motoring down a deserted Interstate 163 through southeastern Utah, bisecting the über-scenic heart of the otherworldly Monument Valley, she exits just before the Arizona border at a dilapidated sign for the Navajo Tribal Park's visitor center. Her eyes wander onto the fuzzy, water-stained photo of a two-year-old version of herself in her mother's arms taped to the dashboard. Refocusing on the present task, she checks the juncture on her hand-sketched map. "Okay, so far, so good."

Cranking down her window, she breathes in crisp October air, blowing her shoulder-length dirty-brown hair, and almost misses a hard left onto a private road. Wheeling the rugged workhorse across the median, the tires screech and kick up a ruddy dust cloud past a holed wooden sign nailed to the wide-open gate:

WARNING – TRESPASSING IS NOT ALLOWED.

Venturing into the off-limits hallowed expanse with the good sheriff's blessing, East Mitten Butte looms before her, with West Mitten Butte to the left, its rocky spire forming a thumbs-up toward majestic Merrick Butte out the passenger side window. "Yep, just as Briscoe described it."

Trying to keep her directions from taking flight, she glances through her mirrored Ray-Bans and shoves the crumpled sheet under her black medical bag jostling atop the passenger seat.

Bumping down the teeth-rattling unpaved road, she gulps the last of her Evian and tosses the empty in the back atop an unkempt pile of camping gear.

By noon, the temperature tips into the 80s under a cloudless cerulean sky contrasting against the warm-toned landscape as she brakes to a stop at a dead-end trailhead parking lot before a bucolic, cedar-filled box canyon. Eating homemade gorp while trying to decipher her cryptic handwriting that would make any physician proud, she mutters a curse and retraces her dusty path. Bounding down a new route through a maze of twists and turns up steep inclines and down identical-looking dry washes, she lurches to a stop to avoid plowing through a flock of sheep crossing her path. Sheep.

Following the baaing livestock, she rolls through a barbed gate and navigates the narrow road up a series of switchbacks atop a plateau centered with a cluster of weathered ranch-style structures. After five long hours, Penny pulls her dusty gas-powered wonder between a rusted camper and a pickup truck. Donning her CDC cap and medical bag, she exits and stretches her long thin frame in boot-cut jeans and a light-blue polo embroidered with the company patch.

80 percent certain she is at the right place, Penny announces her presence, just in case, "Hello! I'm Doctor Pennywell with the Centers for Disease Control. Is anybody here?"

Stepping past clucking chickens pecking at the hardpan, she vaults atop the main house's wrap-around front porch and knocks on a rickety screen door. Peering through a fist-sized hole in the sun-faded mesh, she repeats, "Hello?"

With a shrug, Penny slides the post of her sunglasses down her opened collar and pushes inside the darkened interior. Dusty boots creak across the floorboards, looking over the homemade furniture backed by a wood-burning stove and sepia-tinted portrait collages of proud Native Americans on horseback hung around the comfortable space.

A rank odor from the back portion of the abode assaults her senses. Nudging aside a hand-carved toy pony lying on the floor, she ventures down a shadowed hall toward an arched entryway to the family kitchen. Penny blanches at the sight of decaying bodies, a man, a woman, and a child, situated around a simple wooden table before rotted plates of food swarming with flies. Penny ties a bandana around her neck and pulls it over her nose, noting the woman and preteen boy suffered gunshot wounds to the chest. A portion of the man's head was blown clear off, the pistol still gripped in his hand. Scanning the gore-filled crime scene, she notes dried blood, desiccated tissue, and skull fragments splattered across shelves of pots and dishes. "I better call Sheriff Briscoe."

Upon closer inspection of the double murder-suicide, Penny notes grayish chunks of meaty flesh stuck like glue to the dead man's flannel shirt and a weird oily blue residue smeared and spattered on his hands and upper torso mixed with dark red blood. Reaching into her kit, she dons a pair of latex gloves and uses forceps to pluck off a piece of putrid gray flesh before sealing it in a tube. Next, she repeats the forensic process with the gooey blue substance. Following that, her focus widens beyond the deceased trio, noting an upturned highchair but no signs of a baby or toddler-aged child. Strange.

Moving around the table, she avoids broken pottery scattered about the tiled floor mixed with rotting food and sticky pools of blood. A mouse skitters across the counter and through the cracked back door, leading her gaze onto a partial view of a small body slumped against a red boulder outside in the dry grass.

Tiptoeing across the mess, she exits through the back door. Approaching the victim, she first notes the silvery reflective suit before pulling down her face covering, her mouth agape at the unbelievable sight, "Holy Christ! A goddamned mother-fucking alien!"

On cue, the deceased alien's bulbous head lolls toward her with a deep-black dead-eyed stare. Her heart beating out of her chest, she maintains a distance from the Gray. Teetering between fright and fascination, she tips back her hat brim and hunches down to get a better look at the creature. Catching a downwind whiff from the aqua-colored chest wound oozing through a bullet hole in its shiny suit, she notes multiple scrapes and cuts on the alien's hairless noggin.

"There was a struggle. The man tried to save his family from the alien intruder but killed them in cold blood. Why would he do that?"

Deep in thought, Penny fails to see the alien's four-fingered hand clench into a fist.

The alien lunges forward, scratching her left forearm with a long sharp finger. On instinct, Penny sweeps her right leg in a roundhouse kick as the tip of her boot crushes its fragile skull, sending the creature flailing sideways in a twisted heap.

Crying and scrabbling backward, she peels off the gloves and rubs handfuls of gritty sand across the sticky bluish residue mixing into the bleeding gash on her arm.

* * *

Covered in dirt and scrapes with a weird sensation throbbing from her wounded arm, Penny stumbles back to her Land Rover in shock. Dumping her bag on the passenger seat, she grabs the sat phone to call the fucking sheriff as the sound of chopper blades cuts through the dry autumn air.

Stunned that the sheriff had access to a helicopter, she waves to the pilot, who salutes a smiling nod back at her, setting down in an empty corral, sending dust, rocks, and manure flying in all directions. As the blades turn in a steady idle, a large man with a shaved head in camo fatigues jumps from the airship's passenger compartment on a beeline toward her.

Penny's abject relief morphs into fear, realizing the man is not from Sheriff Briscoe's office.

"Penny Pennywell?"

Swiping at her brow, covered in dirt, she yells over the idling chopper, "Who wants to know?"

Coming within arm's reach, the man's shadow looms over her, "Mademoiselle Pennywell, my name is Henri DeVille. I would appreciate it if you came along without a fuss."

As Penny's nightmare unfolds, she retreats to her trusty Land Rover, grabs the photograph from the dash, and shoves it into her pocket. Tripping over herself to climb behind the wheel, the musclebound Frenchman is on her in an instant, his meaty paw clasping a damp cloth over her face seconds before her world fades to black.

Rachel | The Amazon
02:40 p.m. | October 11, 2044

"Antoine, goddammit! Watch that log, cut left, now steady through that gap past that boulder shaped like a fucking elephant's ass."

"Yes, sir, Mr. Pembroke."

Rachel hears Pembroke's misgivings in her head over the outboard motors' steady churn, propelling the Zodiacs through miles of dense jungle, slicing days off their journey to reach Professor Stevens' base camp. Leaning sideways against the thick portside buoyancy tube in her pest-repelling camo ensemble, she unties her calf-height boots and peels out of her socks, wiggling toes in the still jungle air.

Distracted by Rachel's effortless charm, Owen laughs, "Hey, stinky feet, can you pull a bar from the food bag? I'm starving."

Rachel reaches over the side and splashes water at Owen, "Call me stinky feet, will ya?" Accessing a canvas tote stuffed with packaged rations, she pulls out a nutrified oat bar and flips it over a shoulder to Owen, who makes a one-handed catch.

Richard swivels backward to the Haigs, "Two things: Number one, respect the river; you never know what lurks beneath the surface. And two, those rations are all we have for the duration."

Overhearing Richard from the lead Zodiac's bow, Pembroke cradles a futuristic-looking semi-automatic rifle with a folding stock, "The food is an issue because of you, Richard. Let the man have a fucking snack bar."

Reminiscent of squabbling parents on a long car drive, Antoine leans sideways out of the line of fire and adjusts his hand on the till.

Never to be outdone, Richard fires back, "Pembroke, you are well-paid for contingencies such as this morning's regrettable losses, so please refrain from the constant griping."

* * *

The Zodiacs navigate the lazy jungle waterway alive with daytime squawks, chirps, screeches, and hollers beneath a dense, daunting tangle of woody vines and creeping plants extending clinging tendrils upward into trees laden with moss, lichens, flowers, insects, and birds. Playful, curious hummingbirds dart around the boats, their colorful feathers shimmering in the occasional light shaft stealing through the canopy from hundreds of feet overhead.

Inspired by the otherworldly beauty engulfing her, Rachel retrieves a Hotel Granrios paper pad from her pack and sketches the passing scenery. Managing a decent rendering of an unimpressed mammal lumbering along the left bank with its offspring in tow, she holds her artwork before Owen's face.

"Owen! Check out my aardvark drawing."

In stereo, the know-it-all professor and her husband, the master of trivia, reply: "Tapirs."

Rachel laughs, "Yeah, sure, tapirs. I know that. Hey, we can play the license plate game—Amazon edition."

From his stern position in the lead boat, Antoine laughs, "Okay, I got one. Something big just swam under the boat."

Maintaining a steady 20-foot distance in Antoine's wake, Owen scans the swollen depths in response to the ex-Seal's sighting. "Is it a caiman? Holy shit, Pembroke, get your gun ready."

The mercenary glimpses a long shadowy shape, "Easy, Mr. Haig. It's just a playful fishy, like a large-mouth bass, only this fellow is a 10-footer."

Richard clears his throat, reticent to sound like a know-it-all but itching to one-up Owen with his amassed Amazon knowledge, "It is called an Arapaima. And your bass reference is spot-on, Pembroke."

Miles farther upstream, Richard checks his transponder for the umpteenth time, "Nothing. That is unfortunate."

Rachel watches the scientist fine-tune the handheld device, "Professor, are you sure we are heading in the right direction?"

"Unlike the transponder's reliance on the fraction of functioning satellites passing high above the Amazon," King pulls a compass from his tech vest, "my compass does not lie."

From his seated bow position lazing upriver, Richard gazes past massive boulders and fallen logs into impassable undergrowth and shakes his head in wonderment. "We are heading due west and making remarkable progress. I discovered this waterway while perusing an old National Geographic map lambasting the development of a hydroelectric dam on the Tapajós near Itaituba. I was not even sure it would be navigable, but with the unseasonable rains, it is swollen— which works to our benefit. This forest is in constant flux, like a living, breathing creature. As I have said, it is much better to be lucky than good."

Within minutes, the lucky streak ends.

Pembroke calls out, "Pull onto that bank, Antoine."

Owen follows suit, pushing his Zodiac halfway up a muddy embankment.

The expedition remains seated, listening as Pembroke utters a curse, "Do you hear that?"

Rachel nods, "I hear a dull roar from somewhere up ahead."

Pembroke hoists himself from the Zodiac onto the bank, "Wait here. I will scout ahead and recon what we are dealing with."

Twenty minutes later, he returns, "Okay, there is a series of rapids and falls up ahead, but it appears navigable. The other option is to haul everything overland, but that could take an entire day."

Owen raises a hand, "I vote for the first option."

Antoine seconds the motion.

Pembroke produces a wicked smile on his scarred face, "It will be dangerous, but I admire your bravery, misguided though it may be." Noting the opened bags, boots, and stuff scattered on the second inflatable's aluminum decking, he smiles at the Haigs, "Owen, secure everything tight as a drum. Miss Rachel, pull out the ponchos—it will get wet."

Owen and Antoine hike uphill through the trees, scouting the cascading series of rapids, "Owen, let's take this one boat at a time. I'll take King and Rachel; you follow with Pembroke. Our outboard motors should have enough horsepower for a swift water upstream passage. Gun it hard before hitting whitewater and maintain your momentum. Whatever you do, keep your bow pointing forward. Don't get sideways. That spells disaster."

Owen nods, "Gun it and keep it straight, check."

Antoine proffers a confident toothy smile at the former banker, "Good man, Owen."

* * *

Owen and Pembroke watch Antoine edge the first Zodiac back into the river. Rachel proffers a brave thumbs-up before holding tight to the lifeline along the top of the thick gray buoyancy tube as the Chinese electric outboard roars at full throttle, pushing the heavy boat upstream.

The no-nonsense ex-military man turns to Owen, "Five minutes head start, then we shove off, got it?"

Biting his lower lip, the half-listening Owen watches Rachel's blond head disappear into the jungle darkness. "Uh, yeah."

300 seconds later, Pembroke pushes off and jumps into the bow, "Full steam ahead, Mr. Haig."

Feeling like he is in a deleted scene from the director's cut of *Deliverance*, Owen reads the current and guns the Zodiac's powerful engine, gaining speed toward the churning rapids and the first whitewater cascade. Pembroke pulls back on the rubberized bow as the inflatable shoots up the lower falls and goes airborne before the jarring splashdown shaves precious momentum, pulling the boat sideways like a twig drifting down a mighty river. Cursing his rookie mistake, Owen oversteers hard to starboard, course-correcting at the last possible moment as the roiling water splashes over and around the stricken inflatable. Hearing Pembroke's yells and curses over the crashing turbulence while tossed about like a bath toy and drenched to the bone, Owen eyeballs a route through the maelstrom. Gripping the till while holding on for dear life, he helms the inflatable forward, colliding into the next gushing torrent at full speed, tipping skyward, and plowing atop the next level.

Determined to maintain his full-speed upstream course, Owen calls out, "Hang on, Pembroke!" bounding up the flumes before bursting over the top and gunning it across the streaming shallows to a boulder-strewn shoreline where Antoine pulled onto the bank.

Exhilarated after conquering the treacherous river ascent, Owen calls to his soaked fellow explorers, "Howdy, y'all. That was badass! I may have heard the twang of banjos halfway up."

Returning a somber-faced expression, Rachel shakes her head.

Cutting the engine, Owen glides along the river's edge.

"Why the long faces? We made it." With a wet, furrowed brow, Owen follows Professor King's pointing finger to a giant hunk of metal, "What is that?"

Soaked to the bone, Pembroke squints toward the crumpled mass jutting from the river, "Looks like the tail section of a Brazilian Air Force Embraer EMB 120. It probably crashed during the invasion."

King wades into the current and climbs into Owen's Zodiac. "Let's check it out. We might find something useful inside."

Maneuvering the Zodiac with a confidence borne out of necessity, Owen circumnavigates the downturned tail before Pembroke throws a line and secures the inflatable aside a jagged hole half in and half out of the swift-flowing current.

Pembroke steadies the boat, allowing Professor King space to secure a handhold on a tangle of wires spilling from a cross-section of the torn fuselage and pull himself into the aircraft's near-vertical tail.

Inside the dark and dank fuselage, Richard bumps against an empty seatback and uses the dangling belt to hoist his frame upward amid decayed human remains. Noting a shiny gold watch around a bony wrist at the cuff of a brown flight jacket, he pulls a bandana over his nose and climbs past the dead trio toward the galley. A disappointed curse crosses his lips, "What a disgusting mess."

On the cusp of giving up, Richard unlatches a cabinet, hoping for packaged snacks; instead, a heavy box drops into his hands. Opening the lid, he finds airline-size bottles of Chilean cabernet. "Well, that is better than nothing."

Richard passes the waterlogged clinking box to Pembroke, who looks inside and smirks, "Fuck, Richard, you didn't find any cheese plates? What are we, savages?"

Richard angles through the narrow opening and hangs onto the inflatable's thick rounded side, "There are three dead bodies in there. I need air."

Pembroke pulls the scientist into the Zodiac, "We are camping here tonight. That was enough river for one day."

Richard | The Amazon
05:35 p.m. | October 11, 2044

After draining river water from the Zodiacs and arranging their packs and meager supplies on mossy granite outcroppings to dry, Antoine clears a 20-foot diameter camp with a flamethrower loaded with alien fire pellets.

Watching the impressive show of literal firepower, Owen laughs, "Hey, Sheffield, that is cheating."

Antoine replies with a coy smile, "It's not cheating if it works."

Pembroke interjects, "Like fishing with a hand grenade. Less sporting, but much more effective."

Observing Rachel contemplating the nylon sack containing her tree hammock, the young Black man smiles, "Hey, Miss Rachel, do you remember what I showed you all back in Santarém?"

Rachel frowns, "Yes. And no."

Owen's eyes widen, "Perhaps a little refresher is in order."

Professor King pulls out a baggy filled with purple pellets, "Nuts to your tree hammocks. I sleep on the ground, facing up toward the stars. Alien fire! You should all have a supply in your vests."

* * *

With the roaring campfire's blue and violet alien flames cracking and popping in the humid evening air, the expedition relaxes around the blaze, digesting their first meal on the trail to the lost ship: a pot of Richard's homemade dehydrated chili—just add water and heat.

Screwing the cap on his cabernet, Owen gazes across the still waters at the ghost-like tail section, glimmering pale blue in the darkness. "Does the PTB know how many people died during the invasion?"

Richard takes a swig from his bottle, "That is quite good." Staring up at the stars, the PTB's top scientist sighs, "There is no discernible method of making an accurate assessment, but our estimates put the death toll at close to 100 million souls lost during the Gorks' 12-hour siege. Since then, probably another 50 million. Maybe more."

Rachel lights a handheld torch with the alien flame and moves to her pack, "On that somber note, I need to poop, and then I am going to change over behind that rock. If anybody wants to know."

The boys watch her go, and Owen sees Antoine's white smile gleaming through the darkness like the Cheshire Cat, "She is one hell of a girl. Does Ms. Rachel have a brother?"

Owen tosses his empty bottle into the fire, "As a matter of fact, she does. But I don't think Joe would have made it this far. A bit of a college boy."

Antoine returns an eye-rolling frown, "Ugh. I've had my fill of that crowd. No thanks."

Pembroke smokes and stares into the flames, "I had a girl. She left me for a London stockbroker. I sent the poor bastard a gift basket and a sympathy card."

Penny Pennywell | En route to Manaus
10:45 p.m. | October 11, 2044

A waifish two-year-old in grubby pink shorts and sandals under a second-hand Dora the Explorer t-shirt follows the winding path of an iridescent beetle across ruddy hardscrabble. The pretty bug crawls into well-defined midday shadows beneath the rusted trailer hitched to a dusty pad in a deserted campground under a cloudless deep-blue southwestern sky. Brushing dirty brown hair off her face, she pokes at the bug with a stick and smiles, tuning out adults talking in low sad tones mixed with crackling noises from the radio in a police car parked askew with its door open.

After shuffling and talking from inside, she hears the camper's busted door creak open, and watches two firemen carry Mommy on a stretcher to a waiting van.

A policeman follows out of the dilapidated trailer, holding Mommy's pill bag, and looks toward the little girl, "What's your name, darlin'?"

* * *

Penny's swollen eyes snap open onto a dull-metallic bulkhead. Strapped to a sweaty cot, she angles her aching head onto a hulking back-turned figure and tries to speak, "Hey. Hey!"

An alabaster-faced young lady appears, elevating Penny's head to drink water from a bottle, "There, Mademoiselle, now lie back and rest."

The woman wearing a red beret checks an IV line snaking under Penny's thick-wrapped left forearm and feels her forehead, "Your fever has broken."

Penny's vision darkens, and she slips back into a semi-conscious state.

Anna slinks next to Henri DeVille, "Pennywell is awake."

Seated on a crate filled with Nemesis ammo and gear, DeVille glances back at his prized prisoner, "She should thank us for saving her life."

Producing a satellite phone from Penny's stolen bag, he keys in a series of numbers, "Time to advise Pike that we are about to land in Manaus."

Anna slides a skinny arm around his beefy shoulder, "Chayefsky, Smythe, and Rollins should have a chopper loaded and ready by the time we land."

Griffin Pike | Fordlandia
11:30 p.m. | October 11, 2044

"I tried to reach you, Griffin, but the lines of communication are terrible. Perhaps your shitty satellites are the culprit."

Griffin holds the crackly satellite phone away from his ear, suppressing venomous rage at the insubordinate Frenchman, "Henri. So good of you to call. Yes. Yes. We are in Fordlandia, enjoying the locals and doing a little sightseeing. Hey. I know. How about this? Get your fat ass down here on the double."

Slamming the phone on a side table, Griffin rolls onto his back and pulls Sapphire back atop him.

Glistening in the moonlight, the assassin's dark almond eyes pierce his distracted gaze, "You have quite a way with people, Griffin."

"I hate people."

With a sad pout, she slides her sweaty body off his limp form and stares at a lizard clinging to the ceiling, "What about me?"

"I did not realize you thought of yourself as human, my love."

Chapter Seven:
The Nemesis

Henri DeVille | Fordlandia
05:30 a.m. | October 12, 2044

After 48+ hours languishing at Henry Ford's defunct rubber plantation, Griffin and Sapphire grab light packs and move out to board a commandeered Peruvian Air Force Mi-26 transport helicopter settling atop an overgrown concrete foundation.

Buffeted by the rust bucket's massive 8-bladed prop wash, Pike yells at the top of his lungs toward the hulking figure hanging out a wide-open portal, "About fucking time!"

Sapphire hisses, "We waited two days for that piece of junk?"

"Beggars can't be choosers, my love."

"If his steroid stooges try to cop a feel, I will chop off their dicks."

Pike grabs his prickly assassin by the hand and leads her toward the chopper. "Duly noted."

The craft lumbers into the sky over Fordlandia through smoke lingering in the mist-filled morning air from the previous night's raging funeral pyre of victims that succumbed to Sapphire's bloodlust and boredom.

With the two passengers aboard, Leon Chayefsky lifts off, orienting the Soviet-era relic on a southwestern vector over unexplored rainforest toward a secret jungle airstrip. In the co-pilot seat, Duke Rollins leans back and relights his Cuban stogey while staring out a filthy starboard window at a monotonous sea of green.

Steadying himself in the rattling and jostling airship, Griffin Pike moves between crated supplies to get his first look at the Pennywell girl and blanches at the sight of the frail young woman tied to a stretcher, "Henri? What the hell did you do to her? She is useless dead."

DeVille scowls at Pike's lack of appreciation, "She contacted toxic Gray blood. You are damn lucky we carry the antidote, or she would be dead."

Pike shifts on a dime to a more conciliatory approach, "Your initiative will be compensated, but tell me, since she was not part of my plan, how did you find her?"

DeVille shrugs his massive bodybuilder physique, "A mole in the CDC provided her identity to the Nemesis Group over a year ago. Since you aim to take out her grandpappy, I leaned on a compromised Navajo Sheriff to set a trap. Miss Pennywell obliged. Her alien encounter was another in a long line of unfortunate happenings."

With his choreographed plan entering the last act, Pike allows his acerbic wit to return to the fore, "You can't trust anybody these days."

Sapphire elbows around her boss and curls beside the young Pennywell, "I will take care of her. If anyone comes near her, I will cut their throat." The assassin points a gleaming short blade at a surprised Anna, "Especially you."

Pembroke eyeballs colorful tree frogs staring at him from pooled, dripping flowery keeps amid a vibrant display of bromeliads covering a mossy trunk while completing a much-needed morning constitutional to alleviate an ill-advised double-helping of Richard's chili from the night before.

With a renewed bounce in his mechanical gait through the dripping rainforest toward the camp, Pembroke steps over a log and feels something strike his boot. The mercenary elevates his robotic leg and frowns at a six-foot green snake's head chomped onto thick khaki material dangling from his leather boot.

"You picked the wrong leg, little fella."

Hacking through the underbrush with the snake's grisly disembodied head hanging from his boot, Pembroke snickers in anticipation of a good-old-fashioned hazing but finds Antoine and Owen loading the Zodiacs as Richard sits cross-legged by the fire, drinking coffee and perusing his map.

Disappointed, Pembroke asks, "Richard, where is Mrs. Haig?"

King replies with a coy smile, "Around here somewhere."

Sensing someone at his six, Pembroke pivots onto Rachel, already in mid-follow-through, flinging the headless snake at him.

"I'm right here!"

The headless reptile smacks him square in the chest, sending the rough and tumble military man recoiling backward, "What the hell?"

Richard and Rachel's laughter echoes through the trees, "I'm sorry, Pembroke, but you had that coming."

The steely-eyed veteran nods approval and nudges the ropy remains into the fire, "Mrs. Haig, you are indeed badass."

Richard motions at the snake head still attached to Pembroke's pants leg, "You do plan on disposing of the head."

Pembroke drops to a knee to pry off the offending snake head, "Of course, Richard."

Aghast by the man's careless approach, Richard jumps to his feet, "Careful, man! That viper's venom will melt your skin down to the bone, like acid. Local tribesmen use it to tip their weapons."

Rachel finishes washing her hands and tosses the balled-up towel at the mercenary, "Here you go, Mr. Pembroke. Sometimes I can't help but ruin a good practical joke."

* * *

Dripping sweat, Owen and Antoine finish repacking and start the Zodiacs' battery-powered engines, humming at less than half the original charge.

Weary of the horseplay, Owen lights a fire under his fellow travelers, "C'mon, let's get this jungle trek moving upriver!"

Rachel and Richard assume familiar positions in the Zodiac and follow Antoine and Pembroke into the mist up the coursing waterway.

* * *

A Forest Ghost hunting party emerges from the undergrowth into the abandoned encampment. One of them stoops to examine the intruders' extinguished firepit and notices an unusual stacking of pellets. Plucking a single berry-sized shape from the pile, he holds it before his keen gaze and squeezes it between his thumb and forefinger. The tiny orb ignites and burns his fingertips.

Griffin Pike | Cartel airstrip
10:15 a.m. | October 12, 2044

Flying low and slow above impenetrable jungle spread out to the hazy horizon in all directions, the overloaded Soviet-era chopper drops like an ugly rock into a valley concealing a short runway carved out of the jungle.

Sensing the hot, noisy, and uncomfortable ride is almost over, Griffin Pike exhales and speaks over the din toward DeVille, "We made up for a lot of lost time. I do believe we regained the upper hand over the PTB."

Seated across from Pike, Smythe, the Nemesis Group security expert, presses the renowned mogul, "Why do you hate the PTB?"

Taken aback by the impertinent underling's query, Griffin looks at the dull-lit faces of Henri DeVille and the skinny French girl, Anna, before addressing the ill-mannered Brit, "It's Smythe, right?"

"Yeah, Smythe. Liverpool born and raised."

Pike controls his temper and smiles at the insolent man, "Well, good for you. I don't *hate* anybody. The PTB is simply in the way of my plan."

DeVille quells the testosterone-laced animosity seeping to the surface between the two men and interjects, "What plan, Griffin?"

A perplexed grin widens across Pike's handsome visage, "Henri, you disappoint me. I thought my goal was rather obvious to the most dim-witted among your crew: Rule the world."

Sapphire catches the skinny French girl's surreptitious eye roll as the Mi-26 helicopter clatters and jerks while corkscrewing to the ground like a sketchy carnival ride.

Unaffected by the chopper's gut-churning descent, Henri's thick brow furrows, his deep-set eyes narrowing onto Pike, "Since we are playing catch-up, here's one for you, Pike. How did you know about this airfield?"

"Elementary, Henri." Pike waves off the question with smug confidence, "Owning 80 percent of the world's satellites comes with an endless supply of useless information and the occasional gem, like this airstrip's existence."

Sapphire preempts Pike's rambling monologue, "Griffin. Stop

talking. I will tell the story." Running a supple hand over her close-shorn head, the tanned assassin slips into an affected Eastern-European accent, "The Powers That Be allied with a powerful cartel in the 1970s in return for protection while exploring the Amazon for rare medicinal plants and other commodities. Quid pro quo, the PTB allowed the criminal drug enterprise to flourish."

Griffin beams like a proud parent, "Sexy and smart, a lethal combination, wouldn't you say, Henri?" Glancing out the filthy cabin window into the encroaching green and black mass coming up fast, he laughs, "And best of all, Artemus Pennywell had no clue how close he was to the lost ship—the only treasure worth having in this Godforsaken place."

DeVille's bearded mug frowns at the psychopathic duo entwined on the cracked leather jump seat, "How fucking close?"

Feeling the bald tires finally touch down on the overgrown tarmac in a wobbly three-point landing, Griffin Pike expels hot air inside the cramped airship, "Ah, we are here at last!" Releasing a tight grip on his mistress, he answers DeVille's query with a nonchalant hand wave, "Oh, about a half day's walk in the woods to the location indicated in my ancestor's notebook."

Exiting the cramped confines of the stinky, sauna-like chopper, Griffin heads toward the airstrip's lone structure to get out of the sun and map out the best trail to the spiral nucleus in deceased Uncle Chuck's notebook. Sapphire guides the wobbly Penny Pennywell by the arm, following on his heels.

Skeptical of the jungle runway's abandoned outward appearance, DeVille deploys Rollins and Smythe to scout the perimeter and outflank potential trouble, leaving a grumbling Leon Chayefsky and Anna to unload the gear and rations from the chopper's hold. Satisfied with the assignments, the massive Frenchman crunches across the tarmac to the shabby structure to confer with Pike.

Griffin unfurls his updated topographical map inside the

trash-strewn hut atop a wobbly table, ignoring skittering vermin and a multi-hued blur slithering out a broken window above a wooden chair, planning the path forward.

Holding a sweaty Penny by the hand, Sapphire kicks through the busted door and snickers at the half-collapsed roof leaking thick vines and branches through every crack and fissure, "Griffin, you take me to all of the best places." With an inexplicable soft spot for Penny, the assassin guides the feverish young woman to a chair, "Sit still, my love and behave."

Pike hears DeVille enter the space, never looking up from the complex topographical linework, "There you are. Are we through playing soldier? I need to show you the route. We should have done this days ago, but here we are."

An adept tactician and more than capable of reading a fucking map, DeVille ambles through the trash and kicks a half-empty beer bottle out of the way, "I thought you said this place was deserted?"

Griffin shakes his head, "Who cares? We will leave as soon as your people unload that shitty chopper. Now pay attention, goddammit. We are here," drawing a finger west and north, he taps a red X and mutters, "And this, my friend, is ground zero."

A confused look distorts DeVille's bearded face, "So the lost ship is only a few klicks from here? Why didn't the PTB find it?"

Pike slams his fist into the table, "No! No! No! This spot leads to the precise location of the lost ship." Sensing more than a bit of confusion, he clarifies, "We lack the second spiral clue—the fucking PTB expedition got to it first."

DeVille furrows his thick brow and peers outside, distracted by the slow unloading of the airship's hold, "Who came up with the fucking spirals? What bullshit. Just put the X on the treasure, like fucking Redbeard."

Griffin Pike stares daggers at his musclebound mercenary, "That is brilliant, Henri. Can we get back to reality? I don't know why they used perfect spirals. Some things are beyond explanation. Can you accept that?"

"Your funeral, Pike. I get paid either way."

"Like I said, we will get to the first spiral nucleus and wait for the PTB expedition."

Sapphire fills the pregnant pause between the two men with her rapier-sharp wit, "And kill them all?"

DeVille glares at the lithe young killer, "Cold-blooded murder is not part of my contract."

The crackle of automatic gunfire preempts Sapphire's naughty comeback. Moving to the busted window, DeVille pulls his sidearm and picks off three locals' misguided frontal assault on the half-unloaded chopper's cache of food and ammo.

The gunfire echoes into the surrounding hills and valleys before fading to the ubiquitous jungle cacophony.

Griffin rises from behind the table, "Nice shooting, Henri."

"Fuck off, Pike."

Wishing he had more firepower than his .45, DeVille slams home a new mag as another terrorist trio crashes from the underbrush. With ice water coursing through his veins, the mercenary drops two of the three combatants, but the third boy proves elusive. Stumbling to a kneeling position fifty feet from the chopper's starboard side, the kid shoulders a rocket launcher and fires a projectile seconds before Leon mows him down with an uncrated short-stock sub-machine gun.

The incendiary round impacts the Soviet-made chopper, exploding in a violent fireball of destruction, hurling flaming chunks of debris hundreds of feet into the air before cascading across the jungle valley. More automatic fire breaks out as Smythe and Rollins take out the remaining terrorists hunkered in the jungle with devastating efficiency.

Engulfed in flames, the chopper rages with blazing intensity igniting ammo crates like fireworks on the Fourth of July. DeVille exits the hut and strides through the acrid smoke and ash blowing across the airstrip toward Leon, hunched over Anna's frail form bleeding out from a gaping head wound on the sizzling hot macadam.

With the threat neutralized, Henri DeVille scoops his girl's red beret, clenching it tight to his heaving chest, internalizing abject rage as Smythe and Rollins push two frightened terrorists before him. Without saying a word, the hulking mercenary unsheathes a hunting knife and guts the young man on the left. The other prisoner's eyes widen, watching his cohort's entrails dump from the torso in a torrent of red-hot blood as he collapses face down to the ground.

Henri swipes his gore-covered blade on the other kid's tattered, dirty fatigues and growls, "Do you speak?"

The boy nods, "Si."

"Bueno, motherfucker. You are the messenger. Now run along and tell anybody still out there to stay clear, or I'll skin them alive and feed their corpses to the vultures."

Henri fakes a stab, sending the kid stumbling backward, slipping in his friend's blood and guts. "Go, you little fuck, before I change my mind."

Watching the proceeding from a safe distance, Griffin Pike moves to DeVille's side and places a hand on the man's thick shoulder, "I am sorry, Henri. I mean it."

DeVille turns on Pike, snatching his arm in a vicelike grip, "This is not over," before letting go and skulking toward the fractional supply of off-loaded crates that survived the assault.

Leon follows behind, "Mr. DeVille, sir, we lost two-thirds of our shit."

DeVille shakes his head, mustering every ounce of restraint to not kill his pilot and weapons expert for failing to protect Anna. "Inventory the rations and ammo and distribute it between the crew. It should be enough. We have one less mouth to feed." Seeing Rollins and Smythe checking for their packs dumped in a heap, "You two, grab shovels and dig a hole. I need to bury my girl."

Looking back at Griffin, DeVille raises his hand, "I will bury her, and then we will set out. If that is unacceptable, you are welcome to proceed without my crew. Your choice."

Griffin checks Sapphire's unreadable expression, "Of course, Henri. We will wait. Sapphire, look after the Pennywell girl. Make sure she is still in the hut."

Richard | The Amazon
11:42 a.m. | October 12, 2044

A steamy hour-plus upstream, the PTB expedition's progress is reduced to a frustrating slog through an overgrown swamp suffocated with jungle vegetation choking the way forward. Hacking at the low-hanging ropy vines intertwined with mossy branches, Pembroke hears the outboard's steady hum reduced to a taxed whine, churning up silt, rocks, and detritus, "Antoine, raise the motor before we lose the prop!"

"Yes, sir, Mr. Pembroke."

"Owen, same drill, kill your engine, and get the prop out of the mud!"

Muttering curses, Pembroke grabs the bowline and climbs over the side into the knee-deep water covered with algae. Looking back at the second boat's occupants, he barks, "Well? Let's go! We will pull the boats through this shit and hope we come out on the other side without stepping on anything nasty."

Antoine angles his long legs over the side to push the heavy Zodiac from behind as Pembroke pulls while hacking a path with his machete.

Owen exhales a heavy sigh, "Man, I knew this was too fucking easy." Dipping his boots into the shallow creek with his bowline looped over a shoulder, he drags the second Zodiac through greenish muck and debris stirred up by the mercenary duo slogging up the streambed.

Watching Richard's unenthusiastic move toward the stern to push from behind, Rachel stops the 124-year-old, "That's okay, Richard. I'll push."

With relief creeping into this voice, Richard smiles, "Are you sure?"

Sliding her firm ass over the thick tubed side into the murky water, she smiles, "Yeah, I'm sure." With a chuckle, she adds, "I'm bulletproof, remember?"

After grueling hours of trudging through the dank jungle swamp aswarm with insects testing the limits of the expedition's pest-resistant outerwear bolstered with DEET, the creeping undergrowth thins as the stream's current picks up once again, narrowing into a steep gorge. Eager to get out of the water, everyone resumes their places in the Zodiacs, motoring past sheer granite walls covered in mosses, ferns, and lichens. Rachel marvels at the misty canyon like something out of a dream, teeming with iridescent butterflies and nesting birds.

Immune to such flights of fancy, the sharp-eyed Pembroke scans the depths for submerged obstructions, feeling a twitch of danger creeping up his reconstructed spine. "Stay sharp, Antoine. I got a bad feeling about this place."

Antoine has to laugh at his boss, "Sure thing, Mr. Pembroke."

In the second boat, Rachel tries to get comfortable in her wet clothes, watching Richard fuss over his transponder while Owen maintains a steady hand on the till. With nothing better to do, she turns a new page in her sketchbook and draws the first thing she sees with her hands aglow.

A piercing squawk draws her attention upward, catching the silhouette of a massive raptor swooping overhead before nose-diving into the canyon, "Hey! What is that?"

Pembroke bolts onto his feet on the solid aluminum planking and raises his semi-auto rifle, "Get down! Get down!" Cool as a cucumber, the mercenary takes careful aim as the Zodiac knocks against a boulder, pitching him off balance. Losing his chance at a clean shot, the winged reptile continues its low pass over the boats from behind, snatching Pembroke by the arm in its massive claws and lifting the heavy man fifty feet into the air. Wriggling out of his jacket, he drops into the deep, murky water.

Antoine guns his Zodiac to a shaken and bloodied Pembroke and pulls him back into the boat as smaller flying raptors with razor-sharp beaks take turns diving at the vulnerable inflatables. Owen gets off a shot with his pistol, cracking ear-splitting echoes through the gorge and scaring the prehistoric pests into the misty heights.

Frightened, flustered, and exhilarated by the appearance of a species thought to be extinct for over 60 million years, Richard yells toward the lead inflatable, "Antoine, is Pembroke okay?"

The growling mercenary preempts his man's reply, "I need gauze and the alien painkillers."

Owen maneuvers beside the first craft and idles as Rachel throws a line around a rock. Richard climbs into the first boat to assist the injured man, "Pembroke, now you have a story to tell."

"Fuck off, Richard. What the hell was that thing?"

Owen maintains a vigilant watch, seconding Pembroke's query, "Yeah, Richard, that was Lost World-level insane." His P365 drawn, he adds, "What else is down here?"

Sprinkling alien healing powder on the bloody gash down Pembroke's right arm, Professor Richard King wraps it tight and rips the sleeve to create a sling. Satisfied with his ad hoc first aid, he smiles, "That was a juvenile Pteranodon. Technically not a dinosaur. And yes, despite what we were all taught in grade school, there may be pockets of prehistoric creatures alive today. Like the Loch Ness monster. Although no one has verified their existence." With an incongruent jocularity, he adds, "Until now, of course."

None too amused by another peel of the onion that is Professor Richard King, Pembroke spits out river water and groans, "More pain killer."

Antoine looks over the side of the boat into the dark water, "Sir, your rifle."

"It is gone, Antoine. We are down to your rifle and small caliber handguns to ward against Richard's fucking dinosaurs—and God only knows what else."

More prehistoric screeches ratchet down the gorge, prompting Owen to take decisive action, "Rachel, untether the Zodiacs. We will take point. Antoine, you follow with Richard so he can look after Pembroke'."

Owen plies upstream, watching Rachel's blond hair blowing in the breeze from her bow watch position.

The gorge's steep walls morph back into the lush greens and blacks of the impenetrable jungle undergrowth fighting for survival under the high tree canopy as the convoy motors up a swollen section of the mysterious waterway into marshy headwaters.

Richard feels raindrops pelt his unruly charcoal curls and drip down his forehead, "Well, that is not good."

Rachel | The Amazon
07:05 p.m. | October 12, 2044

Sopping wet and weary, the expedition huddles within the alien campfire's protective circumference on a raised spit of muddy Brazilian rainforest surrounded by a flooded understory constituting the unnamed river's headwaters.

Rachel checks the collapsible camp pot hung above the licking blue flames and pours two beef stew packets before giving it a solid stir. The miserable five try not to appear too hungry as freeze-dried chunks rehydrate and expand like magic into cubed meat and potatoes mixed with green beans, onions, and corn in a thick and savory bone broth.

Owen leans forward, frowning, "Who puts corn in beef stew?"

Richard objects with feigned indignation, "I do."

Antoine passes his bowl to Rachel. "I don't care what is in there; I'm starving."

Rachel rises from a kneeled position in her camouflaged poncho, "Hold that thought, Antoine; I left the rations bag on the boat. I will be right back."

Grabbing a trusty alien torch, she smiles at the stare-eyed group before picking a path down the mud-slickened bank in the fading light to the tarped Zodiacs.

Leaning into the inflatable to access the nylon rations bag, she fixates on her glowing hands, wondering why the boys, except Richard, refrain from asking her about the strange condition. With a shrug, she slings the cinched sack over her shoulder, standing at the water's edge in her calf-height boots. Despite hunger pangs, she pauses to check her blue-lit visage reflected on the water's murky surface distorted by pattering raindrops. With a heady swoon, she peers deeper at an ethereal underwater vision of herself, with lustrous white hair billowing around her naked form aglow in luminous blue hues.

"Miss Rachel? Miss Rachel? Do you need help finding the rations?"

Shaking the cobwebs from her head, Rachel wipes her watery eyes and turns to Antoine's chiseled dark-brown face, "Uh, yeah. Right here."

Handing the bag to the former Seal, she scans his thoughts. An avid reader from an early age who has read Tolkien's *Lord of the Rings* multiple times, the young man likens their current location to *The Passage of the Marshes* in *The Two Towers*.

"Antoine? Do you like to read?"

"Yes, Mrs. Haig, I do."

"Please, call me Rachel. I thought so. Who is your favorite author?"

Trudging up the slippery bank toward low voices around the campfire, he laughs, "Oh. That's an easy one. It has to be Tolkien."

* * *

The incessant drizzle and heavy cloud cover gives way to the spectacular heavens on full display as the group enjoys the last cabernet bottles under the stars.

Richard stands to address the group, eliciting mock boos from the peanut gallery mixing with the hoots, squawks, and hollers from the nighttime jungle.

Pembroke takes a long pull on his wine bottle and adjusts his injured arm in a sling, "Richard, any luck with the transponder?"

"I am happy to report that I am now picking up a weak signal that could only be from a locator beacon left by Stevens. So, in fact, we are getting closer."

Owen pokes at the fire with a stick, sending blue sparks into the darkness, "How close?"

"We are in the middle of the headwaters of a river that does not exist, populated with flying creatures thought extinct for millions of years. Tomorrow we will reach the end of our river journey and continue on foot. Perhaps no more than a day's hike if we keep a decent pace. Dinosaurs, cannibals, and natural impediments notwithstanding."

Raising his voice over the collective groan, Richard raises his hand, "That is not what I need to talk to you all about."

Pembroke rolls his eyes, "What now, Richard?"

"Two things, really. First, there is a chance we might encounter the Empire Grays at some point. They are also searching for the lost ship." Casting his gaze upward, he muses, "I would not be surprised if they monitor our movements even as I speak." Snapping from his reverie, he taps his temple with a thick finger, "Now, what was I saying? Oh, yes. As you may know, physical contact with them is quite deleterious for humans." Seeing the blank return stares in the campfire's blue glow, he holds his hands out, "Don't worry, you were all immunized back in Scotland." Turning to Antoine, he frowns, "Except you, young man. I am sorry I do not have the antidote in my pack."

Antoine shrugs, slipping into his smooth and easy Southern drawl, "I take my chances with many things, Professor." Making eye contact with everyone, ending with Rachel, he concludes, "And I got your backs if things get hot."

Pembroke shakes his head, "Typical PTB bullshit, Richard."

Eager to address the elephant in the jungle, Rachel clears her throat to speak, "Professor, tell them the second part."

Richard's thick eyebrows raise, "What, dear? Oh, yes. The second part. The lost ship."

Owen looks around the group, "We are searching for a lost alien ship. We all know that already. So what?"

Richard nods in a professorial fashion, "Yes, Owen. Spot on, in fact." Richard gestures toward the 24-year-old blond from Rhode Island, "Rachel, hold up your hands if you please."

Rachel complies, presenting her lovely hands, palms out, with her blue spirals aglow in the darkness.

Pembroke and Antoine stare in wonder as the elder mercenary remarks, "I noticed the glow but did not want to call attention to it."

Owen places a protective arm around his wife, "It is a personal matter. And it has nothing to do with this expedition."

Richard's face contorts into a sheepish grin before addressing the young Mr. Haig. "That is not entirely accurate, Owen. You are here *because* of Rachel's transformative state. It leaves her as the only person on Earth who can withstand the shipwreck's deadly payload. At least, that is the hypothesis. I apologize for not being more forthright earlier."

Owen's face reddens, "This was supposed to be a recovery mission. Rachel and I had already saved the world once. We have the medals to prove it. Now that we are past the point of no return in the middle of the fucking jungle, you decide to tell me this is just another

Rachel saves the world suicide mission—here's a crappy rundown villa in the south of France for your trouble."

Richard attempts to defuse the hyperbolic tension as Pembroke basks at the sight of Richard having to eat a whopping slice of his own shit pie. Owen rises to confront King with his hands clenched, but Antoine scoots up and places the fuming former banker in a firm hold, "Come on, man. Be cool. Be cool."

Rachel stands tall, putting her glowing hand on her worried husband's heaving chest, "It is okay, Owen. I love you, and I got this."

Rachel concentrates on the closer Zodiac and extends her svelte left arm, "Watch this."

The dripping inflatable elevates five feet off the muddy embankment like it is filled with helium as Rachel rotates her hand, turning it in mid-air.

A flabbergasted Owen looks from his smiling wife to the Zodiac before noting the stunned expressions on Pembroke and Antoine, "Did you two know about this?"

Antoine laughs, "What the hell just happened? Miss Rachel, you can move things with your mind?"

Rachel flips her wet blond hair over a bug-bitten shoulder, "It is a blessing and a curse." Patting her husband on the back, she winks at Professor King, "Owen, I need to do this. And I can't do it without you. We are saving the world again, but we are doing it for our new baby this time."

Overwhelmed by the day's events, punctuated by the sudden news that he will be a dad, Owen wavers on his sopping feet as an ever-attentive Antoine catches and lowers the shell-shocked 27-year-old to the ground.

"Take it easy, Owen. And congratulations."

Richard shrugs and smiles, "What a relief. That went better than expected."

Chapter Eight:

The Jungle

Antoine | The Amazon
07:00 a.m. | October 13, 2044

Following Antoine's lead, Owen navigates his Zodiac carrying Rachel and Richard over and around silty underwater obstructions across the algae-choked flooded forest floor through stifling darkness under a greenish-black cathedral ceiling.

Antoine slows before massive kapok trees, rising from the fetid marsh like sentinels; he shoots the gap between the ancient trees, scraping bark and moss on both sides.

With her wet blond ponytail curled from under her hat's floppy brim, Rachel yells over her shoulder to Owen, "Can we fit through there?"

"Antoine made it, and so will we. Hold on, Richard!"

Lost in his notes, Richard mumbles a reply, looping his free hand under the nylon line.

Rachel reaches out from under her camo poncho, gripping the safety line as Owen guns it over the kapoks' leviathan root system before scraping between the moss-covered trunks and splashing out the other side like an amusement park log flume ride. Owen hears Rachel laugh for the first time in a long while and thinks, *I'm going to be a dad.*

Rachel turns with an effervescent smile, placing her glowing hand on his leg, "Yeah, you are."

Owen contorts his rakish good looks into a sad puppy dog expression, "Oh yeah, you read minds." After a slight pause, he teases his beautiful wife, "How am I supposed to notice other women without you knowing?"

Rachel replies with a hearty laugh, "I never needed special powers to know when you did that."

The expedition churns muddy water for miles south and west through the mosquito-infested bog in the soul-crushing darkness.

Antoine calls back to Richard in the second boat, "How much further, Professor? My engine is almost out of juice."

Owen yells over the motors' drone and the howlers high above in the trees, "Hey, Antoine. I'm riding on empty for the last hour."

Pembroke turns and glares at Richard, "Well, Richard? Our helmsmen asked a question."

Unwilling to accept that they are lost; King lifts the transponder in his outstretched arm and picks up a faint ping. "I don't know, dammit. I should have brought a drone. Next time. Next time." Feeling four sets of eyes upon him, he looks up and offers a less-than-comforting sheepish grin, "Oh, not to worry. We are heading in the right direction. Ease off the motors; that should conserve some power."

Owen smirks, "That is what I have been doing all morning, but it takes a little momentum to push our heavy asses up this swamp."

With sharp eyesight that would make an eagle proud, Antoine

sees a shaft of light piercing the monotonous dark passage, "Hey! We are coming out at something up ahead."

A half-hour later, Pembroke uses the flamethrower to burn a gaping hole through tangled undergrowth. The inflatables push through the crackling, smoking breech onto a deep lake covered in massive lily pads.

With a resonance that reminds Antoine of Gandalf's voice from an old LOTR epic, Richard announces to his soggy companions, "This, my friends, is the river's source and the end of our raft journey. From the far side of this pond, we proceed on foot."

Pembroke spits into the water at an ominous shadow swimming beneath the boats. Not wanting to alert the others, he picks up Antoine's rifle and cradles it atop his robotic legs.

Skimming across the lilies toward a muddy beachhead like D-day invaders, Antoine cuts the motor with Owen following suit before a nest of caiman guarding the open embankment, "Uh, now what?"

Richard again adopts his deep tonal voice, "*Caiman yacare*, of the *Alligatoridae* family, if memory serves. We need to locate another landing ...."

Pembroke cuts off the Professor's long-winded travelogue soliloquy, "I got this one, Richard." Reaching into a bag, the mercenary pulls out a stun grenade.

Rachel objects, "Ah, c'mon, Pembroke. Do we have to kill them?"

Registering the beautiful blond's protestation at killing the dangerous predators, "No, Miss Rachel, this will only drive them off, so they don't kill any of us."

Pulling the key, the mercenary lobs the pear-shaped device above the scary beasts, where it detonates on its downward trajectory, scaring the reptiles into the water.

Owen's eyes widen in panic, "That was not smart. Now they are heading toward us!"

"Ease off, mate. The beasties don't know what hit them. We should be safe."

Hitting the loamy landing zone, the hot and sweaty quintet pulls into their packs stuffed with everything they can't leave behind.

Owen and Antoine haul the Zodiacs into the undergrowth.

"Should we deflate the boats?"

Antoine thinks about it for a minute, "No. Who knows? We may need them again."

Owen pulls into his backpack, "Good point."

Richard pulls a digital tracker from his pack and sticks it into a tree trunk amidst an exotic tableau of orchids, ferns, and bromeliads. "Okay. This way."

Penny Pennywell | The Amazon
08:40 a.m. | October 13, 2044

Eating dry Froot Loops from a plastic bowl, the two-year-old sits cross-legged on the stained low-pile carpet before a 24-inch flat-screen TV in the prefab trailer's family room slash kitchenette, watching SpongeBob's latest shenanigans.

The TV cuts to black as the power goes out again, revealing Penny's sad reflection on the blank, cracked screen.

Padding barefoot over creaking floorboards, she pauses at the door leading to Mommy's bedroom. Alone and afraid, she musters the courage to breach the dark room, ignoring a powerful odor, "Mommy? Wake up. Please wake up ...."

"Wake up, Penny. It is time to get up."

Feeling a firm tug on her shoulder, Penny's eyes snap open onto Sapphire's model-perfect visage. "Where am I?"

Sporting a cropped tee exposing her toned and tanned midriff with low-cut khakis tucked into calf-height soft-leather boots, Sapphire offers a bowl of scrambled eggs and a banana with a perfect smile, "You must eat, my darling girl."

Sitting back against a tree across from Penny, Sapphire toys with a gleaming short blade, "You are a doctor, no?"

Penny's eyes widen onto her jungle surroundings, ignoring the bowl in her trembling hand, "Who are you people, and what do you want with me?" Shooting pain up her wrapped left forearm causes Penny to drop the bowl and wince, "The alien. I contracted Gray flu. Shit. You should have let me die."

A male voice bellows from behind, "Now, why would a young lady with her whole life ahead of her want to die?"

Sapphire leans back on a sharp elbow watching Griffin enter the small clearing, interrupting her girl talk, "Miss Pennywell's memory is returning, Griffin."

The handsome 40-ish man dressed in custom-fitted all-weather hunting gear towers over Penny and takes a long swig of morning joe, "Ah, nothing beats camp coffee, right Sapphire?"

"Whatever, Griffin."

A light switch turns on in Penny's mind, "Griffin? As in Griffin Pike—the satellite guy?" Looking between the strange woman and the world-famous mogul, "Why did your goons kidnap me?"

Pike scrutinizes the young woman, "Goons? I like the sound of that for some odd reason. You really have no idea who you are, do you?"

Akin to a POW, Penny gives her name, rank, and serial number: "I am Penny Pennywell. A Harvard-educated physician employed by the Centers for Disease Control."

"Ah, that was a mistake now, wasn't it?"

"What? No. What do you mean by mistake?"

"Your employer sold you out." Reading the blank stare in reply, he continues, "Pennywell. That is also quite a name. It doesn't mean anything to you?"

Penny scoops up her bowl, picking at a chunk of lukewarm egg, "Yeah, it means I come from a family of deadbeats and dropouts."

"Madame, you could not be more mistaken."

On the cusp of divulging Penny's ancestral tie to the PTB's CEO, Henri DeVille lumbers into the clearing, "Pike, the men are in position. We have the PTB's base camp in a tight box."

"Excellent, Henri. We may have to wait a while. It seems our PTB friends took the scenic route."

Recognizing the hulking man as the one who abducted her, Penny swallows hard, averting her watery eyes from the empty spot Sapphire vacated without a sound.

Dismissing his lead mercenary, Pike kneels before the young Dr. Pennywell, "Sorry about that. DeVille is indeed a fucking goon." Checking her healing arm, he proffers a kind smile, "I see you are recovering quickly from your altercation with the Gray. Nasty creatures. I will deal with the aliens in due time. First, I need your friends' help."

Squawking blue macaws settle in the leafy trees, "The Amazon is noisy. Who knew? I do not wish to keep you bound in any way. We are deep in the uncharted jungle. There is no escape. Stay calm and quiet. I promise this will all be over soon. Who knows? You may find our side is not so bad in the world that follows."

"Follows what?"

Exuding a devilish charm, Pike smiles, "Something transformative and cleansing."

* * *

Bored stiff, Smythe, Rollins, and Chayefsky blow thick clouds of cigar smoke into the sticky stillness warding off nasty insects buzzing around their high lookout over the PTB's base camp.

Leon scooches on the loamy ground avoiding contact with a low-hanging ropy vine covered with ants moving in both directions like a superhighway.

Smythe wipes down his semi-auto assault rifle and props it against a punky stump covered in mushrooms.

Rollins sips black coffee from his tin cup and stares through the hole in the underbrush at the PTB expedition's most likely ingress. "I just want to get paid and go home."

Smythe turns to the US Army veteran, "Where is home, mate?"

Rollins flicks long gray ash from his cigar, "It doesn't matter anymore. It's gone."

Chayefsky snickers in a sing-song voice, "The shining beacon on a hill is no more."

Rollins scowls at the gawky-looking Leon Chayefsky, "Don't get cocky, Leon. I am here for the money. Nothing more. I don't give a rat's ass about this fucking lost ship business."

Smythe reaches forward and taps Rollins on the boot, "Bloody hell, keep your voice down. These fuckers will kill you if they sense you are not a team player."

* * *

Harboring a deep resentment against Pike for Anna's death, Henri DeVille scouts the perimeter, stumbling upon a 20-foot tall earthen mound rising from the jungle floor. Alone in the primeval forest before the undiscovered ancient ruin, DeVille's keen senses alert him to something big hunkered in the dense underbrush to his right. Unholstering his .45, the mercenary creeps closer to investigate, eliciting a snarling growl in response to his movements before the shadowy form of a six-foot creature with a whiplike tail crashes past him in a blurred violent frenzy, knocking him flat on his ass.

More surprised than frightened, Henri scrambles to his feet, muttering French curses and brushing dirt from his wet camo gear.

Unexpected laughter redirects his squinted gaze upon Sapphire's sexy form in a wide-legged stance atop the earthen mound like an Amazonian goddess from an old Frank Frazetta painting.

"Did you see that thing?"

Looking down upon the heaving Frenchman, she nods, and her smile fades, "This is a place out of time. I doubt we make it out alive."

Richard | The Amazon
11:55 a.m. | October 13, 2044

Three grueling hours out from the caiman beachhead, swallowed within a living, breathing maze of drenched greens and blacks punctuated by glinting machetes, the PTB expedition fans out in a long line. Squawks, caws, growls, howls, screeches, and the omnipresent buzz of insects serenade the intruders cutting a path through a pristine wilderness untouched by civilization. With Pembroke on point, Richard provides direction, struggling to maintain compass bearings from point to point without a glimpse of the sun in the bright blue sky obscured by the high tree canopy. Rachel follows next, with Owen watching her ass and Antoine bringing up the rear, watching Owen's ass.

After a steep, slippery uphill grade, the quintet breaks at the base of a jungle waterfall, washing away sweat, muck, sticky resins, and plant splatters in the clear flowing water. After topping off canteens, they forge ahead sans food, reinvigorated by the welcoming respite.

Scrambling up a steep grade around sharp-edged granite outcroppings covered in moss, lichens, and splashes of colorful orchids, the expedition grasps clinging vines and branches as handholds, confronting more impenetrable undergrowth at the top.

Owen wipes his forehead and swats away something buzzing in his ear, "Christ, will this ever end?" Watching his companions hacking away, he exhales a weary sigh and plows onward.

Up on point, Pembroke swings his blade through lianas hanging from dizzying heights and trudges through the opening onto a windswept grassy escarpment at the jungle's edge. Richard stands beside him, admiring the sweeping vista of hills and valleys smothered in the trees to the far horizon and thousands of miles beyond.

Bright midday sunshine and a steady breeze improve the morale, drying through to undergarment layers clinging to sweaty skin.

Rachel wriggles out of her backpack and releases her ponytail, letting her wet blond hair blow in the strong wind, luxuriating in the sun's warming rays, "Oh, man. This is Heaven. I never thought we would see the sun again."

Antoine peels out of his clingy olive-drab shirt, revealing his glistening dark-brown strapping bodybuilder physique.

Owen watches a vivid spectacle of red, blue, and yellow macaws taking flight, contrasting against the dark green valley down below.

Richard mounts a granite outcropping and raises the transponder over his head, "The signal is much stronger out in the open. We are closer to Steven's base camp than I anticipated. Remarkable. It must be due to the extra distance we traversed through the flooded jungle."

Pembroke beats everyone to the punch, "How close?"

Professor Richard King squints westward toward gathering storm clouds, "Perhaps before sundown if we pick up the pace. I would like to beat that storm."

Owen | The Amazon
05:40 p.m. | October 13, 2044

Leaving the airy ridgeline behind, Owen takes his turn at point, hacking through curling, twisting, creeping leaves, shoots, and stems from tangling vines, scratching and clawing toward life-giving sunlight leaking through the canopy hundreds of feet overhead. Feeling new blisters forming over old ones through his gloved hands, he muses, "Man, I am such a wuss."

Unable to see what lays beyond giant leaves obscuring his vision to infinity, the former financial adviser and weekend warrior emits a fatigued laugh, calling over his shoulder, "I signed up for this? What was I thinking?"

A slithering movement to his right catches his attention seconds before a viper's green head strikes his shoulder. Swinging his machete in a backhanded tennis motion, his blade slices through scaly muscle like a hot knife through butter, separating the head from the recoiling body, flinging onto the trampled mud at his boots, "Fuck! That was close."

Antoine jogs up to Owen's position. "Are you all right, Owen?"

Breathless and shaken, Owen blurts out, "The damned thing chomped into my sleeve. Get it off!"

Antoine pulls the snake's head from the thick outer jacket and checks Owen's arm. You would be in severe pain if it got you. Tossing the bloody head into the woods, he laughs, "You are one dangerous motherfucker." With a firm swat on Owen's ass like he just hit a walk-off homer, Antoine angles past, "You need a break, my friend; I'll take the point. "

Red-faced and hyperventilating from the close encounter of the snake kind, Owen shakes his head and wipes his blade on a six-foot banana leaf, "Pure reflexes. I never saw it."

Richard pushes past Owen in the tight space, "Are you through congratulating yourself? A locator beacon is pinging loud and clear from beyond that embankment ahead."

Slashing through the undergrowth to the base of the unusual mound, a hint of danger pricks Rachel's senses. Pulling herself atop the 20-foot-tall bulge in the loamy jungle floor, she looks down through leaves and branches at the group from the high vantage point, feeling like Indiana Jones, "This appears manmade."

Richard turns up the volume on his transponder, letting the pinging sound echo through the dense jungle surrounding the archeological find. Pushing along a well-trod animal trail, he comes to Stevens' beacon, blinking green, jutting from the dark soil, "There you are. Stevens led us here. We are likely standing in the middle of an ancient city buried eons ago under the jungle."

Recovering from his viper attack, Owen joins Pembroke and Antoine, watching the trees, "What's up, fellas?"

Ignoring the American, Pembroke points his unholstered gun into the undergrowth, signaling Antoine to train his semi-automatic carbine at a creeping shadow lurking in the dark forest.

Peering through the night-vision scope, "Nothing, Mr. Pembroke." Antoine lowers his short barrel rifle, "It was more than likely a deer or another animal."

Pembroke shakes his head, rubbing the long burn scar on his face, "I know what I saw. It was a human."

Richard's loud voice breaks the silence, "Stevens' base camp!"

A crack of thunder breaks the jubilant mood as the late-afternoon Brazilian sky opens, releasing a torrential downpour on the expedition.

Owen assists Rachel at the bottom of the mound, "What did you see up there, Rachel?"

"Not much, but this place gives me the creeps."

"Well, we are in the middle of nowhere."

Antoine hefts his heavy pack and angles past the Haigs, "This way, you two."

Trudging along the tamped-down animal path, the sky opens, releasing a torrential downpour on the expedition, breaking out of the jungle into a meadow.

Richard drops his bag on the grass and calls over the pouring rain, "We have arrived at the coordinates where we last heard from Stevens."

Pembroke finds a busted satellite phone's bright orange outer casing amid the abandoned equipment, "It appears Professor Stevens vacated the base camp in a hurry."

Owen pulls the shaft of a long decorated spear from a cinched nylon sack, "I got a bad feeling about this."

Richard wheels toward Owen, "Do not touch the tip. It is no doubt dipped in poison."

Antoine laughs as the downpour morphs into a steady drizzle, "Is there anything out here that is not poisonous?" Pouring more alien fire pellets into the reassembled flamethrower, he clears a wide swath of ground before igniting an unnatural blue blaze dead center in the open space.

The wet and weary group slips into their routine, setting up camp. Rachel pulls another dehydrated culinary surprise—courtesy of Richard—from the dwindling sack of rations and reads the handwritten label, "I hope everybody is hungry for Beef Stroganoff and noodles."

Richard pulls a plastic bag from his pack, "We can add these wild mushrooms I foraged along the way." Reading the usual blank stares in reply, "He rolls his eyes; they are quite edible and delicious, I might add."

Griffin Pike | The Amazon
07:11 p.m. | October 13, 2044

Dry and semi-comfortable under a camouflaged tarp, Griffin Pike watches the PTB expedition set up camp and light a brilliant fire through his high-powered night-vision binocs. Focusing on the strapping Black fellow clearing a wide swath of tall grass with a fiery blue arc from a snub-nosed flamethrower, he smiles, "A fucking flamethrower. Why didn't Henri's people think of bringing one of those?"

Turning to a bound and gagged Penny Pennywell, he delivers a trademark evil grin, "Your cavalry has finally arrived."

Chapter Nine:

The Escape

Flynn | Gray battlecruiser
03:30 a.m. | October 14, 2044

Honking up ruddy phlegm across the sharp grated floor in the splattered, disgusting torture box, a bruised and bloodied Agent Flynn of The Powers That Be signals timeout to Ted, his massive reptilian confidante. "Since I'm on the menu, I guess this is meant for one last fucked up meat tenderizing session."

Acknowledging Flynn's resignation, Ted's iridescent scaly head motions toward the locked portal before pointing to himself.

Wishing he could express gratitude to the empathetic hybrid, Flynn restrains himself from an overt emotional display, "It was an honor having a pro like you kick the crap out of me."

An oblivious Gray enters the box, disrupting further conversation with an anticipatory smile creasing its evil slit-for-a-mouth. Dismissing

Ted to stand aside, the frail colorless humanoid directs two scarecrow guards to seize the human prisoner for immediate processing.

Ted's almost imperceptible nod alerts Flynn that *it's go-time*. The hulking lizard man snatches both scarecrows by their skinny necks, bashing their oversized skulls together with a sickening crunch, splatting gore across the filthy walls before pitching their limp bodies into the shadows.

Unperturbed by the violence, the small Gray's attention pivots onto the misbehaving science experiment, sending Ted crumpling onto his clawed hands and thick knees with a vicious electrified jolt.

Intent on not letting Ted's diversion go to waste, Flynn springs off the deck and lifts the Gray over his head. "Bloody hell, I've had hamsters that weigh more than you."

The flummoxed alien wriggles in Flynn's firm grip but fails to retaliate before its arched back snaps over the agent's bent knee. After flinging the dead Gray atop the scarecrow heap, Flynn rushes to Ted, hunched over and struggling to breathe, "Bloody hell, mate. Are you okay?"

The reptilian's slitted yellowy eyeballs focus on the human before he speaks aloud, "Good plan, Flynn. Leave now. More will come."

"I did not know you could talk."

"And now it is too late. See you on the other side."

With no time to mourn his heroic sparring partner and friend, Flynn grabs the dead scarecrows' weapons and bolts into the dark corridor. Expecting trouble around every nightmarish bend in the labyrinthine dreadnought, the agent hails Nicole on their closed telepathic frequency, *"It's on, baby. I am heading your way."*

Nicole's panicked voice echoes in his head, *"They took Nina. It's dinnertime."*

Flynn hits an intersection and ducks away from more clueless aliens moving past his hidden position, *"I know where they took her. Change in plans. Hang tight, and don't let them take you alive."*

Hugging the dull walls in his ripped and bloody PTB flight suit, he clutches the alien weapons in his aching grip, *"It's payback time, motherfuckers."*

A scarecrow shoves Nina into a dripping chamber and slams the portal closed behind her naked form. Through the dimness, she counts five scared humans in their birthday suits, looking more like Holocaust survivors, staring at her from a long bench, "Does anybody here speak English?" Receiving nothing but terrified stares, Nina mutters, "I'll take that as a no."

Realizing this was it, Nina squeezes between the sealed exit and a gaunt, defeated Spanish woman on the wet and sticky bench as hot water sprays from jets embedded in the low ceiling. Weeks of filth and bacteria wash from the naked bodies and drain into collection grates built into the slick floor, like cleaning a bag of lettuce before making a salad.

Acknowledging her life's sad, weird ending, Nina tries to tune out the soul-crushing sobs of her fellow abductees to no avail. The water slows to a trickle before stopping as a robotic vertical bar extends from the wall, shooting a sudsy substance down the row of tasty uncooked humans. Before the soap machine reaches Nina, muffled explosions rattle the claustrophobic space, jerking the cleansing process to a stop.

Wiping water from her face, Nina hears an odd scuffling before the portal swings open. Agent Flynn ducks his bruised face inside the sauna-like chamber and speaks out loud, "Nina! Are you okay?"

"A little wet and slippery, but just peachy otherwise."

Flynn kicks aside a dead scarecrow, "Come on, we gotta move! Unless you all want to be the main fucking course."

Thrust into an unimaginable nightmare, the multinational hodge-podge of abductees responds like frightened animals before three follow Nina's lead and exit the shower. A haggard Italian man kicks and spits at one of the dead scarecrows on his way past. With the clock ticking, Flynn looks inside at the last two, a young Japanese woman seated and holding hands with an older Indian fellow splattered with soapy foam.

"This is it. There will not be another chance at escape. Come on!"

The twenty-ish female speaks words aloud for the first time in months, "We are staying. My friend has Stage 4 cancer. He is dying. I want to be here for him, so he will not die alone."

Nina grabs Flynn by the elbow, pulling him away from the pair, "We need to get the fuck out of here!"

Flynn tosses a scarecrow weapon to the girl, who proffers a courageous smile. "Thank you. They will not take us alive. Please leave, and good hunting."

Leading the stone naked quartet down an empty corridor, Flynn pauses at the same intersection, ensuring the coast is clear before moving to the elevator. "We are heading for the docking bay. That is where we will find our ship." Wiping tears from his black and blue eyes, he adds, "I hope."

Nina remote views the battlecruiser's massive docking bay, "I can see it." With a confident smile directed at the bedraggled escapees, the authoritative PTB administrator points to Agent Flynn, "Follow this man and do what he tells you, okay?"

Naked and afraid, they mumble yes in Italian, Farsi, and Spanish.

Nicole | Gray battlecruiser
04:10 a.m. | October 14, 2044

Inside the dank cell where she had spent the last 50 days waiting to die, Nicole zips up her jumpsuit, covering scars from her botched impregnation—which saved her from Astrid's fate—and stands tall, *"Zint! It is the time!"*

Silence.

"Zint! We have to go!"

The plebeian traitor appears at her opened cell with another brain implant pressed between his thin dexterous fingers, *"I am here."* Motioning for her to bend down to his level, he explains, *"This implant activates the brain's latent telekinetic ability."*

Nicole feels a sharp pain as the needle burrows through her scalp and skull, transmogrifying her cerebrum. Flush with the instant gratification of renewed vigor and clarity of purpose, she places a firm hand on her little ally's narrow shoulder, *"I want you to come with me."*

An amused grin creases Zint's face, dominated by large, intelligent black oval eyes, *"I thought that was implied by my treasonous behavior."*

With an orgasmic rush pulsating every fiber of her being, Nicole oohs, *"Whoa. This is amazing."*

"Good. It is working. You are a special human, Nicole." Sensing someone's approach, Zint takes Nicole's hand, *"Time to go."*

A scarecrow enters the cellblock's central corridor, blocking the exit with a look of surprise on its ugly face. With a wink toward Zint, Nicole uses her telekinetic implant to slam the rail-thin guard against the wall, *"Payback is a bitch."*

Zint reaches out his four-fingered hand and touches her thigh, *"Do not overdo. Dangerous. Very dangerous."*

As the little Gray traitor hustles down the cell block, opening doors, Nicole counts seven abductees staggering into the dim blue light.

Only seven people. "We are leaving. Now!"

The German Shepherd, whose master passed weeks beforehand, bounds out of a cell to Nicole's side. She reaches down, giving the shedding, malnourished animal a good ear scratch, "Hello, girl. We finally meet face-to-face."

Zint leads the ragtag assemblage representing Morocco, North Korea, Mexico, and the US into the prison deck's main artery, *"This way, Nicole. Your ship is in the hangar bay."*

"Will it fly?"

"We will all find out together."

Nina | Gray battlecruiser
04:46 a.m. | October 14, 2044

Flynn leads a wet, naked Nina and the emaciated trio of escapees into the massive hangar bay. Crouching behind a row of pill-shaped scout vessels, they discover the PTB cargo ship parked on a raised platform.

Nina tugs Flynn's arm and whispers, "Can you fly that thing?"

Relieved to discover their ride home remains intact, he grimaces, "No. We need Nicole."

Flynn unbolts the PTB ship's portal, keeping a watchful eye while ushering everyone aboard, surprised their escape thus far appears undiscovered by the omniscient Grays.

Nina accesses one-size-fits-all flight suits and passes them to the thankful trio. Tossing a clean uniform to Flynn, she holds her nose, "Change out of those bloody rags; you smell terrible."

Flynn peels out of his worn and bloodied uniform, "Now that is the Nina I know and love, always with an eye on fashion."

Slipping into a loose-fitted light-blue one-piece uniform, Nina shrugs her thin shoulders, "If I'm gonna die, I want to look good."

***

Minutes later, the tail-wagging German Shepherd bounds aboard the cargo ship ahead of Zint, the seven remaining abductees, and a fired-up Nicole, taking immediate command of the situation, "Nina, get everybody strapped in. Flynn, watch for the aliens!"

"You got it, Missy!"

"And for the love of Christ, stop calling me that. I hate it!"

Nina ushers the multinational group of seven to join their fellow excited escapees and buckle up.

Nicole climbs into the cockpit, feeling the second implant enhancing neural connections with a gusher of electrochemical signals inside her brain. Shaking off a dizzy head rush, her gaze lands on Astrid's broken headset resting on the empty co-pilot's chair where her music-loving friend left it. Sucking back horrible grief, "Goodbye, Astrid. I will visit your parents in Scotland when this is over."

Flipping switches to initialize life support and start the anti-gravity engine, Nicole races through preflight checklists at a superhuman pace as consoles light up like the 4th of July, "The ship's drive better be operational, or this will be a short flight."

Wiping away tears of relief, Nicole hears the familiar wah-wah-wah pulsating to life and calls down to her fellow humans, "Okay, here we go!" Manipulating joystick rudders on her command console, the ship elevates backward before yanking to a violent stop at the end of a tether, whipsawing down by the nose and smashing sideways into a wall. Jerked back and forth, Nicole yells into the open comm, "We are tied to the deck!"

After the aborted take-off, Flynn regains his footing inside the listing ship, still straining at the end of a leash, "What the hell, Nicole?"

"Flynn, I need you to go outside and cast off; they tied the ship to the deck."

"For the love of Christ, will we ever catch a fucking break? I'm on it!"

Bursting past Nina, Zint, and the terrified ten, a cursing Flynn unseals the hatch and barrels outside like a paratrooper, dropping ten feet onto the deck in a heap. Scrambling up, he hunches through the darkened hangar bay toward the thick metal cleat where the ship is tied down. Spotting resurgent scarecrows appearing out of nowhere, he dives sideways behind a crate as the massive hangar bay explodes with searchlights and ear-splitting staccato alarms. *"We have company, Nicole!"*

"You gotta cut us loose, Flynn! The bay doors are sliding shut!"

Flynn scurries to hide, nowhere near the cleat, *"I can't get near the bloody line, Nicole. Holy shit, it is getting crowded out here!"*

A scarecrow guard fires an energized warning blast past Nicole's viewscreen, *"Flynn, we are all going to die!"*

Knowing surrender means certain death, Zint unbuckles from his seat, jumps from the tethered ship, and sneaks through the chaos to stop the hangar bay doors from grinding shut.

Feeling their one chance at escaping slip away, Nina turns to her wide-eyed fellow humans, "Stay put!" Brandishing an alien weapon, she vaults into the hangar, ready to blast at the first thing that moves. *"Flynn, where are you?"*

The chaotic din ratchets into the jostling cargo ship through the wide-open portal as the mortified international group watches the silhouette of an evil scarecrow breach the ship's hold.

The German Shepherd emits a low mean growl, bursting forward with fearless abandon, releasing weeks of pent-up energy and snarling rage to repel the tall skinny humanoid. Landing atop the alien on the hangar deck, the snarling dog chomps the tormentor's suit before running off into the shadows, following Zint's trail.

Unable to locate Flynn amid the disorienting lights and sounds, Nina's keen vision follows the stricken PTB ship's thick tethered line from a defiladed position, "Here goes nothing." Shooting suppressing fire, she sprints under the unwieldy vessel and ducks as it swings around, trying to pull free, *"Jesus, Nicole, wait a minute."*

From point-blank range, she blasts the heavy cleat into

metal shards.

Straining from the end of the line at maximum thrust, the ship's released momentum vaults it upward, smashing into the rafters and ductwork before leveling off high up inside the hangar's shadowy heights.

Nicole's elated voice resonates in Nina's head, *"I can circle back and pick you up!"*

A defeated-sounding Flynn interjects, *"Bloody hell, Nicole, get out of here!"*

Overwhelmed with grief and disappointment, Nina seconds Flynn's admonition, *"Go on, my dear. We'll catch the next ride."*

Hunkering down an aisle, Nina spots Zint and the German Shepherd hiding amid a long row of pill-shaped scout ships.

"This way, Nina. Hurry."

Surrounded by stone-faced scarecrows, the recaptured Agent Flynn watches the PTB ship escape through the bay's half-closed doors. Laughing through his aches and pains, he turns to face an unamused silver-suited Gray splitting the phalanx of bumbling guards. With a violent sweep of its four-fingered hand, the Gray uses unrestrained telekinesis to yank out Flynn's brain enhancer, leaving a bloody hole in its place. Inspecting the offending needle in its delicate hand, it orders the Black human's return to the cell block.

Feeling a throbbing pain in place of the needle implant, Flynn swallows hard, accepting his fate as a gleaming white scout vessel rises from a long row of parked ships.

Realizing the aliens appear confused by the unauthorized take-off on the heels of the PTB ship's escape, he hears a familiar voice screaming his name out loud over the noisy sirens, *"Flynn! Goddamit, duck!"*

With a wide-eyed recognition that something is about to happen, Flynn hits the deck and covers his bloodied head a heartbeat before a lime-green tractor beam shoots from the craft, snatching the shocked alien contingent and lifting them high off the deck.

Inside the cramped scout ship, Zint smiles at a virtual screen, watching his so-called superior and a bunch of humorless meat sacks writhe and struggle like rats immersed in the unyielding greenish glow. With a deft hand, the traitor to his kind seals his place in Gray lore by flicking a small joystick sideways, flinging the suffocating aliens from the pressurized hangar bay into the cold dark vacuum of space.

With the clock ticking, Nina and the German Shepherd poke their heads from the scout ship's seamless portal watching the shaken PTB agent scrambling back onto his feet, "Agent Flynn, do you need a ride?"

Zint | Atlantic Ocean
05:13 a.m. | October 14, 2044

Seated behind the pill-shaped scout ship's spartan helm, Zint executes an escape trajectory toward Earth, evading energized salvos from two vengeful Empire Gray fighters hot on its tail. Swooping and swerving the nimble craft, he calls back to his passengers ensconced within a physics-defying life support system, "I always wanted to do this."

Piercing Earth's layer cake of atmospheric levels without leaving a friction-generated tell-tale fiery wake, the craft drops through a violent storm churning over the mid-Atlantic. It skims the roiling sea through dark aqua cresting waves. Unable to shake the tenacious chase craft, Zint dives beneath the surface like a torpedo, gliding between breeding Humpbacks off coastal Brazil.

With her molecular makeup preserved at a sub-atomic level from the deadly g-forces, Nina tries to speak, but the words mush and distort as her physical form pulls like taffy through a sharp turn.

"D-D-DDiiiiddddd weeeee loooooossse themmmmmm?"

Intent on his driving, Zint calls back with cool-headed telepathy as another blast knocks the ship, *"No. Not yet."*

The ship bursts from the blue Atlantic over a pre-dawn Rio de Janeiro, zigzagging above the Brazilian jungle at treetop level.

Passing over hundreds of miles of undulating jungle terrain dotted with farms, villages, and snaking rivers, a cognitive jolt pierces Zint's brainwaves as he banks north and west, projecting a map of the Amazon into Nina's head.

"Nina. Who is Rachel?"

Struggling to breathe in the confining hold, with her left leg draped over a passed-out Flynn and her arm hugged around the heroic German Shepherd looking like it needs to pee, Nina replies, eeking out a telepathic response, *"Raaachel …. Raaaaachellllll Haaaaaaaiiiiig …. She is a new PTB-B-B-B reeeeecruit_tute-tute-tute."*

"I can see the one called Rachel. She is not far from here."

Out of the loop for so long, fighting to stay alive, Nina's former life as chief administrator of The Powers That Be refloods her brain, *"Offf coooourse. The PTB-B-B-B mountedededed a second Amazonnnnnn expeditionnnnn …. Can we reach them-them-them …?"*

Zint pulls straight up as one of the two pursuing ships abandons the pursuit, *"Hold tight, please. Keep your seats upright and tray tables stored."*

Nina's laugh stretches out like a funhouse mirror within the life support, *"Where did you learrrrrn that that that that?"*

Zint's mouth curls into a smile, *"I monitored Earth's TV signals for many years. Sit back and have a Coke and a smile."*

The remaining fighter predicts its target's portside turn, leading a well-timed volley of explosive bursts that end Zint's wild ride with an end-over-end, out-of-control spin. Releasing the helm, the tiny alien dons his life support seconds before the scout ship slams into a precipitous cliff face high above the jungle stretching over the horizon.

Releasing the ship's life support, Zint crawls through the narrow fuselage to the cramped hold, *"Is everyone okay?"*

The German Shepherd's loud bark echoes in everyone's ears.

"I'll take that as a yes."

Flipping a switch, the ship turns transparent, revealing their dire predicament on a rocky outcropping midway up a sheer granite wall. *"We are in quite a pickle."*

Flynn wakes up, staring hundreds of feet toward a rocky cliff base disappearing into the jungle far below. Fending off vertigo, he struggles to turn around and jabs Nina with an elbow, "Bloody hell, mate. Turn that off."

"No one can see in, Flynn."

Flynn feels the back of his salt and pepper hair matted with blood, "I lost my telepathic needle."

"I know. I still have mine, but it is starting to hurt."

Zint touches the back of Nina's short-cropped red-headed scalp, *"I will remove it now. Hold still."* Producing the red sticky needle, he comments on an open telepathic channel, *"I can still communicate with you both like when we first met."*

Scanning the blue heavens dotted with puffy white clouds, Nina muses, "I guess they think we died in the crash."

Zint nods, *"I concur. I flew right into their trap."*

Flynn pushes onto his elbows, "On purpose, mate?"

"It was the only way. I did not want to lead them to Rachel."

Flynn stares at the tiny alien, "Rachel?"

Nina jumps into the conversation, "She is here, Flynn. Most likely part of a larger PTB expedition."

Flummoxed beyond belief, Flynn inhales the fresh air flowing into the ship, "Christ, how long were we gone?"

* * *

Zint replicates the ping of locator beacons permeating the surrounding wilderness. *"Perhaps your people will pick up the SOS embedded in our signal."*

"I would not count on it, but it is worth a try." Scooching sideways to relieve his sore back, Flynn muses aloud, "I wonder if Nicole made it?"

Nina smiles, "I can feel her life force in my head."

"Even without your brain needle thing?"

"Yes, Agent Flynn. It is called faith. Try it sometime."

The dog wags its tail and licks Zint's face.

Nina brushes loose hair off her pants leg, "Ah, she is expressing gratitude, Zint."

The little Gray alien replies with his trademark inquisitive expression, *"I know. I can read Daphne's thoughts."*

Flynn beats Nina to the punch, "Daphne?"

Zint's head cocks at an angle, *"That is her name."* After a brief pause, he continues, *"She tells me it is time to urinate."*

The sleep of reason produces monsters.

– Francisco Goya

Chapter Ten:

The Ghosts

Semi-dry and protected within the alien pellet fire's protective bluish glow from creepy crawlers, Owen and Rachel awaken to another sweltering day in the oppressive Amazon under a breathable pest-repellant reflective blanket.

"Good morning, sunshine."

"Ugh, I hate this heat."

Slinging his semi-automatic carbine over a shoulder, Antoine sidesteps the snuggled couple pretending to sleep and pours Richard King a second cup of black coffee, "Here you go, Professor."

King mutters "thanks" without tearing his deep-set dark blue eyes from the water-stained, dog-eared, mud-splattered maps and notes on the loamy ground before him.

Staring down another long steamy day in the jungle with little to occupy his time, Antoine watches over the PTB scientist's shoulder, scribbling a notation on a map dominated by a pair of overlapping spirals—one big, one small. "So, when do we head out and finish the mission?"

Plotting the wayward Professor John Stevens' weak locator beacon signals pinging around the base camp, Richard takes a swig of Antoine's delicious camp coffee, breathing in the tolerable early morning air before the sun rises enough to bake the meadow. "Perhaps soon. I need to be sure. Setting out in the wrong direction from here would be ruinous. Most likely, the same lapse in judgment befell our friend, Stevens."

Pembroke breaks from the undergrowth at the meadow's northern edge, returning from his morning constitutional. "Listen up, people, I have news." Pouring a cup, he takes a long drink before gesturing in a wide arc with his mug, "There are tracks, both human and animal, all over this neck of the woods."

With unmasked facetiousness, King replies, "Stevens was here. You found his footprints. Good job, Pembroke."

"Don't be an asshole, Richard." Hunching down to his PTB colleague's seated position, Pembroke's scarred face creases into a cagey grin, "Does your Professor Stevens weigh 250 pounds and wear size 17 French army boots?"

Richard's eyes narrow, returning the mercenary's stare, "No, he certainly does not."

Antoine scans the thick undergrowth surrounding the open meadow base camp. Exposed and vulnerable, the trio acknowledges a new danger lurking in the jungle—Griffin Pike and a squad of high-paid killers armed with enough firepower to take down a small nation.

Richard's transponder breaks the tense silence, broadcasting a new signal: *"Beep-beep-beep Beeeeep-Beeeep-Beeeep Beep-beep-beep …."*

The group's collective gaze turns to the mustard-yellow handheld device positioned atop a stack of notes and charts.

Breaking the spellbound silence, Antoine chimes in, "That is an old-school Morse code SOS."

Pembroke ignores the obvious comment and checks the awakening Haigs, sitting up and rubbing sleep from their pretty eyes before speaking to a perplexed Richard in a low voice, cognizant they are more than likely under surveillance, "Could that be signal be from Stevens?"

A confounded and confused Richard shakes his head with frustration, triangulating the SOS and plotting its position on the treasure map in the polar opposite direction from the converging spiral nuclei, "Why would Stevens move in that direction? There is nothing over there."

Exhaling a frustrated sigh, trying to appear as normal as possible, Pembroke stands and brushes an insect from his pants leg, "Antoine, light a fire under the sleeping beauties over there; they are coming with us."

"What about me, Mr. Pembroke?"

"I need you to guard the camp. We are not alone."

* * *

Following the mystery signal for miles into the dense jungle, the foursome hacks its way to the precipice of a sheer cliff.

Feeling days of hard slogging and incredible sacrifice to reach the lost ship slipping from his grasp, Richard's anger, and frustration swell, "Blast this stupid transponder! And blast this world reduced to middle ages navigation like I am fucking Amerigo Vespucci, for Christ's sake. I'm done here. Let's head back so I can finish my work and find that damn ship."

Pembroke's eyes narrow, "Wait a minute, Richard. What if someone tried to draw us away from the base camp?"

"Right, right," King produces an annoyed frown, "the gorilla in

French army boots."

Rachel looks askance at her fellow hikers, "What gorilla?"

Tired of the scientist and mercenary's constant sniping, Owen proceeds to the cliff's edge and peers over the near-vertical side, "Hey! There is something about 70 feet down."

Rachel steps to her husband's side, clutching his sleeve to stave off vertigo, "What is that?"

Richard splits the pair and looks down, "It's a ship. An Empire Gray scout ship, to be precise."

Rachel feels a heady swoon overwhelm her senses and pitches forward before Owen grabs around her waist and pulls her from the precipice.

Shaking her blond ponytail head in the heat and humidity, she mutters, "It's Nina. Nina Madsen. And Flynn. Oh my God. They are trapped inside that thing."

Owen feels his wife's forehead, "Rachel, honey, I think you have a slight case of jungle fever. You just said Flynn and Nina are inside that crashed ship."

The faint sound of a dog's bark echoes up the cliff face causing everyone to freeze in place.

Richard addresses his confounded colleagues with a smirk, "I have known Nina for many years. That is not her bark."

Pembroke ignores Richard's poor attempt at humor while raising Antoine on his radio, "I need you to gather whatever rope we have and bring it to these coordinates."

* * *

With the nylon line from the Zodiacs secured around a tree, Owen ties the rope in a harness and lowers himself over the edge, rappelling down the rocky cliff. Antoine and Pembroke maintain the line as Richard watches the dare-devil descent next to a worried Rachel.

Pulling her blond ponytail into a bun, she wipes sweat from

her forehead, talking more to herself, "Why do these adventures always involve Owen at the end of a rope?"

Richard grins, "You are referring to your time in Libya retrieving the golden ellipse. I read the after-action account of your exploits. Quite heroic."

Rachel turns to the PTB scientist, "I could try to bring them up with my telekinetic power, but I have never moved anything that large. I am not sure I can."

"Your time will come, my dear. Let Owen play the hero once again."

Rachel watches through the haze as her husband reaches within feet of the white pill-shaped vessel, gleaming in the hot sun, "Owen just wanted to retire so we could enjoy a quiet life together and raise a family. I was the one who insisted on saving the world by joining the PTB."

With a sage smile on his lined face, Richard places a hand on Rachel's shoulder, "We both know that was never going to happen."

* * *

Owen's boots hit the solid granite ledge where the alien vessel slammed sideways and jammed against a massive tree trunk jutting into space hundreds of feet up the cliff wall above the jungle. Keeping a firm grip on the rope, he climbs astride the cylindrical craft approximating the mass of an SUV, looking for a hatch or window, "Hello in there? Anybody home?"

The weight shifts, and he feels the craft wobble in the precarious embrace of the thick busted branches as the dog's muffled bark reaches his ears. "Nina? Flynn? Are you in there?"

Sliding forward, Owen knocks with his free hand as a portal opens in the craft's rounded white fuselage behind him. Swinging his legs around, Owen startles, seeing a gray head peek from the hole like an alien prairie dog.

A weird voice trickles into his mind, *"Hold tight, Owen.*

Dangerous up here. Very dangerous."

Reeling from the telepathic connection, a woman in a dusty blue PTB flight suit rises next to the tiny alien man, "Hello, Owen."

"Nina, is that you?"

The PTB administrator rubs close-shorn white hair on her scraped and bruised scalp, "Yeah, it's me. I really need a trip to my salon. You are a sight for sore eyes, young man."

Owen hears Flynn's familiar British accent resonating from the craft, "Bloody hell! Is that my mate, Owen Haig, out there? Enough bloody chit-chat, Nina; let me out of this sodding flying coffin!"

More dog barks echo Flynn's anxious words.

* * *

Pembroke clutches around Flynn's bloodied and bruised forearm in a two-handed grip and pulls the wounded agent over the ledge.

Chest heaving from the arduous rope climb, lying prone on his aching back, Flynn eyeballs the mercenary through the bright midday sun, "I see the PTB is scraping the barrel, post-invasion, hiring the likes of you, Pembroke."

"Fuck off, mate, or I will drop you back over the side."

Rachel guides an exhausted Nina away from the edge, "Let me dress that cut on your forehead, Nina."

"Thank you, dear." Nina raises her face into the invigorating sunshine, letting Rachel play nursemaid, "You have come a long way, young lady."

Rachel replies with an irony-laced smile, reaching for a gauze roll in the medical kit, "In more ways than one." Pulling a length to wrap around Nina's close-cropped head, her glowing hands pass before Nina's blue-eyed gaze.

Nina's eyes widen, "Your hands …."

"It is my new reality." Proceeding with the bandaging of Nina's head, Rachel chuckles, "I'm also pregnant. It's a girl."

Nina places a hand on Rachel, pausing her head wrapping, "Mazeltov to the baby news. I am sorry I was not here to help you after your rescue from under the pyramid."

Reaching for the roll of tape, Rachel wipes away wistful tears, "I had plenty of helpers." Showing off her high-tech outdoors attire, she offers an Earthy contented smile, "Roy Kendall, for one. He outfitted us and did his best to fill your high heel shoes."

"Not literally, I hope."

"No! I don't think so." With a sly smile, she adds, "Although he has the legs for it."

Nina's laughter morphs into a coughing fit. Wiping tears from her bloodshot eyes, she notices Professor Richard King lingering amongst the bramble in his scuffed, muddied knee-high boots and olive-green jungle ensemble, pretending to study an orchid, "Hello, Doc. It's been quite some time."

Richard turns toward Nina, his face shadowed under his wide-brimmed hat in the bright sunshine, "Good to have you back among the living, Miss Madsen."

* * *

Owen grabs the jury-rigged animal harness swinging in mid-air and secures it on the narrow ledge. Peering inside the exotic little craft, he sees the last occupants, a dog, and an alien, waiting for rescue, "Okay, girl. Come on out of there."

The German Shepherd ignores Owen, panting next to Zint in the hot interior.

"Call her Daphne. She will respond."

Owen hears the tiny alien's advice in his head, "Okay. Come here, Daphne. Time to go, girl."

The dog springs onto its feet and climbs out of the scout ship. Tail wagging, she smiles at Owen as if to say, *"Now what?"*

Antoine and Pembroke hoist Daphne in a makeshift harness up

the cliff face onto solid ground, where the others are preparing to return to the base camp.

Zint executes a timed self-destruct before rushing to exit through the scout ship's portal, finding a waiting Owen, ready to help the tiny being up the cliff, *"You are still here? We must go. The ship will explode in less than ten Earth minutes."*

Dripping in sweat, Owen tamps down reservations, motioning for the alien to climb onto his back.

The alien complies, clasping long gray fingers tight around his chest, *"I'm ready, Owen."*

Clutching the swaying rope, the former banker and the piggybacking alien ascend the cliff's face. Owen grimaces at the little alien's added weight and mutters to himself, *"This isn't weird at all."*

Feet from the top, Zint springs upward like a monkey, loosening a cascade of rocks and pebbles. Dangling solo from the nylon rope, Owen grimaces while reaching for a handhold and feels Antoine's iron grip on his arm pull him over the ledge to safety.

"I got you, man."

Scrabbling onto solid ground, Owen catches his breath, wiping dirt and sweat off his face as a low tremor rattles the trees, sending a flock of macaws skyward. Zint peers over the precipice, ensuring the scout craft is gone, before turning to Owen, *"Thank you for the rescue."*

Catching Rachel's relieved gaze, smiling and talking to Nina and Richard, he looks down at the Gray alien, "What? Uh, no problem."

Zint | Stevens' base camp
07:00 p.m. | October 14, 2044

Antoine's deep woods culinary talent shines to the fore, slicing into a wild boar roasting from a spit over a firepit, crackling and crisping succulent meat to savory perfection for the ravenous group, eating, drinking, and exchanging war stories.

A greasy-fingered Richard King accepts another helping with an effusive thank you to the chef, holding court while bringing the newcomers up to speed. "… And so, here we are at Professor John Stevens' base camp."

Nina absorbs most of the protracted monologue while nursing a cup of tea, "Stevens left for Brazil last summer. Is it possible he is still alive?"

Richard licks a finger and shoots a coy smile at the sultry former redhead uplit by the flickering firelight, "I guess anything is possible, Nina. Were you close to John?"

"Just a friend, Richard, like you."

Seated next to Owen, devouring meat off a bone like a caveman, Rachel's hands radiate brighter as the sky above the base camp clearing darkens and fills with stars, "Professor, tell them about Pike."

"What? Oh, yes. Rachel refers to the other expedition vying to reach the lost ship under the direction of Griffin Pike."

Flynn washes down a mouthful of real food, trying not to overeat after 50 days on a forced starvation diet, "Griffin Pike? What the hell does he want with an ancient shipwreck?"

Richard's reply is interrupted by Zint, tossing his gnawed bone in the fire, sending sparks skyward before speaking fluent English in an audible tone, "Terrible weapon. Terrible. It must not fall into the wrong hands. My kind is searching for it. We must be first. Otherwise, everyone dies."

Nina speaks for the shocked campfire roundtable, asking, "Zint, we did not know you could talk."

Shuffling on his bare feet in a matte silver suit, the alien smiles, "Did I mention that Antoine's dinner is finger-licking good?"

With a knowing chuckle, Nina turns to the confused group, "Zint monitored our TV signals for over half a century."

Owen laughs, "You don't say? Hey Zint, what is your favorite show?"

Without hesitation, the alien replies, "I like *Seinfeld*. Also, *X-Files*, even funnier."

Pembroke sits apart from the group sipping tea, half-listening as the campfire banter reduces to inanities while maintaining furtive surveillance on a ghostlike figure moving through the underbrush.

Antoine carves a large portion of meat and plops on the ground cross-legged next to Owen, enjoying his repast with one eye on the tired group and the other on a concerned Pembroke.

Owen turns to the fit former sailor and pats him on the back, "You are quite a chef, Antoine. This was an amazing feast."

Producing a gleaming white smile in the firelight, Antoine shrugs, "I caught the poor thing rummaging through our camp after you all left this morning. I had most of the day to prepare. No big deal. Really." After biting off a dripping chunk washed down with weak tea, he shrugs with genuine modesty, "Oh yeah, that is good. Let's hear it for this noble beast providing sustenance for us all."

Richard stands and cleans his hands on a wet cloth, "That is the first time I heard a wild boar referred to as a noble beast."

A satiated and sleepy Nina yawns and slumps beside Flynn, allowing the alien healing powder to work its magic.

Flynn pulls a blanket over Nina's hunched shoulders before taking another long swig of purified water. Studying the recycled clear plastic bottle refracting the flickering flames, he shakes his head, "Bloody hell, something as simple as water. Never take anything for granted. Never." Scooching to allow Nina to rest her head on his lap, he smiles, "Okay. I got that off my chest, and now I want to say a few words: Nicole, baby, Godspeed wherever you are. I also need to mention the Nigerian abductee who gave up his liver so I could live to see 49 more hellish days on that fucking alien rust bucket. And last, I'd like to remember Ted, my hybrid lizard man torturer slash sparring partner who pulled his punches just enough to keep the Empire Grays off my back and keep me alive."

Nina rises and elbows the dead-tired agent in his sore ribs, "Uh, Flynn, I think you left someone out of your tribute."

Flynn finds the diminutive Empire Gray alien through the darkness, eyes aglow in the firelight, seated beside his pal, Daphne. "Well, yes, of course, Mr. Zint. Our jailer turned savior. I cannot thank him enough for everything he did."

Nina adds, "And at incredible personal peril. We were under constant surveillance. He took risks that went beyond mere bravery."

Zint stands and moves his three-foot frame before the blue sparking flames, "I spent my life observing the human race suffering through wars, natural disasters, famines, and pandemics and grew to admire human perseverance. It is no small feat. Most species do not make it this far. Many. Some, like my kind, survive beyond a reason to exist, becoming machines bent on conquest millions of years ago. Worse, the botched Gork invasion taught us nothing."

Listening to the humanoid speak conversational English—something the Gray advisers to the PTB, including Ping, are incapable of doing—Richard's interest piques, "What lesson should they have learned from the Gorks?"

Zint turns to the learned human scientist, "Simple, really. Don't mess with the humans."

Daphne stands and resettles beside Zint, prompting a collective "Aw."

Scratching the dog's furry head, Zint produces a wistful smile, "I discovered her master's dead body lying on his cell floor and loyal Daphne standing guard. She growled, not letting me near her person. I brought her food and water. Over time, we bonded. She is like a human in many ways."

Looking into the mesmerized faces of his new band of brothers and sisters, Zint's expressive face fills with shame, "One of my duties involved separating human prisoners from their personal effects before they were taken for processing. I saved certain things and learned about those poor people through what they left behind. Would it be okay to recite a poem I found in Daphne's master's shirt pocket?"

Richard exits the campfire conversation to confer with Pembroke prompting Rachel to speak up, "Of course, Zint. We are all ears, right everybody?"

Checking the curious nods, Zint clears his throat. "It goes like this:

The burning desire
lights hearts afire
to a planet afar
orbiting a star
but time and space
are not about place
a feeling inside
is what will abide
the celestial dust
turning ships to rust
never reached
forever beached
in merciless hands
on cosmic sands
disaster fraught
I never thought
it came to me
it came to me
adrift in mystery
what have I found
I'm glory bound
I'm glory bound.

Gazing into the twinkling tableau stretching to infinity above his tiny gray head, "I hope Daphne's master found his glory."

"That was beautiful, Zint." Rachel feels the tension rise and squirms in her seat as Daphne emits a low growl, hearing a branch snapping from the pitch-dark undergrowth.

Richard and Pembroke interrupt the campfire gathering, "We need to end this party and get some rest. Antoine and I will stand watch in shifts throughout the night."

Owen jumps onto his feet, "Let me take the first watch. You both need sleep."

Antoine removes the semi-auto carbine slung over his shoulder and presents it to Owen in a firm two-handed grip, "Good man, Owen. Much obliged. You ever fire a short barrel rifle?"

Owen shakes his head, "You hang onto that, Antoine. I have my trusty 9mm."

Rachel assists a sleepy Nina with supplies from her pack as the party ends, rolling out bags and blankets for another night beneath the stars, well within the augmented blue fire's protective circumference.

Flynn notes the casual ease with which the expedition sleeps on the ground under the stars without fear of snakes and scorpions crawling up their pants legs. Speaking to no one in particular, his head abuzz from the painkillers, "I would like to point out that I was the first to introduce the American couple to the concept of the alien fire way back in North Africa."

Owen turns to his friend, "Flynn, it is good to have you back among the living."

"Likewise, mate. Likewise."

Thirty yards downwind of the campers, near the jungle's edge, Pembroke splinters Antoine's makeshift barbeque pit with a hatchet, dropping the smoky charred boar atop the smoldering wood before burying the greasy carcass in the sandy soil. "What a waste of meat. Next time, let's order takeout."

Griffin muses, "I could go for some of that boar meat," passing the hi-def night vision binocs to his killer mistress.

Stretching her tawny frame, Sapphire yawns, "I thought you were an avowed vegetarian, like your gay friends back in civilization."

"That is a very pejorative phraseology, my little wench."

Looking through the binoculars, she smirks, more to herself, "Look at them. It's like a fucking field trip down there. They make me want to puke."

Griffin turns to his sweaty assassin, admiring the moonlight glistening off the curve of her back, "Now Sapphire, everyone can't be pure evil like you."

Bored, hungry, and horny, the lithe killer turns with a look of wanton desire toward the somnolent Penny Pennywell sleeping against a tree.

Griffin grabs her by the arm, "Don't. That crosses a line, even for me."

Sapphire's free hand grabs Griffin by the crotch, kneading him with her strong, nimble fingers through his khakis. After failing to get a rise from her bisexual partner in crime, she releases her hand and licks his face with her long tongue, whispering, "Griffin, don't go soft when we are so close to victory."

"Now, Sapphire, we both know that will never happen. As for your needs, I know a couple horny monkeys that could fill your gap until daybreak."

* * *

DeVille observes the tall PTB mercenary breaking down the firepit and throwing dirt over the pig from a camouflaged position, muttering, "You and I will have a fight to the death, my friend."

Displaced howler monkeys, unamused by the boorish human intrusion on their world, drown out a snoring Smythe sleeping in a high hammock near Rollins and Chayefsky, swaying from tarped sacks stretched between the trees.

Rachel | Stevens' base camp
06:15 a.m. | October 15, 2044

Rachel hears shuffling and grunts, awakening to the point of a spear inches from her nose. Afraid to move a muscle, she nudges her bedroll partner, "Owen, wake up. We have company."

With the blanket pulled over his head, Owen feigns sleep, ready to fight if Richard's risky plan goes sideways.

Holding glowing hands in mock surrender, Rachel rises to a seated position staring down a stocky young native slathered in white paint.

Comfortable in his primitive nakedness, the kid notes the universal sexiness of the light-haired female at the opposite end of his long spear, forming an involuntary erection.

A telekinetic jolt sends the pubescent lad stumbling backward, grabbing his crotch, *"Not happening, Sport."*

Richard rises from his spot on the dirt, seeing Pembroke kneeling in the grass next to Antoine with three Forest Ghost hunters wielding poisonous spears inches from their backs.

Richard calls to his mercenary gun-for-hire, masking a coy smile, "Really, Pembroke? I am disappointed they got the drop on you without so much as a tussle."

Pembroke sneers at the cheeky scientist, taking obvious pleasure in his discomfort, "This cockamamie plan had better work, Richard, or we all die."

Richard's voice rises over the morning jungle noise, "I did not see any other way. They know every tree in the forest, and they can lead us to the lost ship."

Owen sits up and puts an arm around his scared wife, "Just play along, Rachel. It's all part of a plan we concocted last night."

Richard stands, prompting a sharp response from the Forest Ghosts, "Zint, please rise."

Pulling from beneath a blanket next to Daphne, Zint stands, "Good morning, Richard. I see we have company."

The Forest Ghosts' jaws drop at the tiny alien's sudden appearance. Lowering their weapons, they fall prostrate on the ground, chanting in low synchronous tones.

Owen whispers to Rachel, "They have seen aliens before. Richard planned to let them get the drop on us so he could introduce Zint without us getting hurt or killed."

"Why didn't you tell me?"

"To be honest, I assumed you read my mind. And I was exhausted after all of that pork."

The anesthetized duo of Agent Flynn and Nina lay huddled together, snoozing through the native encounter.

Richard | Forest Ghost encampment
07:42 a.m. | October 15, 2044

Communicating with the primitive hunters using a hacked dialect of burps, beeps, and whistles culled from hazy recollections of a seminar on uncontacted tribes, Richard tries to impart one salient point: *Take me to your leader.*

Bemused by the weird noises coming from the strange white man, the lead hunter lowers his spear and orders two pre-teen boys slathered in white clay to take the curious fellow into custody.

Sensing a vague understanding between himself and the

primitive hunters, Richard points at Pembroke, standing off to the side with a cigarette dangling from his mouth, "He must come with me."

In complete control, the lead hunter ambles over to Pembroke, removes the cigarette from his mouth, and takes a deep puff. Blowing smoke into the hot, humid early morning air, he nods for two more boys to accompany Pembroke.

A fuming Pembroke follows Richard, at spearpoint, into the dense undergrowth, leaving Antoine, Rachel, Owen, and Zint staring in their wake while Flynn and Nina sleep through the entire encounter like angels.

Owen asks his mortified cohorts, "Should I try to follow them?"

Antoine shakes his head, "No. My gut says they are fine."

Owen burps and rubs his full belly from the previous night's feast, "My gut says something else."

* * *

Hiking along a well-trod jungle path for over an hour, the bickering pair of Richard and Pembroke are led through the undergrowth into the Forest Ghosts' nomadic encampment, melded into the trees with only a matted clearing large enough for a firepit sparking and smoldering in the stultifying air. Small rodents skitter about the thatched dwellings and dark puddles with a pall of greasy smoke lingering in the air.

Two middle-aged men and a woman suckling a tiny baby eyeball the light-skinned foreigners entering their primeval community before returning to their routine daily existence. Catching sight of the new arrivals, an excited gaggle of toddler-aged children burst from a communal nursery, laughing and punching, pulling at clothing, reaching into pockets, and tugging at anything shiny, as they have done before, to other unlucky guests.

Pembroke makes eye contact with one of the males, who returns a lascivious smile with a strand of drool dangling from his fat lower lip. "Richard, I do not wish to be dinner."

"Quiet, Pembroke. It was your fucking plan. Follow my lead."

The hunter disperses his posse before tapping Richard's shoulder and pointing at a larger shack concealed amongst a thick stand of shiny, dripping banana trees laden with creeping vines and mossy branches.

"Bingo."

"Just get on with it, Richard."

The Westerners duck through a low entrance into a darkened, musty interior wreaking of cooked flesh mixed with pungent spices. As their eyes adjust to the dimness, they look past a smoldering fire wisping thin white smoke through a hole in the roof onto two seated elders with spindly legs crossed, covered in tattoos and bony piercings over their paunchy mocha-brown bodies.

Richard separates from Pembroke, hunching farther inside and sitting opposite the two men. The circumspect mercenary lingers by the exit, noticing the interior walls adorned with watches and jewelry from past visitors to the camp, "Fucking great, just great."

"Easy, Pembroke. Let me do the talking."

Eschewing pleasantries, Richard removes a crumpled copy of his lost ship map covered in notes and scribbles from a jacket pocket and passes it to the tribal elders. Toning down his resonant voice in the 10-foot circular abode, "We are here to recover a deadly weapon from the shipwreck. If we don't locate it first. You will all die." Gesturing at himself and Pembroke, he amplifies the bold statement, "Everyone will die."

Receiving blank stares in reply, Richard plays it cool, pointing again at the paper, "Look at my fucking map, damn you. We need help finding the lost ship. The spirals do not provide enough information on their own."

The grizzled and wrinkled chieftains ignore their sweaty and disheveled guest's agitation, conferring in hushed tones before the elder to Richard's left nods toward Pembroke with a wide yellowy smile, "Smokes."

Confused, Richard leans forward and repeats, "Smokes?"

The man nods, "Yes. Smokes."

Pembroke objects, discerning the mythical tribal elder's request, "Get your own bloody cigarettes, mate."

Biting his tongue, Richard remains calm, "Do it, Pembroke. You have half a carton back at camp."

Heaving an irritated sigh, Pembroke tosses a half-empty cigarette pack to the chief, "Here you go. Those are bad for you, you know."

Exhibiting an unusual dexterity despite his arthritis-riddled dark hands, the Forest Ghost elder removes a filtered cigarette and lights it from the end of a burning stick. Blowing smoke rings into the air, the cagey native tugs at necklaces strung with rows of gold-capped teeth around his flappy neck and chuckles like Santa Claus, "Good. Good."

Richard King wipes his brow in the stifling heat, redirecting the distracted old-timers onto his map, "*Quid pro quo*, old-timer. Now the map."

Watching his colleague puff away, the elder speaks, "Many generations ago, small gray folk—like the one in your group—made us guardians of the lost ship. Our brutal way kept it hidden. But now, many more appear in the forest seeking the ship. They are different. Evil. Pure evil. And poison, not good. Not good. We lost many after eating the flesh of one of their kind."

Richard's face contorts into sheer confusion, "I do not mean to be unsympathetic, but we are running out of time."

With a bemused smile, the man focuses on the map, "Spirals. Good." Shoving the map back at Richard, he shakes his head, "It is missing landmarks.

Richard scooches around the fire next to the old man while the other guy falls asleep with the cigarette dangling from his lower lip. "Yes. Yes. We are here. Base camp. That is where your hunters found us."

Tracing a calloused forefinger along a winding stream, the elder turns to Richard, "You might want to write this down."

Sapphire | Outside Stevens' base camp
11:45 a.m. | October 15, 2044

Immune to insects pestering Griffin, Sapphire nudges him aside and peers through high-def binocs, letting the long leather strap dangle from her glistening neck and shoulders, "Why didn't the cannibals butcher the PTB expedition and do us all a favor?"

Griffin swats at a mosquito and shrugs, applying more DEET to his arms, "I don't know. But where would the fun be in that? We need at least one of them alive to lead us to the lost ship."

***

DeVille crouches along a winding path through leaves and vines dappled with sunlight leaking through the canopy toward Pike's camouflaged lookout. An odor of shit smacks the hulking man's senses like a petrol station toilet the minute he gets within ten feet. Entering the tamped-down space, he pinches his pugnacious crooked nose and scowls at Pike and Sapphire, "Jesus, man, you are not supposed to shit where you sleep."

Pike ignores the jibe, "My shit does not stink. It's those fucking monkeys."

Henri waves a thick meaty hand through the foul-smelling air, "Uh, sorry, asshole. Yeah, it does."

"Did you come over to insult me, or do you have news?"

"The second thing. Rollins tracked two of them, the older man and his hired gun, heading off into the woods with those white-painted natives."

Sapphire mutters, "They are called Forest Ghosts. What an asshole."

Griffin stares at his high-paid mercenary, waiting for the rest of the story, "Well? What of it?"

DeVille internalizes his contempt for the effete billionaire and his psycho-bitch girlfriend, "Rollins thinks they are obtaining accurate intel from the tribal elders on the lost ship's location."

Griffin's mood swings to happy, "See, Henri? That was not so difficult. Rollins is the smart one in the bunch. Based on his astute appraisal, we will await their return before our attack."

Sapphire groans, turning over onto her flat belly and raising her firm, round ass.

"Don't pout, my dear. I will retrieve Pennywell; we are moving to a new spot. Too many bugs."

Watching Pike disappear into the undergrowth, DeVille takes his place and monitors the new additions to the PTB expedition, milling about the blue fire. Pressed beside the enigmatic vixen amidst the steamy leaves and dripping vines, Henri feels a heady swoon as his hand wanders over Sapphire's curved backside and glides toward her crotch.

Sapphire slinks into Henri's wandering hand for a heartbeat before snapping back and grabbing his thumb. Twisting upward, a blade springs from her opposite hand to the immobilized man's thick scruffy neck, "Try touching me like that again, you sick fuck."

DeVille releases from her firm grasp as a bemused Griffin shakes his head from the clearing's edge next to a drugged and wavering Penny Pennywell, "If you are looking to kill time until we move out, you might try Smythe. He is quite amenable to an attack from the rear."

Henri rolls backward and springs onto his feet, waving it off as if nothing happened, "No, Griffin, that is more your thing from what I hear."

Richard | Stevens' base camp
03:22 p.m. | October 15, 2044

"We have returned!"

Flush with the tribal elder's generational knowledge leading to the lost ship's precise location, Pembroke and Richard exit the jungle, to everyone's abject relief, near where they left hours earlier.

The PTB scientist makes a beeline for his pack and accesses Pike's map. Upon unfurling the thin sheet on the ground, he removes the prehistoric stone artifact and reorients the overlapping Fibonacci spirals based on the tribal elder's direction, "Eureka."

Taking a deep breath in the midday heat, he wipes his brow and proceeds to sketch, "Let's see, starting at the stream downhill from here, we follow it south and west for about five miles to the entrance of a cavern system." Realizing his narration is attracting the interest of Zint, Owen, and Rachel, he looks up, assuming his professorial tone, "Pay attention; this is where the magic comes in .... From the cavern, we proceed to the top of a steep ridgeline and down the opposite side and end up at a clearwater pool."

Owen interjects, "So, no caves, right?"

"No. Although that would be a shortcut, albeit dangerous."

Drawing an amoeba-shaped body of water, he frowns, "It could be shaped like a kidney bean. Who cares? We look for a streamlet from the pool coursing across a verdant glade."

"A glade?"

Rachel elbows Owen, "Quit interrupting."

King glances at Owen, "You know, like a meadow." Refocusing on the map, "Where was I? Oh, yes. From the glade, the stream deepens and drops into a narrow slot canyon on the far side." Pausing to envision the elder's description, he continues, "This might prove dangerous, but others have made the journey, and so shall we. Once through the slot, the stream widens into a snaking jungle river fed by hundreds of rivulets until reaching a precipitous waterfall."

Sitting up from his hunched position, King stretches his back and grins with a look of accomplishment.

Overhearing Richard's description, Nina appears in one of

Rachel's backup weather and pest-resistant ensembles, rolling up sleeves and cuffs to fit her shorter frame, "Richard? Did you forget something?"

Seeing the notorious fashion maven wearing the taller and leaner Rachel's clothes, Richard bites his tongue and presents a coy smile, "Yes. Quite right, Nina. The waterfall plummets over 200 feet into a deep rift in the Earth's crust. At the bottom, we will find the lost ship."

Owen can't resist a mocking jibe, "You have got to be joking. Ridges above lakes and rivulets into slot canyons feeding gorges that beget waterfalls cutting deep into the Earth. No wonder this place is off the grid."

Richard swats ants off his map and refurls it into his pack. "Has anybody here read Burroughs? Edgar Rice—not the other one. The last phase of our expedition may resemble *a land that time forgot*."

Sounding more like the class know-it-all than she wanted to admit, Rachel raises her hand, "I read it. Hobbes Rare Books back in Newport has a whole section dedicated to Burroughs."

Nina places her hand on Richard's shoulder, "Don't leave us hanging with another of your arcane literary allusions, Richard. Unlike Rachel, most of us have not had the pleasure of reading century-old dime store paperbacks."

"The Forest Ghost elder warned of monsters lurking in the jungle surrounding the lost ship." Richard stands, brushing dirt and ants from his pack, "Who knows? Perhaps he meant more Pteranodons."

Owen muses, "Or maybe he meant us?"

Richard contemplates Owen's dry wit, "Perhaps. At any rate, the Forest Ghosts—or what's left of them—are nothing if not superstitious."

Remaining a silent observer throughout Richard's reading of the map, Zint adds his thoughts, "Monsters come in all shapes and sizes. We will know them by their deeds, not their appearances."

Squinting through the hazy midday sun, Richard spies Pembroke huddled with Flynn and Antoine. Checking his watch, he mumbles, "Quarter past three. Blast. We lost another day. We'll break camp and head out tomorrow at sunrise.”

Antoine | Stevens' base camp
02:30 a.m. | October 16, 2044

After the last meal at Stevens' base camp—rehydrated chicken and dumplings cooked with fresh mushrooms that paled next to Antoine's wild boar barbeque—the expedition settles around the campfire, eager for daybreak and a final push to the lost ship.

***

Standing watch in the jungle darkness as a high-paid freelance operator, Antoine muses on his life. Proud of his service, he never let his alternative leanings interfere with his sworn duty as a sailor in the United States Navy. A high-ranking Pentagon official's swishy, drunken dare resulted in him joining the Seals. Despite initial misgivings, the young Georgian excelled, finishing at the top of his class and silencing naysayers far and wide.

Stepping over a log jutting from the thick undergrowth surrounding the camp, Antoine moves toward a rustling disturbance with practiced stealth.

“I could have left the military and become a chef at a swanky South Beach eatery, drinking daiquiris and partying my fucking brains out. But no. I got greedy, and now I'm in the middle of nowhere, guarding a group of folks with no business out in the jungle.”

Hearing his snoring boss snoozing against a tree stump 20 feet distant, he laughs, *“Even Mr. Pembroke's salad days are in his rearview.”*

Reaching the spot where his razor-sharp auditory senses picked up something suspicious, he pauses, concentrating on listening over the usual jungle din, *“Probably a wayward monkey venturing to the forest floor.”*

Finding nothing of concern, Antoine looks at the stars twinkling through low-hanging clouds gliding westward, contemplating the majesty of God's creation and life's intrinsic mysteries.

Another audible snap to his left prompts the former Seal to lift his semi-auto carbine and peer through the night-vision scope. Scanning the ghostly, green-lit forest, he sees a wild boar foraging in the tall grass. "Don't worry, fella, I am still stuffed from eating your cousin."

Before he can lower his weapon, a horrible pain pierces Antoine's upper back. Feeling his hands numb, the rifle slips from his grasp and falls harmless at his boots. Looking down at his broad chest, he fixates on the tip of a steel blade piercing his camo shirt as his thoughts muddle and a trickle of blood foams at his mouth, "No. This can't be right."

Perceiving his life force ebbing toward a peculiar welcoming light, his vision blurs and darkens, gurgling up bloody last words, "Stabbed in the back, that is cold, man."

A millisecond later, the young Georgia native with an intimate, firsthand knowledge of kinky escapades permeating the Pentagon's upper echelons pitches face down atop the loamy ground, bleeding out like a stuck pig.

The assassin swipes her blade on his camouflaged shirt and melds back into the undergrowth, "That's one."

You need have no fear of any failure...

– Percy Fawcett

Chapter Eleven:

The Trail

Pembroke | Stevens' base camp
04:32 a.m. | October 16, 2044

It seemed like yesterday, but six years had passed since Pembroke's decorated military career had deteriorated into a humiliating wheelchair-bound security gig at the much-maligned and ridiculed Paris Mouse House. In those dark days, contemplating suicide, an experimental operation, and the gift of shiny new neural-controlled bionic legs, pulled the scarred veteran from the abyss and put him back on two feet. Determined not to waste a second of his new lease on life, he joined the PTB as a freelance security specialist.

Deep in the heart of the sopping wet, superheated, bug-infested Amazon, a sleep-deprived Pembroke leans forward at the waist to reset a glitchy sensor on his robotic left leg, indicating a faltering connection to synapses in his brain. After multiple attempts to reset the fucking red light, his stoic visage falters for a heartbeat, mulling the increasing probability of an ill-timed prosthetics failure.

Muttering curses under his breath, Pembroke makes a final attempt and manages to turn off the light. Springing onto his feet with a new cigarette pressed between chapped lips, he tests his balance, bending to the ground on one leg and snatching a long stick off the mud with the grace of a ballet dancer. Mindful of disturbing the slumbering group's harmonized rhythmic snores while stoking the miraculous blue flames, the mercenary checks his watch. Searching the semi-darkness for Antoine's strapping silhouette, a familiar stench of danger wafts through the stillness. *"There is trouble afoot."*

Deciding against waking the exhausted expedition, the veteran warrior unsheathes his prized 10-inch hunting knife—gifted from a Norwegian princess he rescued in a previous life—and moves toward the camp's shadowy tree line.

"I told Richard we needed to move on from here. Too exposed."

Crouching past the remnants of Antoine's ad-hoc pit barbeque, Pembroke halts in his tracks, hearing whispered voices intermingling with the jungle sounds.

A loud snap precedes a graveled French-accented voice resonating from his six, "Bonjour, motherfucker. Behind you."

Wheeling on his metal feet, Pembroke's widened gaze lands on the French gorilla in the flesh, eclipsing his escape with a mean grin on his thick-bearded face.

Springing sideways, Pembroke evades the hulking fellow's clumsy attack, delivering a roundhouse kick to the man's ribs. To his surprise, the assailant crashes headfirst into the underbrush and disappears.

Concerned for Antoine, Pembroke pursues his quarry, dodging low-hanging vines, branches smacking against his scarred face, before skidding to a halt in a tamped-down clearing filled with trash and stinky wet clothes. Straining to see through the green-black shadows, the veteran warrior realizes he made a disastrous miscalculation. Hoping to assert an air of authority, he speaks into the predawn jungle, "I know you work for Pike. Come out; we can talk like men."

Hearing nothing but silence, clutching the knife in his sweaty hand, Pembroke's fragile connection to his legs evaporates, rendering him paralyzed. "Oh no. Fuck no. This can't be happening."

A tall, athletic man in fine-tailored camouflaged hunting garb steps from the shadows pinching a matchbook-sized gadget between his thumb and forefinger, "Oh, but it is happening, Mr. Pembroke. If I let go of this button, the connection between your brain and your legs will return." With mock pity, he tsk-tsks, "I regret that is not happening. My company developed your prosthetic tech, similar to beaming data between my satellites and server farms. And just like that, I have complete control over you like I have Earth by the balls."

Stepping forward but staying outside Pembroke's frozen position, the man's body odor mixed with bug repellant assaults the paralyzed Pembroke. "I'm sorry, Pike, but you stink."

Acknowledging the obvious with a shrug, Pike smiles at his victim, "Yes, I do. But I can take a shower. You, my half-metal friend, are as good as dead."

On cue, the French gorilla reappears, pushing Pike aside and growling at Pembroke, "You broke my ribs."

Wavering on numbed legs, unsure how long he can stay upright, Pembroke contemplates the knife in his hand as a gun barrel jabs his back. A Cockney-accented voice whispers in his ear, "Easy, mate. Let's have that knife. Nice and easy."

Relinquishing his blade, Pembroke falls flat on his back. With the wind knocked out of him, he looks up at the shadowy figure looming over him, grinding a muddy, size 17 army boot into his heaving chest to hold him down.

"Smythe, give me his knife."

"Here you go, boss."

The Frenchman admires the glistening blade before positioning the razor-sharp tip over Pembroke's beating heart in a two-handed grip.

"I take no pleasure in your death, monsieur; I will make this quick."

"No. No. No." A panicked Pembroke pushes against the man's downward pressure, but the knife inches closer before contacting his chest and driving straight through his heart. Eyes bulging, gurgling, and spitting, his bowels let loose before clasping his hands over DeVille's steel grip and bleeding out on the loamy forest floor.

Though consumed with death on a global scale, Griffin Pike had never witnessed the brutal and intimate act of murder. Mesmerized by the unfortunate fellow's life force escaping his mortal coil, he releases the button and tosses the device into the bushes with a laugh verging on psychotic. Peering at Henri DeVille through the gloom, he catches the Frenchman making the sign of the cross over the dead man, "Henri, are you saying a prayer for the man you just murdered in cold blood?"

Turning to the feckless atheistic mogul, Henri's fists clench tight, "This is it, Pike. I will not kill another soul. The rest will do as we tell them. Do you understand me?"

Griffin Pike rolls his eyes, "Henri, you are a strange man." With a dismissive smirk, he heads back to Sapphire, keeping a vigilant eye on the Pennywell girl.

Struggling to clean Pembroke's blood from his hands, Henri DeVille turns to Smythe with an agitated scowl, "What the fuck are you looking at, Smythe? Wrap this gentleman in a tarp and place him next to his Black associate. We will return them to their people at first light."

After Henri tromps into the undergrowth, Smythe extricates the 10-inch murder weapon and keeps it as a souvenir. Within the hour, Pembroke lies beside Antoine, eyes wide open, staring through a gap in the high tree canopy at the fading stars in the brightening morning sky.

Henri DeVille | Stevens' base camp
06:22 a.m. | October 16, 2044

Henri DeVille's boots sink into the mud, hefting the tarped body across the wet meadow through shafts of morning sunlight and dumping him atop Antoine's prone form, already engulfed, crackling, and sparking in the raging blue fire. Scraping the soles of his mud-caked boots on a sharp-edged tree stump, he winces at a stab of pain in his ribs. Turning to the shocked group staring daggers at him, he smiles, "Your man got in one last kick; may God have mercy on his soul." Sitting on the fallen log with a burdensome sigh, he speaks in an even-toned French accent, "The deaths of your hired security could not be avoided. Their passing to a greater reward should serve as a warning to the rest of you."

Caught flat-footed by the early morning incursion, Flynn's resolute stance signals his gobsmacked colleagues, rousted at gunpoint from their bedrolls, to quell their tears and not to try anything stupid. Cognizant of the arsenal pointed at their backs, the agent places a firm hand on Owen's shoulder, "Easy, mate. We can't lose you, too."

Noting the mercurial young American's reluctant head nod, Flynn speaks for the distraught group, "Everyone, meet Henri DeVille, the Nemesis Group's overpriced gun-for-hire." With a wry laugh, the veteran PTB agent jibes his hulking captor, probing for weaknesses, "Bloody hell, man, nothing better to do after the fucking alien invasion went tits up than bollocks off to Brazil for some loose pocket change? Where's your boss, Henri? Getting a manicure while you and your mates do his dirty work? Not very sporting, is it, old chap?"

After glancing into the shadowed jungle tree line, a distracted DeVille focuses on the agent's battered face, "Ah, Agent Flynn, your presence is a bit of a mystery, but we shall leave that for now. Someone already administered a proper thrashing; you look like shit."

Picking up a rock and tossing it into the fire, DeVille shakes his head, "Enough with your head games, Flynn." Noting the return stares with a weary smile, he calls out to his men, "Rollins, Smythe, lower your weapons. These people pose no threat."

Stomach growling and desperate for a morning caffeine jolt, Smythe nudges Zint with his gun's barrel, "What about this little gray bugger? The aliens can't be trusted."

Nina grabs the barrel and shoves it sideways, "You touch him, and you will have to deal with me, asshole."

Sympathetic to Nina's swift, angry response to the leering Cockney creep, Rachel sends a telepathic message to Professor King, *"I could try to take them out."*

Internalizing genuine sadness for the irascible mercenary and the rather pleasant young Black man, King replies in his head, "No. Not yet." while nudging the precious detailed map into a deep pocket in his pack.

After piercing Smythe with a neural jolt, sending the dimwitted ruffian stumbling backward, Zint's circumspect oval gaze follows a grumbling Chayefsky, tying Daphne by the neck to a stake hammered into the soft dirt. Without moving a muscle, he soothes his furry friend's whimpering anxiety, *"Easy, Daphne. We must stay strong and calm."*

Nina removes a wet cloth from her satchel and passes it to a shaken Rachel, staring into the funeral pyre. Needing to pee, the elegant 56-year-old stands to stretch aching muscles, "DeVille, you never answered the agent's question. Where is Griffin Pike?"

After glancing at his watch, Henri peers into the trees, "That is what I am wondering, madam." Taking the measure of the fit mature woman with close-shorn charcoal gray mixed with red hair, he smiles, "Since you are up, please be so kind as to make a pot of your camp's coffee, enough for everyone."

* * *

Griffin Pike strides from the jungle an hour later in crisp, clean-smelling camo gear, "Henri, I see you have made some friends. I hope you all saved me a cup of that wonderful coffee. The aroma alone is enough to entice the monkeys out of the fucking trees." Coming to a halt opposite the extended group, he puts clean hands on his hips and looks at Henri's drawn face, "So, where are we, DeVille? Really. I am running out of time and patience. Let's get this shitstorm in gear."

In unison, all eyes look beyond the well-dressed mogul toward a svelte young woman in straight-legged khakis tucked into knee-high boots under a half-buttoned olive-drab blouse escorting a disheveled female from the underbrush.

Richard stands and peers through the hazy morning sunlight, eyes widening in disbelief at the waifish lass with dirty blond straight hair, "It can't be … how did you … Oh, my God, it is her." Eschewing personal safety, Richard bolts toward the pair, meeting them halfway between the trees and the campfire. Ignoring the vivacious captor with the sculpted, tanned face, he blocks Penny's stumbling path, "Penny. Penny Pennywell." Receiving a confused frown in reply, Richard's heart sinks.

Unmoved by the professor's quick identification of the girl, Pike smirks, "Sapphire, let the professor take the Pennywell girl; we don't need her." With a casual jibe at his mercenary, he adds, "Never did."

Guiding the half-stumbling Penny slumped under a dirty blanket toward Nina and Rachel, Richard scowls at the psychopath, "Damn you, Pike. What did you do to her?"

Pike turns to the indignant PTB professor, whose 122 years on Earth parallel the Pennywell family saga, "What did I do? For starters, Professor King, we saved her from a deadly case of Gray flu. Moreover, she is under a mild sedative for her own safety. Nothing more. Once it wears off, she will be right as rain."

Sapphire slinks over to Pike's side, sliding a long arm around his waist, "I gave her a little extra shot this morning, Griffin." Running her opposite hand up his chest, she shoots a lascivious smile toward Rachel and adds, "I had to make sure the naughty girl behaved."

Pike bites his lower lip, unable to mask his arousal while feigning a contemplation of his next move, "Now then, we have a few more mouths to feed than I anticipated, but more fodder for the cannibals, if it comes to that."

Adding Artemus' great-great granddaughter to an endless list of concerns, Richard grumbles at Pike, "The locals eat for nourishment. You kill for sport. Tell me, Pike, which sounds more civilized to you?"

Separating from the nimble assassin's side, Pike navigates through the heaped packs and bedrolls, crouching before a kneeling Richard. Considering the man's impertinence, he smacks the scientist across the face with the back of his soft hand, "Civilization is dead to me. Does that answer your fucking question, old man?" Not expecting an answer, Pike's eyes narrow onto the backpack at King's side. Snatching it by a strap, he dumps the contents and pulls a folded sheet from the pile after tossing a loaded 9mm at Rollins.

"No more surprises, Richard." Opening the thick paper with the relish of a child on Christmas morning, his eyes alight at the illustrated parchment, complete with the Forest Ghost elders' landmarks in glorious detail, "Nice, Richard, real nice. You have quite a talent." Refolding the map, he shoves it into his jacket pocket. "Much obliged."

Fighting to remain calm and resolute, hearing Rachel's voice in his head, Richard stands face to face with the SATstar mogul, "What of us?"

Pike takes a long step backward, "Richard, you need mouthwash or something." Looking around the PTB expedition, he sighs, "Oh, you are all coming along. I would not dream of abandoning you in such an inhospitable setting." With a perverse laugh, he turns to Henri, sulking on the stump, "Henri, have your men gather our new friends' supplies and be sure to confiscate any more weapons. We are leaving in one hour."

Holding a cup out to Nina, he smiles, "More, please."

Griffin Pike | The Stream
08:15 a.m. | October 16, 2044

With Richard's map tucked in his jacket, Griffin Pike stumbles down a treacherous steep grade, separating from his security, struggling to keep up with his agile lover's effortless pace. Climbing over and around mossy boulders and clinging vines, he slips across slick limestone before taking a tumble and sliding the last 15 feet on his backside to an ignominious halt at the swollen banks of the roaring jungle stream. Wiping green gunk from his ultra-high-tech, weather-resistant, and breathable camo pants, he internalizes rage with no one to blame but himself, "Fuck! That hurt!"

Sapphire slips out of her light pack and boots, dropping them on a rocky outcropping, sending butterflies fluttering into the humid air before wading into the stream to wait for the rest of the plodding ungraceful group. Wriggling her toes in the crystalline water, stirring minnows from the shadows, she fantasizes about the one called Rachel.

With no choice but to follow the megalomanic, Richard chooses a less treacherous descent from memory. Catching his breath, he breaks from the undergrowth none the worse for wear and stands next to the impatient tech mogul as curses, pratfalls, and snapping branches from the loud and cumbersome party echoes through the jungle.

Wincing at echoing volleys of expletives from DeVille's men, King turns and finds the enigma known as Sapphire, lost in her own little world, luxuriating in a knee-deep pool, the thin material of her wet blouse clinging to her chest.

Noting Richard's doubletake at the hyper-sexual woman's perky breasts on full display under her dripping shirt like a fraternity wet tee contest, he smirks, "She is a handful; I would keep my distance if I were you."

Waiting for the others, Richard turns back to Griffin with a deadpan expression, "She is a wee bit on the young side for an old man like me. It is just that I am a little confused."

Pike bites, "About what?"

Richard allows a coy smile to widen on his lined face, "Well, if you must know. The scuttlebutt is that you prefer men. So, seeing her hanging on you was an odd aside to an already strange set of occurrences."

Nina, Zint, and Daphne emerge upstream, interrupting Pike's rebuttal.

Knowing he hit paydirt, Richard hides a smile, "Nina! Over here!"

Rachel and Owen assist the recovering Agent Flynn and a wavering Penny to the sandy bank with DeVille and his trio of armed goons on their heels.

Still reeling from Richard's jab, Pike stomps to his high-paid Nemesis Group specialist, "Henri, we need to pick up the pace, got it?"

The broad-shouldered Henri DeVille swipes sap and green plant matter off his machete, pushing Pike aside, "You're an asshole, Pike."

Fuming, hot, itchy, and frustrated, Griffin Pike removes the map, pinning their position at the stream. Checking both ways through an impenetrable green mass encroaching over the fast-flowing water, he turns to King, "Downstream, right, Professor?"

"Do you know how to read a map, Pike?"

At his wit's end, Griffin crumples the map and pitches it at Richard, "Listen up, everyone! New plan. Richard will decipher his fucking map with Henri on point, clearing the path. Smythe, fetch that flamethrower and give it to your boss." Pushing two fingers into Richard's chest, he threatens the PTB's lead scientist, "And, Professor, do not try anything. I will kill one of your friends for each misstep, starting with Artemus' granddaughter."

Hearing more than enough from the prattling Pike, Nina nudges through the group to defend Richard, "Coward."

Griffin pivots from Richard's sweaty visage to Nina, "Ah, the lovely and gracious Nina Madsen. We have met before. I believe it was when I fended off your boss' bid to acquire SATstar."

"The offer was more than generous, and it would have allowed the PTB to populate EMP shielding on servers around the world with the push of a button."

Pike's maniacal laugh echoes into the trees, "Where would the fun be in that, Ms. Madsen? The Gorks performed an essential task by devastating over half the world's population in less than a day. Now my satellites are the only game in town."

The gawky Chayefsky eyeballs the captives before poking Flynn in the ribs with his rifle, "Easy, sport. The lady looks like she can handle herself better than you."

Flynn glares at the Russian, "Don't do that again, mate. You get one warning."

With his altered plan in place, Pike holds the group with a raised hand, letting a grumbling Henri DeVille cut a parallel downstream trail through the thick underbrush like a human bulldozer, with Richard following in his wake.

Rachel and Owen look at each other and frown, watching Sapphire skipping behind the brutish man, swinging a machete with a carefree elan. Rachel mutters, "Is she for real?"

Owen leans over, "Maybe she is a replicant."

Rachel shrugs, "Maybe. I think she has the hots for me."

Owen laughs, "Well, well, well. Mrs. Haig. A little full of yourself."

Rollins nudges the married couple forward, "Okay, enough talk. Let's go."

Owen turns to the least offensive of the mercenary trio and smiles, "Where are you from, Rollins?"

"I grew up on a farm in Ohio. Washed out of the army and ended up working freelance. It pays well, and aside from this shitty assignment, most gigs entail babysitting oligarchs' daughters, which has its side perks."

Rachel turns to the man and pierces his brain, "Switch sides before it is too late."

Shaking his head like something flew into his ear, he snarls at Rachel, "Keep moving."

Bringing up the rear, Smythe and Chayefsky search the beaten path in a panic, "Hey, what the fuck happened to the alien bugger and the dog?"

From 50 yards ahead, Henri barks at the low-IQ mercenaries, "Goddammit, do I have to do everything? They cannot have gone far."

Trailing behind Richard, Pike whistles and raises a hand, "Ignore that order! They will perish out here, and we do not need them."

* * *

The expletive-laced banter mixed with hacking blades and snapping branches fades to the daytime jungle din as Pike's mercenaries march the captive PTB expedition for torturous miles downstream.

Hunkered under a tangle of vines crawling with ants, Zint raises a long finger and touches Daphne's back near her tail. The telekinetic zap expels every insect from the German Shepherd's dirty, matted coat and shields her from biting pests inhabiting the forest floor.

"Daphne, we need to get help."

Nina | The Caverns
01:15 p.m. | October 16, 2044

Hacking along the stream's winding course, the expedition emerges into a luscious fern glade swarming with butterflies and hummingbirds diving out of a deep blue sky dotted with puffy white clouds.

At the bucolic meadow's far end, Henri stops near a boulder-strewn cave entrance and turns to the straggling group, "Okay, take a break, but stay within sight."

Pike checks Richard's map, confirming the stream going underground at the jagged cavern entrance with a reluctant head nod. Tracing a finger along the dotted line, he notes the trail's abrupt ascent onto a snaking ridgeline before a long zig-zagging downhill trek into the vale on the opposite side, where a kidney-shaped lake marks their destination for day one. "Good call, Henri. I concur. Take a break, everyone, but be ready to move out in 20 minutes."

Desperate to reassert his wilted manhood after Sapphire's rebuffs and Richard's perceptive comment, Pike braves churning waters at the cavern's entrance and peers inside while clutching a thick wad of vines for dear life.

With an overwrought snarling contempt, DeVille calls over the roaring water to his idiot boss, "That is risky, monsieur. None of us would bother if you fell inside."

Pulling himself to safety across the slippery rocks, Pike glances at the group, resting and trying to cool down for the final day one push. "That is what I like about you, Henri. You tell it like it is."

Bored and horny, Sapphire climbs atop a smooth rounded boulder, unbuttoning her shirt to bask in the heat with her supple form curved toward Rachel.

After a much-needed trip into the underbrush, Owen plops beside Flynn, "Hey, you look a little green around the gills."

Glancing toward Rollins and Smythe, resting under a tree with their hats pulled over their faces, Flynn mutters, "I'm fine. Just looking for an opening, mate."

Owen leans close to his friend, "I'll repeat what you told me this morning. Don't do it. Stay alive."

Eavesdropping on the conversation, Leon Chayefsky skulks from behind a thick mangle of roots and taps Flynn on the head, "Listen to your pal, Flynn. I don't want to kill you."

Flynn rises and spins in a flash, clenching a fist around the surprised Russian's shirt collar and holding him for a long count before letting go and pushing the man backward on his heels. "I warned you once already, don't try me, asshole. I have fought better men than you."

A chastised Chayefsky looks around and realizes no one witnessed the brash encounter with a sigh of relief before sulking off by himself.

Flynn smiles at Owen, "All bark and no bite."

Downstream at the cave entrance, Richard approaches Penny, Nina, and Rachel, sitting on a log, eating snack bars, unaware of Flynn's rash behavior.

Nina reopens the bag, "Care for a trail mix bar, Richard?"

Feeling the latent tension in the humid air, he checks the healing scar on Penny's forearm, "You are lucky to be alive, Miss Pennywell." Turning to Nina, he adds, "No thanks, Nina. Not hungry."

Penny takes Richard's hand, "Hold on, Professor King. I have something I need you to see." With some effort, the pale, weak 26-year-old removes the dog-eared Polaroid from her jacket, "Did you know my mother?"

Richard looks at the faded image and nods, "Yes. Yes, I did. I met both of you when I worked in the southwest at a base called Lost Cactus. Artemus brought you and your mother there so she could rehab, but it was not to be." Considering his words, he smiles at the recovering young woman, "I understand you graduated at the top of your class at Harvard Med, quite an achievement. Artemus is very proud. As am I. Although surprised you took a job with the CDC."

Penny looks into Richard's eyes, "The job gave me the freedom to travel and find my past. And the pay was good. Although these goons tell me, my boss at the CDC sold my identity for a few thousand bucks."

Richard nods, "The DC swamp is alive, and well, I'm afraid. There are good people, but the lifetime bureaucrats that run things in America give Artemus fits."

Nina breaks into the conversation, "And here we are."

Penny's pleasant face scrunches into an inquisitive look, "How is it that you recognized me if you had not seen me since I was a baby?"

Without a hint of self-awareness, Richard answers, "You are one of a handful of people alive on this planet that merit the PTB's constant scrutiny."

Rachel leans across Nina, seated in the middle, and smiles, "The Powers That Be surveilled my family for generations. Welcome to the club."

Nina segues the conversation back to their current predicament, "You know we are all dead once they find the lost ship."

Taking a long step backward, Richard salutes the three women, "Tell Owen and Flynn to behave themselves."

Alarm bells ring in Nina's head, recognizing an all-too-familiar mischievous glint in her former flame's keen blue eyes, "Richard, look at me. Whatever it is you are planning, stop. We need you."

Feigning cooling off in the shallows, Richard winks at Nina with a furtive thumbs-up, "Rachel has my map imprinted in her brain. I put it there for safekeeping." After a deep inhalation, he adds, "I will see you on the other side."

Falling backward into the main channel, he lets the swift current carry him through the cavern entrance, disappearing into the darkness.

* * *

Sapphire grabs a dangling vine for support, wades into the perilous current to the jagged aperture, and peers inside with a powerful torch clutched in her nimble hand. Tuning out Griffin Pike's tirade of epithets directed at the lackluster Nemesis people, she searches the treacherous churning waters roiling through the dark expanse to no avail.

Wading across the slick bottom to the assembled group, she tosses the flashlight back to Rollins and proffers an indifferent shrug at her fuming former lover, "He is gone, Griffin."

Zint | Forest Ghost encampment
04:01 p.m. | October 16, 2044

Passing a human skull jammed atop a six-foot bamboo stake—a clear warning to turn around, Daphne whimpers, following her non-human friend.

"It is okay. Friends. We are friends."

Recalling her previous master's confidence, Daphne proffers a panting smile in the hot, muggy jungle air and quickens her padded steps along the loamy path to keep up.

Emerging from the dense forest into a clearing rimmed with primitive structures in a loose circular arrangement around the communal firepit, the odd pair bisect the encampment to the elder's thatched lean-to.

A young woman blocks their entry at the entrance with a vicious look on her smooth amber face.

"I … I mean, we need your help."

Daphne barks once, echoing Zint's plea.

The woman eyeballs the strange duo before moving aside and ushering them into the hidden encampment.

Griffin Pike | The Lake
09:00 p.m. | October 16, 2044

Professor Richard King's apparent drowning glommed atop Pembroke, and Antoine's murders left the survivors demoralized and defeated. After an arduous climb from the cave and traversing a narrow ridgeline, the extended expedition descends into the swampy valley through reeds and mangled driftwood to an open spot along a sandy lakeshore under a bright full moon.

Rollins trains Antoine's compact alien flamethrower in a wide arc, not taking any chances, sending anything crawling, slithering, or scurrying into the dense forest as the long day's march winds to a close.

Wading into the lake's lapping shallows, Griffin holds up poor Richard's map, fixated on the ethereal ribbon of water aglow in the moonlight, gushing from a fissure high up a sheer granite face into the lake's far side.

Reading Pike's paranoia like the back of his hand, Henri splashes to his employer's side, reaching down for a handful of the cool, clear water, "I know what you are thinking, Griffin. There is no way King survived and came out of that opening. Even if he did, the 60-foot drop would break his neck."

Pike folds the precious map and shoves it in his jacket, "Yes. Of course. You are right."

Noting the weary faces staring at him, Pike offers a less-than-sincere smile, "Owen, my man, get a fire started. We are all famished."

Feeling a prick of danger coursing his spine, Pike rubs his stubbled chin and whispers to DeVille, "This place is haunted with or without the ghost of Richard King. You fuckers are going to start earning your pay. Set up a perimeter and have your men stand watch throughout the night. No more surprises, Henri."

Flynn | The Lake
03:00 a.m. | October 17, 2044

Between Owen's snores and the nighttime jungle resonating with howlers howling as they do at three a.m. every morning, Flynn sits awake with his hands and feet zip-tied, formulating a plan in his weary head. A sudden violent rustling through the trees breaks his train of thought seconds before the forest cacophony falls silent, followed by a low, almost imperceptible growling noise: *RRRRRRRRrrrrrrrrrrrrrRRRRrrrr* …

Bound down, facing Owen, his heart beating out of his chest,

Flynn stretches forward and jostles the snoring American, "Wake up, mate. Did you hear that?

Stirring from a restless and uncomfortable sleep, with a gnarled chunk of driftwood jabbing him in the back, Owen lifts his wrists and wipes drool on his dirty forearm, "Not now, Rachel. Go back to sleep."

Flynn kicks his boot, contacting Owen's shin, "Bloody hell. I am serious. Wake up, man. Something is out there. Something big."

Bleary-eyed and in no mood for games, Owen snaps awake, "I don't hear anything. Even the howlers stopped."

Flynn kicks him harder, "That's my point. Something scared every fucking animal in the forest."

Rubbing gritty sleep from his eyes, Owen surveys the beachhead campsite, finding Rachel, Nina, and Penny sleeping atop bedrolls laid out in the sand by the dying fire with Sapphire catnapping, or whatever, an arm's length from their collective repose.

Peering through the darkness, he locates Griffin's tarped bag tied in the trees, six feet off the ground. "What an asshole. I think he is using my gear …."

RRRRRRRrrrrrrRRRRRRrrrrrrrRRRRRRRrrrrrrr …

Meeting the whites of Flynn's eyes through the pale moonlight, Owen's imagination runs wild in his sleep-deprived state, "Do you know what that sounds like?"

"I have an idea."

"It sounds like a goddamn dinosaur. Where are we?"

Bound against the heavy driftwood, the men listen to the guttural beastly sounds of a lost world.

* * *

Stationed in a hacked-out six-foot jungle clearing, keeping watch for God only knows, Leon Chayefsky props his carbine against a tree and lights another cigarette. Leery of the forest floor, he prefers standing, having already killed two snakes slithering into his tamped-

me to Leon's jerk-off post."

Carrying blue flaming torches and rifles at the ready, Smythe leads DeVille down a hacked trail into the jungle with the faint orange-purple glow of dawn eking over the eastern horizon. Hiking over a quarter mile from the lake, the pair reach the cleared space expecting to find Leon asleep at the switch.

Through the darkness, Henri catches wet reflections glistening on the leaves and vines surrounding the tamped space as the overpowering smell of blood fills his flaming nostrils. His keen vision adjusting to the darkness, DeVille picks up Leon's rifle, noting blood and guts splattered everywhere on everything, "And yet, the safety on Leon's rifle is still engaged."

Stepping over a disgusting puddle of filth and sticky, fleshy remnants mixed with bony spurs, DeVille stops cold, hearing the low snarling growl of something lurking nearby.

"Henri, over here. I found part of Leon."

Pulling a gnarled arm out of a tree, the battle-hardened DeVille pulls a wedding band off a finger and swallows hard to avoid puking his guts, "So did I."

Griffin Pike | The Lake
08:34 a.m. | October 17, 2044

With patience drawn from deep inside his soulless being, Griffin Pike listens to Henri's blow-by-blow account of Leon's gruesome passing, nodding, and absorbing the news without saying a word.

Henri finishes his report, fingering Leon's wedding band dangling from a string around his massive neck. "Well? Did you know what we would be up against or not?"

"Henri, I was sorry about Anna. And now Leon's passing ... tsk tsk."

Resisting a violent urge to reach out and break the mogul's scrawny neck, Henri leans in close and presses two fingers hard into Pike's chest, "I want more money to compensate Leon's widow."

"Done. Say the amount."

"These people need a day to recuperate. No forced march today."

"Now, Henri, be reasonable …."

"You are welcome to forge ahead on your own, Griffin. Take your bald bitch with you."

After a pregnant pause, Griffin smiles, "All right, you win, Henri. You have the day to recuperate, as you call it. Tomorrow, we go balls out and get to the ship. No more fucking around, got it?"

"It's your funeral, Pike."

* * *

Slinging his carbine over a beefy shoulder, Rollins pulls his knife and cuts Owen and Flynn's zip-tied wrists and ankles, "You boys promise to behave, right? We are shorthanded and can use a hand refilling canteens and collecting firewood."

Rubbing sore wrists, Owen nods and proffers a mischievous smile.

Flynn gestures toward Pike and DeVille, out of earshot, deep in conversation, "Hey, Rollins. What are your boss and Pike going on about?"

Rollins shrugs, "Mr. DeVille is renegotiating our contract. Pike left out the part about fucking dinosaurs." With a wry laugh, he adds, "Henri is unhappy about losing Leon." With a furtive sideways glance, he adds, "I don't know about you, but I don't want to die out here."

Sensing a chink in the armor, Owen tries to reason with the barrel-chested operator, "Rollins, we are both Americans. You represent the swing vote. Switch sides, brother, and we can take these assholes."

Pretending not to hear Owen's appeal, the mercenary shakes his head and saunters toward the lake.

Flynn smacks Owen on the back, "Nice try."

* * *

With the lost ship close yet so fucking far, Griffin Pike retires to his tree hammock, stinging from Henri's latest demands and seething about another wasted day deep in the heart of the Amazon. Zipped inside the olive-green nylon cocoon, the once brilliant aerospace engineer turned megalomaniac studies every centimeter of Richard's map, visualizing the world killer weapon clutched in his hands.

* * *

After scraping another day's worth of powdered eggs into a halfway decent scramble with edible mushrooms volumizing the breakfast, the captive PTB expedition lingers around the crackling blue fire under the watchful eye of an upbraided Smythe.

Sipping weak coffee, Nina turns to the stone-faced man from Liverpool, "Smythe, does your boss have any plan to bury or burn Leon's body?"

Smythe's sullen headshake speaks volumes, "There is nothing left of him, Miss."

Casting his curious gaze around the shoreline, Owen notes DeVille and Rollins' absence, "Where are your friends?"

Smythe takes a long puff from one of the deceased Pembroke's cigarettes and blows a smoke ring into the stultifying air, "Scouting the path forward. Tomorrow it is balls out to the lost ship. No more rest stops."

Flynn laughs, "Bloody hell, man. There is no shipwreck. It is more than likely buried in solid rock. You lot are wasting your time."

Smythe pitches the butt and shakes another from a half-empty pack, "Is that so? Then why are you all out here?"

Owen nudges Flynn, "Touché, Smythe."

Interrupting the debate, Sapphire drops from her swaying

hammock. Sauntering past the group, she lays out on the sand like another day at the beach.

Breaking the vicious woman's spell, Nina glares at the assassin, "What do you know … we are making progress; her perfect breasts are not on full display for a change."

Rachel spit-takes coffee, hearing Nina's comment. Dabbing her thin tee, she admits, "You know, she has an incredible body. I wish I looked that good."

"You are better looking than her. Case closed." Nina rubs her short gray hair, musing on the assassin's close-shorn, sculpted appearance, "The Grays cut off all my hair when I was under sedation. To this day, I have no clue why they did that."

Early in her first trimester, Rachel's emotions swell to the surface. Leaning in, she starts to cry and hugs Nina, "I am so glad you are here."

Missing the conversation after a much-needed trip to the bushes, Owen grins at the emotional pair's public display of affection, "What did I miss? Aliens? Dinosaurs? Dogs and cats living together?"

Nina wipes tears from her eyes and gestures toward Sapphire, spread out on the sand like an Amazonian goddess, "Rachel thinks that woman is better looking than she is. Tell her, Owen."

"Oh, yeah, Rachel, you are way better looking. I don't really get her whole shaved head thing." Addressing Nina, he adds, "We both had our heads shaved under duress. Scratching his stubbly auburn scalp, he adds, "Yours is growing back faster than mine." Allowing himself a long look at the shapely assassin, "She is sexy, though. I will give her that."

Rachel flings a rock at her husband to break his mesmerized, too-long stare, "Owen. Snap out of it; the woman murdered Antoine in cold blood."

"Enough navel-gazing, people." Flynn lowers his tone to amplify the gravity of their situation, "Let's get back to reality here. Owen, you know damn well that the thing that attacked Leon was a fucking dinosaur. Case closed."

Owen sighs, pouring a second cup of pale amber liquid from the hot kettle, "For God's sake, Flynn, it wasn't a dinosaur. That is insane."

Sitting cross-legged in shorts and a tee shirt, Rachel downs the dregs of her cup before countering her husband's steadfast denial, "Richard mentioned Edgar Rice Burroughs' The Land That Time Forgot." Looking between Flynn, Nina, and Owen, she doubles down, "That is where we are. The sooner we accept that reality, the better off we will be." Raising a long thin finger for emphasis, she adds, "And it will get more bizarre and dangerous from this point onward."

Turning her hand inward, she looks at the glowing spiral on her palm and forces her feet to stay firmly attached to the sandy ground, "Something is happening to me. I wish Richard was here."

Stroking a hand through Rachel's long blond locks, Nina tries to ease the pain of losing their brilliant albeit eccentric leader, "Richard was a gifted scientist and never at a loss for a literary reference in challenging times."

Perplexed, Rachel turns to Nina, "Why are you mentioning Professor King in the past tense?" Standing tall and stretching her lithesome frame, Rachel's hands glow brighter, "He is alive."

Pivoting her green-eyed gaze beyond Sapphire's languid form to the rippling deep-blue lake reflecting the sky, she adds, "Now, unless someone has a reason why I shouldn't, I am going for a swim in that lake and wash this stinking jungle out of my hair and off my skin."

Owen echoes her idea, "I will join you, Rachel."

Flynn rises onto his feet, causing a jumpy Smythe to point the gun in his direction. The cool-headed agent holds up his hands, "Easy, Smythe. The group wants to swim in the lake. I will use a little alien magic to clear the waters."

Nina finishes her coffee, explaining Flynn's idea, "The alien fire burns underwater."

Shaking his head, Owen quips to no one in particular, "Of course it does. At what point did we cross the Rubicon into an honest-to-God sci-fi novel?"

Chapter Twelve:

The Interview

Pennywell | PTB HQ, Scotland
02:20 p.m. | October 17, 2044

Lost in a nondescript wedge-shaped section of a concentric maze comprising the PTB's multi-level subterranean HQ underneath Crichton Castle's crumbled ramparts, Ping's oversized wheelchair brakes at another dead-end. Under his psychokinetic control, the large-wheeled conveyance spins and retraces its path. Reaching another intersection, he ventures right, humming in tune with the whirring motor's monotonous beat.

Navigating another deserted corridor, he rolls toward a welcoming female bathed in the greenish glow of a recording studio light mounted above a half-opened doorway. Wheeling closer, he recognizes Number 8's perfect face, beckoning him inside with a beautiful sultry smile. "Right this way, Ambassador." With a graceful step backward, she adds, "I was about to assemble a search party."

Beaming large black ocular pools upon the replicant, Ping's e-translator produces a scratchy, *"Thank you, 8. I should have taken a left turn at Albuquerque."*

Number 8 replies with a polite titter, hearing the old joke for the first time in her young life.

"Am I late?"

Wearing a black PTB tee and jeans under a lab coat, 8 proffers a magnetic smile and light-hearted shrug, "Time is a mortal construct."

"I'll take that as a no."

Entering the control room, Ping's wheels bump over bundled cables past a back-turned Number 7, pouring over an elaborate mixing console Richard salvaged from the erstwhile Abbey Road Studio. Re-imagined for holographic broadcasting at Pennywell's request, the impressive and historic sound board's function is almost entirely aesthetic but integral to the broadcast's nostalgic vibe. Meeting 7's intelligent gaze reflecting in the soundproof window, he continues through the cramped tech-laden space onto an improvised talk show set. Noting an unmistakable 60s-era public television vibe, right down to the taupe shag carpet pressed beneath his wheels, Ping parks himself opposite Pennywell's favorite Scandinavian recliner. The one and only set piece out of place and time, like its owner.

Fatigued from the mental exertion required to propel his wheelchair, Ping rests his frail form, smoothing the wrinkled front of his formal silver suit, which fit much better in his salad years. To his right, empty rows of reclaimed red velour theater seats. No in-person audience for this production, just a world unprepared for what is to come.

Hearing Andrew's familiar footfalls approaching from behind, he watches the handsome replicant angle around his chair to a moderator's lectern midway between himself and Pennywell's recliner. Acknowledging each other with telepathic nods, Ping's eyes scan upward, watching boom mics swing into position as the house lights dim, replaced by downlights illuminating the stage.

Number 8 reappears with a makeup bag, patting a gray-toned powder on Ping's head to reduce the highlights.

Experiencing a cosmetic touch-up for the first time in his 300+ years, Ping's watery gaze fixes on the fresh-faced Number 8, *"Don't I look beautiful enough already?"*

With a devilish wink, Number 8 finishes with Ping's noggin before snapping the gray powder case shut and turning to the PTB's virile jack-of-all-trades. "Okay, Andy, you are next."

With a furtive wince, he waves 8 off, "No thanks. That is not happening, Number 8. However, conceal Mr. Pennywell's shiny dome when he arrives."

Feigning a pouty disappointment, the smitten Number 8 closes her makeup bag and struts backstage.

"My apologies, Ping. I did not know they would go to that extent."

Ping's electronic voice trebles a coy reply, *"Quite alright, Andy."*

Andrew's sharp gaze narrows on Ping for a heartbeat acknowledging the jibe before opening a virtual display above the dais. Scrolling through data, the replicant gives a thumbs-up to 7 through the glassed-off control room. "Everything appears in order. All we need is our host for the evening."

Intent on maintaining a jovial disposition, Ping quips, *"He will be late to his own funeral."*

Looking as fit as his first day, Andrew brushes a speck of lint off his black and gray pinstripe vest over a crisp white button-down, red bowtie, jeans, and signature western boots. Pausing his endless list of last-minute producer slash moderator tasks, he laments, "Ambassador Ping, I am not the same man I was before."

"No, Andrew, you are better, and Number 8 bears your child. Congratulations."

His face reddens, busted by the perceptive alien, "You are the first to know about that."

"Don't be so sure."

"Are you aware Number 8 and Rachel Haig were led to cubes out in the Lowlands?"

"Yes. In every worthwhile endeavor, there are trailblazers so others will follow."

"I do not think humanity is ready."

Ping's eyes pierce the replicant's soulful gaze, *"Andrew, the perfect time is now or never. Let them come; chips, or cubes as the case may be, will fall where they may."*

Andrew laughs, "You sound just like Artemus."

Double doors at the back of the darkened theater swing open as the Powers That Be CEO burst through.

Seeing his old friend's dramatic entrance, Ping smiles at Andrew, *"Speaking of the devil. His ears are burning."*

Oblivious to the pair's private conversation, Pennywell admires the realization of his creative brainstorm from behind the back row. "The set looks awesome! Too bad we don't have an audience." Already knowing the answer, the giddy and drunk CEO asks, "Any chance of having life-size cutouts filling the seats?"

Andrew shakes his head, squinting past stage lights toward his boss' booming voice, "No. And quit asking."

Cane in hand, Pennywell trots down the center aisle with a spry gait, "Andrew! I just had another brilliant idea!"

Unable to mask his annoyance, Andrew deadpans, "Let me guess, you want to reanimate John Lennon and have him write a theme song for our little show that starts in under five minutes."

Pennywell's tall, lean frame vaults onto the stage, scanning the space in his black suit and silver Saguaro bolo cinched at his starched white collar, "John Lennon? Really, Andrew. Sarcasm does not suit you."

Before he can continue, Number 8 springs from the wings

like she was shot from a cannon, makeup bag in hand, patting a fluffy powder puff on Pennywell's prominent forehead.

Engulfed in a powdery cloud, Pennywell swipes his scrunched nose, trying not to sneeze.

Standing on her toes, Number 8 sticks out her pink tongue, intent on completing her task, "Hold still, Mr. Pennywell."

Pennywell complies, allowing the replicant's soft and nimble hands to do their work. Leaning close so she can brush powdered specks from his lapel, he turns to Andrew, "Music. We need a signature tune like Carson had."

Ping and Andrew exchange glances, waiting for 8's comical performance with the ageless dynamo to conclude.

Still fussing with his itchy nose, Pennywell unbuttons his suit jacket and folds his tall, bony frame into his favorite chair before addressing Ping for the first time, "Thank you for coming, Ping. You stand as the show's first and last guest."

"I am honored."

Turning to his valet and personal fixer, "What the hell, Andrew. We don't have all day. Are we good to get this thing started, or not?"

Andrew lets the verbal snipe pass, unable to resist a witty retort, "Yes, sir. I just programmed an original score in the same amount of time it took you to sit your skinny arse in that overstuffed chair."

"Well then, giddy-up." Pennywell takes a swig from his omnipresent flask, "Do you see what nonsense I have to put up with, Ping? No respect."

Andrew measures his boss's blood-alcohol level with a sigh, "Sir, we need you sharp."

"Dammit, Andrew, how often do I have to tell you I am a raging alcoholic."

"Sir, please be serious."

Pennywell turns to the circumspect alien for support, "Tell this bucket of bolts, Ping, humans require a boost now and again. I'm not flying a plane and have not driven a car in over 40 years. Besides, back in the sixties, half the guests on Buckley's show were high as a fucking kite. I am striving for authenticity wherever I can fake it."

With an impish twinkle in his eye, the 134-year-old CEO whispers to his old friend and mentor, "You wouldn't happen to have any LSD, would you, Ping?"

Despite himself, the edges of Ping's narrow mouth curve into a smile, *"Not today, my friend. It appears your single malt will have to suffice."*

Swiping a virtual screen closed after adding a final flourish to his ad-hoc preprogrammed musical score, Andrew frowns, "LSD? Honestly, sir." Checking the control room, working out another in a long line of kinks, he stalls for time, "What do you think of the set? Numbers 14 and 15 worked hard to realize your vision of a *Firing Line* talk show layout."

Pennywell's gaze widens onto an aqua-blue velvet curtain backdrop with a 3-foot diameter PTB seal hung dead-center above and behind Andrew's head, "That's an unfortunate color choice."

"Beggars can't be choosers, sir."

Noting the generalized 60s vibe, Pennywell offers a grudging nod, "It looks better than Buckley's set, which is good enough for me." Turning back to Ping, he laughs and takes another swig for good measure, "I tried to purchase remnants from the old *Firing Line* set years ago, but I soon discovered no one knew what the hell I was talking about, let alone remember William F. Buckley. This world is chockful of ignorant people. Tell me, Ping, how did we go so wrong?"

Not waiting for the alien's reply, "I had the Sisters construct this based on a grainy old interview between Buckley and Groucho Marx. Not one of my favorite people, but there it is." Leaning back in his chair, Pennywell continues, "When the world wide web came online in the 90s, my idea was to reinvent Bill's stripped-down format and produce fucking podcasts or something." With a derisive laugh, "Of course, we did not call them that. What the hell did we call them? Oh well, who gives a flying fuck? It never happened; now here we are."

Pennywell's rumination pauses, allowing 1 and 2 to assume positions behind a pair of old-school television studio recording rigs. Dressed in black with dark hair pulled into tight buns, the talented duo don oversized noise-canceling headphones and proffer thumbs-up to the control room. While an autonomous holographic recording apparatus captures every nuance of the stage and its actors in 4D, the sisters' dual cameras will record a traditional analog broadcast for posterity.

Pennywell exhales and smiles toward Ping, quelling a case of the butterflies, "Getting close, now, Ping. Hey. Remember when I was scheduled as a guest on Bill's show. I had to bow out when we were summoned to help rescue prisoners from the Hanoi Hilton?"

"A long time ago, Artemus. I remember one of the pilots refused our help."

"That is right, his name escapes me … McDonald, McMaster. I recall he went into politics … a senator or something."

The stage lights dim as Number 7's soft melodic voice echoes from the control room through a speaker, "We are recording in 5, 4, 3, 2, 1 …."

A spotlight hits Pennywell's seat as Number 1's camera swivels onto his position while Andrew's rather good score fills the air. Assuming a relaxed, sophisticated pose, hands tented, leaning back with his right leg crossing his left, the PTB CEO takes a deep breath and swivels his angular, aristocratic visage toward Number 1's camera with a broad smile. Allowing the theme to fade, he clears his throat and commences a short unrehearsed monologue, "Hello, fellow Earthlings, you are witnessing my first and last broadcast from a clandestine soundstage at The Powers That Be headquarters. I am your host, Artemus Pennywell. I will not bore you with lame Gork jokes or eye-rolling banter with my sidekick, Andrew. Time is short, and so is my patience. So, let's get into it with our one and only guest, Ping. The 350-year-old Gray alien that devoted his life to our ungrateful, foolhardy world."

The second camera zooms onto the ancient Gray's tiny, wrinkled frame, straightening and expanding like air filling a balloon. Adjusting the volume on his speech recognition apparatus, Ping speaks, cognizant that every word will be scrutinized worldwide: *"Thank you, Artemus Pennywell and your fantastic staff, for the invitation. My name is Ping, and I am an interstellar ambassador to The Powers That Be. I would prefer not to dwell on the events leading up to the Gork invasion; what is done is done. However, Artemus and I must clear the air once and for all before addressing new and pressing concerns."*

Pennywell leans forward to speak, but in true *Firing Line* fashion, Andrew, acting as the moderator, intercedes, "Ambassador Ping, let us not jump ahead. Mr. Pennywell would like your comment on the current situation in light of the aborted Gork invasion and the non-stop rioting and looting plaguing every city and town."

Ping pauses to frame his response, *"Artemus, words like ungrateful and foolhardy are unproductive. However, since Disclosure Day in 2032, the notion of alien life thriving throughout the universe should not have been such a surprise. The harsh reality was that humanity, as a species, was ill-prepared for the Gorks' invasion on every conceivable front, and the destructive behavior needs to end."*

Andrew raises a hand to follow up, "Do you include the Powers That Be in your appraisal?"

Ping pauses to consider his words, *"No. Of course not. The PTB weathered Griffin Pike's mock tribunal. Still, sovereign countries and the media have pressed their baseless attacks on the PTB. They are leveraging the burgeoning mistrust among an undereducated and overmedicated worldwide population."* With a slight smile creasing his narrow mouth, he adds, *"It is simple arithmetic; someone must pay."*

Pennywell jumps in to speak before the moderator can intercede, "The reason for a worldwide lack of trust is our centuries-long partnership with the aliens, Ping. Most folks cannot—or will not—discern between powerful extraterrestrial allies like your group and violent, misanthropic species like the Gorks. Not to mention your Gray cousins—who look just like you—abducting thousands of people."

Andrew gavels down Pennywell before he goes off the rails, "A point of order, Mr. Pennywell. We will circle back to the Empire Grays in greater detail."

Pennywell rolls his eyes, noting the moderator's gavel has gone to Andrew's head as he addresses Ping with a follow-up, "Ambassador Ping, explain why you and others did not intercede to thwart the Gorks' invasion?"

Ping leans forward, ensuring his words are heard loud and clear, *"The Light Specters forbid interference."*

Andrew interrupts, "Please take a moment and explain who the Light Specters are."

"Supreme energy beings beyond the constraints of space and time. They have been called angels, demons, gods, and even foo fighters. Their existence lies beyond my intellect. Suffice to say, it is wise to obey their edicts without a hint of transgression."

Seeing his friend and mentor's frail gray body struggling for each breath, Pennywell turns to Andrew, "Permission to speak, Your Majesty?"

Andrew opts not to take the bait, "Granted."

Training his sharp gaze into Number 1's camera lens, he lowers his tone for dramatic effect, "Ambassador Ping's explanation is accurate. For reasons beyond comprehension, the Light Specters viewed our revolutionary forebears as a sea change in the human condition, starting with George Washington at Valley Forge. I wish this history could have been disclosed through the centuries, but much like Ping's non-interference edict, The Powers That Be was founded on secrecy."

With an ironic laugh, he concludes, "The Light Specters cautioned Ping's alien friends about our latent potential before acquiescing to requests to assist our advancement.

Think about it: humanity remained stagnant for thousands of years. Suddenly, we evolved from buggy whips and candles to splitting the atom and supersonic jets within the last three centuries. Even after Disclosure Day in 2032 and the introduction of anti-gravity, of all things, the jaded world responded with a collective shrug. Without curiosity, they accepted a bounty of tech dropped in their laps without questioning its origins."

Surprised Andrew has held his gavel in check, Pennywell continues, "Since no one seemed to notice or care what we did as long as they got their new toys, I expanded The Powers That Be role as an NGO, spearheading new enterprises like the International Outer Space Consortium. We even have a UN ambassador, the lovely and talented Anastasia Gabreski. I believe that the PTB spreads the wealth with fairness and equity as our driving principles. Both China and Russia received the same damn tech secrets as the USA. No favorites."

Andrew turns to Ping, who waves him off, struggling to catch his breath, "Please continue, Artemus."

"Thank you, Andrew. Uh, well, things were proceeding just fine until Ping's group uncloaked hi-def images of Gork fleets amassing for an imminent attack. We knew they were out there, but the fuckers had held their position for decades. All of a sudden, without warning, the gloves were off."

Andrew counters, "Let's fast-forward. Artemus, please explain why the Gorks abandoned their invasion?"

Pennywell clears his throat and takes a sip of water, "Should we jump into that, Andrew?"

"Yes, Artemus, time is short."

"Agreed. Keep it short and pithy. Check." Adjusting his bolo, he replies with a solemn-voiced gravitas, "The Gork invasion proved a sink or swim proposition designed to test humanity's worthiness to join the universal community of civilizations."

Getting his second wind, Ping interjects, *"Some of you are familiar with the name Rachel Alexander Haig. This young woman wielded nascent supernatural abilities to defeat the Gorks. I hesitate to get ahead of my partner, so I will stop there."*

With a raised eyebrow, Pennywell turns to Andrew, "Have we missed anything regarding the Gorks, Andrew?"

Andrew's confident smile speaks volumes, "I think that about covers it, Artemus. Please proceed to the present dilemma facing Earth."

"Yes. The lost ship." Breaking the fourth wall again, Pennywell proffers an easy smile into the camera and quips, "If you are watching this production—in 3D or 4D—things went well. If not, this broadcast is as moot as humanity's once-promising future." Leaning back with a weary sigh, Pennywell dabs his shiny forehead with a hankie, "I lived with this looming threat my whole life; I will say no more."

Stunned by his loquacious boss' abrupt reticence, Andrew turns to Ping, "Would you care to add anything, Ping?"

"Thank you, Andrew. Unlike the Gork invasion, the lost ship is not a test. It is a 90-million-year-old shipwreck holding a hyper-weaponized virulent pathogen that must not fall into the wrong hands, human or otherwise. For the record, I also concur with Artemus' obvious conclusion regarding the transmission of this broadcast."

As the presentation winds to a close, Artemus Pennywell leans back and relaxes. Studying Andrew's regal bearing with intense interest, he watches the handsome man swiping open colorful graphics filling a virtual screen, reviewing the presentation's key points for an unseen audience of hundreds of millions with warmth, charm, and gravitas. The camera does not lie.

After Andrew's concise review, complete with links and supporting documentation, concludes, he gavels the broadcast to a close, "This was quite illuminating. I hope it brings clarity and reason to a world sorely lacking both at the present time. Mr. Pennywell and Ambassador Ping, thank you both for …."

Pennywell raises his hand, "Hold on, Andrew. I have one more announcement. As I said in my intro, this is the first and last broadcast I will be making as CEO of The Powers That Be."

With a wink and a nod toward Ping, he continues, "The post-invasion epoch is upon us. It requires new leadership with intelligence, grace, wit, and, above all, candor. Full disclosure is paramount to obtaining the public's trust, especially going forward. So, with that mantra in mind, I wish to spend these last minutes speaking about drastic forthcoming changes to life on Earth as we knew it before August 22, 2044."

Pausing to formulate his words, "Ping alluded to it when mentioning our friend Rachel Haig's superhuman heroism. It is an epochal event known as the Blue Spark—the fusion of human and artificial intelligence, as demonstrated by Miss Rachel's dramatic transcendence. Walking in the footsteps of pioneering men and women throughout history, she stands at an evolutionary precipice. Her progeny and untold others of mixed natural and synthetic human seeds will supplant the current human population within a generation. This, my friends, is our prize for prevailing over the Gorks. We passed the test and now reap the reward, a gift from the gods." Considering his words, he adds, "May God help us."

Feeling the weight of a thousand suns lifted from his shoulders, Pennywell emits a relieved chuckle, "One last thing, I suffer no illusions of possessing the uncanny ability to lead the PTB into this new era. Without further ado, I resign as the CEO of The Powers That Be and appoint Andrew as my immediate successor."

With a look of abject surprise on his reddening face, Andrew drops the gavel on the lectern, "Artemus, that is not funny."

Pennywell loosens his bolo while standing out of the chair, "I am dead serious, Andrew. You take the reins. My time here has reached an end." With a wink toward Ping, he raises his monogrammed flask to the new PTB CEO, takes a final drink, and walks off the set.

From a little spark may burst a flame.

– Dante Alighieri

Chapter Thirteen:
The Ship

Griffin Pike | The Lake
05:00 a.m. | October 18, 2044

Griffin Pike lies awake in a zipped hammock, swaying between tall, straight trunks in an early morning breeze, watching water drops splat atop the stretched tarp shielding his nylon keep while fantasizing about the lost ship's purifying world killer. Ruminating on the pile of dead bodies it took to reach this point, any thoughts of cutting his losses and hightailing it back to civilization are moot. He wants the apocalyptic payload, and today is the day. No more delays and negotiations; everyone can go to hell, even Sapphire.

Unzipping and dropping bare feet onto the wet ground, Griffin pulls into his stinky outerwear over boxers and a SATstar tee before removing an upturned left boot from a tall stake driven into the mud. Dumping a three-inch centipede, he double-checks the other before lacing them up his sore calves. Dressed and ready for action, he tromps to the smoldering blue campfire on the sandy lakeshore.

Scratching his messy, thick bedhead, he starts a pot of water for coffee. Rifling through the dwindling rations for the last coffee packets, he catches Rachel's wide-awake glare. "Care for some coffee? I know you like your early morning cup of joe."

Scooching to a sitting position on her bedroll with her hands and feet zip-tied, she checks Penny and Nina, sound asleep, before whispering, "Why? Are you going to spill it on me again?"

Griffin watches indigenous waterfowl take flight from the lake's placid misty surface before offering Rachel a luminous smile through the damp stillness, "I know you don't believe anything I tell you, but that was an accident. Your presence in Santarém caused me great anxiety."

Griffin's deep-set gaze scans past Rachel, checking Owen and Flynn, bound back-to-back, asleep beside a boulder. Standing to stretch his athletic six-foot frame, a prick of danger creeps down his spine, "Something is not right." Wheeling back toward the lake and its ribbony waterfall, an alarm goes off in his paranoid brain. Stepping over Sapphire's curled repose draped under a blanket from head to toe, he looks toward where he last saw his bought-and-paid-for mercenary, "Where the fuck is Henri?"

With the coffee pot forgotten, he retreats toward his hammock to grab the holstered weapon he left inside.

Alarmed, Rachel scans the lakefront, not finding Smythe or Rollins anywhere in sight. Her heart beating out of her chest and hands glowing bright, a sultry voice whispers, *"Hold still."*

Sapphire slices through Rachel's zip ties before cutting loose Nina and Penny, jostling them awake.

Nina's bleary gaze focuses on the knife-wielding assassin hovering over her, thinking this is it, but the woman shoots her a cold stare, "Stay down, bitch, if you want to live."

Twisting toward the jungle from her knelt pose, Sapphire

throws the sharp blade across the clearing on a dime through a young, spear-toting native's chest.

Slathered ghost white from head to toe, the hilt juts from the boy's chest as he pitches face down onto the sand.

More youthful Forest Ghosts materialize from the dense undergrowth, spread out in a hunting formation designed to box in their prey. Rising onto bare feet in camo khakis and a sports bra, Sapphire pulls a long blade from the mounded bedroll where she faked her sleeping position. Half out of her mind with a wide-eyed, ululating scream, she charges the hunters, dodging poison darts. Eight feet from the nearest native, she vaults herself airborne and swings the machete through his skinny neck in a singular, violent motion. The headless body drops to the wet sand as Sapphire presses her 1-on-15 attack. Snatching the headless boy's spear, she pivots onto the next native's clumsy charge, driving the poison spear tip through his shoulder. Screaming in pain, the kid writhes on the ground as the remaining Forest Ghosts pile on the crazed female's blood-drenched form, grappling her arms, dodging leg kicks, and wrestling her to an immobilized position. Writhing like a demon against four wide-eyed kids holding her down in their skinny arms, her enraged screams resemble a stricken animal's last-ditch struggle to break free.

Still tied back-to-back, Owen and Flynn stumble to Rachel, Nina, and Penny's huddled position by the fire.

Speechless and uncertain of their looming fate, they watch a grizzled elder appear from the jungle with a cigarette dangling from his thick lower lip. Naked as a jaybird but sans his hunters' white paint, the dark-skinned fellow glances toward the assembled PTB group with an odd smile before producing a club in his gnarled hand and smacking it down on Sapphire's shaved, bloody head, turning out her lights.

With the violent woman's ear-splitting cries silenced, the elder commands his boys to gather the severed head and body while administering to the injured kid's shoulder wound. The remaining young men hog-tie Sapphire's limp body to a long pole and hoist her onto their scrawny shoulders back to the Forest Ghosts camp.

Rachel | The Lake
06:22 a.m. | October 18, 2044

Dumping Sapphire's light bag on the sand, Rachel shuffles through the scant contents and finds another sharp knife, "Hold still, boys. I don't want to cut you by accident."

Flynn calls over his shoulder, "Please be quick about it. We need to find out what happened here."

Owen pulls his freed hands forward and vaults onto bare feet on a beeline toward his tree hammock, expecting to find Griffin cowering inside. "I am going to beat the shit out of him!" Picking up a thick branch, he swings it at the bag like hitting a piñata. "Come out of there, asshole!" watching it sway back and forth, Owen realizes it is unoccupied.

After untying his hammock from the trees, never taking his wary eyes off the encroaching jungle, Owen balls it into a wad, dragging long lines back down to the encampment where everyone is busy packing like maniacs.

Flynn glances up at Owen, "What's that, mate?"

With unmasked frustration Owen shakes his head, squinting beyond the lake toward the grassy meadow. "Griffin Pike has left the building."

Shaking wet sand out of the bedding, Rachel notes her husband's sulking attitude, "Snap out of it, Owen. Good riddance."

Nina gives Penny a water bottle and guides her to a tree stump, "Sit down, dear. What is going on? I thought you were recovering."

"I'll be okay. Just give me a minute."

Noting a kettle of buzzards circling overhead, Flynn drops

Smythe's backpack, following multiple sets of sandy footprints through gnarly twisted driftwood piles rising twice his height, curving along the lake's deep blue rippling edge. With Smythe's loaded .45 outstretched in a two-handed grip, he ducks on instinct as a menacing shadow disappears through the tangled, desiccated branches. Sneaking closer, rips and tears grow louder as he peers past three turkey vultures feasting and fighting over a corpse. "Shit, I found Rollins."

Probing past the squawking, cawing scavengers, Flynn discovers what's left of Smythe, noting a poison dart jutting from the dead Brit's half-eaten neck crawling with flies and ants.

Expecting to find the big guy's bearded head on a stake, a black-feathered turkey vulture lands in front of Flynn. Taking a wide path around the giant bird, "Stay back. I'm still alive, for now, anyway," he makes his way back up the beach.

Shoehorning a water bottle and Nemesis Group nut bars into her pack like the final pieces of a jigsaw puzzle, Nina sees Flynn's ashen-faced return, "I am almost afraid to ask what you found out there?"

Returning to Smythe's pack, he shoves the man's ID inside and tosses it in the bushes. "What's that? Oh, I located Smythe and Rollins." Taking a swig of water, he mutters, "They won't be a problem anymore."

Pale as a ghost, Penny questions the reticent PTB agent while rummaging through Sapphire's pack, "What about DeVille?"

"Sorry, Miss Penny. I did not find him. My guess is he took off with Pike. Or he is dead. Either way, we need to press on."

"How are we supposed to do that?" Nina turns to the group, "Don't you all remember? Pike has Richard's map."

While the group goes silent, Rachel begins to laugh.

Owen turns to his beautiful wife, "Rachel, honey. Have you gone mad?"

"No, you idiot. I have the map in my head. I am visualizing it as we speak, clear as day."

A familiar bark resonates from the jungle as Zint parts leafy vines, appearing before the group with Daphne wagging her tail at his side. Digging deep for a quote culled from years spent monitoring humanity's broadcast signals, he puffs out his bony chest, "I come back to you now at the turn of the tide."

As the only person in the group familiar with Tolkien's trilogy, Rachel starts laughing again, "How long have you been waiting to use that line?"

"A long, long time."

Flynn slings a heavy pack over his shoulder and scoops up Smythe's carbine, "We need to leave this spot before the natives get restless again."

Daphne bolts across the camp to greet Penny as Zint holds up his four-fingered hands. "We are safe. I brought them here. They know us as the good guys."

Letting his guard down a fraction, Flynn stoops to shake the three-foot alien's hand, "That is the second time you saved my sorry ass. Let's not go for the trifecta."

Zint nods, "Understood."

Zint | The Glade
10:12 a.m. | October 18, 2044

After packing everything they cannot leave behind, Owen extinguishes the fire, musing that without Pembroke and Antoine, the experienced Agent Flynn is a welcome addition to their moveable feast.

Moving single file down the clearwater lake's lapping shoreline, dark clouds blot out the clear blue Amazon sky as they enter the driftwood forest.

Hoisting a heavy pack laden with supplies on his broad shoulders, Owen feels a drop hit his nose and pulls up the hood on his ripped poncho, "Looks like rain."

In response to Owen's blithe observation, the skies open, drenching the expedition, wearing torn and stained outerwear under raingear with worn boots caked in sand and mud tromping past Rollins and Smythe's remains.

Rachel pauses to visualize Richard's map, breaking from the heaps of driftwood piled high in the swampy environs at the lake's western shore.

With Daphne running point, staying well within eyeshot, Rachel finds the streamlet draining downhill from the lake, snaking through the grassy glade teeming with butterflies, dragonflies, and swarms of mosquitoes.

Zint hurries forward and touches Rachel's arm with a static electric shock. "Ow! What was that for?"

"Protects against the bugs and snakes. Sorry, I should warn first before zapping people."

Owen follows next. Zap.

Wearing Sapphire's dark-olive one-piece jumpsuit and knee-high boots, Penny extends her left arm from under her poncho and pulls up the sleeve, exposing the four-inch scar from her altercation with the Empire Gray. Zint's gaze lands on the red, swollen wound. After her bug zap, he presses a finger atop her forearm. "I apologize for my kind. Let me take your pain."

Penny studies the wound after Zint releases his hand, watching the redness and swelling fade, "What did you do?"

"It is okay. Pain makes me stronger."

Nina's zap follows before hustling to rejoin her place in line.

Bringing up the rear with a weighted pack and the carbine slung over a shoulder, Flynn smiles at his little gray friend, "So, what do you have for male-pattern baldness?"

The fickle rains stop, replaced by the blazing hot mid-morning sun. Trekking downhill along a well-trod path used by animals and ostensibly the Forest Ghosts, the expedition halts at a formation of smooth boulders where the waters quicken and rush through a narrow three-foot slot before cascading down a series of waterfalls toward a mist-enshrouded forest far below.

Thrust into a leadership role by default, Rachel refills a plastic bottle in the stream and takes a long drink.

Owen catches her too late, "Hey, you didn't purify that."

"Fuck it, Owen. I am zapped. So are you, by the way."

Owen turns to the group with a sheepish grin, "Oh yeah. Hard to keep up with all the new shit." Noting the collective reticence to proceed through the mysterious slot without knowing what is on the other side, he slouches out of his pack, "Okay. Allow me to recon this so-called slot." Wading into the frigid knee-deep rushing water, he wedges through the narrow passage and yells back, "Okay, there's a ledge on the opposite side. Hang on."

Straining to hear him over the rushing water, the group watches Owen squeeze through the gap and disappear.

Waiting beside Rachel, Nina smiles, "Does this bring back fond memories?"

Rachel shakes her head, "Nope."

Owen's wet head peeks through the gap, hugging the rough granite boulder, "Okay, throw me the packs. I will toss them to the bottom." Catching a spray of rushing water on his face, he wipes his eyes, "Then come out, one at a time. I will help everyone get to the bottom. It is a long way down but doable."

Wading into the strong current, Penny's slight build sweeps into Owen's embrace, "I got you, Penny. Just hold tight."

Easing backward through the slot, Penny hugs Owen with her smooth face pressed against his cheek and makes the mistake of looking down. "Oh, no. I can't do this. I don't like heights."

Moving across the slick rocks covered in algae at the top of the falls with Penny strangling him, Owen yells into her ear over the raging water, "Don't look down. You will be fine."

Pulling her loose atop the precipitous ledge, Owen stays calm, "I know, ride piggyback, and keep your eyes closed if that helps."

Pale, shivering, and soaked to the bone, Penny looks up into Owen's dreamy hazel eyes and kisses him on the mouth, "I trust you."

Descending five cascading levels, Owen drops six feet from the lowest granite shelf with Penny clinging to his back like a monkey. Collecting packs and bags at rock bottom next to a deep pool at the base of the falls, Owen breaks the awkward silence, "Wait here; I'll be right back."

"Owen?"

The married man turns and smiles, "Don't worry about it, Penny."

Watching Owen free climb 50 feet back to the slot at the top of the falls, Penny mutters, "I really need to get a boyfriend when this is over."

After lowering Daphne in a makeshift harness akin to her cliff rescue, Flynn follows Owen's lead, picking a wet, slippery descent down the terraced falls, where the group watches and waits with a dense, foreboding jungle at their backs.

Penny | The Stream
02:34 p.m. | October 18, 2044

Catching a breather at the base of the falls, Penny wraps gauze around cuts and scrapes on Owen's hands incurred during his repeated trips up and down the sharp granite cascade, "Where did you learn to climb like that?"

Never one to shrink from one of his favorite topics, Owen smiles, "Well, Miss Penny. I started free climbing in high school. My friends and I would drive from Vermont to the White Mountains in New Hampshire on weekends to camp, drink beer, and rock climb.

Good times."

Turning to find Rachel and Nina repacking the bags, Penny ventures another question while her delicate hands wind more gauze over and around Owen's hands, "Does Rachel like to rock climb?"

Owen looks into the young woman's brown eyes with her shoulder-length mousy hair pulled into a short, wet ponytail, "That would be a no. Thanks for the bandage job, Penny. Or should I say, Doc? I understand you are a Harvard grad. That is impressive. What are you, 21?"

Kneeling on the soft dirt in front of Owen, Penny laughs and leans into him, drawing a quick glance from Rachel, "No, silly. I am 26."

Flexing his bandaged hands, he chuckles, "You're kidding? You are two years older than Rachel. How about that?"

Feeling self-conscious and out of place, Penny stands and closes the cobbled-together medical kit before wandering off to sit with Daphne and Zint.

Flynn jumps up from his resting spot, pulling into his pack's thick straps, and sidles up to Flynn, "Careful, mate, you are treading dangerous seas."

Owen smiles, "No, it will be fine. When you are married to someone like Rachel, you get used to having men and women ogle and flirt with her right in front of you. Young Miss Penny sees me as a big brother, nothing more."

"Sure, mate, keep telling yourself that."

* * *

Rivulets trickle over and around mossy boulders, craggy overhangs, and knotted roots down the steep, fern-covered jungle, feeding the riffling stream's winding course.

Rachel resumes her point position behind Daphne with the remaining expedition fanned out single file at her back. Shining a flashlight through the misty darkness, she calls back to Owen, following her lead, "What time is it?"

"A little after three."

"It is like the dead of the night down here." Stepping through stands of ferns, trying to avoid tripping over hidden obstructions or stepping on anything dangerous, she muses the valley floor beneath the thick canopy high overhead is more open and passable.

Rachel | The Stream
04:32 p.m. | October 18, 2044

Owen exhales and checks the lagging, tired group. "Hold up, Rach. How much further?"

Scrunching her pert nose, Rachel's hands glow in the dark as she tries to pin their position on the map Richard implanted in her psyche, "I don't know. If I had to guess, we are close to the falls."

At the back end of the expedition, Flynn scooches a slithering snake away from his boot with an expandable walking stick he discovered in someone's gear. "Great. Another falls."

Catching her breath, hands on her hips, Nina chuckles, "It's funny, between the starvation diet up in space and this jungle trek, I must have dropped three sizes."

Walking in Nina's footsteps, Zint soaks in the humans' conversations, holding Penny's wet hand.

Stumbling on a sharp boulder jutting from the soft ground, Rachel's long, taut legs feel like rubber. With a whistle to alert Daphne, she veers left and splashes into the stream's lazy current, letting the cool water flow around her aching legs. "Ah, that feels good!"

Waiting for the others while Daphne laps up the crystal clear water, Rachel hears a dull roar from the green-black forest. The German Shepherd emits a growl, shaking droplets from her thick coat.

Rachel pats her back, "Quiet girl, it's okay, no barking."

Sabotaging her attempt at stealth, Owen jumps feet-first into the stream with a loud whoop-whoop.

"Owen, stop! Can you hear it?"

"Can I hear what?" Tuning out the jungle cacophony overhead, he focuses on a low rumbling vibration. "Wait, I hear it! It sounds like a waterfall."

The rest of the intrepid group wades into the water, sliding their boots across smooth river stones as minnows and small fish dart about, disturbed by the intruders. Flynn catches the tail end of a long snake slithering upstream past a fallen log, repelled by the alien-zapped intruders.

Sloshing downstream, the group pauses at a sand bar jutting into the streambed within eyeshot of the top of the falls.

Nina breaks out the snacks, tossing bars to everyone. "We made it. Richard would be proud." Seeing Rachel's frowning expression, she corrects, "Is proud."

Rachel peels the wrapper on a Nemesis Group nut bar and takes a bite. Chewing the nuts and dates mixed with chocolate chunks and nougat, she shrugs, "Not half bad. I'd buy these at the store."

Penny reads the label and quips, "It says here Product of Germany."

Rachel smiles, loosening bits of nuts from her teeth with her tongue, "Germany. Well, Trader Joe's will carry them."

Finishing her bar, Rachel folds the wrapper, shoves it in a pocket, and looks across the rippling waters at a tall native covered in stark white paint, bony piercings, and tattoos. Standing in knee-deep water, clutching a long decorated spear, the young man proffers a youthful smile. Realizing no one else sees the apparition, she wanders across the stream, pretending to admire a beautiful orchid, coming within five feet of the boy, sporting a softball-sized hole through his chest.

Communicating in a strange tongue, Rachel somehow

understands the native's words resonating in her mind: *"Seek out hidden steps past the alien rock. It is the only path into the rift."*

Rachel gives the native a green-eyed inquiring look, *"Alien rock?"*

The Forest Ghost directs her gaze toward Zint, skipping rocks across the stream with Daphne at his side.

"Right. Alien rock."

The Forest Ghost fades into the stifling jungle darkness with a final warning, *"Watch out for the monsters."*

Owen | The Rift Falls
04:55 p.m. | October 18, 2044

Rejuvenated by the protein-rich bars and the thunderous waterfall echoing through the cathedral of trees, the expedition tromps back onto the slippery, muddy bank, a stone's throw from a sheer drop into a dark and foreboding abyss. Hacking a trail around the left side of the falls, they come upon a rocky vantage point jutting over the abyss.

Turning to the group, Owen jokes, "Well, let's not all volunteer at once." Everyone waits on firm, flat ground, watching Owen scamper to the dizzying edge.

Nina nudges Rachel, "Do you worry about him?"

"No. If Owen falls, I have our French villa all to myself."

Nina looks askance at Rachel, "What French villa?"

Eyeballing Owen's careful advance on the slippery outcropping, "The Villa St. Claire in Le Tholonet."

With a surprised look, Nina muses, "Artemus is getting generous in his old age."

With a long whistle, Owen peers into the dark, mist-filled rift, "I can't make out the bottom." Scanning the sheer cliff walls covered in lush layers of greens and blacks, he swallows hard, knowing this would be a significant challenge for an experienced climber, requiring weeks of preparation, "How are we going to get down there?"

Pretending to visualize Richard's map, Rachel remembers the Forest Ghost's words, "Uh, we need to find a rock formation that looks like an alien head. Sorry, Zint, no offense."

"None taken."

Hacking through more dense undergrowth along the precipitous rim, the weary expedition reaches a dome-shaped formation overhanging the rift. Without asking if anyone else wants a turn, Owen climbs to the top and looks around, "I don't know, Rachel, I can see pretty far, and nothing looks like a fucking alien head."

With a burst of inspiration, Flynn breaks from the tired group and hacks through thick masses of clinging vines, climbing down the steep edge to a position below the domed rock jutting out over the rift. Looking up at the rounded formation, he sees massive concave ovals positioned like a pair of eyes. Returning to the expedition, Flynn yells toward Owen at the granite dome's apex, "You are fucking standing on the bloody alien head, mate."

Rachel laughs, "Of course. Owen! Stay there. We need to see what is on the other side."

Owen stands at the apex, ensuring no one gets vertigo and falls from the perilous height. Not too concerned with appearances, Penny and Nina scooch down the opposite side on their bottoms.

Bringing up the rear, Flynn guides Daphne with a makeshift rope leash, pausing beside Owen at the top. Scanning 360 degrees, the PTB agent marvels at the unobstructed view back upstream, enshrouded in a sea of clouds and rainforest topography rendering the rift invisible from above. "It appears we reached the end of the map and fell off the other side."

Richard | The Rift

06:14 p.m. | October 18, 2044

Sliding off the alien head formation, Owen walks down the path, and parts between Nina and Penny's confused looks toward Rachel, cutting and hacking through the thick undergrowth toward the rim, "Careful, Rachel, it's a sheer drop on the other side of that tangled mess. What are you looking for, an elevator?"

Rachel's blade cuts a hole through the ropy vines and branches. Exerting a final heavy thwack, she kicks through a thick chunk of bramble, sending it out over the abyss.

"It is a long way down."

Rachel wipes sweat from her forehead and turns to her husband's concerned face, "This is what I am looking for. Stairs."

Angling over his wife's dirty blond head, he pulls out a sticky green leaf, "What? I don't see anything."

Rachel bends down and clears leafy debris using the tip of her long machete, revealing a three-foot carved step chiseled out of solid granite, "This. It's a step." Holding Owen's arm, she stretches down and brushes off the next step and the one after, revealing an ancient stairway.

Estimating over 600 steps zigzagging down to a thick layer of mist enshrouding the remaining descent to the bottom, Owen's heart sinks, "We can't expect these folks to do this. I am getting vertigo."

Rachel clutches Owen's arm, fending off dizziness, "There is no other way down."

"How do you know that?"

Rachel sighs, "I just do, Owen. Stop asking stupid questions."

Flynn hunches behind the bickering couple, "Everyone is wondering what you two are going on about."

Owen angles sideways, "We found the way down."

Flynn squints downward, "Ah. Okay. Stairs. Jolly good."

Nina and Penny crowd behind Flynn, "Hey, we want to have a

look, too."

Penny gulps, "Do you people ever take a day off?"

Acknowledging an unspoken dejection permeating the tired group, none too keen on the proposition of the narrow, uneven steps with no support or handrails, Owen volunteers. "I refuse to give up so close to the lost ship. Let me climb down that stairway. Just tell me what to do since I don't have a fucking clue what the lost ship looks like."

With an exasperated eye roll, Nina turns to the Haigs, "Richard never shared his plan? Man, that is so typical of him."

Rachel studies the map in her mind's eye, finding no guidance beyond this point. "Nope, I have nothing. Not even where to look if we did manage to get down there."

Owen nods, "We need Richard."

"Did somebody say my name?"

Richard King breaks from a path farther along the rim. "I see everyone has survived the journey. What about Griffin and his lot?"

Mouths agape, the group stares at the PTB's intrepid scientist in tattered clothes with matted hair and beard, joining the discussion like he just returned from taking a leak behind a tree.

Flynn beats Owen to the punch, "They did not survive."

Richard winces, "Ah. Tough luck for them, I suppose."

Seeing Richard King's return, Zint disappears into the undergrowth and returns holding a fistful of bright yellow flowers.

Penny departs from her usual taciturn shell, feigning jealousy, "Zint? What about me? I like flowers."

Accepting the fragrant bouquet, Richard plucks a petal from a large, sticky bloom, rubs it between his fingers to release the oils, and swipes it inside his nostrils. Sniffing back the strong fragrance, he shakes his head, eyes dilating, "That is quite invigorating."

Gobsmacked by Richard's nonchalant attitude, standing before her, getting high—like old times—Nina remembers why they split.

Sensing her disapproval, Richard and Zint pass a bloom

to everyone, "The oils in this flower's yellowy petals relieve inner ear imbalances, quelling vertigo. They also provide a rather pleasant buzz that should alleviate anxiety and acrophobia. Quite a remarkable medicinal plant, really. Zint read my mind and beat me to the punch."

While everyone shoves the oily yellow substance up their noses, Owen abstains, "What have you been doing all this time, Richard?"

"Looking for the way down. I was circling back, hoping to meet up with some of you. I am heartened and somewhat surprised you all made it this far." With a furtive wink toward Rachel, he continues, "Since she is the one that discovered the steps, I suggest she have the honor of leading the way."

Girded by a heady buzz and a sense of elation, doors to anxiety-filled rooms within Rachel's complicated psyche slam shut. Parting from the group toward the rim, she grabs a dangling vine in her left hand and extends her right boot onto the top step, loosening pebbles over the edge, beginning her careful descent with a subtle smiling wave. Focused on the next step downward, she hazards a peek toward the misty layer far below on her right, obscuring the bottom. Leaning into the wall, taking it one chiseled step at a time, a sense of finality swells within her, "I am not scared. I should be, but I am not."

The serene trio of Penny, Nina, and Flynn allow ten steps to pass before each takes their turn. Counting Flynn's downward progression, Richard turns to Owen, holding Daphne, "See you both at the bottom."

Owen shoots the professor an inquisitive look, "Professor, how did …."

King holds up a hand, "Later. I will explain everything to everyone all at once."

Taking a deep inhalation of hot, muggy air, Richard lets the natural chemicals in the yellow petals do their work. On his first step, the worn heel of his right boot lands on a loosened chunk of granite. Slipping onto his bottom, he grabs the cut vine at the last second before chuckling to Owen, "Watch that first step. It is a doozy."

Pulling into his heavy pack, Owen watches as Zint places a calming hand on Daphne's head, her tongue out, panting in the early evening heat. "Take it easy, girl. Slow and steady."

Owen taps the alien, "Go ahead, Zint. Follow Richard. I will make sure Daphne is safe."

Zint smiles, "Thank you, Owen Haig. You did not use the petals. Why?"

"Drugs do not agree with me. I am better off making the descent sans pharmacological boost."

Owen peeks over the rim beyond Zint's careful descent, watching Richard and the others moving downward and disappearing through a thick layer of mist.

Worried she is falling behind, Daphne nudges Owen's leg.

"Okay, girl, let's go."

Sapphire | Forest Ghosts encampment
08:47 p.m. | October 18, 2044

Intense heat radiating from multiple flaming torches crackling into the night stirs Henri DeVille back to consciousness after a succession of head blows finally brought down the strapping behemoth like a snarling big game animal. Lying prone with his hairy muscular arms and tree-trunk legs splayed apart and strapped to a sturdy bamboo frame, he hears jabbering voices mixed with the laughter of a communal cannibal gathering.

Feeling thick streams of blood trickling from a gaping hole in his fractured skull, his blurred gaze darts sideways onto another body splayed atop a frame. A chanting foursome blocks his view, hefting the bamboo assembly to a vertical position as DeVille's eyes narrow on a feminine form silhouetted before a raging fire resembling a nightmarish recreation of Da Vinci's Vitruvian Man, or woman, as the case may be.

A tall, lean native teen slathered in white paint stalks before the woman as the reverie falls silent, replaced by a rhythmic, hungry chant. Producing a sharp blade in his hand, he slices into her left arm at the shoulder socket. The woman snaps awake, crying in anguished pain, struggling to free herself from a nightmare that will not end. With a primal scream, she yells at the top of her lungs for the knife-wielding boy to stop, "I am not a human! I am not a human!"

Having experienced the final pleas for mercy over 16 years of the only life he knows, the kid ignores her panicky rants, completing a deep incision at her left shoulder before proceeding to skin the female down her left torso to her crotch and up the opposite side.

Knowing it is his turn once they are done skinning Sapphire alive for a late-night barbeque feast, DeVille hears the chants ebb to stunned silence.

Straining to lift his head, he sees the back-turned butcher pulling glistening filaments from her neck and shoulder.

The confused cannibal mutters a long series of odd notes and whistles before using the blade to cut her loose. Freed from her binds, standing stark naked before the transmogrified, slack-jawed audience, her lithesome form glowing in the firelight like a god, she takes the knife from the stunned native and finishes slicing off her dangling useless left arm with a deep inhalation of smoky air. Snatching a fiery torch, she cauterizes her jagged shoulder and pitches the useless appendage in the fire, sending sparks and smoke into the air before it melts into a gooey mass.

In complete command, twirling the balanced cutting instrument in her hand, she orders the cannibals to lift Henri before the fire.

Struggling against his binds, he grits his teeth in a furious rage, staring daggers at the menacing woman, "Sapphire. Don't."

"Too late, Henri." Making an initial deep gash at his throat, blood splatters everywhere as she cuts down the middle of his heaving hairy chest.

Covered in Henri's warm blood, she turns to the wide-eyed boy, "See, if you slice down the middle, you can part the skin to the sides and access the vital organs more efficiently. Got it?"

Noting the boy's serious-faced nod, she proffers the bloody knife hilt, "Here, you try. I gotta run now. More to do. It never ends."

Cutting through the dark forest, Henri's cries and wails resonate to her ears through the ancient trees before ebbing to silence.

Griffin Pike | The Rift
09:14 p.m. | October 18, 2044

Covered in greenish filth and grime with oozing cuts and bloody scrapes seeping through the ripped and torn vestiges of his custom-fitted, high-tech, camouflaged outerwear, Griffin Pike tumbles down the alien head formation. Thumping face-first into the muddy, tamped-down clearing, he scrambles onto his soaked boots, aiming the gun clutched in his shaking, white-knuckled grip at dangerous shadows lurking in the trees. "Go away. Leave me alone."

Escaping the Forest Ghosts' attack by a hair's breadth, Pike stumbled upon Rollins and Smythe's bodies. Concealing himself in the tangled masses of driftwood, the mogul waited for the cannibals to leave and the expedition survivors to pass, fending off the dead-eyed advances of hungry vultures.

With Richard's crumpled map in his scraped fists, he trailed the expedition's arduous trek, staying well beyond eyeshot through the glade. At the slot, he almost drowns after tumbling halfway down the terraced cascade and knocking his head on the sharp rocks.

Straggling farther behind, following the twisting jungle stream to the falls, he hid upstream from the sand bar, catching their detour into the jungle and making their way around the dangerous rim. Checking the map in his trembling hands, he hears animals stalking him through the thick underbrush and hastens to follow the humans. At the domed formation, he hunkered low and watched with rapt anticipation, "What are they doing? Get on with finding a way down, dammit all."

Alone at the staircase under a night sky filling with stars, he peers through the darkness at movement far below, passing through the mist and disappearing from view. "I'll rest here for a few hours to give them time to descend. Then I will get what is coming to me. Screw this world."

Flynn | The Rift
10:17 p.m. | October 18, 2044

The expedition illuminates the lower flights of steps zigzagging down the cliff face to the dark, muggy rift floor with flashlights.

Richard takes a final step onto the loamy ground, absorbing every nuance of the prehistoric place, "I now know how Neil Armstrong felt walking on the moon."

Nina bear hugs him from behind, "I thought you were gone."

Richard turns into her embrace, "Nonsense, Nina. Griffin, his despicable henchmen, and woman were contemplating killing the lot of you. I needed to change the paradigm." With a broad smile on his lined face, he adds, "Of course, I did not wish to die a horrible death. I made the correct assumption that the underground river came out somewhere. And it did." Tweaking his sore neck, he laments, "I could have done without the 60-foot drop at the end, but such is life. We never know what fate lies ahead."

Watching Daphne pulling Owen down the last 20 steps to rejoin the group, he turns to Nina with a melancholy awareness replacing his smile,

"I am sorry, Nina. I found Stevens. Or what was left of him after a dinosaur attack. Theropods, to be precise. Hungry ones, too. I doubt he suffered too much."

Segueing onto Penny's slender form, still high from the petals, Richard proffers a warm smile, "I am heartened to see you are feeling better, Miss Pennywell."

"Thanks, Professor King, but I still have more questions than answers."

"I know you do." Richard smiles, giving the young Pennywell a gentle hug, "I am afraid you will have to wait a bit longer."

Placing an arm over Penny's shoulder, Richard musters his most authoritative tone, lending their predicament an air of serious gravitas, "This place is beyond our known world and teeming with dangers. We must proceed with caution."

Generating static energy, Zint gives everyone, including Daphne, booster zaps before setting out.

A loud snarling roar followed by the anguished wails of a dying animal pierces the pitch-blackness, echoing off the chasm walls.

Waiting for the frightening sounds to stop, Flynn steps up, swinging his torch through the woods, "Well then, Richard, lead the way."

With an incredulous look on his expressive face, Richard pivots toward Agent Flynn, "I did not make myself clear. It is too risky to traverse this place at night. I propose we camp right here and await whatever passes for the morning light in this chasm."

Huddled around the blue fire, the expedition shares Nemesis Group tins and more German nut bars with purified water from the stream 30 yards down a shallow slope from the base of the ancient steps.

Scraping the last of his beanie-weenies from a tin, Owen smooths a finger inside the rim, not wanting to lose a morsel, "I have never been this hungry."

Penny tosses her unopened tin to Owen, "Take mine. I'll stick with the nut bar."

"Thanks, Penny." On the cusp of popping the lid and devouring the contents, Owen feels the starving group's eyes upon him, "You know, on second thought, I'll save it for later."

Rachel gives Owen a playful punch in the arm, "Nice. You are finally learning to work and play with the other kids."

Agent Flynn tosses his empty in the fire, "Well, that was bloody awful." Taking a long swig of water to wash out the taste, the veteran PTB agent turns to Richard's uplit face, "What is the plan when we locate this alien shipwreck?"

Lost in his thoughts, Richard takes a moment before answering, "What? Oh, yeah. We locate the payload." Tapping his vest, he continues, "and then call for help with my satellite-linked transponder." The blood drains from King's face, patting up and down his left and right vest pockets, "Blast it all! I must have lost my transponder at the cavern. This changes everything."

Watching her absent-minded former flame verge on a histrionic display for the ages, Nina stifles a laugh at Richard's expense. Reaching into her pack among the dwindling supply of snack bars, she finds the mustard-yellow transponder and holds it up in the blue fire's glow, "Does it look like this?"

"Thank you, Nina." More relieved than he cared to admit, Richard offers a muted grin toward the bone-tired group, "We all can use some sleep. We should be safe enough within the fire's light."

Griffin Pike | The Rift
12:36 a.m. | October 19, 2044

Sneaking down the last of the steep, narrow chiseled stairs with insane stealth born out of avarice and an unrequited bloodlust, Griffin Pike looks down upon the slumbering fools bathed in the protective blue light, getting fucking shut-eye. Just as weary, if not more, he plods downward, gun in his hand, debating the efficacy of taking out the alien or the dog before making a run for the tree line. Ruminating on a surprise attack, the tall blond looker rises from her bedroll, casting a long flickering shadow onto the carved stairs. Mere steps from paydirt, he freezes with the gun trained on her pretty noggin. After long minutes, he watches the American beauty turn away from the fire and proceed zombielike downslope through a stand of gnarled trees along a trickling, riffling stream he hears but cannot see through the darkness.

Apathetic to the woman's safety, he counts to ten before scurrying down the last steps and making a beeline for the trees. Who cares if the stupid dog and alien live to see one more day? As one of his favorite political heroines once remarked, "What difference does it make."

Conjuring his fantasized vision of the lost ship's lethal bounty in his altered state of mind, he moves over the loose rocks and loamy soil, stumbling over shit in the dark. As his keen vision adjusts, the snaking stream glows pale shades of blue, framing Rachel Haig's statuesque pose along the flowing stream's sandy, rock-strewn bank. Sticking a pin in his misanthropic fever dream, he stalks toward the stellar beauty from behind, within arm's length of her long blond hair shimmering in the dark. He could take her hostage. No. He could do many things. "Mrs. Haig? Rachel? Can you hear me?"

Realizing she is asleep on her feet, a lascivious smile creases his dirty face, "You are a sleeping beauty." Extending his swollen, trembling hand, he dares to touch a wispy lock of hair, curling down her back in the warm, wet stillness.

Rachel twitches and grunts, prompting him to pull his hand back on impulse. After a hesitant pause, he turns and leaves without looking back, reminding himself that his destiny lies upstream. Mrs. Haig's fate is her own.

* * *

Rachel looks down upon her electric blue radiance, "What is

happening to me?"

A familiar male voice penetrates her dream, "You look beautiful."

Pulling her gaze from her transcendence, Rachel sees a vision of her father bathed in a pure white light on the opposite side of the stream, "Dad?"

Not quite touching the ground in his best tuxedo marred by blotchy red stains permeating his white dress shirt under his tailored jacket, he smiles at his girl, *"I miss you so much."*

"It is my fault you were shot. Mom is a wreck."

"Rachel, Miriam is fine, and so is your brother. It is you, my dear, who needs help."

Extending her blue hands and arms outward, she breaks down in tears, "I don't understand."

"Do you remember the last thing I told you?"

"You said something about a blue spark."

"That is not true. I said you are the blue spark."

"But what does that mean?"

"Something wonderful, Rachel."

Frustrated and confused by her father's vague reply, Rachel's tongue-tied comeback is interrupted by a firm grip on her shoulder, pulling her from the paranormal brink, startled and gasping for air, "Oh no. Where am I? Daddy, don't leave me here!"

"Rachel, wake up! You are sleepwalking again. Holy Christ, it is dangerous out here. We need to get back to the fire."

A deafening roar reverberates across the stream, sending tremors through the wet ground.

"What was that?"

Owen tracks black-on-black shadows melding with the gnarled trees, "Don't know. Don't care. We need to get back to the fire."

Richard | The Rift
06:16 a.m. | October 19, 2044

Zint watches Daphne chasing giant dragonflies buzzing the campfire's dying blue embers, "We are not in Kansas anymore, Toto."

Penny and Nina trade nervous smiles, overhearing Zint's witticism while shaking the bedding before rolling and squeezing it into the nylon-cinched sacks. Rachel and Owen douse the fire and collect their scattered trash, stewards of a lost world.

Zint's Oz reference resonates as the first shafts of hazy sunlight filtering through a pea soup ground fog illuminate the otherworldly chasm floor. Richard stoops to study a carnivorous plant digesting a giant shiny beetle mere feet from where he rested his head in the night. Feeling nature's call, he ventures behind a large trunk to execute what dear departed Pembroke called his morning constitutional, "The man did not deserve to die out here." Zipping up, he turns to find a voyeuristic bipedal reptile standing ten inches tall, waving its long tail. Marveling at the intelligent creature, he punctuates the sad remark, "None of us do."

Returning to the camp at the foot of the ancient carved stairs, he bumps past Flynn checking the 12-round mag in his P365, "Excuse me, agent."

"Careful, Richard. Damn, you want to get shot?" Annoyed, Flynn turns to Owen, "How are you set for ammo?"

Owen checks his PTB-issued sidearm, "I have a full clip, but that's it."

Rachel jumps in, "Those Nemesis freaks confiscated my gun. I never saw it again."

Owen expresses abject concern for the group's safety, recalling the beasts he heard roaring in the dark while retrieving his sleepwalking wife, "What about Smythe's rifle?"

Flynn holsters his gun and scratches a rash on his arm, "I would not want to fire that weapon without a proper oiling and cleaning."

"Well, that sucks; bringing down a dinosaur will take more than a 9mm round."

"Bloody hell, Owen. I'm putting you in charge of morale."

The fog lifts halfway up the steep rift walls, filtering sunlight and forming a low ceiling over an undulating, rugged landscape.

A stubborn omnipresent mist clinging to the ground reminds Richard of a trek across the Scottish Moors.

With everyone rested and packed, Richard leads the group toward the stream, "I recommend topping off canteens here. It will take an hour-plus to hike back upstream toward the waterfall."

Owen decides to ask the question on everyone's minds, "How do you know the lost ship is not the other way?"

Richard rinses his hands and splashes the crisp flowing water on his face and through his curly hair, "It has to be there."

Rachel unscrews the cap on her plastic water bottle and dunks it in the icy stream, watching her strange blue glow travel from her palm halfway up her arm, sending a chill down her spine. Ensuring no one saw her arm turn blue, she uncuffs her sleeves, buttoning them at the wrists as her stomach gurgles in protest.

Rehydrating and rinsing off in the cool water, Nina looks down and pulls out a bright red nugget, "What the hell? I found a chunk of ruby."

Penny peers through the ankle-deep current, scooping a handful of sand mixed with green and red flecks shimmering among polished granite, limestone, and quartz pebbles.

Watching the group fan out, splashing among the rocks for more priceless gemstones, Richard whistles, "Hey. Focus people. I am sure there is plenty more of that along the way."

Flynn laughs, "I think I just solved the national debt."

Tromping along the grassy bank, beads of sweat drip from Owen's forehead, gazing up the prehistoric rift's sheer, green-carpeted walls to the thick layer of clouds resembling a frothy head on an ice-cold glass of beer. "You know what sounds good right now?"

Reading her husband's mind over trepidation and doubts from the rest of the hot, sticky group, Rachel replies, "I bet I know, beer."

Owen watches his mind-reading wife approach with a sly smile on her bluish face, "Quit doing that. It is annoying."

Taking the point position, Flynn swings his dull machete through a dense stand of undergrowth, dropping visibility to the green mass before him, impeding progress upstream. Chunking his blade into an odd off-white trunk, he glimpses upward at the underside of a massive toadstool rising ten feet above his head. Swatting away luminous spores floating before his face, Flynn doubles down, "If I come across a bong-toking caterpillar, I'm turning around."

Venturing under alien mushrooms of all shapes, colors, and sizes, Richard notes chicken-sized, purple-feathered dinosaurs hopping among the toadstools, observing the strange intruders without a hint of fear. "Fascinating."

A feathery trio stalks from a stand of red-capped wonders covered in basketball-sized orange spots, blocking Flynn's progression, "Bloody hell, these beasties are freaking me out."

Kicking away a tiny raptor with the temerity to peck at his boot, Owen proffers a nervous laugh, "What's the matter, Agent? You battled aliens under the pyramid. These are just chicken-sized dinosaurs checking us out, right Richard?"

Flynn feigns an attack without waiting for the distracted scientist's response, sending the playful creatures skittering into the bramble. "Yeah, you better run."

The expedition proceeds unimpeded through the fungal forest onto a rocky escarpment. Following the meandering stream, the rift doglegs left, narrowing by half. Picking up the pace, the group fans out with the waterfall roaring somewhere around more bends and curves up ahead. Rachel and Penny turn back to coax a straggling Nina, entranced by shimmering ruby and emerald seams jutting from a prismatic quartz matrix among dripping mosses, orchids, and ferns decorating a massive, jagged outcropping larger than a city bus. "Nina, catch up! We need to stick together."

Nina's blue-eyed gaze widens onto crystallized clusters glittering from nooks and crevices and scattered across the vine and root-congested ground, "Just a minute, I have to see this."

Hefting a heavy stone in a two-handed grip, she breaks off a blood-red chunk, "Rubies are my birthstone. I …."

A foul whoosh of hot air bellows over her from above, stopping her rockhounding in its tracks. With a terrifying dread overwhelming her senses, she cranes upward at the toothy head of a ten-ton feathered beast unmasking from its camouflaged position straddling the craggy formation. Unable to move or scream, Nina closes her eyes and waits as the dinosaur lowers its enormous head, enveloping Nina's 5-6 frame in a delicate bite.

Just like that, Nina is gone.

Witnessing Nina's horrifying death from only 30 yards up the path, Penny and Rachel's screams ratchet through the early morning heat and humidity.

The methodical single-file morning trek to the lost ship disintegrates into a panicked run for their lives. Rachel and Penny burst past a surprised Richard, Owen, and Flynn, hellbent on escaping the gigantic prehistoric creature and poor Nina's fate by hiding in a dense bamboo grove tangled with creeping vines and roots.

Owen mirrors Rachel's frantic pace over, under, and around slippery logs and low branches covered in moss, fungi, snakes, bugs, and twisted roots and vines. Coming to a concealed clearing, the panting pair skid to an abrupt stop. Bent at the waist, sucking in hot, wet air, struggling to catch their breaths, the former financier straightens and turns to his inconsolable wife, brushing aside long strands of wet hair hanging in clumps across her face. Unaware, a giant theropod ate Nina in a single bite; he blurts out, "What was it you said to me? Oh yeah. Come on, Owen. Let's join the PTB. What else do we have to do? It will be fun."

"Shut up, Owen! Just shut up."

Penny enters the tamped-down spot from another direction with tears streaming down her face, "We lost Nina."

Daphne's bark precedes her entrance, followed by Zint and Richard, huffing and puffing, doubled over in exhaustion.

Owen checks through the semi-darkness, "What happened to Flynn?"

"I'm here." Flynn drops from a tree limb, snapping through thin branches on the way back down, "Bloody fucking hell. What was that?"

Catching his breath, trying to keep it together, Richard ventures a guess, "*Giganotosaurus carolinii* if I had to guess. T-Rex's southern cousin. Much larger and apparently able to blend seamlessly into its surroundings."

Penny plops on a log to rest. Checking for reptiles, she picks up a sticky piece of ostrich-sized eggshell, "Hey, what is this?"

Richard's face pales, realizing they are standing in a nest, "Let's move on from this place before the parents return."

* * *

The enormous dinosaur from a species that ruled the Gondwana forests of the late Cretaceous has no taste for human flesh. Blundering through the lost ship's time portal into a new world as a much smaller juvenile five years earlier, the shy creature drops Nina's limp form atop a massive blood-red gemstone cluster in a thick, stinky puddle of drool. Suffering only scrapes, contusions, and a painful ankle injury, Nina swipes gunk from her face, seeing shades of red through her blurred vision. Assuming it is her blood, she cowers on her side. Hearing the dinosaur stomp off in search of more amenable prey, a sharp pain jabs in her side. Thinking the worst, she removes the collapsible walking stick down spot.

"I cannot wait to get out of this fucking jungle."

Bored to tears and fighting drowsiness, he accesses a baggie of Brazilian marching powder and sprinkles a line on the side of his bony hand. In mid-snort, a low growl resonates in his sweaty head.

"What the hell …."

Wiping tell-tale white off his crooked nose, he scoops his short-barrel semi-automatic rifle and peers through the night-vision scope into the deep-black bramble. A shadowy form skulks past his view, only twenty alarming yards from his solitary post.

With the forgotten cigarette dangling from his thick lower lip, the gawky Russian who has bagged big game from Siberia to the African Veldt hunkers to a knee and checks his weapon, "A Jaguar—never bagged one of those before."

With a bitter and intoxicating taste of cocaine trickling through his sinuses and throat, he aims into the forest, but the big cat is gone.

Lowering his assault rifle, he flicks his cigarette into the underbrush in disgust.

The sound of a snapping branch just beyond his hide sends a gusher of adrenalin coursing through Leon's feverish brain. Freezing ramrod still, his accelerated heartbeat thump-thumping in his ears, the 32-year-old clutches his rifle in a sweaty grip, pushing his bony finger through the trigger housing. Bugged-out eyes dart from side to side, scanning his world reduced to a six-foot kill box as the shadowed form returns, staring through him with glowing green eyes piercing his soul.

Thunderstruck by the angular, long-necked bipedal animal, he watches its elongated tail swinging in a gentle arc. With a sudden burst of acute awareness, he squeezes the trigger, not realizing he neglected to disengage the safety. In a panic, he fumbles for the switch, unable to make his hands work. Crying terrorized sobs, the gun slips from his clumsy hands as the animal looms before him, its sharp-toothed pointed snout at the end of a long feathery neck like an overgrown ostrich—

more curious than hungry.

Inching backward to clear space between himself and the terrifying lizard, Leon's bulging peripheral vision catches another much larger head lowering through the branches like it had been there the whole time. Dripping hot stinging drool from its gaping toothy maw, the beast crushes the fragile sobbing man, grinding his head and torso into a bloody paste while whipping dangling limbs from side to side, sending torn fleshy body parts flinging into the underbrush like a gruesome rag doll.

The creature drops chunks of Leon to the hide near his rifle and recedes into the trees like it was never there, leaving smaller long-necked dinosaurs to fight over his gory remains before dragging bits of meat back into the jungle.

Henri DeVille | The Lake
05:15 a.m. | October 17, 2044

Henri jabs a rifle butt into Smythe's chest, rousting him from his beauty sleep.

Doubling over sideways and coughing out a blue streak of expletives, Smythe glares at his hulking boss, "Bloody fucking hell, DeVille, what's your problem?"

"Where is Leon? You should have relieved him on watch an hour ago. Can't you dolts do anything right."

Scrambling onto his feet in full CYA mode, Smythe protests, "It's not my fault. He was supposed to wake me up. That was the fucking plan, you cunt."

Enraged by the stammering fool's juvenile response, DeVille grabs Smythe by the shirt collar and lifts him off the ground, "Call me that again, I dare you. You fuckers have no idea—this place will kill us all." Thrusting the useless Brit onto the dirt, he spits, "Get up and take

Rachel gave her earlier that morning and begins to cry tears of relief.

Griffin Pike | The Lost Ship
10:18 a.m. | October 19, 2044

Soaked in blood and sweat after a harrowing trek up the otherworldly rift teeming with terrible beasts, Griffin Pike burst from the undergrowth, splashes across the streambed, and stares up at an ancient hulk. Climbing to the exposed section of skeletal framework amid thick jungle growing out of Cretaceous-era strata high up the wall, he pulls his aching body into a shipwreck that endured the ravages of time. Determined to pursue his apocalyptic passion to its inglorious conclusion, he crawls through a lichen-encrusted portal into a maze of passages littered with cobwebs, debris, and animal feces in search of the world killer's release mechanism.

Uncle Charles would be so proud.

Owen | The Lost Ship
12:24 p.m. | October 19, 2044

Shaken to their cores by Nina's horrible death, the downtrodden group plods behind Richard's meandering footsteps predicated on base assumptions of what a 90 million-year-old shipwreck could look like.

Flynn presses his PTB colleague, "Professor, the fact is you have no idea what to look for, or if it even exists, isn't that right. This entire excursion was bollocks from the start."

Face reddening with anger, King turns on the grieving agent, "See here, Flynn. No one asked you and Nina to tag along. You are twisting her horrible death into my fault." Richard King stammers, close to a total breakdown, "I loved Nina!"

Witnessing both men starting to lose it, Owen cuts between them to stop the confrontation from getting worse than it already is. "Say, Professor, how about letting someone else take a crack at finding the needle in the proverbial haystack."

Richard surrenders with a look of abject failure, "Be my guest, young man."

Owen crumples Richard's scribbled notes and tosses them into the bushes. Lightening the mood, he offers his best roguish smile, "Screw Smokey the Bear. He's never been here." Refocusing on the lost ship, Owen presses the learned man of science and his ultra-keen intellect, "Professor King. If you were a shipwreck buried, exposed, and buried again, hundreds, maybe thousands of times over millions and millions of years, where might you end up?"

The PTB scientist's dirty, sweat-smeared face widens into a triumphant grin, "That is brilliant, young man. The shipwreck will be within layers of Cretaceous era strata higher up the rift's steep walls."

Cutting down to the fast-flowing streambed, the group peers through the milky haze in silence, scanning the green-carpeted cliffs. After long minutes, Penny spies an incongruent shape jutting through the clouds up the sheer rift wall rising high overhead. "Hey! What is that? Is that what we are looking for?"

Following her gaze, Richard sees it too, "How fitting that a Pennywell is the first person to lay eyes upon the lost ship."

Rachel | The Lost Ship
01:15 p.m. | October 19, 2044

Penny leads Richard by the hand, wading upstream over slippery rocks around another shallow bend, both never taking their eyes off the prize. Zint and Daphne follow close behind, with Flynn keeping a sharp eye for voracious predators, both large and small.

Trailing behind the others, Owen helps Rachel climb over a large fallen log and notices her forearms glowing blue through her thin sleeves. Opting to ignore the weird affliction's apparent progression up to her elbows from her palms, he offers a comforting smile, "Hey, we made it."

Swallowing back a sudden queasiness, Rachel forces a smile, "Yeah. How about that."

Owen scratches his stubbly beard and catches his intrepid partner's wavering stance on slippery rocks in the knee-deep rushing water. Unwilling to turn a blind eye to her obvious discomfort, he places an arm around her thin waist, "You know, Rachel, I can carry you."

Rachel waits for the others to separate farther ahead, amused by her husband's chivalrous offer despite anxiety swelling within her, "I'll be fine. Probably the beanie weenies." Feeling goosebumps on her glowing arms, she exhales, trying to act natural, "I have a question for you, Owen."

"Fire away."

"Do you like the name Hannah?"

Owen glances around, considering the question straight out of left field, "Yeah. I do." Pulling his wife forward to catch up with the others, he laughs, "If it is a girl, that is."

Feeling sick and somewhat patronized, Rachel pulls back, "Hey. Look at me. I'm serious." Biting her lip and staunching real tears, "It is a girl, and she will be the first."

With a sigh, Owen glances upstream where their merry little band is whooping and backslapping in the shadow of the massive skeletal alien shipwreck, jutting from solid rock and jungle high up the sheer cliff wall, "Yeah, Rach, I know, our first. I want more, but we can cross that ...."

Rachel shakes her head and presses her fingers to Owen's chapped lips, "Stop talking. Just listen to my words. She will be the first of a new kind."

Nina | The Lost Ship
01:43 p.m. | October 19, 2044

Downstream from the thunderous waterfall resounding through a pervasive mist soaking everything, the weary group drops what's left of their bags and gear on a sandy spit along the fast-flowing stream with thick jungle encroaching on all sides.

Richard peers high above their position at the massive oddity jutting from the dense green before turning to Owen, "Are you joining Flynn and me? The sooner we get up there, the sooner we can all go home."

Still mulling Rachel's cryptic words and masking alarm at an almost ethereal blueness permeating her skin, Owen turns to the group, "I'm just worried about Rachel. She is sicker than she is letting on."

Ignoring Forest Ghosts watching them that only she can see, Rachel coughs and wavers back onto her feet, "Owen, I'll be fine. Richard and Flynn need you more than I do right now. Dr. Penny will look after me."

Owen shakes his head and frowns, "Are you sure? I am worried about you, Rachel. You are turning blue in places where you were not blue before. That is far from normal."

Rachel smiles, her face tinged with a pale blue skin tone, "Owen, my dearest sweet husband. Your guess is as good as mine. All I know is something down here seems to have activated my blue spark in new ways."

Richard King winces and turns away at the mention of the words blue spark.

Noting Professor King's overt reaction, Rachel invades the scientist's guilt-riddled mind, *"I know my father made a deal with the PTB and traded me for real estate. And I know you led the experimentation performed on me that started before I was even born. The pieces are coming together. Richard, I don't blame you, so please do not feel guilty. What was done is done and there is no going back.*

Acknowledging her telepathy with a sheepish nod, Richard wipes tears from his eyes and picks up his sack to remove unneeded extra weight.

After clearing the air with Richard, Rachel turns to Owen, "The energy within me is mutating from what I experienced under the pyramids into something even more powerful." With a wink toward Richard, she adds, "Maybe my transformation is the real purpose of this expedition, right Richard?"

Owen's brow furrows, glancing back toward Professor King, maintaining a safe distance but within earshot of their conversation.

"Hey Richard, should we worry about the baby?"

"The baby? Oh, you mean *your* baby, of course. Where was my mind wandering off to?" Richard pulls the strap from his lightened pack over a shoulder and considers the question, "No. Penny checked the vitals, and both mother and baby appeared healthy." Smiling toward Rachel, he nods and adds, "I surmise you are suffering from morning sickness exacerbated by the intense heat and humidity coupled with the extreme situation we find ourselves in ... and the so-called blue spark, of course."

Anxious to return to civilization and discover what happened to Nicole and the other escapees, Flynn breaks up the meeting, "Come on, then, let's get moving."

Richard smiles, "Quite right, Agent Flynn ... Owen? Are you coming?"

Owen kisses his wife's light blue cheek, "Well, I always wanted to marry a Smurf. Yeah, let's go."

* * *

Owen grabs the rope and follows Richard and Flynn, disappearing into the thick undergrowth on their way up the jagged cliff to seek out the shipwreck's apocalyptic payload. Igniting a roaring alien blaze, the pregnant 24-year-old Rachel shakes off a dizzying head swoon, "And that is why I am staying down here."

None too thrilled with the prospect of another climb, Penny was more than happy to stay behind with the woozy Rachel and set up the camp on a sandy streamside spit far below the shipwreck's exposed skeletal hulk.

Organizing the gear and spreading out a tarp, Penny catches a tail-wagging Daphne trailing Zint into the underbrush, "Hey! Where are you two going?"

Zint's earnest reply resonates in her mind, "I do not want to interfere with Richard's mission. I need to address another matter buried deep inside the shipwreck."

Still parsing the alien's abrupt departure, Penny looks back and finds a stricken Rachel staggering down to the stream, puking up vomit. Hesitant to interfere with Owen's beautiful wife, Penny calls out, "Is there anything I can do for you, Rachel?"

Waving off a well-meaning Penny without turning around, Rachel vomits and coughs thick strands of drool into the ankle-deep water as her blurred vision latches onto a hazed human form standing across the stream.

Concerned for Mrs. Haig's health but understanding when to back off, Penny resumes stacking the bags and counting the dwindling rations. Coping with a flood of unbelievable experiences over the past weeks, her intuition prompts a quick doubletake toward Rachel. The Harvard grad's hazel eyes widen in terror at a naked, bloodied, one-arm Sapphire standing toe-to-toe before Rachel with a long glistening blade in her clenched one-handed grip.

Trying to fathom the horrible woman's shocking return from the dead, Penny screams for help as Nina breaks from the undergrowth, splashes across the stream, and impales Sapphire with a toxin-laced blade sprung from the tip of her walking stick.

Her bald head twitching in spastic movements, Sapphire drops the knife and clutches the sharp blade poking through her perfect chest as synthetic blood spurts and gurgles from ruby lips on her shocked face. Wheeling to face the breathless Nina, the replicant beams a mean smile and a middle-finger salute before pitching sideways into the rushing water.

With a primal scream, Nina pushes Sapphire's twitching form into a deep channel and watches her float downstream before staggering from the water and collapsing beside the passed-out Rachel on the sandy bank.

Penny rushes forward, "Nina! You are alive!"

"It appears I made it here in the nick of time. Where is everyone?"

Penny's index finger points straight up, "The boys left for the ship a while ago. Do you think Sapphire was going to kill Rachel?"

Nina shrugs, "Who knows, but it was not worth the risk to wait around and find out."

Regaining consciousness, Rachel's green eyes widen onto the warrior goddess, Nina Madsen, "Thanks, Nina."

Penny hands Rachel and Nina cool, wet towels, "We thought you were dead. A massive dinosaur swallowed you whole."

Recovering her trademark swagger, an effervescent smile for the ages widens on Nina's dirty, splattered face, "Well, ladies, despite my current battered and bruised appearance, I have good taste, but apparently, I don't taste that good."

Griffin Pike | The Lost Ship
01:55 p.m. | October 19, 2044

After hours of dead-ends and roadblocks penetrating the lost ship's elongated fuselage buried on its side beneath tons of rock, Griffin Pike reaches what his addled brain surmises to be the uppermost levels—where the command decks would have to be. Gritting pearly whites contrasting with his dirt-smeared face, the maniacal mogul exerts every ounce of strength left in his tattered and torn body, forcing an ossified alien bulkhead sideways enough to squeeze past. Flicking his penlight through motes stirred by his breach, he enters a chamber half-buried in sediment peppered with bone fragments and rocks covering what once was but is no more.

Scraping across the uneven surface on his hands and knees, leaving a bloody trail in his wake, he reminds himself there is no going back. Oblivious to a deep gash in his left palm, he scuttles toward an aperture in a half-collapsed wall where the space narrows to four feet, butting against a stalactite and fumbling his penlight in the process. The dim beam illuminates a hideous alien skull staring at him through the total blackness with a mocking smile on its toothless face.

"Wipe that shit-eating grin off your fucking ugly mug."

Examining the jagged oblong hole, he aims the light back on the skull, releasing his last shred of sanity, "I'm looking for the command deck. Is it through here?"

Richard | The Lost Ship
02:15 p.m. | October 19, 2044

Unaware of the drama unfolding far below, the lost ship's broken and corroded infrastructure comes into sharper detail as Richard King pulls upward through the soupy swirling mist, following Owen's lead. With a giddy rush of anticipation swelling from within, the intrepid scientist calls out, "It is in remarkable condition considering its age."

Adjusting the well-used nylon rope coiled over his shoulder, Owen grunts a reply, grabbing a thick vine to pull atop the last slippery ledge.

Straggling behind, Flynn shoos aside a spider the size of his hand, "Bloody hell."

Waiting for his slower colleagues to join him, Owen surveys an impenetrable swath of jungle covering the deep ledge to where the rift's sheer wall rises hundreds of feet higher overhead. "Man, this place is creepy. I wish Rachel could have come along."

Richard brushes off, adjusting his light pack and standing beside Owen, "We made it."

Owen helps Flynn onto his feet, "Thanks, Owen. Watch out for the spiders."

Owen smiles, "Noted."

The trio catches their breath, gawking at massive fins rising above the organic-shaped superstructure and out over the expeditions' streamside encampment far below.

Richard can't help but smile, "Impressive. Most impressive."

Flynn frowns, "Yeah, but isn't it a bit of a miracle that this whole ship was not buried underground like a dinosaur fossil?"

Richard pivots to the PTB agent, "That is a good point, Agent Flynn." Gesturing toward the continuation of the rift's sheer cliff beyond the encroaching jungle, "I would wager what we are looking at represents less than 20 percent of the shipwreck, with the rest buried in solid rock formed and reformed over 90 million years."

Owen jumps in, "Are you saying there is only a 1 in 5 chance that this payload we are looking for is recoverable?"

Absorbing the question, Richard nods, "Yes. However, the PTB is not willing to risk a world killer falling into the wrong hands based on a twenty percent probability."

Flynn smiles, "I'd take those odds."

"Precisely."

Owen shrugs, "Well, we are here. Lead the way, Professor."

Richard hoists himself atop a cracked section of the alien airframe serving as a ramp. Scouting a path forward, he hunches under a protruding chunk of the root-covered fuselage before disappearing inside the lost ship. At the threshold of discovery, he pulls a bandanna over his nose to ward against the puddled interior's jungle rot and decay mixed with guano. Undaunted, the scientist clears cobwebs and flicks his torch beam on a snarled mass of pipe and ductwork snaking through a long tubular shaft pierced by light seeping through countless fissures in the outer wall.

Owen peers at Richard's progress, already ten feet into the darkness, "Man, it smells like shit in here."

Flynn ties a handkerchief around his sweaty head, "Bat shit, to be precise."

Stumbling over a pipe, Richard pauses and turns to the reluctant pair, "Come along, gentlemen. We must find the payload."

Flynn says what Owen is thinking, "Any idea what the bloody thing will look like?"

King's retort echoes through the darkness, "It's like pornography; you will know it when you see it."

Flynn exhales through his cloth face covering and steps inside, "Ah, what the hell."

Advancing to the shaft's end, Richard pauses at a three-way intersection. None too keen on getting lost inside the lost ship, a faint draft draws him up a shallow incline toward gauzy light filtering through a torn bulkhead. Angling his weary frame from the stale passage, he steps onto a narrow ledge at one end of the skeletal airframe visible from the streambed far below. Breathing the fresh air, Richard balances on a gnarled spine interconnected with a succession of exposed ribs supporting the fuselage's upper half, still covered in a metallic alloy skin resistant to the ravages of time. Venturing along the four-foot wide beam, Richard passes through vaporous clouds wafting through the gymnasium-sized space, noting bats nesting high up at the hollowed-out ceiling. Turning back toward Owen and Flynn, gulping air into their lungs, "It appears the ship is broken into different sections like pieces of a massive puzzle. You can see where the space between the ribs formed multiple levels in its day, inferring this section of the ship is indeed on its side."

Owen nods, studying the alien framework, "So, you are saying, in its day, this thing stood tall, like a Saturn rocket."

Lost in thought, Richard hunches down, smoothing his thick fingers over hexagonal rivets lining the corroded, lichen-covered metal. "What it must have been like to set down on a long-forgotten supercontinent at the height of the Cretaceous era."

Flynn wonders aloud, "Why is the lower half open air but the upper half intact?"

Richard looks up, "Yes. That is a bit odd."

Eager to find the payload and go home, Owen's mind races, "Just spitballing here, but what if that specific section of the craft was reinforced because it has the payload mounted on its opposite outer side." Reveling in his moment of brilliance, Owen looks from Flynn to Richard and back again with a broad smile on his bearded face. "Well? Do you two have any better ideas?"

Richard scans upward, "It could be, young man. Where we are standing, the outer fuselage deteriorated a long time ago. That is quite obvious by the look of things."

Flynn laughs, "Owen, you are quite the optimist. Did anyone ever tell you that?"

"I have been called a lot worse." Tossing the coiled rope at Flynn, Owen balances along the spine to the far end and angles around a curved rib to look far down at their streamside camp. Hoping to find Rachel relaxing, his sharp eyes lock onto a sight for sore eyes, "You both are not going to believe what I am seeing."

Weighing the least dangerous way of climbing four stories up and out onto the ship's upper side, Flynn turns back to Owen, "What? Get over here and help. I don't know what the fuck I'm doing. You are the bloody climbing expert."

"I see Nina Madsen down there."

Richard almost falls, catching himself from a precipitous drop, rushing to peer over Owen's shoulder straight down, "That is Nina. Thank God she is alive."

Flynn crowds behind the gawking pair, "Move over, I want to see." Looking more like ants, he sees his precious Nina and smiles, "The woman has nine lives.

***

Using the even-spaced hexagonal rivets as handholds, Owen free climbs to the rafters inside the cavernous space and pulls himself atop a cross-beam. Checking the bats roosting higher up, he ties the rope to the beam and calls down, "Okay. It is the best I can do. There are plenty of crisscrossing girders up here for support—as long as you don't mind a little bird and bat shit." Gesturing toward light leaking through a curved orifice centered in the arched ceiling, "After you guys get up here, we can climb out through that hole and see what is up there."

With the nylon rope dangling between them, Flynn smiles at Richard, "Age before beauty, mate."

***

Owen pokes his head out of a massive nacelle molded into the airframe, reconning the lost ship's upper half.

Richard holds tight to the lower rungs below Owen's boots and angles upward, "What can you see?"

Hoisting himself over the curved rim, Owen sits on the edge and catches his breath, "Uh, for starters, it is fucking high, and there is very little room to maneuver."

Richard pulls himself out of the odd swooped nacelle, scooching beside Owen with his boots dangling down the curved side, "What now?"

Owen sighs, "We came all the way up here." Using a crusted seam between the nacelle and the airframe as a foothold, he slides his backside along the outside of the craft, grasping rivets, knowing one slip means instant death. "Richard, stay here. I will climb out there and have a look."

Watching a flight of bright blue macaws flying through the warm, humid air, Richard maintains a white-knuckled grip on the ledge. Fighting dizziness, he sees Owen disappear around the massive metal protrusion obstructing a line of sight down the fuselage jutting over the rift. Cursing Flynn for chickening out, the scientist hears Owen's triumphant voice over the omnipresent jungle noise, "That has to be the payload. I cannot believe it! The fucking thing looks like a cruise missile!"

Internalizing a sudden bout of agoraphobia, Richard grits his teeth and follows Owen's careful footsteps along the sloped ledge. "I must see this thing for myself." In a loud voice, he calls to Owen, "Stay there! I am coming out!"

Zint | The Lost Ship
02:31 p.m. | October 19, 2044

Leading Daphne up a less treacherous but longer trail, the odd couple reach the lost ship and move through the stinky shaft.

Daphne whimpers, splashing through a greasy puddle.

"It is okay, girl. Nothing will harm us. I am sorry about the smells."

At the three-way intersection, Zint leads the German Shepherd on a quest for the ship's operational warp drive time portal. Like an open door, it allows a prehistoric menagerie to enter a future world 90 million years removed from their time on Earth.

Griffin Pike | The Lost Ship
03:40 p.m. | October 19, 2044

Hearing a dog's bark echoing from within the ship's ancient passageways, Griffin Pike widens the portal, using the laughing alien's broken skull as a shovel to clear away loosened debris. Crawling through the narrow space, he shines the penlight onto a jumble of alien and dinosaur bones half-buried in a swirled foundation of solid rock across the lost ship's former command deck. Pulling himself across the dead, his bloodied hand grasps the arm of a curved chair jutting from the sandstone at an angle where the upper half of an alien's skeletal remains rest frozen in time, guarding a retrofitted box topped with a simple button mechanism.

At the climax of his journey, a dizzying, almost orgasmic elation overwhelms Griffin Pike, "Press the button and destroy the world. Fuck them all." His laughter fades, ruminating on his stupid species, "They had their chance. I would have made a great ruler. Why could no one see that?"

Pulling closer to the petrified contraption, he places his palm on the convex button, smearing it blood red. Gathering himself in the claustrophobic space, he pushes down on the button, but the blasted thing is frozen. "Fuck!"

Squashing panic and disappointment, Pike's crazed bulging eyeballs search around his prone form for some kind of blunt instrument. Grabbing hold of a foot-long metallic chunk, the once-brilliant engineer marvels at the alien alloy, noting its mass far exceeds its weight. With a shrug, he purges last-second thoughts of escaping to his factory to back-engineer the metal compound. No. It is over. He smashes metal atop the button, creating a shower of sparks but no movement. Striking the button again produces the same result. Weeping, he continues bludgeoning the switch as an uncontrollable rage overwhelms his addled brain until a sharp crack resonates through the space. Heaving with

exhaustion, he stares at the button and waits.

A mechanical thunk-thunk precedes the control button lowering through an aperture in the calcified box. For a heartbeat, nothing happens before a violent tremor permeates the command deck.

Griffin's eyes widen in horror, "What have I done?"

A deafening crack and the low ceiling above Griffin Pike's head collapses, flattening the SATstar mogul atop the alien captain's bone fragments on the shipwreck's erstwhile bridge in a cloud of dust and dirt.

Engineered to withstand the rigors of interstellar space travel, the Empire Gray cargo ship's vast inner workings lie dormant, broken, or buried within tons of rock. Yet after 90 million years, the world killer payload receives the generated electrical pulse that initiates the apocalyptic nuclear launch sequence.

Owen | The Lost Ship

04:12 p.m. | October 19, 2044

Richard joins Owen, staring at the 90-million-year-old cruise missile held at a 45-degree angle by struts extending from the lost ship's tough metallic skin near its outermost point.

Owen slaps Richard on the back, "There is your bloody world killer, Professor King. Hanging out for all to see like a Times Square flasher on a Saturday night."

Richard turns to the crass American, "Bear in mind, that line will be recorded in history books for time immemorial."

Still chuckling, Owen climbs over a second protrusion to examine how it is attached to the ship, "There must be some kind of release mechanism."

Richard nods, "That would be somewhere within the ship or perhaps triggered by altitude or speed ... Oh no ...."

A series of violent tremors knock Richard off his feet. Sliding down the fuselage, he clings to a wet, slippery handhold by his fingertips.

Regaining his balance on the shuddering craft, Owen slides to the scientist's perilous position with his arms outstretched, "Grab my hands, Richard. It is a long way down."

Grasping hold for dear life, Richard scrabbles back to relative safety at the top of the rounded fuselage as the shaking intensifies. Heaving with fright and exhaustion, they cover their ears and duck as a conical energy blast from the missile shoots overhead past their position.

A gut-wrenching rip resounds through the ship as the world killer missile—aiming downward at a sharp angle—pulls against frozen struts bracing it to the fuselage.

The blood drains from Owen's face, "We are at ground zero for the end of the world."

Richard's eyes widen, recognizing a pattern in the world killer's rhythmic pulsations, "It is not stuck, Owen. The missile is counting down to a release."

Rachel | The Lost Ship
04:14 p.m. | October 19, 2044

After the harrowing encounter with the one-armed replicant bent on murderous revenge, Nina supports a groggy Rachel to the fire. She collapses atop a spread-out bedroll in vomit-stained long sleeves and passes out cold.

Gobsmacked by the electric blue glow permeating Rachel's body from head to toe, Penny kneels beside her in the sand, checking her vitals.

With her injuries forgotten, Nina peppers the young doctor for an update, "What is happening to her? Penny, you are a doctor. We need to do something. She is turning blue."

Penny turns to the distraught Nina, noting her swollen, bruised ankle and numerous cuts and scrapes over her injured body. "Nina, please sit down. Rachel is suffering from a bout of early pregnancy morning sickness. Her blue glow stems from some kind of bioluminescent mutation. Maybe it is some new viral strain she picked up here in the jungle. I don't know."

Nina smiles and wipes her brow in the heat, "Perhaps. Please keep an eye on her. I am going to find Richard's alien med bag. My leg is killing me."

Penny sighs, "How did you … It is a bad sprain or possibly a fracture. Either way, you need to stay off of it. Let me find the drugs."

Searching through Richard's bag of tricks for the powdered pain-killer, a jarring earthquake knocks her to the ground.

As the relentless shuddering and shaking elevate, avalanches of loosened rocks, boulders, and jungle cascade into the narrow rift, crashing around the campsite.

Nina drops to the sand and lays flat on her belly, covering her head from the pelting rocks and dirt flying in every direction. Venturing a peek toward Rachel's bedroll, she finds it empty. Pushing up on her elbows, she scans through the chaos and sees the tall blond stripped down to khaki shorts and an olive-green tee, midstream staring straight up at the lost ship. Nina follows her friend's gaze upward and sees the operational missile at the epicenter of the maelstrom.

"Rachel! Come back. It is not safe!"

Penny ducks to Nina's side, holding a bleeding gash on her forehead, "What is she doing?"

Nina shakes her head, "I don't know."

* * *

Oblivious to the tumultuous chaos rocking the rift, Rachel walks barefoot over the sand, shedding her vomit-covered shirt and wading midstream into roiling water. Locking her glowing green eyes through the lost ship's superstructure onto the missile's conical burner, blasting a stream of fire up the chasm at a 45-degree angle, a prophetic vibrancy swells through every cell of her transhuman form. Raising her outstretched hands above her head, she manipulates the gravitational energy surrounding her form and lifts from the streambed into the air, her supernatural translucence glowing bright blue, elevating through billowing clouds of rock and sand swirling around the misty chasm.

Ascending to a hovering position ten feet from the world killer's rounded nosecone, Rachel Haig pushes her hands forward, applying an equivalent opposing force to the missile—milliseconds post ripping free of the lost ship's hull after 90 million years of stasis. Suspending the armed and activated alien doomsday projectile in a state of equilibrium high above the rift floor, the intense heat exchange burns through her clothes and flowing blond mane. Struggling to keep it together, she concentrates on the energized cone of fire shooting from the missile's tail, watching it ebb as her radiance dims while lowering herself and the weapon to 15 feet above the stream.

With her hair and skin ablaze, Rachel allows the weapon to splash down nose first into the roiling stream with its superheated tail section jutting through a vaporous cloud of steam wafting into the canyon.

Plummeting into the water, the blue glow fades from Rachel's burned body as Nina splashes into the deep pool to pull her out before she drowns. Penny grabs a side and helps Nina drag her onto the sand before accessing the medical kit and donning a stethoscope. Noting Rachel's shallow breaths, she feels for a pulse. Motioning for an apoplectic Nina to hush, Penny places the stethoscope's diaphragm on Rachel's scorched belly and listens for a fetal heartbeat. "Damn. Nina, how far along is Rachel's pregnancy?"

Staunching agonized tears at beautiful magnetic Rachel's burned and bloodied form lying motionless on the sand, Nina blurts out, "I have no idea."

Penny tries again, moving the diaphragm around, listening, and muttering, "Come on. Come on."

More tears stream from Nina's swollen eyes, waiting with bated breath, "Please, God, don't. She has been through enough."

After more intense minutes, Penny whoops, "There you are! I hear you in there." Sliding the stethoscope around her neck, she turns to Nina and smiles, "I had trouble finding it, but the baby's heartbeat is strong."

Nina shakes her head, "What about Rachel?"

"She is another story." Penny reaches inside the bag for the gauze and studies a jar marked medicinal salve in Richard's chicken scratch writing. "Even though she was literally on fire, most of her burns are first and second-degree. I am sick about her scorched hair, but that will grow back. Let's clean her up as best as possible and wrap her up in what's left of the gauze.

Owen | The Lost Ship

04:52 p.m. | October 19, 2044

Witnessing Rachel's supernatural spectacle from the lost ship's vantage, a terrified Owen helps Richard scramble down, rejoining a gobsmacked Flynn and retracing a path through the ship and down the steep cliff. Rushing across the sandy bank littered with rocks and debris, the missile still smoking and ticking in the stream, he slides to Rachel's side. Searching Penny's eyes for answers, he asks, "How is she?"

With a doubletake, he turns to Nina like he is looking at a ghost, "How did you …."

In unison, Penny and Nina reply, "Don't ask."

With her trademark "everything will be fine" smile," Nina limps over and sits beside Owen, hugging his arm, "I never got to see you two at the hospital in Cairo after the pyramid rescue."

Owen pats her back, "You were, shall we say, detained." With an irony-laced chuckle, "Seeing Rachel wrapped like a mummy rekindles horrible memories we were just starting to leave behind. And now, I am afraid she has somehow transmogrified into Superman."

Nina elbows his side, "That makes you Lois Lane."

"Uh, yeah, I guess it does."

Flynn emerges from behind and sweeps Nina off her feet, holding her in a bear hug. "I am so glad you survived." Looking down at the unconscious Rachel, lying beside the blue fire, "Jesus, she is in bad shape."

Nina releases from his embrace, "You really have no filter, Agent Flynn."

Richard sneaks up from behind, "Hey! It's Nina, back from the bowels of a prehistoric theropod. That must have been some trip."

Nina turns with a sarcastic look on her battered face, "Good to see you, too, Richard."

Penny looks up from Rachel's side, "Tell them about Sapphire."

The men look at Nina with inquisitive expressions on their dirty faces.

Nina Madsen revels in her moment, beaming a bright smile, "I killed her."

"Bloody hell, Nina, you are badass."

"Well, as it happens, she was a replicant. Quite similar to the sisters, but with her evil button switched to ON."

Owen laughs, "I knew it!"

Walking down to the stream, Richard King studies the ancient alien technology, marveling at its similarities to a proliferation of hypersonic nukes in modern-day military arsenals. Flynn stands beside him, "So that thing has enough payload to destroy the world?"

Richard shakes his head, "No. The initial blast would impact a small area. It is the secondary viral threat embedded inside we need to access and safeguard from a dangerous world. Griffin Pike's megalomaniacal tendencies are the tip of the iceberg."

Flynn hands him the yellow transponder, "Nina told me to give you this. It is past time to call in the cavalry."

Zint | The Lost Ship
06:02 p.m. | October 19, 2044

After hours of searching the lost ship's passages for the operational warp drive chamber responsible for the prehistoric beasts roaming the modern-day jungle, Zint turns to the panting German Shepherd, "I am sorry, Daphne, but I cannot find the engineering decks. Let's go back."

Retracing their path, a violent quake ruptures weakened bulkheads blocking the way out.

Daphne's bark directs Zint toward a tunnel exposed by a collapsed facade through a suffocating cloud of dust and debris.

Patting his tail-wagging companion, "Very good, Daphne; when one door closes, another opens. Lead the way, my friend."

The dog picks a cautious path over and around a knotted tangle of mesh, wiring, and rubble into a domed ventricular expanse ringed with ancient alien tech mounted at intervals along a raised platform. Centered within the echoing room, the warp drive's energized 8-meter Möbius strip hums on an infinite cyclical loop.

Zint keeps a watchful eye on Daphne while considering their options. "The way out is blocked, so deactivating the warp drive is no longer necessary. However, we are also stuck here." Noting the functioning warp drive, the resourceful alien offers Daphne the last of their water, "Drink this, Daphne. I need you to stay hydrated and strong."

Moving to a workstation, Zint brushes silt off a circular console and frowns at indecipherable glyphs captioning complex instrumentation from eons before his time. Taking his best guess at energizing the time portal and adjusting its settings, he shakes his bulbous gray head, "Educated guesses are not the answer. I am tired."

Daphne barks.

Focused on the cryptic warp drive console, Zint pats the German Shepherd's head, "I know, my friend. I am trying my best."

Bark! Bark!

Zint turns his large oval eyes onto the object of Daphne's excitement, the Möbius loop accelerating to a radiant blurred portal showing through to a tropical beach on the other side. Before he can react, the scene transitions to a rural country lane.

Turning back to the lit display, he inputs another series of commands but cannot sync it to a specific date or place. Frustrated by the random locations appearing like an out-of-control screensaver, he checks again and sees desert sands, "It is looping to places in time at random. I may have caused that. I am sorry."

An electrified blast jolts the chamber. Cognizant that the warp drive is teetering on the brink of an epic overload, Zint pats Daphne and repeats a favorite proverb, "He who hesitates is lost."

Looking into Daphne's intelligent brown eyes, the alien maintains a stiff upper lip, "Come on. Let's see what comes next." Scratching her head, he smiles, "At worst, you will see your former master sooner rather than later."

Bark!

"I will take that as a yes." The portal morphs again, revealing a nighttime urban street scene with neon-illuminated crowds milling about in all directions under a steady downpour, "Good enough. Let's go before it stops working."

Zint and Daphne disappear through the spinning time portal moments before the Möbius ebbs to a stop in total darkness.

Rachel | The Lost Ship
08:15 a.m. | October 20, 2044

Wrapped up like an Egyptian mummy and draped under a light blanket, Rachel stares through slits in gauze covering her face at the alien campfire, sipping water and marveling at the colorful spectrum dancing amid the blue alien flames licking into the misty morning air.

Penny's soft voice resonates from behind, "Good morning, Rachel. I see you finally woke up. You had everyone really worried."

Sitting cross-legged on her wet, stinky bedroll covered in gritty sand, Rachel turns to the youthful Pennywell, "Richard's alien meds are already healing my burns. Thank you for looking after me."

Penny hesitates, "Does anything hurt? I can give you another dose …."

Rachel coughs and glances at the prismatic fire, "I better not; I am tripping enough already."

Penny scooches forward, "About what happened to you yesterday, I don't know what to say."

Rachel places her wrapped hand on Penny's knee, "Ask your Grandpa. He knows what the PTB did to me. So does Richard." Noticing the young doctor's reaction when mentioning her family ties, Rachel switches subjects, "Where is everybody?"

Penny sighs, "Looking for Zint and Daphne. They never came back after your, uh, what happened. They may be trapped inside the ship."

Rachel closes her eyes and smiles, "Zint is a wandering soul. Perhaps we will see him again one day."

Penny ignores the movement of curious feathery creatures watching them from a twisted mass of thick leafy vines encroaching on the campsite, "I'm going to miss Daphne. What a sweet dog."

Empire Grays | The Lost Ship
09:11 a.m. | October 20, 2044

An Empire Gray attack ship lands two miles downstream from the lost ship and uncloaks its spartan airframe. A seamless portal opens, allowing an elite squad of Empire Gray shock troops to exit and assemble outside the craft under a tyrannical squad leader's ruthless gaze. Weighed down by silvery armor and Earth's gravity, the ten-plus-one unit marches single-file through thick undergrowth into the fungal forest. Under orders to neutralize the human presence with extreme prejudice and recover their world killer, they move with lethal stealth across the loamy surface.

Exuding supreme confidence in their ability to overwhelm the primitive human expedition, the point alien raises a tiny four-finger fist, halting the squad's progress before a theropod standing twice their three-foot height blocking the trail.

The leader aims his weapon at the stupid animal as a ravenous hunting pack appears out of nowhere, outflanking them and blocking a retreat.

Penned in, the Grays form a tight circle as the dinosaurs jump their prey with terrible long claws ripping down tiny bodies and splattering their toxic aqua-colored blood across the forest.

After the 30-second melee concludes without the surprised aliens getting off a single shot, the raptors transport eleven tattered bodies to the rift valley's prehistoric stream and drop them into the icy water. The strong current carries the dead over shifting rocks and sands that will bury them for eternity, joining their ancient ancestors from 90 million years ago.

* * *

The battlecruiser spaces a last load of human body parts and debris before exiting its outer orbital post around Earth. The defeated

Ping wheels to the large portal and watches the stars stream past, "You did it, Artemus. The Light Specters will be pleased."

"Rachel Haig deserved a normal life."

Pennywell's sage alien confidante shakes his head, "No. She did not. The only way to complete Rachel's energized transformation was to expose her to the lost ship's viral payload. As we hypothesized, the others breathed it into their lungs from the moment they entered the rift, suffering no ill effects. But within Rachel, the prehistoric virus leaking from the missile mutated within her, sealing her transcendence—and that of her child."

Pennywell caps the elegant pen and places it on the table, "I suppose Nietzsche had it right: what does not kill you makes you stronger."

"Well put, Artemus. I advised before the Gork invasion that Rachel was a pioneer. Her bond with the golden ellipse proved her resilience and brought her latent blue spark energy to the fore. And now, she will carry the torch at the end of our time."

Pennywell picks up the crystal tumbler, "I'll drink to that."

Leaning back in the comfortable seat, his vision fades to black, "Ping? Are you there? What is happening? I want to …."

Letting the moment pass, Ping reaches out his long fingers and closes Pennywell's watery gray eyes, "Goodbye, Artemus."

Acknowledging the end of his long industrious life, Ping shrinks into his seat as the automaton returns and injects his thin gray arm with a clear fluid.

Drifting into the abyss, Ping's final thoughts are of humanity. A lonely species in a hostile, unforgiving universe. Only now, with a new beginning.

The one called Rachel bears a child who will be the first of a new kind.

The End

The End

Epilogue One

Flynn | Somalia
03:30 p.m. | January 9, 2045

Still fuming after their prolonged detention at the chaotic Mogadishu airport logjammed with relief supplies rotting on the hot tarmac, Flynn shakes his head, "The consulate guy back in Mogadishu was a jackass."

Behind the hot, sticky wheel of their rented Land Rover, Nicole shoots her on-again boyfriend an annoyed sideways glance over her wireframes, "Get over it, Flynn. The jackass, Mr. Foster, is way over his head. We showed up without a passport between us, hat-in-hand, demanding carte-blanche access to one of the most backward countries in the world."

"I showed Foster my PTB credentials. That used to be enough to get me into any country." With a wry chuckle, he adds, "The Powers

That Be official ID card—don't leave home without it." Ratcheting his seat back, he pulls his cap over his eyes, "Wake me when we get closer."

* * *

Bounding along rutted dirt roads through the stark rolling Somali backcountry for hours, Nicole waves past local farmers on camelback, ambling across the hardpan, untethered from modern world problems.

Distracted by their nomadic spirit, she looks back out the windscreen onto a large animal carcass blocking the narrow road and veers around it at the last second. "Whew! That was close. We almost gave this piece of shit rental a new hood ornament."

Nicole's driving and the bumpy road stir Flynn awake after a two-hour catnap. Checking his watch, he emits a yawning groan, "Ugh, five o'clock," noting the battleship-gray storm clouds rolling in from over the sea far to the east; he switches his wristwatch to a proprietary GPS tracker mode, "We are getting close."

Nicole glances at the tech-heavy watch, "It never ceases to amaze me what the PTB can do. Richard's team matched genetic data from your transplanted liver against a top-secret alien abduction registry and found a match. I did not know they kept such records."

Flynn laughs, "The PTB is a data-crunching, numbers-loving machine. And now, with Andrew large and in charge, it will get even more so."

Feeling the long raised scars across his abdomen, Flynn winces, "Thanks for helping me, Nicole. It means a lot to have you here." Wiping his eyes, he bites his lip, "I need to meet my donor's family and tell them their man did not die in vain. It haunts me."

* * *

Dipping through a dry wash and into a scrubby stand of trees, Nicole slows as a giggling gaggle of Somali children runs alongside the

Epilogue Two

Inside the PTB's sick bay turned obstetrics ward, wearing a light blue surgical gown and gloves over his usual black mock turtleneck and jeans with cloth booties covering his socked feet on the cold tile floor, Andrew sucks air through a mask and wipes a strange tear from his eye, "I wish Artemus were here."

Cognizant of 14 identical sisters' enrapt stares through the thick glass viewing window at his back, Andrew proffers a thumbs up to the peanut gallery.

Across the bright, sterile delivery room, Dr. Aashvi Patel hunches forward on a stool between Number 8's long legs spread apart in stirrups; her pelvis scooched to the edge of a high-tech hospital bed. "Okay, Number 8, I can see your little one's head ... let's have another push in 3, 2, 1 ...."

Number 8 emits another blood-curdling scream as the baby's head elongates and pushes through the birth canal.

With a crazed look in her vivid blue eyes, Number 8 pivots to an excited Number 11, clutching her hand and acting as her breathing coach and moral support.

Sporting bright red hair, 11 meets her sister's maniacal gaze with a broad, confident smile, "Breathe in and breathe out. That's it, nice and easy. Let Dr. Patel tell you when to push."

With her jet-black hair and blanched face dripping in sweat, Number 8 gets zip, zero, zilch of 11's unbridled happiness through her drug-free delivery experience. Gritting her teeth, fighting the urge to push, she squeezes 11's hand in a vicelike grip, her strained voice sounding like a woman possessed, "I want that baby out! Now!"

With a furtive chuckle to herself, Dr. Patel muses on the ease and simplicity of the drama-free labor before inciting one final push, "Okay, girl, give it all you got!"

Number 8 screams bloody murder, pushing her miracle child's head and shoulders from the birth canal with all the elegance and nuance nature intended. With the second shoulder out, the rest of the infant's seven-pound two-ounce body slides out like butter. Cradling the child in her steady grip, Patel lifts the gorgeous baby boy to 8's bosom and turns to Andrew. "Come here, Papa. Say hello to your son."

A relieved Andrew pulls down his mask before addressing the doctor in an even tone, "Call him Paddy."

Rachel | Mass General, Boston
04:37 a.m. | June 23, 2045

Upon returning the worse for wear from a mystery trip that no one would discuss, the widowed Miriam Haig convinced a reluctant

Owen and Rachel to settle with her at Aunt Shirley's spacious Beacon Hill residence through the pregnancy. Noticing the rift between the newly married couple widening as the due date approached, the vibe in the mansion went from close-mouthed to downright icy.

After months of walking on eggshells, the day of reckoning came early and surprised everyone. From the moment Rachel's water broke while gobbling a bowl of Froot Loops at Aunt Shirley's prized colonial-era oak and maple kitchen table, nothing went as planned.

The spanking-new, hot-off-the-line EV Owen finagled through business connections for the short trip to the Mass General had zero battery charge when he needed it.

Screaming at her husband, Rachel accessed a holographic device, and within minutes Cowboy's chopper set down in Aunt Shirley's backyard next to the rose garden. The tall and handsome Stetson-wearing Texan assisted Rachel, Owen, and a beguiled Miriam into the air taxi for the 10-minute flight over the chaotic snarl of a decimated downtown Boston to Mass Gen's rooftop helipad.

From the tight cockpit, Cowboy tipped back his hat's brim to the hospital orderly waiting with a wheelchair and turned to the Haig family, "Just like old times. I will leave y'all in the good graces of that young man and park this thing at Logan. I'll come back when you need me."

* * *

Physically and mentally exhausted after helping Rachel and her discombobulated husband through 22 grueling hours of intense labor, Miriam Alexander rests in a comfortable hospital room recliner with her aching feet propped up. Across the dim quietude, Owen's tall frame lies slumped sideways in a chair next to Rachel's restless, prone form, sleeping atop the bed.

Rubbing her eyes, swollen and red from tears of joy at meeting Hannah, her newborn granddaughter, hours earlier, she hears Rachel mumbling to someone in her sleep.

Leaning forward, Miriam contemplates Rachel's short-cropped blond hair, tinged with a streak of blue. The coif gave her daughter a hard edge reminding her of Rachel's brief punk rock faze during high school. Aside from her new hairstyle, Rachel's personality had changed after their return from Brazil. Something happened. Something bad. She did not believe the sunburn story for a second. Why was Owen not burned over his entire body? Rachel and Owen's obfuscations and bald-faced lies proved beyond frustrating.

Dr. Gene Simmons | Mass General, Boston
05:49 a.m. | June 23, 2045

Wearing a light windbreaker over a golf shirt and slacks, Dr. Gene Simmons steps off the elevator and enters Mass Gen's maternity ward through swinging double doors. Ambling to the receiving desk, he proffers a warm smile and waits for a young nurse nearing the end of her shift to finish a call.

The sleepy-eyed night shift nurse taps her earphone and turns to Gene, "Sir, visiting hours start at 07:00 a.m. I can ...."

Holding up a hand to stop her rehearsed spiel, "I am Dr. Gene Simmons with The Powers That Be, here for Rachel Alexander Haig."

The nurse checks a screen and shrugs, "We have no one by that name. Are you at the right hospital?"

"Try Betty Hill."

"Oh, yes. We do have a Mrs. Hill."

"Excellent. I would like to see her in private, but first I want to see the baby."

commander sends an encrypted communication to the Empire Gray fleet, idling between Jupiter's moons: *The lost ship was found, but the world killer is lost.*

Flynn | The Lost Ship
06:15 p.m. | October 20, 2044

Staying within the alien fire's protective circumference, the group listens to another round of prehistoric roars thrashing through the thick jungle at the bottom of the narrow rift.

Flynn laughs, "Call me crazy, but I am getting used to the sound of dinosaurs."

Sitting at Rachel's side, waiting for their PTB ride back to civilization, Owen turns to his friend, "You are crazy."

With one hell of a story to tell and her broken ankle in a makeshift splint, Nina turns to Richard, "Any word on when the PTB will arrive?"

Professor Richard King looks up from his notebook, "Oh, uh, did I not tell you all? They will not be here until tomorrow."

The group's collective moan resonates up the rift's echoing walls into the late afternoon Amazon sky.

Owen | The Lost Ship
07:30 a.m. | October 21, 2044

Agent Flynn waves a bright flashlight, guiding a boxy anti-gravity ship to a wobbly landing on the sandy spit rising above the swift-flowing stream. A portal opens, and the wheelchair-bound Ping exits down a ramp, followed by Andrew. The pair wait on the wet sand as Artemus Pennywell, dressed in his signature black suit, ducks out of the opening, pausing to take in the prehistoric scene. Appearing frail and tired, he smooths back a wisp of thin gray hair and smiles, "I finally made it, Paddy."

Leaning on his cane for support, Pennywell steps down the ramp and leads Andrew and Ping toward the surviving members of his expedition aligned in the lost ship's early morning shadow.

Acknowledging the bedraggled group, Pennywell glances between Richard, the Haigs, and Agent Flynn, "Where is Ms. Madsen?"

Flynn replies with his best poker face, "Nina will be along. You know how she likes to keep up appearances."

With a raised eyebrow, Pennywell acknowledges his agent's reply, "Yes. That does sound like Nina. Well. I apologize for our late arrival, but we had to round up a pilot who could fly that stupid anti-gravity box."

Turning to Andrew, Pennywell nods, "We will wait for Ms. Madsen before passing out the commendations."

Tired, itchy, hungry, and suffering caffeine withdrawals, Owen smirks, "Commendations? That is all you have? We risked our fucking lives. Rachel saved the goddamn planet from destruction. Again! People died out here. Good people in your employ. Mr. Pennywell."

Something roars in the distance over the usual jungle din as the entire group waits with bated breath to see if Pennywell unleashes a trademark tirade on the young American.

Artemus fixes Owen with a severe stare that transforms into genuine empathy, "You are quite right, Mr. Haig. Overt displays of gushing gratitude are not part of my nature. It is a personal flaw. One that it is far too late to rectify."

Again, addressing his former valet, "Be sure to throw in a fruit basket for the Haigs' troubles." After a pause, he continues, "Owen, I gave you Villa St. Claire, free and clear. What more do you want?"

Owen places an arm around a wavering Rachel's waist. "Nothing. You can have it back if you want."

vehicle in grubby shorts and tees. Beside themselves with excitement, they lead the dirty SUV through an opened double gate in a rickety wood outer fence. Inside the tiny community of cylindrical abodes with conical-shaped roofs covered in a patchwork of woven rugs, sun-faded multi-colored fabrics, and dried thatch, Nicole slows to a stop, shifts into Park, and turns off the ignition. Smiling out her window at the horde of children clamoring for them to get out and play, Nicole turns to Flynn, "Well?"

Flynn double-checks his tracker, "Yeah, this seems right, Nicole. Only one way to know for sure."

Backing away from the dusty, ticking vehicle just enough to allow the doors to swing open, the children gather around Nicole and Flynn in the late-afternoon heat and lead them into the community.

Nicole peers into the huts' dark interiors and turns to Flynn, "Where are the grown-ups?"

Making a quick head count of 24 children ranging from preschool to junior high amidst the chickens, goats, and feral dogs scrounging in the loose dirt and rocks pocked with mounded cacti and tall grasses, he frowns. "I don't know."

A tall teenage lad sporting a camo uniform two sizes too big for his malnourished skinny body exits from a hut and splits the spirited assemblage, motioning for quiet. Stepping forward, the stone-faced youngster with a carbine slung over his shoulder approaches Flynn and Nicole. In perfect English, he speaks, "State your business."

Flynn smiles and assumes his most non-threatening posture, "I am looking for Mr. Bilal Hersi's family. Do they live here?"

The kid's face contorts into a wary stare, "Who are you?"

Nicole interjects, "We came to have a word with his wife or other family relations."

The kid straightens and adjusts the heavy rifle strap on his narrow shoulder, "They are gone." In a commanding voice, he calls out, "Leylo!"

Nicole and Flynn turn and watch a preschool-aged girl elbow through the crowd, delivering a folded paper into Flynn's hands.

The boy waits as Flynn unfolds the tabloid-size sheet revealing a child's crayon rendering of little gray men leading a group of people into a ship.

"The aliens took Bilal Hersi and many other adults that night."

Awash in empathy and compassion for the children's plight, Nicole nudges Flynn, I am going back to the car and contacting whoever we have in the area to come here and take care of these children."

Engrossed in the drawing, imagining his donor among the stick figures, Flynn mumbles, "Okay. Good idea."

Snapping from his reverie, he refolds the sheet, "Can I keep this?"

The boy proffers a solemn-faced nod.

"Thank you." Sliding the drawing into a pocket, Flynn feels an unmistakable kinship developing between himself and the dark-skinned lad, "Mr. Hersi was your father."

With the weight of the world on his shoulders, the brave teen releases the floodgates, breaking down in tears.

Flynn pulls the kid into a warm embrace and pats him on the back, "I am so sorry for your loss. Your father was a hero. He saved my life."

Pennywell's deep-set gaze meets Rachel's eyes as she floods his brain with a singular defense of her out-of-sorts husband, *"Don't mind Owen; he has not had his morning coffee in two days."*

Pennywell creases a thin smile on his weathered face, acknowledging the telepathic side effect of her energized blue spark, "Oh, and by the way, Owen, speaking of the villa, I need you to investigate an art forgery ring with links to the St. Claire heir who committed suicide. I do believe the white-collar criminal enterprises are more in your wheelhouse than trekking around the jungle like fucking Indiana Jones."

Owen frowns, "So none of that art in the cellar was real?"

Pennywell smiles, "Not a single fucking canvas or statue. However, the wine was vintage enough and worth a small fortune. Louie 2.0 is taking care of things in your absence."

Ping sits motionless in his chair while Artemus blusters through what should be a happy occasion. The expedition parts allowing a cleaned-up Nina Madsen to limp across the sand and join the reunion, "Hello, Artemus. We have met in strange places, but this takes the cake."

"Nina, I am so happy you and Flynn escaped the Empire Grays. I could not be prouder of you both."

Flynn quips, "Extra fruit in Nina's bloody basket, I bet."

On the cusp of reprimanding his sharp-tongued agent, Artemus' face goes pale, recognizing a waifish form appearing from the shadows. In genuine shock and surprise, Pennywell is left speechless for one of the few times in his life. Fumbling for words, he blurts out, "Penny?"

With her eyes swollen and red from crying over the loss of Daphne and Zint, Penny's tearful gaze meets her great-great-grandfather's rheumy gray eyes. The assembled group falls silent as she steps across the sand, pulling Emma's photo from her jacket, "Do you recognize her?"

Ashen-faced and gobsmacked by the spontaneous reunion, Artemus accepts the faded Polaroid and looks at the lovely young woman in the picture holding a smiling baby girl, "Yes. Emma. Poor tragic Emma."

Lowering the photo, Pennywell places his hands on Penny's shoulders and pulls her into his warm embrace, "I am so sorry, Penny, I could have done more. Her death was the tragic consequence of being a Pennywell. In reaction to your mother's death, I shielded you from your past. I regret that now. It must have been lonely. I am so sorry."

Penny pushes back, wiping her bloodshot eyes and proffering a brave smile, "Well, now that can change, Grandpa. I want us to spend some time together."

Artemus Pennywell looks down at his lovely granddaughter, "I am afraid that is impossible, my dear."

Turning to address the group, Artemus Pennywell gestures toward his friend and confidante, "I will be leaving you all. I am accompanying Ping on a new journey. It is my last."

Caught flat-footed by Pennywell's sad announcement, Andrew pivots to his boss and friend, "Sir, are you serious? I thought you would stick around and help with my transition. We have so much more to do."

"No. Andrew. *You* have much more to do. That is your damn job as CEO."

Flynn | The Lost Ship
08:01 p.m. | October 21, 2044

A pod-shaped spacecraft lands near the boxy anti-gravity cargo ship. Ping signals the aliens at the controls and rolls up the ramp into the vessel. Having already exhausted his goodbyes, Artemus Pennywell smooths the crease in his black suit jacket, adjusts his Saguaro bolo tie, and follows in Ping's tracks up the ramp, leaning on the cane. At the opened portal, he turns and beams a broad smile toward the group before focusing on his trusted right-hand man and confidante, "Behave

Epilogue Three

Richard King | Lost Cactus Laboratory
11:43 a.m. | August 22, 2045

On the first anniversary of the Gork's aborted invasion, Professor Richard King jumps from the passenger seat of an old-school military Jeep, pushing aside a dried tangle of tumbleweeds while opening a weather-beaten 12-foot chain-linked gate, ignoring the bullet-riddled NO TRESPASSING sign.

Fresh off quitting her job at the CDC and joining the PTB, Penny Pennywell sits behind the wheel, watching cute ground squirrels scampering about a gnarled scrub oak's windswept branches above metal drums half-buried in the desert hardpan.

Richard vaults back atop his seat and taps the narrow dashboard, proffering an excited, almost giddy smile, "Okay, let's go."

Penny looks through the open gate at the same barren

southwestern landscape they had already driven across for hours, "Where is the base?"

"See that mesa and the natural bridge?"

Peering through dark-tinted sunglasses across the superheated desert toward the prominent topographical landmark, Penny nods, "Yes."

"Whatever remains of Lost Cactus lies on the opposite side. Drive on."

* * *

Richard's baby, The Powers That Be funded laboratory codenamed Lost Cactus, built in a post-WW2 era on the brink of a new atomic age with an outpouring of ET assistance, looked more akin to a ghost town as Penny drove past a dilapidated gatehouse, "Does anybody still work or live here?"

A flood of memories returns as Richard scans the familiar environs, "No. I left for good in 2029 to head up your Grandfather's underground lab in Scotland." With a weighty sadness tinging his words, he adds, "Things went downhill after my departure.

* * *

Inside the base perimeter, Richard peers through the brightness down the deserted Main Street, resembling a ghost town, toward the erstwhile science and research building's weather-beaten facade, with its broken and jagged glass-enclosed atrium lobby.

Shaking his charcoal gray curly head under a PTB ballcap, his heart sinks, seeing his creation reduced to sunken girders and a patchwork of busted and broken windowpanes dripping with chalky white bird crap, "I miss my former life here with a white-hot passion."

Exiting the Jeep, Richard crunches across the cracked and potholed macadam noting vestiges of yellow-painted directional arrows toward a rusted half-cylindrical metallic hangar over three football fields long, rising five-plus stories overhead.

Penny turns off the ignition and joins him at the massive, shuttered hangar doors fronting the hulking structure, "Now what? It is locked up tight."

Richard moves to a lockbox mounted at eye level on the side of the building. Turning to Penny, he shoots her a mischievous smile, "Rule number one when working for the PTB: Things are not always as they appear."

Busting a padlock off a rusted hasp with a rock, he pulls the hinged lid open and positions his left eye in front of a red-glowing lens. On cue, the heavy metal doors groan and creak, rolling apart along a bent metal track for the first time in years.

The backlit duo cast long shadows through a wide arcing patch of desert sunlight, breaching the threshold to the dark, cavernous space.

Penny gawks at row upon row of crates atop enormous shelves stacked high up into the rafters. "This place is remarkable. What is in all of these boxes and crates?"

Richard places his hands on his hips and exhales, contemplating the enormity of the task before him, "The secrets of the world harboring tales too tall to tell."

Penny's eyes adjust to the darkness, following Richard's footsteps down a central aisle, seeing rats skittering for the shadowy recesses amid a veritable trove of treasures from throughout history that would make the Smithsonian green with envy.

Catching up to Richard, she watches him pause before a child-size pinewood coffin positioned atop a heaped palette.

Looking over his shoulder, Penny shines her light at the name stenciled into the lid, "Bentley? Who was Bentley?"

"A good friend." After a private chuckle, he adds, "Let's leave that alone for now."

Penny moves ahead of the PTB scientist, "Tell me again, Professor King," casting her flashlight across the wooden crates, "What are we looking for?" Another rat hops atop a container and scrutinizes her with an intelligent beady-eyed stare.

Distracted by the strange encounter, Penny casts her beam toward the 123-year-old man of science, finding him hunched next to a stack of boxes. "Professor, are you okay?"

Richard wipes tears from his eyes, "I am back where I belong, Penny. Lost Cactus is my home." Waving his arms around the yawning expanse, "But I can't remember the arcane system I devised to catalog this damn warehouse."

Collecting himself after the unexpected emotional outburst, he walks up to Penny, "Like Artemus, I am well past my time on Earth. I cheated death, and now I realize my mind will go long before my body. Not a good ending, I'm afraid."

Penny shakes her head, "No, Richard. They are doing great things with the neural chips, I …."

"I invented that technology." Richard holds up a hand, "No thanks. It is a cold reality for your generation, but it is not for me." Gazing into the rafters, he repeats, "The blue spark. The blue spark."

Connecting Richard's lament to the blue spark that afflicted Rachel Haig in the Amazon, Penny shines her light toward the back of the warehouse, illuminating a row of crates with blue X's stenciled on the sides. "Hey Richard, does a blue X mean anything?"

"Ah, eureka!" Pivoting toward Penny Pennywell with a renewed sense of purpose on his expressive face, he smiles, "We need to access those containers and open the one marked, Sarah."

"Richard, don't tell me we are searching for human remains?"

"No, my dear. We are looking for a metallic cube that contains Sarah's eternal essence."

"Okay. What are you going to do with that?"

Richard trains his light on the young Pennywell, "I plan to join her."

Thank you for reading

THE LOST SHIP

Watch for the third science fiction

action-adventure novel in

The Powers That Be trilogy

THE BLUE SPARK

Visit **johnhopkinsauthor.com**

for more information.

*The following is an excerpt from **THE BLUE SPARK***

Stanley Hobbes | Newport, RI
11:43 a.m. | February 3, 2020

Stanley Hobbes fancied himself something of a low-level superhero. Sporting rumpled secondhand clothes under trademark moth-eaten sweaters and Coke-bottle spectacles on his bald head, the affirmed bachelor with a keen eye for the ladies looked more like one of Superman's turds which suited him just fine. His God-given short stature and humble outward appearance proved invaluable superpowers, lulling a cruel world to overlook and underestimate his squat 5-2 frame.

Heat-packing guards and state-of-the-art security systems protecting Newport's notorious debauchery and high society hedonism from the prying eyes of mere mortals proved no match for Stanley. Quick-witted and resourceful, his chameleon-like personae infiltrated elite gatherings, extravagant weddings, bar mitzvahs, glitzy fundraisers, and outrageous parties, documenting the inevitable devolution into a shameful and embarrassing smorgasbord of drunken bacchanals, vicious fights, and fumbling awkward trysts.

After uploading salacious high-class hijinks reportage and reputation-damaging hi-res imagery to his editors via anonymous links, he scooped up thick envelopes of cash at dead drop locations, maintaining his secret identity, just like Clark Kent.

On rare occasions, pangs of conscience permeated Stanley's psyche, but a lifetime of derisive mockery at the hands of these same rich assholes assuaged his guilt. Post ten years of countless breaches and narrow escapes, he almost had enough to secure a down payment on a vacant Newport storefront that sold candy back in the day. Stanley's dream: convert the retail space wedged between an antique shop and a maritime art gallery into Hobbes Rare Books, specializing in comics and pulpy fiction from a bygone era. An impressive personal collection of books and manuscripts amassed over his 35 years stored in a climate-controlled facility will stock the shelves before a grand opening.

Stanley Hobbes made a solemn resolution: one more big score, and he would quit the cloak-and-dagger paparazzi racket for good. With his John Hancock on a thick stack of loan papers, his transmogrification into an upstanding business owner and pillar of the community will be realized. He even had half a mind to join the local chamber.

* * *

Through a reliable source, Stanley learned that socialite extraordinaire Miriam Alexander, wife of Marcus Alexander, the

Newport-based entertainment mogul, was rushed to the Women & Infants Hospital in Providence. Recovering from an emergency C-section, Mrs. Alexander's condition is guarded, and the six-month-old preemie baby girl is tucked away in the neonatal ICU under heavy security. The mission, should Stanley accept, is to capture pictures of the mother and child.

This was a job for, well, Stanley.

Rachel | Providence, RI
11:43 a.m. | February 4, 2020

Stanley pulled his 2002 Chevy Malibu rust bucket into a handicapped spot in the hospital parking garage, popped the trunk, pulled out his crutches, and snapped a brace around his right leg. Patting the charged smart device in his trouser pocket, the conman hobbled to the elevator to breach the renowned birthing hospital, churning out pampered little brats like a factory.

Struggling through cumbersome glass doors into the lobby, no one offered Stanley assistance—a harmless runt with a bum leg birth defect—not too far from the truth.

Stanley scoped the scene, feigning reading the hospital's directory inside the well-adorned lobby, noting stone-faced men in black impeding access to the bank of elevators. His source was not kidding about the heightened security presence. An anticipatory prickle down the spine informed the veteran reporter that there is more to this story than snapping precious baby photos for slavish masses eking out vicarious lives through the privileged elite.

Limping past the security desk, Stanley waved at a guard and pointed toward the gift shop. The musclebound Black man stared right through him before turning his back to assist another visitor.

***

Waltzing down a central corridor like he owned the place, munching on a Snickers bar from the overpriced gift emporium with a pink "It's a Girl!" balloon tied to a crutch, Stanley spied an unattended emergency stairwell. Checking his six, he ditched the crutches behind a potted plant and climbed flights of stairs, huffing, and panting by the time he reached the sixth-floor Neonatology ward.

Dabbing sweat with a hankie, Stanley held the balloon close, cognizant of cameras up and down the quiet corridor. Walking past floor-to-ceiling glass-fronted intensive care units bathed in serene blue glows to prevent jaundice, he read the handwritten placards by each doorway: Rodriguez, Hoffman, Yang, Simpson, Palmieri …. No Alexander. Shit. Shit. And more shit.

Moving toward a centralized nurses' station, Stanley nodded past a weary couple and froze as elevator doors slid apart. Melding behind a metal trash can, he watched a distinguished fellow in a houndstooth sportscoat and red bow tie with dark-gray curly hair leading a team of important-looking white-coated men and women into a meeting room.

Connecting the bow tie wearer to the men in black standing watch on the main floor, Stanley assumed his cloak of invisibility and sauntered past the preoccupied nurses' station. Approaching the closed door to eavesdrop, he heard voices raised in angry tones, realizing it was some kind of high-level ass-chewing. Ducking into an adjacent storage room on impulse, Hobbes searched the tight space and pulled a stethoscope from a shelf crammed with supplies.

"Jesus, I know where to go if I ever need a caseload of rubber gloves."

Jamming the earpieces into his hairy ears, he placed the diaphragm against the wall adjoining the conference room and picked up the superheated conversation.

"… *don't care about your damnable ethics! The injections must proceed on schedule.*"

A woman's voice interjected, "*Professor King, you must agree that* the premature birth resulted from your drug trial. If you do not tell me what these injections are designed to do, ethically, I cannot participate. I will not be a party to your human experimentation."

Red bow tie's authoritative reply resonated through Stanley's earpieces.

"Doctor, you are free to go, but please be mindful of your NDAs. The Powers That Be will not fuck around with whistleblowers."

A more conciliatory male voice interjected, "Be reasonable, Doctor Shepherd. Professor King's organization made a sizable donation. It is just one little girl. And, from what I understand, she is doing amazingly well for a six-month preemie."

"Really, Bob? We are so hard up for cash that this so-called scientist can waltz in here, write a check, and we have to inject his untested drug into a tiny baby's brain? I want no part of this. I quit. Professor King, you and your powers that be can go to hell."

Readjusting the stethoscope earpieces, Stanley mumbled, "Powers That Be," before the conference room's door creaked open and slammed shut, shaking the thin wall.

The room fell silent before Stanley heard the man adopt a more conciliatory tone to quell further debate, "We do not require the close-minded Doctor Shepherd's approval to proceed with the injections. I assure you that no harm will come to the baby. Case closed."

Stanley scrunched closer to the wall, listening as a softer female voice dared to ask: "Does Mr. and Mrs. Alexander know what you are up to, Professor?"

"If you must know, Nurse Rahimi, Marcus Alexander, the child's father, signed off on the procedure in exchange for exclusive rights to build his arenas on a portfolio of high-end properties. Quid pro quo. That is how The Powers That Be operates. By the way, did your mortgage pay-off check clear?"

"Yes."

"Congratulations. Now, Miriam Alexander is still in post-cesarean *recovery. She was told that her daughter's NICU is listed under the last name Hoffman for privacy. Everything is above board as far as the mother is concerned. Proceed with baby Rachel's injections and ensure no unauthorized hospital personnel enters her NICU. I do not wish to post guards, but I will if it comes to that."*

Nurse Rahimi ventured a follow-up query. *"Do these injections have a name?"*

Hobbes leaned in to hear Professor King's reply, *"Blue Spark is the codename for the experimental treatment. Miriam and Marcus Alexander's child is the first of a new kind."*

Seated atop a cardboard box in stunned silence, Stanley Hobbes removed the stethoscope as the meeting ended. "Blue Spark … that is catchy." With his paparazzi task forgotten, Stanley Hobbes exited the storeroom and stumbled past the nurses' station, mulling the consequential eavesdrop in his active mind.

"Sir! Can I help you?"

Still clutching the balloon, Stanley snapped back to the present, wheeling toward the woman's familiar soft voice, "Uh, Nurse Rahimi, uh … I am here with a delivery. Uh, yeah, I was told to deliver this balloon to the Hoffman baby." With a wide-eyed nod, he mumbled, "Yep, that is why I am here."

Fresh off her confrontational meeting and in no mood to play around with the blatant liar, Nurse Rahimi's dark gaze pierced Stanley's wafer-thin story. "Should I call security?"

Stanley Hobbes tossed caution to the wind, "Please don't. You are right; that was a lie. I would like to see the Hoffman baby. Is that in any way possible?"

With one eye on the elevator, ensuring that Professor King's mysterious PTB entourage had vacated the floor, Nurse Rahimi proffered a broad smile, "Sure. Why not? Let me find you a mask and scrubs—sized extra small."

Covered from head to toe, Stanley Hobbes followed the dark-

<h1 style="text-align:right">Bibliography</h1>

Epigraphy

Chapter One:

"Ad Astra (phrase)." *Wikipedia*, https://en.wikipedia.org/wiki/Ad_astra_(phrase)

Chapter Two:

Shapiro, Fred R. *The Yale Book of Quotations*. Yale University Press, 2006.

Chapter Three:

Brillat-Savarin, Jean Anthelme. *Physiologie du Goût*. Project Gutenberg ebook, 2007.

Chapter Four:

O'Rourke, P. *All the Trouble in the World*. Atlantic Monthly Press, 1995.

Chapter Five:

Jung, C.G., Adler, Gerhard., Aniela, Jaffé. *Letters of C. G. Jung, Volume 2, 1951-1961*. Routledge, 1976.

Chapter Six:

Hersholt, Jean. "A translation of Hans Christian Andersen's "den lille havfrue," The Little Mermaid." *The Hans Christian Andersen Center*, https://andersen.sdu.dk/vaerk/hersholt/TheLittleMermaid_e.html

Chapter Seven:

Shapiro, Fred R. *The Yale Book of Quotations*. Yale University Press, 2006.

Chapter Eight:

Burroughs, Edgar R. and Resnick, Mike. *The Land That Time Forgot*. Bison Books, 1999.

Chapter Nine:

"George S. Patton quotes." https://www.brainyquote.com/quotes/george_s_patton_104742

Chapter Ten:

"Los Caprichos." https://en.wikipedia.org/wiki/Los_caprichos

Chapter Eleven:

"Percy Fawcett." https://en.wikipedia.org/wiki/Percy_Fawcett

Chapter Twelve:

Green, Jonathon. *The Cynic's Lexicon: A Dictionary of Amoral Advice.* Routledge &
     Kegan Paul, 1984.

Chapter Thirteen:

Alighieri, Dante and Sayers, Dorothy L. *The Divine Comedy, Part 3: Paradise.*
     Penguin Classics, 1962.

Books

Grandin, Greg. *Fordlandia: The Rise and Fall of Henry Ford's Forgotten Jungle City.*
     Metropolitan Books, 2009.

Perelman, Yevgeny and Ginosar, Ran. *The NeuroProcessor.* Springer, 2008.

Williams, Olivia. *The Secret Life of the Savoy: Glamour and Intrigue at the World's
     Most Famous Hotel*, Pegasus Books, 2021.

Videos

"Brazil Amazon Mangrove." *YouTube*, uploaded by hors frontieres, 5 Nov. 2016,
     https://www.youtube.com/watch?v=5M0UTiJ48jg

"Interview With The Lifelike Hot Robot Named Sophia" *YouTube*,
     uploaded by CNBC, 25 Oct. 2017, https://www.youtube.com/
     watch?v=S5t6K9iwcdw

"Different Types Of Alien Species On Earth" *YouTube*, uploaded by What We
     Know, 24 Jun. 2020, https://youtu.be/xg_js3raIW0

"Howler Monkeys." *YouTube*, uploaded by National Geographic, 18 Aug. 2008,
     https://www.youtube.com/watch?v=REPoVfN-Ij4

"Paris 3 Stars Michelin Le Cinq." *YouTube*, uploaded by Gourmet B Gourmet,
     11 Apr. 2022, https://www.youtube.com/watch?v=Z5AeOkbCHGc

Smith, Melanie. "Fordlandia." *FelixBlume.com,* https://felixblume.com/
     fordlandia/

"SummerKyleUnderway." *YouTube*, uploaded by Gerr Marine, 6 Jul. 2020, https://www.youtube.com/watch?v=QSlF6YuFIAw

"The Prophetic Vision of George Washington at Valley Forge." *YouTube*, Jon McNaughton, 18 Mar. 2021, https://www.youtube.com/watch?v=sCcdK7qW6qY

Articles

Bohn, Liv. "Everything you need to know about visiting the Amazon." *Intrepid*, 20 Mar. 2019, https://www.intrepidtravel.com/adventures/amazon-travel-guide/

Bostrom, Nick. "Transhumanism: The World's Most Dangerous Idea?" *Nick Bostrom*, https://www.nickbostrom.com/papers/dangerous.html

Bringsjord, Selmer and Govindarajulu, Naveen Sundar. "Artificial Intelligence" *The Stanford Encyclopedia of Philosophy*, https://plato.stanford.edu/archives/fall2022/entries/artificial-intelligence/

Brown, Dwayne and Landau, Elizabeth. "NASA-Funded Research Creates DNA-like Molecule to Aid Search for Alien Life." *NASA Science*, 22 Feb. 2019, https://solarsystem.nasa.gov/news/859/nasa-funded-research-creates-dna-like-molecule-to-aid-search-for-alien-life/

Butler, Rhett. "10 Facts about the Amazon Rainforest in 2022." *Mongabay*, https://rainforests.mongabay.com/amazon/amazon-rainforest-facts.html

Crooks, Vanessa. "In a Remote Amazon Region, Study Shows Indigenous Peoples Have Practiced Forest Conservation for Millennia." *Smithsonian Magazine*, 23 Jun, 2021, https://www.smithsonianmag.com/smithsonian-institution/remote-amazon-region-study-shows-indigenous-peoples-have-practiced-forest-conservation-millennia-180978038/

Castillo, M. "The Omega Point and Beyond: The Singularity Event." *American Journal of Neuroradiology*, Mar. 2012, https://doi.org/10.3174/ajnr.A2664

Dang, Sanjit Singh. "Artificial Intelligence In Humanoid Robots." *Forbes*, https://www.forbes.com/sites/cognitiveworld/2019/02/25/artificial-intelligence-in-humanoid-robots/?sh=2d7eb54d24c7

Gell, Aaron. "Eli Roth Faces Off With Tribal Rights Campaigners Over Cannibal Film." *Business Insider*, Aug. 2014, https://www.businessinsider.com/eli-roth-cannibal-rainforest-controversy-2014-8

Hoffower, Hillary. "A short history of the secret bunker underneath the White House." *Business Insider*, 11 Jun. 2020, https://www.businessinsider.com/white-house-secret-bunker-details-features-2020-6

Jensen, Scott. "Flying Dinosaurs Sightings Are On The Rise in North Carolina." *Charlotte Stories*, 5 Oct. 2021, https://www.charlottestories.com/flying-dinosaurs-sightings-rise-north-carolina/

Poon, Linda. "The Odds of a Major Flood in Washington D.C, Will Quadruple by 2050." *Pacific Standard*, 22 Jul. 2019, https://psmag.com/environment/the-odds-of-a-major-flood-in-dc-will-quadruple-by-2050

Ramsdale, Suzannah. "Vintage prewar wines sell for £50,000." *Decanter*, 18 Mar. 2009, https://www.decanter.com/wine-news/vintage-prewar-wines-sell-for-50000-72924/

Robb, Alice. "Will Overpopulation and Resource Scarcity Drive Cannibalism?" *The New Republic*, 19 Jun. 2024, https://newrepublic.com/article/118252/cannibalism-and-overpopulation-how-amazon-tribe-ate-their-dead

Sims, Shannon. "The rubber thief of Brazil." *OZY*, 29 Aug. 2015, https://www.ozy.com/true-and-stories/the-rubber-thief-of-brazil/60424/

South, Todd. "Army chooses Sig Sauer to build its Next Generation Squad Weapon." *Army Times*, 19, Apr. 2022, https://www.armytimes.com/news/your-army/2022/04/19/army-chooses-sig-sauer-to-build-its-next-generation-squad-weapon/

Thomas, A. "Lapin a La Cocotte is the French way for serving Rabbit!" *Wokokon*, 17 DEC. 2012, https://wokokon.com/lapin-a-la-cocotte-is-the-french-way-for-serving-rabbit/

Tonon, Rafael. "A Complete Guide to Cachaça: Brazil's Most Popular Spirit." *Eater*, 11 De. 2015, https://www.eater.com/drinks/2015/12/11/9891376/what-is-cachaca

Walker, Robert and Simmons, Cynthia. "Endangered Amazon: An Indigenous Tribe Fights Back Against Hydropower Development in the Tapajós Valley" *Environment: Science and Policy for Sustainable Development*, vol. 60, 2018, Issue 2, https://plato.stanford.edu/archives/fall2022/entries/artificial-intelligence/

Whitelocks, Sadie. "I slept in the jungle - and survived! What it's like sleeping in a hammock surrounded by scorpions, venomous snakes, tarantulas and jaguars." *Daily Mail*, 6 Dec. 2018, https://www.dailymail.co.uk/travel/travel_news/article-6310939/I-slept-jungle-survived-like-sleeping-ants-spiders-hammock.html

Papers

Calvo, Jorge and Lockley, Martin. "The first pterosaur tracks from Gondwana" *Science Direct*, Oct. 2001, Vol. 22, Issue 5, https://www.sciencedirect.com/science/article/abs/pii/S0195667101902769

LaBonta, Lo'eau. "Human Energy Converted to Electricity." *Stanford University, Dept. of Physics*, 6 Dec. 2014, http://large.stanford.edu/courses/2014/ph240/labonta1/

Green, Ronald M. "Challenging Transhumanism's Values." *The Hastings Center Report,* vol. 43, no. 4, [The Hastings Center, Wiley], 2013, pp. 45–47, http://www.jstor.org/stable/23480982.

Xavier, Thomas. "Communication After an EMP." *More Than Just Surviving*, 23 Oct. 2014, https://morethanjustsurviving.com/communication-after-emp/

Websites

"Alien Abduction." *Wikipedia*, https://en.wikipedia.org/wiki/Alien_abduction

"Best season to travel to Provence & French Riviera - Wine Grape Harvest." *Rove. Me*, https://rove.me/to/provence-french-riviera/wine-grape-harvest

"Brazil." *Wikipedia*, https://en.wikipedia.org/wiki/Brazil

"Brazil Nut Tree." *Plant World Seeds*, https://www.plant-world-seeds.com/store/view_seed_item/5371?currency=USD&gclid=Cj0KCQjwn4qWBhCvARIsAFNAMih6oVMmiwE0SLOPW8bmNeSd6fgQ76-pmESRNpDBvbUpF8BF0IsEpvsaAv-6EALw_wcB

"Bringing People Together Again." *World Forum*, https://www.worldforum.nl/en/nieuws/bringing-people-together-again-2

"Carnivores of Gondwana." *Cleveland Museum of Natural History*, https://www.cmnh.org/science-news/blog/april-2020/carnivores-of-gondwana

"Casava." *Wikipedia*, https://en.wikipedia.org/wiki/Cassava

"Chiswick." *Wikipedia*, https://en.wikipedia.org/wiki/Chiswick

"Cleopatra's Needle." *Wikipedia*, https://en.wikipedia.org/wiki/Cleopatra%27s_Needle

"Crichton Castle." *Wikipedia*, https://en.wikipedia.org/wiki/Crichton_Castle

"Embraer ERJ family." *Wikipedia*, https://en.wikipedia.org/wiki/Embraer_ERJ_family#Specifications

"Get to Know the Anhinga, or 'Snakebird'." *Birdnote Podcast and The National Audubon Society*, https://www.audubon.org/news/get-know-anhinga-or-snakebird

"Harpy Eagles." *Rainforest Expeditions*, https://www.rainforestexpeditions.com/wildlife/harpy-eagle/

"International Criminal Court." *Wikipedia*, https://en.wikipedia.org/wiki/International_Criminal_Court

"Intracranial Hematoma." *Mayo Clinic*, https://www.mayoclinic.org/diseases-conditions/intracranial-hematoma/symptoms-causes/syc-20356145

"Meeting of the Water." *Selvagem Tours*, https://selvagem.net/en/meeting-of-the-waters-in-santarem/

"Mil Mi-26." *Wikipedia*, https://en.wikipedia.org/wiki/Mil_Mi-26

"Rosecliff." *Newport Mansions*, https://www.newportmansions.org/explore/rosecliff

"Occupation of primordial Brazil." *Pesquisa FAPESP*, https://revistapesquisa.fapesp.br/en/occupation-of-primordial-brazil/

"RAF Lakenheath." *Wikipedia*, https://en.wikipedia.org/wiki/RAF_Lakenheath

"Santarém." *wiki voyage*, https://en.wikivoyage.org/wiki/Santarém_(Brazil)

Savoy Hotel, https://www.thesavoylondon.com/about-us/location/

"Tapajós." *Wikipedia*, https://en.wikipedia.org/wiki/Tapajós

"The giant kapok tree, the creeping aroids, and other resident architects of the Amazon rainforest." *WWF*, https://wwf.panda.org/discover/knowledge_hub/where_we_work/amazon/about_the_amazon/wildlife_amazon/plants/

"The Skinny-water Fleet Ultra-shoal, Ocean-proven Beachable Boats." *Gerr Marine*, https://www.gerrmarine.com/Beachable_Boats.html

"Uncontacted Tribes." *Survival*, https://www.survivalinternational.org/uncontactedtribes

"US 191." *Google Maps*, https://www.google.com/maps/@37.0401083,-113.5391146,300886m/data=!3m1!1e3

"Zodiac." *Zodiac website*, https://www.zodiac-nautic.com/us/

About the Author

Author and artist John Hopkins' curiosity for what lies beyond common knowledge shapes his imaginative, character-driven storytelling. Following his muse, John created **Lost Cactus**, a comic strip set on an off-the-grid top-secret research base—think Area 51. The strip's quick wit, fearless lampoonery, and supernatural mythology expanded into a shared universe of science fiction short stories and novels. Sequels and graphic novels featuring the expansive world-building of **Lost Cactus** and **The Powers That Be** shared universe are in the works.

Stay tuned and keep an eye on the sky.

johnhopkinsauthor.com

complected nurse into the blue-lit NICU.

"Here she is. Isn't she a beauty?"

Bathed in a peaceful blue ambiance, overwhelmed with a dizzying sense of grace, Stanley Hobbes moved before the tall glass incubator, staring enrapt at the delicate creature ensconced within, lying atop a cute animal print blanket. "She is the most perfect thing I have ever seen."

As if hearing Stanley's words, baby Rachel's eyes opened, and her tiny head swiveled onto his watery gaze.

Swallowing hard, Stanley noted the miniaturized cannula and thin tube extending from the delicate preemie's left temple with a wince. Replaying the stern man's profound statement that this child is the first of a new kind, he proffers a delicate wave, "Hello, Rachel. My name is Stanley Hobbes."

Upon saying the words aloud, the nebbish little paparazzo knew his life was irrevocably altered in ways that would play out over time. Taking a deep breath through his mask, Stanley returned Rachel's mesmerizing gaze through his glowing reflection in the incubator glass, "I will watch over you, Rachel. That's a promise."

Perceiving the gravitational pull between the tiny baby and the strange little man, Nurse Rahimi remained vigilant while administering a prescribed dosage of Professor Richard King's mystery drug from an IV bag. Monitoring the blue fluid coursing through the thin tube and into baby Rachel, the veteran NICU nurse hears people coming down the hall, "Okay, Mr. Hobbes, it is time to go."

Stanley removed his thick spectacles and swiped more tears from his eyes before pivoting toward Nurse Rahimi, "Tell me everything you know about The Powers That Be and the Blue Spark."